Praise for Walter Mosley

'A wonderful new talent . . . we sense that here is a real world we are hearing about for the first time. The most exciting arrival in the genre for years'

Financial Times

'Astonishing virtuosity . . . upending Chandler's LA to show a dark side of a different kind'

Sunday Times

'So hot it burns the fingers, with blistering dialogue and multi-coloured images. Highly addictive'

Evening Standard

'One of the finds of the 1990s'

Daily Telegraph

Walter Mosley

Walter Mosley was born in Los Angeles in 1952.
He currently lives in New York

• THE •
WALTER MOSLEY
OMNIBUS

Devil in a Blue Dress

A Red Death

White Butterfly

PICADOR

Devil in a Blue Dress first published 1990 by W. W. Norton & Company, Inc., New York
First published in Great Britain 1991 by Serpent's Tail
First published in an imprint of Macmillan Publishers Ltd 1992 by Pan Books

A Red Death first published 1991 by W. W. Norton & Company, Inc., New York
First published in Great Britain 1992 by Serpent's Tail
First published in an imprint of Macmillan Publishers Ltd 1994 by Pan Books

White Butterfly first published 1992 by W. W. Norton & Company, Inc., New York
First published in Great Britain 1993 by Serpent's Tail
First published in an imprint of Macmillan Publishers Ltd 1994 by Picador

This combined edition first published 1995 by Picador

This edition published 1996 by Picador
an imprint of Macmillan Publishers Ltd
25 Eccleston Place, London SW1W 9NF
and Basingstoke

Associated companies throughout the world

ISBN 0 330 33626 6

This is a work of fiction.
Any similarity of persons, places, or events depicted herein to actual
persons, places, or events is purely coincidental.

1 3 5 7 9 8 6 4 2

A CIP catalogue record for this book is available from
the British Library.

Phototypeset by Intype London Ltd
Printed and bound in Great Britain by
Mackays of Chatham plc, Chatham, Kent

Contents

• I •

DEVIL IN A BLUE DRESS

For

Joy Kellman, Frederic Tuten,

and Leroy Mosley

• 1 •

I was surprised to see a white man walk into Joppy's bar. It's not just that he was white but he wore an off-white linen suit and shirt with a Panama straw hat and bone shoes over flashing white silk socks. His skin was smooth and pale with just a few freckles. One lick of strawberry-blond hair escaped the band of his hat. He stopped in the doorway, filling it with his large frame, and surveyed the room with pale eyes; not a color I'd ever seen in a man's eyes. When he looked at me I felt a thrill of fear, but that went away quickly because I was used to white people by 1948.

I had spent five years with white men, and women, from Africa to Italy, through Paris, and into the Fatherland itself. I ate with them and slept with them, and I killed enough blue-eyed young men to know that they were just as afraid to die as I was.

The white man smiled at me, then he walked to the bar where Joppy was running a filthy rag over the marble top. They shook hands and exchanged greetings like old friends.

The second thing that surprised me was that he made Joppy nervous. Joppy was a tough ex-heavyweight who was comfortable brawling in the ring or in the street, but he ducked his head and smiled at that white man just like a salesman whose luck had gone bad.

I put a dollar down on the bar and made to leave, but before I was off the stool Joppy turned my way and waved me toward them.

"Com'on over here, Easy. This here's somebody I want ya t'meet."

I could feel those pale eyes on me.

"This here's a ole friend'a mines, Easy. Mr. Albright."

"You can call me DeWitt, Easy," the white man said. His grip was strong but slithery, like a snake coiling around my hand.

"Hello," I said.

"Yeah, Easy," Joppy went on, bowing and grinning. "Mr. Albright and me go way back. You know he prob'ly my oldest friend from L.A. Yeah, we go ways back."

"That's right," Albright smiled. "It must've been 1935 when I met Jop. What is it now? Must be thirteen years. That was back before the war, before every farmer, and his brother's wife, wanted to come to L.A."

Joppy guffawed at the joke; I smiled politely. I was wondering what kind of business Joppy had with that man and, along with that, I wondered what kind of business that man could have with me.

"Where you from, Easy?" Mr. Albright asked.

"Houston."

"Houston, now that's a nice town. I go down there sometimes, on business." He smiled for a moment. He had all the time in the world. "What kind of work you do up here?"

Up close his eyes were the color of robins' eggs; matte and dull.

"He worked at Champion Aircraft up to two days ago," Joppy said when I didn't answer. "They laid him off."

Mr. Albright twisted his pink lips, showing his distaste. "That's too bad. You know these big companies don't give a damn about you. The budget doesn't balance just right and they let ten family men go. You have a family, Easy?" He had a light drawl like a well-to-do southern gentleman.

"No, just me, that's all," I said.

"But they don't know that. For all they know you could have ten kids and one on the way but they let you go just the same."

"That's right!" Joppy shouted. His voice sounded like a regiment of men marching through a gravel pit. "Them people own them big companies don't never even come in to work, they just get on the telephone to find out how they money is. And you know they better get a good answer or some heads gonna roll."

Mr. Albright laughed and slapped Joppy on the arm. "Why don't you get us some drinks, Joppy? I'll have scotch. What's your pleasure, Easy?"

"Usual?" Joppy asked me.

"Sure."

When Joppy moved away from us Mr. Albright turned to look around the room. He did that every few minutes, turning slightly, checking to see if anything had changed. There wasn't much to see though. Joppy's was a small bar on the second floor of a butchers' warehouse. His only usual customers were the Negro butchers and it was early enough in the afternoon that they were still hard at work.

The odor of rotted meat filled every corner of the building; there were few people, other than butchers, who could stomach sitting in Joppy's bar.

Joppy brought Mr. Albright's scotch and a bourbon on the rocks for me. He put them down and said, "Mr. Albright lookin' for a man to do a lil job, Easy. I told him you outta work an' got a mortgage t'pay too."

"That's hard." Mr. Albright shook his head again. "Men in big business don't even notice or care when a working man wants to try to make something out of himself."

"And you know Easy always tryin' t'be better. He just got his high school papers from night school and he been threatenin' on some college." Joppy wiped the marble bar as he spoke. "And he's a war hero, Mr. Albright. Easy went in with Patton. Volunteered! You know he seen him some blood."

"That a fact?" Albright said. He wasn't surprised. "Why don't we go have a chair, Easy? Over there by the window."

Joppy's windows were so dingy that you couldn't see out onto 103rd Street. But if you sat at a small cherry table next to them, at least you had the benefit of the dull glow of daylight.

"You got a mortgage to meet, eh, Easy? The only thing that's worse than a big company is the bank. They want their money on the first and if you miss the payment, they will have the marshal knocking down your door on the second."

"What's my business got to do with you, Mr. Albright? I don't wanna be rude, but I just met you five minutes ago and now you want to know all my business."

"Well, I thought that Joppy said you needed to get work or you were going to lose your house."

"What's that got to do with you?"

"I just might need a bright pair of eyes and ears to do a little job for me, Easy."

"And what kind of work is it that you do?" I asked. I should have gotten up and walked out of there, but he was right about my mortgage. He was right about the banks too.

"I used to be a lawyer when I lived in Georgia. But now I'm just another fella who does favors for friends, and for friends of friends."

"What kind of favors?"

"I don't know, Easy." He shrugged his great white shoulders. "Whatever somebody might need. Let's say that you need to get a message to someone but it's not, um, convenient for you to do it in person; well, then you call me and I take the job. You see I always do the job I'm asked to do, everybody knows that, so I always have lots of work. And sometimes I need a little helper to get the job done. That's where you come in."

"And how's that?" I asked. While he talked it dawned on me that Albright was a lot like a friend I had back in Texas—Raymond Alexander was his name but we called him Mouse. Just thinking about Mouse set my teeth on edge.

"I need to find somebody and I might need a little help looking."

"And who is it you want to—"

"Easy," he interrupted. "I can see that you're a smart man with a lot of very good questions. And I'd like to talk more about it, but not here." From his shirt pocket he produced a white card and a white enameled fountain pen. He scrawled on the card and then handed it to me.

"Talk to Joppy about me and then, if you want to try it out, come to my office any time after seven tonight."

He downed the shot, smiled at me again, and stood up, straightening his cuffs. He tilted the Panama hat on his head and saluted Joppy, who grinned and waved from behind the bar. Then Mr. DeWitt Albright strolled out of Joppy's place like a regular customer going home after his afternoon snort.

The card had his name printed on it in flourished letters. Below that was the address he'd scribbled. It was a downtown address; a long drive from Watts.

I noted that Mr. DeWitt Albright didn't pay for the drinks he ordered. Joppy didn't seem in a hurry to ask for his money though.

• 2 •

"Where'd you meet this dude?" I asked Joppy.

"I met him when I was still in the ring. Like he said, before the war."

Joppy was still at the bar, leaning over his big stomach and buffing the marble. His uncle, a bar owner himself, had died in Houston ten years earlier, just when Joppy decided to give up the ring. Joppy went all the way back home to get that marble bar. The butchers had already agreed to let him open his business upstairs and all he could think of was getting that marble top. Joppy was a superstitious man. He thought that the only way he could be successful was with a piece of his uncle, already a proven success, on the job with him. Every extra moment Joppy had was spent cleaning and buffing his bar top. He didn't allow roughhousing near the bar and if you ever dropped a pitcher or something heavy he'd be there in a second, looking for chips.

Joppy was a heavy-framed man, almost fifty years old. His hands were like black catcher's mitts and I never saw him in shirt-sleeves that didn't strain at the seams from bulging muscle. His face was scarred from all the punishment he had taken in the ring; the flesh around his big lips was jagged and there was a knot over his right eye that always looked red and raw.

In his years as a boxer Joppy had had moderate success. He was ranked number seven in 1932 but his big draw was the violence he brought to the ring. Joppy would come out swinging wildly, taking everything any boxer could dish out. In his prime no one could knock Joppy down and, later on, he always went the distance.

"He got something to do with the fights?" I asked.

"Wherever they's a little money to be made Mr. Albright got his nose to the ground," Joppy said. "An' he don't care too much if that money got a little smudge or sumpin' on it neither."

"So you got me tied up with a gangster?"

"Ain't no gangster, Ease. Mr. Albright just a man with a finger in a whole lotta pies, thas all. He's a businessman and you know when you in business sellin' shirts and a man come up to you with a box he say done falled off'a truck, well . . . you just give that man a couple'a dollars and look t'other way." He waved his catcher's mitt at me. "Thas business."

Joppy was cleaning one area on his counter until it was spotless, except for the dirt that caked in the cracks. The dark cracks twisting through the light marble looked like a web of blood vessels in a newborn baby's head.

"So he's just a businessman?" I asked.

Joppy stopped wiping for a moment and looked me in the eye. "Don't get me wrong, Ease. DeWitt is a tough man, and he runs in bad company. But you still might could get that mortgage payment an' you might even learn sumpin' from 'im."

I sat there looking around the small room. Joppy had six tables and seven high stools at his bar. A busy night never saw all his chairs full but I was jealous of his success. He had his own business; he owned something. He told me one night that he could sell that bar even though he only rented the room. I thought he was lying but later on I found out that people will buy a business that already has customers; they wouldn't mind paying the rent if there was money coming in.

The windows were dirty and the floor was rutted but it was Joppy's place and when the white butcher-boss came up to collect the rent he always said, "Thank you, Mr. Shag." Because he was happy to get his money.

"So what he want with me?" I asked.

"He just want you t'look for somebody, leastwise that what he said."

"Who?"

"Some girl, I dunno." Joppy shrugged. "I ain't ax him his business if it don't gotta do wit' me. But he just payin' you to *look*, ain't nobody says you gotta find nuthin'."

"And what's he gonna pay?"

"Enough fo' that mortgage. That's why I called you in on this, Easy, I know'd you need some fast money. I don't give a damn 'bout that man, or whoever it is he lookin' fo' neither."

The thought of paying my mortgage reminded me of my front yard and the shade of my fruit trees in the summer heat. I felt that I was just as good as any white man, but if I didn't even own my front door then people would look at me like just another poor beggar, with his hand outstretched.

"Take his money, man. You got to hold on to that little bit'a property," Joppy said as if he knew what I was thinking. "You know all them pretty girls you be runnin' wit' ain't gonna buy you no house."

"I don't like it, Joppy."

"You don't like that money? Shit! I'll hold it for ya."

"Not the money . . . It's just . . . You know that Mr. Albright reminds me of Mouse."

"Who?"

"You remember, he was a little man lived down in Houston. He married EttaMae Harris."

Joppy turned his jagged lips into a frown. "Naw, he must'a come after my time."

"Yeah, well, Mouse is a lot like Mr. Albright. He's smooth and a natty dresser and he's smilin' all the time. But he always got his business in the front'a his mind, and if you get in the way you might come to no good." I always tried to speak proper English in my life, the kind of English they taught in school, but I found over the years that I could only truly express myself in the natural, "uneducated" dialect of my upbringing.

" 'Might come to no good' is a bitch, Easy, but sleepin' in the street ain't got no 'might' to it."

"Yeah, man. I'm just feelin' kinda careful."

"Careful don't hurt, Easy. Careful keep your hands up, careful makes ya strong."

"So he's just a businessman, huh?" I asked again.

"Thas right!"

"And just exactly what kind of business is it he does? I mean, is he a shirt salesman or what?"

"They gotta sayin' for his line'a work, Ease."

"What's that?"

"Whatever the market can bear." He smiled, looking like a hungry bear himself. "Whatever the market can bear."

"I'll think about it."

"Don't worry, Ease, I'll take care'a ya. You just call old Joppy now and then and I'll tell ya if it sounds like it's gettin' bad. You just keep in touch with me an' you be just fine."

"Thanks for thinkin'a me, Jop," I said, but I wondered if I'd still be thankful later on.

3

I drove back to my house thinking about money and how much I needed to have some.

I loved going home. Maybe it was that I was raised on a sharecropper's farm or that I never owned anything until I bought that house, but I loved my little home. There was an apple tree and an avocado in the front yard, surrounded by thick St. Augustine grass. At the side of the house I had a pomegranate tree that bore more than thirty fruit every season and a banana tree that never produced a thing. There were dahlias and wild roses in beds around the fence and African violets that I kept in a big jar on the front porch.

The house itself was small. Just a living room, a bedroom, and a kitchen. The bathroom didn't even have a shower and the back yard was no larger than a child's rubber pool. But that house meant more to me than any woman I ever knew. I loved her and I was jealous of her and if the bank sent the county marshal to take her from me I might have come at him with a rifle rather than to give her up.

Working for Joppy's friend was the only way I saw to keep my house. But there was something wrong. I could feel it in my fingertips. DeWitt Albright made me uneasy; Joppy's tough words, though they were true, made me uneasy. I kept telling myself to go to bed and forget it.

"Easy," I said, "get a good night's sleep and go out looking for a job tomorrow."

"But this is June twenty-five," a voice said. "Where is the sixty-four dollars coming from on July one?"

"I'll get it," I answered.

"How?"

We went on like that but it was useless from the start. I knew I was going to take Albright's money and do whatever he wanted me to, providing it was legal, because that little house of mine needed me and I wasn't about to let her down.

And there was another thing.

DeWitt Albright made me a little nervous. He was a big man, and powerful by the look of him. You could tell by the way he held his shoulders that he was full of violence. But I was a big man too. And, like most young men, I never liked to admit that I could be dissuaded by fear.

Whether he knew it or not, DeWitt Albright had me caught by my own pride. The more I was afraid of him, I was that much more certain to take the job he offered.

The address Albright had given me was a small, buff-colored building on Alvarado. The buildings around it were taller but not as old or as distinguished. I walked through the black wrought-iron gates into the hall of the Spanish-styled entrance. There was nobody around, not even a directory, just a wall of cream-colored doors with no names on them.

"Excuse me."

The voice made me jump.

"What?" My voice strained and cracked as I turned to see the small man.

"Who are you looking for?"

He was a little white man wearing a suit that was also a uniform.

"I'm looking for, um . . . ah . . ." I stuttered. I forgot the name. I had to squint so that the room wouldn't start spinning.

It was a habit I developed in Texas when I was a boy. Sometimes, when a white man of authority would catch me off guard, I'd empty head of everything so I was unable to say anything. "The less you know, the less trouble you find," they used to say. I hated myself for it but I also hated white people, and colored people too, for making me that way.

"Can I help you?" the white man asked. He had curly red hair and a pointed nose. When I still couldn't answer he said, "We only take deliveries between nine and six."

"No, no," I said, trying to remember.

"Yes we do! Now you better leave."

"No, I mean I . . ."

The little man started backing toward a small podium that stood against the wall. I figured that he had a nightstick back there.

"Albright!" I yelled.

"What?" he yelled back.

"Albright! I'm here to see Albright!"

"Albright who?" There was suspicion in his eye, and his hand was behind the podium.

"Mr. Albright. Mr. DeWitt Albright."

"Mr. Albright?"

"Yes, that's him."

"Are you delivering something?" he asked, holding out his scrawny hand.

"No. I have an appointment. I mean, I'm supposed to meet him." I hated that little man.

"You're supposed to meet him? You can't even remember his name."

I took a deep breath and said, very softly, "I am supposed to meet Mr. DeWitt Albright tonight, any time after seven."

"You're supposed to meet him at seven? It's eight-thirty now. He's probably gone."

"He told me *any time* after seven."

He held out his hand to me again. "Did he give you a note saying you're to come in here after hours?"

I shook my head at him. I would have liked to rip the skin from his face like I'd done once to another white boy.

"Well, how am I to know that you aren't just a thief? You can't even remember his name and you want me to take you somewhere in there. Why you could have a partner waiting for me to let you in . . ."

I was disgusted. "Forget it man," I said. "You just tell him, when you see him, that Mr. Rawlins was here. You tell him that the next time he better give me a note because you cain't be lettin' no street niggahs comin' in yo' place wit' no notes!"

I was ready to leave. That little white man had convinced me that I was in the wrong place. I was ready to go back home. I could find my money another way.

"Hold on," he said. "You wait right there and I'll be back in a minute." He sidled through one of the cream-colored doors, shutting it as he went. I heard the lock snap into place a moment later.

After a few minutes he opened the door a crack and waved at me to follow him. He looked from side to side as he let me through the door; looking for my accomplices I suppose.

The doorway led to an open courtyard that was paved with dark red brick and landscaped with three large palm trees that reached out beyond the roof of the three-story building. The inner doorways on the upper two floors were enclosed by trellises that had vines of white and yellow sweetheart roses cascading down. The sky was still light at that time of year but I could see a crescent moon peeking over the inner roof.

The little man opened another door at the other side of the courtyard. It led down an ugly metal staircase into the bowels of the building. We went through a dusty boiler room to an empty corridor that was painted drab green and draped with gray cobwebs.

At the end of the hall there was a door of the same color that was chipped and dusty.

"That's what you want," the little man said.

I said thank you and he walked away from me. I never saw him again. I often think of how so many people have walked into my life for just a few minutes and kicked up some dust, then they're gone away. My father was like that; my mother wasn't much better.

I knocked on the ugly door. I expected to see Albright, but instead the door opened into a small room that held two strange-looking men.

The man who held the door was tall and slight with curly brown hair, dark skin like an India Indian, and brown eyes so light they were almost golden. His friend, who stood against a door at the far wall, was short and looked a little like he was Chinese around the eyes, but when I looked at him again I wasn't so sure of his race.

The dark man smiled and put out his hand. I thought he wanted to shake but then he started slapping my side.

"Hey, man! What's wrong with you?" I said, pushing him away. The maybe-Chinese man slipped a hand in his pocket.

"Mr. Rawlins," the dark man said in an accent I didn't know. He was still smiling. "Put your hands up a little from your sides, please. I'm just checking." The smile widened into a grin.

"You could just keep your hands to yourself, man. I don't let nobody feel on me like that."

The little man pulled something, I couldn't tell what, halfway out of his pocket. Then he took a step toward us. The grinner tried to put his hand against my chest but I grabbed him by the wrist.

The dark man's eyes glittered, he smiled at me for a moment, and then said to his partner, "Don't worry, Manny. He's okay."

"You sure, Shariff?"

"Yeah. He's alright, just a little shaky." Shariff's teeth glinted between his dusky lips. I still had his wrist.

Shariff said, "Let him know, Manny."

Manny put his hand back in his pocket and then took it out again to knock on the door behind.

DeWitt Albright opened the door after a minute.

"Easy," he smiled.

"He doesn't want us to touch him," Shariff said as I let him go.

"Leave it," Albright answered. "I just wanted to make sure he was solo."

"You're the boss." Shariff sounded very sure of himself; even a little arrogant.

"You and Manny can go now," Albright smiled. "Easy and I have some business to talk over."

Mr. Albright went behind a big blond desk and put his bone shoes up next to a half-full bottle of Wild Turkey. There was a paper calendar hanging on the wall behind him with a picture of a basket of blackberries as a design. There was nothing else on the wall. The floor was bare too: plain yellow linoleum with flecks of color scattered through it.

"Have a seat, Mr. Rawlins," Mr. Albright said, gesturing to the chair in front of his desk. He was bare-headed and his coat was nowhere in sight. There was a white-leather shoulder holster under his left arm. The muzzle of the pistol almost reached his belt.

"Nice friends you got," I said as I studied his piece.

"They're like you, Easy. Whenever I need a little manpower I give them a call. There's a whole army of men who'll do specialized work for the right price."

"The little guy Chinese?"

Albright shrugged. "No one knows. He was raised in an orphanage, in Jersey City. Drink?"

"Sure."

"One of the benefits of working for yourself. Always have a bottle on the table. Everybody else, even the presidents of these big companies, got the booze in the bottom drawer, but I keep it right out in plain sight. You want to drink it? That's fine with me. You don't like it? Door's right there behind you." While he talked he poured two shots into glasses that he had taken from a desk drawer.

The gun interested me. The butt and the barrel were black; the only part of DeWitt's attire that wasn't white.

As I leaned over to take the glass from his hand he asked, "So, you want the job, Easy?"

"Well, that depends on what kind of job you had in mind?"

"I'm looking for somebody, for a friend," he said. He pulled a photograph from his shirt pocket and put it down on the desk. It was a picture of the head and shoulders of a pretty young white woman. The picture had been black and white originally but it was touched up for color like the photos of jazz singers that they put out in front of nightclubs. She had light hair coming down over her bare shoulders and high cheekbones and eyes that might have been blue if the artist got it right. After staring at her for a full minute I decided that she'd be worth looking for if you could get her to smile at you that way.

"Daphne Monet," Mr. Albright said. "Not bad to look at but she's hell to find."

"I still don't see what it's got to do with me," I said. "I ain't never laid eyes on her."

"That's a shame, Easy." He was smiling at me. "But I think you might be able to help me anyway."

"I can't see how. Woman like this don't hardly know my number. What you should do is call the police."

"I never call a soul who isn't a friend, or at least a friend of a friend. I don't know any cops, and neither do my friends."

"Well then get a—"

"You see, Easy," he cut off, "Daphne has a predilection for the company of Negroes. She likes jazz and pigs' feet and dark meat, if you know what I mean."

I knew but I didn't like to hear it. "So you think she might be down around Watts?"

"Not a doubt in my mind. But, you see, I can't go in those places looking for her because I'm not the right persuasion. Joppy knows me well enough to tell me what he knows but I've already asked him and all he could do was to give me your name."

"So what do you want with her?"

"I have a friend who wants to apologize, Easy. He has a short temper and that's why she left."

"And he wants her back?"

Mr. Albright smiled.

"I don't know if I can help you, Mr. Albright. Like Joppy said, I lost a job a couple of days ago and I have to get another one before the note comes due."

"Hundred dollars for a week's work, Mr. Rawlins, and I pay in advance. You find her tomorrow and you keep what's in your pocket."

"I don't know, Mr. Albright. I mean, how do I know what I'm getting mixed up in? What are you—"

He raised a powerful finger to his lips, then he said, "Easy, walk out your door in the morning and you're mixed up in something. The only thing you can really worry about is if you get mixed up to the top or not."

"I don't want to get mixed up with the law is what I mean."

"That's why I want you to work for me. I don't like the police myself. Shit! The police enforce the law and you know what the law is, don't you?"

I had my own ideas on the subject but I kept them to myself.

"The law," he continued, "is made by the rich people so that the poor people can't get ahead. You don't want to get mixed up with the law and neither do I."

He lifted the shot glass and inspected it as if he were checking for fleas, then he put the glass on the desk and placed his hands, palms down, around it.

"I'm just asking you to find a girl," he said. "And to tell me where she is. That's all. You just find out where she is and whisper it in my ear. That's all. You find her and I'll give you a bonus mortgage payment and my friend will find you a job, maybe he can even get you back into Champion."

"Who is it wants to find the girl?"

"No names, Easy, it's better that way."

"It's just that I'd hate to find her and then have some cop come up to me with some shit like I was the last one seen around her—before she disappeared."

The white man laughed and shook his head as if I had told a good joke.

"Things happen every day, Easy," he said. "Things happen every day. You're an educated man, aren't you?"

"Why, yes."

"So you read the paper. You read it today?"

"Yes."

"Three murders! Three! Last night alone. Things happen every day. People with everything to live for, maybe they even got a little money in the bank. They probably had it all planned out what they'd be doing this weekend, but that didn't stop them from dying. Those plans didn't save them when the time came. People got everything to live for and they get a little careless. They forget that the only thing you have to be sure of is that nothing bad comes to you."

The way he smiled when he sat back in his chair reminded me of Mouse again. I thought of how Mouse was always smiling, especially when misfortune happened to someone else.

"You just find the girl and tell me, that's all. I'm not going to hurt her and neither is my friend. You don't have a thing to worry about."

He took a white secretary-type wallet from a desk drawer and produced a stack of bills. He counted out ten of them, licking his square thumb for every other one, and placed them in a next stack next to the whiskey.

"One hundred dollars," he said.

I couldn't see why it shouldn't be my one hundred dollars.

When I was a poor man, and landless, all I worried about was a place for the night and food to eat; you really didn't need much for that. A friend would always stand me a meal, and there were plenty of women who would have let me sleep with them. But when I got that mortgage I found that I needed more than just friendship. Mr. Albright wasn't a friend but he had what I needed.

He was a fine host too. His liquor was good and he was pleasant enough. He told me a few stories, the kind of tales that we called "lies" back home in Texas.

One story he told was about when he was a lawyer in Georgia.

"I was defending a shit-kicker who was charged with burning down a banker's house," DeWitt told me as he stared out toward the wall behind my head. "Banker had foreclosed on the boy the minute the note was due. You know he didn't even give him any chance to make extra arrangements. And that boy was just as guilty as that banker was."

"You get him off?" I asked.

DeWitt smiled at me. "Yeah. That prosecutor had a good case on Leon, that's the shit-kicker. Yeah, the honorable Randolph Corey had solid proof that my client did the arson. But I went down to Randy's house and I sat at his table and pulled out this here pistol. All I did was talk about the weather we'd been having, and while I did that I cleaned my gun."

"Getting your client off meant that much to you?"

"Shit. Leon was trash. But Randy had been riding pretty high for a couple'a years and I had it in mind that it was time for him to lose a case." Albright straightened his shoulders. "You have to have a sense of balance when it comes to the law, Easy. Everything has to come out just right."

After a few drinks I started talking about the war. Plain old man-talk, about half of it true and the rest just for laughs. More than an hour went by before he asked me, "You ever kill a man with your hands, Easy?"

"What?"

"You ever kill a man, hand-to-hand?"

"Why?"

"No reason really. It's just that I know you've seen some action."

"Some."

"You ever kill somebody up close? I mean so close that you could see it when his eyes went out of focus and he let go? When you kill a man it's the shit and piss that's worst. You boys did that in the war and I bet it was bad. I bet you couldn't dream about your mother anymore, or anything nice. But you lived with it because you knew that it was the war that forced you to do it."

His pale blue eyes reminded me of the wide-eyed corpses of German soldiers that I once saw stacked up on a road to Berlin.

"But the only thing that you have to remember, Easy," he said as he picked up the money to hand me across the table, "is that some of us can kill with no more trouble than drinking a glass of bourbon." He downed the shot and smiled.

Then he said, "Joppy tells me that you used to frequent an illegal club down on Eighty-ninth and Central. Somebody saw Daphne at that very same bar not long ago. I don't know what they call it but they have the big names in there on weekends and the man who runs it is called John. You could start tonight."

The way his dead eyes shined on me I knew our party was over. I couldn't think of anything to say so I nodded, put his money in my pocket, and moved to leave.

I turned back at the door to salute him goodbye but DeWitt Albright had filled his glass and shifted his gaze to the far wall. He was staring into someplace far from that dirty basement.

• 4 •

John's place was a speakeasy before they repealed Prohibition. But by 1948 we had legitimate bars all over L.A. John liked the speakeasy business though, and he had been in so much trouble with the law that City Hall wouldn't have given him a license to drive, much less to sell liquor. So John kept paying off the police and running an illegal nightclub through the back door of a little market at the corner of Central Avenue and Eighty-ninth Place. You could walk into that store any evening up until three in the morning to find Hattie Parsons sitting behind the candy counter. They didn't have many groceries, and no fresh produce or dairy goods, but she'd sell you what was there and if you knew the right words, or were a regular, then she'd let you in the club through the back door. But if you thought that you should be able to get in on account of your name, or your clothes or maybe your bankbook, well, Hattie kept a straight razor in her apron pocket and her nephew, Junior Fornay, sat right behind the door.

When I pushed open the door to the market I ran into my third white man that day. This one was about my height with wheat-brown hair and an expensive dark blue suit. His clothes were disheveled, and he smelled of gin.

"Hey, colored brother," he said as he waved at me. He walked straight toward me so that I had to back out of the store if I didn't want him to run me down.

"How'd ya like t'make twenty dollars fast?" he asked when the door swung shut behind him.

They were just throwing money at me that day.

"How's that?" I asked the drunk.

"I need to get in here . . . lookin' fer someone. Girl in there won't let me in." He was teetering and I was afraid he'd fall down. "Why'ont you tell'em I'm fine."

"I'm sorry, but I can't do that," I said.

"Why's that?"

"Once they tell you no at John's they stick to it." I moved around him to get into the door again. He tried to turn and grab my arm but all he managed was to spin around twice and wind up sitting against the wall. He put up his hand as if he wanted me to bend down so he could whisper something but I didn't think that anything he had to offer could improve my life.

"Hey, Hattie," I said. "Looks like you got a boarder out on your doorstep."

"Drunk old white boy?"

"Yep."

"I'll have Junior look out there later on. He can sweep 'im up if he still there."

With that I put the drunk out of my mind. "Who you got playin' tonight?" I asked.

"Some'a your homefolks, Easy. Lips and his trio. But we had Holiday, Tuesday last."

"You did?"

"She just come breezin' through." Hattie's smile revealed teeth that were like flat gray pebbles. "Must'a been 'bout, I don't know, midnight, but the birds was singin' wit 'er 'fore we closed for the night."

"Oh man! Sorry I missed that," I said.

"That'a be six bits, baby."

"What for?"

"John put on a cover. Cost goin' up an' he tryin' t'keep out the riff-raff."

"And who's that?"

She leaned forward showing me her watery brown eyes. Hattie was the color of light sand and I doubt if she ever topped a hundred pounds in her sixty-some years.

"You heard about Howard?" she asked.

"What Howard?"

"Howard Green, the chauffeur."

"No, uh-uh. I haven't seen Howard Green since last Christmas."

"Well you ain't gonna see him no more—in this world."

"What happened?"

"He walked outta here about three in the mo'nin' the night Lady Day was here and wham!" She slammed her bony fist into an open palm.

"Yeah?"

"They din't hardly even leave a face on 'im. You know I tole 'im that he was a fool t'be walkin' out on Holiday but he didn't care. Said he had *business* t'see to. Hmm! I tole him he hadn't oughtta left."

"Killed him?"

"Right out there next to his car. Beat him so bad that his wife, Esther, said the only way she could identify the body was cuz of his ring. They must'a used a lead pipe. You know he had his nose in somebody's nevermind."

"Howard liked to play hard," I agreed. I handed her three quarters.

"Go right on in, honey," she smiled.

When I opened the door I was slapped in the face by the force of Lips' alto horn. I had been hearing Lips and Willie and Flattop since I was a boy in Houston. All of them and John and half the people in that crowded room had migrated from Houston after the war, and some before that. California was like heaven for the southern Negro. People told stories of how you could eat fruit right off the trees and get enough work to retire one day. The stories were true for the most part but the truth wasn't like the dream. Life was still hard in L.A. and if you worked every day you still found yourself on the bottom.

But being on the bottom didn't feel so bad if you could come to John's now and then and remember how it felt back home in Texas, dreaming about California. Sitting there and drinking John's scotch you could remember the dreams you once had and, for a while, it felt like you had them for real.

"Hey, Ease," a thick voice crackled at me from behind the door.

It was Junior Fornay. He was a man that I knew from back home too. A big, burly field hand who could chop cotton all day long and then party until it was time to climb back out into the fields. We had had an argument once, when we were both much younger, and I couldn't help thinking that I'd've probably died if it wasn't for Mouse stepping in to save my bacon.

"Junior," I hailed. "What's goin' on?"

"Not too much, yet, but stick around." He was leaning back on a stool, propping himself against the wall. He was five years older than I, maybe thirty-three, and his gut hung over his jeans, but Junior still looked to be every bit as powerful as when he put me on the floor all those year before.

Junior had a cigarette between his lips. He smoked the cheapest, foulest brand that they made in Mexico—Zapatas. I guess that he was finished smoking it because he let it fall to the floor. It just lay on the oak floor, smoldering and burning a black patch in the wood. The floor around Junior's chair had dozens of burns in it. He was a filthy man who didn't give a damn about anything.

"Ain't seen ya 'round much, Ease. Where ya been?"

"Workin', workin', day and night for Champion, and then they let me go."

"Fired?" There was a hint of a smile on his lips.

"On my ass."

"Shit. Sorry t'hear it. They got layoffs?"

"Naw, man. It's just that the boss ain't happy if you just do your job. He need a big smack on his butt too."

"I hear ya."

"Just this past Monday I finished a shift and I was so tired I couldn't even walk straight . . ."

"Uh-huh," Junior chimed in to keep the story going.

". . . and the boss came up and say that he need me for an extra hour. Well I told him that I was sorry but I had a date. And I did too, with my bed."

Junior got a kick out of that.

"And he got the nerve to tell me that *my people* have to learn to give a little extra if we wanna advance."

"He said that?"

"Yeah." I felt the heat of my anger returning.

"And what is he?"

"Italian boy, I think his parents the ones came over."

"Man! So what you say?"

"I told him that my people been givin' a little extra since before Italy was even a country. 'Cause you know Italy ain't even been around that long."

"Yeah," Junior said. But I could see that he didn't know what I was talking about. "So what happened then?"

"He just told me to go on home and not to bother coming back. He said that he needed people who were willing to work. So I left."

"Man!" Junior shook his head. "They do it to ya every time."

"That's right. You want a beer, Junior?"

"Yeah." He frowned. "But can you buy it with no job and all?"

"I can always buy a couple'a beers."

"Well then, I can always drink 'em."

I went over to the bar and ordered two ales. It looked like half of Houston was there. Most tables had five or six people. People were shouting and talking, kissing and laughing. John's place felt good after a hard day's work. It wasn't quite legal but there was nothing wrong with it either. Big names in Negro music came there because they knew John in the old days when he gave them work and didn't skimp on the paycheck. There must've been over two hundred regulars that frequented John's and we all knew each other, so it made a good place for business as well as a good time.

Alphonso Jenkins was there in his black silk shirt and his foot-high pompadour hairdo. Jockamo Johanas was there too. He was wearing a wooly brown suit and bright blue shoes. Skinny Rita Cook was there with five men hanging around her table. I never did understand how an ugly, skinny woman like that attracted so many men. I once asked her how she did it and she said, in her high whiny voice, "Well, ya know, Easy, it's only half the mens is int'rested in how a girl look. Most'a your colored mens is lookin' for a woman love 'em so hard that they fo'gets how hard it is t'make it through the day."

I noticed Frank Green at the bar. We called him Knifehand because he was so fast to pull a knife that it seemed he always had one in his hand. I stayed away from Frank because he was a gangster. He hijacked liquor trucks and cigarette shipments all over California, and Nevada too. He was serious about everything and just about ready to cut any man he met.

I noted that Frank was wearing all dark clothes. In Frank's line of business that meant he was about to go out to work—hijacking or worse.

The room was so crowded that there was barely any space to dance, but there were a dozen or so couples wrestling out there between the tables.

I carried the two mugs of ale back to the entrance and handed Junior his. One of the few ways I know to make a foul-tempered field hand happy is to feed him some ale and let him tell a few tall tales. So I sat back and sipped while Junior told me about the goings-on at John's for the previous week or so. He told me the story about Howard Green again. When he told it he added that Green had been doing some illegal work for his employers and, Junior thought, "It's them white men kilt 'im."

Junior liked to make up any old wild story, I knew that, but there were too many white people turning up for me to feel at ease.

"Who was he workin' for?" I asked.

"You know that dude dropped outta the mayor's race?"

"Matthew Teran?"

Teran had a good chance at winning the mayor's race in L.A. but he'd just withdrawn his name a few weeks before. Nobody knew why.

"Yeah, that's him. You know all them politicians is just robbers. Why I remember when they first elected Huey Long, down in Louisiana—"

"How long Lips gonna be here?" I asked, to cut him off.

"Week or so." Junior didn't care what he talked about. "They bring back some mem'ries, don't they. Shit, they was playin' that night Mouse pulled me off your ass."

"Thas right," I said. I can still feel Junior's foot in my kidney when I turn the wrong way.

"I should'a thanked 'im for that. You know I was so drunk an' so mad that I might'a kilt you, Easy. And then I'd still be on the chain gang."

That was the first real smile he showed since I'd been with him. Junior was missing two teeth from the lower row and one upper.

"What ever happened to Mouse?" he asked, almost wistfully.

"I don't know. Today's the first time I even thought about him in years."

"He still down there in Houston?"

"Last I heard. He married to EttaMae."

"What's he doin' when you seen 'im last?"

"Been so long I don't even remember," I lied.

Junior grinned. "I remember when he killed Joe T., you know the pimp? I mean Joe had blood comin' from everywhere an' Mouse had on this light blue suit. Not a spot on it! You know that's why the cops didn't take Mouse in, they didn't even think he could'a done it 'cause he was too clean."

I was remembering the last time I had seen Raymond Alexander, and it wasn't something to make me laugh.

•

I hadn't seen Mouse in four years when we ran into each other one night, outside of Myrtle's saloon, in Houston's Fifth Ward. He was wearing a plum-colored suit and a felt brown derby. I was still wearing army green.

"'S'appenin', Easy?" he asked, looking up at me. Mouse was a small, rodent-faced man.

"Not much," I answered. "You look jus' 'bout the same."

Mouse flashed his gold-rimmed teeth at me. "Ain't so bad. I got the streets tame by now."

We smiled at each other and slapped backs. Mouse bought me a drink in Myrtle's and I bought him another. We traded back and forth like that until Myrtle locked us in and went up to bed. She said, "Leave the money fo' what you'all drink under the counter. Do' lock itself on the way out."

"'Member that shit wit' my stepdaddy, Ease?" Mouse asked when we were alone.

"Yeah," I said softly. It was early morning and empty in the bar but I still looked around the room; murder should never be discussed out loud, but Mouse didn't know it. He had killed his stepfather five years earlier and blamed it on another man. But if the law ever found out the true circumstances he'd have been hanging in a week.

"His real son, Navrochet, come lookin' fo' me last year. He didn't think that boy Clifton done it even though the law said he did." Mouse poured a drink and knocked it back. Then he poured another one. "You get any white pussy in the war?" he asked.

"All they got is white girls. What you think?"

Mouse grinned and sat back, rubbing his crotch. "Shit!" he said, "that might be worf a couple'a potshots, huh?" And he slapped my knee like in the old days when we were partners, before the war.

We were drinking for an hour before he got back to Navrochet. Mouse said, "Man come down here, right in this saloon, and come up on me wit' his high boots on. You know I had t'look straight up t'see that boy. He had on a nice suit wit' them boots, so I jus' slipped down my zipper when he walk in. He say he wanna talk. He says les step outside. And I go. You might call me a fool but I go. And the minute I get out there and turn around he got a pistol pointed at my fo'head. Can you imagine that? So I play like I'm scared. Then ole Navro wanna know where he could fine you . . ."

"Me!" I said.

"Yeah, Easy! He heard you was wit' me so he gonna kill you too. But I'as workin' my stomach in and out and you know I had some beer in me. I'as actin' like I'as scared and had Navro thinkin' he so bad 'cause I'm shakin' . . . Then I pulls out Peter and open up the dam. Heh, heh. Piss all over his boots. You know Navrochet like t'jump three feet." The grin faded from his lips and he said, "I shot him four times 'fore he hit the floor. Same amount'a lead I put in his fuckin' son-of-a-whore daddy."

I had seen a lot of death in the war but Navrochet's dying seemed more real and more terrible; it was so useless. Back in Texas, in Fifth Ward, Houston, men would kill over a dime wager or a rash word. And it was always the evil ones that would kill the good or the stupid. If anyone should have died in that bar it should have been Mouse. If there was any kind of justice he should have been the one.

"He caught me one in the chest though, Ease," Mouse said, as if he could read my mind. "You know I was layin' up against the wall wit' no feelin' in my arms or legs. Everything was kinda fuzzy an' I hear this voice and I see this white face over me." He sounded almost like a prayer. "And that white face told me that he was death an' wasn't I scared. And you know what I told him?"

"What?" I asked, and at that same moment I resolved to leave Texas forever.

"I tole 'im that I had a man beat me four ways from sundown my whole life and I sent him t'hell. I say, 'I sent his son after 'im, so Satan stay wit' me and I whip yo' ass too.' "

Mouse laughed softly, laid his head on the bar, and went to sleep. I pulled out my wallet, quietly as if I were afraid to waken the dead, left two bills, and went down to the hotel. I was on a bus for Los Angeles before the sun came up.

*

But it seemed like a lifetime had passed since then. I was a landowner that night and I was working for my mortgage.

"Junior," I said. "Many white girls been in here lately?"

"Why? You lookin' fo' one?" Junior was naturally suspicious.

"Well . . . kinda."

"You kinda lookin' fo' one! When you gonna find out?"

"You see, uh, I heard about this girl. Um . . . Delia or Dahlia or sumpin'. I know it starts with a 'D.' Anyway she has blond hair and blue eyes and I been told that she was worth lookin' at."

"Cain't say I remember, man. I mean some white girls come in on the weekends, you know, but they don't never come alone. And I lose my job wolfin' after some other brother's date."

I had the notion that Junior was lying to me. Even if he knew the answer to my question he would have kept it quiet. Junior hated anybody who he thought was doing better than he was. Junior hated everybody.

"Yeah, well, I guess I'll see her if she comes in." I looked around the room. "There's a chair over there next to the band, think I'll grab it."

I knew Junior was watching me as I left him but I didn't care. He wouldn't help me and I didn't give a damn about him.

• 5 •

I found a chair next to my friend Odell Jones.

Odell was a quiet man and a religious man. His head was the color and shape of a red pecan. And even though he was a God-fearing man he'd find his way down to John's about three or four times a week. He'd sit there until midnight nursing a bottle of beer, not saying a word unless somebody spoke to him.

Odell was soaking up all the excitement so he could carry it around with him on his job as a janitor at the Pleasant Street school. Odell always wore an old gray tweed jacket and threadbare brown woolen pants.

"Hey, Odell," I greeted him.

"Easy."

"How's it going tonight?"

"Well," he said slowly, thinking it over. "It's goin' alright. It sure is goin'."

I laughed and slapped Odell on the shoulder. He was so slight that the force pushed him to the side but he just smiled and sat back up. Odell was older than most of my friends by twenty years or more; I think he was almost fifty then. To this day he's outlived two wives and three out of four children.

"What's it look like tonight, Odell?"

"'Bout two hours ago," he said while he scratched his left ear, "Fat Wilma Johnson come in with Toupelo and danced up a storm. She jump up in the air and come down so hard this whole room like t'shook."

"That Wilma like to dance," I said.

"Don't know how she keep that much heft, hard as she work and hard as she play."

"She probably eat hard too."

That tickled Odell.

I asked him to hold a seat for me while I went around saying hello.

I made the rounds shaking hands and asking people if they had seen a white girl, Delia or Dahlia or something. I didn't use her real name because I didn't want anybody to connect me with her if Mr. Albright turned out to be wrong and there was trouble. But no one had seen her. I would have even asked Frank Green but he was gone by the time I worked my way to the bar.

When I got back to my table Odell was still there and smiling.

"Hilda Redd come in," he said to me.

"Yeah?"

"Lloyd try to make a little time an' she hit him in that fat gut so hard he a'most went down." Odell acted out Lloyd's part, puffing his cheeks and bulging his eyes.

We were still laughing when I heard a shout that was so loud even Lips looked up from his horn.

"Easy!"

Odell looked up.

"Easy Rawlins, is that you?"

A big man walked into the room. A big man in a white suit with blue pinstripes and a ten-gallon hat. A big black man with a wide white grin who moved across the crowded room like a cloudburst, raining hellos and howyadoin's on the people he passed as he waded to our little table.

"Easy!" he laughed. "You ain't jumped outta no windahs yet?"

"Not yet, Dupree."

"You know Coretta, right?"

I noticed her there behind Dupree; he had her in tow like a child's toy wagon.

"Hi, Easy," she said in a small voice.

"Hey, Coretta, how are ya?"

"Fine," she said quietly. She spoke so softly that I was surprised I understood her over the music and the noise. Maybe I really didn't hear her at all but just understood what she meant by the way she looked at me and the way she smiled.

Dupree and Coretta were as different as any two people could be. He was muscular and had an inch or two on me, maybe six-two, and he was loud and friendly as a big dog. Dupree was a smart man as far as books and numbers went but he was always broke because he'd squander his money on liquor and women, and if there was any left over you could talk him out of it with any old hard-luck story.

But Coretta was something else altogether. She was short and round with cherry-brown skin and big freckles. She always wore dresses that accented her bosom. Coretta was sloe-eyed. Her gaze moved from one part of the room to another almost aimlessly, but you still had the feeling that she was watching you. She was a vain man's dream.

"Miss ya down at the plant, Ease," Dupree said. "Yeah, it just ain't the same wit'out you down there t'keep me straight. Them other niggahs just cain't keep up."

"I guess you have to do without me from now on, Dupree."

"Uh-uh, no. I can't live with that. Benny wants you back, Easy. He's sorry he let you go."

"First I heard of it."

"You know them I-talians, Ease, they cain't say they sorry 'cause it's a shame to'em. But he wants you back through, I know that."

"Could we sit down with you and Odell, Easy?" Coretta said sweetly.

"Sure, sure. Get her a chair, Dupree. Com'on pull up here between us, Coretta."

I called the bartender to send over a quart of bourbon and a pail of chipped ice.

"So he wants me back, huh?" I asked Dupree once we all had a glass.

"Yeah! He told me this very day that if you walked in that door he'd take you back in a minute."

"First he want me to kiss his be-hind," I said. I noticed that Coretta's glass was already empty. "You want me to freshen that, Coretta?"

"Maybe I'll have another lil taste, if you wanna pour." I could feel her smile all the way down my spine.

Dupree said, "Shoot, Easy, I told him that you was sorry 'bout what happened an' he's willin' t'let it pass."

"I'm a sorry man alright. Any man without his paycheck is sorry."

Dupree's laugh was so loud that he almost knocked poor Odell over with the volume. "Well see, there you go!" Dupree bellowed. "You come on down on Friday an' we got yo' job back for sure."

I asked them about the girl too, but it was no use.

At midnight, exactly, Odell stood up to leave. He said goodnight to Dupree and me, then he kissed Coretta's hand. She even kindled a fire under that quiet little man.

Then Dupree and I settled in to tell lies about the war. Coretta laughed and put away whiskey. Lips and his trio played on. People came in and out of the bar all night but I had given up on Miss Daphne Monet for the evening. I figured that if I got my job back at the plant I could return Mr. Albright's money. Anyway, the whiskey made me lazy—all I wanted to do was laugh.

Dupree passed out before we finished the second quart; that was about 3 A.M.

Coretta twisted up her nose at the back of his head and said, "He use' to play till the cock crowed, but that ole cock don't crow nearly so much no mo'."

• 6 •

"They done throwed him outta his place cuz he missed the rent," Coretta said.

We were dragging Dupree from the car to her door; his feet trailed two deep furrows in the landlord's lawn.

She went on to say, "First-class machinist at almost five dollars a hour but he cain't even pay his bills."

I couldn't help thinking that she wouldn't have been so put out if Dupree held his liquor a little better.

"Throw 'im in there on the bed, Easy," she said after we got him through the front door.

Dupree was a big man and he was lucky that I could pile him in the bed at all. By the time I was through pulling and pushing his dead weight I was exhausted. I stumbled from Coretta's tiny bedroom to her even smaller living room.

She poured me a little nightcap and we sat on her sofa. We sat close to each other because her room wasn't much larger than a broom closet. And if I said something halfway funny she'd laugh and rock until she bent down to clutch my knee for a moment and then she'd look up to shine her hazel eyes on me. We spoke softly and Dupree's deep snoring drowned out a good half of whatever we said. Every time Coretta had something to say she whispered it in a confidential way and shifted a little closer to me, to make sure I heard her.

When we were so close that we were passing the same breath back and forth between us, I said, "I better be goin', Coretta. Sun catch me tiptoein' out your door and no tellin' what your neighbors say."

"Hmm! Dupree fall asleep on me an' you jus' gonna turn your back, walk out the door like I was dog food."

"You got another man right in the next room, baby. What if he hears sumpin'?"

"Way he snorin'?" She slid her hand into her blouse, lifting the bodice to air her breasts.

I staggered to my feet and took the two steps to the door.

"You be sorry if you go, Ease."

"I be more sorry if I stay," I said.

She didn't say anything to that. She just laid back on the sofa, fanning her bosom.

"I gotta go," I said. I even opened the door.

"Daphne be 'sleep now," Coretta smiled, and popped open a button. "You cain't get none'a that right now."

"What you call her?"

"Daphne. Ain't that right? You said Delia but that ain't her real name. We got real tight last week when her date an' my date was at the Playroom."

"Dupree?"

"Naw, Easy, it was somebody else. You know I never got just one boyfriend."

Coretta got up and walked right into my arms. I could smell the scent of cool jasmine coming in through the screen door and hot jasmine rising from her breast.

I had been old enough to kill men in a war but I wasn't a man yet. At least I wasn't a man the way Coretta was a woman. She straddled me on the couch and whispered, "Oh yeah, daddy, you hittin' my spot! Oh yeah, yeah!" It was all I could do not to yell. Then she jumped off of me saying, in a shy voice, "Oooo, that's jus' *too* good, Easy." I tried to pull her back but Coretta never went where she didn't want to go. She just twisted down to the floor and said, "I cain't get up off'a that much love, daddy, not the way things is."

"What things?" I cried.

"You know." She gestured with a twist of her head. "Dupree's right there in the next room."

"Fo'get about him! You got me goin', Coretta."

"It just ain't right, Easy. Here I am doin' this right in the next room and all you doin' is nosin' after my friend Daphne."

"I ain't after her, honey. It's just a job, that's all."

"What job?"

"Man wants me to find her."

"What man?"

"Who cares what man? I ain't nosin' after nobody but you."

"But Daphne's my friend . . ."

"Just some boyfriend, Coretta, that's all."

When I started to lose my excitement she gave me her spot again and let me hit it some more. In that way she kept me talking until the sky turned light. She *did* tell me who Daphne's boyfriend was; I wasn't happy to hear it, but it was better that I knew.

When Dupree started coughing like a man about to wake up I hustled on my pants and made to leave. Coretta hugged me around the chest and sighed, "Don't ole Coretta get a little ten dollars if you fines that girl, Easy? I *was* the one said about it."

"Sure, baby," I said. "Soon as I get it." When she kissed me goodbye I could tell the night was over. Her kiss would have hardly roused a dead man.

• 7 •

When I finally made it back to my house, on 116th Street, it was another beautiful California day. Big white clouds sailed eastward toward the San Bernadino mountain range. There were still traces of snow on the peaks and there was the lingering scent of burning trash in the air.

My studio couch was in the same position it had been in the morning before. The paper I'd been reading that morning was still folded neatly on my upholstered chair. The breakfast plates were in the sink.

I opened the blinds and picked up the stack of mail the mailman had dropped through the door slot. Once I'd become a homeowner I got mail every day—and I loved it. I even loved junk mail.

There was a letter promising me a free year of insurance and one where I stood a chance of winning a thousand dollars. There was a chain letter that prophesied my death if I didn't send six exact copies to other people I knew and two silver dimes to a post office box in Illinois. I supposed that it was a white gang preying on the superstition of southern Negroes. I just threw that letter away.

But, on the whole, it was pretty nice sitting there in the slatted morning light and reading my mail. The electric percolator was making sounds from the kitchen and birds were chirping outside.

I turned over a big red packet full of coupons to show a tiny blue envelope underneath. It smelled of perfume and was written in a fancy woman's hand. It was postmarked from Houston and the name over the address read "Mr. Ezekiel Rawlins." That got me to move to the light of the kitchen window. It wasn't every day that I got a letter from home, by someone who knew my given name.

I looked out of the window for a moment before I read the letter. There was a jay looking down from the fence at the evil dog in the yard behind mine. The mongrel was growling and jumping at the bird. Every time he slammed his body against the wire fence the jay started as if he were about to fly off, but he didn't. He just kept staring down into those deadly jaws, mesmerized by the spectacle there.

Hey Easy!

Been a dog's age brother. Sophie give me your address. She come back down to Houston cause she say it's too much up there in Hollywood. Man, you know I asked her what she mean by too much but she just say, "Too much!" And you know every time I hear that I get a kind of chill like maybe too much is just right for me.

Everybody down here is the same. They tore down the Claxton Street Lodge. You should have seen the rats they had under that place!

Etta's good but she throwed me out. I come back from Lucinda's one night so drunk that I didn't even wash up. I sure am sorry about that. You know you gotta respect your woman, and a shower ain't too much to ask. But I guess she'll take me back one day.

You gotta see our boy, Easy. LaMarque is beautiful. You should see how big he is already! Etta says that he's lucky not to have my ratty look. But you know I think I see a little twinkle in his eye though. Anyway, he got big feet and a big mouth so I know he's doing okay.

I been thinking that maybe we ain't seen each other in too long, Ease. I been thinking maybe now I'm a bachelor again that maybe I could come visit and we burn down the town.

Why don't you write me and tell me when's a good time. You can send the letter to Etta, she see that I get it.

See you soon,

P.S. I got Lucinda writing this letter for me and I told her that if she don't write down every word like I say then I'm a beat her butt down Avenue B so hold onto it, alright?

At the first words I went to my closet. I don't know what I wanted to do there, maybe pack my bags and leave town. Maybe I just wanted to hide in the closet, I don't know.

When we were young men, in Texas, we were the best of friends. We fought in the streets side by side and we shared the same women without ever getting mad about it. What was a woman compared to the love of two friends? But when it came time for Mouse to marry EttaMae Harris things began to change.

He came to my house late one night and got me to drive him, in a stolen car, down to a little farming town called Pariah. He said that he was going to ask his stepfather for an inheritance his mother had promised him before she died.

Before we left that town Mouse's stepfather and a young man named Clifton had been shot dead. When I drove Mouse back to Houston he had more than a thousand dollars in his pocket.

I had nothing to do with those shootings. But Mouse told me what he did on the drive back home. He told me that he and Clifton held up daddyReese because the old man wouldn't relent to Mouse's claim. He told me that when Reese got to a gun Clifton was cut down, and then Mouse killed Reese. He said all that in complete innocence as he counted out three hundred dollars, blood money, for me.

Mouse didn't ever feel bad about anything he'd done. He was just that kind of man. He wasn't confessing to me, he was telling his story. There was nothing he ever did in his life that he didn't tell at least one person. And once he told me he gave me three hundred dollars so he would know I thought he had done right.

It was the worst thing I ever did to take that money. But my best friend would have put a bullet in my head if he ever thought that I was unsure of him. He would have seen me as an enemy, killed me for my lack of faith.

I ran away from Mouse and Texas to go to the army and then later to L.A. I hated myself. I signed up to fight in the war to prove to myself that I was a man. Before we launched the attack on D-Day I was frightened but I fought. I fought despite the fear. The first time I fought a German hand-to-hand I screamed for help the whole time I was killing him. His dead eyes stared at me a full five minutes before I let go of his throat.

The only time in my life that I had ever been completely free from fear was when I ran with Mouse. He was so confident that there was no room for fear. Mouse was barely five-foot-six but he'd go up against a man Dupree's size and you know I'd bet on the Mouse to walk away from it. He could put a knife in a man's stomach and ten minutes later sit down to a plate of spaghetti.

I didn't want to write Mouse and I didn't want to let it lie. In my mind he had such power that I felt I had to do whatever he wanted. But I had dreams that didn't have me running in the streets anymore; I was a man of property and I wanted to leave my wild days behind.

I drove down to the liquor store and bought a fifth of vodka and a gallon of grapefruit soda. I positioned myself in a chair at the front window and watched the day pass.

Looking out of the window is different in Los Angeles than it is in Houston. No matter where you live in a southern city (even a wild and violent place like Fifth Ward, Houston) you see almost everybody you know by just looking out your window. Every day is a parade of relatives and old friends and lovers you once had, and maybe you'd be lovers again one day.

That's why Sophie Anderson went back home I suppose. She liked the slower life of the South. When she looked out her window she wanted to see her friends and her family. And if she called out to one of them she wanted to know that they'd have the time to stop for a while and say hello.

Sophie was a real Southerner, so much so that she could never last in the workaday world of Los Angeles.

Because in L.A. people don't have time to stop; anywhere they have to go they go there in a car. The poorest man has a car in Los

Angeles; he might not have a roof over his head but he has a car. And he knows where he's going too. In Houston and Galveston, and way down in Louisiana, life was a little more aimless. People worked a little job but they couldn't make any real money no matter what they did. But in Los Angeles you could make a hundred dollars in a week if you pushed. The promise of getting rich pushed people to work two jobs in the week and do a little plumbing on the weekend. There's no time to walk down the street or make a bar-b-q when somebody's going to pay you real money to haul refrigerators.

So I watched empty streets that day. Every once in a while I'd see a couple of children on bicycles or a group of young girls going to the store for candy and soda pop. I sipped vodka and napped and reread Mouse's letter until I knew that there was nothing I could do. I decided to ignore it and if he ever asked I'd just look simple and act like it never got delivered.

By the time the sun went down I was at peace with myself. I had a name, an address, a hundred dollars, and the next day I'd go ask for my old job back. I had a house and an empty bottle of vodka that had made me feel good.

The letter was postmarked two weeks earlier. If I was very lucky Etta had already taken Mouse back in.

When the telephone woke me it was black outside.

"Hello?"

"Mr. Rawlins, I've been expecting your call."

That threw me. I said, "What?"

"I hope you have some good news for me."

"Mr. Albright, is that you?"

"Sure is, Easy. What's shaking?"

It took me another moment to compose myself. I had planned to call him in a few days so it would seem like I had worked for his money.

"I got what you want," I said, in spite of my plans. "She's with—"

"Hold on to that, Easy. I like to look a man in the face when we do business. Telephone's no place for business. Anyway, I can't give you your bonus on the phone."

"I can come down to your office in the morning."

"Why don't we get together now? You know where the merry-go-round is down at Santa Monica pier?"

"Well, yeah, but . . ."

"That's about halfway between us. Why don't we meet there?"

"But what time is it?"

"About nine. They close the ride in an hour so we can be alone."

"I don't know . . . I just got up . . ."

"I *am* paying you."

"Okay. I'll get down there soon as I can drive it."

He hung up in my ear.

• 8 •

There was still a large stretch of farmland between Los Angeles and Santa Monica in those days. The Japanese farmers grew artichokes, lettuce, and strawberries along the sides of the road. That night the fields were dark under the slight moon and the air was chill but not cold.

I was unhappy about going to meet Mr. Albright because I wasn't used to going into white communities, like Santa Monica, to conduct business. The plant I worked at, Champion Aircraft, was in Santa Monica but I'd drive out there in the daytime, do my work, and go home. I never loitered anywhere except among my own people, in my own neighborhood.

But the idea that I'd give him the information he wanted, and that he'd give me enough money to pay the next month's mortgage, made me happy. I was dreaming about the day I'd be able to buy more houses, maybe even a duplex. I always wanted to own enough land that it would pay for itself out of the rent it generated.

When I arrived the merry-go-round and arcade were closing down. Small children and their parents were leaving and a group of young people were milling around, smoking cigarettes and acting tough the way young people do.

I went across the pier to the railing that looked down onto the beach. I figured that Mr. Albright would see me there as well as any place and that I was far enough away from the white kids that I could avoid any ugliness.

But that wasn't my week for avoiding anything bad.

A chubby girl in a tight-fitting skirt wandered away from her friends. She was younger than the rest of them, maybe seventeen, and it seemed like she was the only girl without a date. When she saw me she smiled and said, "Hi." I answered and turned away to look out over the weakly lit shoreline north of Santa Monica. I was hoping that she'd leave and Albright would come and I'd be back in my house before midnight.

"It's pretty out here, huh?" Her voice came from behind me.

"Yeah. It's all right."

"I come from Des Moines, in Iowa. They don't have anything like the ocean back there. Are you from L.A.?"

"No. Texas." The back of my scalp was tingling.

"Do they have an ocean in Texas?"

"The Gulf, they have the Gulf."

"So you're used to it." She leaned on the rail next to me. "It still knocks me out whenever I see it. My name's Barbara. Barbara Moskowitz. That's a Jewish name."

"Ezekiel Rawlins," I whispered. I didn't want her so familiar as to use my nickname. When I glanced over my shoulder I noticed that a couple of the young men were looking around, like they'd lost someone.

"I think they're looking for you," I said.

"Who cares?" she answered. "My sister just brought me 'cause my parents made her. All she wants to do is make out with Herman and smoke cigarettes."

"It's still dangerous for a girl to be alone. Your parents are right to want you with somebody."

"Are you going to hurt me?" She stared into my face intently. I remember wondering what color her eyes were before I heard the shouting.

"Hey you! Black boy! What's happening here?" It was a pimply-faced boy. He couldn't have been more than twenty years and five and a half feet but he came up to me like a full-grown soldier. He wasn't afraid; a regular fool of a youth.

"What do you want?" I asked as politely as I could.

"You know what I mean," he said as he came within range of my grasp.

"Leave him alone, Herman!" Barbara yelled. "We were just talking!"

"You were, huh?" he said to me. "We don't need ya talking to our women."

I could have broken his neck. I could have put out his eyes or broken all of his fingers. But instead I held my breath.

Five of his friends were headed toward us. While they were coming on, not yet organized or together, I could have killed all of them too. What did they know about violence? I could have crushed their windpipes one by one and they couldn't have done a thing to stop me. They couldn't even run fast enough to escape me. I was still a killing machine.

"Hey!" the tallest one said. "What's wrong?"

"Nigger's trying to pick up Barbara."

"Yeah, an' she's just jailbait."

"Leave him alone!" Barbara shouted. "He was just saying where he was from."

I guess she was trying to help me, like a mother hugging her child when he's just broken his ribs.

"Barbara!" another girl shouted.

"Hey, man, what's wrong with you?" the big one asked in my face. He was wide-shouldered and a little taller than I; built like a football player. He had a broad, fleshy face. His eyes, nose, and mouth were like tiny islands on a great sea of white skin.

I noticed that a couple of the others had picked up sticks. They moved in around me, forcing me back against the rail.

"I don't want any problem, man," I said. I could smell the liquor on the tall one's breath.

"You already got a problem, boy."

"Listen, all she said was hi. That's all I said too." But I was thinking to myself, Why the hell do I have to answer to you?

Herman said, "He was telling' her where he lived. She said so herself."

I was trying to remember how far down the beach was. By then I knew I had to get out of there before there were two or three dead bodies, one of them being mine.

"Excuse me," a man's voice called out.

There was a slight commotion behind the football player and then a Panama hat appeared there next to him.

"Excuse me," Mr DeWitt Albright said again. He was smiling.

"What do you want?" the footballer said.

DeWitt just smiled and then he pulled the pistol, which looked somewhat like a rifle, from his coat. He leveled the barrel at the large boy's right eye and said, "I want to see your brains scattered all over your friends' clothes, son. I want you to die for me."

The large boy, who was wearing red swimming trunks, made a sound like he had swallowed his tongue. He moved his shoulder ever so slightly and DeWitt cocked back the hammer. It sounded like a bone breaking.

"I wouldn't move if I were you, son. I mean, if you were to breathe too heavily I'd just kill you. And if any of you other boys move I'll kill him and then I'll shoot off *all* your nuts."

The ocean was rumbling and the air had turned cold. The only human sound was from Barbara, who was sobbing in her sister's arms.

"I want you boys to meet my friend," DeWitt said. "Mr. Jones."

I didn't know what to do so I nodded.

"He's a friend'a mine," Mr. Albright continued. "And I'd be proud and happy if he was to lower himself to fuck my sister *and* my mother."

No one had anything to say to that.

"Now, Mr. Jones, I want to ask you something."

"Yes, sir, Mr., ah, Smith."

"Do you think that I should shoot out this nasty's boy's eyeball?"

I let that question hang for a bit. Two of the younger boys had been weeping already but the wait caused the footballer to start crying.

"Well," I said, after fifteen seconds or so, "if he's not sorry for bullying me then I think you should kill him."

"I'm sorry," said the boy.

"You are?" Mr. Albright asked.

"Y-y-yes!"

"How sorry are you? I mean, are you sorry enough?"

"Yessir, I am."

"You're sorry enough?" When he asked that question he moved the muzzle of the gun close enough to touch the boy's tiny, flickering eyelid. "Don't twitch now, I want you to see the bullet coming. Now are you sorry enough?"

"Yessir!"

"Then prove it. I want you to show him. I want you to get down on your knees and suck his peter. I want you to suck it good now . . ."

The boy started crying outright when Albright said that. I was pretty confident that he was just joking, in a sick kind of way, but my heart quailed along with the footballer.

"Down on your knees or you're dead, boy!"

The other boys had their eyes glued to the footballer as he went to his knees. They tore out running when Albright slammed the barrel of his pistol into the side of the boy's head.

"Get out of here!" Albright yelled. "And if you tell some cops I'll find every one of you."

We were alone in less than half a minute. I could hear the slamming of car doors and the revving of jalopy engines from the parking lot and the street.

"They got something to think about now," Albright said. He returned his long-barreled .44–caliber pistol to the holster inside his coat. The pier was abandoned; everything was dark and silent.

"I don't think that they'd dare call the cops on something like this but we should move on just in case," he said.

Albright's white Cadillac was parked in the lot down under the pier. He drove south down along the ocean. There were few electric lights from the coast, and just a sliver of moon, but the sea glittered with a million tiny glints. It looked like every shiny fish in the sea had come to the surface to mimic the stars that flickered in the sky. There was light everywhere and there was darkness everywhere too.

He switched on the radio and tuned in a big-band station that was playing "Two Lonely People," by Fats Waller. I remember because as soon as the music came on I started shivering. I wasn't afraid; I was angry, angry at the way he humiliated that boy. I didn't care about the boy's feelings, I cared that if Albright could do something like that to one of his own then I knew he could do the same, and much worse, to me. But if he wanted to shoot me he'd just have to do it because I wasn't going down on my knees for him or for anybody else.

I never doubted for a minute that Albright would have killed that boy.

"What you got, Easy?" he asked after a while.

"I got a name and an address. I got the last day she was seen and who she was with. I know the man she was seen with and I know what he does for a living." I was proud of knowledge when I was a young man. Joppy had told me just to take the money and to pretend I was looking for the girl, but once I had a piece of information I had to show it off.

"All that's worth the money."

"But I want to know something first."

"What's that?" Mr. Albright asked. He pulled the car onto a shoulder that overlooked the shimmering Pacific. The waves were really rolling that night, you could even hear them through the closed windows.

"I want to know that no harm is going to come to that girl, or anybody else."

"Do I look that much like God to you? Can I tell you what will happen tomorrow? I don't plan for the girl to be hurt. My friend thinks he's in love with her. He wants to buy her a gold ring and live happily ever after. But, you know, she might forget to buckle her shoes next week and fall down and break her neck, and if she does you can't hold me up for it. But whatever."

I knew that was the most I would get out of him. DeWitt made no promises but I believed that he meant no harm to the girl in the photograph.

"She was with a man named Frank Green, Tuesday last. They were at a bar called the Playroom."

"Where is she now?"

"Woman who told me said she thought that they were a team, Green and the girl, so she's probably with him."

"Where's that?" he asked. His smile and good manners were gone; this was business now—plain and simple.

"He's got an apartment at Skyler and Eighty-third. Place is called the Skyler Arms."

He took out the white pen and wallet and scribbled something on the notepad. Then he stared at me with those dead eyes while he tapped the steering wheel with the pen.

"What else?"

"Frank's a gangster," I said. That got DeWitt to smile again. "He's with hijackers. They take liquor and cigarettes; sell 'em all over southern California."

"Bad man?" DeWitt couldn't keep his smile down.

"Bad enough. He somethin' with a knife."

"You ever see him in action? I mean, you see him kill somebody?"

"I saw him cut a man in a bar once; loudmouth dude didn't know who Frank was."

DeWitt's eyes came to life for a moment; he leaned across the seat so far that I could feel his dry breath on my neck. "I want you to remember something, Easy. I want you to think about when Frank took his knife and stabbed that man."

I thought about it a second and then I nodded to let him know that I was ready.

"Before he went at him, did he hesitate? Even for a second?"

I thought about the crowded bar down on Figueroa. The big man was talking to Frank's woman and when Frank walked up to him he put his hand against Frank's chest, getting ready to push him away, I suppose. Frank's eyes widened and he threw his head around as if to say to the crowd, "Look at what this fool is doin'! He deserve t'be dead, stupid as he acts!" Then the knife appeared in Frank's hand

and the big man crumpled against the bar, trying to ward off the stroke with his big fleshy arms . . .

"Maybe just a second, not even that," I said.

Mr. DeWitt Albright laughed softly.

"Well," he said. "I guess I have to see what I shall see."

"Maybe you could get to the girl when he's out. Frank spends a lot of time on the road. I saw him the other night, at John's, he was dressed for hijacking, so he might be out of town for a couple of more days."

"That would be best," Albright answered. He leaned back across the seat. "No reason to be any messier than we have to, now. You got that photograph?"

"No," I lied. "Not on me. I left it at home."

He only looked at me for a second but I knew he didn't believe it. I don't know why I wanted to keep her picture. It's just that the way she looked out at me made me feel good.

"Well, maybe I'll pick it up after I find her; you know I like to make everything neat after a job . . . Here's another hundred and take this card too. All you have to do is go down to that address and you can pick up a job to tide you over until something else comes up."

He handed me a tight roll of bills and a card. I couldn't read the card in that dim light so I shoved it and the money in my pocket.

"I think I can get my old job back so I won't need the address."

"Hold on to it," he said, as he turned the ignition. "You did alright by me, getting this information, and I'm doing right by you. That's the way I do business, Easy; I always pay my debts."

The drive back was quiet and brilliant with night lights. Benny Goodman was on the radio and DeWitt Albright hummed along as if he had grown up with big bands.

When we pulled up to my car, next to the pier, everything was as it had been when we left. When I opened the door to get out Albright said, "Pleasure working with you, Easy." He extended his hand and when he had the snake grip on me again his look because quizzical and he said, "You know, I was wondering just one thing."

"What's that?"

"How come you let those boys get around you like that? You could have picked them off one by one before they got your back to the rails."

"I don't kill children," I said.

Albright laughed for the second time that night.

Then he let me go and said goodbye.

• 9 •

Our team worked in a large hangar on the south side of the Santa Monica plant. I got there early, about 6 A.M., before the day shift began. I wanted to get to Benny, Benito Giacomo, before they started working.

Once Champion designed a new aircraft, either for the air force or for one of the airlines, they had a few teams build them for a while to get out the kinks in construction. Benito's team would, for instance, put together the left wing and move it on to another group in charge of assembly for the entire aircraft. But instead of assembling the plane a group of experts would go over our work with a magnifying glass to make sure that the procedures they set up for production were good.

It was an important job and all the men were proud to be on it but Benito was so high-strung that whenever we had a new project he'd turn sour.

That's really why he fired me.

I was coming off a hard shift, we had two men out with the flu and I was tired. Benny wanted us to stay longer just to check out our work but I didn't want any of it. I was tired and I knew that anything I looked at would have gotten a passing grade, so I said that we should wait until morning. The men listened to me. I wasn't a team leader but Benny relied on me to set an example for others because I was such a good worker. But that was just a bad day. I needed sleep to do the job right and Benny didn't trust me enough to hear that.

He told me that I had to work hard if I wanted to get the promotion we'd talked about; a promotion that would put me just a grade below Dupree.

I told him that I worked hard every day.

A job in a factory is an awful lot like working on a plantation in the South. The bosses see all the workers like they're children, and everyone knows how lazy children are. So Benny thought he'd teach me a little something about responsibility because he was the boss and I was the child.

The white workers didn't have a problem with that kind of treatment because they didn't come from a place where men were always called boys. The white worker would have just said, "Sure, Benny, you called it right, but damn if I can see straight right now." And Benny would have understood that. He would have laughed and realized how pushy he was being and offered to take Mr. Davenport, or whoever, out to drink a beer. But the Negro workers didn't drink with Benny. We didn't go to the same bars, we didn't wink at the same girls.

What I should have done, if I wanted my job, was to stay, like he asked, and then come back early the next day to recheck the work. If I had told Benny I couldn't see straight he would have told me to buy glasses.

So there I was at the mouth of the man-made cave of an airplane hangar. The sun wasn't really up but everything was light. The large cement floor was empty except for a couple of trucks and a large tarp over the wing assembly. It felt good and familiar to be back there. No jazzy photographs of white girls anywhere, no strange white men with dead blue eyes. I was in a place of family men and working men who went home to their own houses at night and read the newspaper and watched Milton Berle.

"Easy!"

Dupree's shout always sounded the same whether he was happy to see you or he was about to pull out his small-barreled pistol.

"Hey, Dupree!" I shouted.

"What you say to Coretta, man?" he asked as he came up to me.

"Nuthin', nuthin' at all. What you mean?"

"Well, either you said sumpin' or I got bad breath because she tore out yesterday mornin' an' I ain't seen 'er since."

"What?"

"Yeah! She fixed me some breakfast an' then said she had some business so she'd see me fo' dinner and that's the last I seen of 'er."

"She din't come home?"

"Nope. You know I come in an' burnt some pork chops to make up for the night before but she din't come in."

Dupree had a couple of inches on me and he was built like Joppy when Joppy was still a boxer. He was hovering over me and I could feel the violence come off of him in waves.

"No, man, I didn't say a thing. We put you in the bed, then she gave me a drink and I went home. That's all."

"Then where is she?" he demanded.

"How you expect me t'know? You know Coretta. She likes to keep her secrets. Maybe she's with her auntie out in Compton. She could be in Reno."

Dupree relaxed a little and laughed. "You prob'ly right, Easy. Coretta hear them slot machines goin' an' she leave her own momma."

He slapped me on the back and laughed again.

I swore to myself that I'd never look at another man's woman. I've taken that pledge many times since then.

"Rawlins," came a voice from the small office at the back of the hangar.

"There you go," Dupree said.

I walked toward the man who had called me. The office he stood before was a prefabricated green shell, more like a tent than a room. Benny kept his desk in there and only went in himself to meet with the bosses or to fire one of the men. He called me in there four days before to tell me that Champion couldn't use men that didn't give "a little extra."

"Mr. Giacomo," I said. We shook but there was no friendliness in it.

Benny was shorter than I but he had broad shoulders and big hands. His salt-and-pepper hair had once been jet black and his skin color was darker than many mulattos I'd known. But Benny was a white man and I was a Negro. He wanted me to work hard for him and he needed me to be grateful that he allowed me to work at all. His eyes were close-set so he looked intent. His shoulders were slightly hunched, which made him seem like an advancing boxer.

"Easy," he said.

We went into the shell and he pointed at a chair. He took a seat behind the desk, kicked his foot up on it, and lit a cigarette.

"Dupree says that you want back on the job, Easy."

I was thinking that Benny probably had a bottle of rye in the bottom drawer of his desk.

"Sure, Mr. Giacomo, you know I need this job to eat." I concentrated on keeping my head erect. I wasn't going to bow down to him.

"Well, you know that when you fire somebody you have to stick to your guns. The men might get to thinkin' that I'm weak if I take you back."

"So what am I doin' here?" I said to his face.

He leaned farther back in his chair and hunched his large shoulders. "You tell me."

"Dupree said that you would give me my job back."

"I don't know who gave him the authority to say that. All I said was that I'd be glad to talk to you if you had something to say. Do you have something to say?"

I tried to think about what Benny wanted. I tried to think of how I could save face and still kiss his ass. But all I could really think about was that other office and that other white man. DeWitt Albright had his bottle and his gun right out there in plain view. When he asked me what I had to say I told him; I might have been a little nervous, but I told him anyway. Benny didn't care about what I had to say. He needed all his children to kneel down and let him be the boss. He wasn't a businessman, he was a plantation boss; a slaver.

"Well, Easy?"

"I want my job back, Mr. Giacomo. I need to work and I do a good job."

"Is that all?"

"No, that's not all. I need money so that I can pay my mortgage and eat. I need a house to live in and a place to raise children. I need to buy clothes so I can go to the pool hall and to church . . ."

Benny put his feet down and made to rise. "I have to get back to my job, Easy . . ."

"That's Mr. Rawlins!" I said as I rose to meet him. "You don't have to give me my job back but you have got to treat me with respect."

"Excuse me," he said. He made to go past me but I was blocking his way.

"I said, you have got to treat me with respect. Now I call you Mr. Giacomo because that's your name. You're no friend to me and I got no reason to be disrespectful and call you by your first name." I pointed at my chest. "My name is Mr. Rawlins."

He balled his fists and looked down at my chest the way a fighter does. But I think he heard the quaver in my voice. He knew that one or two of us would be broken up if he tried to go through me. And who knows? Maybe he realized that he was in the wrong.

"I'm sorry, Mr. Rawlins," he smiled at me. "But there are no openings right now. Maybe you could come back in a few months, when production on the new fighter line begins."

With that he motioned for me to leave his office. I went without another word.

I looked around for Dupree but he was nowhere to be seen, not even at his station. That surprised me but I was too happy to worry about him. My chest was heaving and I felt as if I wanted to laugh out loud. My bills were paid and it felt good to have stood up for myself. I had a notion of freedom when I walked out to my car.

• 10 •

I was home by noon. The street was empty and the neighborhood was quiet. There was a dark Ford parked across the street from my house. I remember thinking that a bill collector was making his rounds. Then I laughed to myself because all my bills were paid well in advance. I was a proud man that day; my fall wasn't far behind.

As I was closing the gate to the front yard I saw the two white men getting out of the Ford. One was tall and skinny and he was wearing a dark blue suit. The other one was my height and three times my girth. He had on a wrinkled tan suit that had greasy spots here and there.

The men strode quickly in my direction but I just turned slowly and walked toward my door.

"Mr. Rawlins!" one of them called from behind.

I turned. "Yeah?"

They were approaching fast but cautiously. The fat one had a hand in his pocket.

"Mr. Rawlins, I'm Miller and this is my partner Mason." They both held out badges.

"Yeah?"

"We want you to come with us."

"Where?"

"You'll see," fat Mason said as he took me by the arm.

"Are you arresting me?"

"You'll see," Mason said again. He was pulling me toward the gate.

"I've got the right to know why you're taking me."

"You got a right to fall down and break your face, nigger. You got a right to die," he said. Then he hit me in the diaphragm. When I doubled over he slipped the handcuffs on behind my back and together they dragged me to the car. They tossed me in the back seat where I lay gagging.

"You vomit on my carpet and I'll feed it to ya," Mason called back.

They drove me to the Seventy-seventh Street station and carried me in the front door.

"You got 'im, huh, Miller?" somebody said. They were holding me by my arms and I was sagging with my head down. I had recovered from the punch but I didn't want them to know it.

"Yeah, we got him coming home. Nothing on 'im."

They opened the door to a small room that smelled faintly of urine. The walls were unpainted plaster and there was only a bare wooden chair for furniture. They didn't offer me the chair though, they just dropped me on my knees and walked out, closing the door behind them.

The door had a tiny peephole in it.

I pushed my shoulder against the wall until I was standing. The room didn't look any better. There were a few bare pipes along the ceiling that dripped now and then. The edge of the linoleum floor was corroded and chalky from the moisture. There was only one window. It didn't have glass but only a crisscross of two two-inch bars down and two bars across. Very little light came in through the window due to the branches and leaves that had pushed their way in. It was a small room, maybe twelve by twenty, and I had some fear that it was to be the last room I ever inhabited.

I was worried because they didn't follow the routine. I had played the game of "cops and nigger" before. The cops pick you up, take your name and fingerprints, then they throw you into a holding tank with other "suspects" and drunks. After you were sick from the vomit and foul language they'd take you to another room and ask why you robbed that liquor store or what did you do with the money?

I would try to look innocent while I denied what they said. It's hard acting innocent when you are but the cops know that you aren't. They figure that you did something because that's just the way cops think, and you telling them that you're innocent just proves to them that you have something to hide. But that wasn't the game that we were playing that day. They knew my name and they didn't need to scare me with any holding tank; they didn't need to take my fingerprints. I didn't know why they had me, but I did know that it didn't matter as long as they thought they were right.

I sat down in the chair and looked up at the leaves coming in through the window. I counted thirty-two bright green oleander leaves. Also coming in through the window was a line of black ants that ran down the side of the wall and around to the other side of the room where the tiny corpse of a mouse was crushed into a corner. I speculated that another prisoner had killed the mouse by stamping it. He probably had tried in the middle of the floor at first but the quick rodent had swerved away two, maybe even three times. But finally the mouse made the deadly mistake of looking for a crevice in the wall and the inmate was able to block off his escape by using both feet. The mouse looked papery and dry so I supposed that the death had occurred at the beginning of the week; about the time I was getting fired.

While I was thinking about the mouse the door opened again and the officers stepped in. I was angry at myself because I hadn't tried to see if the door was locked. Those cops had me where they wanted me.

"Ezekiel Rawlins," Miller said.

"Yes, sir."

"We have a few questions to ask. We can take off those cuffs if you want to start cooperating."

"I am cooperating."

"Told ya, Bill," fat Mason said. "He's a smart nigger."

"Take off the cuffs, Charlie," Miller said and the fat man obliged.

"Where were you yesterday morning at about 5 A.M.?"

"What morning is that?" I stalled.

"He means," fat Mason said as he planted his foot in my chest and pushed me over backwards, "Thursday morning."

"Get up," Miller said.

I got to my feet and righted the chair.

"That's hard to say." I sat down again. "I was out drinking and then I helped carry a drunk friend home. I could'a been on my way home or maybe I was already in bed. I didn't look at a clock."

"What friend is that?"

"Pete. My friend Pete."

"Pete, huh?" Mason chuckled. He wandered over to my left and before I could turn toward him I felt the hard knot of his fist explode against the side of my head.

I was on the ground again.

"Get up," Miller said.

I got up again.

"So where was you and your peter drinkin'?" Mason sneered.

"Down at a friend's on Eighty-nine."

Mason moved again but this time I turned. He just looked at me with an innocent face and his palms turned upward.

"Would that be an illegal nightclub called John's?" Miller asked.

I was quiet.

"You got bigger problems than busting your friend's bar, Ezekiel. You got bigger troubles than that."

"What kinda troubles?"

"Big troubles."

"What's that mean?"

"Means we can take your black ass out behind the station and put a bullet in your head," Mason said.

"Where were you at five o'clock on Thursday morning, Mr. Rawlins?" Miller asked.

"I don't know exactly."

Mason had taken off his shoe and started swatting the heel against his fat palm.

"Five o'clock," Miller said.

We played that game a little while longer. Finally I said, "Look, you don't have to beat up your hand on my account; I'm happy to tell you what you wanna know."

"You ready to cooperate?" Miller asked.

"Yes, sir."

"Where did you go when you left Coretta James' house on Thursday morning?"

"I went home."

Mason tried to kick the chair out from under me but I was on my feet before he could.

"I had enough'a this shit, man!" I yelled, but neither cop seemed very impressed. "I told you I went home, and that's all."

"Have a seat, Mr. Rawlins," Miller said calmly.

"Why'm I gonna sit and you keep tryin' to knock me down?" I cried. But I sat down anyway.

"I told ya he was crazy, Bill," Mason said. "I told ya this was a section eight."

"Mr. Rawlins," Miller said. "Where did you go after you left Miss James' house?"

"I went home."

No one hit me that time; no one tried to kick the chair.

"Did you see Miss James later that day?"

"No, sir."

"Did you have an altercation with Mr. Bouchard?"

I understood him but I said, "Huh?"

"Did you and Dupree Bouchard have words over Miss James?"

"You know," Mason chimed in. "Pete."

"That's what I call him sometimes," I said.

"Did you," Miller repeated, "have an altercation with Mr. Bouchard?"

"I didn't have nuthin' with Dupree. He was asleep."

"So where did you go on Thursday?"

"I went home with a hangover. I stayed there all day and night and then I went to work today. Well"—I wanted to keep them talking so that Mason wouldn't lose his temper with the furniture again—"not to work really because I got fired Monday. But I went to get my job back."

"Where did you go on Thursday?"

"I went home with a hangover . . ."

"Nigger!" Mason tore into me with his fists. He knocked me to the floor but I grabbed onto his wrists. I swung around and twisted so that I was straddling his back, sitting on his fat ass. I could have killed him the way I'd killed other white men in uniforms, but I could feel Miller behind me so I stood straight up and moved to the corner.

Miller had a police special in his hand.

Mason made like he was going to come after me again but the belly-flop had winded him. From his knees Mason said, "Lemme have 'im alone for a minute."

Miller weighed the request. He kept looking back and forth between me and the fat man. Maybe he was afraid that I'd kill his partner or maybe he didn't want the paperwork; it could have been that Miller was a secret humanitarian who didn't want bloodshed and ruin on his hands. Finally he whispered, "No."

"But . . ." Mason started.

"I said no. Let's move."

Miller hooked his free hand under the fat man's armpit and helped him to his feet. Then he holstered his pistol and straightened his coat. Mason sneered at me and then followed Miller out of the cell door. He was starting to remind me of a trained mutt. The lock snapped behind them.

I got back in the chair and counted the leaves again. I followed the ants to the dead mouse again. This time though, I imagined that I was the convict and that mouse was officer Mason. I crushed him so that his whole suit was soiled and shapeless in the corner; his eyes came out of his head.

There was a light bulb hanging from a wire at the ceiling but there was no way to turn it on. Slowly the little sun that filtered in through the leaves faded and the room became twilight. I sat in the chair pressing my bruises now and then to see if the pain was lessening.

I didn't think a thing. I didn't wonder about Coretta or Dupree or how the police knew so much about my Wednesday night. All I did was sit in darkness, trying to become the darkness. I was awake but my thinking was like a dream. I dreamed in my wakefulness that I could become the darkness and slip out between the eroded cracks of that cell. If I was nighttime nobody could find me; no one would even know I was missing.

I saw faces in the darkness; beautiful women and feasts of ham and pie. It's only now that I realize how lonely and hungry I was then.

It was fully black in that cell when the light snapped on. I was still trying to blink away the glare when Miller and Mason came in. Miller closed the door.

"You think of anything else to say?" Miller asked me.

I just looked at him.

"You can go," Miller said.

"You heard him, nigger!" Mason shouted while he was fumbling around to check that his fly was zipped up. "Get outta here!"

They led me into the open room and past the desk watch. Everywhere people turned to stare at me. Some laughed, some were shocked.

They took me to the desk sergeant, who handed me my wallet and pocketknife.

"We might be in touch with you later, Mr. Rawlins," Miller said. "If we have any questions we know where you live."

"Questions about what?" I asked, trying to sound like an honest man asking an honest question.

"That's police business."

"Ain't it my business if you drag me outta my own yard an' bring me down here an' throw me around?"

"You want a complaint form?" Miller's thin, gray face didn't change expression. He looked like a man I once knew, Orrin Clay. Orrin had a peptic ulcer and always held his mouth like he was just about to spit.

"I wanna know what's goin' on," I said.

"We'll be coming 'round if we need you."

"How am I supposed to get home from way out here? The buses stop after six."

Miller turned away from me. Mason was already gone.

• 11 •

I left the station at a fast walk but I wanted to run.

It was fifteen blocks to John's speak and I had to keep telling myself to slow down. I knew that a patrol car would arrest any sprinting Negro they encountered.

The streets were especially dark and empty. Central Avenue was like a giant black alley and I felt like a small rat, hugging the corners and looking out for cats.

Every once in a while a car would shoot past. Maybe I'd catch a snatch of music or laughter and then they'd be gone. There wasn't another soul out walking.

I was three blocks from the station when I heard, "Hey you! Easy Rawlins!"

A black Cadillac had pulled up beside me and matched my pace. It was a long automobile; long enough to be two cars. A white face in a black cap stuck out of the driver's window. "Come on, Easy, over here," the face said.

"Who are you?" I asked over my shoulder, then I turned to keep on walking.

"Come on, Easy," the face said again. "Somebody in the back wants to talk to you."

"I don't have the time right now, man. I gotta go." I had doubled my pace so that I was nearly running.

"Jump in. We'll take you where you're going," he said, and then he said "What?" not to me but to whoever his passenger was.

"Easy," he said again. I hate it when someone I don't know knows me by name. "My boss wants to give you fifty dollars to take a ride."

"Ride where?" I didn't slow my stride.

"Wherever you want to go."

I stopped talking and kept on walking.

The Cadillac sped on ahead and pulled onto the curb about thirty feet ahead of me. The driver's door swung open and he came out. He had to unfold his long legs from his chest to climb out from the seat. When he stood up I could see that he was a tall man with a thin, almost crescent face and light hair that was either gray or blond—I couldn't tell which by lamplight.

He held his hands out in front of him, about shoulder height. It was a strange gesture because it looked like he was asking for peace but I knew he could have grabbed me from that pose too.

"Listen here, man," I said. I crouched back thinking that it would be easiest to take a tall man down at the knee. "I'm goin' home. That's all I'm doin'. Your friend wanna talk, then you better tell 'im to get me on the phone."

The tall driver pointed behind with his thumb and said, "Man told me to tell you that he knows why the police took you in, Easy. He says he wants to talk about it."

The driver had a grin on his face and faraway look in his eye. While I looked at him I got tired. I felt that if I lunged at him I'd just fall on my face. Anyway, I wanted to find out why the police had taken me in.

"Just talk, right?" I asked.

"If he wanted to hurt you you'd already be dead."

The driver opened the door to the back seat and I climbed in. The moment the door shut I gagged on the odors. The smells were sweet like perfume and sour, an odor of the body that I recognized but could put no name to.

The car took off in reverse and I was thrown into the seat with my back to the driver. Before me sat a fat white man. His round white face looked like a moon in the flashes of passing lamplight. He was smiling. Behind his seat was a shallow storage area. I thought I saw something moving around back there but before I could look closer he spoke to me.

"Where is she, Mr. Rawlins?"

"'Scuse me?"

"Daphne Monet. Where is she?"

"Who's that?"

I never got used to big lips on white people, especially white men. This white man had lips that were fat and red. They looked like swollen wounds.

"I know why they took you in there, Mr. Rawlins." He gestured with his head to say the police station behind. But when he did that I looked in the storage area again. He looked pleased and said, "Come on out, honey."

A small boy climbed over the seat. He was wearing soiled briefs and dirty white socks. His skin was brown and his thick straight hair was black. The almond-shaped eyes spoke of China but this was a Mexican boy.

He climbed down to the floor and curled around the fat man's leg.

"This is my little man," the fat man said. "He's the only reason I can keep on going."

The sight of that poor child and the odors made me cringe. I tried not to think about what I was seeing because I couldn't do anything about it—at least not right then.

"I don't know what you want with me, Mr. Teran," I said. "But I don't know why the police arrested me and I don't know no Daphne nobody. All I want is to get home and put this whole night behind me."

"So you know who I am?"

"I read the paper. You were running for mayor."

"Could be again," he said. "Could be again. And maybe you could help." He reached down to scratch the little boy behind the ear.

"I don't know what you mean. I don't know nuthin'."

"The police wanted to know what you did after you had drinks with Coretta James and Dupree Bouchard."

"Yeah?"

"I don't care about that, Easy. All I want to know is if somebody used the name Daphne Monet."

I shook my head, no.

"Did anybody," he hesitated, "strange . . . want to talk to Coretta?"

"What you mean, strange?"

Matthew Teran smiled at me for a moment, then he said, "Daphne is a white girl, Easy. Young and pretty. It means an awful lot to me if I can find her."

"I can't help ya, man. I don't even know why they pulled me in there. Do you know?"

Instead of answering me he asked, "Did you know Howard Green?"

"I met 'im once or twice."

"Did Coretta say anything about him that night?"

"Not a word." It felt good to tell the truth.

"How about your friend Dupree? Did he say anything?"

"Dupree drinks. That's what he does. And when he's finished drinking, then he goes to sleep. That's what he did. That's all he did."

"I'm a powerful man, Mr. Rawlins." He didn't need to tell me. "And I wouldn't want to think that you were lying to me."

"Do you know why the cops took me in?"

Matthew Teran picked up the little Mexican boy and hugged him to his chest.

"What do you think, honey?" he asked the boy.

Thick mucus threatened to flow from the boy's nose. His mouth was open and he stared at me as if I were a strange animal. Not a dangerous animal, maybe the corpse of a dog or porcupine run over and bleeding on the highway.

Mr. Teran picked up an ivory horn that hung next to his head and spoke into it. "Norman, take Mr. Rawlins where he wants to go. We're finished for the time being." Then he handed the horn to me. It smelled strongly of sweet oils and sour bodies. I tried to ignore the smells as I gave Norman the address of John's speak.

"Here's your money, Mr. Rawlins," Teran said. He was holding a few damp bills in his hand.

"No thanks." I didn't want to touch anything that that man had touched.

"My office is listed in the book, Mr. Rawlins. If you find something out I think you might find me helpful."

When the car stopped in front of John's I got out as fast as I could.

"Easy!" Hattie yelled. "What happened to you, baby?"

She came around the counter to put her hand on my shoulder.

"Cops," I said.

"Oh, baby. Was it about Coretta?"

Everyone seemed to know about my life.

"What about Coretta?"

"Ain't you heard?"

I just stared at her.

"Coretta been murdered," she said. "I hear the police took Dupree outta his job 'cause he been out there with her. And I knowed you was with 'em on Wednesday so I figured the police might'a s'pected you."

"Murdered?"

"Just like Howard Green. Beat her so bad that it was her mother who had to tell 'em."

"Dead?"

"What they do to you, Easy?"

"Is Odell here, Hattie?"

"Come in 'bout seven."

"What time is it?"

"Ten."

"Could you get Odell for me?" I asked.

"Sure can, Easy. You just let me get Junior t'do it."

She stuck her head in the door and then came back. In a few minutes Odell came out. I could see that I must've looked bad by the expression on Odell's face. He rarely showed any emotion at all but right then he looked like he'd seen a ghost.

"Could you give me a ride home, Odell? I don't have my car."

"Sure thing, Easy."

Odell was quiet for most of the ride but when we got close to my house he said, "You better get some rest, Easy."

"I sure intend to try, Odell."

"I don't mean just sleep, now. I mean some real rest, like a vacation or somethin'."

I laughed. "A woman once told me that poor people can't afford no vacations. She said that we gotta keep workin' or we end up dead."

"You don't have to stop workin'. I mean more like a change. Maybe you should go on down t'Houston or maybe even Galveston where they don't know you too good."

"Why you say that, Odell?"

We pulled up to my house. My Pontiac was a welcome sight, parked there and waiting for me. I could have driven across the nation with the money Albright had given me.

"First Howard Green gets killed, then Coretta goes the same way. Police do this to you and they say Dupree's still in jail. Time to go."

"I can't go, Odell."

"Why not?"

I looked at my house. My beautiful home.

"I just can't," I said. "But I do think you're right."

"If you don't leave, Easy, then you better look for some help."

"What kind'a help you mean?"

"I don't know. Maybe you should come on down to church on Sunday. Maybe you could talk to Reverend Towne."

"Lord ain't got no succor fo' this mess. I'm'a have to look somewhere else."

I got out of his car and waved him goodbye. But Odell was a good friend; he waited there until I had hobbled to my door and stumbled into the house.

• 12 •

I put away a pint and a half of bourbon before I could get to sleep. The sheets were crisp and dry and the fear was far enough away in the alcohol, but whenever I closed my eyes Coretta was there, hunching over me and kissing my chest.

I was still young enough that I couldn't imagine death really happening to someone I knew. Even in the war I expected to see friends again, though I knew they were dead.

The night carried on like that. I'd fall asleep for a few minutes only to wake up calling Coretta's name or to answer her calling me. If I couldn't fall back to sleep I'd reach for the bottle of whiskey next to the bed.

Later that night the phone rang.

"Huh?" I mumbled.

"Easy? Easy, that you?" came a rough voice.

"Yeah. What time is it?"

"'Bout three. You 'sleep, man?"

"What you think? Who is this?"

"Junior. Don't you know me?"

It took me a while to remember who he was. Junior and I had never been friends and I couldn't even think of where he might have found my phone number.

"Easy? Easy! You fallin' back asleep?"

"What you want this time'a mornin', Junior?"

"Ain't nuthin'. Nuthin'."

"Nuthin'? You gonna get me outta my bed at three fo' nuthin'?"

"Don't go soundin' off on me now, man. I just wanted to tell you what you wanted t'know."

"What you want, Junior?"

"'Bout that girl, thas all." He sounded nervous. He was talking fast and I had the feeling that he kept looking over his shoulder. "Why was you lookin' fo' her anyway?"

"You mean the white girl?"

"Yeah. I just remembered that I saw her last week. She come in with Frank Green."

"What's her name?"

"I think he called her Daphne. I think."

"So how come you just tellin' me now? How come you callin' me this late anyway?"

"I'ont get off till two-thirty, Easy. I thought you wanted to know, so I called ya."

"You jus' figgered you'd call me in the middle'a the night an' tell me 'bout some girl? Man, you fulla shit! What the hell do you want?"

Junior let out a couple of curses and hung the phone in my ear.

I got the bottle and poured myself a tall drink. Then I lit up a cigarette and pondered Junior's call. It didn't make any sense, him calling me in the night just to tell me about some girl I wanted to play with. He had to know something. But what could a thick-headed field hand like Junior know about my business? I finished the drink and the cigarette but it still didn't make sense.

The whiskey calmed my nerves, though, and I was able to fall into a half sleep. I dreamed about casting for catfish down south of Houston when I was just a boy. There were giant catfish in the Gatlin River. My mother told me that some of them were so big that the alligators left them alone.

I had caught on to one of those giants and I could just make out its big head below the surface of the water. Its snout was the size of a man's torso.

Then the phone rang.

I couldn't answer it without losing my fish so I shouted for my mother to get it but she must not have heard because the phone kept on ringing and that catfish kept trying to dive. I finally had to let it go and I was almost crying when I picked up the receiver. "Hello."

"'Allo? Thees is Mr. Rawlins? Yes?" The accent was mild, like French, but it wasn't French exactly.

"Yeah," I exhaled. "Who's that?"

"I am calling you about a problem with a friend of yours."

"Who's that?"

"Coretta James," she said, enunciating each syllable.

That set me up straight. "Who is this?"

"My name is Daphne. Daphne Monet," she said. "Your friend, Coretta, no? She came to see me and asked for money. She said that you were looking for me and if I don't give it to her she goes to tell you. Easy, no?"

"When she say that?"

"Not yesterday but the day before that."

"So what'd you do?"

"I give to her my last twenty dollars. I don't know you, do I, Mr. Rawlins?"

"What she do then?"

"She goes away and I worry about it and my friend is away and doesn't come back home so then I think maybe I find you and you tell me, yes? Why you want to find me?"

"I don't know what you mean," I said. "But your friend, who's that?"

"Frank. Frank Green."

I reached for my pants out of reflex; they were on the floor, next to the bed.

"Why do you look for me, Mr. Rawlins? Do I know you?"

"You must'a made some kinda mistake, honey. I don't know what she was talkin' 'bout . . . Do you think Frank went lookin' for her?"

"I don't tell Frank about her coming 'ere. He was not 'ere but then he does not come home."

"I don't know a thing about where Frank is, and Coretta's dead."

"Dead?" She sounded as if she was really surprised.

"Yeah, they think it happened Thursday night."

"This is terrible. Do you think maybe something 'as 'appened with Frank?"

"Listen, lady, I don't know what's goin' on with Frank or anybody else. All I know is that it ain't none'a my business and I hope you do okay but I have to go right now . . ."

"But you must help me."

"No thanks, honey. This is too much fo' me."

"But if you do not help I will 'ave to go to the police to find my friend. I will 'ave to tell them about you and this woman, this Coretta."

"Listen, it was prob'ly your friend that killed her."

"She was stabbed?"

"No," I said, realizing what she meant. "She was beaten to death."

"That ees not Frank. He 'as the knife. He does not use his fists. You will help me?"

"Help you what?" I said. I put up my hands to show how helpless I was but no one could see me.

"I 'ave a friend, yes? He may know where to find Frank."

"I don't need to go lookin' fo' Frank Green but if you want 'im why don't you just call this friend?"

"I, I must go to him. He 'as something for me and . . ."

"So why do you need me? If he's your friend just go to his house. Take a taxi."

"I do not 'ave the money and Frank 'as my car. It is far away, my friend's house, but I could tell you 'ow to go."

"No thanks, lady."

"Please help me. I do not want to call the police but I 'ave no other way if you do not help."

I was afraid of the police too. Afraid that the next time I went down to the police station I wouldn't be getting out. I was missing my catfish more and more. I could almost smell it frying; I could almost taste it.

"Where are you?" I asked.

"At my house, on Dinker Street. Thirty-four fifty-one and a 'alf."

"That's not where Frank lives."

"I 'ave my own place. Yes? He is not my lover."

"I could bring you some money and put you in a cab over on Main. That's all."

"Oh yes, yes! That would be fine."

• 13 •

At four in the morning the neighborhoods of Los Angeles are asleep. On Dinker Street there wasn't even a dog out prowling the trash. The dark lawns were quiet, dotted now and then with hushed white flowers that barely shone in the lamplight.

The French girl's address was a one-story duplex; the porch light shone on her half of the porch.

I stayed in my car long enough to light up a cigarette. The house looked peaceful enough. There was a fat palm tree in the front yard. The lawn was surrounded by an ornamental white picket fence. There were no bodies lying around, no hard-looking men with knives on the front porch. I should have taken Odell's advice right then and left California for good.

When I got to the door she was waiting behind it.

"Mr. Rawlins?"

"Easy, call me Easy."

"Oh, yes. That is what Coretta called you. Yes?"

"Yeah."

"I am Daphne, please to come in."

It was one of those houses that used to be for one family but something happened. Maybe a brother and sister inherited it and couldn't come to a deal so they just walled the place in half and called it a duplex.

She led me into the half living room. It had brown carpets, a brown sofa with a matching chair, and brown walls. There was a bushy potted fern next to the brown curtains that were closed over the entire front wall. Only the coffee table wasn't brown. It was a gilded stand on which lay a clear glass tabletop.

"A drink, Mr. Rawlins?" Her dress was the simple blue kind that the French girls wore when I was a GI in Paris. It was plain and came down to just below her knee. Her only jewelry was a small ceramic pin, worn over her left breast.

"No thanks."

Her face was beautiful. More beautiful than the photograph. Wavy hair so light brown that you might have called it blond from a distance, and eyes that were either green or blue depending on how she held her head. Her cheekbones were high but her face was full enough that it didn't make her seem severe. Her eyes were just a little closer than most women's eyes; it made her seem vulnerable, made me feel that I wanted to put my arms around her—to protect her.

We looked at each other for a few moments before she spoke. "Would you 'ave something to eat?"

"No thanks." I realized that we were whispering and asked, "Is there anybody else here?"

"No," she whispered, moving close enough for me to smell the soap she used, Ivory. "I live alone."

Then she reached out a long delicate hand to touch my face.

"You 'ave been fighting?"

"What?"

"The bruises on your face."

"Nuthin'."

She didn't move her hand.

"I could clean them for you?"

I put my hand out to touch her face, thinking, This is crazy.

"It's okay," I said. "I brought you twenty-five dollars."

She smiled like a child. Only a child could ever be that happy.

"Thank you," she said. She turned away and seated herself on the brown chair, clasping her hands on her lap. She nodded at the couch and I lowered myself.

"I got the money right here." I went for my pocket but she stopped me with a gesture.

"Couldn't you take me to him? I'm just a girl, you know. You could stay in the car and I would only take a little time. Five minutes maybe."

"Listen, honey, I don't even know you . . ."

"But I need 'elp." She looked down at the knot of hands and said, "You do not want to be bothered by the police. I do not either . . ."

I'd heard that line before. "Why don't you just take the taxi?"

"I am afraid."

"But why you gonna trust me?"

"I 'ave no choice. I am a stranger 'ere and my friend is gone. When Coretta tells me that you are looking for me I ask her if you are a bad man and she says no to me. She says that you are a good man and that you are just looking, how you say, innocent."

"I just heard about ya," I said. "That's all. Bouncer at John's said that you were something to see."

She smiled for me. "You will help me, yes?"

The time for me to say no was over. If I was going to say no, it should have been to DeWitt Albright or even to Coretta. But I still had a question to ask.

"How'd you know where to call me?"

Daphne looked down at her hands for maybe three seconds; long enough for the average person to formulate a lie.

"Before I gave Coretta her money I said that I wanted to 'ave it, so I could talk to you. I wanted to know why you look for me."

She was just a girl. Nothing over twenty-two.

"Where you say your friend lives?"

"On a street above Hollywood, Laurel Canyon Road."

"You know how to get there?"

She nodded eagerly and then jumped up saying, "Just let me get one thing."

She ran out of the living room into a darkened doorway and returned in less than a minute. She was carrying an old beaten-up suitcase.

"It is Richard's, my friend's," she smiled shyly.

I drove across town to La Brea then straight north to Hollywood. The canyon road was narrow and winding but there was no traffic at all. We hadn't even seen a police car on the ride and that was fine with me, because the police have white slavery on the brain when it comes to colored men and white women.

At every other curve, near the top of the road, we'd catch a glimpse of nighttime L.A. Even way back then the city was a sea of lights. Bright and shiny and alive. Just to look out on Los Angeles at night gave me a sense of power.

"It is the next one, Easy. The one with the carport."

It was another small house. Compared with some of the mansions we'd seen on the ride it was like a servant's house. A shabby little A-frame with two windows and a gaping front door.

"Your friend always leave his door open like that?" I asked.

"I do not know."

When we parked I got out of the car with her.

"I will only be a moment." She caressed my arm before turning toward the house.

"Maybe I better go with ya."

"No," she said with strength that she hadn't shown before.

"Listen. This is late at night, in a lonely neighborhood, in a big city. That door is open and that means something's wrong. And if something happens to one more person I know the police are gonna chase me down into the grave."

"Okay," she said. "But only to see if it is alright. Then you go back to the car."

I closed the front door before turning on the wall switch. Daphne called out, "Richard!"

It was one of those houses that was designed to be a mountain cabin. The front door opened into a big room that was living room, dining room, and kitchen all in one. The kitchen was separated from the dining area by a long counter. The far left of the room had a wooden couch with a Mexican rug thrown across it and a metal chair with tan cushions for the seat and back. The wall opposite the front door was all glass. You could see the city lights winking inside the mirror image of the room, Daphne, and me.

At the far left wall was a door.

"His bedroom," she said.

The bedroom was also simple. Wood floor, window for a wall, and a king-sized bed with a dead man on it.

He was in the same blue suit. He lay across the bed, his arms out like Jesus Christ—but the fingers were jangled, not composed like they were on my mother's crucifix. He didn't call me "colored brother" but I recognized the drunken white man I'd met in front of John's place.

Daphne gasped. She grabbed my sleeve. "It is Richard."

There was a butcher's knife buried deep in his chest. The smooth brown haft stood out from his body like a cattail from a pond. He'd fallen with his back on a bunch of blankets so that the blood had flowed upwards, around his face and neck. There was a lot of blood around his wide-eyed stare. Blue eyes and brown hair and dark blood so thick that you could have dished it up like Jell-O. My tongue grew a full beard and I gagged.

The next thing I knew I was down on one knee but I kept myself from being sick. I kneeled there in front of that dead man like a priest blessing a corpse brought to him by grieving relatives. I didn't know his family name or what he had done, I only knew that he was dead.

All the dead men that I'd ever known came back to me in that instant. Bernard Hooks, Addison Sherry, Alphonso Jones, Marcel Montague. And a thousand Germans named Heinz, and children and women too. Some were mutilated, some burned. I'd killed my share of them and I'd done worse things than that in the heat of war. I'd seen open-eyed corpses like this man Richard and corpses that had no heads at all. Death wasn't new to me and I was to be damned if I'd let one more dead white man break me down.

While I was down there, on my knees, I noticed something. I bent down and smelled it and then I picked it up and wrapped it in my handkerchief.

When I got to my feet I saw that Daphne was gone. I went to the kitchen and rinsed my face in the sink. I figured that Daphne had run to the toilet. But when I was through she hadn't returned. I looked in the bathroom but she wasn't there. I ran outside to look at my car but she was nowhere to be seen.

Then I heard a ruckus from the carport.

Daphne was there pushing the old suitcase into the trunk of a pink Studebaker.

"What's goin' on?" I asked.

"What'a ya think's goin' on! We gotta get out of here and it's best if we split."

I didn't have the time to wonder at her loss of accent. "What happened here?"

"Help me with my bag!"

"What happened?" I asked again.

"How the hell do I know? Richard's dead, Frank's gone too. All I know is that I have to get out of here and you better too, unless you want the police to prove you did it."

"Who did it?" I grabbed her and turned her away from the car.

"I do not know," she said quietly and calmly into my face. Our faces were no more than two inches apart.

"I cain't just leave it like this."

"There's nothing else to do, Easy. I'll take these things so nobody will know that I was ever here and you just go on home. Go to sleep and treat it like a dream."

"What about him?" I yelled, pointing at the house.

"That's a dead man, Mr. Rawlins. He's dead and gone. You just go home and forget what you saw. The police don't know you were here and they won't know unless you shout so loud that someone looks out here and sees your car."

"What you gonna do?"

"Drive his car to a little place I know and leave it there. Get on a bus for somewhere more than a thousand miles from here."

"What about the men lookin' for you?"

"You mean Carter? He doesn't mean any harm. He'll give up when they can't find me." She smiled.

Then she kissed me.

It was a slow, deliberate kiss. At first I tried to pull away but she held on strong. Her tongue moved around under mine and between my gums and lips. The bitter taste in my mouth turned almost sweet from hers. She leaned back and smiled at me for a moment and then she kissed me again. This time it was fierce. She lunged so deep into my throat that once our teeth collided and my canine chipped.

"Too bad we won't have a chance to get to know each other, Easy. Otherwise I'd let you eat this little white girl up."

"You can't just go," I stammered. "That's murder there."

She slammed the trunk shut and went around me to the driver's side of the car. She got in and rolled down the window.

"Bye, Easy," she said as she popped the ignition and threw it into reverse.

The engine choked twice but not enough to stall.

I could have grabbed her and pulled her out of the car but what would I have done with her? All I could do was watch the red lights recede down the hill.

Then I got into my car thinking that my luck hadn't turned yet.

• 14 •

"You lettin' them step on you, Easy. Lettin' them walk all over you and you ain't doin' a thing."

"What can I do?"

I pulled onto Sunset Boulevard and turned left, toward the band of fiery orange light on the eastern horizon.

"I don't know, man, but you gotta do somethin'. This keep up and you be dead 'fore next Wednesday."

"Maybe I should just do like Odell says and leave."

"Leave! Leave? You gonna run away from the only piece'a property you ever had? Leave," he said disgustedly. "Better be dead than leave."

"Well, you say I'ma be dead anyway. All I gotta do is wait fo' nex Wednesday."

"You gotta stand up, man. Lettin' these people step on you ain't right. Messin' with French white girls, who ain't French; workin' fo' a white man kill his own kind if they don't smell right. You gotta find out what happened an' set it straight."

"But what can I do with the police or Mr. Albright or even that girl?"

"Bide yo' time, Easy. Don't do nuthin' that you don't have to do. Just bide yo' time an' take advantage whenever you can."

"What if . . ."

"Don't ask no questions. Either somethin' is or it ain't. 'What if 'is fo' chirren, Easy. You's a man."

"Yeah," I said. Suddenly I felt stronger.

"Not too many people wanna take down a man, Easy. They's too many cowards around for that."

The voice only comes to me at the worst times, when everything seems so bad that I want to take my car and drive it into a wall. Then this voice comes to me and gives me the best advice I ever get.

The voice is hard. It never cares if I'm scared or in danger. It just looks at all the facts and tells me what I need to do.

The voice first came to me in the army.

When I joined up I was proud because I believed what they said in the papers and newsreels. I believed that I was a part of the hope of the world. But then I found that the army was segregated just like the South. They trained me as a foot soldier, a fighter, then they put me in front of a typewriter for the first three years of my tour. I had gone through Africa and Italy in the statistics unit. We followed the fighting men, tracing their movements and counting their dead.

I was in a black division but all the superior officers were white. I was trained how to kill men but white men weren't anxious to see a gun in my hands. They didn't want to see me spill white blood. They said we didn't have the discipline or the minds for a war effort, but they were really scared that we might get to like the kind of freedom that death-dealing brings.

If a black man wanted to fight he had to volunteer. Then maybe he'd get to fight.

I thought the men who volunteered for combat were fools.

"Why I wanna die in this white man's war?" I'd say.

But then one day I was in the PX when a load of white soldiers came in, fresh from battle outside Rome. They made a comment about the Negro soldiers. They said that we were cowards and that it was the white boys that were saving Europe. I knew they were jealous because we were behind the lines with good food and conquered women, but it got to me somehow. I hated those white soldiers and my own cowardice.

So I volunteered for the invasion of Normandy and then later I signed on with Patton at the Battle of the Bulge. By that time the Allies were so desperate that they didn't have the luxury of segregating the troops. There were blacks, whites, and even a handful of Japanese-Americans in our platoon. And the major thing we had to worry about was killing Germans. There was always trouble between the races, especially when it came to the women, but we learned to respect each other out there too.

I never minded that those white boys hated me, but if they didn't respect me I was ready to fight.

It was outside Normandy, near a little farm, when the voice first came to me. I was trapped in the barn. My two buddies, Anthony Yakimoto and Wenton Niles, were dead and a sniper had the place covered. The voice told me to "Get off yo' butt when the sun comes down an' kill that motherfucker. Kill him an' rip off his fuckin' face with yo' bayonet, man. You cain't let him do that to you. Even if he lets you live you be scared the rest'a yo' life. Kill that motherfucker," he told me. And I did.

The voice has no lust. He never told me to rape or steal. He just tells me how it is if I want to survive. Survive like a man.

When the voice speaks, I listen.

• 15 •

There was another car parked in front of my house when I got home. A white Cadillac. No one was in it but this time it was my front door that was open.

Manny and Shariff were loitering just inside the door. Shariff grinned at me. Manny looked at the floor so I still couldn't tell about his eyes.

Mr. Albright was standing in the kitchen, looking out over the backyards through the window. The smell of coffee filled the house. When I came in he turned to me, a porcelain cup cradled in his right hand. He wore white cotton pants and a cream sweater, white golf shoes, and a captain's cap with a black brim.

"Easy." His smile was loose and friendly.

"What you doin' in my house, man?"

"I had to talk to you. You know I expected you to be home." There was the slightest hint of threat in his voice. "So Manny used a screwdriver on the door, just to be comfortable. Coffee's made."

"You got no excuse to be breakin' into my house, Mr. Albright. What would you do if I broke into your place?"

"I'd tear your nigger head out by its root." His smile didn't alter in the least.

I looked at him a minute. Somewhere in the back of my mind I thought, Bide your time, Easy.

"So what you want?" I asked him. I went to the counter and poured a cup of coffee.

"Where have you been this time of morning, Easy?"

"Nowhere got to do with your business."

"Where?"

I turned to him saying, "I went to see a girl. Don't you git none, Mr Albright?"

His dead eyes turned colder and the smile left his face. I was trying to say something that would get under his skin and then I was sorry I had.

"I didn't come here to play with you, boy," he said evenly. "You got my money in your pocket and all I got is an earful of smartass."

"What do you mean?" I stopped myself from taking a step backward.

"I mean, Frank Green hasn't been home in two days. I mean that the superintendent at the Skyler Arms tells me that the police have been around his place asking about a colored girl that was seen with Green a few days before she died. I want to know, Easy. I want to know where the white girl is."

"You don't think I did my job? Shit, I give you the money back."

"Too late for that, Mr. Rawlins. You take my money and you belong to me."

"I don't belong to anybody."

"We all owe out something, Easy. When you owe out then you're in debt and when you're in debt then you can't be your own man. That's capitalism."

"I got your money right here, Mr. Albright." I reached for my pocket.

"Do you believe in God, Mr. Rawlins?"

"What do ya want, man?"

"I want to know if you believe in God."

"This here is bullshit. I gotta go to bed." I made like I was going to turn away but I didn't. I would have never knowingly turned my back on DeWitt Albright.

"Because you see," he continued, leaning slightly toward me, "I like to look very close at a man I kill if he believes in God. I want to see if death is different for a religious man."

"Bide your time," the voice whispered.

"I seen her," I said.

I went to the chair in the living room. Sitting down took a great weight off me.

Albright's henchmen moved close to me. They were roused, like hunting dogs expecting blood.

"Where?" DeWitt smiled. His eyes looked like those of the undead.

"She called me. Said that if I didn't help her she'd tell the police about Coretta . . ."

"Coretta?"

"A dead girl, friend'a mine. She prob'ly the one that the police askin' 'bout. She the one was with Frank an' your girl," I said. "Daphne gave me an address over on Dinker and I went there. Then she had me drive up in the Hollywood Hills to a dude's house."

"When was all this?"

"I just got back."

"Where is she?"

"She took off."

"Where is she?" His voice sounded as if it came from out of a well. It sounded dangerous and wild.

"I don't know! When we found the body she split in his car!"

"What body?"

"Dude was dead when we got there."

"What was this guy's name?"

"Richard."

"Richard what?"

"She just called him Richard, that's all." I saw no reason to tell him that Richard had been nosing around John's place.

"You sure he was dead?"

"Had a knife right through his chest. There was a fly marchin' right across his eye." I felt bile in my throat remembering it. "Blood everywhere."

"And you just let her go?" The threat in his voice was back so I got up and moved toward the kitchen for more coffee. I was so worried about one of them coming behind me that I bumped into the doorjamb trying to get through the door.

"Bide your time," the voice whispered again.

"You din't hire me fo' no kidnappin'. The girl grabbed his keys and split. What you want me to do?"

"You call the cops?"

"I tried my best to keep in the speed limit. That's all I did."

"Now I'm going to ask you something, Easy." His gaze held my eye. "And I don't want you to make any mistakes. Not right now."

"Go on."

"Did she take anything with her? A bag or a suitcase?"

"She had an ole brown suitcase. She put it in his trunk."

DeWitt's eyes brightened and all the tension went out of his shoulders. "What kind of car was that?"

"Forty-eight Studebaker. Pink job."

"Where'd she go? Remember, now, you're still telling me everything."

"All she said was she was gonna park it somewhere, but she didn't say where."

"What's the address she was at?"

"Twenty-six—"

He waved at me impatiently and, to my shame, I flinched.

"Write it down," he said.

I got paper from the drawer of my end table.

He sat across from me on the couch scrutinizing that little slip of paper. He had his knees wide apart.

"Get me some whiskey, Easy," he said.

"Get it yourself," the voice said.

"Get it yourself," I said. "Bottle's in the cabinet."

DeWitt Albright looked up at me, and a big grin slowly spread across his face. He laughed and slapped his knee and said, "Well, I'll be damned."

I just looked at him. I was ready to die but I was going to go down fighting.

"Get us a drink, will you, Manny?" The little man moved quickly to the cabinet. "You know, Easy, you're a brave man. And I need a brave man working for me." His drawl got thicker as he talked. "I've already paid you, right?"

I nodded.

"Well, the way I figure it, Frank Green is the key. She will be around him or he will know where she's gone to. So I want you to find this gangster for me. I want you to set me up to meet him. That's all. Once I meet him there I'll know what to say. You find Frank Green for me and we're quits."

"Quits?"

"*All* our business, Easy. You keep your money and I leave you alone."

It wasn't an offer at all. Somehow I knew that Mr. Albright planned to kill me. Either he'd kill me right then or he'd wait until I found Frank.

"I'll find him for ya, but I need another hundred if you want my neck out there."

"You my kinda people, Easy, you sure are," he said. "I'll give you three days to find him. Make sure you count them right."

We finished our drinks with Manny and Shariff waiting outside the door.

Albright pushed open the screen to leave but then he had a thought. He turned back to me and said, "I'm not a man to fool with, Mr. Rawlins."

No, I thought to myself, neither am I.

• 16 •

I slept all that day and into the evening. Maybe I should have been looking for Frank Green but all I wanted was to sleep.

I woke up sweating in the middle of the night. Every sound I heard was someone coming after me. Either it was the police or DeWitt Albright or Frank Green. I couldn't throw off the smell of blood that I'd picked up in Richard's room. There was the hum of a million flies at the window, flies that I'd seen swarming on our boys' corpses in North Africa, in Oran.

I was shivering but I wasn't cold. And I wanted to run to my mother or someone to love me, but then I imagined Frank Green pulling me from a loving woman's arms; he had his knife poised to press into my heart.

Finally I jumped up from my bed and ran to the telephone. I didn't know what I was doing. I couldn't call Joppy because he wouldn't understand that kind of fear. I couldn't call Odell because he'd understand it too well and just tell me to run. I couldn't call Dupree because he was still locked up. But I couldn't have talked to him anyway because I would have had to lie to him about Coretta and I was too upset to lie.

So I dialed the operator. And when she came on the line I asked her for long distance, and then I asked for Mrs. E. Alexander on Claxton Street in Houston's Fifth Ward.

When she answered the phone I closed my eyes and remembered her: big woman with deep brown skin and topaz eyes. I imagined her frown when she said "Hello", because EttaMae never liked the telephone. She always said, "I like to see my bad news comin'; not get it like a sneak through no phones."

"Hello," she said.

"Etta?"

"Who's this?"

"It's Easy, Etta."

"Easy Rawlins?" And then a big laugh. The kind of laugh that makes you want to laugh along with it. "Easy, where are you, honey? You come home?"

"I'm in L.A., Etta." My voice was quavering; my chest vibrated with feeling.

"Sumpin' wrong, honey? You sound funny."

"Uh . . . Naw, ain't nuthin', Etta. Sure is good to hear you. Yeah, I can't think of nuthin' better."

"What's wrong, Easy?"

"You know how I can reach Mouse, Etta?"

There was silence then. I thought of how they said in science class that outer space was empty, black and cold. I felt it then and I sure didn't want to.

"You know Raymond and me broke up, Easy. He don't live here no more."

The idea that I made Etta sad was almost more than I could take.

"I'm sorry, baby," I said. "I just thought you might know how I could get to him."

"What's wrong, Easy?"

"It's just that maybe Sophie was right."

"Sophie Anderson?"

"Yeah, well, you know that she's always sayin' that L.A. is too much?"

Etta laughed in her chest. "I sure do."

"She might just be right." I laughed too.

"Easy . . ."

"Just tell Mouse that I called, Etta. Tell him that Sophie might have been right about California and maybe it is a place for him."

She started to say something else but I made like I didn't hear her and said, "Goodbye." I pushed down the button of the receiver.

I put my chair in front of the window so I could look out into my yard. I sat there for a long time, balling my hands together and taking deep breaths when I could remember to. Finally the fear passed and I fell asleep. The last thing I remember was looking at my apple tree in the pre-dawn.

• 17 •

I put the card that De Witt Albright had given me on the dresser. It read:

MAXIM BAXTER
Personnel Director
Lion Investments

In the lower right-hand corner there was an address on La Cienega Boulevard.

I was dressed in my best suit and ready to ride by 10 A.M. I thought that it was time to gather my own information. That card was the one of two things I had to go on, so I drove across town again to a small office building just below Melrose, on La Cienega. The whole building was occupied by Lion Investments.

The secretary, an elderly lady with blue hair, was concentrating on the ledger at her desk. When my shadow fell across her blotter she said, to the shadow, "Yes?"

"I came to see Mr. Baxter."

"Do you have an appointment?"

"No. But Mr. Albright gave me his card and told me to come down whenever I had a chance."

"I know no Mr. Albright," she said, again to the shadow on her desk. "And Mr. Baxter is a very busy man."

"Maybe he knows Mr. Albright. He gave me this card." I tossed the card down onto the page she was reading and she looked up.

What she saw surprised her. "Oh!"

I smiled back down. "I can wait if he's busy. I got a little time off'a work."

"I, ah . . . I'll see if he can make time, Mr.—?"

"Rawlins."

"You just have a seat over on the couch and I'll be right back."

She went through a doorway behind the desk. After a few minutes another elderly lady came out. She looked at me suspiciously and then took up the work that the other one had left.

The waiting room was nice enough. There was a long, black leather couch set up against a window that looked out onto La Cienega Boulevard. Through the window was a view of one of those fancy restaurants, the Angus Steak House. There was a man standing out front in a Beefeater's uniform, ready to open the door for all the nice people who were going to drop a whole day's salary in forty-five minutes. The Beefeater looked happy. I wondered how much he made in tips.

There was a long coffee table in front of the couch. It was covered with business newspapers and business magazines. Nothing for women. And nothing for men who might have been looking for something sporty or entertaining. When I got tired of watching the Beefeater open doors I started looking around the room.

On the wall next to the couch was a bronze placard. At the top there was a raised oval that had the form of a swooping falcon carved into it. The falcon had three arrows in its talons. Below that were the names of all the important partners and affiliates of Lion Investments. I recognized some of the names as celebrities that you read about in the daily *Times*. Lawyers, bankers, and just the plain old wealthy folks. The president's name was at the bottom of the plaque as if he were a shy man who didn't want his name placed too obviously as the one in charge. Mr. Todd Carter wasn't the kind of man who wanted his name spread around, I figured. I mean, what would he say if he knew that a strange French girl, who went in the night to steal a dead man's car, was using his name? I laughed loud enough for the old woman behind the desk to look up and scowl.

"Mr. Rawlins," the first secretary said as she walked up to me. "You know Mr. Baxter is a very busy man. He doesn't have a lot of time . . ."

"Well, then maybe he better see me quick so he can get back to work."

She didn't like that.

"May I ask what is the nature of your request?"

"Sure you can, but I don't think your boss wants me to talk to the help about his business."

"I assure you, sir," she said, barely holding in her anger, "that whatever you have to say to Mr. Baxter is safe with me. Also, he cannot see you and I am the only person with whom you may speak."

"Naw."

"I'm afraid so. Now if you have some sort of message please tell me so I can get back to my work." She produced a small pad and a yellow, wooden pencil.

"Well, Miss—?" For some reason I thought that it would be nice if we traded names.

"What is your message, sir?"

"I see," I said. "Well, my message is this: I have news for a Mr. Todd Carter, the president of your company, I believe. I was given Mr. Baxter's card to forward a message to Mr. Carter about a job I was employed to do by a Mr. DeWitt Albright." I stopped there.

"Yes? What job is that?"

"Are you sure you want to know?" I asked.

"What job, sir?" If she was nervous at all I couldn't see it.

"Mr. Albright hired me to find Mr. Carter's girlfriend after she ditched him."

She stopped writing and peered at me over the rim of her bifocals. "Is this some sort of joke?"

"Not that I know of, ma'am. As a matter of fact, I haven't had a good laugh since I went to work for your boss. Not one laugh at all."

"Excuse me," she said.

She slammed the pad down hard enough to startle her helper and disappeared through the back door again.

She wasn't gone for more than five minutes when a tall man in a dark gray suit came out to see me. He was thin with bushy black hair and thick black eyebrows. His eyes seemed to pull back into shadows under those hefty brows.

"Mr. Rawlins." His smile was so white that it would have looked at home on DeWitt Albright.

"Mr. Baxter?" I rose and grabbed his extended hand.

"Why don't you come with me, sir?"

We went past the two scowling women. I was sure that they'd put their heads together and start gabbing as soon as Mr. Baxter and I had gone through the door.

The hallway we entered was narrow but well carpeted and the walls were papered with a plush blue fabric. At the end of the hall was a fine oak door with "Maxim T. Baxter, Vice-President," carved into it.

His office was modest and small. The ash desk was good but not big or fancy. The floor was pine and the window behind his desk looked out onto a parking lot.

"Not very smart talking about Mr. Carter's business to the front desk," Baxter said the moment we were both seated.

"I don't wanna hear it, man."

"What?" It was a question but there was a kind of superiority in his tone.

"I said I don't wanna hear it, Mr. Baxter. It's just too much goin' on fo' me t'be worried 'bout what you think ain't right. Ya see, if you'd let that woman out there know that she should let me talk to you, then—"

"I *asked* her to get a message from you, Mr. Rawlins. It is my understanding that you're looking for employment. I could set up an appointment for you through the mails . . ."

"I'm here to talk to Mr. Carter."

"That's impossible," he said. Then he stood up as if that would scare me.

I looked up at him and said, "Man, why don't you sit down and get your boss on the line."

"I don't know who you think you are, Rawlins. Important men don't even barge in on Mr. Carter. You're lucky that I took the time to see you."

"You mean the poor nigger lucky the foreman take out the time t'curse 'im, huh?"

Mr. Baxter looked at his watch instead of answering me. "I have an appointment, Mr. Rawlins. If you just tell me what you want to say to Mr. Carter he'll call you if it seems appropriate."

"That's what the lady out there said, and you go blamin' me for shootin' off my mouth."

"I'm aware of Mr. Carter's situation; the ladies outside are not."

"You might be aware of what he told you but you ain't got no idea of what I gotta say."

"And what might that be?" he asked, sitting back down.

"All I'm'a tell ya is that he might be runnin' Lion from a jail cell if he don't speak to me, and real quick too." I didn't exactly know what I meant but it shook up Baxter enough for him to pick up his phone.

"Mr. Carter," he said. "Mr. Albright's operative is here and he wants to see you... Albright, the man we have on the Monet thing... He sounds as though it's urgent, sir. Maybe you should see him..."

They talked a little more but that was the gist of it.

Baxter led me back down the hall but made a left turn before we went through the door that led to the secretaries. We came to a darkwood door that was locked. Baxter had a key for it and when he pulled it open I saw that it was the door to a tiny, padded elevator.

"Get in, it will take you to his office," Baxter said.

There was no feeling of motion, only the soft hum of a motor somewhere below the floor. The elevator had a bench and an ashtray. The walls and ceiling were covered in velvety red fabric that was cut into squares. Each square had a pair of dancing figures in it. The waltzing men and women were dressed like courtiers of the French court. The wealth made my heart beat fast.

The door came open on a small, red-headed man who wore a tan suit that he might have bought at Sears Roebuck and a simple white shirt that was open at the collar. At first I thought he was Mr. Carter's servant but then I realized that we were the only ones in the room.

"Mr. Rawlins?" He fingered his receding hairline and shook my hand. His grip felt like paper. He was so small and quiet that he seemed more like a child than a man.

"Mr. Carter. I came to tell you—"

He put up a hand and shook his head before I could go on. Then he led me across the wide room to the pair of pink couches that stood in front of his desk. The desk was the color and size of a grand piano. The great brocade curtains behind the desk were open to a view of the mountains behind Sunset Boulevard.

I remember thinking that it was a long way from vice-president to the top.

We sat at either end of one of the couches.

"Drink?" He pointed at a crystal decanter that held a brown liquid on an end table near me.

"What is it?" My voice sounded strange in the large room.

"Brandy."

That was the first time I ever had a really good liquor. I liked it just fine.

"Mr. Baxter said that you had news from that man Albright."

"Well, not exactly, sir."

He frowned when I said that. It was a little boy's frown; it made me feel sorry for him.

"You see, I'm a little unhappy about how things are going with Mr. Albright. As a matter of fact, I'm unhappy about almost everything that's happened to me since I met the man."

"And what's that?"

"A woman, a friend of mine, was killed when she started asking questions about Miss Monet and the police think I had something to do with it. I've been mixed up with hijackers and wild people all over town and all because I asked a couple'a questions about your friend."

"Has anything happened to Daphne?"

He looked so worried that I was happy to say, "The last time I saw her she looked just fine."

"You saw her?"

"Yeah. Night before last."

Tears welled up in his pale, child's eyes.

"What did she say?" he asked.

"We were in trouble, Mr. Carter. But you see that's how it's crazy. The first time I saw her she was talking like she was a French girl. But then, after we found the body, she sounded like she could have come from San Diego or anywhere else."

"Body? What body?"

"I'm'a get to that but first we got to come to some kinda understanding."

"You want money."

"Uh-uh, no. I been paid already an' I guess that comes from you anyway. But what I need is for you to help me understand what's happening. You see, I don't trust your man Albright at all and you can forget the police. I got this one friend, Joppy, but this is too much for him. So I figure you the only one can help. I gotta figure that you want the girl 'cause you love 'er and if I'm wrong 'bout that then my ass is had."

"I love Daphne," he said.

I was almost embarrassed to hear him. He wasn't trying to act like a man at all. He was wringing his hands trying to keep from asking about her while I talked.

"Then you gotta tell me why Albright is lookin' for her."

Carter ran his finger along his hairline again and looked out at the mountains. He waited another moment before saying, "I was told, by a man I trust, that Mr. Albright is good at doing things, confidentially.

There are reasons that I don't want this affair in the papers."

"You married?"

"No, I want to marry Daphne."

"She didn't steal anything from you?"

"Why do you ask?"

"Mr. Albright seems real concerned about her luggage and I thought she had something you wanted back."

"You might call it stealing, Mr. Rawlins, it doesn't matter to me. She took some money when she left but I don't care about that. I want her. You say she was fine when you saw her?"

"How much money?"

"I don't see where that matters."

"If you want me to answer questions then you give too."

"Thirty thousand dollars." He said it as if it was just some pocket change on the bathroom shelf. "I had it at home because we were giving the people in our various concerns half-a-day holiday as a sort of bonus but the day we chose was a payday and the bank couldn't deliver the cash that early so I had them deliver it to my home."

"You let the bank deliver that much money to your house?"

"It was only once, and what were the odds I'd be robbed that night?"

"About one hundred percent, I guess."

He smiled. "The money means nothing to me. Daphne and I had a fight and she took the money because she thought I'd never talk to her again. She was wrong."

"Fight about what?"

"They tried to blackmail her. She came to me and told me about it. They wanted to use her to get at me. She made up her mind to leave, to save me."

"What they got on her?"

"I'd rather not say."

I let it pass. "Albright know about the money?"

"Yes. Now I've answered your questions, I want to know about her. Is she all right?"

"Last I saw of her she was fine. She was looking for her friend—Frank Green."

I thought that a man's name might shake him up but Todd Carter didn't even seem to hear it. "What did you say about a body?"

"We went to another friend of hers, a man named Richard, and we found him dead in his bed."

"Richard McGee?" Carter's voice went cold.

"I don't know. All I know is Richard."

"Did he live on Laurel Canyon Road?"

"Yeah."

"Good. I'm glad he's dead. I'm glad. He was an awful man. Did she tell you that he dealt in young boys?"

"All she said was that he was a friend'a hers."

"Well he did. He was a blackmailer and a homosexual pimp. He worked for rich men with sick appetites."

"Well he's dead and Daphne took his car, that was the night before last. She said that she was gonna leave the city. That was the last I heard of her."

"What was she wearing?" His eyes were glistening, expectant.

"A blue dress and blue heels."

"Was she wearing stockings?"

"I think so." I didn't want him to think I was looking too closely.

"What color?"

"Blue too, I think."

He smiled with all his teeth. "That's her. Tell me, did she wear a pin here, on her chest?"

"On the other side, but yeah. It was red with little green dots in it."

"You want another drink, Mr. Rawlins?"

"Sure."

He poured that time.

"She's a beautiful woman, isn't she?"

"You wouldn't be lookin' for her if she wasn't."

"I never knew a woman who could wear perfume where the smell was so slight that you just wanted to get closer to tell what it was."

Ivory soap, I thought to myself.

He asked me about her makeup and her hair. He told me that she was from New Orleans and that her family was an old French family that traced their heritage to Napoleon. We talked about her eyes for a half hour. And then he started to tell me things that men should never say about their women. Not sex, but he talked about how she'd hold him to her breast when he was afraid and how she'd stand up for him when a shopkeeper or waiter tried to walk over him.

Talking with Mr. Todd Carter was a strange experience. I mean, there I was, a Negro in a rich white man's office, talking to him like we were best friends—even closer. I could tell that he didn't have the fear or contempt that most white people showed when they dealt with me.

It was a strange experience but I had seen it before. Mr. Todd Carter was so rich that he didn't even consider me in human terms. He could tell me anything. I could have been a prized dog that he knelt to and hugged when he felt low.

It was the worst kind of racism. The fact that he didn't even recognize our difference showed that he didn't care one damn about me. But I didn't have the time to worry about it. I just watched him move his lips about lost love until, finally, I began to see him as some strange being. Like a baby who grows to man-size and terrorizes his poor parents with his strength and his stupidity.

"I love her, Mr. Rawlins. I'd do anything to get her back."

"Well I wish ya luck on that. But I think you better get Albright away from her. He wants that money."

"Will you find her for me? I'll give you a thousand dollars."

"What about Albright?"

"I'll tell my associates to fire him. He won't go against us."

"Suppose he does?"

"I'm a rich man, Mr. Rawlins. The mayor and the chief of police eat at my house regularly."

"Then why can't they help you?"

He turned away from me when I asked that.

"Find her for me," he said.

"If you gimme something to hold, say two hundred dollars, I'll give it a try. I ain't sayin' nuthin's gonna come from it. She could be back in New Orleans for all I know."

He stood up smiling. He touched my hand with his papery grip. "I'll have Mr. Baxter draw up a check."

"Uh, sorry, but I need cash."

He pulled out his wallet and flipped through the bills. "I have a hundred and seventy-some-odd in here. They could write you a check for the rest."

"I'll take one-fifty," I said.

He just took all the money from his wallet and handed it over, mumbling, "Take it all, take it all."

And I took it too.

Somewhere along the way I had developed the feeling that I wasn't going to outlive the adventure I was having. There was no way out but to run, and I couldn't run, so I decided to milk all those white people for all the money they'd let go of.

Money bought everything. Money paid the rent and fed the kitty. Money was why Coretta was dead and why DeWitt Albright was going to kill me. I got the idea, somehow, that if I got enough money then maybe I could buy my own life back.

• 18 •

I had to find Frank Green.

Knifehand held the answer to my problems. He knew where the girl was, if anybody did, and he knew who killed Coretta; I was sure of that. Richard McGee was dead too, but I didn't care about that death because the police couldn't connect me to it.

It's not that I had no feelings for the murdered man; I thought it was wrong for a man to be murdered and, in a more perfect world, I felt that the killer should be brought to justice.

But I didn't believe that there was justice for Negroes. I thought that there might be some justice for a black man if he had the money to grease it. Money isn't a sure bet but it's the closest to God that I've ever seen in this world.

But I didn't have any money. I was poor and black and a likely candidate for the penitentiary unless I could get Frank to stand between me and the forces of DeWitt Albright and the law.

So I went out looking.

The first place I went was Ricardo's Pool Room on Slauson. Ricardo's was just a hole-in-the-wall with no windows and only one door. There was no name out front because either you knew where Ricardo's was or you didn't belong there at all.

Joppy had taken me to Ricardo's a few times after we locked up his bar. It was a serious kind of place peopled with jaundice-eyed bad men who smoked and drank heavily while they waited for a crime they could commit.

It was the kind of place you could get killed in but I was safe as long as I was with a tough man like Joppy Shag. Still, when Joppy would leave the pool table to go to the toilet I could almost feel the violence pulsing in the dark.

But I had to go to places like Ricardo's to look for Frank Green. Because Frank was in the hurting trade. Maybe there was somebody who had taken his money, or messed with his girl, and Frank needed a gunman to back him up in the kill—Ricardo's was where he'd go. Maybe he just needed an extra hand in taking down a cigarette shipment. The men in Ricardo's were desperate; they lived for hurting.

It was a large room with four pool tables, a green lamp shade hanging above each one. The walls were lined with straight-back chairs where most of the customers sat, drinking from brown paper bags and smoking in the dim light. Only one skinny youth was shooting pool. That was Mickey, Rosetta's son.

Rosetta had run the place ever since Ricardo got diabetes and lost both his legs. He was upstairs someplace, in a single bed, drinking whiskey and staring at the walls.

When I'd heard about Ricardo's illness I said to her, "I'm sorry t'hear it, Rose."

Rosetta's face was squat and wide. Her beady eyes pressed down into her chubby brown cheeks. She squinted at me and said, "He done enough ho'in 'round fo' two men and then some. I guess he could rest now." And that's all she said.

She was sitting at the only card table at the far side of the room. I walked over to her and said, "Evenin', Rosetta, how you doin' t'nite."

"Joppy here?" she asked, looking around me.

"Naw. He still workin' at the bar."

Rosetta looked at me as if I were a stray cat come in after her cheese.

The room was so dark and smoky that I couldn't make out what anyone was doing, except for Mickey, but I felt eyes on me from the haze. When I turned back to Rosetta I saw that she was staring too.

"Anybody been sellin' some good whiskey lately, Rose?" I asked. I had hoped to have some light talk with her before asking my question but her stare unsettled me and the room was too quiet for just talk.

"This ain't no bar, honey. You want whiskey you better go see yo' friend Joppy." She glanced at the door, telling me to leave, I suppose.

"I don't want a drink, Rose. I'm lookin' t'buy a case or two. Thought maybe you might know how I could get some."

"Why'ont you ast yo' friend anyway? He know where the whiskey grow."

"Joppy send me here, Rose. He say you the one t'know."

She was still suspicious but I could see that she wasn't afraid. "You could try Frank Green if you want t'buy by the box."

"Yeah? Where can I get a'hold of'im?"

"I ain't seen 'im in a few days now. Either he shacked up or he out earnin' his trade."

That was all Rosetta had to say on the subject. She lit up a cigarette and turned away. I thanked her back and wandered over to Mickey.

"Eight ball?" asked Mickey.

It really didn't matter what we played. I put a five down and lost it, then I lost five more. That took me about a half an hour. When I figured I'd paid enough for my information I saluted the hustler and walked out into the sun.

I had a feeling of great joy as I walked away from Ricardo's. I don't know how to say it, exactly. It was as if for the first time in my life I was doing something on my own terms. Nobody was telling me what to do. I was acting on my own. Maybe I hadn't found Frank but I had gotten Rosetta to bring up his name. If she had known where he was I would have gotten to him that day.

There was a big house on Isabella Street, at the end of a cul-de-sac. That was Vernie's place. Lots of working men would drop by there now and then, to visit one of Vernie's girls. It was a friendly place. The second and third floors had three bedrooms each and the first floor was a kitchen and living room where the guests could be entertained.

Vernie was a light-skinned woman whose hair was frosted gold. She weighed about three hundred pounds. Vernie would stay in the kitchen cooking all day and all night. Her daughter, Darcel, who was the same size as her mother, would welcome the men into the parlor and collect a few dollars for their food and drinks.

Some men, like Odell, would be happy to sit around and drink and listen to music on the phonograph. Vernie would come out now and then to shout hello at old friends and introduce herself to newcomers.

But if you were there for companionship there were girls upstairs who sat out in front of their doors if they weren't occupied with a customer. Huey Barnes sat in the hall on the second floor. He was a wide-hipped, heavy-boned man who had the face of an innocent child. But Huey was fast and vicious despite his looks, and his presence caused all business at Vernie's to run smoothly.

I went there in the early afternoon.

"Easy Rawlins." Darcel reached her fat hands out to me. "I did believe that you had died and left us for heaven."

"Uh-uh, Darcie. You know I just been savin' it up for ya."

"Well bring it on in here, baby. Bring it on in."

She led me by the hand to the living room. A few men were sitting around drinking and listening to jazz records. There was a big bowl of dirty rice on the coffee table and white porcelain plates too.

"Easy Rawlins!" The voice came from the door to the kitchen.

"How you, baby?" Vernie asked as she ran up to me.

"Just fine, Vernie, just fine."

The big woman hugged me so that I felt I was being rolled up in a feather mattress.

"Uh," she groaned, almost lifting me from the floor. "It's been too long, honey. Too long!"

"Yeah, yeah," I said. I hugged her back and then lowered onto the couch.

Vernie smiled on me. "You stay put now, Easy. I want you to tell me how things is goin' before you go wandrin' upstairs." And with that she went back to the kitchen.

"Hey, Ronald, what's goin' on?" I said to the man next to me.

"Not much, Ease," Ronald White answered. He was a plumber for the city. Ronald always wore his plumber's overalls no matter where he was. He said that a man's work clothes are the only real clothes he has.

"Takin' a break from all them boys?" I liked to kid Ronald about his family. His wife dropped a son every twelve or fourteen months. She was a religious woman and didn't believe in taking precautions. At the age of thirty-four Ronald had nine sons, and one on the way.

"They like to tear the place down, Easy. I swear." Ronald shook his head. "They'd be climbin' 'cross the ceilin' if they could get a good hold. You know they got me afraid to go home."

"Oh com'on now, man. It can't be that bad."

Ronald's forehead wrinkled up like a prune, and he had pain in his face when he said, "No lie, Easy. I come on in and there's a whole army of 'em, runnin' right at me. First the big ones come leapin'. Then the ones can hardly walk. And while the little ones come crawlin' Mary walks in, so weak that she's like death, and she's got two babies in her arms.

"I tell ya, Easy. I spend fifty dollars on food and just watch them chirren destroy it. They eat every minute that they ain't yellin'." There were actually tears in Ronald's eyes. "I swear I can't take it, man. I swear."

"Darcel!" I yelled. "Come bring Ronald a drink, quick. You know he needs it too."

Darcel brought in a bottle of I. W. Harpers and poured all three of us a drink. I handed her three dollars for the bottle.

"Yeah," Curtis Cross said. He was sitting in front of a plate of rice at the dining table. "Chirren is the most dangerous creatures on the earth, with the exception of young girls between the ages of fifteen and forty-two."

That even got Ronald to smile.

"I don't know," Ronald said. "I love Mary but I think I'm'a have to run soon. Them kids a'kill me if I don't."

"Have another drink, man. Darcie, just keep 'em comin', huh? This man needs to forget."

"You already paid for this bottle, Easy. You can waste it any way you want." Like most black women Darcel wasn't happy to hear about a man who wanted to abandon his wife and kids.

"Just three dollars and you still make some money?" I acted like I was surprised.

"We buy bulk, Easy." Darcie smiled at me.

"Could I buy it like that too?" I asked, as if it was the first time I had ever heard of buying hijack.

"I don't know, honey. You know Momma and me let Huey take care of the shoppin'."

That was it for me. Huey wasn't the kind of man to ask about Frank Green. Huey was like Junior Fornay—mean and spiteful. He was no one to tell my business.

I drove Ronald home at about nine. He was crying on my shoulder when I let him out at his house.

"Please don't make me go in there, Easy. Take me with you, brother."

I was trying to keep from laughing. I could see Mary at the door. She was thin except for her belly and there was a baby boy in each of her arms. All their children crowded around her in the doorway pushing each other back to get a look at their father coming home.

"Come on now, Ron. You made all them babies, now you got to sleep in your bed."

I remember thinking that if I lived through the troubles I had then, my life would be pretty good. But Ronald didn't have any chance to be happy, unless he broke his poor family's heart.

During the next day I went to the bars that Frank sold hijack to and to the alley crap games that he frequented. I never brought up Frank's name though. Frank was skitterish, like all gangsters, and if he felt that people were talking about him he got nervous; if Frank was nervous he might have killed me before I had time to make my pitch.

It was those two days more than any other time that made me a detective.

I felt a secret glee when I went into a bar and ordered a beer with money someone else had paid me. I'd ask the bartender his name and talk about anything, but, really, behind my friendly talk, I was working to find something. Nobody knew what I was up to and that made me sort of invisible; people thought that they saw me but what they really saw was an illusion of me, something that wasn't real.

I never got bored or frustrated. I wasn't even afraid of DeWitt Albright during those days. I felt, foolishly, safe from even his crazy violence.

• 19 •

Zeppo could always be found on the corner of Forty-ninth and McKinley. He was half Negro, half Italian, and palsied. He stood there looking to the world like a skinny, knotted-up minister when the word of the Lord gets in him. He'd shake and writhe with all kinds of frowns on his face. Sometimes he'd bend all the way down to the ground and place both palms on the pavement as if the street were trying to swallow him and he was pushing it away.

Ernest, the barber, let Zeppo stand out in front of his shop to beg because he knew that the neighborhood children wouldn't bother Zeppo as long as he stood in front of the barber's pane.

"Hey, Zep, how you doin'?" I asked.

"J-j-ju-j-just fi-f-f-fi-f-fine, Ease." Sometimes words would come easy to him and other times he couldn't even finish a sentence.

"Nice day, huh?"

"Y-y-y-yeah. G-go-g-g-go-good d-day," he stammered, holding his hands before his face, like claws.

"Alright," I said, and then I walked into the barbershop.

"Hey, Easy," Ernest said as he folded his newspaper and stood up from his barber's chair. I took his place and he blossomed the crisp white sheet over me, knotting the bib snug at my throat.

"I thought you come in on Thursdays, Ease?"

"Man can't always be the same, Ernest. Man gotta change with the days."

"Hotcha! Lord, give me that seven!" someone shouted from the back of the narrow shop. There was always a game of craps at the back of Ernest's shop; a group of five men were on their knees back beyond the third barber chair.

"So you looked in the mirror this mo'nin' and saw a haircut, huh?" Ernest asked me.

"Grizzly as a bear."

Ernest laughed and took a couple of practice snips with his scissors.

Ernest always played Italian opera on the radio. If you asked him why he'd just say that Zeppo liked it. But Zeppo couldn't hear that radio from the street and Ernest only had him in the shop once a month, for his free haircut.

Ernest's father had been a drinking man. He beat poor little Ernest and Ernest's mother until the blood ran. So Ernest didn't have much patience with drinkers. And Zeppo was a drinker. I guess all that shaking didn't seem so bad if he had a snout full of cheap whiskey. So he'd beg until he had enough for a can of beans and a half-pint of scotch. Then Zeppo would get drunk.

It was because Zeppo was almost always drunk, or on the way to being drunk, that Ernest wouldn't allow him in the shop.

I once asked him why he'd let Zeppo hang out in front of the store if he hated drunks so much. And he told me, "The Lord might ask one day why I didn't look over my little brother."

We shot the breeze while the men threw their bones and Zeppo twisted and jerked in the window; *Don Giovanni* whispered from the radio. I wanted to find out the whereabouts of Frank Green but it had to come up in normal conversation. Most barbers know all the important information in the community. That's why I was getting my hair cut.

Ernest was brushing the hot lather around my ears when Jackson Blue came in the door.

"Happenin', Ernest, Ease," he hailed.

"Jackson," I said.

"Lenny over there, Blue," Ernest warned.

I glanced over at Lenny. He was a fat man, on his knees in a gardener's suit and a white painter's cap. He was biting a cigar butt and squinting at Jackson Blue.

"You tell that skinny bastard t'get away from here, Ernie. I kill the mothahfuckah. I ain't foolin'," Lenny warned.

"He ain't messin' wit' you, Lenny. Get back to your game or get outta my shop."

One nice thing about barbers is that they have a dozen straight razors that they will use to keep order in their shops.

"What's wrong with Lenny?" I asked.

"Just a fool," Ernest said. "Thas all. Jackson here is too."

"What happened?"

Jackson was a small man and very dark. He was so black that his skin glinted blue in the full sun. He cowered and shone his big eyes at the door.

"Lenny's girlfriend, you know Elba, left him again," Ernest said.

"Yeah?" I was wondering how to turn the conversation to Frank Green.

"And she come purrin' 'round Jackson just t'get Lenny riled."

Jackson was looking at the floor. He wore a loose, striped blue suit and small-brimmed brown felt hat.

"She did?"

"Yeah, Easy. And you know Jackson stick his business in a meat grinder if it winked at him."

"I 'idn't mess wit' her. She jus' tole 'im that." Jackson was pouting.

"I guess my stepbrother be lyin' too?" Lenny was right there with us. It was like a comic scene in the movies because Jackson looked scared, like a cornered dog, and Lenny, with his fat gut hanging down, was like a bully dog bearing down on him.

"Back off!" Ernest shouted, putting himself between the two men. "Any man can come in here wit'out fightin' if he wants."

"This skinny lil booze hound gonna have to answer on Elba, Ernie."

"He ain't gonna do it here. I swear you gonna have t'come through me t'get Jackson and you know he ain't worth that kinda pain."

I remembered then how Jackson sometimes made his money.

Lenny reached out at Jackson but the little man got behind Ernest and Ernest stood there, like a rock. He said, "Go back to your game while the blood still in your veins, man," then he pulled a straight razor from the pocket of his blue smock.

"You ain't got no cause to threaten me, Ernie. I ain't shit on no man's doorstep." He was moving his head back and forth trying to see Jackson behind the barber's back.

I started to get nervous sitting there between them and took off the bib. I used it to wipe the lather from my neck.

"See that, Lenny. You botherin' my customer, brother." Ernest pointed a finger thick as a railroad tie at Lenny's belly. "Either you get back in the back or I'm'a skin ya. No lie."

Anybody who knew Ernest knew that that was his last warning. You had to be tough to be a barber because your place was the center of business for a certain element in the community. Gamblers, numbers runners, and all sorts of other private businessmen met in the barbershop. The barbershop was like a social club. And any social club had to have order to run smoothly.

Lenny tucked in his chin and shifted his shoulders this way and that, then he shuffled backwards a few steps.

I got out of the chair and slapped six bits down on the counter. "There you go, Ernie," I said.

Ernie nodded in my direction but he was too busy staring Lenny down to look at me.

"Why don't we split," I said to the cowering Jackson. Whenever Jackson was nervous he'd have to touch his thing; he was holding on to it right then.

"Sure, Easy. I think Ernie got it covered here."

We turned down the first corner we came to and then down an alley, half a block away. If Lenny was to come after us he'd have to want us bad enough to hunt.

He didn't find us, but as we were walking down Merriweather Lane someone shouted, "Blue!"

It was Zeppo. He hobbled after us like a man on invisible crutches. At every step he teetered on the edge of falling over but then he'd take another step, saving himself, just barely.

"Hey, Zep," Jackson said. He was looking over Zeppo's shoulder to see if Lenny was coming.

"J-Jackson."

"What you want, Zeppo?" I wanted something from Jackson myself and I didn't need an audience.

Zeppo craned his head back further than I thought was possible, then he brought his wrists to his shoulder. He looked like a bird in agony. His smile was like death itself. "L-L-Lenny show i-is m-m-m-m-ad." Then he started coughing, which for Zeppo was a laugh. "Y-y-you-ou s-sellin', B-Blue?"

I could have kissed the cripple.

"Naw, man," Jackson said. "Frank gone big time now. He only sell by the crate to the stores. He say he don't want no nickels and dimes."

"You don't sell fo' Frank any more?" I asked.

"Uh-uh. He too big fo' a niggah like me."

"Shit! An' I was lookin' fo' some whiskey too. I gotta party in mind that need some booze."

"Well maybe I could set a deal, Ease." Jackson's eyes lit up. He was still turning now and then to see if Lenny was coming.

"Like what?"

"Maybe if you buy enough Frank'a cut us a deal."

"Like how much?"

"How much you need?"

"Case or two of Jim Beam be fine."

Jackson scratched his chin. "Frank'a sell by the case t'me. I could buy three an' sell one by the bottle."

"When you gonna see 'im?" I must've sounded too eager because a caution light went on in Jackson's eye. He waited a long moment then said, "Whas up, Easy?"

"What you mean?"

"I mean," he said, "why is you lookin' fo' Frank?"

"Man, I don't know what you mean. All I know is I got people comin' to the house on Saturday and the cupboard is bare. I got a couple'a bucks but I was laid off last Monday and I can't spend it all on whiskey."

All this time Zeppo was shimmying there next to us. He was waiting to see if a bottle would materialize out of our talk.

"Yeah, well, if you need it fast," Jackson said, still suspicious, "what if I get you a deal somewhere's else?"

"I don't care. All I want is some cheap whiskey and I thought that was the business you did."

"It is, Easy. You know I usually buy from Frank but maybe I could go someplace he sells ta. Cost a little more but you still save some money."

"Anything you say, Jackson. Just lead me to the well."

"M-m-m-m-me too," Zeppo added.

• 20 •

When we got to my car I drove down Central to Seventy-sixth Place. I was nervous being so close to the police station but I had to find Frank Green.

Jackson took Zeppo and me down to Abe's liquor store. I was glad that Zeppo had come along with us because people who didn't know Zeppo kept their eyes and attention on him. I was banking on that to hide any questions I asked about Frank.

On the way down to the liquor store Jackson told me the story of the men that owned it.

Abe and Johnny were brothers-in-law. They came from Poland, most recently from the town of Auschwitz; Jews who survived the Nazi camps. They were barbers in Poland and they were barbers in Auschwitz, too.

Abe was part of the underground in the camp and he saved Johnny from the gas chamber when Johnny was so sick that the Nazi guard had selected him to die. Abe dug a hole in the wall next to his bed and he put Johnny there, telling the guard that Johnny had died and was picked up, by the evening patrol, for cremation. Abe collected food from his friends in the resistance and fed his ailing brother-in-law through a hole in the wall. That went on for three months before the camp was liberated by the Russians.

Abe's wife and sister, Johnny's wife, were dead. Their parents and cousins and everyone else they had ever known or had ever been related to had died in the Nazi camps. Abe took Johnny on a stretcher and dragged him to the GI station where they applied to immigrate.

Jackson wanted to tell me more stories he'd heard about the camps but I didn't need to hear them. I remembered the Jews. Nothing more than skeletons, bleeding from their rectums and begging for food. I remembered them waving their weak hands in front of themselves, trying to keep modest; then dropping dead right there before my eyes.

Sergeant Vincent LeRoy found a twelve-year-old boy who was bald and weighed forty-six pounds. The boy ran to Vincent and hugged his leg, like the little Mexican boy clung to Matthew Teran. Vincent was a hard man, a gunner, but he melted for that little boy. He called him Tree Rat because of the way the boy crawled up on him and wouldn't let go.

The first day Vincent carried Tree Rat on his back while we evacuated the concentration camp survivors. That night he made Tree Rat go with the nurses to the evacuation center, but the little boy got away from them and made it back to our bivouac.

Vincent decided to keep him after that. Not the way Matthew Teran kept the Mexican boy, but like any man whose heart goes out to children.

Little Tree, as I called him, rode on Vincent's back all the next day. He ate a giant chocolate bar that Vincent had in his pack and other sweets the men gave him.

That night we were awakened by Tree's moaning. His little stomach had distended even more and he couldn't even hear us trying to soothe him.

The camp doctor said that he died from the richness of the food he'd been eating.

Vincent cried for a whole day after Tree Rat died. He blamed himself, and I suppose he had a share of the blame. But I'll never forget thinking how those Germans had hurt that poor boy so terribly that he couldn't even take in anything good. That was why so many

Jews back then understood the American Negro; in Europe the Jew had been a Negro for more than a thousand years.

Abe and Johnny came to America and had a liquor store in less than two years. They worked hard for what they got but there was just one thing wrong: Johnny was wild.

Jackson said, "I don't know if he got like that in that hole in the wall or he was always like that. He said that he went crazy for a night, once, because him an' Abe had to cut the hair from they own wives' heads fo' they went to the gas chambers. Imagine that? Cuttin' yo' own wife's hair an' then sendin' her ta die? . . . Anyway, maybe he went crazy for the night an' now that's why he's so wild."

"What you mean, wild?" I asked him.

"Just wild, Easy. One night I goes down there with this high school girl, Donna Frank, an' I'm lookin' to impress her wit' some liquor and Abe is already gone. So Johnny acts like I'm not even there an' he start tellin' her how pretty she is an' how he'd like t'give her sumpin'."

"Yeah?"

"He give her five dollars an' had me stand at the register while he fuckin' her right there behind the counter!"

"You lyin'!"

"Naw, Easy, that boy gotta screw loose, couple of 'em."

"So you go inta business then?"

"Shit no, that dude scared me. But I told Frank about it and he made the connection. You see, Frank had gone to Abe one time but Abe didn't want nuthin' t'do wit' no hijack. But Johnny love it, all he sells is hijack after Abe go home at night."

"Frank delivers here regular?" I asked.

"Yeah."

"Just like a delivery truck, huh?" I laughed. "He drive up on Wednesday afternoon an' unload."

"Us'ly it's Thursday," Jackson said, but then he frowned.

It was just a hole-in-the-wall liquor store. They had one rack for cakes, potato chips, and bagged pork rinds in the middle of the floor.

There was a long candy counter and behind that were the shelves of liquor and the cash register. At the back wall was a glass-door refrigerator where they had mixers and soda pop.

Johnny was a tall man with sandy hair and glassy brown eyes. There was a look on his face halfway between a smile and wonderment. He looked like a young boy who had already gone bad.

"Hiya, Johnny," Jackson said. "This here's my friends Easy an' Zeppo."

Zeppo came twisting in behind us. Johnny's smile hardened a little when he saw Zeppo. Some people are afraid of palsy, maybe they're afraid they'll catch it.

"Good day, sirs," he said to us.

"You gonna have to start givin' me a percent, Johnny, much business as I bring you. Easy gettin' ready fo' a party an' Zeppo need his milk ev'ry day."

Johnny laughed, keeping his eyes on Zeppo. He asked, "What do you need, Easy?"

"I need a case'a Jim Beam an' Jackson say you could get it a little cheaper than normal."

"I can give it discount if you buy by the box." His accent was heavy but he understood English well enough.

"What can you do for two cases?"

"Three dollars the bottle, anywhere else you pay four."

"Yeah, that's good, but just a touch over my budget. You know I lost my job last week."

"Oh, that's too bad," Johnny said, and turned to me. "Here it is your birthday and they throw you out."

"Just a party. How 'bout two-seventy-five?"

He brought up his right hand rubbing the fingers. "I'd be giving it to you for that, my friend. But I tell you what," he said. "Two cases at three dollars is fifty-four. I let you have them for fifty."

I should have haggled for more but I was impatient to get out of there. I could tell Albright that Frank would be there Friday and on Thursday Frank and I would make a deal.

"Deal," I said. "Can I pick it up tomorrow?"

"Why can't we do business now?" he asked suspiciously.

"I ain't got no fifty dollars on me, man. I could get it by tomorrow."

"I can't do it until Friday. I have another delivery Friday."

"Why not tomorrow?" I asked just to throw him off.

"I can't sell all my whiskey to one man, Easy. Tomorrow I will get two cases but what if a customer comes in and wants Jim Beam? If I don't have it he goes to another store. Not good for business."

We settled the deal with a ten-dollar deposit. I bought Zeppo a half-pint of Harpers and I gave Jackson a five.

"Whas happenin', Easy?" Jackson said to me after Zeppo had gone off.

"Nuthin'. What you talkin' 'bout?"

"I mean you ain't givin' no party. An' you ain't usually gettin' no haircut on a Wednesday neither. Sumpin's up."

"You dreamin', man. Party gonna be Saturday night an' you welcome t'come."

"Uh-huh." He eyed me warily. "Whas all this got to do with Frank?"

My stomach filled with ice water but I didn't let it show. "This ain't got nuthin' t'do with Frank Green, man. I just want some liquor."

"Alright. Sounds good. You know I be around if they's a party t'be had."

"See ya then," I said. I was hoping that I'd still be alive.

All I had to do was live for twenty-four hours, until Frank made his weekly rounds.

• 21 •

I stopped by Joppy's on the way back from the liquor store.

It felt like home to see him buffing that marble top. But I was uncomfortable. I had always respected Joppy as a friend. I was also a little wary of him because you had to be careful around a fighter.

When I got to the bar I dug both hands into the pockets of my cotton jacket. I had so much to say that, for a moment, I couldn't say anything.

"What you starin' at, Ease?"

"I don't know, Jop."

Joppy laughed and ran his hand over his bald head. "What you mean?"

"That girl called me the other night."

"What girl is that?"

"The one your friend's lookin' for."

"Uh-huh." Joppy put down his rag and placed his hands on the bar. "That's pretty lucky, I guess."

"I guess so."

The bar was empty. Joppy and I were studying each other's eyes.

"But I don't think it was luck, really," I said.

"No?"

"No, Joppy, it was you."

The muscles in Joppy's forearms writhed when he clenched his fists. "How you figure?"

"It's the only answer, Jop. You and Coretta were the only ones who knew I was lookin' for her. I mean DeWitt Albright knew but he'd'a just gone after the girl if he knew where she was. And Coretta was still lookin' to get money from me, so she wouldn't want me knowin' she talked to Daphne. It was you, man."

"She could'a looked you up in the phone book."

"I ain't in the book, Joppy."

I didn't know for sure if I was right. Daphne could have found me some other way, but I didn't think so.

"Why, man?" I asked.

Joppy's hard face never let you know what he was thinking. But I don't think he suspected the lead pipes I had clenched in my pockets either.

After a long minute he gave me a friendly smile and said, "Don't get all hot, man. It ain't so bad."

"What you mean, ain't so bad?" I yelled. "Coretta's dead, your friend Albright is on my ass, the cops already brought me down once—"

"I din't mean for none'a that t'happen, Easy, you gotta believe it."

"Now Albright got me chasin' Frank Green," I blurted out.

"Frank Green?" Joppy's eyes tightened to birds' eyes.

"Yeah. Frank Green."

"Okay, Easy. Lemme tell ya how it is. Albright come here lookin' for that girl. He showed me the picture and right away I knew who it was . . ."

"How'd you know that?" I asked.

"Sometimes Frank bring her along when he deliverin' liquor. I figured she was his girl or sumpin'."

"But you didn't say nuthin' to Albright?"

"Naw. Frank's my supply, I ain't gonna get in bad with him. I just waited until he come back with her and I let her know, on the sly, that I got some information that she want to know. She called me and I give it to her."

"Why? Why you want to help her?"

Joppy flashed a smile at me that was as close to shy as he was likely to get. "She's a pretty girl, Easy. Very pretty. I wouldn't mind her bein' my friend."

"Why not just tell Frank?"

"And have him come in here swingin' that knife? Shit. Frank is crazy."

Joppy relaxed a little when he saw that I was listening. He picked up his rag again. "Yeah, Ease, I thought I could get you some money and send Albright on a wrong trail. It would'a all been fine if you had listened t'me and laid off lookin'."

"Why you had her call me?"

Joppy clamped his jaw so that the bones stood out under his ears. "She called me and wanted me to help her go somewhere, to some friend she said. But I didn't want none of it. You know I could help as long as all I had to do was from behind the bar, but I wasn't goin' nowhere."

"But why me?"

"I told her t'call ya. She wanna know what DeWitt want, and you the one workin' fo' him." Joppy hunched his shoulders. "I give her your number. I couldn't see where it hurt."

"So you just playin' me for the fool and then, when you finished, you gimme t'her."

"Nobody made you take that man's money. Nobody made you see that girl."

He was right about that. He talked me into it, but I was hungry for that money too.

"Her friend was dead," I said.

"White guy?"

"Uh-huh. And Coretta James is dead, and whoever killed her also got to Howard Green."

"That's what I heard." Joppy threw the rag under the counter and brought out a short glass. While pouring my whiskey he said, "I din't mean fo' all this, Easy. Just tryin' t'help you and that girl."

"That girl is the devil, man," I said. "She got evil in every pocket."

"Maybe you should get out of it, Ease. Take a trip back east or down south or sumpin'."

"That's what Odell told me. But I ain't gonna run, man."

I knew what I had to do. I had to find Frank and tell him about the money that Carter offered. Frank was a businessman at heart. And if DeWitt Albright stood in the way of Frank's business I'd just stand to the side and let them fight it out.

Joppy filled my glass again. It was a kind of peace-offering. He really hadn't tried to hurt me. It was just the lie that stuck in my craw.

"Whyn't you tell me 'bout the girl?" I asked him.

"I don't know, Easy. She wanted me t'keep it quiet like and"—Joppy's face softened—"I wanted to keep her . . . secret. To myself, ya know?"

I took my drink and offered Joppy a cigarette. We smoked our peace and sat in friendship. We didn't speak again for a long time.

Later on Joppy asked, "Who you think been killin' all them folks?"

"I don't know, man. Odell told me that the cops think it might be a maniac. And maybe it was with Coretta and Howard but I know who killed that Richard McGee."

"Who?"

"I can't see where it helps either of us for me to tell you. Best t'keep that to myself."

I was thinking these things as I walked through the gate and up the path to my house. It wasn't until I was almost to the door that I realized that the gate wasn't double-latched, the way the postman usually left it.

Before I turned back to look an explosion went off in my head. I started a long fall through the twilight toward the cement stair of my front porch. But for some reason I didn't hit the stair. The door flung open and I found myself face down on the couch. I wanted to get up but the loud noise in my head made me dizzy.

Then he turned me over.

He was wearing a dark blue suit, so dark that you might have mistaken it for black. He wore a black shirt. His black shoe was on the cushion next to my head. There was a short-rimmed black Stetson on his head. His face was as black as the rest of him. The only color to Frank Green was his banana-colored tie, loosely knotted at his throat.

"Hi, Frank." The words shot pain through my head.

Frank's right fist made a snickering sound and a four-inch blade appeared, like a chrome-colored flame.

"Hear you been lookin' fo' me, Easy."

I tried to sit up but he shoved my face back down onto the couch. "Hear you been lookin' fo' me," he said again.

"That's right, Frank. I need to talk to you. I gotta deal for you, make us both five hundred dollars."

Frank's black face cracked into a white grin. He put his knee against my chest and pressed the tip of his knife, just barely, into my throat. I could feel the flesh prick and the blood trickle.

"I'm'a have t'kill you, Easy."

My first reaction was to look around to see if there was something that might save me but there was nothing except walls and furniture. Then I noticed something strange. The straight-back wood chair that I kept in the kitchen was pulled up to my sofa chair as if someone had used it for a footrest. I don't know why I concentrated on that; for all I knew Frank had pulled it out while I was still out of it.

"Hear me out," I said.

"What?"

"I might could make it seven-fifty."

"How a mechanic gonna get that kinda money?"

"Man wanna talk to a girl you know. Rich man. He pay that much just to talk."

"What girl?" Frank's voice was almost a growl.

"White girl. Daphne Monet."

"You a dead man, Easy," Frank said.

"Frank, listen to me. You got me wrong, man."

"You been nosin' all 'round after me. I been hearin' it. You even goin' where I'm doin' business and where I be drinkin'. I come back from my little business trip and now Daphne's gone and you in every hole I shit in." His hard yellow eyes were staring right into mine.

"The cops lookin' fo' me too, Easy. Somebody kilt Coretta and I hear you was around 'fore she died."

"Frank . . ."

He pressed the blade a little harder. "You dead, Easy," he said and then he shifted the weight of his shoulder.

The voice said, "Don't cry or beg, Easy. Don't give this nigger the satisfaction."

"Evenin', Frank," somebody said in a friendly tone. It wasn't me. I could tell that it was real because Frank froze. He was still staring at me but his attention was at his back.

"Who's that?" he croaked.

"Been a long time, Frank. Must be ten years."

"That you, Mouse?"

"You got a good mem'ry, Frank. I always like a man got a good memory, cause nine times outta eleven he's a smart man could 'preciate a tough problem. 'Cause you know I got a problem here, Frank."

"What's that?"

Right then the phone rang, and I'll be damned if Mouse didn't answer it!

"Yeah?" he said. "Yeah, yeah, Easy's here but he kinda busy right now. Uh-huh, yeah, sure. Could he call you right back? No? Okay. Yeah. Yeah, try back in 'bout a hour, he be free by then."

I heard him put the phone back on the hook. I couldn't see past Frank Green's chest.

"Where was I . . . oh yeah, I was gonna tell ya my problem. You see, Frank, I got this here long-barreled forty-one-caliber pistol pointed at the back'a yo' head. But I cain't shoot it 'cause I'm afraid that if you fall you gonna cut my partner's throat. Thas some problem, huh?"

Frank just stared at me.

"So what you think I should do, Frank? I know you just itchin' t'cut on poor Easy but I don't think you gonna live t'smile 'bout it, brother."

"Ain't none'a yo' business, Mouse."

"I tell you what, Frank. You put down that knife right there on the couch an' I let you live. You don't an' you dead. I ain't gonna count or no bullshit like that now. Just one minute and I'm'a shoot."

Frank slowly took the knife from my throat and placed it on the couch, where it could be seen from behind.

"Okay now, stand away and sit over in this here chair."

Frank did as he was told and there was Mouse, beautiful as he could be. His smile glittered. Some of the teeth were rimmed with gold and some were capped. One tooth had a gold rim with a blue jewel in it. He wore a plaid zoot suit with Broadway suspenders down the front of his shirt. He had spats on over his patent leather shoes and the biggest pistol I had ever seen held loosely in his left hand.

Frank was staring at that pistol too.

Knifehand was a bad man but there wasn't a man in his right mind who knew Mouse who didn't give him respect.

"'S'appenin', Easy?"

"Mouse," I said. Blood covered the front of my shirt; my hands were shaking.

"Want me t'kill 'im, Ease?"

"Hey!" Frank yelled. "We hadda deal!"

"Easy my oldest partner, man. I shoot yo' ugly face off and ain't nuthin' you gonna say t'stop me."

"We don't need t'kill 'im. All I need is a couple of answers." I realized that I didn't need Frank if I had Mouse on my side.

"Then get t'askin', man," Mouse grinned.

"Where's Daphne Monet?" I asked Green. He just stared at me, his eyes sharp as his knife.

"You heard 'im, Frank," Mouse said. "Where is she?"

Frank's eyes weren't so sharp when he looked at Mouse but he stayed quiet anyway.

"This ain't no game, Frank." Mouse let the pistol hang down until the muzzle was pointing at the floor. He walked up to Frank; so close that Knifehand could have grabbed him. But Frank stayed still. He knew that Mouse was just playing with him.

"Tell us what we wanna know, Frankie, or I'm'a shoot ya."

Frank's jaw set and his left eye half closed. I could see that Daphne meant enough to him that he was ready to die to keep her safe.

Mouse raised the pistol so that it was pointing to the soft place under Frank's jaw.

"Let 'im go," I said.

"But you said you had a five-hundred-dollar deal." Mouse was hungry to hurt Frank, I could hear it in his tone.

"Let'im go, man. I don't want him killed in my house." I thought maybe Mouse would sympathize with keeping blood off the furniture.

"Gimme your keys then. I take him for a drive." Mouse smiled an evil grin. "He'll tell me what I wanna know."

Without warning Mouse pistol-whipped Frank three times; every blow made a sickening thud. Frank fell to his knees with the dark blood coming down over his dark clothes.

When Frank fell to the floor I jumped between him and Mouse.

"Let 'im go!" I cried.

"Get outta my way, Easy!" There was bloodlust in Mouse's voice.

I grabbed for his arm. "Let him be, Raymond!"

Before anything else could happen I felt Frank pushing me from behind. I was propelled onto Mouse and we fell to the floor. I hugged Mouse to break my fall but also to keep him from shooting Frank. By the time the wiry little man got out from under me Frank had bolted out the door.

"Dammit, Easy!" He turned with the pistol loosely aimed at me. "Don't you never grab me when I got a gun in my hand! You crazy?"

Mouse ran to the window but Frank was gone.

I hung back for a moment while Mouse calmed down.

After a minute or two he turned away from the window and looked down at his jacket. "Look at the blood you got on my coat, Easy! Why you wanna go and do that?"

"I need Frank Green alive. You kill him and one of my sources dries up."

"What? What that got to do with this mess?" Mouse took off his jacket and draped it over his arm. "That the bathroom?" he asked, pointing to the door.

"Yeah," I said.

He hung the pistol in his belt and carried the stained jacket to the toilet. I heard the water running.

When Mouse returned I was staring out the front window, through the slatted blinds.

"He ain't gonna be back t'night, Easy. Tough man like Frank seen too much death to want it on him."

"What you doin' here, Mouse?"

"Din't you call Etta?"

"Yeah?"

Mouse was looking at me, shaking his head and smiling.

"Easy, you changed."

"How's that?"

"You use' t'be kinda scared of everything. Take them little nigger jobs like gardenin' and cleanin' up. Now you got this nice house and you fuckin' some white man's girl."

"I ain't touched her, man."

"Not yet."

"Not ever!"

"Com'on Easy, this is the Mouse you talkin' to. A woman look twice at you an' you cain't say no. I should know."

I had messed around with Etta behind Mouse's back when they were just engaged. He found out about it but he didn't care. Mouse never worried about what his women did. But if I'd touched his money he'd have killed me straight away.

"So what you doin' here?" I asked to change the subject.

"First thing I want to figure is how I can get that money you told Frank about."

"No, Mouse. That has nuthin' t'do with you."

"You gotta man comin' here wanna kill you, Easy. Yo' eye look like hamburger. Man, I could see why you called me, you could use some help."

"No, Raymond, I did call ya, but that was when I was low. I mean I'm glad you saved me, man, but your kinda help ain't nuthin' I could use."

"Com'on Easy, you let me in on it an' we both come outta this wit' sumpin'."

He had said about exactly the same words to me eight years before. When everything was over I had two dead men on my soul.

"No, Raymond."

Mouse stared at me for a minute. He had light gray eyes; eyes that seemed to see through everything.

"I said no, Mouse."

"Tell me 'bout it, Easy." He leaned back into his chair. "Ain't no other way, brother."

"What you mean?"

"Nigger cain't pull his way out the swamp wit'out no help, Easy. You wanna hole on t'this house and git some money and have you some white girls callin' on the phone? Alright. That's alright. But, Easy, you gotta have somebody at yo' back, man. That's just a lie them white men give 'bout makin' it on they own. They always got they backs covered."

"All I want is my chance," I said.

"Yeah, Easy. Yeah, that's all."

"But let me tell ya," I said. "I'm scared t'get mixed up wit' you, man."

Mouse flashed his golden smile at me. "What?"

"You remember when we went to Pariah? To get yo' weddin' money?"

"Yeah?"

"Daddy Reese an' Clifton died, Ray. They died 'cause'a you."

When Mouse stopped smiling the light in the room seemed to go dim. All of a sudden he was pure business; he'd just been playing with Frank Green.

"What you mean?"

"You kilt 'em, man! You, an' me too! Clifton came to me two nights fo' he died. He wanted me t'tell 'im what t'do. He tole me how you planned t'use him." I felt the tears pressing my eyes but held them back. "But I didn't say nuthin'. I just let that boy go. Now ev'rybody think he killed Reese but I know it was you. And that hurts me, man."

Mouse rubbed his mouth, never even blinking.

"That been botherin' you all this time?" He sounded surprised.

"Yeah."

"That was a lotta years ago, Easy, an' you wasn't even there, really."

"Guilt don't tell time," I said.

"Guilt?" He said the word as if it had no meaning. "You mean like what *I* did makes you feel bad?"

"That's right."

"I tell you what then," he said, putting his hands up at his shoulders. "You let me work on this with you and I let you run the show."

"Whas that mean?"

"I ain't gonna do nuthin' you don't tell me t'do."

"Everything I say?"

"Whatever you say, Easy. Maybe you gonna show me how a poor man can live wit'out blood."

We didn't touch the whiskey.

I told Mouse what I knew; it wasn't much. I told him that DeWitt Albright was up to no good. I told him that I could get a thousand dollars for information about Daphne Monet because there was a price on her head.

When he asked me what she had done I looked him in the eye and said, "I don't know."

Mouse puffed on a cigarette while he listened to me. "Frank come back here an' you might not get out again," he said when I stopped talking.

"We ain't gonna be here neither, man. We both leave in the morning an' follow this thing down." I told him where he could find DeWitt Albright. I also told him how he could get in touch with Odell Jones and Joppy if he needed help. The plan was to put Mouse on Frank's trail and I'd look into the places I had seen Daphne. We'd come up with the girl and improvise from there.

It felt good to be fighting back. Mouse was a good soldier, though I worried about him following orders. And if I had the whole thing scammed out right we'd both come out on top; I'd still be alive and have my house too.

Mouse fell asleep on my living room sofa. He was always a good sleeper. He once told me that they'd have to wake him for his execution because "the Mouse ain't gonna miss his rest."

• 22 •

I didn't tell Mouse everything.

I didn't tell him about the money Daphne stole or the rich white man's name; or that I knew his name. Mouse probably meant to keep his word to me; he could keep from killing if he tried. But if he got a whiff of that thirty thousand dollars I knew that nothing would hold him back. He would have killed *me* for that much money.

"All you have to do is worry about Frank," I told him. "Just find out where he goes. If he leads you to the girl then we got it made. Understand me, Raymond, I just wanna find the girl, there ain't no reason to hurt Frank."

Mouse smiled at me. "Don't worry, Ease. I was just mad when I seen 'im over you like that. You know, it made me kinda wanna teach him a lesson."

"You gotta watch him," I said. "He know how to use that knife."

"Shit!" Mouse spat. "I'as born wit' a knife in my teefs."

The police met us as we were leaving the house at eight in the morning.

"Shit."

"Mr. Rawlins," Miller said. "We came to ask you a few more questions."

Mason was grinning.

"Guess I better be goin', Easy," Mouse said.

Mason put a fat hand against Mouse's chest. "Who are you?" he asked.

"Name is Navrochet," Mouse said. "I just come by t'get some money he owe me."

"Money for what?"

"Money I lent him over a year ago." Mouse produced a wad of bills, the topmost of which was a twenty.

The broad grin on Mason's fat face didn't make him any prettier. "And he's just got it now?"

"Better have," Mouse said. "Or you officers would be comin' fo' me."

The cops exchanged meaningful glances.

"Where do you live, Mr. Navrochet?" Miller asked. He took out a pad and a pen.

"Twenty-seven thirty-two and a half, down on Florence. It's upstairs in the back," Mouse lied.

"We might have some questions for you later," Miller informed him as he wrote down the address. "So you should stick around town."

"Anything you boys want. I work at that big World Carwash on Crenshaw. You know I be there if I ain't at my house. See ya, Easy." Mouse went swinging his arms and whistling. I never did figure out how he knew the streets so well to lie like that.

"Shall we go in?" Miller gestured back toward the house.

They put me in a chair and then they stood over me, like they meant business.

"What do you know about this Richard McGee?" Miller asked me.

When I looked up I saw them searching my face for the truth.

"Who?" I said.

"You heard me," Miller said.

"I don't know who you said." I was stalling for time to figure out what they knew. Mason laid a heavy hand on my shoulder.

"LAPD found a dead man in his house in Laurel Canyon last night," Miller told me. "Richard McGee. He had a hand-written note on his table."

Miller held out the scrap of paper to me. On it was scrawled "C. James."

"Sound familiar?" Miller asked.

I tried to look stupid; it wasn't very difficult.

"How about Howard Green? You know him?" Miller put his foot on my table and leaned forward so far that his gaunt face was no more than a few inches from mine.

"No."

"You don't? He goes to that nigger bar you were at with Coretta James. That place just isn't big enough to hide in."

"Well, maybe I'd know his face if you showed me," I said.

"That would be kinda hard," Mason growled. "He's dead and his face looks like hamburger."

"What about Matthew Teran, Ezekiel?" Miller asked.

"Course I know him. He was runnin' for mayor up till a few weeks ago. What the hell is this, anyway?" I stood up, faking disgust.

Miller said, "Teran called us the night we arrested you. He wanted to know if we'd found out who killed his driver, Howard Green."

I gave him a blank stare.

"We told him no," Miller continued. "But there had been another murder. Coretta James' murder, that had the same kind of violence related to it. He was real interested, Easy. He wanted to know all about you. He even came down to the station and had us point you out to him and his new driver."

I remembered the peephole in the door.

"I ain't never even met the man," I said.

"No?" Miller said. "Teran's body was found in his downstairs office this morning. He had a nice little bullet hole through his heart."

The spike through my head drove me back into the chair.

"We don't think you had anything to do with it, Ezekiel. At least, we can't prove anything. But you have to know something . . . and we have all day to ask you questions."

Mason grinned wide enough to show me his flaring red gums.

"I don't know what you guys are talking about. Maybe I know this dude Howard Green. I mean if he goes to John's I prob'ly know what he looks like but I don't know nuthin' else."

"I think you do, Ezekiel. And if you do but you don't tell us then things are going to get bad. Real bad for you."

"Man, I don't know a thing. People gettin' killed ain't got a thing to do with me. You took me in. You know I ain't got no record. I had me a drink with Dupree and Coretta and that's all. You cain't hang me for that."

"I can if I prove that you were in McGee's house."

I noticed that Miller had a small crescent scar under his right eye. It seemed to me that I always knew he had that scar. Like I knew it and I didn't know it at the same time.

"I ain't been there," I said.

"Where?" Miller asked eagerly.

"I ain't been to no dead man's house."

"There's a big fat fingerprint on the knife, Ezekiel. If it's yours then you're fried."

Mason took my jacket from a chair and held it out to me, like a butler might. He thought he had me so he could afford being polite.

They took me back down to the station for fingerprinting, then they sent the prints downtown to be compared against the one found on the knife.

Miller and Mason took me to the little room again for another round of questions.

They kept asking the same things. Did I know Howard Green? Did I know Richard McGee? Miller kept threatening to go down to John's and find somebody who could tie me to Green but we both knew that he was throwing a bluff. Back in those days there wasn't one Negro in a hundred who'd talk to the police. And those that did were just as likely to lie as anything else. And John's crowd was an especially close one so I was safe, at least from the testimony of friends.

But I was worried about the fingerprint.

I knew that I hadn't touched the knife but I didn't know what the police were up to. If they really wanted to catch who did the killing then they'd be fair and check my prints against the knife's and let me go. But maybe they needed a culprit. Maybe they just wanted to close the books because their record hadn't been so good over the year. You never could tell when it came to the cops and a colored neighborhood. The police didn't care about crime among Negroes. I mean, some soft-hearted cops got upset if a man killed his wife or did any such harm to a child. But the kind of violence that Frank Green dished out, the business kind of violence, didn't get anybody worried. The papers hardly ever even reported a colored murder. And when they did it was way in the back pages.

So if they wanted to get me for Howard Green's death, or Coretta's, then they might just frame me to cut down the paperwork. At least that's what I thought at the time.

The difference was that two white men had died also. To kill a white man was a real crime. My only hope was that these cops were interested in finding the real criminal.

I was still being questioned that afternoon when a young man in a loose brown suit entered the small room. He had a large brown envelope that he handed to Miller. He whispered something into Miller's ear and Miller nodded seriously as if he had heard something that was very important. The young man left and Miller turned to me; it was the only time I ever saw him smile.

"I got the answer on the fingerprints right here in this package, Ezekiel," he grinned.

"Then I guess I can go now."

"Uh-uh."

"What's it say?" Mason was frisking from side to side like a dog whose master had just come home.

"Looks like we got our killer."

My heart was beating so fast that I could hear the pulse in my ear. "Naw, man. I wasn't there."

I looked into Miller's face, not giving away an ounce of fear. I looked at him and I was thinking of every German I had ever killed. He couldn't scare me and he couldn't bring me down either.

Miller pulled out a white sheet from the envelope and looked at it. Then he looked at me. Then to the paper again.

"You can go, Mr. Rawlins," he said after a full minute. "But we're going to get you again. We're going to bring you down for something, Ezekiel, you can bank on that."

"Easy! Easy, over here!" Mouse hissed to me from my car across the street.

"Where'd you get my keys?" I asked him as I climbed in the passenger's side.

"Keys? Shit, man, all you gotta do is rub a couple'a sticks together an' you could start this thing."

The ignition had a bunch of taped wires hanging from it. Some other time I might have been mad but all I could do then was laugh.

"I was startin' t'think that I'd have t'come in after you, Ease," Mouse said. He patted the pistol that sat between us on the front seat.

"They don't have enough to hold me, yet. But if something don't happen fo' them real soon they might just take it in their heads to fo'get ev'rybody else an' drag me down."

"Well," Mouse said, "I found out where Dupree is holed up. We could go stay with him and figger what's next."

I wanted to talk to Dupree but there was something that was more important.

"We go over there a little later, but first I want you to drive somewhere."

"Where's that?"

"Go up to the corner and take a left," I said.

• 23 •

Portland Court was a horseshoe of tiny apartments not far from Joppy's place, near 107th and Central. There were sixteen little porches and doorways staggered in a semicircle around a small yard that has seven stunted magnolia trees growing in brick pots. It was early evening and the tenants, mostly old people, were sitting inside the screened doorways, eating their dinners off of portable aluminum stands. Radios played from every house. Mouse and I waved to folks and said hello as we made it back to number eight.

That door was closed.

I knocked on it and then I knocked again. After a few minutes we heard something crash and then heavy footsteps toward the door.

"Who's that?" an angry voice that might have had some fear in it called out.

"It's Easy!" I shouted.

The door opened and Junior Fornay stood there, in the gray haze of the screen door, wearing blue boxer shorts and a white tee-shirt.

"What you want?"

"I wanna talk about your call the other night, Junior. I gotta couple'a things I wanna ask."

I reached to pull the door open but Junior threw the latch from the inside.

"If you wanted t'talk you should'a done it then. Right now I gotta get some sleep."

"Why'ont you open the do', Junior, fo' I have t'shoot it down,"

Mouse said. He had been standing to the side of the door, where Junior couldn't see, but then he stood out in plain sight.

"Mouse," Junior said.

I wondered if he was still anxious to see my friend again.

"Open up, Junior, Easy an' me ain't got all night."

We went in and Junior smiled as if he wanted to make us feel at home.

"Wanna beer, boys? I gotta couple'a quarts in the box."

We got drinks and lit up cigarettes that Junior offered. He seated us on folding chairs he had placed around a card table.

"What you need?" he asked after a while.

I took a handkerchief from my pocket. It was the same handkerchief that I used to pick up something from the floor at Richard McGee's.

"Recognize this?" I asked Junior as I opened it on his table.

"What's a cigarette butt gotta do with me?"

"It's yours, Junior, Zapatas. You the only one I know cheap enough to smoke this shit. And you see how somebody just let it drop to the floor and burn so that the paper on the bottom is just charred but not ash?"

"So what? So what if it's mine?"

"I found this here on the floor of a dead man's house. Richard McGee was his name. Somebody had just given him Coretta James' name; somebody who knew that Coretta was with that white girl."

"So what?" Like magic, sweat appeared on Junior's brow.

"Why'd you kill Richard McGee?"

"Huh?"

"Ain't no time to play, Junior. I know you the one killed him."

"Whas wrong wit' Easy, Mouse? Somebody hit him in the head?"

"This ain't no time to play, Junior. You killed him and I need to know why."

"You crazy, Easy. You crazy!"

Junior jumped up out of his chair and made like he was about to leave.

"Sit down, Junior," Mouse said.

Junior sat.

"Tell me what happened, Junior."

"I don't know what you talkin' 'bout, man. I don't even know what you mean."

"All right," I said, showing him my palms. "But if I go to the police they gonna find out that that fingerprint they got on the knife belong to you."

"What knife?" Junior's eyes looked like moons.

"Junior, you got to listen real close to this. I got troubles of my own right now and I ain't got the time to worry 'bout you. The night I was at John's that white man was there. Hattie had you carry him home and then he must'a paid you for Coretta's name. That's when you killed him."

"I ain't killed nobody."

"That fingerprint gonna prove you wrong, man."

"Shit!"

I knew I was right about Junior but that wasn't going to help me if he didn't want to talk. The problem was that Junior wasn't afraid of me. He was never afraid of any man that he felt he could best in a fight. Even though I had the information that would prove him guilty he didn't worry because I was his inferior in combat.

"Kill 'im, Raymond," I said.

Mouse grinned and stood up. The pistol was just there, in his hand.

"Wait a minute, man. What kinda shit you tryin' t'pull here?" Junior said.

"You killed Richard McGee, Junior. And the next night you called me 'cause it had somethin' to do with that girl I was lookin' for. You wanted to find out what I knew but when I didn't tell you anything you hung up. But you killed him and you gonna tell me why or Mouse is gonna waste your ass."

Junior licked his lips and threw himself around in his chair like a child throwing a fit.

"What you wanna come messin' wit' me fo', man? What I do to you?"

"Tell it the way it happened, Junior. Tell me and maybe I forget what I know."

Junior threw himself around some more. Finally he said, "He was down at the bar the night you come in."

"Yeah?"

"Hattie didn't want him inside so she told him to go. But he must'a already been drunk 'cause he kinda like passed out on the street. So Hattie got me to go out an' check on 'im 'cause she didn't want no trouble with him out there. So I go out to help him to his car, or whatever."

Junior stopped to take a drink of beer but then he just stared out the window.

"Get on with it, Junior," Mouse said at last. He wanted to move on.

"He say he give me twenty dollars for to know 'bout that girl you was askin' on, Easy. He said that he give me a hundred if I was to drive him home and tell 'im how to find the white girl."

"I know you took that." Mouse was working a toothpick between his front teeth.

"Lotta money," Junior smiled hopefully at the warmth Mouse showed. "Yeah, I drove him home. And I told 'im that I seen the girl he was lookin' for, with Coretta James. Just a white girl anyway, why should I care?"

"Then why you kill 'im?" I asked.

"He wanted me to give Frank Green a message. He says that he give me the money after I do that."

"Yeah?"

"I tole him that he could fuck dat! I did what he wanted and if he needed sumpin' else we could talk about that after I got paid." Junior got a wild look in his eyes. "He told me I could walk home with my twenty if that's how I felt. Then he bad-mouth me some an' turn off into the other room. Shit! Fo' all I know'd he had a pistol in there. I got a knife from the sink an' goes in after 'im. He could'a had a gun in there, ain't that right, Raymond?"

Mouse sipped his beer and stared at Junior.

"What he want you to say to Frank?" I asked.

"He want me t'tell 'im that him an' his friends had sumpin' on the girl."

"Daphne?"

"Yeah," Junior said. "He say that they got sumpin' on 'er and they should all talk."

"What else?"

"Nuthin'."

"You just killed him 'cause he might'a hadda gun?"

"You ain't got no cause to tell the cops, man," Junior said.

He was sunken in his chair, like an old man. He disgusted me. He was brave enough to take on a smaller man, he was brave enough to stab an unarmed drunk, but Junior couldn't stand up to answer for his crimes.

"He ain't worf living," the voice whispered in my head.

"Let's go," I said to Mouse.

• 24 •

Dupree was at his sister's house, out past Watts, in Compton. Bula had a night job as a nurse's assistant at Temple Hospital so it was Dupree who answered our knock.

"Easy," he said in a quiet voice. "Mouse."

"Pete!" Mouse was bright. "That pigtails I smell?"

"Yeah, Bula made some this mo'nin'. Black-eyes too."

"You don't need to show me, I just run after my nose."

Mouse went around Dupree toward the smell. We stood in the tiny entrance looking at each other's shoulders. I was still half outside. Two crickets sounded from the rose beds that Bula kept.

"I'm sorry 'bout Coretta, Pete. I'm sorry."

"All I wanna know is why, Easy. Why somebody wanna kill her like that?" When Dupree looked up at me I saw that both of his eyes were swollen and dark. I never asked but I knew that those bruises were part of his police interrogation.

"I don't know, man. I can't see why someone wanna do that t'anybody."

Tears were coming down Dupree's face. "I do it to the man done it to her." He looked me in the eye. "When I find out who it was, Easy, I'm'a kill that man. I don't care who he is."

"You boys better com'on in," Mouse said from the end of the hall. "Food's on the table."

*

Bula had rye in the cabinet. Mouse and Dupree drank it. Dupree had been crying and upset the whole evening. I asked him some questions but he didn't know anything. He told us about how the police had questioned him and held him for two days without telling him why. But when they finally told him about Coretta he broke down so they could see that it wasn't him.

Dupree drank steady while he told his story. He got more and more drunk until he finally passed out on the sofa.

"That Dupree is a good man," Mouse slurred. "But he jus' cain't hold his liquor."

"You got your sails pretty far up too, Raymond."

"You callin' me drunk?"

"All I'm sayin' is that you been puttin' it away along wit' im and you could be sure that you wouldn't pass no breath test neither."

"If I was drunk," he said, "could I do this?"

Mouse, moving as fast as I've ever seen a man move, reached into his fancy jacket and came out with that long-barreled pistol. The muzzle was just inches from my forehead.

"Ain't a man in Texas could outdraw me!"

"Put it down, Raymond," I said as calmly as I could.

"Go on," Mouse dared, as he put the pistol back in his shoulder holster. "Go fo' your gun. Les see who gets kilt."

My hands were on my knees. I knew that if I moved Mouse would kill me.

"I don't have a gun, Raymond. You know that."

"You fool enough to go without no piece then you must wanna be dead." His eyes were glazed and I was sure that he didn't see me. He saw somebody, though, some demon he carried around in his head.

He drew the pistol again. This time he cocked the hammer. "Say your prayers, nigger, 'cause I'm'a send you home."

"Let him go, Raymond," I said. "He done learned his lesson good enough. If you kill 'im then he won't have got it." I was just talking.

"He fool enough t'call me out an' he ain't even got no gun! I kill the motherfucker!"

"Let him live, Ray, an' he be scared'a you whenever you walk in the room."

"Motherfucker better be scared. I kill the motherfucker. I kill 'im!"

Mouse nodded and let the pistol fall down into his lap. His head fell to his chest and he was asleep; just like that!

I took the gun and put it on the table in the kitchen.

Mouse always kept two smaller pistols in his bag. I knew that from our younger days. I got one of them and left a note for Dupree and him. I told them that I had gone home and that I had Mouse's gun. I knew he wouldn't mind as long as I told him about it.

I drove down my block twice before I was sure no one was waiting for me in the street. Then I parked around the corner so that anyone coming up to my place would think I was gone.

When I had the key in my lock the phone started ringing. It was on the seventh ring before I got to it.

"Easy?" She sounded as sweet as ever.

"Yeah, it's me. I thought you'd be halfway to New Orleans by now."

"I've been calling you all night. Where have you been?"

"Havin' fun. Makin' all kinds'a new friends. The police want me to come down there and live wit 'em."

She took my joke about friends seriously. "Are you alone?"

"What do you want, Daphne?"

"I have to talk with you, Easy."

"Well go on, talk."

"No, no. I have to see you. I'm scared."

"I don't blame ya for that. I'm scared just talkin' to ya on the phone," I said. "But I need to talk to ya though. I need to know some things."

"Come meet me and I'll tell you everything you need to know."

"Okay. Where are you?"

"Are you alone? I only want you to know where I am."

"You mean you don't want your boyfriend Joppy to know where you hidin'?"

If she was surprised that I knew about Joppy she didn't show it.

"I don't want *anybody* to know where I am, but you. Not Joppy and not that other friend that you said was visiting."

"Mouse?"

"Nobody! Either you promise me or I hang up right now."

"Okay, okay fine. I just got in and Mouse ain't even here. Tell me where you are and I'll come get ya."

"You wouldn't lie to me, would you, Easy?"

"Naw. I just wanna talk, like you."

She gave me the address of a motel on the south side of L.A.

"Hurry up, Easy. I need you," she said before hanging up. She got off the phone so quickly that she didn't give me the number of her room.

I scribbled a note, making my plans as I wrote. I told Mouse that he could find me at a friend's house, Primo's. I wrote RAYMOND ALEXANDER in bold letters across the top of the note because the only words Mouse could read were his own two names. I hoped that Dupree came with Mouse to read him the note and show him the way to Primo's house.

Then I rushed out the door.

I found myself driving in the L.A. night again. The sky toward the valley was coral with skinny black clouds across it. I didn't know why I was going alone to get the girl in the blue dress. But for the first time in quite a while I was happy and expectant.

• 25 •

The Sunridge was a smallish pink motel, made up of two rectangular buildings that came together in an "L" around an asphalt parking lot. The neighborhood was mostly Mexican and the woman who sat at the manager's desk was a Mexican too. She was a full-blooded Mexican Indian; short and almond-eyed with deep olive skin that had lots of red in it. Her eyes were very dark and her hair was black, except for four strands of white which told me that she had to be older than she looked.

She stared at me, the question in her eyes.

"Lookin' for a friend," I said.

She squinted a little harder, showing me the thick webbing of wrinkles at the corner of her eyes.

"Monet is her last name, French girl."

"No men in the rooms."

"I just have to talk with her. We can go out for coffee if we can't talk here."

She looked away from me as if to say our talk was over.

"I don't mean to be disrespectful, ma'am, but this girl has my money and I'm willing to knock on every door until I find her."

She turned toward the back door but before she could call out I said, "Ma'am, I'm willing to fight your brothers and sons to talk to this woman. I don't mean her any harm, or you neither, but I have got to have words with her."

She sized me up, putting her nose in the air like a leery dog checking out the new mailman, then she measured the distance to the back door.

"Eleven, far end," she said at last.

I ran down to the far end of the building.

While I knocked on number eleven's door I kept looking over my shoulder.

She had on a gray terrycloth robe and a towel was wrapped into a bouffant on her head. Her eyes were green right then and when she saw me she smiled. All the trouble she had and all the trouble I might have brought with me and she just smiled like I was a friend who was coming over for a date.

"I thought you were the maid," she said.

"Uh-uh," I mumbled. She was more beautiful than ever in the low-slung robe. "We should get outta here."

She was looking past my shoulder. "We better talk to the manager first."

The short woman and two big-bellied Mexican men were coming our way. One of the men was swinging a nightstick. They stopped a foot from me; Daphne closed the door a little to hide herself.

"Is he bothering you, miss?" the manager asked.

"Oh no, Mrs. Guitierra. Mr. Rawlins is a friend of mine. He's taking me to dinner." Daphne was amused.

"I don't want no men in the rooms," the woman said.

"I'm sure he won't mind waiting in the car, would you, Easy?"

"I guess not."

"Just let us finish talking, Mrs. Guitierra, and he'll be a good man and go wait in his car."

One of the men was looking at me as if he wanted to break my head with his stick. The other one was looking at Daphne; he wanted something too.

When they moved back toward the office, still staring at us, I said to Daphne, "Listen. You wanted me to come here alone and here I am. Now I need the same feeling, so I want you to come with me to a place I know."

"How do I know that you aren't going to take me to the man Carter hired?" Her eyes were laughing.

"Uh-uh. I don't want any piece of him . . . I talked to your boyfriend Carter."

That took the smile from her face.

"You did! When?"

"Two, three days ago. He wants ya back and Albright wants that thirty thousand."

"I'm not going back to him," she said, and I knew that it was true.

"We can talk about that some other time. Right now you've got to get away from here."

"Where?"

"I know a place. You've got to get away from the men looking for you and I do too. I'll put you someplace safe and then we can talk about what we can do."

"I can't leave L.A. Not before I talk to Frank. He should be back by now. I keep calling though, and he's not home."

"The police tied him into Coretta, he's probably lyin' low."

"I have to talk to Frank."

"Alright, but we've got to get away from here right now."

"Wait a second," she said. She went into the room for a moment. When she reappeared she handed me a piece of paper wrapped around a wad of cash. "Go pay my rent, Easy. That way they won't bother us when they see us moving my bags."

Landlords everywhere love their money. When I paid Daphne's bill the two men left and the little woman even managed to smile at me.

Daphne had three bags but none of them was the beat-up old suitcase that she carried the first night we met.

We drove a long way. I wanted far from Watts and Compton so we went to East L.A.; what they call El Barrio today. Back then it was just another Jewish neighborhood, recently taken over by the Mexicans.

We drove past hundreds of poor houses, sad palm trees, and thousands of children playing and hollering in the streets.

We finally came to a dilapidated old house that used to be a mansion. It had a great cement porch with a high green roof and two big picture windows on each of the three floors. Two of the windows had been broken out; they were papered with cardboard and stuffed with rags. There were three dogs and eight old cars scattered and lounging around the red clay yard under the branches of a sickly and failing oak tree. Six or seven small children were playing among the wrecks. Hammered into the oak was a small wooden sign that read "rooms."

A grizzled old man in overalls and a tee-shirt was sitting in an aluminum chair at the foot of the stairs.

"Howdy, Primo,' I waved.

"Easy," he said back to me. "You get lost out here?"

"Naw, man. I just wanted a little privacy so I figured to give you a try."

Primo was a real Mexican, born and bred. That was back in 1948, before Mexicans and black people started hating each other. Back then, before ancestry had been discovered, a Mexican and a Negro considered themselves the same. That is to say, just another couple of unlucky stiffs left holding the short end of the stick.

I met Primo when I became a gardener for a while. We worked together, with a team of men taking on the large jobs in Beverly Hills and Brentwood. We even took care of a couple of places downtown, off of Sixth.

Primo was a good guy and he liked to run with me and my friends. He told us that he'd bought that big house so that he could turn it into a hotel. He was always begging us to come out and rent a room from him or to tell our friends about him.

He stood up when I came up the path. He only came up to my chest. "How's that?" he asked.

"You got somethin' with some privacy?'

"I got a little house out back that you and the señorita can have." He bent down to look at Daphne in the car. She smiled nicely for him.

"How much?"

"Five dollars for a night."

"What?"

"It's a whole house, Easy. Made for love." He winked at me.

I could have argued him down and I would have done it for fun, but I had other things on my mind.

"Alright."

I gave him a ten-dollar bill and he showed us to the path that led around the big house to the house out back. He started to come with us but I stopped him.

"Primo, my man," I said. "I'll come on up tomorrow an' we do some damage to a fifth of tequila. Alright?"

He smiled and thumped my arm before he turned to leave. I wished that my life was still so simple that all I was after was a wild night with a white girl.

The first thing we saw was a mass of flowering bushes with honeysuckle, snapdragons, and passion fruit weaving through. A jagged, man-sized hole was hacked from the branches. Past that doorway was a small building like a coach house or the gardener's quarters on a big estate. Three sides of the house were glass doors from ceiling to floor. All the doors could open outward onto the cement patio that surrounded these three sides of the house, but they were all shut. The front door was wood, painted green.

Long white curtains were drawn over all the windows.

Inside, the house was just a big room with a fallen-down springbed on one side and a two-burner gas range on the other. There was a table with a toaster on it and four spindly chairs. There was a big stuffed sofa upholstered with a dark brown material that had giant yellow flowers stitched into it.

"It's just beautiful," Daphne exclaimed.

My face must've said that she was crazy because she blushed a little and added, "Well it could use some work but I think we could make something out of it."

"Maybe if we tore it down . . ."

Daphne laughed and that was very nice. As I said before, she was like a child and her childish pleasure touched me.

"It is beautiful," she said. "Maybe not rich but it's quiet and it's private. Nobody else could see us here."

I put her bags down next to the sofa.

"I gotta go out for a little while," I said. Once I had her in place I saw how to get things moving.

"Stay."

"I got to, Daphne. I got two bad men and the L.A. police on my trail."

"What bad men?" She sat at the edge of the bed and crossed her legs. She had put on a yellow sundress at the motel, and it showed off her tan shoulders.

"The man your friend hired and Frank Green, your other friend."

"What does Frankie have to do with you?"

I went up to her and she stood to meet me. I pulled my collar down and showed her my gashed throat, saying, "That's what *Frankie* done to Easy."

"Oh, honey!" She reached out gently for my neck.

Maybe it was just the touch of a woman that got to me or maybe it was finally realizing all that happened to me in the previous week; I don't know.

"Look at that! That's the cops!" I said, pointing at the bruise on my eye. "I been arrested twice, blamed for four murders, threatened by people I wished I never met, and . . ." I felt that my liver was going to come out between my teeth.

"Oh my poor man," she said as she took me by the arm and led me to the bathroom. She didn't let go of my arm while she turned on the water for the bath. She was right there with me, unbuttoning my shirt, letting down my pants.

I was sitting there, naked on the toilet seat, and watching her go through the mirror-doored medicine cabinet. I felt something deep down in me, something dark like jazz when it reminds you that death is waiting.

"Death," the saxophone rasps. But, really, I didn't care.

• 26 •

Daphne Monet, a woman who I didn't know at all personally, had me laid back in the deep porcelain tub while she carefully washed between my toes and then up my legs. I had an erection lying flat against my stomach and I was breathing slowly, like a small boy poised to catch a butterfly. Every once in a while she'd say, "Shh, honey, it's all right." And for some reason that caused me pain.

When she finished with my legs she washed my whole body with a rough hand towel and a bar of soap that had pumice in it.

I never felt drawn to a woman the way I was to Daphne Monet. Most beautiful women make me feel like I want to touch them, own them. But Daphne made me look inside myself. She'd whisper a sweet word and I was brought back to the first time I felt love and loss. I was remembering my mother's death, back when I was only eight, by the time Daphne got to my belly. I held my breath as she lifted the erection to wash underneath it; she looked into my face, with eyes that had become blue over the water, and stroked my erection up and down, twice. She smiled when she finished and pressed it back down against my flesh.

I couldn't say a word.

She stepped back from the tub and shrugged off her yellow dress in one long stretch then tossed it in the water over me and pulled down her pants. She sat on the toilet and urinated so loud that it reminded me more of a man.

"Hand me the paper, Easy," she said.

The roll was at the foot of the bathtub.

She stood over the tub, with her hips pressed outward, looking down on me. "If my pussy was like a man's thing it'd be as big as your head, Easy."

I stood out of the tub and let her hold me around the testicles. As we went into the bedroom she kept whispering obscene suggestions in my ear. The things she said made me ashamed. I never knew a man who talked as bold as Daphne Monet.

I never liked it when women talked like that. I felt it was masculine. But, beneath her bold language, Daphne seemed to be asking me for something. And all I wanted was to reach as far down in my soul as I could to find it.

We yelled and screamed and wrestled all night long. Once, when I had fallen asleep, I woke to find her rubbing an ice cube down my chest. Once, at about 3 A.M., she took me out to the cement patio behind the bushes and made love to me as I lay back against a rough tree.

When the sun came up she nestled against my side on the bed and asked, "Does it hurt, Easy?"

"What?"

"Your thing, does it hurt?"

"Yeah."

"Is it sore?"

"It's more like the blood vessels ache."

She grabbed my penis. "Does it hurt for you to love me, Easy?"

"Yeah."

Her grip tightened. "I love it when you hurt, Easy. For us."

"Me too," I said.

"Do you feel it?"

"Yeah, I feel it."

She released me. "I don't mean that. I mean this house. I mean us here, like we aren't who they want us to be."

"Who?"

"They don't have names. They're just the ones who won't let us be ourselves. They never want us to feel this good or close like this. That's why I wanted to get away with you."

"*I* came to you."

She put her hand out again. "But I called you, Easy; I'm the one who brought you to me."

When I look back on that night I feel confused. I could say that Daphne was crazy but that would mean that I was sane enough to say, and I wasn't. If she wanted me to hurt, I loved to hurt, and if she wanted me to bleed, I would have been happy to open a vein. Daphne was like a door that had been closed all my life; a door that all of a sudden flung open and let me in. My heart and chest opened as wide as the sky for that woman.

But I can't say that she was crazy. Daphne was like the chameleon lizard. She changed for her man. If he was a mild white man who was afraid to complain to the waiter she'd pull his head to her bosom and pat him. If he was a poor black man who had soaked up pain and rage for a lifetime she washed his wounds with a rough rag and licked the blood till it staunched.

It was mid-afternoon when I gave out. We had spent every moment in each other's arms. I didn't think about the police or Mouse or even DeWitt Albright. All I cared about was the pain I felt loving that white girl. But finally I pulled away from her and said, "We gotta talk, Daphne."

Maybe I was imagining it but her eyes flashed green for the first time since the bath.

"Well, what?" She sat up in the bed covering herself. I knew that I was losing her, but I was too satisfied to care.

"There's a lot of dead people, Daphne, and the police want me behind that. There's that thirty thousand dollars you stole from Mr. Carter and DeWitt Albright is on my ass for that."

"Any money I have is between me and Todd and I don't have anything to do with dead people or that Albright man. Nothing at all."

"Maybe you don't think so but Albright has the talent to make your business his . . ."

"So, what do you want from me?"

"Why'd Howard Green get killed?"

She stared through me as if I were a mirage. "Who?"

"Come on."

She looked away for a moment and then sighed. "Howard worked for a rich man named Matthew Teran. He was Teran's driver, chauffeur. Teran wanted to run for mayor but in that crowd you have to ask permission like. Todd didn't want Teran to do it."

"How come?" I asked.

"A while ago I met him, Teran I mean, and he was buying a little Mexican boy from Richard."

"The man we found?"

She nodded.

"And who was he?"

"Richard and I were"—she hesitated for a moment—'friends.' "

"Boyfriend?"

She nodded slightly. "Before I met Todd we spent some time together."

"The night I first started lookin' for you I ran into Richard in front of John's speak. Was he lookin' for you?"

"He might have been. He didn't want to let me go so he got together with Teran and Howard Green, to cause me trouble so they could get at Todd."

"What kind of trouble?" I asked.

"Howard knew something. Something about me."

"What?"

But she wouldn't answer that question.

"Who killed Howard?" I asked.

She didn't answer at first. She just played with the blankets, letting them fall down below her breasts.

"Joppy did," she said at last. She wouldn't meet my eye.

"Joppy!" I cried. "Why'd he want to do somethin' like that?" But I knew it was the truth even before I asked the question. It would take the kind of violence Joppy had to beat someone to death.

"Coretta too?"

Daphne nodded. The sight of her nakedness nauseated me right then.

"Why?"

"Sometimes I would go to Joppy's place with Frank. Just because Frank liked people to see me with him. And the last time I went there Joppy whispered that someone had been asking for me and that I should call him later to find out who. That's when I found out about that Albright man."

"But what about Howard and Coretta? What about them?"

"Howard Green had already come to me and told me that if I didn't do what he and his boss said they would ruin me. I told Joppy that I could get him a thousand dollars if he could make sure that Albright didn't find me and if he could talk with Howard."

"So he killed Howard?"

"It was a mistake, I think. Howard had a fast tongue. Joppy just got mad."

"But what about Coretta?"

"When she came to me I told Joppy about it. I told him that you were asking questions and"—she hesitated—"he killed her. He was scared by then. He'd already killed one man."

"Why didn't he kill you?"

She raised her head and threw her hair back. "I hadn't given him the money yet. He still wanted the thousand dollars. Anyway, he thought I was Frank's girl. Most people respect Frank."

"What's Frank to you?"

"Not anything you'd ever understand, Easy."

"Well, do you think he knows who killed Matthew Teran?"

"I don't know, Easy. I haven't killed anybody."

"Where's the money?"

"Somewhere. Not here. Not where you can get it."

"That money's gonna get you killed, girl."

"You kill me, Easy." She reached over to touch my knee.

I stood up. "Daphne, I gotta talk to Mr. Carter."

"I won't go back to him. Not ever."

"He just wants to talk. You don't have to be in love with him to talk."

"You don't understand. I do love him and because of that I can't ever see him." There were tears in her eyes.

"You makin' this hard, Daphne."

She reached for me again.

"Cut it out!"

"How much will Todd give you for me?"

"Thousand."

"Get me to Frank and I'll give you two."

"Frank tried to kill me."

"He won't do anything to you if I'm there."

"Take more than your smile to stop Frank."

"Take me to him, Easy; it's the only way you'll get paid."

"What about Mr. Carter and Albright?"

"They want me, Easy. Let Frank and me take care of it."

"What's Frank to you?" I asked again.

She smiled at me then. Her eyes turned blue and she laid back against the wall behind the bed. "Will you help me?"

"I don't know. I gotta get outta here."

"Why?"

"It's just too much," I said, remembering Sophie. "I need some air to breathe."

"We could stay here, honey; this is the only place for us."

"You wrong, Daphne. We don't have to listen to them. If we love each other than we can be together. Ain't no one can stop that."

She smiled, sadly. "You don't understand."

"You mean all you want from me is a roll in the hay. Get a little nigger-love out back and then straighten your clothes and put on your lipstick like you didn't ever even feel it."

She put out her hand to touch me but I moved away. "Easy," she said. "You have it wrong."

"Let's go get somethin' to eat," I said, looking away. "There's a Chinese place a few blocks from here. We could walk there through a shortcut out back."

"It'll be gone when we get back," she said.

I imagined that she had said that to lots of men. And lots of men would have stayed rather than lose her.

We dressed in silence.

When we were ready to go a thought came to me.

"Daphne?"

"Yes, Easy?" Her voice was bored.

"I wanted to know somethin'."

"What's that?"

"Why'd you call me yesterday?"

She turned green eyes on me. "I love you, Easy. I knew it from the first moment we met."

• 27 •

Chow's Chow was a kind of Chinese diner that was common in L.A. back in the forties and fifties. There were no tables, just one long counter with twelve stools. Mr. Ling stood behind the counter in front of a long black stove on which he prepared three dishes: fried rice, egg foo yong, and chow mein. You could have any one of these dishes with chicken, pork, shrimp, beef, or, on Sunday, lobster.

Mr. Ling was a short man who always wore thin white pants and a white tee-shirt. He had the tattoo of a snake that coiled out from under the left side of his collar, went around the back of his neck, and ended up in the middle of his right cheek. The snake's head had two great fangs and a long, rippling red tongue.

"What you want?" he yelled at me. I had been in Mr. Ling's diner at least a dozen times but he never recognized me. He never recognized any customer.

"Fried rice," Daphne said in a soft voice.

"What kind?" Mr. Ling shouted. And then, before she could answer, "Pork, chicken, shrimp, beef!"

"I'll have chicken and shrimp, please."

"Cost more!"

"That'll be alright, sir."

I had egg foo yong with pork.

Daphne seemed a little calmer. I had the feeling that if I could get her to open up, to talk to me, then I could talk some sense into her. I didn't want to force her to see Carter. If I forced her I could have been arrested for kidnapping and there was no telling how Carter would have reacted to her being manhandled. And maybe I loved her a little bit right then. She looked very nice in that blue dress.

"You know, I don't want to force anything on you, Daphne. I mean, the way I feel you don't ever have to kiss Carter again and it's okay with me."

I could feel her smile in my chest and in other parts of my body.

"You ever go to the zoo, Easy?"

"No."

"Really?" She was astonished.

"No reason t'see animals in cages far as I can see. They cain't help me and I cain't do nuthin' fo' them neither."

"But you can learn from them, Easy. The zoo animals can teach you."

"Teach what?"

She sat back and looked into the smoke and steam raised by Mr. Ling's stove. She was looking back into a dream.

"The first time my father took me to the zoo, it was in New Orleans. I was born in New Orleans." As she spoke she developed a light drawl. "We went to the monkey house and I remember thinking it smelled like death in there. A spider monkey was swinging from the nets that hung from the top of his cage; back and forth. Anyone with eyes could see that he was crazy from all those years of being locked away; but the children and adults were nudging each other and sniggering at the poor thing.

"I felt just like that ape. Swinging wildly from one wall to another, pretending I had somewhere to go. But I was trapped in my life just like that monkey. I cried and my father took me out of there. He thought that I was just sensitive to that poor creature. But I didn't care about a stupid animal.

"From then on we only went to the cages where the animals were more free. We watched the birds mainly. Herons and cranes and pelicans and peacocks. The birds were all I was interested in. They were so beautiful in their fine plumes and feathers. The male peacocks would spread out their tail feathers and rattle them at the hens when they wanted to mate. My daddy lied and said that they were just playing a game. But I secretly knew what they were doing.

"Then, at almost closing time, we passed the zebras. No one was around and Daddy was holding my hand. Two zebras were running back and forth. One was trying to avoid the other but the bully had cut off every escape. I yelled for my daddy to stop them because I worried that they were going to fight."

Daphne had grabbed on to my hand, she was so excited. I found myself worried; but I couldn't really tell what bothered me.

"They were right there next to us," she said. "At the fence, when the male mounted the female. His long, leathery thing jabbing in and out of her. Twice he came out of her completely, and spurted jissum down her flank.

"My daddy and I were holding hands so tight that it hurt me but I didn't say anything about it. And when we got back to the car he kissed me. It was just on the cheek at first but then he kissed me on the lips, like lovers do." Daphne had a faraway smile on her face. "But when he finished kissing me he started to cry. He put his head in my lap and I had to stroke his head for a long time and tell him that it was just fine before he'd even look up at me again."

The disgust must've shown on my face because she said, "You think that it was sick, what we did. But my daddy loved me. From then on, my whole fourteenth year, he'd take me to the zoo and the park. Always at first he'd kiss me like a father and his little girl but then we'd get alone someplace and act like real lovers. And always, always after he'd cry so sweet and beg me to forgive him. He brought me presents and gave me money, but I'd've loved him anyway."

I wanted to run away from her but I was too deep in trouble to act on my feelings so I tried to change the subject. "What's all that got to do with you goin' t'see Carter?" I asked.

"My daddy never took me anywhere again after that year. He left Momma and me in the spring and I never saw him again. Nobody ever knew about him and me and what had happened. But I knew. I knew that that was why he left. He just loved me so much that day at the zoo and he knew me, the real me, and whenever you know somebody that well you just have to leave."

"Why's that?" I wanted to know. "Why you have t'leave someone just when you get close?"

"It's not just close, Easy. It's something more."

"And that's what you had with Carter?"

"He knows me better than any other man."

I hated Carter then. I wanted to know Daphne like he did. I wanted her, even if knowing her meant that I couldn't have her.

Daphne and I took the back path, through the bushes, to the little house. Everything was fine.

I opened the door for her. She hadn't had anything else to say after her story about the zoo. I don't know why but I didn't have anything else to say either. Maybe it was because I didn't believe her. I mean, I believed that she believed the story, or, at least, she wanted to believe it, but there was something wrong with the whole thing.

Somewhere between the foo yong and the check I decided to cut my losses. Daphne was too deep for me. Somehow I'd call Carter and tell him where she was. I'd wash my hands of the whole mess. I'm just in it for the money, I kept thinking to myself.

I was so busy having those thoughts that I didn't think to check the room. What was there to worry about anyway? So when Daphne gasped I was surprised to see DeWitt Albright standing at the stove.

"Evening, Easy," he drawled.

I reached for the pistol in my belt but before I could get to it an explosion went off in my head. I remember the floor coming up to my face and then there was nothing for a while.

• 28 •

I was on a great battleship in the middle of the largest fire fight in the history of war. The cannons were red hot and the crew and I were loading those shells. Airplanes strafed the deck with machine-gun fire that stung my arms and chest but I kept on hefting shells to the man in front of me. It was dusk or early dawn and I was exhilarated by the power of war.

Then Mouse came up to me and pulled me from the line. He said, "Easy! We gotta get outta here, man. Ain't no reason t'die in no white man's war!"

"But I'm fighting for freedom!" I yelled back.

"They ain't gonna let you go, Easy. You win the one and they have you back on the plantation 'fore Labor Day."

I believed him in an instant but before I could run a bomb rocked the ship and we started to sink. I was pitched from the deck into the cold cold sea. Water came into my mouth and nose and I tried to scream but I was underwater. Drowning.

When I came awake I was dripping from the bucket of water that Primo had dumped on me. Water was in my eyes and down my windpipe.

"What happened, amigo? You have a fight with your friends?"

"What friends?" I asked suspiciously. For all I knew at that minute it was Primo who suckered me.

"Joppy and the white man in the white suit."

"White man?" Primo helped me to a sitting position. I was on the ground right outside the door of our little house. My head started clearing.

"Yeah. You okay, Easy?"

"What about the white man? When did he and Joppy get here?"

"About two, three hours ago."

"Two, three hours?"

"Yeah. Joppy asked me where you were and when I told him he drove the car back around the house. Then they took off about a little bit after that."

"The girl with 'em?"

"I don't see no girl."

I pulled myself up and went through the house, Primo at my heels. No girl.

I went out back and looked around but she wasn't there either. Primo came up behind me. "You guys have a fight?"

"Not much'a one. Can I use your phone, man?"

"Yeah, sure. It's right inside."

I called Dupree's sister but she said that he and Mouse had left in the early morning. Without Mouse I didn't know what to do. So I went out to my car and drove toward Watts.

The night was fully black with no moon and thick clouds that hid the stars. Every block or so there'd be a street lamp overhead, shining in darkness, illuminating nothing.

"Get out of it, Easy!"

I didn't say anything.

"You gotta find that girl, man. You gotta make this shit right."

"Fuck you!"

"Uh-uh, Easy. That don't make you brave. Brave is findin' that white man an' yo' friend. Brave is not lettin' them pull this shit on you."

"So what can I do?"

"You got that gun, don't ya? You think them men's gonna beat bullets?"

"They armed too both of 'em."

"All you gotta do is make sure they don't see ya comin'. Just like in the war, man. Make believe you is the night."

"But how I even find 'em t'sneak up on? What you want me t'do? Look in the phone book?"

"You know where Joppy live, right? Les go look. An' if he ain't there you know they gotta be with Albright."

Joppy's house was dark and his bar was padlocked from the outside. The night watchman on duty at Albright's building, a fat, florid-faced man, said that Albright had moved out.

So I made up my mind to call information for every town north of Santa Monica. I got lucky and found DeWitt Albright on my first try. He lived on Route 9, in the Malibu Hills.

• 29 •

I drove past Santa Monica into Malibu and found Route 9. It was just a graded dirt road. There I found three mailboxes that read: Miller, Korn, Albright. I passed the first two houses and drove a full fifteen minutes before getting to Albright's marker. It was far enough out that any death cry would go unheard.

It was a simple, ranch-style house, not large. There were no outside lights except on the front porch so I couldn't make out the color. I wanted to know what color the house was. I wanted to know what made jets fly and how long sharks lived. There was a lot I wanted to know before I died.

I could hear loud male voices and the woman's pleading before I got to the window.

Over the sill I saw a large room with a darkwood floor and a high ceiling. Before the blazing hearth sat a large couch covered with something like bear skin. Daphne was on the couch, naked, and the men, DeWitt and Joppy, stood over her. Albright was wearing his linen suit but Joppy was stripped to the waist. His big gut looked obscene hanging over her like that and it took everything I had not to shoot him right then.

"You don't want any more of that now do you, honey?" Albright was saying. Daphne spat at him and he grabbed her by the throat. "If I don't get that money you better believe I'll get the satisfaction of killing you, girl!"

I like to think of myself as an intelligent man but sometimes I just run on feelings. When I saw that white man choking Daphne I eased the window open and crawled into the room. I was standing there, pistol in hand—but DeWitt sensed me before I could draw a bead on him. He swung around with the girl in front of him. When he saw me he threw her one way and he leaped behind the couch! I moved to shoot but then Joppy bolted for the back door. That distracted me, and in my one moment of indecision the window behind me shattered and a shot, like a cannon roar, rang out. As I dove for cover behind a sofa chair I saw that DeWitt Albright had drawn his pistol.

Two more shots ripped through the back of the fat chair. If I hadn't moved to the side, down low, he would have gotten me then.

I could hear Daphne crying but there was nothing I could do for her. My big fear was that Joppy would come around outside and get me from behind. So I moved into a corner, still hidden, I hoped, from Albright's sight and in a position to see Joppy if he stuck his head in the window.

"Easy?" DeWitt called.

I didn't say a word. Even the voice was silent.

We waited two or three long minutes. Joppy didn't appear at the window. That bothered me and I began to wonder what other way he might come. But just as I was looking around I heard a noise as if DeWitt had lurched up. There was a dull thud and the sofa chair came falling backwards. He'd heaved a lamp at the top of its high back. The lamp shattered and, even as I pulled off a shot where I expected him to be, I saw DeWitt rise up a few feet farther on; he had that pistol leveled at me.

I heard the shot, and something else, something that seemed almost impossible: DeWitt Albright grunted, "Wha?"

Then I saw Mouse! The smoking pistol in his hand!

He'd come into the room through the door Joppy had taken.

More shots exploded. Daphne screamed. I jumped to cover her with my body. Splinters of wood jumped from the wall and I saw Albright hurl himself through a window at the other side of the room.

Mouse took aim but his gun wouldn't fire. He cursed, threw it down, and got a snub-nose from his pocket. He ran for the window but in that time I heard the Caddy's engine turn over; tires were slithering in the dirt before Mouse could empty his second chamber.

"DAMN!!" Mouse yelled. "DAMN DAMN DAMN!!!"

A cold draft, sucked in through the shattered window, washed over Daphne and me.

"I hit him, Easy!" He was grinning down on me with all those golden teeth.

"Mouse," was all I could say.

"Ain't ya glad t'see me, Ease?"

I got up and took the little man in my arms. I hugged him like I would hug a woman.

"Mouse," I said again.

"Com'on man, we gotta get yo' boy back here." He jerked his head toward the door he'd come through.

Joppy was on the floor in the kitchen. His arms and legs were behind him, hog-tied by an extension cord. There was thick blood coming from the top of his bald head.

"Les get him to the other room," Mouse said.

We got him to the chair and Mouse strapped him down. Daphne wrapped herself in a blanket and shied to the end of the couch. She looked like a frightened kitten on her first Fourth of July.

All of a sudden Joppy's eyes shot open and he shouted, "Cut me aloose, man!"

Mouse just smiled.

Joppy was sweating, bleeding, and staring at us. Daphne was staring at the floor.

"Lemme go," Joppy whimpered.

"Shut up, man," Mouse said and Joppy quieted down.

"Can I have my clothes now?" Daphne's voice was thick.

"Sure, honey," Mouse said. "Right after we take care on some business."

"What's this?" I asked.

Mouse leaned forward to put his hand on my knee. It felt good to be alive and to be able to feel another man's touch. "I think you an' me deserve a little sumpin' fo' all this mess, don't you, Easy?"

"I give you half of everything I made, Ray."

"Naw, man," he said. "I don't want your money. I wanna piece'a that big pie Ruby over here sittin' on."

I didn't know why he called her Ruby, but I let it pass.

"Man, that's stolen money."

"That's the sweetest kind, Easy." He turned to her and smiled. "What about it, honey?"

"That's all Frank and I have. I won't give it up." I would have believed her if she wasn't talking to Mouse.

"Frank's dead," Mouse's face was completely deadpan.

Daphne looked at him for a moment and then she crumpled, just like a tissue, and started shaking.

Mouse went on, "Joppy the one did it, I figure. They found him beat to death in a alley just down from his bar."

When Daphne raised her head she had hate in her eyes, and there was hate in her voice when she said, "Is that the truth, Raymond?" She was a different woman.

"Now am I gonna lie to you, Ruby? Your brother is dead."

I had only been in an earthquake once but the feeling was the same: The ground under me seemed to shift. I looked at her to see the truth. But it wasn't there. Her nose, cheeks, her skin color—they were white. Daphne was a white woman. Even her pubic hair was barely bushy, almost flat.

Mouse said, "You gotta hear me, Ruby, Joppy killed Frank."

"I ain't kilt Frankie!" Joppy cried.

"Why you keep callin' her that?" I asked.

"Me an' Frank known each other way back, Ease, 'fore I even met you. I remember old Ruby here from her baby days. Half-sister. She more filled out now but I never forget a face." Mouse pulled out a cigarette. "You know you a lucky man, Easy. I got it in mind to follah this mothahfuckah when I seen 'im comin' outta yo' house this afternoon. I'as lookin' fo' you when I seen 'im. I had Dupree's car so

I follahed him downtown and he hooked up with whitey. Once I seed that you know I was on his ass for the duration."

I looked at Joppy. His eyes were big and he was sweating. Watery blood was dripping from his chin. "I ain't killed Frank, man. I ain't had no cause. Why I wanna kill Frank? Lissen, Ease, only reason I got you in this was so you could get some money—fo' that house."

"Then why you wit' Albright now?"

"She lied, man. Albright come t'me and he told me 'bout that money she got. She lied! She said she ain't hardly had no money!"

"Alright, thas enough talk," Mouse said. "Now, Ruby, I don't wanna scare ya but I will have that money."

"You don't scare me, Ray," she said simply.

Mouse frowned for just a second. It was like a small cloud passing quickly on a sunny day. Then he smiled.

"Ruby, you gotta worry 'bout yourself now, honey. You know men can get desperate when it comes to money . . ." Mouse let his words trail off while he took the pistol from his waistband.

He turned casually to his right and shot Joppy in the groin. Joppy's eyes opened wide and he started honking like a seal. He rocked back and forth trying to grab his wound but the wires held him to the chair. After a few seconds Mouse leveled his pistol and shot Joppy in the head. One moment Joppy had two bulging eyes, then his left eye was just a bloody, ragged hole. The force of the second shot threw him to the floor; spasms went through his legs and feet for minutes afterward. I felt cold then. Joppy had been my friend but I'd seen many men die and I cared for Coretta too.

Mouse stood up and said, "So let's go get that money, honey." He picked up her clothes from behind the couch and dropped the heap in her lap. Then he went out the front door.

"Help me, Easy." Her eyes were full of fear and promise. "He's crazy. You still have your gun."

"I can't," I said.

"Then give it to me. I'll do it."

That was probably the closest Mouse had ever come to a violent death.

"No."

"I found some blood in the road," Mouse said when he returned. "I tole ya I got 'im. I don't know how bad it is but he gonna remember me." There was a childish glee in his voice.

While he talked I untied Joppy's corpse. I took Mouse's jammed pistol and put it in Joppy's hand.

"What you doin', Easy?" Mouse asked.

"I don't know, Ray. Just confusing things I guess."

Daphne rode with me and Mouse followed in Dupree's car. When we were a few miles away I threw Joppy's extension cord bonds down an embankment.

"Did you kill Teran?" I asked as we swung onto Sunset Boulevard.

"I guess so," she said, so softly that I had to strain to hear her.

"You guess? You don't know?"

"I pulled the trigger, he died. But he killed himself really. I went to him, to ask him to leave me alone. I offered him all my money but he just laughed. He had his hands in that little boy's drawers and he laughed." Daphne snorted. I don't know if it was a laugh or a sound of disgust. "And so I killed him."

"What happened to the boy?"

"I brought him to my place. He just ran in the corner and wouldn't even move."

Daphne had the bag in a YWCA locker.

Back in East L.A. Mouse counted out ten thousand for each of us. He let Daphne keep the bag.

She called a cab and I went out with her to wait by the granite lamppost at the curb.

"Stay with me," I said. Moths fluttered around us in that small circle of light.

"I can't, Easy, I can't stay with you."

"Why not?" I asked.

"I just can't."

I put my hand out but she moved away saying, "Don't touch me."

"I've done more than touch you, honey."

"That wasn't me."

"What you mean? Who was it if it wasn't you?" I moved toward her and she got behind her bag.

"I'll talk to you, Easy. I'll talk to you till the car comes but just don't touch me. Don't touch me or I'll yell."

"What's wrong?"

"You know what's wrong. You know who I am; what I am."

"You ain't no different than me. We both just people, Daphne. That's all we are."

"I'm not Daphne, My given name is Ruby Hanks and I was born in Lake Charles, Louisiana. I'm different than you because I'm two people. I'm her *and* I'm me. I never went to the zoo, she did. She was there and that's where she lost her father. I had a different father. He came home and fell in my bed about as many times as he fell in my mother's. He did that until one night Frank killed him."

When she looked up at me I had the feeling that she wanted to reach out to me, not out of love or passion but to implore me.

"Bury Frank," she said.

"Okay. But you could stay here with me and we could bury him together."

"I can't. Do me one other favor?"

"What's that?"

"Do something about the boy."

I didn't really want her to stay. Daphne Monet was death herself. I was glad that she was leaving.

But I would have taken her in a second if she'd asked me to.

The cab driver could tell something was wrong. He kept looking around as if he expected to be mugged any second. She asked him to carry her bag. She put her hand on his arm to thank him but she wouldn't even shake my hand goodbye.

"Why'd you kill him, Mouse?"

"Who?"

"Joppy!"

Mouse was whistling and wrapping his money in a package fashioned from brown paper bags.

"He the cause of all yo' pain, Easy. And anyway, I needed to show that girl how serious I was."

"But she already hated him fo' Frank; maybe you could'a worked on that."

"It was me killed Frank," he said. This time it was Mouse reminding me of DeWitt Albright.

"You killed him?"

"So what? What you think he gonna do fo' you? You think he wasn't gonna kill you?"

"That don't mean I had t'kill 'im."

"Hell it don't!" Mouse flashed his eyes angrily at me.

It was murder and I had to swallow it.

"You just like Ruby," Mouse said.

"What you say?"

"She wanna be white. All them years people be tellin' her how she light-skinned and beautiful but all the time she knows that she can't have what white people have. So she pretend and then she lose it all. She can love a white man but all he can love is the white girl he think she is."

"What's that got to do with me?"

"That's just like you, Easy. You learn stuff and you be thinkin' like white men be thinkin'. You be thinkin' that what's right fo' them is right fo' you. She look like she white and you think like you white. But brother you don't know that you both poor niggers. And a nigger ain't never gonna be happy 'less he accept what he is."

• 30 •

They found DeWitt Albright slumped over his steering wheel just north of Santa Barbara; it took him that long to bleed to death. I could hardly believe it. A man like DeWitt Albright didn't die, couldn't die. It frightened me even to think of a world that could kill a man like that; what could a world like that do to me?

Mouse and I heard it on the radio when I was driving him to the bus station the next morning. I was happy to see him off.

"I'm'a give all that money to Etta, Easy. Maybe she take me back now that I done saved yo' ass and come up rich." Mouse smiled at me and climbed on the bus. I knew I'd see him again and I didn't know how I felt about that.

That same morning I went to Daphne's apartment where I found the little boy. He was filthy. His underwear hadn't been changed in weeks and mucus was caked in his nose and on his face. He didn't say anything. I found him eating from a bag of flour in the kitchen. When I walked up to him and held out my hand he just took it and followed me to the bathroom. After he was clean I brought him out to Primo's place.

"I don't think he understands English," I said to Primo. "Maybe you could get something out of him."

Primo was a father at heart. He had as many children as Ronald White and he loved them all.

"I could give some mommasita a few hundred bucks over the next year or two while she looked after him," I said.

"I'll see," Primo said. He already had the boy in his lap. "Maybe I know someone."

The next person I went to see was Mr. Carter. He gave me a cool eye when I told him that Daphne was gone. I told him that I'd heard from Albright about the killings Joppy and Frank had done. I told him about Frank's death and that Joppy had disappeared.

But what really got to him was when I told him that I knew Daphne was colored. I told him that she wanted me to tell him that she loved him and wanted to be with him but that she would never know any kind of peace as long as she was with him. I laid it on kind of thick but he liked it that way.

I told him about her sundress, and while I talked I thought about making love to her when she was still a white woman. He had a look of ecstasy on his face; I had a darker feeling, but just as strong, inside.

"But I've got a problem, Mr. Carter, and you do too."

"Oh?" He was still savoring the last glimpse of her. "What is that?"

"I'm the only suspect that the police have," I told him. "And unless sumpin' happens I'm'a have to tell 'em 'bout Daphne. And you know she gonna hate you if you drag her through the papers. She might even kill herself," I said. I didn't think it was a lie.

"What can I do about that?"

"You the one braggin' 'bout all your City Hall connections."

"Yes?"

"Then get 'em on the phone. I got a story t'tell 'em but you gotta back me up in it. 'Cause if I go in there on my own you know they gonna sweat me till I tell about Daphne."

"Why should I help you, Mr. Rawlins? I lost my money and my fiancée. You haven't done a thing for me."

"I saved her life, man. I let her get away with your money and her skin. Any one of the men involved with this would have seen her dead."

That very afternoon we went to City Hall and met with the assistant to the chief of police and the deputy mayor, Lawrence Wrightsmith.

The policeman was short and fat. He looked to the deputy mayor before saying anything, even hello. The deputy mayor was a distinguished man in a gray suit. He waved his arm through the air while he talked and he smoked Pall Malls. He had silver-gray hair and I thought for a moment that he looked the way I imagined the president to be when I was a child.

Officers Mason and Miller were called when I mentioned them.

We were all sitting in Mr. Wrightsmith's office. He was behind his desk and the deputy police chief stood behind him. Carter and I sat before the desk and Carter's lawyer was behind us. Mason and Miller sat off to the side, on a couch.

"Well, Mr. Rawlins," Mr. Wrightsmith said. "You have something to tell us about all these murders going on?"

"Yessir."

"Mr. Carter here says that you were working for him."

"In a way, sir."

"What way is that?"

"I was hired by DeWitt Albright, through a friend of ours, Joppy Shag. Mr. Albright hired Joppy to locate Frank and Howard Green. And later on Joppy got him to hire me."

"Frank and Howard, eh? Brothers?"

"I've been told that they were distant cousins, but I couldn't swear to that," I said. "Mr. Albright wanted me to find Frank for Mr. Carter here. But he didn't tell me why he wanted them, just that it was business."

"It was for the money I told you about, Larry," Carter said. "You know."

Mr. Wrightsmith smiled and said to me, "Did you find them?"

"Joppy had already got to Howard Green, that's when he found out about the money."

"And what exactly was it that he found out, Mr. Rawlins?"

"Howard worked for a rich man, Matthew Teran. And Mr. Teran was mad because Mr. Carter here messed him up on running for mayor," I smiled. "I guess he was looking to be your boss."

Mr. Wrightsmith smiled too.

"Anyway," I continued, "he wanted Howard and Frank to kill Mr. Carter and make it look like a robbery. But when they got in the house and found that thirty thousand dollars they got so excited that they just ran without even doin' the job."

"What thirty thousand dollars?" Mason asked.

"Later," Wrightsmith said. "Did Joppy kill Howard Green?"

"That's what I think now. You see, I didn't get in it until they were looking for Frank. You see, DeWitt was checking out Mr. Teran because Mr. Carter suspected him. Then DeWitt got interested in the Greens when he checked out Howard and came up with Frank's name. He wanted somebody to look for Frank in the illegal bars down around Watts."

"Why were they looking for Frank?"

"DeWitt wanted him because he was lookin' for Mr. Carter's money, and Joppy wanted him for that thirty thousand dollars, for himself."

The sun was coming in on Mr. Wrightsmith's green blotter. I was sweating as if it was coming in on me.

"How did you find all this out, Easy?" Miller asked.

"From Albright. He got suspicious when Howard turned up dead and then he was certain when Coretta James was killed."

"Why's that?" Wrightsmith said. Every man in the room was staring at me. I had never been on trial but I felt I was up against the jury right then.

"Because they were looking for Coretta too. You see, she spent a lot of time around the Greens."

"Why didn't you get suspicious, Easy?" Miller asked. "Why didn't you tell us about this when we brought you in?"

"I didn't know none'a this when you talked to me. Albright and Joppy had me looking for Frank Green. Howard Green was already dead and what did I know about Coretta?"

"Go on, Mr. Rawlins," Mr. Wrightsmith said.

"I couldn't find Frank. No one knew where he was. But I heard a story about him though. People were sayin' that he was mad over the death of his cousin and that he was out for revenge. I think he went out after Teran. He didn't know nuthin' 'bout Joppy."

"So you think that Frank Green killed Matthew Teran?" Miller couldn't hide his disgust. "And Joppy got to Frank Green and DeWitt Albright?"

"All I know is what I just said," I said as innocently as I could.

"What about Richard McGee? He stab himself?" Miller was out of his chair.

"I don't know 'bout him," I said.

They asked me questions for a couple of hours more. The story stayed the same though. Joppy did most of the killing. He did it out of greed. I went to Mr. Carter when I heard about DeWitt's death and he decided to come to the police.

When I finished Wrightsmith said, "Thank you very much, Mr. Rawlins. Now if you'll just excuse us."

Mason and Miller, Jerome Duffy—Carter's lawyer, and I all had to go.

Duffy shook my hand and smiled at me. "See you at the inquest, Mr. Rawlins."

"What's that mean?"

"Just a formality, sir. When a serious crime is committed they want to ask a few questions before closing the books."

It didn't sound any worse than a parking ticket if you listened to him.

He got in the elevator to leave and Mason and Miller went with him.

I took the stairs. I thought I might even walk all the way home. I had two years' salary buried in the back yard and I was free. No one was after me; not a worry in my life. Some hard things had happened but life was hard back then and you just had to take the bad along with the worse if you wanted to survive.

Miller came up to me as I descended the granite stair of City Hall.

"Hi, Ezekiel."

"Officer."

"You got a mighty powerful friend up there."

"I don't know what you mean," I said, but I did know.

"You think Carter gonna come save your ass when we arrest you every other day for jaywalking, spitting, and creating a general nuisance? Think he's gonna answer your calls?"

"Why I have to worry about that?"

"You have to worry, Ezekiel"—Miller pushed his thin face right up to mine, he smelled of bourbon, wintermint, and sweat—"because I have to worry."

"What do you have to worry about?"

"I got a prosecutor, Ezekiel. He's got a fingerprint that don't belong to anybody we know."

"Maybe it's Joppy's. Maybe when you find him you'll have it."

"Maybe. But Joppy's a boxer. Why'd he stop boxing to use a knife?"

I didn't know what to say.

"Give it to me, son. Give it to me and I'll let you off. I'll forget about the *coincidence* of you being involved in all this and having drinks with Coretta the night before she died. Mess with me and I'll see that you spend the rest of your life in jail."

"You could try Junior Fornay against that print."

"Who?"

"Bouncer at John's. He might fit it."

It might be that the last moment of my adult life, spent free, was in that walk down the City Hall stairwell. I still remember the stained-glass windows and the soft light.

• 31 •

"I guess things turned out okay, huh, Easy?"

"What?" I turned away from watering my dahlias. Odell was nursing a can of ale.

"Dupree's okay and the police got the killers."

"Yeah."

"But you know, something bothers me."

"What's that, Odell?"

"Well, it's been three months, Easy, an' you ain't had a job or looked for one far as I can see."

The San Bernadino range is the most beautiful in the fall. The high winds get rid of all the smog and the skies take your breath away.

"I been workin'."

"You got a night job?"

"Sometimes."

"What you mean, sometimes?"

"I work for myself now, Odell. And I got two jobs."

"Yeah?"

"I bought me a house, on auction for unpaid taxes, and I been rentin' it and—"

"Where you get that kinda money?"

"Severance from Champion. And you know them taxes wasn't all that much."

"What's your other job?"

"I do it when I need a few dollars. Private investigations."

"Git away from here!"

"No lie."

"Who you work for?"

"People I know and people they know."

"Like who?"

"Mary White is one of 'em."

"What you do for her?"

"Ronald run off on her two months back. I tailed him up to Seattle and gave her the address. Her family brought him back down."

"What else?"

"I found Ricardo's sister in Galveston and told her what Rosetta was doin' with 'im. She gave me a few bucks when she come up and set him free."

"Damn!" That was the only time I ever heard Odell curse. "That sounds like some dangerous business, man."

"I guess. But you know a man could end up dead just crossin' the street. Least this way I say I earned it."

Later on that evening Odell and I were having a dinner I threw together. We were sitting out front because it was still hot in L.A.

"Odell?"

"Yeah, Easy."

"If you know a man is wrong, I mean, if you know he did somethin' bad but you don't turn him in to the law because he's your friend, do you think that's right?"

"All you got is your friends, Easy."

"But then what if you know somebody else who did something wrong but not so bad as the first man, but you turn this other guy in?"

"I guess you figure that the other guy got ahold of some bad luck."

We laughed for a long time.

• II •

A RED DEATH

Dedicated to the memory of

Alberta Jackson and Lillian Keller

with special thanks to

Daniel and Elizabeth Russell

If it wasn't for back luck
I wouldn't have no luck at all . . .

—old blues refrain

• 1 •

I always started sweeping on the top floor of the Magnolia Street apartments. It was a three-story pink stucco building between Ninety-first Street and Ninety-first Place, just about a mile outside of Watts proper. Twelve units. All occupied for that month. I had just gathered the dirt into a neat pile when I heard Mofass drive up in his new '53 Pontiac. I knew it was him because there was something wrong with the transmission, you could hear its high singing from a block away. I heard his door slam and his loud hello to Mrs. Trajillo, who always sat at her window on the first floor—best burglar alarm you could have.

I knew that Mofass collected the late rent on the second Thursday of the month; that's why I chose that particular Thursday to clean. I had money and the law on my mind, and Mofass was the only man I knew who might be able to set me straight.

I wasn't the only one to hear the Pontiac.

The doorknob to Apartment J jiggled and the door came open showing Poinsettia Jackson's sallow, sorry face.

She was a tall young woman with yellowish eyes and thick, slack lips.

"Hi, Easy," she drawled in the saddest high voice. She was a natural tenor but she screwed her voice higher to make me feel sorry for her.

All I felt was sick. The open door let the stink of incense from her prayer altar flow out across my newly swept hall.

"Poinsettia," I replied, then I turned quickly away as if my sweeping might escape if I didn't move to catch it.

"I heard Mofass down there," she said. "You hear him?"

"I just been workin'. That's all."

She opened the door and draped her emaciated body against the jamb. The nightcoat was stretched taut across her chest. Even though Poinsettia had gotten terribly thin after her accident, she still had a large frame.

"I gotta talk to him, Easy. You know I been so sick that I can't even walk down there. Maybe you could go on down an tell 'im that I need t'talk."

"He collectin' the late rent, Poinsettia. If you ain't paid him all you gotta do is wait. He'll be up here soon enough to talk to you."

"But I don't have it," she cried.

"You better tell 'im that," I said. It didn't mean anything, I just wanted to say the last word and get down to work on the second floor.

"Could you talk to him, Easy? Couldn't you tell 'im how sick I am?"

"He know how sick you are, Poinsettia. All he gotta do is look at you and he could tell that. But you know Mofass is business. He wants that rent."

"But maybe you could tell him about me, Easy."

She smiled at me. It was the kind of smile that once made men want to go out of their way. But Poinsettia's fine skin had slackened and she smelled like an old woman, even with the incense and perfume. Instead of wanting to help her I just wanted to get away.

"Sure, I'll ask 'im. But you know he don't work for me," I lied. "It's the other way around."

"Go on down there now, Easy," she begged. "Go ask 'im to let me slide a month or two."

She hadn't paid a penny in four months already, but it wouldn't have been smart for me to say that to her.

"Lemme talk to 'im later, Poinsettia. He'd just get mad if I stopped him on the steps."

"Go to 'im now, Easy. I hear him coming." She pulled at her robe with frantic fingers.

I could hear him too. Three loud knocks on a door, probably unit B, and then, in his deep voice, "Rent!"

"I'll go on down," I said to Poinsettia's ashen toes.

I pushed the dirt into my long-handled dustpan and made my way down to the second floor, sweeping off each stair as I went. I had just started gathering the dirt into a pile when Mofass came struggling up the stairs.

He'd lean forward to grab the railing, then pull himself up the stairs, hugging and wheezing like an old bulldog.

Mofass looked like an old bulldog too; a bulldog in a three-piece brown suit. He was fat but powerfully built, with low sloping shoulders and thick arms. He always had a cigar in his mouth or between his broad fingers. His color was dark brown but bright, as if a powerful lamp shone just below his skin.

"Mr. Rawlins," Mofass said to me. He made sure to be respectful when talking to anyone. Even if I actually had been his cleanup man he would have called me mister.

"Mofass," I said back. That was the only name he let anyone call him. "I need to discuss something with you after I finish here. Maybe we could go somewhere and have some lunch."

"Suits me," he said, clamping down on his cigar.

He grabbed the rail to the third floor and began to pull himself up there.

I went back to my work and worry.

Each floor of the Magnolia Street building had a short hallway with two apartments on either side. At the far end was a large window that let in the morning sun. That's why I fell in love with the place. The morning sun shone in, warming up the cold concrete floors and brightening the first part of your day. Sometimes I'd go there even when there was no work to be done. Mrs. Trajillo would stop me at the front door and ask, "Something wrong with the plumbing, Mr. Rawlins?" And I'd tell her that Mofass had me checking on the roof or that Lily Brown had seen a mouse a few weeks back and I was checking the traps. It was always best if I said something about a rodent or bugs, because Mrs. Trajillo was a sensitive woman who couldn't stand the idea of anything crawling down around the level of her feet.

Then I'd go upstairs and stand in the window, looking down into the street. Sometimes I'd stand there for an hour and more, watching the cars and clouds making their ways. There was a peaceful feeling about the streets of Los Angeles in those days.

Everybody on the second floor had a job, so I could sit around the halls all morning and nobody would bother me.

But that was all over. Just one letter from the government had ended my good life.

Everybody thought I was the handyman and that Mofass collected the rent for some white lady downtown. I owned three buildings, the Magnolia Street place being the largest, and a small house on 116th Street. All I had to do was the maintenance work, which I liked because whenever you hired somebody to work for you they always took too long and charged too much. And when I wasn't doing that I could do my little private job.

On top of real estate I was in the business of favors. I'd do something for somebody, like find a missing husband or figure out who's been breaking into so-and-so's store, and then maybe they could do me a good turn one day. It was a real country way of doing business. At that time almost everybody in my neighborhood had come from the country around southern Texas and Louisiana.

People would come to me if they had serious trouble but couldn't go to the police. Maybe somebody stole their money or their illegally registered car. Maybe they worried about their daughter's company or a wayward son. I settled disputes that would have otherwise come to bloodshed. I had a reputation for fairness and the strength of my convictions among the poor. Ninety-nine out of a hundred black folk were poor back then, so my reputation went quite a way.

I wasn't on anybody's payroll, and even though the rent was never steady, I still had enough money for food and liquor.

"What you mean, not today?" Mofass' deep voice echoed down the stairs. After that came the strained cries of Poinsettia.

"Cryin' ain't gonna pay the rent, Miss Jackson."

"I ain't got it! You know I ain't got it an' you know why too!"

"I know you ain't got it, that's why I'm here. This ain't my reg'lar collectin' day, ya know. I come to tell you folks that don't pay up, the gravy train is busted."

"I can't pay ya, Mofass. I ain't got it and I'm sick."

"Lissen here." His voice dropped a little. "This is my job. My money comes from the rent I collect fo' Mrs. Davenport. You see, I bring her a stack'a money from her buildin's and then she counts it. And when she finishes countin' she takes out my little piece. Now when I bring her more money I get more, and when I bring in less . . ."

Mofass didn't finish, because Poinsettia started crying.

"Let me loose!" Mofass shouted. "Let go, girl!"

"But you promised!" Poinsettia cried. "You promised!"

"I ain't promised nuthin'! Let go now!"

A few moments later I could hear him coming down the stairs.

"I be back on Saturday, and if you ain't got the money then you better be gone!" he shouted.

"You can go to hell!" Poinsettia cried in a strong tenor voice. "You shitty-assed bastard! I'ma call Willie on yo' black ass. He know all about you! Willie chew yo' shitty ass off!"

Mofass came down the stair holding on to the rail. He was walking slowly amid the curses and screams. I wondered if he even heard them.

"BASTARD!!" shouted Poinsettia.

"Are you ready to leave, Mr. Rawlins?" he asked me.

"I got the first floor yet."

"Mothahfuckin' bastard!"

"I'll be out in the car then. Take your time." Mofass waved his cigar in the air, leaving a peaceful trail of blue smoke.

When the front door on the first floor closed, Poinsettia stopped shouting and slammed her own door. Everything was quiet again. The sun was still warming the concrete floor and everything was as beautiful as always.

But it wasn't going to last long. Soon Poinsettia would be in the street and I'd have the morning sun in my jail cell.

• 2 •

"You got your car here?" Mofass asked when I climbed into the passenger's side of his car.

"Naw, I took the bus." I always took the bus when I went out to clean, because my Ford was a little too flashy for a janitor. "Where you wanna go?"

"You the one wanna talk to me, Mr. Rawlins."

"Yeah," I said. "Let's go to that Mexican place then."

He made a wide U-turn in the middle of the street and drove off in the direction of Rebozo's.

While Mofass frowned and bit down on his long black cigar I stared out the window at the goings-on on Central Avenue. There were liquor stores and small clothes shops and even a television repair shop here and there. At Central and Ninety-ninth Street a group of men sat around talking—they were halfheartedly waiting for work. It was a habit that some Southerners brought with them; they'd just sit outside on a crate somewhere and wait for someone who needed manual labor to come by and shout their name. That way they could spend the afternoon with their friends, drinking from brown paper bags and shooting dice. They might even get lucky and pick up a job worth a couple of bucks—and maybe their kids would have meat that night.

Mofass was driving me to his favorite Mexican restaurant. At Rebozo's they put sliced avocado in the chili and peppered potato chunks in the burritos.

We got there without saying any more. Mofass got out of the car and locked his door with the key, then he went around to my side and locked that door too. He always locked both doors himself. He never trusted that someone else could do it by holding the door handle so that the lock held. Mofass didn't trust his own mother; that's what made him such a good real estate agent.

Another thing I liked about Mofass was that he was from New Orleans and, though he talked like me, he wasn't intimate with my friends from around Houston, Galveston, and Lake Charles, Louisiana. I was safe from idle gossip about my secret financial life.

Rebozo's was a dark room with a small bar at the back and three booths on either side. There was a neon-red jukebox next to the bar that was almost always playing music full of brassy horns, accordions, and strumming guitars. But even if the box was silent when we walked in Mofass would always drop a few nickels and push some buttons.

The first time he did that I asked him, "You like that kinda music?"

"I don't care," he answered me. "I just like to have a little noise. Make our talk just ours." Then he winked, like a drowsy Gila monster.

Mofass and I stared at each other across the table. He had both hands out in front of him. Between the fingers of his left hand that cigar stood up like a black Tower of Pisa. On the pinky of his right hand he wore a gold ring that had a square onyx emblem with a tiny diamond embedded in its center.

I was nervous about discussing my private affairs with Mofass. He collected the rent for me. I gave him nine percent and fifteen dollars for each eviction, but we weren't friends. Still, Mofass was the only man I could discuss my business with.

"I got a letter today," I said finally.

"Yeah?"

He looked at me, patiently waiting for what I had to say, but I couldn't go on. I didn't want to talk about it yet. I was afraid that saying the bad news out loud would somehow make it real. So instead I asked, "What you wanna do 'bout Poinsettia?"

"What?"

"Poinsettia. You know, the rent."

"Kick her ass out if she don't pay."

"You know that gal is really sick up there. Ever since that car crash she done wasted away."

"That don't mean I got to pay her rent."

"It's me gonna be payin' it, Mofass."

"Uh-uh, Mr. Rawlins. I collect it and until I put it in yo' hands it's mine. If that gal go down and tell them other folks that I don't take her money they gonna take advantage."

"She's sick."

"She got a momma, a sister, that boy Willie she always be talkin' 'bout. She got somebody. Let them pay the rent. We in business, Mr. Rawlins. Business is the hardest thing they make. Harder than diamonds."

"What if nobody pays for her?"

"You will done fo'got her name in six months, Mr. Rawlins. You won't even know who she is."

Before I could say anything more a young Mexican girl came up to us. She had thick black hair and dark eyes without very much white around them. She looked at Mofass and I got the feeling that she didn't speak English.

He held up two fat fingers and said, "Beer, chili, burrito," pronouncing each syllable slowly so that you could read his lips.

She gave him a quick smile and went away.

I took the letter from my breast pocket and handed it across the table.

"I want your opinion on this," I said with a confidence I did not feel.

While I watched Mofass' hard face I remembered the words he was reading.

Reginald Arnold Lawrence
Investigating Agent
Internal Revenue Service

July 14, 1953

Mr. Ezekiel Rawlins:

It has come my attention, sir, that between August 1948 and September of 1952 you came into the possession of at least three real estate properties.

> I have reviewed your tax records back to 1945 and you show no large income, in any year. This would suggest that you could not legally afford such expenditures.
>
> I am, therefore, beginning an investigation into your tax history and request your appearance within seven days of the date of this letter. Please bring all tax forms for the time period indicated and an *accurate* record of all income during that time.

As I remembered the letter I could feel ice water leaking in my bowels again. All the warmth I had soaked up in that hallway was gone.

"They got you by the nuts, Mr. Rawlins," Mofass said, putting the letter back down between us.

I looked down and saw that a beer was there in front of me. The girl must've brought it while I was concentrating on Mofass.

"If they could prove you made some money and didn't tell them about it, yo' ass be in a cast-iron sling," Mofass said.

"Shit! I just pay 'em, that's all."

He shook his head, and I felt my heart wrench.

"Naw, Mr. Rawlins. Government wants you t'tell 'em what you make. You don't do that and they put you in the fed'ral penitentiary. And you know the judge don't even start thinkin' 'bout no sentence till he come up with a nice round number—like five or ten."

"But you know, man, my name ain't even on them deeds. I set up what they call a dummy corporation, John McKenzie helped me to do it. Them papers say that them buildin's 'long to a Jason Weil."

Mofass curled his lip and said, "IRS smell a dummy corporation in a minute."

"Well then I just tell 'em I didn't know. I didn't."

"Com'on, man." Mofass leaned back and waved his cigar at me. "They just tell ya that ignorance of the law ain't no excuse, thas all. They don't care. Say you go shoot some dude been with your girl, kill 'im. You gonna tell 'em you didn't know 'bout that killin' was wrong? Anyway, if you went to all that trouble t'hide yo' money they could tell that you was tryin' t'cheat 'em."

"It ain't like I killed somebody. It ain't right if they don't even give me a chance t'pay."

"On'y right is what you get away wit', Mr. Rawlins. And if they find out about some money, and they think you didn't declare it . . ." Mofass shook his head slowly.

The girl returned with two giant white plates. Each one had a fat, open-ended burrito and a pile of chili and yellow rice on it. The puffy burritos had stringy dark red meat coming out of the ends so that they looked like oozing dead grubs. The chili had yellowish-green avocado pieces floating in the grease, along with chunks of pork flesh.

One hundred guitars played from the jukebox. I put my hand over my mouth to keep from gagging.

"What can I do?" I asked. "You think I need a lawyer?"

"Less people know 'bout it the better." Mofass leaned forward, then whispered, "I don't know how you got the money to pay for those buildin's, Mr. Rawlins, and I don't think nobody should know. What you gotta do is find some family, somebody close."

"What for?" I was also leaning across the table. The smell of the food made me sick.

"This here letter," Mofass said, tapping the envelope. "Don't say, fo'a fact, that he got no proof. He just investigatin', lookin'. You sign it over t'some family, and backdate the papers, and then go to him, prove that it ain't yours. Say that they was tryin' t'hide what they had from the rest of the family."

"How I back-whatever?"

"I know a notary public do it—for some bills."

"So what if I had a sister or somethin'? Ain't the government gonna check her out? 'Cause you know ev'rybody I know is poor."

Mofass took a suck off his cigar with one hand and then shoveled in a mouthful of chili with the other.

"Yeah," he warbled. "You need somebody got sumpin' already. Somebody the tax man gonna believe could buy it."

I was quiet for a while then. Every good thing I'd gotten was gone with just a letter. I had hoped that Mofass would tell me that it was alright, that I'd get a small fine and they'd let me slide. But I knew better.

Five years before, a rich white man had somebody hire me to find a woman he knew. I found her, but she wasn't exactly what she seemed to be, and a lot of people died. I had a friend, Mouse, help me out though, and we came away from it with ten thousand dollars apiece. The money was stolen, but nobody was looking for it and I had convinced myself that I was safe.

I had forgotten that a poor man is never safe.

When I first got the money I'd watched my friend Mouse murder a man. He shot him twice. It was a poor man who could almost taste that stolen loot. It got him killed and now it was going to put me in jail.

"What you gonna do, Mr. Rawlins?" Mofass asked at last.

"Die."

"What's that you say?"

"On'y thing I know, I'ma die."

"What about this here letter?"

"What you think, Mofass? What should I do?"

He sucked down some more smoke and mopped the rest of his chili with a tortilla.

"I don't know, Mr. Rawlins. These people here don't have nothin', far as I can see. And you got me t'lie for ya. But ya know if they come after my books I gotta give 'em up."

"So what you sayin'?"

"Go on in there and lie, Mr. Rawlins. Tell 'em you don't own nuthin'. Tell 'em that you a workin' man and that somebody must have it out for you to lie and say you got that property. Tell 'em that and then see what they gotta say. They don't know your bank or your banker."

"Yeah. I guess I'ma have to feel it out," I said after a while.

Mofass was thinking something as he looked at me. He was probably wondering if the next landlord would use him.

• 3 •

It wasn't far to my house. Mofass offered to drive, but I liked to use my legs, especially when I had thinking to do.

I went down Central. The sidewalks were pretty empty at midday, because most people were hard at work. Of course, the streets of L.A. were usually deserted; Los Angeles has always been a car-driving city, most people won't even walk to the corner store.

I had solitude but I soon realized that there was nothing for me to consider. When Uncle Sam wanted me to put my life on the line, fighting the Germans, I did it. And I knew that I'd go to prison if he told me to do that. In the forties and fifties we obeyed the law, as far as poor people could, because the law kept us safe from the enemy. Back then we thought we knew who the enemy was. He was a white man with a foreign accent and a hatred for freedom. In the war it was Hitler and his Nazis; after that it was Comrade Stalin and the communists; later on, Mao Tse-tung and the Chinese took on an honorary white status. All of them bad men with evil designs on the free world.

My somber mood lifted when I came to 116th Street. I had a small house, but that made for a large front lawn. In recent years I had taken to gardening. I had daylilies and wild roses against the fence, and strawberries and potatoes in large rectangular plots at the center of the yard. There was a trellis that enclosed my porch, and I always had flowering vines growing there. The year before I had planted wild passion fruit.

But what I loved the most was my avocado tree. It was forty feet high with leaves so thick and dark that it was always cool under its shade. I had a white cast-iron bench set next to the trunk. When things got really hard, I'd sit down there to watch the birds chase insects through the grass.

When I came up to the fence I had almost forgotten the tax man. He didn't know about me. How could he? He was just grabbing at empty air.

Then I saw the boy.

He was doing a crazy dance in my potato patch. He held both hands in the air, with his head thrown back, and cackled deep down in his throat. Every now and then he'd stamp his feet, like little pistons, and reach both hands down into the soil, coming out with long tan roots that had the nubs of future potatoes dangling from them.

When I pushed open the gate it creaked and he swung around to look at me. His eyes got big and he swiveled his head to one side and the other, looking for an escape route. When he saw that there was no escape he put on a smile and held the potato roots out at me. Then he laughed.

It was a ploy I had used when I was small.

I wanted to be stern with him, but when I opened my mouth I couldn't keep from smiling.

"What you doin', boy?"

"Playin'," he said in a thick Texas drawl.

"That's my potatas you stampin' on. Know that?"

"Uh-uh." He shook his head. He was a small, very dark boy with a big head and tiny ears. I figured him for five years old.

"Whose potatas you think you got in your hands?"

"My momma's."

"Yo' momma?"

"Um-huh. This is my momma's house."

"Since when?" I asked.

The question was too much for him. He scrunched his eyes and hunched his boy shoulders. "It just is, thas all."

"How long you been here kickin' up my garden?" I looked around to see daylilies and rose petals strewn across the yard. There wasn't a red strawberry in the patch.

"We just come." He gave me a large grin and reached out to me. I picked him up without thinking about it. "Momma losted her key so I had to go in da windah an' open up the door."

"What?"

Before I could put him down I heard a woman humming. The timbre of her voice sent a thrill through me even though I didn't recognize it yet. Then she came around from the side of the house. A sepia-colored woman—large, but shapely, wearing a plain blue cotton dress and a white apron. She carried a flat-bottomed basket that I recognized from my closet, its braided handle looped into the crook of her right arm. There were kumquats and pomegranates from my fruit trees and strawberries from the yard on a white handkerchief that covered the bottom of the basket. She was a beautiful, full-faced woman with serious eyes and a mouth, I knew, that was always ready to laugh. The biceps of her right arm bulged, because EttaMae Harris was a powerful woman who, in her younger years, had done hand laundry nine hours a day, six days a week. She could knock a man into next Tuesday, or she could hold you so tight that you felt like a child again, in your mother's loving embrace.

"Etta," I said, almost to myself.

The boy tittered like a little maniac. He squirmed around in my arms and worked his way down to the ground.

"Easy Rawlins." Her smile came into me, and I smiled back.

"What . . . I mean," I stammered. The boy was running around his mother as fast as he could. "I mean, why are you here?"

"We come t' see you, Easy. Ain't that right, LaMarque?"

"Uh-huh," the boy said. He didn't even look up from his run.

"Stop that racin' now." Etta reached out and grabbed him by the shoulder. She spun him around, and he looked up at me and smiled.

"Hi," he said.

"We met already." I motioned my head toward the lawn.

When Etta saw the damage LaMarque had done her eyes got big and my heart beat a little faster.

"LaMarque!"

The boy lowered his head and shrugged.

"Huh?" he asked.

"What you do to this yard?"

"Nuthin'."

"Nuthin'? You call this mess nuthin'?"

She reached out to grab him, but LaMarque let himself fall to the ground, hugging his knees.

"I's just gard'nin' in the yard," he whimpered. "Thas all."

"Gard'nin'?" Etta's dark face darkened even more, and the flesh around her eyes creased into a devil's gaze. I don't know how LaMarque reacted to that stare, but I was so worried that I couldn't find my breath.

She balled her fists so that her upper arms got even larger, a tremor went through her neck and shoulders.

But then, suddenly, her eyes softened, she even laughed. Etta has the kind of laugh that makes other people happy.

"Gard'nin?" she said again. "Looks like you a reg'lar gard'nin' tornado."

I laughed along with her. LaMarque didn't exactly know why we were so cheery but he grinned too and rolled around on the ground.

"Get up from there now, boy, and go get washed."

"Yes, Momma." LaMarque knew how to be a good boy after he had been bad. He ran toward the house, but before he got past Etta she grabbed him by one arm, hefted him into the air, and gave him a smacking kiss on the cheek. He was grinning and wiping the kiss from his face as he turned to run for the door.

Then Etta held her arms out and I walked into her embrace as if I had never heard of her husband, my best friend, Mouse.

I buried my face in her neck and breathed in her natural, flat scent; like the smell of fresh-ground flour. I put my arms around

EttaMae Harris and relaxed for the first time since I had last held her—fifteen years before.

"Easy," she whispered, and I didn't know if I was holding her too tight or if she was calling my name.

I knew that embrace was the same thing as holding a loaded gun to my head, because Raymond Alexander, known to his friends as Mouse, was a killer. If he saw any man holding his wife like that he wouldn't even have blinked before killing him. But I couldn't let her go. The chance to hold her one more time was worth the risk.

"Easy," she said again, and I realized that I was pressing against her with my hips, making it more than obvious how I felt. I wanted to let go but it was like early morning, when you first wake up and just can't let go of sleep yet.

"Let's go inside, honey," she said, putting her cheek to mine. "He wants his food."

The smells of southern cooking filled the house. Etta had made white rice and pinto beans with fatback. She'd picked lemons from the neighbor's bush for lemonade. There was a mayonnaise jar in the center of the table with pink and red roses in it. That was the first time that there were ever cut flowers in my house.

The house wasn't very big. The room we were in was a living room and dining room in one. The living room side was just big enough for a couch, a stuffed chair, and a walnut cabinet with a television in it. From there was a large doorless entryway that led to the dinette. The kitchen was in the back. It was a short alley with a counter and a stove. The bedroom was small too. It was a house big enough for one man; and it held me just fine.

"Get up from there, LaMarque," Etta said. "The man always sit at the head of the table."

"But . . ." LaMarque began to say, and then he thought better of it.

He ate three plates of beans and counted to one hundred and sixty-eight for me—twice. When he finished Etta sent him outside.

"Don't be doin' no more gard'nin', though," she warned him.

"'Kay."

We sat across the table from each other. I looked into her eyes and thought about poetry and my father.

I was swinging from a tree on the tire of a Model A Ford. My father came up to me and said, "Ezekiel, you learn to read an' ain't nuthin' you cain't do."

I laughed, because I loved it when my father talked to me. He left that night and I never knew if he had abandoned me or was killed on his way home.

Now I was half the way through Shakespeare's sonnets in my third English course at LACC. The love that poetry espoused and my love for EttaMae and my father knotted in my chest so that I could hardly even breathe. And EttaMae wasn't something slight like a sonnet; behind her eyes was an epic, the whole history of me and mine.

Then I remembered, again, that she belonged to another man; a murderer.

"It's good to see you, Easy."

"Yeah."

She leaned forward with her elbows on the table, placed her chin in the palm of her hand, and said, "Ezekiel Rawlins."

That was my real name. Only my best friends used it.

"What are you doing here, Etta? Where's Mouse?"

"You know we broke up years ago, honey."

"I heard you took him back."

"Just a tryout. I wanted to see if he could be a good husband and a father. But he couldn't, so I threw him out again."

The last moments of Joppy Shag's life flashed through my mind. He was lashed to an oaken chair, sweat and blood streamed from his bald head. When Mouse shot him in the groin he barked and strained like a wild animal. Then Mouse calmly pointed the gun at Joppy's head . . .

"I didn't know," I said. "But why are you up here?"

Instead of answering me Etta got up and started clearing the table. I moved to help her, but she shoved me back into the chair, saying, "You just get in the way, Easy. Sit down and drink your lemonade."

I waited a minute and then followed her out to the kitchen.

"Men sure is a mess." She was shaking her head at the dirty dishes I had piled on the counter and in the sink. "How can you live like this?"

"You come all the way from Texas to show me how to wash dishes?"

And then I was holding her again. It was as if we had taken up where we'd left off in the yard. Etta put her hand against the bare back of my neck, I started running two fingers up and down either side of her spine.

I had spent years dreaming of kissing Etta again. Sometimes I'd be in bed with another woman and, in my sleep, I'd think it was Etta; the kisses would be like food, so satisfying that I'd wake up, only to realize that it was just a dream.

When Etta kissed me in the kitchen I woke up in another way. I staggered back from her mumbling, "I cain't take too much more of this."

"I'm sorry, Easy. I know I shouldn't, but me and LaMarque been in a bus for two days—all the way from Houston. I been thinkin' 'bout you all that time and I guess I got a little worked up."

"Why'd you come?" I felt like I was pleading.

"Mouse done gone crazy."

"What you mean, crazy?"

"Outta his mind," Etta continued. "Just gone."

"Etta," I said as calmly as I could. The desire to hold her had subsided for the moment. "Tell me what he did."

"Come out to the house at two in the mo'nin' just about ev'ry other night. Drunk as he could be and wavin' that long-barreled pistol of his. Stand out in the middle'a the street yellin' 'bout how he bought my house and how he burn it down before he let us treat him like we did."

"Like what?"

"I don't know, Easy. Mouse is crazy."

That had always been true. When we were younger men Mouse carried a gun and a knife. He killed men who crossed him and others who stood in the way of him making some coin. Mouse murdered his own stepfather, daddyReese, but he rarely turned on friends, and I never expected him to go against EttaMae.

"So you sayin' he run you outta Texas?"

"Run?" Etta was surprised. "I ain't runnin' from that little rat-faced man, or no other one'a God's creatures."

"Then why come here?"

"How it gonna look to LaMarque when he grow up if I done killed his father? 'Cause you know I had him in my sight every night he was out there in the street."

I remembered that Etta had a .22-caliber rifle and a .38 for her purse.

"After he done that for ovah a month I made up my mind to kill 'im. But the night I was gonna do it LaMarque woke up an' come in the room. I was waitin' for Raymond to come out. LaMarque asked me what I was doin' with that rifle, and you know I ain't never lied to that boy, Easy. He asked me what I was fixin' t' do with that rifle and I told him that I was gonna pack it and we was goin' to California."

Etta reached out and took both of my hands in hers. She said, "And that was the first thing I said, Easy. I didn't think about goin' to my mother or my sister down in Galveston. I thought'a you. I thought about how sweet you was before Raymond and me got married. So I come to you."

"I just popped into your head after all these years?"

"Well." Etta smiled and looked down at our tangled fingers. "Corinth Lye helped some."

"Corinth?" She was a friend from Houston. If I happened to run into her at Targets Bar I'd buy a bottle of gin and we'd put it away; sit there all night and drink like men. I'd told her many deep feelings and secrets in the early hours. It wasn't the first time that I was betrayed by alcohol.

"Yeah," Etta said. "I wrote her about Mouse when it all started. She wrote me about how much you still cared for me. She said I should come up here, away from all that."

"Then why ain't you wit' her?"

"I wus s'posed to, honey. But you know I got t' thinkin' 'bout you on that ride, an' I tole LaMarque all about you till we decided that we was gonna come straight here."

"You did?"

"Mmm-hm," Etta hummed, nodding her head. "An' you know I was glad we did." Etta's grin was shameless.

She smiled at me and the years fell away.

The one night I had spent with Etta, the best night of my life, she woke up the next morning talking about Mouse. She told me how wonderful he was and how lucky I was to have him for a friend.

LaMarque had never seen a television. He watched everything that came on, even the news. Some poor soul was in the spotlight that night. His name was Charles Winters. He was discovered stealing classified documents at his government job. The reporter said that Winters could get four ninety-nine-year sentences if he was found guilty.

"What's a comanisk, Unca Easy?"

"What, you think that just 'cause this is my TV that I should know everything it says?"

"Uh-huh," he nodded. LaMarque was a treasure.

"There's all kindsa communists, LaMarque."

"That one there," he said, pointing at the television. But the picture of Mr. Winters was gone. Instead there was a picture of Ike in the middle of a golf swing.

"That kind is a man who thinks he can make things better by tearin' down what we got here in America and buildin' up like what they got in Russia."

LaMarque opened his eyes and his mouth as far as he could. "You mean they wanna tear down Momma house and Momma TV up here in America?"

"The kinda world he wants, nobody owns anything. It's like this here TV would be for everybody."

"Uh-uh!"

LaMarque jumped up, balling his little fists.

"LaMarque!" Etta shouted. "What's got into you?"

"Commanisk gonna take our TV!"

"Time for you to go t'bed, boy."

"Nuh-uh!"

"I say yes," Etta said softly. She cocked her head to the side and tilted a little on the couch. LaMarque lowered his head and moved to turn off the set.

"Tell Unca Easy g'night."

"G'night, Unca Easy," LaMarque whispered. He climbed on the couch to kiss me, then he crawled into Etta's lap. She carried him into my bedroom.

We'd decided after the meal that they'd take my bed and I'd take the couch.

• 4 •

I was resting on the couch at about midnight, watching a bull's-eye pattern on the TV screen. I was smoking Pall Malls, drinking vodka with grapefruit soda, and wondering if Mouse could kill me even if I was in a federal jail. In my imagination, he could.

"Easy?" she called from the bedroom door.

"Yeah, Etta?"

Etta wore a satiny gown. Coral. She sat down in the chair to my right.

"You sleepin', baby?" she asked.

"Uh-uh, no. Just thinkin'."

"Thinkin' what?"

"'Bout when I went down to see you in Galveston. You know, when you an' Mouse was just engaged."

She smiled at me, and I had to make myself stay where I was.

"You remember that night?" I asked.

"Sure do. That was nice."

"Yeah." I nodded. "You see, that's what's wrong, Etta."

"I don't follah." Even her frown made me want to kiss her.

"That was best night of my life. When I woke up in the morning I was truly surprised, because I knew I had to die, good as that felt."

"Ain't nuthin' wrong with that, Easy."

"Ain't nuthin' wrong with it until you tell me that 'it was nice' stuff. You know what you said to me when you got up?"

"That was fifteen years ago, baby. How'm I s'posed to 'member that?"

"I remember."

Etta looked sad. She looked like she'd lost something she cared for. I wanted to stop, to go hold her, but I couldn't. I'd been waiting all those years to tell her how I felt.

I said, "You told me that Mouse was the finest man you ever knew. You said that I was truly lucky to have a man like that for a friend."

"Baby, that was so long ago."

"Not fo' me. Not fo' me." When I sat up I realized that I had an erection. I crossed my legs so that Etta wouldn't see it pressing against my loose pants. "I remember like it was only this mo'nin. When we got up you started tellin' me how lucky I was to have a man like Mouse fo'a friend. You told me how great he was. I loved you; I still do. An' all you could think of was him. You know I had plenty'a women tell me that they love me when we get up in the mo'nin. But it only made me sick 'cause they wasn't you sayin' it. Every time I hear them I hear you talkin' 'bout Mouse."

Etta shook her head sadly. "That ain't me, Easy. I loved you, I did, as a friend. An' I think you's a beautiful man too. I mean, yeah, I shouldn'ta had you over like that. But you came t'me, honey. I was mad 'cause Raymond was out ho'in just a couple a days after I said I'd marry him. I used you t'try an' hurt him, but you knew what I was doin'. You knew it, Easy. You knew what I was givin' you was his. That's why you liked it so much.

"But that was a long time ago, an' you should be over it by this time. But, you know, it's just that some men be wantin' sumpin' from women; sumpin' like a woman shouldn't have no mind of her own. It's like when LaMarque want me t'tell 'im that he's the strongest man in the world if I let him carry my pocketbook. I tell 'im what he wants t'hear 'cause he just a baby. But you's a man, Easy. If I lied t'you it would be a insult."

"I know, I know," I said. "I knew it then. I never said nuthin', but now here you are again. An' here I am wit' my nose open.

"You know somebody saw you get on that bus, Etta. Somebody told somebody else that they heard you went to California. And Mouse could be outside that door at this very minute. Or maybe he be here tomorrah. He's comin', though, you could bet on that. An' if he finds you been in my bed we gonna have it out." I didn't add that I knew Mouse well enough to be afraid. I didn't need to.

"Raymond don't care 'bout if I got boyfriends, Easy. He don't care 'bout that."

"Maybe not. But if Mouse think I done taken his wife an' child fo' my own he see red. And now here you are talkin' 'bout him bein' crazy—how I know what he might do?"

Etta didn't say anything to that.

Mouse was a small, rodent-featured man who believed in himself without question. He only cared about what was his. He'd go against a man bigger than I was with no fear because he knew that nobody was better than him. He might have been right.

"And here I am again," I said. "Tryin' to keep offa you when I got so many problems I shouldn't even think about it."

Etta leaned forward in the chair, resting her elbows on her knees, revealing the dark cleft of her breasts. "So what you wanna do, Easy?"

"I . . ."

"Yeah?" she asked after I stalled.

"I know a man named Mofass."

"Who's he?"

"He manages some units up here and I work fo'im."

When Etta shifted, her gown slid and tremors went down my back.

"Yeah?" she asked.

"I think I could get him to find a place for you and LaMarque. You know, some place fo' you t'live. Without no rent, I mean." I was talking but I didn't want to say it: I wanted her for myself.

Etta sat up and her gown rose over her breasts. Her nipples were hard dimes against the slick material.

"So that's it? I come all this way an' now you gonna put us out." She stuck her lower lip out and shrugged, ever so slightly. "LaMarque an' me be ready by noon."

"You don't have t'rush, Etta . . ."

"No, no," she said, rising and waving her hand at me. "We gotta settle in someplace, and the sooner the better. You know chirren need a home."

"I'll give you money, Etta. I got lotsa money."

"I'll pay you back soon as I find work."

We looked at each other awhile after that.

Etta was the most beautiful woman I'd ever known. I'd wanted her more than life itself, once. And the fact that I had let that go was worse than the fear of the penitentiary.

"'Night, Easy," she whispered.

I made to get up, to kiss her good night, but she held her hand against me.

"Don't kiss me, honey," she said. "'Cause you know I been thinkin' 'bout you long as you been thinkin' 'bout me."

Then she went off to bed.

I didn't sleep that night. I didn't worry or think about taxes either.

• 5 •

The government building was on Sixth Street, downtown. It was small, four stories, and built from red brick. It almost looked friendly from the outside, not like the government at all.

But once you got past the front door all the friendliness was gone. A woman sat at the information desk. Her blond hair was pulled back so tight that it pained my scalp just to look at her. She wore a gray businesslike jacket and dark horn-rimmed glasses. She squinted at me, wincing as if her skull might have actually hurt.

"May I assist you, sir?" she asked.

"Lawrence," I said. "Agent Lawrence."

"FBI?"

"Naw. Revenue."

"IRS?"

"I guess that's what you call it. Spells taxes no matter what way you say it."

As government workers went she was polite, but she wasn't going to smile for my joke.

"Go down to the end of this hall." She pointed it out for me. "And take the elevator to the third floor. The receptionist there will assist you."

"Thanks," I said, but she had turned back to something important on her desk. I peeked over the little ledge and saw the magazine, *The Saturday Evening Post.*

Agent Lawrence's office was just down the hall from the reception desk on the third floor, but when the woman called him he told her that I had to wait.

"He's going over your case," the fat brunette told me.

I sat down in the most uncomfortable straight-backed chair ever made. The lower back of the chair stuck out farther than the top so I had the feeling that I was hunched over as I sat there watching the big woman rub pink lotion into her hands. She frowned at her hands, and then she frowned again when she saw me staring through her glistening fingers.

I wondered if she would have been performing her toilet like that in front of a white taxpayer.

"Rawlins?" a military-like voice inquired.

I looked up.

There I saw a tall white man in a crayon-blue suit. He was of a good build with big hands that hung loosely at his sides. He had brown hair, and small brown eyes and was clean shaven, though there would always be a blue shadow on his jaw. But for all his neat appearance Agent Lawrence seemed to be somehow unkempt, disheveled. I took him in for a few seconds. His bushy eyebrows and the dark circles under his eyes made him seem pitiful and maybe even a little inept.

It was my habit to size up people quickly. I liked to think I had an advantage on them if I had an insight into their private lives. In the tax man's case I figured that there was probably something wrong at home. Maybe his wife was fooling around, or one of his kids had been sick the night before.

I dropped my speculations after a few moments, though. I had never met a government man who admitted to having a private life.

"Agent Lawrence?" I asked.

"Follow me," he said with a gawky nod. He turned around, avoiding eye contact, and went down the hall. Agent Lawrence might have been a whiz at tax calculations but he couldn't walk worth a damn; he listed from side to side as he went.

His office was a small affair. A green metal desk with a matching filing cabinet. There was a big window, though, and the same morning sun that came into the Magnolia Street apartments flowed across his desk.

There was a bookcase with no books or papers in it. There was nothing on his desk except a half-used packet of Sen-Sen. I had the feeling that if I rapped my knuckles on his cabinet it would resound hollow as a drum.

He took his place behind the desk and I sat before him. My chair was of the same uncomfortable make as the one in the hall.

Taped to a wall, far to my left, was a crumpled piece of paper on which was scrawled "I LOVE YOU DADDY" in bold red letters that took up the whole page. It was as if the child were screaming love, testifying to it. There was a photograph in a pewter frame standing on his windowsill. A small red-haired woman with big frightened eyes and a young boy, who looked to be the same age as LaMarque, both cowered under the large and smiling figure of the man before me.

"Nice-lookin' fam'ly," I said.

"Um, yes, thank you," he mumbled. "I assume that you received my letter and so you know why I wanted to meet with you. I couldn't find your home address in our files, and so I had to hope that the address we found in the phone book was yours."

I was never listed in a phone book from that year on.

"The only address we had for you," Lawrence continued, "was the address of a Fetters Real Estate Office."

"Yeah, well," I said. "I been in that same house for eight years now."

"Be that as it may, I'd like you to write your current address and phone number on this card. Also any business number if I need to get in touch with you during the day."

He produced a three-by-five lined card from a drawer and handed it to me. I took it and put it down on the desk. He didn't say anything at first, just stared until finally he asked, "Do you need a pencil?"

"Um, yeah, I guess. I don't carry one around with me."

He took a short, eraserless pencil from the drawer, handed it to me, and waited until I had written the information he wanted. He read it over two or three times and then returned the pencil and card to the drawer.

I didn't want to start the conversation. I had taken the position of an innocent man, and that's the hardest role to play in the presence of an agent of the government. It's even harder if you really are innocent. Police and government officials always have contempt for innocence; they are, in some way, offended by an innocent man.

But I was guilty, so I just sat there counting the toes of my right foot as I pressed them, one by one, into the sole of my shoe. It took great concentration for the middle toes.

I had reached sixty-four before he said, "You've got a big problem, son."

The way he called me *son* instead of my name returned me to southern Texas in the days before World War Two; days when the slightest error in words could hold dire consequences for a black man.

But I smiled as confidently as I could. "It must be some mistake, Mr. Lawrence. I read your note and I don't own nuthin', 'cept fo' that li'l house I done had since 'forty-six."

"No, that's not right. I have it, from reliable sources, that you purchased apartment buildings on Sixty-fourth Place, McKinley Drive, and Magnolia Street in the last five years. They were all auctioned by the city for back taxes."

He wasn't even reading from notes, just rattling off my life as if he had my whole history committed to memory.

"What sources you talkin' 'bout?"

"Where the government gets its information is none of your concern," he said. "At least not until this case goes to court."

"Court? You mean like a trial?"

"Tax evasion is a felony," he said, and then he hesitated. "Do you understand the severity of a felony charge?"

"Yeah, but I ain't done nuthin' like that. I'm just a maintenance man for Mofass."

"Who?"

"Mofass, he's the guy I work for."

"How do you spell that?"

I made up something, and he pulled out the card with my information on it and jotted it down.

"Did you bring the documents I asked for in the letter?" he asked. He could see I didn't have anything.

"No, sir," I said. "I thought that it was all a mistake and that you didn't have to be bothered with it."

"I'm going to need all your financial information for the past five years. A record of all your income, all of it."

"Well," I said, smiling and hating myself for smiling, "that might take a few days. You know I got some shoe boxes in the closet, and then again, some of it might be in the garage if it goes all that far back. Five years is a long time."

"Some people make an awful lot of noise about equality and freedom, but when it comes to paying their debt they sing a different song."

"I ain't singin' nuthin', man," I said. I would have said more but he cut me off.

"Let's get this straight, Rawlins. I'm just a government agent. My job is to find out tax fraud if it exists. I don't have any feeling about you. I've asked you here because I have reason to believe that you cheated the government. If I'm right you're going to trial. It's not personal. I'm just doing my job."

There was nothing for me to say.

He looked at his watch and said, "I have a lot of business to see to today and tomorrow. You've served in the army, haven't you, son?"

"Say what?"

He stroked the lower half of his face and regarded me. I noticed a small, L-shaped scab on the forefinger knuckle of his right hand.

"I'm going to call you this afternoon at three sharp," he said. "Three. And then I'm going to tell you when I can meet with you to go over your income statements. I want all your tax returns, and I want to see bank statements too. Now, it might not be regular office hours, because I'm doing a lot of work this month. There's a lot of bigger fish than you trying to cheat Uncle Sam, and I'm going to catch them all."

If there was something wrong at home for Agent Lawrence, he was going to make sure that the whole world paid for it.

"So it may not be until tomorrow evening that I can see you." He stood up with that.

"Tomorrow! I can't have all that by tomorrow!"

"I have an appointment at the federal courthouse in half an hour. So if you'll excuse me." He held his open hand toward the door.

"Mr. Lawrence . . ."

"I'll call you at three. An army man will know how to be at that phone."

• 6 •

The first thing I did after leaving the tax man was to go to a phone. I called Mofass and told him to have somebody get the empty apartment at the Sixty-fourth Street building ready for two tenants. Then I called Alfred Bontemps at his mother's house.

She answered sweetly, "Yes?"

"Mrs. Bontemps?"

"Is that you, Easy Rawlins?"

"Uh-huh, yeah. How you been, ma'am?"

"Just fine," she said. There was gratitude in her voice. "You know Alfred's come back home 'cause of you."

"I know that. I went up there an' got 'im. I could see how you missed him."

Mrs. Bontemps' son, Alfred, stole three hundred dollars from Slydell, a neighborhood bookie, and then he ran out to Compton because he was afraid that Slydell wanted him dead—which he did. Alfred stole the money because his mother was sick and needed a doctor. Slydell hired me to find the boy and his money. I went straight to Mrs. Bontemps and told her that if she didn't tell me about Alfred, Slydell would kill him.

She gave me the address after I told her how Slydell had once torn off a man's ear for stealing the hubcaps from his car.

"But you workin' fo' that man," she'd told me. Tears were in her eyes.

"That's just business though, ma'am. If I could get what Slydell wants I could maybe cut a deal with him."

She was so scared that she told me the address. Woman's love has killed many a man that way.

I found Alfred, threw him in the back of my Ford, and drove him to a hotel on Grand Street in L.A. Then I drove over to the bookie shop; that was the back room of a barbershop on Avalon.

I gave Slydell the forty-two dollars Alfred had left and told him, "Alfred's gonna give you fifteen dollars a month until that money is paid, Slydell."

"The hell he is!"

I had no intention of letting that boy get killed after I'd found him, so I brought out my pistol and held it to the bookie's silver-capped tooth.

"I said I'd bring you yo' money, man. You know Alfred cain't pay you if he's dead."

"I cain't let that boy get away wit' stealin' from me. I got a reputation t'think of, Easy."

Slydell was only tough with a man who cowered at threats of violence. And he knew I wasn't the kind of man who bowed down.

"Then it's either you or him, man," I said. "You know I don't look kindly on killin' boys."

We settled it without bloodshed. Alfred got a good job with the Parks Department, paid Slydell, and got his mother on his health insurance.

Mrs. Bontemps kind of took me on as her foster son after that.

"You ever gonna get married, Easy?" she asked.

"If I ever find somebody t'take me."

"Oh, you'd be a good catch, honey," she said. "I know lotsa good women give they eyeteeth fo' you."

But all I was interested in was Alfred at that moment. He was a small boy, barely out of his teens, and skitterish, but he felt he owed me a debt of honor for standing up against Slydell. And I think he might have been happy to get back home to his mother too.

"Could I talk with Alfred, ma'am?"

"Sure, Easy, an' maybe you could come over fo' dinner sometimes."

"Love it," I said.

After a few moments Alfred came on the line.

"Mr. Rawlins?"

"Listen up, Alfred. I gotta move somebody t'day an' I need a helper ain't gonna go runnin' his mouth after it."

"You got it, Mr., um, Easy. When you need the help?"

"You know my house on 116th Street?"

"Not really."

I gave him the address and told him to be there at about one-thirty.

"But first go over to Mofass' office an' tell 'im that you gonna use his truck fo' the move," I said.

All the time I was on the phone the idea of the government taking my money and my freedom was gnawing at me. But I didn't even let that become a thought. I was afraid of what might happen if I did.

So instead I went to Targets Bar after my phone calls. It was still early in the day, but I needed some liquor and some peace.

John McKenzie was the bartender at Targets. He was also the cook and the bouncer, and, though his name wasn't on the deed, John was also the owner. He used to own a speakeasy down around Watts but the police finally closed that down. An honest police captain moved into the precinct, and because of the differences between honest cops and honest Negro entrepreneurs, he put all our best businessmen out of trade.

John couldn't get a liquor license because he had been a bootlegger in his youth, so he took an empty storefront and set out a plank of mahogany and eighteen round maple tables. Then he gave nine thousand dollars to Odell Jones, who in turn made a down payment to the bank. But it was John's bar. He managed it, collected the money, and paid the mortgage. What Odell got was that he could come in there anytime he wanted and drink to his heart's content.

It was John who gave me the idea of how to buy my own buildings through a dummy corporation.

Odell worked at the First African Baptist Day School, which was around the corner from his bar. He was the custodian there.

Odell was at his special table the day I came from the IRS. He was eating his regular egg-and-bacon sandwich for lunch before going back to work. John was standing at the far end of the bar, leaning against it and staring off into the old days when he was an important man.

"Easy."

"Mo'nin'. John."

We shook hands.

John's face looked like it was chiseled in ebony. He was tall and hard. There wasn't an ounce of fat on John, but he was a big man, still and all. He was the kind of man who could run a bar or speakeasy, because violence came to him naturally, but he preferred to take it easy.

He put a drink down in front of me and touched my big knuckle. When I looked up into his stark white-and-brown eyes he said, "Mouse been here t'day, Easy."

"Yeah?"

"He askin' fo' EttaMae, an' when that failed he asted 'bout you."

"Like what?"

"Where you been, who you been wit'. Like that. He was wit' Rita Cook. They was goin' t'her house fo' a afternoon nap."

"Yeah?"

"I just thought you wanna know 'bout yo' ole friend bein' up here, Easy."

"Thanks, John," I said, and then, "By the way . . ."

"Yeah?" He looked at me with the same dead-ahead look that he had for a customer ordering whiskey or an armed robber demanding what was in the till.

"Some people been talkin' 'bout them buildin's I bought a while back."

"Uh-huh."

"You tell anybody 'bout them papers we did?"

At first he moved his shoulders, as if he were going to turn away without a word. But then he straightened up and said, "Easy, if I wanted to get you I could put sumpin' in yo' drink. Or I could get one'a these niggahs in here t'cut yo' th'oat. But now you know better than that, don't you?"

"Yeah, I know, John. But you know that I had t'ask."

We shook hands again, still friends, and I moved away from the bar.

I said hello to Odell. We made plans to get together in the next couple of days. It felt like I was back in the war again. Back then I'd see somebody and make plans, just a few hours away, but I wondered if I'd be alive to make the date.

"Hi, Easy," Etta said in a cool voice when I got to the door. The potatoes were replanted and the flower beds were tended. My house smelled cleaner than it ever had, and I was sorry, so sorry that I wanted to cry.

"Hi, Unca Easy," LaMarque yelled. He was jumping up and down on my couch. Up and down, over and over, like a little madman, or a little boy.

"Mouse went to John McKenzie's bar t'day. He was lookin' fo' you an' askin' 'bout me," I told Etta.

"He be here tomorrow then, an' me an' LaMarque be gone."

"How you know he ain't on his way here right now?"

"You say he was in John McKenzie's bar just today?"

"Yeah."

"So he had t'be either wit' a girl or after one."

I didn't say anything to that, so Etta went on, "Raymond always gotta get his thing wet when he get to a new place. So he be here tomorrah, after he get that pussy."

I was ashamed to hear her talk like that and looked around to see where LaMarque was. But something about her bold talk excited me too. I didn't like to feel anything about Mouse's woman, but things were going so poorly in my life that I was feeling a little reckless.

Luckily Alfred drove up then. He was a tiny young man, hardly larger than a punk kid, but he could work. We put Etta's bags and a bed from my garage in the truck. I also gave her a chair and a table from my store of abandoned furniture.

Etta softened a little before she left.

"You gonna come an' see us, Easy?" she asked. "You know LaMarque likes you."

"Just gotta get this tax man offa my butt an' I be by, Etta. Two days, three at top."

"You tell Raymond that I don't wanna see 'im. Tell 'im that I tole you not t'give 'im my address."

"What if he pulls a gun on me? You want me to shoot 'im?"

"If he pulls his gun, Easy, then we all be dead."

• 7 •

After everyone was gone I sat down by the phone. That was five minutes to three. If Lawrence had called me when he said he was I might have been okay. But the minutes stretched into half an hour and then to an hour. During that time I thought about all that I was going to lose; my property, my money, my freedom. And I thought about the way he called me *son* so easily. In those days many white people still took it for granted that a black man was little more than a child.

It was well after four by the time Lawrence called.

"Rawlins?"

"Yeah."

"I want you to come to my office at six-thirty this evening. I've notified someone downstairs so you shouldn't have any trouble getting in."

"Tonight? I cain't have all that by then, man."

But I was wasting my words, because he had already hung up.

I went to the garage and pulled out my box of papers. I had paid taxes on the money I paid myself through Mofass, but I didn't pay taxes on the stolen money because it was still hot in 1948 and after that it was already undeclared. Most of the profit from the rent went into buying more real estate. It was just easier to let the money ride without telling the government about my income.

Then I drove out to see Mofass. My choices were few and none of them sounded any too good.

On the drive over I heard a voice in my head say, "Mothahfuckah ain't got no right messin' like that, man. No right at all."

But I ignored it. I grabbed the steering wheel a little tighter and concentrated on the road.

"It don't look good, Mr. Rawlins," Mofass said behind his fat cigar.

"What about that thing you said with backdatin' them papers?" I asked. We were sitting in his office in a haze of tobacco smoke.

"You said it yourself, they ain't nobody got enough money for you to give it to."

"What about you?"

Mofass eyed me suspiciously and pushed back in his swivel chair.

He sat there, staring at me for a full minute before shaking his head and saying, "No."

"I need it, Mofass. If you don't do this I'm goin' to jail."

"I feel for ya but I gotta say no, Mr. Rawlins. It ain't that I don't care, but this is business. And when you in business there's just some things that you cain't do. Now look at it from my side. I work for you, I collect the rent and keep things smooth. Now all of a sudden you wanna sign ev'rything over t'me. I own it," he said, pointing all eight of his fingers at his chest. "But you get the money."

"John McKenzie do it with Odell Jones."

"From what you told me it sounds like Odell just likes his drink. I'm a businessman and you cain't trust me."

"The hell I cain't!"

"You see"—Mofass opened his eyes and puffed out his cheeks, looking like a big brown carp—"you'd come after me if you thought I was messin' wit' yo' money. Right now that's okay 'cause we got a legal relationship. But I couldn't be trusted if all that was yours suddenly became mines. What if all of a sudden I feel like I deserve more but you say no? In a court of law it would be mine."

"We couldn't go to no courts after we done faked the ownership papers, man."

"That's just it, Mr. Rawlins. If I say yes to you right now, then the only court of appeal we got is each other. We ain't blood. All we is is business partners. An' I tell ya this." He pointed his black stogie at me. "They ain't no greater hate that a man could have than the hate of someone who cheated him at his own business."

Mofass sat back again, and I knew he had turned me down.

"So that's it, huh?" I said.

"You ain't even tried t'lie yet, Mr. Rawlins. Go in there wit' yo' papers and yo' lie and see what you could get."

"He's talkin' court, Mofass."

"Sho he is. That's what they do, try an' scare ya. Go in there wit' yo' income papers an' ast 'im where he think you gonna come up wit' the kinda cash it takes t'buy apartments. Act po', thas what you do. Them white people love t'think that you ain't shit."

"An' if that don't work," a husky voice in my head said, "kill the mothahfuckah."

I tried to shake the gloom that that voice brought on me. I wanted to drive right out to the IRS, but instead I went home and dug my snub-nose out of the closet. I cleaned it and oiled it and loaded it with fresh cartridges. It scared me, because I would carry the .25 for a little insurance, but my .38 was a killing gun. I kept thinking about that clumsy white man, how he had a house and a family to go to. All he cared about was that some numbers made up zero on a piece of paper.

"This man is the government," I said in order to convince myself of the foolishness of going armed.

"Man wanna take from you," the voice replied, "he better be ready to back it up."

The front door of the government building was locked and dark, but a small Negro man came to answer my knock. He was wearing gray gardening overalls and a plaid shirt. I wondered if he owned any property.

"You Mr. Rawlins?" he asked me.

"That's right," I said.

"You could just go on upstairs then."

I was in such a state that all I paid any attention to was the blood pounding in my head. Loud and insistent. And what it was insisting on was more blood, tax man blood. I was going to tell him about the money I was paid and he was going to believe it or I was going to shoot him. If they wanted me in jail I was going to give them a good reason.

Maybe I'd've shot him anyway.

Maybe I would've shot the Negro in the overalls too, I don't know. It's just that sometimes I get carried away. When the pressure gets to me this voice comes out. It saved my life more than once during the war. But those were hard times where life-and-death decisions were simple.

I might have gone lighter if Lawrence had treated me with the same kind of respect he showed others. But I am no white man's *son*.

On approaching the door I threw off the safety on my gun. I heard voices as I pushed the door open but I was still surprised to see someone sitting with him. My finger clutched the trigger. I remember worrying that I might shoot myself in the foot.

"Here he is now," Lawrence was saying. He was the only man I had ever seen who sat in a chair awkwardly. He was tilting to the side and holding on to the arm to keep from falling to the floor. The man sitting across from him stood up. He was shorter than either Lawrence or I, maybe five-ten, and wiry. He was a pale-skinned man with bushy brown hair and hairy knuckles. I noticed these latter because he walked right up to me and shook my hand. I had to release hold of the pistol in my pocket in order to shake his hand; that's the only reason I didn't shoot Reginald Lawrence.

"Mr. Rawlins," the wiry white man said. "I've heard a lot about you and I'm happy to make your acquaintance."

"Yes, sir," I said.

"Craxton!" he shouted. "Special Agent Darryl T. Craxton! FBI."

"Pleased to meet you."

"Agent Craxton has something to discuss with you, Mr. Rawlins," Lawrence said.

When I took my hand off the pistol my chance for murder was through. I said, "I got the papers you wanted right here."

"Forget that." Craxton waved a dismissing hand at the shoe box under my arm. "I got something for you to do for your country. You like fighting for your country, don't you, Ezekiel?"

"I done it when I had to."

"Yeah." Craxton's smile revealed crooked teeth that had wide spaces between them. But they looked strong, like brown-and-white tree stumps that you'd have to dynamite to remove. "I've been discussing your case with Mr. Lawrence here. I've been looking for somebody to help me with a mission, and you're the best candidate I've seen."

"What kind of a mission?"

Craxton smiled again. "Mr. Lawrence tells me that you overlooked paying some taxes for the past few years."

"This man is suspected of tax evasion," Lawrence interrupted. "That is what I said."

"Mr. Rawlins here is a war hero," Craxton answered. "He loves this country. He hates our enemies. A man like that doesn't shirk his responsibility, Mr. Lawrence. I believe that he just made an error."

Lawrence pulled out a white handkerchief and dabbed at his lips.

Craxton turned back to me. "I could fix it so that you just pay your back taxes, by installment if you don't have the cash. All I need is a little help. No. No. Change that. All your country needs is a little help."

That set Lawrence up straight.

He said, "I thought you just wanted to talk with him?"

Before he could say any more I jumped in. "Well, you know I'm always ready to be a good citizen, Mr. Craxton. That's why I'm here this time of night. I want to show that I'm a good citizen." I knew how to be good too; LaMarque didn't have a thing on me.

"See, Mr. Lawrence, see? Mr. Rawlins is eager to help us out. No reason for you to pursue your current course. I tell you what. Mr.

Rawlins and I will do some work together and then I'll come back and have his paperwork transferred to Washington. That way you won't have to worry about his settlement."

Reginald Lawrence grabbed onto the arm of his chair a little tighter.

"This is not proper procedure, Agent Craxton," the IRS man complained.

Craxton just smiled.

"I'll have to speak with my supervisor," Lawrence continued.

"You do what you think is appropriate, Mr. Lawrence." Craxton never stopped smiling. "I appreciate that a man has to do his job, he has to do what he thinks is right. If everybody just does that this country will be fine and healthy."

The blood rose to Lawrence's face. My heart was going like a bird in flight.

• 8 •

Special agent Craxton was saying, "Nice place, Hollywood," as he sipped a glass of 7-Up.

I was nursing a screwdriver. We had driven to a small bar called Adolf's on Sunset Boulevard near La Cienega. Adolf's was an old place, established before the war, so it held on to that unpopular name.

When we got to the door a man in a red jacket and top hat barred our way.

"May I help you gentlemen?"

"Stand aside," Craxton said.

"Maybe you don't understand, mister," the doorman replied, raising his hand in a tentative gesture. "We're a class place and not everyone can cut it."

He was looking directly into my face.

"Listen, bud." Craxton peeled back his left lapel. Pinned to the inside of the jacket was his FBI identification. "Either you open the door now or I shut you down—for good."

After that the manager came over and seated us near the piano player. He also offered us free drinks and food, which Craxton turned down. Nobody bothered us after that. I remember thinking that those white people were just as afraid of the law as any colored man. Of course, I always knew that there was no real difference between the races, but still, it was nice to see an example of that equality.

I was thinking about that and how I had been suddenly saved from the gas chamber. Because it was a certainty that I would have murdered Agent Lawrence if the ugly man in front of me hadn't shaken my hand.

"What do you know about communism, Mr. Rawlins?" Craxton asked. His tone was like a schoolteacher's—I was being quizzed.

"Call me Easy. That's the name I go by."

He nodded and I said, "I figure the Reds to be one step worse than the Nazis unless you happen to be a Jew. To a Jew they ain't nuthin' worse than a Nazi."

I said that because I knew what the FBI man wanted to hear. My feelings were really much more complex. In the war the Russians were our allies; our best friends. Paul Robeson, the great Negro actor and singer, had toured Russia and even lived there for a while. Joseph Stalin himself had Robeson as his guest at the Kremlin. But when the war was through we were enemies again. Robeson's career was destroyed and he left America.

I didn't know how we could be friends with somebody one day and then enemies the next. I didn't know why a man like Robeson would give up his shining career for something like politics.

Agent Craxton nodded while I answered and tapped his cheekbone with a hairy index finger. "Lots of Jews are communists too. Marx was a Jew, grandfather to all the Reds."

"I guess there's all kindsa Jews just like ev'rybody else."

Craxton nodded, but I wasn't so sure that he agreed with me.

"One thing you have right is how bad the Reds are. They want to take the whole world and enslave it. They don't believe in freedom like Americans do. The Russians have been peasants so long that that's the way they see the whole world—from chains."

It was strange talk, I thought, a white man lecturing me about slavery.

"Yeah, some folks learn how to love their chains, I guess."

Craxton gave me a quick smile. In that brief second a shine of admiration flashed across his walnut eyes.

He said, "I knew we'd understand each other, Easy. Soon as I saw your police file I knew you were the kind of man for us."

"What kinda man is that?"

The pianist was playing "Two Sleepy People" on a bright and lively note.

"Man who wants to serve his country. Man who knows what it is to fight and maybe take a couple of chances. Man who doesn't give in to some foreign power saying that they have a better deal."

I had the feeling that Craxton didn't see the man sitting before him, but I'd seen pictures of Leavenworth in *Life* magazine so I pretended to be the man he described.

"Chaim Wenzler," Craxton said.

"Who?"

"One of those communist kind of Jews. Union persuasion. Calls himself a *worker*. Building chains is what he's doing. He's been organizing unions from Alameda County on down the line to Champion Aircraft. You know Champion, don't you, Easy?"

The last real job I had was at Champion.

"I worked production there," I said. "Five years ago."

"I know," Craxton said. He pulled a manila folder from his jacket pocket. The folder was soiled, creased, and pleated down the center. He smoothed it out in front of me. The block red letters across the top said: "LAPD Special Subject." And below that: "subj—Ezekiel P. Rawlins, aka—Easy Rawlins."

"Everything we need to know in here, Easy. War record, criminal associations, job history. One police detective wrote a letter in 1949 saying that he suspected you of being involved in a series of homicides the previous year. Then in 1950 you turn around and help the police find a rapist working the Watts community.

"I'd been looking for a Negro to work for us. Somebody who might have a little trouble but nothing so bad that we couldn't smooth it over if somebody showed a little initiative and some patriotism. Then Clyde Wadsworth called about you."

"Who?"

"Wadsworth, he's Lawrence's head. Clyde saw an inquiry for your file go across his desk a few weeks back. He knew the neighborhood you lived in and gave me a call. Lucky for everybody."

He tapped the folder with a clean, evenly manicured fingernail.

"We need you to get to know this Wenzler, Easy. We need to know if it's the left or right leg he puts into his pants first in the morning."

"How could I do that and the whole FBI cain't do it?"

"This is a sly Jew. We know that he's up to his shoulders in something bad, but damned if we can do anything about it. You see, Wenzler never really gets involved with the place he's organizing. He won't work there. But he finds his fair-haired boy and grooms him to be his mouthpiece. That's what he did with Andre Lavender. Know him?"

Craxton stared me straight in the eye awaiting the answer.

I remembered Andre. A big, sloppy man. But he had the energy of ten men for all his weight. He always had a plan to get rich quick. For a while he sold frozen steaks and then, later on, he tried construction. Andre was a good man but he was too excitable; even if he made a couple of bucks he'd spend them just that quick. "Rich an' important men gotta spend money, Easy," he told me once. He was driving a leased Cadillac at the time, delivering frozen steaks from door to door.

"I don't remember him," I said to Special Agent Craxton.

"Well, maybe he wasn't so loud when you were at Champion, but now he's a union man. Chaim Wenzler's boy."

Craxton sat back for a moment and appraised me. He put his hand flat against my file like a man swearing on a sacred text. Then he leaned across the table and began to whisper, "You see, Easy, in many ways the Bureau is a last line of defense. There are all sorts of enemies we have these days. We've got enemies all over the world; in Europe, in Asia, everywhere. But the real enemies, the ones we really have to watch out for, are people right here at home. People who aren't Americans on the inside. No, not really."

He drifted off into a kind of reverie. The confusion must have shown on my face, because he added, "And we have to stop these people. We have to bring them to the attention of the courts and the

Congress. So even if I have to overlook some lesser crimes"— he paused and stared at me again—"like petty tax theft, I will do that in order to get the bigger job done."

"Listen, man," I said. "You got me by the nuts on this one, so I'ma do what you want. But get to it, alright? I'm a little nervous with all this talk an' these files an' shit."

"Okay," he said, and then he took a deep breath. "Chaim Wenzler has been organizing people through the unions. He's been giving them ideas about this country that are lies and unpatriotic. There's more to it, but I can't tell you what because we can't get anybody close enough to him to really find out what it is that he's up to."

"Why don't you just arrest him? Cain't you do that?"

"He's not what we want, Easy. It's what he represents, the people he works with—that's what we need to know."

"An' you cain't make him tell you all this stuff?" I was well aware of the persuasive powers of the law.

"Not this man." There was a hint of admiration in Craxton's tone. "And it's worth our time to find out who he's working with, without him knowing it, that is. You see, Wenzler is bad, but where you can see someone like him you know that there's serious rot underneath."

"Uh-huh." I nodded, trying to look like I was right up there with him. "So what do you need me for if you already know that this guy is the center of the problem? I mean, what could I do?"

"Wenzler is small potatoes. He's a fanatic, thinks that America isn't free and the Reds are. All by himself he's nothing, just a malcontent with a dull ax to grind. But it's just that kind of man that gets duped into doing the worst harm."

"But I don't even know this guy, how you expect me to get next to him?"

"Wenzler works in the Negro churches. We figure that he's making his contacts down there."

"Yeah?"

"He's working three places right now. One of them is the First African Baptist Church and Day School. That's your neighborhood, right? You probably know some of that flock."

"So what does he do at the church?"

"Charity," Agent Craxton sneered. "But that's just a front. He's looking for others who are like him; people who feel that this country has given them a raw deal. He feels like that, doesn't hardly trust a soul. But the thing is, he'll trust you. He's got a soft spot for Negroes."

It was at that moment I decided not to trust Agent Craxton.

"I still don't see why you need me. If the FBI wants something on him why don't you just make it up?" I was serious.

Agent Craxton took my meaning and laughed. It sounded like an asthmatic's cough.

"I don't have a partner, Easy. Did you notice that?"

I nodded.

"There's no crime here, Mr. Rawlins. We're not trying to put somebody in jail for tax evasion. What we are doing is shedding light on a group of people who use the very freedom we give them in order to burn down what we believe."

I wondered if Agent Craxton had political aspirations. He sounded like a man running for office.

"There is no crime to arrest him for. No crime that we know of, that is. But if you get next to him you might find out something. You might see where we could come in and arrest him for a crime the courts would recognize. You might be our means to his end."

"Uh-huh," I grunted. "But what do you mean about not havin' no partner?"

"I'm a special kind of agent, Easy. I don't just look for evidence. Some agents are in the business of solving crimes. My job is to avoid the damage before it's done."

"Yeah," I said, nodding. "But now lemme get this straight. You want me to get to know this Wenzler guy, then get him to trust me so I find out if he's a spy?"

"And then you find out all you can, Easy. We let you pay your taxes and go back home."

"And what if I don't find out somethin' that you could use? What if it's just that he complains a lot but he don't do nuthin' really?"

"You just report to me. Say once a week. I'll know how to read it.

And when you're through the IRS will let you alone."

"All that sounds good, but I need to know somethin' first."

"What's that?"

"Well, you talkin' 'bout my own people with this conspiracy stuff. An' if you want my opinion, all that is just some mistake. You know I live down there an' I ain't never heard that we some kinda communist conspiracy or whatever."

Craxton just smiled.

"But if you wanna believe that." I continued, "I guess you can. But you cain't get me t' go after my own people. I mean, if these guys broke the law like you say, I don't mind that, but I don't wanna hurt the people at First African just 'cause they run a charity drive or somethin'."

"We see eye to eye, Easy," Craxton said. "I just want the Jew, and whatever it is he's up to. You won't even know I was there."

"So what's this stuff about this other guy, Lavender?"

"You remember him?"

"No."

"We need to find Lavender. He's worked closer with Wenzler than anyone. If we could get him into custody I'm sure that he'd be able to help."

"You sound like he's missin'?"

"He quit Champion three weeks ago and nobody has seen him since. We'd appreciate a line on him, Easy. Finding Lavender would go a long way toward settling your taxes."

"But you just wanna talk to 'im?"

"That's right." Craxton was leaning so far across the table that he could have jumped down my throat.

I knew that he was lying to me, but I needed him, so I said, "Okay," and we shook hands.

The orange juice in my screwdriver was canned, it left a bitter metallic taste in my mouth. But I drank it anyway. Screwdriver was what I asked for; I guess I asked for Craxton too.

• 9 •

I left Adolf's and drove straight to John's bar. I wanted a good-tasting drink in the bar of my own choosing.

That was about nine o'clock, so lots of people were there. Odell was at his regular seat, near the wall. Pierre Kind was with him. Bonita Smith danced slowly in the middle of the floor with Brad Winston in her arms. The bar was lined with men and women, and John worked hard meeting their demands. "Good Night, Irene," the original version by Leadbelly, played on the jukebox, and a haze of cigarette smoke dimmed the room.

I saw Mouse sitting at a table with Dupree Bouchard and Jackson Blue; as unlikely a trio as I could imagine.

Jackson had on jeans and a dark blue button-down shirt. He also wore a baby-blue jacket with matching pointy-toed shoes. Jackson's skin was so black that it glinted blue when in the full sun. He was a small man, smaller than Mouse even, and as cowardly as they come. He was a petty thief and a lackey to the various numbers runners and gangsters. He would have been what we called trash back then, but that wasn't all there was to Jackson Blue. He was the closest I ever came to knowing a genius. Jackson could read and write as well as anybody I knew, including the professors at Los Angeles City College. He'd tell you all kinds of things about history and science and things that happened in places elsewhere in the world. At first I didn't believe the things he'd tell me, but then I bought an old encyclopedia set from him. No matter how I tested him, Jackson knew every fact in those books. From then on I just took it on faith that everything else he said was true, too.

But Jackson didn't just read and remember, he could also tell what people were thinking and what they were likely to do, by just talking to them. Jackson would walk into a room and come out the other side knowing everybody's secrets from just watching their eyes or hearing them talk about the weather.

He was a valuable asset to a man like me; even more so because Jackson never used his ability except to rat back and forth between factions of the criminal element. Give Jackson five dollars and he'd sell out his best friend. And you never had to worry about Jackson lying to you, because he was so cowardly and because he had great pride in the fact that he was right about whatever he said.

Dupree dwarfed his companions. He was a head taller than I and built to split stones. He was wide and burly with close-cropped hair and a great propensity for laughter. Right when I walked in he let go a terrific gust of guffaws. Mouse had probably been telling one of his grim tales.

Dupree wore drab green overalls with CHAMPION sewn into the back in dull red thread. We both worked at the airplane manufacturer for some years, before the untimely death of his girlfriend, Coretta James, and my entrée into the world of real estate and favors.

But for all their showy qualities, Dupree and Jackson were dim lights compared with Mouse.

He wore a cream double-breasted suit with a felt brown derby and brown, round-toed shoes. His white shirt looked to be satin. His teeth were all aglitter with gold edgings, silver caps, and one lustrous blue jewel. He didn't wear rings or bracelets, because they got in the way of weapons handling. Mouse's color was a dusky pecan and his eyes were light gray. He was smiling and talking. People from other tables leaned away from their drinks to hear what he had to say.

"Yeah, man," Mouse drawled. "He waits till the bitch an' me was *in the bed*, not gettin' ready mind ya, but *in the fuckin' bed*. Then he jump out an' say, 'Ah-hah.' "

Mouse opened his eyes wide just the way the jealous lover must've done it. Everybody was laughing.

Jackson asked, "What you do then?" in a way that let you know he felt he might need that trick one day.

"Shit!" Mouse spat. "I kicked off the blankets an' jumped up t' face the mothahfuckah. I say, 'What the fuck is this shit?' That boy was rowdy, but you know he took out a moment t' look down at my big hard dick. 'Cause you know I got sumpin' give any man pause."

Mouse was a master storyteller. He had every man there wondering about his thing just like that jealous lover was supposed to have done.

"Then I go upside the dude's head wit' a lamp from the night table. Heavy clay job, man, it was so thick that it didn't even break. Shit. That boy hit the flo' hard."

"I bet you got yo' ass outta there in a hurry," Jackson laughed. You could tell that Jackson had his hand on his own business under the table; that's how some men maintain their security.

"Run? Hell no! Man, I was really ready t'fuck then, I pulled that bitch down in the bed an' got me some pussy like most men on'y dream of. Run? Shit."

Mouse sat back and drank his beer. The men around were all laughing. Most people there were from Texas originally, but many of them didn't know Mouse. They laughed because they loved a well-told lie. And Raymond didn't mind, because he liked to make people laugh. But I wasn't laughing. Neither was John behind his bar, or Odell over on his side.

Mouse never lied. That wasn't his way. I mean, he'd lie to you if it was business of some sort, but sitting around a bar Mouse told true stories.

What I wondered was how hard he hit that man.

"Easy." Mouse smiled at me out past the edge of his audience.

My heart thrilled and quailed at the same time. Mouse was the truest friend I ever had. And if there is such a thing as true evil, he was that too.

"Raymond," I said. I moved past the others to sit at the small table. "How ya doin', Jackson, Dupree?"

They both said my name and touched my hand.

"You heard I was here?" Mouse asked me.

"Yeah," I answered. "I wondered why you didn't come by t'see me."

Mouse and I were talking to each other. It was like no one else was in the room. Dupree was calling John to get more drinks and Jackson turned away, telling a story to somebody at another table.

"I been out at Dupree's house. I'm out there stayin' wit' him."

"You coulda come t' my house, Ray. I got room, you know that."

"Yeah, yeah. Coulda done, but . . ." He paused and smiled at me. "But I don't like t' be surprised, Easy. It's like that dude come bustin' in the bedroom. You see, if I had seen my ole lady fuckin' somebody in my own bed, well, they both need the undertaker by then."

I felt the weight of that .38 through my jacket and on my right thigh. But my arms felt weak and I remembered how awful it was for my Great-Uncle Halley when he got so old that he couldn't even feed himself.

"Ain't none of us gotta worry 'bout gettin' old, Mouse," I said.

He laughed and slapped my thigh. It was a good laugh. Happy.

"But," I went on, "that ain't no reason fo' you to go to Dupree when I got room right in my own house."

"You seen Etta?"

I wanted to, but I couldn't lie in his face.

"She come yesterday, stayed the night, and moved to a place t'day. Her an' LaMarque."

When I said LaMarque's name Mouse jerked his head up. He looked me in the eye for a moment, and what I saw there scared me.

Most violent and desperate men have a kind of haunted look in their eyes. But never Mouse. He could smile in your face and shoot you dead. He didn't feel guilt or remorse. He was different from most men. What he did, he did because of a set of rules that only applied to him. He loved some people; his mother, dead by then, Etta and LaMarque, and me too. He loved us in the strange way that he felt everything.

So I was unsettled when I saw the remorse and bitterness in

Mouse's gaze. A man who is already insane was frightening enough, but when he goes crazy . . .

"Where she go?"

"She asked me not to tell ya, Raymond. She said t'tell her how she could call you an' she'd do it—when she was ready."

Mouse just stared at me. His eyes were clear again. He might have killed me then. Who knows? Maybe if it all happened at a different time I would have acted differently. But I didn't know how to give in to my fear. In two days I had prepared to lose all my property and my freedom, I had settled on becoming a murderer, and I had become a flunky for the FBI. I decided to let fate hold my cards.

"You ain't gonna tell me where she is?"

"She upset, Raymond. If you don't let her do it her way she gonna blow up at you, an' me too."

Mouse watched me like a little boy might watch a butterfly. John hovered behind him while he put down short glasses filled with various amber liquors and ice.

"Easy got yo' number, Dupree?" Mouse asked at last.

"Ain't ya, Ease?" Dupree asked me.

"Yeah, yeah. I got it."

Mouse laughed. "Well then, that's business. Let's have some drinks."

Dupree got drunk and told stories after a while. Wholesome stories about foolish men at Champion Aircraft. The kind of stories that workmen tell. How somebody lost count when assembling a jet engine and how that engine blew the roof off of the construction bungalow. And when the boss asked what happened the perpetrator just opened his eyes and said something like "Somebody musta lit a match."

At one point I asked Dupree, "You seen Andre Lavender 'round there lately?"

"Uh-uh, man. He got the politics bug pretty bad there for a while. Union. But then he just disappeared one day."

"Disappeared?"

"Yeah, man. Gone. I think he stole sumpin', 'cause they had all kindsa cops there. But no one know what happened."

"Didn't his li'l girlfriend . . ." I snapped my fingers trying to remember.

"Juanita," Dupree said, frowning.

"Yeah, Juanita. Didn't she know where he was?"

"Nope. She come around the plant lookin' fo'im the next day, but nobody could help. But you know I did hear that Andre blew town with Winthrop Hughes' ole lady."

"You mean Shaker's girl?"

"Uh-huh. They say Andre took her, his bank book, an' his car."

"No shit?" I let it drop there. Andre could wait for a while.

When Dupree passed out (which is what he did whenever he drank) we carried him out to the car. We piled him in the back and Jackson jumped into the passenger's seat. Before Mouse pulled in behind the wheel he leaned very close to my face and said, "If you see 'er, you tell 'er that I give it a couple'a days. You tell 'er that I won't be denied. I will not be denied." Then he grabbed my shirt with thin fingers that were hard as nails. "An' if you get in my way, Easy, or if you take her side, I kill you too."

As I watched them drive away I breathed a quiet sigh of relief that Etta had moved out of my house. I figured that EttaMae could handle Mouse, especially if she wasn't with me.

• 10 •

The next morning I called Etta to tell her about my talk with Mouse. She snorted once and had nothing else to say. I offered to escort her to church on Sunday. She accepted and excused herself, polite and cold.

As a kind of treat for my new freedom from the IRS and Raymond Alexander I decided to let myself loll in the sunny halls of the Magnolia Street apartments.

Mrs. Trajillo was at her window rolling out corn tortillas on a breadboard balanced on the windowsill. Her skin was a deep olive color dappled with various-sized freckles and one large mole at the center of her chin. Her long hair was salt and pepper and hung in one thick braid down to about the middle of her thigh. She was short but sturdily built, and though she had never had a job, her hands were strong from years of doing housework, raising children, and making food from scratch.

"Good morning, Mr. Rawlins," she greeted me.

"Hello, ma'am. How're you today?"

"Oh, pretty good I guess. My granddaughter had her confirmation last Sunday."

"That a fact?"

"You look good," she said. "I was worried about you and poor Mr. Mofass the other day. You weren't smiling at all, and that terrible girl . . ." She brought her fingers to her chest and made an O-shape with her lips. "The things she yelled at him. You know I was glad the children were still in school."

"I guess Poinsettia was upset. You know how she's sick and all."

"God gives you what you earn, Mr. Rawlins."

That seemed like a terrible curse coming from such a kind woman.

"What do you mean?" I asked.

"The way she was with men before. No girl of mine would be like that. I'm not telling you anything, Mr. Rawlins, but God knows."

It didn't bother me much. I know that older women often forget how it is to be loved by young men. Or maybe they do remember and hate it all the more.

I went upstairs and stood on the second floor for an hour or more just feeling the sun and looking at nothing. But after a while I picked up the trace of a foul scent.

The sun was shining in on the third floor too. It was beautiful but the smell was bad. The door to Apartment J was ajar; that's where the smell came from.

Really what I should call it is smells. There was the sweet smell of three or four kinds of incense that she used in her prayer altar and the odor of sickness that had been bottled up in her small rooms for the most part of six months. There were all kinds of rotting odors beyond that smell.

But now, I figured, she was gone, moved out after Mofass had threatened her with eviction. The door was open and I knew she had probably left me a major cleaning job.

Poinsettia had gone off for a vacation weekend six months before and come back two weeks later in a private ambulance. The attendants had told Mrs. Trajillo that Poinsettia had been in a bad car accident and that her boyfriend had paid to have her moved from the hospital back home. Her bones and bruises healed, but something happened to her nerves. She couldn't work anymore or even walk right. Somewhere in her late twenties, she had been a beautiful woman until that accident. It was a shame to see her come down so far. But what could I do about it? Mofass was hard but he was right when he said that I couldn't pay her rent.

The living room was a mess. The shades were drawn and the

curtains pulled, so it was twilight in the musty rooms. Ghostly white cartons of Chinese food were open and moldering on the table, trash everywhere. I flicked the light switch, but the bulb had burned out. Against a far wall there sat an altar she had made from a small alcove. Inside she had glued a picture of Jesus. It was painted like a mosaic. He had a halo and held two fingers and a thumb above three saints who were bowing to receive his blessing. All around the painting there were old flowers wired to the walls. They were unidentifiable brown things that she'd probably brought home from mass or after a funeral.

At the foot of the painting was the bronze dish that she also used to burn the incense. The sweet smell was much stronger there. Little ashes, like white maggots, were littered around the brimming dish. And there was a black, gummy substance on the ledge and down the wall to the floor.

The bathroom was disgusting. All kinds of cosmetic bottles open and dried until the liquids had caked and cracked. Mildewed towels on the floor. A spider spun its web over the bathtub faucet.

The worst smells came from the bedroom, and I hesitated to go in there. It's a funny thing how smell is such an animal instinct. The first thing a dog will do is sniff. And if it doesn't smell right there's a natural reluctance to get any closer.

Maybe I should have been a dog.

Poinsettia was hanging from the light fixture in the middle of the ceiling. She was naked and her skin sagged so that it seemed as if it would come right off the bone any second. Directly under her was the cause of the worst smells. Even as I watched a thick drop of blood and excrement fell from her toe.

I don't remember going down to Mrs. Trajillo's apartment. I have a feeling that I tried to use Poinsettia's phone, but it had been disconnected.

"Sure," said Officer Andrew Reedy, a rangy and towheaded policeman. "She kicks over the chair after tying the knot." He was looking at the overturned chair that lay halfway across the room, then continued, "And bingo! She's hung. You said she was despondent, right, Mr. Rawlins?"

"Yeah," I answered him. "She was being evicted by Mofass."

"Who's that?" asked Quinten Naylor. He was Reedy's partner and the only Negro policeman I'd ever seen, up to that time, in plainclothes. He was also looking at that chair.

"He manages the place, collects the rent and the like."

"Who does he manage for?" Naylor asked me.

While I was considering how to answer, Reedy said, "Who cares? This is a suicide. We just tell 'em that she killed herself and that's that."

Naylor was of medium height but he was wide and so gave the feeling of largeness and strength. He was the opposite of his partner in every way, but they seemed to have a kind of rapport.

Naylor walked up to, almost under the hanging corpse. It seemed as if he were sniffing for something wrong.

"Aw, com'on, Quint," Reedy whined. "Who wants to murder this girl? I mean all sneaky-like, pretending she killed herself? Did she have any enemies, Mr. Rawlins?"

"Not that I know of."

"Look at her face, though, Andy. Those could be fresh bruises," Naylor said.

"Sometimes strangulation from hanging does that, Quint," Reedy pleaded.

"Hey listen," the fat ambulance attendant shouted from the hall. I'd called the hospital too, even though I knew she was dead. "When can we cut 'er down an' get outta here?"

He was not my favorite kind of white man.

"Hold up on that," Naylor said. "We got an investigation going here and we can't have the evidence disturbed. I want someone to photograph the room first."

"Aw, geez," Reedy sighed.

"Shit," the fat man said. Then, "Okay, we go, but who signs for the call?"

"We didn't call so you can't charge us," Naylor said.

"What about you, son?" the ambulance attendant asked me. He looked to be in his mid-twenties, almost ten years younger than I.

"Can't say that I know. I just called the police," I lied. It was a kind of warm-up lie. I was getting ready for the real lies I'd have to tell later.

The fat man glared at me but that's all he could do.

When the ambulance men left I turned away and saw Poinsettia hanging there. She seemed to be swaying slightly and my stomach started to move with her, so I turned to leave.

Naylor touched my arm and asked, "Who did you say that Mr. Mofass represented?"

"It's just Mofass. He don't go by no other name."

"Who does he represent?" Naylor insisted.

"Can't say I know. I just clean fo' him."

"Geez, Quint," Reedy said. He'd taken out a handkerchief and covered his mouth and nose. That seemed like a good idea, so I pulled out my own rag.

Reedy was an older man, past fifty. Naylor was young, the ambulance attendant's age. He had probably been a noncommissioned officer in Korea. We got all kinds of things out of that war. Integration, advancement of some colored soldiers, and lots of dead boys.

"Don't look right, Andy," Naylor said. "Let's give it a little bit more."

"Who's gonna care about this one girl, Quint?"

"I care," was all the young policeman answered. And it made me proud. It was the first time I had ever seen civilian blacks and whites dealing with each other in an official capacity. I mean, the first time I'd seen them acting as equals. They were really working together.

"You need me for that?" I asked.

"No, Mr. Rawlins," Reedy sighed. "Just give me your address and phone number and we'll call you for a statement if we need to."

I gave him my address and phone. He wrote them down in a leather-bound note pad that he took from his pocket.

Downstairs, I told Mrs. Trajillo what was happening with the police. She was not only the burglar alarm but she was also a kind of newsletter for the neighborhood.

• 11 •

I lamented Poinsettia's death. She'd come down in the world, but that was no reason to wish her ill. It was a senseless and brutal death whether she killed herself or somebody else did it. But if it was suicide I dreaded the thought that she did herself in over the threat of eviction; an eviction I knew was wrong. I tried to put that thought out of my mind but it burrowed there, in the back of my thoughts, like a gopher tunneling under the ground.

But, no matter how I felt, life had to go on.

I picked EttaMae up on Sunday morning. She was wearing a royal-blue dress with giant white lilies stitched into it. Her hat was eggshell-white, just a layered cap on the side of her head. Her shoes were white too. Etta never wore high heels because she was a tall woman, just a few inches shorter than I.

On the way I asked her, "You talk to Mouse?"

"I called him yesterday, yeah."

"An' what he say?"

"Just like always. He start out fine, but then he get that funny sound in his voice. Then he talkin' 'bout how he *will not be denied*, like I owe 'im sumpin'. Shit! I'ma have t'kill Raymond if he start comin' round scarin' LaMarque like he did in Texas."

"He say anything to LaMarque?"

"Naw. He won't even talk to the boy no more. Why you ask?"

"I dunno."

First African Baptist Church was a big salmon-colored building, built on the model of an old Spanish monastery. There was a large mosaic that stood out high on the wall. Jesus hung there, bleeding red pebbles and suffering all over the congregation. Nobody seemed to notice, though. All the men and women, and children too, were dressed in their finest. Gowns and silk suits, patent-leather shoes and white gloves. The smiles and bows that passed between the sexes on Sunday would have been scandalous anywhere else.

But Sunday was a time to feel good and look good. The flock was decked out and bouncy, waiting for word from the Lord.

Rita Cook came with Jackson Blue. He probably sniffed after her and moved in when Mouse got bored. That's the way most men do it, they let other men break the ice, then they have clear sailing.

Dupree and his new wife, Zaree, were there. She had once told me that her name was from Africa and I asked her from what part of Africa. She didn't know and was angry at me for making her look foolish—after that we never got along too well.

I saw Oscar Jones, Odell's older brother, on the stairs to the church. Etta was saying hello to all the people she hadn't seen yet, so I moved toward where Oscar stood.

As I suspected, Odell was there standing in the shadow of a stucco pillar facade.

"Easy," Oscar said.

"Howdy, Oscar. Odell."

They were brothers, and closer than that. Two men with slightly different faces whose clothes hung on them the same way. They were both soft-spoken men. I'd seen them talking but I'd never heard a word that one said to the other.

"Odell," I said. "I got to talk to you."

"Why don't you come over here."

I waved at Oscar and he bowed to me, that was about a year of conversation for us.

Odell and I walked around the side of the church, down a narrow cement path.

When we were alone I told him, "Listen, man, I got some business with a white man work here."

"Chaim Wenzler?"

"How you know 'bout it?"

"He the only white man here, Easy. I don't mean here today, 'cause he a Jew an' they worship on Saturday—or so I hear."

"I need to get next to 'im."

"What do you mean, Easy?"

"I gotta find out about him fo' the law. Tax man got my by the nuts on this income tax thing an' if I don't do this he gonna bust me."

"So what you want?"

"A li'l introduction is all. Maybe something like workin' fo' the church. I could take it from there."

He didn't answer right away. I knew that he was uncomfortable with me nosing around his church. But Odell was a good friend and he proved it by nodding and saying, "Okay," when he had thought it out.

But then he said, "I heard about Poinsettia Jackson."

We stood before a small green door. Odell had his hand on the knob but he was waiting for my reply before he'd open up.

"Yeah." I shook my head. "Cops wanna chase it down, but I can't see that somebody killed her. Who'd wanna kill a sick woman like that?"

"I don't know, Easy. All I do know is that you talkin' 'bout all kindsa trouble you in an' the next thing I see one'a the people live in your buildin' is dead."

"Ain't got nuthin' to do with me, Odell. It's just a crazy coincidence is all." That is what I believed, and so Odell believed it too.

He led me down the stairs to the basement of the church, where the deacons gathered and suited up before the service. We came upon five men wearing identical black suits and white gloves. Above the left-hand breast pocket of each jacket was sewn a green flag that said *First African* in bright yellow letters. Each man carried a dark walnut tray with a green felt center.

The tallest man was olive brown and had a pencil-thin mustache. His hair was cut short but it was straightened so that he could comb a part on the left side of his head. He smelled of pomade. This man was handsome in a mean sort of way. I knew that the women of the congregation all coveted his attention. But once they got it, Jackie Orr left them at home crying. He was the head deacon at First African and women were only the means to his success.

"How ya doin', Brother Jones?" Jackie smiled. He came over to us and grabbed Odell's right hand with his two gloved ones.

"Brother Rawlins," he said to me.

"Mo'nin, Jackie," I said. I didn't like the man, and one thing I can't stand is calling a man you don't like "brother."

Odell said, "Easy say he wanna do some work fo' the church, Jackie. I tole 'im 'bout Mr. Wenzler, you know how you said Chaim might need a driver."

It was the first I'd heard of it.

But Jackie said, "Yeah, yeah, that's right. So you wanna help out, huh, Brother Rawlins?"

"That's right. I heard that you been doin' some good work wit' old people an' the sick."

"You got that right! Reverend Towne don't believe that charity is just a word. He knows what the Lord's work is, amen on that."

A couple of the deacons seconded his amen.

Two of the deacons were just boys. I guess they had to join a gang one way or another, and the church won out.

The other two were old men. Gentle, pious men who could hold a jostling, impetuous baby boy in their arms all day and never complain, or even think about complaining. They'd never want Jackie's senior position, because that was something outside their place.

Jackie was a political man. He wanted power in the church, and being deacon was the way to get it. He might have been thirty but he held himself like a mature man in his forties or fifties. Older men gave him leeway because they could sense his violence and his vitality. The women sensed something else, but they let him get away with his act too.

I said, "I got a lotta free time in the day, Jackie, and I could get my evenings pretty free if I had t'. You know Mofass an' me got a understandin' so that I can always make a little time. An' Odell says that's what you need, a man who could make some free time."

"That's right. Why'ont you come over tomorrow, around four. That's when we have the meetin'."

We shook hands and I went away.

Etta was looking for me. She was ready for the word of God.

I could have used a drink.

• 12 •

First African was a beautiful church on the inside too. A large rectangular room with a thirty-foot ceiling that held two hundred chairs on a gently sloping floor. The rows of seats came down in two tiers toward the pulpit. The podium that stood up front was a light ash stand adorned with fresh yellow lilies and draped with deep purple banners. Behind the minister's place, slightly off to the left, rose thirty plush velvet chairs, in three rows, for the choir.

There were six stained-glass windows on either side of the room. Jesus at the mountain, John the Baptist baptizing Jesus, Mary and Mary Magdalen prostrate before the Cross. Bright cellophane colors: reds, blues, yellows, browns, and greens. Each window was about fifteen feet high. Giants of the Bible shining down on us mortals.

We might have been poor people but we knew how to build a house of prayer, and how to bury our loved ones.

Etta and I went to seats toward the middle of the room. She sat next to Ethel Marmoset and I sat on the aisle. Odell and Mary sat in front of us. Jackson and Rita stood at the back. People were coming in through the three large doors at the back of the church, and they were all talking, but in hushed tones so that there was a feeling of silence against the hubbub of voices.

When everybody was seated or situated in back, Melvin Pride came down the center aisle with Jackie Orr at his heel. Melvin was what First African called a senior deacon, a man who has paid his dues. While they came in I noticed that the other deacons had spaced themselves evenly along either side of the congregation. The choir, dressed in purple satin gowns, entered from behind the pulpit and stood before the red velvet chairs.

Finally, Winona Fitzpatrick came down the aisle, twenty feet behind Melvin and Jackie. She was the chairwoman of the church council. Winona was large woman in a loose black gown and a wide-brimmed black hat that had a sky-blue satin band. The room was so quiet by then that you could hear the harsh rasp of Winona's stockinged thighs.

As I watched her progress I noticed a large young man watching me from across the aisle. He was wearing a decent brown suit that had widely spaced goldenrod stripes. His broad-rimmed fedora was in his lap. His stony dull eyes were on me.

Jackie took his place as lead singer of the choir, and Melvin stood before the group with his hands upraised. Then he looked down behind him, and for the first time I saw a small woman sitting at a large organ just below the podium.

Then there was music. The deep strains of the organ and Jackie's high tenor voice. The choir sang in back of that.

"Angels," Etta muttered. "Just angels."

They sang "A Prayer to Sweet Baby Jesus." After Melvin was sure he'd guided them into harmony he turned to add his bass to Jackie's high voice.

Melvin was Jackie's height, but he was black and craggy. When he sang he grimaced as if in pain. Jackie seemed more like a suitor trying to talk his way into the bedroom.

The song filled the church and I loved it even though I was there for something else. Even though I was going to go against a member, or at least a helper, of that flock, still the love of God filled me. And that was strange, because I had stopped believing in God on the day my father left me as a child in poverty and pain.

"Brothers and sisters!" Reverend Towne shouted. I hadn't been looking when he came to the dais. He was a very tall man with a big belly that bulged out from his deep blue robes. He was dark brown with strong African features and dense, straightened hair that was greased and combed back away from his forehead.

He ran his left hand over his hair as the last members of the crowd went silent, then he looked out over the faces and grinned and shook his head slowly as if he had seen someone who had been missing for years.

"I'm happy to see you all here this Sunday morning. Yes I am."

No one spoke but there was a kind of shudder in the room.

He held his big open hands out toward us, relishing our human warmth as if he stood before a fire.

"Was a time once when I saw a lotta empty chairs out there."

"Amen," one of the elder deacons intoned.

"Was a time," the minister said, and then he paused. "Yes. Was a time that we didn't have no peanut gallery in the back. Was a time ev'rybody could sit and listen to the word of the Lord. They could sit and meditate on his spirit.

"But no more."

He looked around the room, and I did too. Everyone else had their eyes on him. The women had a kind of stunned look on the whole, their heads tilted upwards in order to bask in the peculiar and cool light that flowed from the stained-glass windows. The men were serious, by and large. They were concentrating every fiber of their wills to understand the ways of righteousness and the Lord in their everyday lives. All except the man in the brown suit. His stony glare was still on my profile, and I was wondering about him.

"No, no more," the minister almost sang. "Because now he is marching."

"Yes, Lord!" an old woman shouted from down front.

"That's right," the minister spoke. "We are going to have to go to the church council to expand the roof of the Lord. Because you know he wants all of you in his flock. He wants all of you to praise his name. Say it. Say, yes Je-sus."

We did, and the sermon started in earnest.

Towne didn't quote from the Bible or talk about salvation. The whole sermon was aimed at the dead and maimed boys coming back home from Korea. Reverend Towne worked in a special clinic that tended to the severely wounded. He spoke especially long and poignantly about Wendell Boggs, a young man who'd lost his legs, most of his fingers, one eye, the other eyelid, and his lips in the service of America. Bethesda Boggs, a member of the congregation, wailed as if to underscore his terrible litany.

Together they, mother and minister, had us all squirming in our chairs.

After a while he started talking about how war was a product of man and of Satan, not God. It was Satan who waged war against God in his own home. It was Satan who had men kill when they could turn the other cheek. And it was Satan who led us in war against the Koreans and the Chinese.

"Satan will take on the guise of a good man," Reverend Towne intoned. "He will appear as a great leader, and you will be blinded by what looks like the fireworks of glory. But when the smoke clears and you squint around to see, you will be surrounded by the wages of sin. Dead men will be your stepping-stones and blood will be your water. Your sons will be wounded and dead, and where will God be?"

He had me back on the front lines. I was choking the life out of a blond teenage boy and crying and laughing, and ready for a woman too.

He ended the sermon like this:

"My question to you is, what are you going to do about Wendell Boggs? What can you do?" Then he made a gesture toward the choir, and Melvin lifted his hands again. The organ started up and the choir rose in song. The music was still beautiful but the sermon had turned it sour. There was a collection by the deacons, but many people left even before the plate got to them.

Everywhere people were grumbling.

"What do he mean? What can I do?"

"A minister ain't no politician, that's illegal."

"We cain't help it."

"Communists are against God. We gotta fight 'em."

Etta turned to me and took hold of my hand. She said, "Take me home, Easy."

• 13 •

Towne was out in front of the church with Winona, Melvin, Jackie, and a couple I didn't know. The couple were older and they looked uncomfortable. They'd probably shaken the minister's hand every Sunday for twenty or more years and they weren't going to stop just because Towne gave one sour sermon.

"Easy," Melvin said. We knew each other from the old days back in the Fifth Ward, in Houston, Texas.

"Melvin."

Jackie was wringing his hands. Winona was gazing at Reverend Towne. It was only then that I noticed Shep, Winona's little husband, standing in the doorway. I hadn't seen him in church.

"That was a powerful and brave sermon, minister," Etta said. She walked up to him and shook his hand so hard that his jowls shook.

"Thank you, thank you very much," he replied. "It's good t'have you up here, Sister Alexander. I hope you're planning to stay for a while."

"That all depends," Etta said, and then she stole a quick glance at me.

Winona stepped up and said something to Towne, I couldn't make out what, then Etta asked, "How is that boy's folks? You think I could he'p 'em?"

I had to laugh at those women fighting over the minister. I think Etta was doing it just because she didn't like to see Winona flirting there in front of her own husband.

I saw Jackie and Melvin move to the bottom of the stairway. There they began to argue. Jackie was waving his hands in the air and Melvin was making placating gestures, holding his palms toward the handsome man as if he were trying to press Jackie's anger down.

I would have liked to know what they were fighting about, but that was merely curiosity, so I turned back to EttaMae.

She had linked arms with the minister and they were walking away. Etta was saying, "Why don't you introduce me to the poor woman, I could maybe do the cooking on some days."

I got to look over my shoulder to see Melvin and Jackie still arguing at the bottom of the stair. Melvin was stealing glances up at me.

"Go get the car, Shep," Winona said, casual and cruel.

"Okay," he answered. Then little brown Shep, in his rayon red-brown suit, went away to the parking lot.

"Etta with you, Easy?" Winona asked before Shep disappeared around the building.

"Say what?"

"You heard me, Easy Rawlins. Is EttaMae your woman?"

"Etta ain't rightly nobody's, Winona. She don't hardly even like t'think she belongs t'Jesus."

"Don't fool with me," she warned. "That bitch is givin' the minister the eye, an' if she free it's gonna have t'stop."

"He married?" I asked, shocked.

"'Course not!"

"Well, Etta ain't neither."

I shrugged and Winona gnashed her teeth. She went down the stairway in a huff.

I looked down at the bottom of the stairs, but Jackie and Melvin were gone, so I turned to enter the church. I found myself at about chest level with a brown suit that had golden stripes. He was standing on a higher stair but even if we stood toe to toe he would have towered over me.

"You Rawlins, ain't you?" he asked in a voice that was either naturally rough or husky with emotion.

"That's right," I said, taking a step backward so I could see his face and move out of range.

His brown face, which clashed with his suit, was smallish, perfectly round, childlike and mean.

"I want you t'take me to yo' boss."

"And why is that?" I asked.

"I got business with 'im."

"This is Sunday, son. On today we s'posed t'rest."

"Listen, man," he threatened. His voice cracked. "I know all about you . . ."

"Yeah?"

"You di'n't lift a finger." He was quoting someone. "She tole me 'bout how he used her, how he took her fo' money an' then he just let her slide when she got sick. She could just die an' all you care 'bout was yo'self."

"What's your name, man?"

"I'm Willie Sacks." He puffed up his shoulders. "Now let's go." He put his hand on my shoulder but I brushed it off.

"You Poinsettia's boyfriend?" I asked. I wasn't going anywhere.

He threw a punch at me that would have put a hole in a brick wall. I crouched down under it though, grabbing his wrist as I did, and came up behind him twisting his arm and wrenching his giant thumb.

Willie said, "Oh!" and knelt on the stair.

"I don't wanna hurt ya, boy," I whispered in Willie's ear. "But you make me damage this suit an' I'm a do some damage on you."

"I kill you!" he shouted. "I kill all'a you!"

I let him go and moved down a few stairs.

"What's your problem, Willie?"

"Take me t'Mofass!"

He stood up. In that shade I felt like David without his slingshot.

It's hard for a big man to throw a punch downward. I let his fist snap somewhere off to the west and then I gave him one and two in the lower gut. Willie folded like a peel bug and rolled down the stairs.

He got right up though, so I ran down and hit him again, on the side of his head that time. I hit him hard enough to hurt a normal man, but Willie was more like a buffalo. I hit him as hard as I could and all he did was sit down.

"I don't wanna hurt you, Willie," I said, more to distract me from the pain in my hand than to worry him.

"When I get up from here we gonna see who gonna be hurt." There were patches of bloody flesh on his face, scrapes from the granite stairs.

"Poinsettia ain't nobody's fault, Willie," I said. "Let it go."

But he lurched to his feet and came shambling up the stair. I lost patience and broke his nose. I could feel the bone give under my knuckle. I was considering his left ear when I felt a blow to my back. It wasn't hard, but I was tensed for a fight, so I swung around, only to be hit in the face with something like a pillow. A tiny woman in a frilly pink dress was swinging her woven string purse at my head. She didn't say a word, saving all of her energy for the fight.

She might have kept it up, but when Willie yelled, "Momma!" she forgot about me and ran to his side.

He was cupping his hands under the bloody faucet of his nose.

"Willie! Willie!"

"Momma!"

"Willie!"

She pushed him until he was up off his knees and then dragged him away, down the street.

Twice the pink-and-brown woman glared at me. She was tiny and wore white-rimmed glasses. Her lips caved inward where teeth once held them firm. Mrs. Sacks couldn't lift her son's arm, but I was more frightened of those killer stares than I would have been of a whole platoon of Willies.

"Sit down on the couch here next to me, honey, not way over there." Etta patted the green fabric next to her.

We were in her new apartment on Sixty-fourth Street. It was a nice six-unit apartment building. Her place had two bedrooms, a shower, and blue wall-to-wall shag carpets. LaMarque was with Lucy Rideau and her two girls. They had all gone to Bible school and now they were having Sunday supper.

"I should really get on to work, Etta."

"On Sunday?"

"I'ma be doin' some extra work fo' the church so I gotta make up my time on the weekend."

"Now what you gonna be doin' fo' the Lord, Easy Rawlins?"

"We all do our li'l piece, Etta. We all do our li'l piece."

"Like you makin' so LaMarque an' me ain't gotta pay no rent to that terrible man?"

"Mofass ain't so bad. He lettin' you stay here, ain't he?"

"He give me this furniture too?"

"We had an eviction last year an' this stuff been in my garage. I tole 'im I'd haul it off to the dump."

"You coulda sold this stuff, Easy. That bed in there is mahogany."

When I didn't answer she said, "Come here, baby, sit down."

I did.

"What's wrong, Easy?"

"Nuthin', Etta, nuthin'."

"Then why you ain't come by? You got me a house an' furniture. You must like us t'do all that."

"Sure I like you."

"Then why'ont you come over an' show me how much?"

Her hand was on my neck. She was much warmer than I was.

Etta's dress was silken and flimsy under her jacket. The bodice was low-cut and her breasts bulged upward when she leaned toward me.

"I thought you didn't wanna see me no mo'," I said.

"I's jus' mad, honey," she said as she leaned toward me. "Thas all."

For some reason I imagined what Wendell Boggs must have looked like on his deathbed. There was fresh blood on his half-face and a whitish scab where one of his eyes should have been.

"Easy?"

"Yeah, Etta?"

"I got the papers to my divorce in the other room."

She shifted slightly to bring her left knee over her right one, nudging my leg. Her dress looked very tight, like it wanted to burst.

"I don't need to see 'em," I said.

"Yes you do."

"No."

"Yes, Easy. You need to see that I'm a free woman and that I can have what I want."

"It ain't you, Etta, it's me," I said, but I kissed her anyway.

"You got me all riled up though, honey." She kissed me back. "Gettin' my house an' my bed, takin' me t' church, mmm, I love that."

We didn't talk for a little while then.

When she leaned back, and I got a moment to breathe, I asked, "But what about Raymond?"

Etta took my hand and put it on her chest, then she gazed at me with eyes that I dream about to this very day.

"Do you want me?" she asked.

"Yeah."

She pressed a finger against my shirt, where my nipple was.

"Then I tell you what," she whispered.

"What?" Just that one word drained all the breath out of me.

"You don't talk about him now an' I won't say nuthin' 'bout him when we wake up."

• 14 •

I got home in the early evening. The phone was ringing as I got to the door. I tried to get the key into the lock but I was too much in a hurry and dropped it in a pile of fallen passion-fruit leaves. The phone kept ringing, though, and it rang until I rummaged around, found the key, and made it inside the door. But I tripped on the doormat and by the time I got off the floor and limped to the coffee table the ringing had finally ceased.

Then I massaged my bruised knee and went to the bathroom. Just as I began to relieve myself the phone started ringing again. But I had learned my lesson. The phone rang while I rinsed my hands and dried them. It rang until I had made it back to the coffee table and then it stopped again.

I was in the kitchen with a quart bottle of vodka in one hand and a tray of ice in the other when he called again. I considered yanking the line out of the wall, thought better of it, and finally I answered the phone.

The first thing I heard was a child screaming. "No! No!" he, or she, yelled. And then, "No," still a yell but muted as if someone had closed a door on a torture room.

"Mr. Rawlins?" IRS Agent Reginald Lawrence asked.

"Yeah?"

"I wanted to ask you a couple of questions and to give you some advice."

"What questions?"

"What was the deal that Agent Craxton offered you?"

"I don't know if I can really say, sir. I mean, he said that it was government business and that I had to be quiet on that."

"We all work for the same government. I'm a government man too."

"But he's the FBI. He's the law."

"He's just represents another *branch* of the government. And his branch doesn't have anything to do with mine."

"Then why you askin' 'bout what he wants?"

"I want to know what he's offered you, because he cannot offer anything on behalf of the Internal Revenue. Once our office commits itself we have to see an investigation through. We have no other choice. You see, I have to follow this investigation or my records—" he paused for a moment, looking for the right words—"my records will be incomplete. So you see, no matter what anyone says, I will have to draw up papers for the court case tomorrow morning."

"What can I do about that?" I asked. "He got me on a federal case an' I'm doin' it. If I tell you his business I'll be in even more trouble than I am already."

"I cannot speak for the FBI, all I can tell you is that if you attempt to avoid paying your taxes, even by working for the FBI, we will still be there when everything is over. I have spoken to my supervisor and he agrees with me on this point. You will have to submit your tax records to me by Wednesday of next week or we will have to subpoena you."

"So you talked this over with Wadsworth, huh?" I asked when he'd run out of wind.

"Who told you . . ." he started to ask, but I guess the answer came to him.

"I'm sorry, but I can't help you, Mr. Lawrence. I got my cards and you got yours. I guess we'll just have to play it out."

"I know that you think you're helping yourself, Mr. Rawlins, but you're wrong. You cannot escape your responsibilities to the government." He sounded like a textbook.

"Mr. Lawrence, I don't know about you, but I take Sundays off."

"This problem won't go away, son."

"Okay, that's it. I'm puttin' the phone down now."

Before I could Mr. Lawrence hung up in my ear.

I went back to the kitchen and put the vodka away. I got my bottle of thirty-year-old imported Armagnac from behind a loose board in the closet. There was snifter sitting next to it. I learned how to drink good liquor from a rich white man I worked for once. I found that if you could savor the booze, I mean if you took longer to drink it, then the intoxication was more pleasurable. And I liked drinking alone when I wanted to be drunk. No loud stories or laughing; all I wanted was oblivion.

The tax man wanted to send me to jail, it was personal with him. And Craxton was lying, I was sure about that, so I had no idea what it was he really wanted. I might not find a thing on his communists, and then he'd just throw me back to the dogs, he might have done so anyway. I considered trying to sign my property over to someone in the meanwhile, just to cover my bases. But I didn't like that idea because I wanted to put my name on the deeds. I wanted EttaMae. I wanted her with all my heart. If she was to be mine then I had to be a man of substance to buy her clothes and make her home.

Of course, that meant that either Mouse or I had to die, I knew that. I knew it but I didn't want to admit it.

On Monday I went to Mofass's office. He was sitting behind the desk glowering at a plate of pork chops and eggs. A boy in the neighborhood brought up his breakfast every morning at about eleven. Mofass stared at the food for sometimes up to half an hour before eating. He never told me why, but I always imagined that he was afraid that the boy spat in it. That's the kind of insult that Mofass always feared.

"Mornin', Mofass."

"Mr. Rawlins."

He picked up a chop by its fatty bone and took a bite out of the eye.

"I ain't gonna be 'round much for the next three or four weeks. I got business t'take care of."

"I'm doin' business ev'ry day, Mr. Rawlins. I can't take no vacation or you'd go broke," he chided through a mass of mashed meat.

"That's why you get paid, Mofass."

"Yeah, I guess," he said. He scooped a good half of the scrambled egg into his mouth.

"Anything happenin' that I need to know about?" I asked.

"Not that I know of. The police come and asked about Poinsettia." A brief shadow worked its way across Mofass' face. I remember thinking that even a hard man like that could feel pain at a young woman's demise. "I told 'em that I only knew that she was five months behind on the rent. That Negro cop didn't like my attitude, so I advised him to come back when he had a warrant."

"I wanted to talk to you about her," I said.

He looked at me with only mild interest.

"Her boyfriend, Willie Sacks, tried t'knock my head off in front of First African Sunday."

"How come?" Mofass asked.

"He wanted you, and I didn't wanna tell 'im where you was."

Mofass took a mouthful of egg and nodded. As soon as he got the mess down to the size of a golf ball he said, "Okay."

"But he was sayin' somethin' like whatever happened to her, I mean like her accident, had sumpin' t'do with you."

"That boy's jes' grievin', Mr. Rawlins. He done left 'er when she got sick and now he wanna blame somebody else when she up and kills herself." He shrugged slightly. Harder than diamonds is right.

Mofass was contemptuous but I still felt bad. I knew what it was to be the cause of another human being's demise. I had felt that guilt myself.

"You want me to hire somebody to take care of the work 'round the places while you on vacation?" Mofass asked.

He knew I didn't like to be called lazy.

"I'm just doin' some extra work, man. Somethin' gotta do with that tax thing."

"What?"

He stopped eating and picked up a cigar that had been in a glass ashtray on his desk.

"They got me doin' 'em a li'l favor. I do that right an' the taxes get easier."

"What could the IRS need from you?"

"Not them exactly." I didn't want to tell him that I was working for the FBI. "Anyway they want me t'find a guy gotta do with the minister down at First African. Maybe he owes 'em mo' taxes than me."

Mofass just shook his head. I could tell he didn't believe me.

"So you be at church the next couple of weeks?"

"More or less."

"I guess you gonna be *prayin'* off them taxes instead'a payin' 'em."

He made a sound like coughing. At first I thought he was choking but then as it got louder I realized that Mofass was laughing. He put his cigar down and pulled out the whitest pocket handkerchief I'd ever seen. He blew his nose and wiped tears from his eyes and he was still laughing.

"Mofass!" I yelled, but he just kept on laughing. "Mofass!"

He added a little catch in his throat, sort of like a far-off goose calling her mate. The tears flowed.

Finally I gave up and walked out.

I stood outside for a few minutes, listening behind the closed door, he laughed the whole time I stood there.

In the later afternoon, I went to First African.

The front of the church was on 112th Street and went all the way through the block to 112th Place. The back entrance was just a door in a rough stucco wall, like a small office building, maybe a dentist's office. On the first floor there was an entrance and a short hall with a few plywood doors on either side. At the end of the tan-carpeted hall was a stairwell that went up and down. Odell had told me that the minister had his office and apartment on the upper floor and that there was a kitchen and cafeteria space in the basement.

I went down to the basement.

There I saw a scene that had been a constant in my life since I was a small boy. Black women. Lots of them. Cooking in the industrial-size kitchen and talking loud, laughing and telling stories. But all I really saw was their hands. Working hands. Laying out plates, peeling yams, folding sheets and tablecloths into perfect squares, washing, drying, stacking and pushing from here to there. Women who lived by working. Brushing the hair of their own children, or brushing the hair of some neighborhood child whose parents were gone, either for the night or for good. Cooking, yes, but there was lots of other work for a Negro woman. Dressing wounds of the men they started out being so proud of. Punishing children, white and black. And working for God in His house and at home.

My own mother, sick as she was, made sweet-potato pies for a church dinner on the night she died. She was twenty-five years old.

"Evenin', Easy," Parker Lamont said. He was one of the elder deacons. I hadn't seen him when I walked in.

"Parker."

"Odell and the others are out in the back," he said and began to lead me through the crowd of working women.

Many of them said hello to me. I moved around the neighborhoods quite a bit in those days and if I saw that one of the ladies needed some help I was happy to oblige; there's all kinds of truth and insight in gossip, and the only key you need is a helping hand.

Winona Fitzpatrick was there. She was bright and full of life even though she didn't smile at me. She was wearing a flattering white dress that wasn't made for the kind of work people were doing. But she wasn't working either. The chairwoman of the church council, she was the power behind the throne, as it were.

"What's goin' on here?" I asked Parker.

"What?"

"All this cookin' an' stuff."

"Gonna be a meetin' of the N double-A C P. Ev'ry chapter in southern California."

"Tonight?"

"Yeah."

He led me through a maze of long dining tables and through an open doorway in the back. This led to a closed door. I could smell the smoke even before we went in.

There I found a room full of black men. All of them smoking and sitting in various positions of ease.

It was a smallish room with a threadbare light green carpet and a few folding tables that the men used to hold their ashtrays. There were checkerboards and dominoes out but nobody was playing. There was a sour smell under the smoky odor. The smell of men's breath.

Odell rose to meet me.

"Easy," he said. "I want you to meet Wilson and Grant."

We nodded at each other.

"Pleased t'meetcha," I said.

Dupree was there and some other men I knew.

"Melvin and the minister be down in a few minutes. They upstairs right now," he said. "And this here is Chaim, Chaim Wenzler."

The white man had been sitting on the other side of Dupree, so I hadn't seen him. He was short and hunched over in a serious conversation with a man I didn't know.

But when he heard his name he straightened up and looked at me.

"This is Easy Rawlins, Chaim. He's got some free time in the week an' wants t' help out."

"Wonderful," Chaim said in a strong voice. He stood up to shake my hand. "I need the help, Mr. Rawlins. Thank you."

"Easy. Call me Easy."

"We are doing work in the neighborhood," he said. He indicated a chair for me and sat himself. We'd gone right to work. I liked him even though I didn't want to.

"Food for old people, some driving maybe. I don't drive and it's hard to get a ride when you need it. Sometimes my daughter drives me, but she works, we all work." He winked on that. "And sometimes we need to take messages about meetings here at the church and some other places."

"What kinda meetin's?"

He hunched his thick shoulders. "Meetings about work. We do lots of work, Mr. Rawlins."

I smiled. "Well, what kind of work you want from me?"

He gave me the once-over then and I took him in. Chaim was short and powerful. His head was bald and I would have put his age at about fifty-five. His eyes were gray, about the same color as Mouse's eyes, but they looked different in Chaim. Chaim's eyes were piercing and intelligent but they were also generous, rather than cruel. Generosity was a feeling that Mouse only had after someone he didn't like had died.

You could see something else in Chaim's eyes. I didn't know what it was at the time but I could see that there was a deep pain in that man. Something that made me sad.

"We need to get clothes," he said at last.

"Say what?"

"Old clothes for the old people. I get people to donate them and then we have a sale."

He leaned toward me in a confidential manner and said, "You know we have to sell it to them because they don't like to be given wit'out paying."

"What you do with the money?"

"A little lunch wit' the sale and it's gone." He slapped his hands together indicating breaking even.

"Yeah, okay," I said. But there must've been a question in my voice.

"You have something to ask, maybe?" He smiled into my eyes.

"Naw, not really . . . it's just that . . ."

"Yes?"

There were people around us but they weren't listening.

"Well, it's like this," I said. "I cain't see why somebody ain't even from down there wanna do all this an' they ain't even bein' paid."

"You are right, of course," he said. "A man works for money or family or," he shrugged, "some men work for God."

"That what move you? You a religious man?"

"No." He shook his head grimly. "No, I'm not a religious man, not anymore."

"So here you don't even believe in God but you gonna do charity for the church?"

I was pushing him and wishing I wasn't. But something bothered me about Chaim Wenzler and I wanted to find out what it was.

He smiled again. "I believe, Mr. Rawlins. Even more—I know. God turned his back on me." The way he looked at me reminded me of something, or someone. "He turned his back on all the Jews. He set the demons on us. I believe, Mr. Rawlins. There could not be such evil as I have seen wit'out a God."

"I guess I could see that."

"And that's why I'm here," Wenzler said. "Because Negroes in America have the same life as the Jew in Poland. Ridiculed, segregated. We were hung and burned for just being alive."

It was then that I remembered Hollis Long.

Hollis was a friend of my father. They used to get together every Saturday afternoon on the front porch. Being the only two black men in the parish that could read, they would smoke pipes and discuss all the newspaper articles that they had read in the past week.

Hollis was a big man. I remember him laughing and bringing me presents of fruit or hard candy. I'd sit on the floor between the two men and listen to them talk about events in New Orleans, Houston, and other southern capitals. Sometimes they'd talk about northern cities or even foreign lands like China or France.

Then one weekday I came home from school to find my mother standing over the wood stove crying. My father stood next to her with his arm around her shoulders. Hollis Long was sitting at the table drinking straight whiskey from a clay jug. The look in his eyes, the same look that Chaim Wenzler had when he was talking about God, told of something terrible.

No one spoke to me, so I ran out of the house down to the sugarcane field that bordered our land.

That night Hollis slept at our house. He stayed there for two weeks before going away to Florida for good. And every night I could hear him moaning and crying. Sometimes I'd be wrenched out of sleep because Hollis would get from his bed hollering and smashing the walls with his fists.

After the first night my mother told me that there was a fire while Hollis was gone lumbering with my father. His wife and sons and mother all perished in the flames.

"When I had given up everything," Chaim said, "men came and saved me. They helped me to take vengeance. And now it is my turn to help."

All I could do was nod. When God abandoned Hollis Long there was no one to save him.

"We must help each other, Easy. Because there are men out there who would steal the meat from your bones."

I thought about agents Lawrence and Craxton and I looked away.

He put his hand on my shoulder and said, "We will work together."

I said, "Alright."

"You got time tomorrow?" he asked, and then he touched the back of my hand the way John had when he was concerned for me.

"Maybe not tomorrow, but in a couple'a days."

And it was done. Chaim and I were partners working for the poor and elderly. Of course, I was trying to hang him too.

Towne and Melvin came in with a beautiful young woman. Her black skin and bright white dress were a shocking contrast. Tall and shapely, she had straightened brown hair that was shot through with golden strands. Her lips were bright orange and her big brown eyes were on Towne. It was the passion of her gaze that made her beautiful. You could see that she held nothing back.

The minister said a few words to Parker, and then he turned to whisper something to the girl. The way he put his palm against her side I knew they were lovers. It wasn't much but it was very familiar. When I looked away from them I saw Melvin staring hard at me.

They left almost immediately. I could see that this disturbed the men. They expected the minister to represent their church at the meeting. But he had other fish to fry. I did too.

Odell asked me, "You stayin', Ease?"

I said, "No, man, I got some calls t'make."

When I turned to go he grabbed me by the arm. That was the only time he'd ever done anything like that. He said, "Don't be messin' wit' us now, Ease. Get what you want from that man, but don't hurt the church."

I smiled as reassuringly as I could and said, "Don't worry, Odell, all I need is some information. That's all. You won't even notice I was here."

The phone only rang once before he answered.

"Craxton."

"I met 'im."

"Good. What did he say?"

"Nuthin' really. He wants me to get clothes for old people."

"Don't fall for it, Mr. Rawlins. He's only helping those people for his own ends."

Just like I am, I thought. "So what next?"

"String him along for a few weeks, see if he brings you to the others. Milk him for information. Try to sound like you're unhappy with white people and America, he eats that stuff up. Maybe find out if he knows where Andre Lavender is."

I made sounds like I'd do what he wanted and then I asked, "Mr. Craxton?"

"Yes?"

"I got a call from Agent Lawrence the other day."

"About what?"

"He wanted to know what I am going to do about my taxes."

"He did?" Craxton laughed. "You have to hand it to him, the man is loyal to his work."

"His loyal be my jail term."

"Don't worry, Mr. Rawlins. J. Edgar Hoover pulls every string in Washington. If he says you're alright, then you are."

Mr. Hoover hadn't said a thing to me, but I didn't mention it.

"What was Wenzler doing at the church?" Craxton asked.

"Helpin' with the N double-A C P meeting."

"Yeah, I thought so."

I could almost hear him nodding.

"You thought what?"

"NAACP. That's one of them. One of the so-called civil rights organizations that are full of Reds and people who will one day be Reds."

I thought that he was crazy and then I thought, I'm working for him, so what does that make me?

• 15 •

Chaim Wenzler was a strange one. But he called up memories in me and I found myself hoping that he wasn't the bad guy Agent Craxton claimed. I figured that as long as Craxton didn't know where to find Andre, that's what I should concentrate on. I suspected that the FBI man wasn't telling me the whole story about what had happened at Champion. And it didn't make sense that he would go to all the trouble of springing me from the IRS just to see what might be happening with some union organizer. I needed more information and Andre was my best bet, but getting to him was a crooked road.

Craxton was smart to get a man like me, because the FBI couldn't really mount an investigation in the ghetto. The colored population at that time wasn't readily willing to tell a white man anything resembling the truth; and the FBI was made up exclusively of white men.

I also had the added advantage of knowing Andre and the company he kept.

Andre had gotten a little girl, Juanita Barnes, pregnant and Juanita had a baby boy. I knew that she was living in a little place off Florence and that she wasn't working. Andre was proud of his son and so I figured he went off with Linda because she flattered his manhood, such as it was, and because he could get a few dollars away from her to send for his son. Not to mention whatever trouble he had gotten into with Champion Aircraft and Chaim Wenzler.

Winthrop Hughes, Linda's husband, knew most of that too, but he wouldn't get one word out of Juanita.

It was the kind of job I liked.

I dropped by Juanita's filthy one-room efficiency apartment the next morning with some patch-up work. Juanita liked to think she was good with needle and thread. She told everybody that she earned her board and keep by sewing, but I didn't believe that lie.

Anyway, I went over there with some torn clothes and asked her could she fix them up.

"You might as well throw this stuff out, Easy," she said, holding the crotch up to the window. You could see the birds congregating on the telephone line through the holes in those pants. "They ain't hardly worth the work," she said.

"You mean you don't need t'work?"

"Naw, it ain't like that."

"Look like it t'me. Here I bring you my work pants and you cain't even be bothered with it."

She cowered a little under my gaze. "I just sayin' that you could maybe buy sumpin' better fo' almost much as you gonna pay me."

"Why'ont you let me say how the money goes," I said. I was standing over her. She had little Andre Jr. in her arms.

Andre Jr. was about fourteen months old. He was walking by then and showing some individuality. His mother was a small, hard-looking girl, about the color of a cougar. She was eighteen with small eyes and skinny legs. But even though she was ugly, Juanita had the dazed look of love in her eyes. The look that many women have with their firstborn.

I took Andre Jr. from her and cuddled him to my chest.

"I'll look after the baby while you fix my clothes," I said. I tried to sound like a father and she played the obedient child. When I think on it now I realize that I must've been almost twice her age.

Little Andre and I had a good time. I let him walk on me and sleep on me, I even heated his bottle, letting Juanita check it to see that I wasn't going to scald her baby's tongue. She gave me a few shy smiles while I sat in her padded chair and she sat on the kitchen counter, working at my rags. But what really got her to glow was when I changed his diapers. I laid him out on the counter next to her and played with him so he didn't even cry.

I showed her that I knew how you could put Vaseline on a baby to keep him from chafing. While I was rubbing the stuff on Andre's buttocks Juanita uncrossed her legs, licked her sliver lips, and asked, "You hungry, Easy?" and before I could answer, "'Cause I'm starved."

I couldn't see where I was doing anything wrong.

Juanita didn't have any close family, so she was alone with Andre Jr. most of the time. And everybody knows how a gabbling baby will drive the strongest will to distraction after a while. All I did was keep her company when she needed a man around.

I got steaks, cornbread mix, and greens from the Safeway and made dinner, because Juanita couldn't really cook. After dinner she put Andre Jr. in a cardboard box on a table next to the couch, which she proceeded to unfold into a bed.

Then Juanita took the bottle of Vaseline and showed me some things she knew how to do. She might have been eighteen, and unacquainted with many ways of the world, but Juanita was full of love. Powerful love. And she had the ability to call forth the love in me.

She pushed me down in that bed and wrapped her arms around me and told me all the things she had dreamed since Andre Sr. had left.

In the middle of the night the baby cried and Juanita tended to him. Then she whispered something to me and before long I was on my knees begging and praying to her like she was a temple and a priestess rolled up into one.

At four in the morning I woke again. I didn't even know where I was. Every tender spot on my body was sore and when I looked at that little girl I felt a kind of awe that verged on fear.

The shades were torn. Light from the granite-columned streetlamp shone on Andre Jr. in his cardboard cradle. I could see his tiny lips pushing in and out.

I looked around the rest of the house. Even in the dark it felt dirty. Juanita never really cleaned the floors or walls. There was dirt in that house that had been there before her; it would be there after she had gone.

When I saw the drawers in the kitchen counter I remembered what I was doing there.

In the very bottom drawer, under a few rolls of wrapping paper, was a stack of envelopes held together with a wide rubber band. The postmark, which was all but impossible to make out in the dim light, was from Riverside, and Juanita's name and address were written in a junior high school scrawl. But it was the return address that interested me. I tore off the upper left corner of one letter, shoved it back into the middle of the stack, and pushed the drawer closed.

"What you want, Easy?"

"Tryin' t'get some water but I didn't wanna turn on the light and wake ya," I said, straightening up quickly.

"You lookin' on the floor fo' some water?"

"I kicked my damn toe!" I tried to sound angry so that she'd let it go.

"Glasses in the cabinet right over your head, honey, get me some too."

When I climbed back into bed Juanita reached for the jar of Vaseline again.

"I'm a little tired, baby," I said.

"Don't worry, Easy, I'ma get you up."

A few hours later sunlight came in through the shade. Juanita was sitting up against the head of the couch with a knowing look in her eye. She had the baby, suckling on his bottle, in her arms.

"How long Andre's father been gone?" I asked.

"Too long," she said.

I lit a cigarette and handed it to her.

"You hear from him at all?"

"Uh-uh. He just gone, thas all." Then she smiled at me. "Don't worry, honey, he ain't gonna come in here. He ain't even in L.A."

"I thought you didn't even know where he was?"

"I heard he was gone."

"From who?"

"I just heard it, thas all."

Her mouth formed a little thin-lipped pout.

I took her foot and rubbed it until she smiled again. Then I asked, "You think you might want him back?"

She said no. But she didn't say it right away. She looked at her baby first and she made like she wanted to pull her foot away from my hand.

I got up and put on my pants.

"Where you goin'?" asked Juanita.

"I gotta meet Mofass at one'a his places at eight," I said.

I went home and napped for a few hours, then I drove out to Riverside.

Riverside was mainly rural then. No sidewalks or street signs to speak of. I had to go to three gas stations before I found out how to get to Andre's address.

I staked out their place until early evening, when I saw Winthrop's Plymouth coming up the road. It was a turquoise job.

Linda was a big woman, heftier than EttaMae and looser in the flesh. Her skin color was high yellow, that's why Shaker, that is to say Winthrop, took to her in the first place. Her face was lusty and sensual, and poor Andre didn't seem as if he could bear the weight of her arm around his shoulders. His shirttails flapped behind him and I could see the lace string of his right shoe dancing freely. Andre Lavender was a bug-eyed, orange-skinned man. He wasn't fat but he was meaty. He had a good-natured and nervous air about him; Andre would shake your hand three times at any one meeting.

I watched them stagger up the dirt driveway to the house. Linda was singing and Andre sagged sloppily in the mud.

I could have gone up against him then, but I wanted him to talk to me. I needed Andre to be scared, but not of me, so I drove back to L.A., back to a little bar I knew.

• 16 •

That night I went to the Cozy Room on Slauson. It was a small shack with plaster walls that were held together by tar paper, chicken wire, and nails. It stood in the middle of a big vacant lot, lopsided and ungainly. The only indication you got that it was inhabited was the raw pine plank over the door. It had the word "Entrance" painted on it in dripping black letters.

It was a small room and very dark. The bar was a simple dictionary podium with a row of metal shelves behind it. The bartender was a stout woman named Ula Hines. She served gin or whiskey, with or without water, and unshelled peanuts by the bag. There were twelve small tables hardly big enough for two. The Cozy Room wasn't a place for large parties, it was there for men who wanted to get drunk.

Because it wasn't a social atmosphere Ula didn't invest in a jukebox or live music. She had a radio that played cowboy music and a TV, set on a chair, that only went on for boxing.

Winthrop was at a far table drinking, smoking, and looking mean.

"Evenin', Shaker," I said. Shaker Jones was the name he went by when we were children in Houston. It was only when he became an insurance man that he decided he needed a fancy name like Winthrop Hughes.

Shaker didn't feel very fancy that night.

"What you want, Easy?"

I was surprised that he even recognized me, drunk as he was.

"Mofass sent me."

"Wha' fo'?"

"He need some coverage down on the Magnolia Street apartments."

Shaker laughed like a dying man who gets in the last joke.

"He got them naked gas heaters, he could go to hell," Shaker said.

"He got sumpin' you want though, man."

"He ain't got nuthin' fo' me. Nuthin'."

"How 'bout Linda an' Andre?"

My Aunt Vel hated drunks. She did because she claimed that they didn't have to act all sloppy and stupid the way they did. "It's all in they minds," she'd say.

Shaker proved her point by straightening up and asking, in a very clear voice, "Where are they, Easy?"

"Mofass told me t'get them papers from you, Shaker. He told me t'drive you out almost to 'em an' then you give me the papers an' I take you the whole way."

"I pay you three hundred dollars right now and we cut Mofass out of it."

I laughed and shook my head.

"I'll see ya tomorrow, Shaker." I knew he was sober because he bridled when I called him that. "Front'a Vigilance Insurance at eight-fifteen."

I turned back to look at him before I went out of the door. He was sitting up and breathing deeply. I knew when I saw him that I was all that stood between Andre and an early grave.

I was in front of his office at the time I said. He was right out there waiting for me. He wore a double-breasted pearl-gray suit with a white shirt and a maroon tie that had dozens of little yellow diamonds printed on it. His left pinky glittered with gold and diamonds and his fedora hat had a bright red feather in its band. The only shabby thing about Shaker was his briefcase; it was frayed and cracked across the middle. That was Shaker to a T: he worried about his appearance but he didn't give a damn about his work.

"Where we headed, Easy?" he asked before he could slam the door shut.

"I tell ya when we get there." I smiled at his consternation. It did me good to see an arrogant man like Shaker Jones go with an empty glass.

I drove north to Pasadena, where I picked up Route 66, called Foothill Boulevard in those days. That took us through the citrus-growing areas of Arcadia, Monrovia, and all the way down to Pomona and Ontario. The foothills were wild back then. White stone and sandy soil knotted with low shrubs and wild grasses. The citrus orchards were bright green and heavy with orange and yellow fruit. In the hills beyond roamed coyotes and wildcats.

The address for Linda and Andre was on a small dirt road called Turkel, just about four blocks off the main drag, Alessandro Boulevard. I stopped a few blocks away.

"Here we are," I said in a cheery voice.

"Where are they?"

"Where them papers Mofass wanted?"

Shaker stared death at me for a minute, but then, when I didn't keel over, he put his hand into the worn brown briefcase and came out with a sheaf of about fifteen sheets of paper. He shoved the papers into my lap, turning a few pages back so he could point out a line that said "Premiums."

"That's what he wanted when we talked last December. Now where's Linda and Andre?"

I ignored him and started flipping through the documents.

Shaker was huffing but I took my time. Legal documents need a close perusal; I'd seen enough of them in my day.

"Man, what you doin'?" Shaker squealed at me. "You cain't read that kinda document. You need to have law trainin' for that."

Shaker was no lawyer. As a matter of fact, he hadn't finished the eighth grade. I had two part-time years of Los Angeles City College under my belt. But I scratched my head to show that I agreed with him.

I said, "Maybe so, Shaker. Maybe. But I jus' got a question t'ask you here."

"Don't you be callin' me Shaker, Easy," he warned. "That ain't my name no mo'. Now what is it you wanna know?"

I turned to the second-to-the-last sheet and pointed to a blank line near the bottom of the page.

"Whas this here?"

"Nuthin'," he said quickly. Too quickly. "The president of Vigilance gotta sign that."

"It says, 'the insurer or the insurer's agent.' Thas you, ain't it?"

Shaker stared death at me a little more, then he snatched the papers and signed them.

"Where is she?" he demanded.

I didn't answer but I pulled back into the road and drove toward Andre and Linda's address.

Shaker's Plymouth was in the yard, hubcap-deep in mud.

"There you go," I said, looking at the house.

"Alright," Shaker said. He got out of the car and so did I.

"Where you goin', Easy?"

"With you, Shaker."

He bristled when I called him that again.

Then he said, "You got what you want. It's my business here on out."

I noticed that his jacket pocket hung low on the right side. That didn't bother me, though. I had a .25 hooked behind my back.

"I ain't gonna leave you t'kill nobody, Shaker. I ain't no lawyer, like you said, but I know that the police love what they call accessory before the fact."

"Just stay outta my way," he said. Then he turned toward the house, striding through the mud.

I stayed behind him, walking a little slower.

When he pushed through the front door I was seven, maybe eight, steps behind. I heard Linda scream and Andre make a noise something like a hydraulic lift engaging. The next thing I heard was crashing furniture. By that time I was going through the door myself.

It was a mess. A pink couch was turned on its back and big Linda was on the other side of it, sitting down and practicing how wide she could open her eyes. She was screaming too; loud, incoherent shrieks. Her wiry, straightened hair stood out from the back of her head so that she resembled a monstrous chicken.

Shaker had a blackjack in one hand and he had Andre by the scruff of the neck with the other. Poor Andre sagged down trying to protect himself from the blows Shaker was throwing at him.

"Lemme go!" Andre kept shouting. Blood spouted from the center of his forehead.

Shaker obliged. He let Andre slump to the floor and dropped the sap. Then went for his jacket pocket. But by that time I was behind him. I grabbed his arm and pulled the pistol out of his pocket.

"What? What? What?" he asked.

I almost laughed.

"You ain't gonna kill nobody t'day, Shaker."

"Get get get." His eyes were glazed over, I don't think he had any idea of what was happening.

"You got some whiskey?" I asked Andre.

"In the kitchen." Andre blinked his enormous eyes at me and made to rise. He was so shaken it took him two attempts to make it to his feet. Blood cascaded down his loose blue shirt. He was a mess.

"Get it," I said.

Linda was still screaming. Her voice was already gone, though. Instead of a chicken she'd begun to sound like an old, hoarse dog barking at clouds.

I grabbed her by the shoulders and shouted, "Shut up, woman!"

I heard something fall, and when I turned around I saw Shaker going at Andre again. He had him by the throat this time.

I boxed Shaker's ears, then I sapped him with the barrel of his gun. He hit the ground faster than if I had shot him.

"He was gonna kill me." Andre sounded surprised.

"Yeah," I said. "You spendin' his money, drivin' his car, an' fuckin' his wife. He was gonna kill you."

Andre looked like he didn't understand.

I went over to Linda and asked, "How much of Shaker's money you got left?"

"'Bout half." The fear of death had knocked any lies she might have had right out of her head.

"How much is that?"

"Eighteen hundred."

"Gimme sixteen."

"What?"

"Gimme sixteen an' then you take two an' get outta here. That is, 'less you wanna go back with him?" I motioned my head toward Shaker's body.

Andre got the money. It was in a sock under the mattress.

While I counted out Linda's piece she was throwing clothes into a suitcase. She was scared because Shaker showed signs of coming to. It didn't fluster me, though. I would have liked to sap him again.

"Come on, baby," Linda said to Andre once she was packed. She wore a rabbit fur and a red box hat.

"I just come from Juanita, Andre," I said. "Li'l Andre want you back, an' you know this trick is over."

Andre hesitated. The side of his face was beginning to swell, it made him resemble his own infant son.

"You go on, Linda," I said. "Andre already got a family. And you cain't hardly take care of both of you on no two hundred dollars."

"Andre!" Linda rasped.

He looked at his toes.

"Shit!" was the last word she said to him.

I said, "There's a bus stop 'bout four blocks up, on Alessandro."

She cursed me once and then she was gone.

"My car is the Ford out front," I said to Andre after I watched Linda slog through the mud toward the end of their street. "You go get in it an' I'll talk to the man here."

Andre took a small bag from the closet. I laughed to myself that he was already packed to leave.

I sat and watched Shaker writhing on the floor and rolling his eyes. He wasn't aware yet. While enjoying the show I took three hundred dollars from the wad that Linda left. He came to his senses about fifteen minutes later. I was sitting in front of him, hugging the back of a folding chair. He looked up at me from his knees.

"Thirteen hundred was all they had left. Here you go," I said, throwing the sock in his face.

"Where Linda?"

"She had somewhere to go."

"Wit' Andre?"

"He's wit' me. I'ma take him home to his family."

"I'ma kill that boy, Easy."

"No you not, Shaker," I said. "'Cause Andre is under my protection. You understand me? You best to understand, 'cause I will kill you if anything happens to him. I will kill you."

"We had a deal, Easy."

"An' I met it. You got your car, you got all the money that's left, an' yo' wife don't want you; killin' Andre ain't gonna stop that. So leave it be or we gonna have it out, an' you know you ain't gonna win that one neither."

Shaker believed me, I could see it in his eyes. As long as he thought I was a poor man he'd be scared of me. That's why I kept my wealth a secret. Everybody knows that a poor man's got nothing to lose; a poor man will kill you over a dime.

• 17 •

Winthrop Hughes got to his feet and I walked him to his car. I kept his pistol and his blackjack in case he saw Linda or he decided to come against me and Andre.

He drove off, cursing and threatening to complain to Mofass. Andre and I took off about twenty minutes later.

"Thank you, Easy," Andre said as we pulled onto the highway. The fright had made him courteous. "You really saved my butt back there."

I didn't say anything. Andre held my handkerchief to the gash in his forehead as he looked from side to side like a dog who needed to be let out.

After a while I asked him, "Where you wanna go, Andre?"

"Um, well." He hesitated. "Maybe you could drop me off at my auntie's over on Florence."

I shook my head. "Police already got that covered, man."

"Say what?"

I was quiet again. I wanted Andre to be scared for his life.

"What you mean 'bout the cops, Easy?"

"They been lookin' for you, Andre. They been askin' 'bout you."

"Who?"

"The police," I said.

Andre seemed to relax.

"And some man from the FBI."

I might as well have thrown hot oil in his face.

"No!"

"It's the truth, man," I said. "You know Shaker got me to look for you 'cause he wanted Linda back and he told me the government might pay somethin' for you. You lucky that I didn't want to play his game. I went over t'ask Juanita what I should do an' she said that yo' boy needed his daddy."

"Thanks," Andre said, but he was looking out of the window. Maybe he was thinking of throwing himself into the road.

"What them cops want?" I asked.

"I dunno, man. They musta made some mistake or sumpin'."

"You gonna tell me?"

"Tell you what? I ain't seen no cops. I just been out here wit' Linda, that's all."

"You want me to drive you to the cops, Andre? 'Cause you know I will."

"Why you wanna mess wit' me, Easy? I ain't done nuthin' t'you."

There were cows leaving a pasture we passed. Black-and-white cows winding their way up a narrow pathway cut into the side of the hill. Their hold on the ground seemed precarious, but they were standing on bedrock compared to the cow-eyed man sitting next to me.

"You tell me what's up an' maybe I could help ya," I said.

"How could you help me?"

"I could find you a place t'stay. Maybe I could get your girlfriend and her baby out to you. I might even buy you some groceries until this thing blows over."

"Ain't nuthin' gonna blow over."

"Tell me the story," I said in a low, reassuring voice.

Andre sat back and wiped his palms against his pants. He was grimacing, showing a mouthful of teeth and moaning.

"I got set up!" he shouted. "Set up!"

"By who?"

"Them people at Champion, man. They put them papers in a envelope that wasn't marked. It was in a blue folder, the same color folder they use for the distribution list."

"What you talkin' 'bout, man?"

"They set me up!" he shouted again. "Mr. Lindquist's secretary told me I could wait fo' 'im in his office. I'm shop steward an' I meet wit' the VP every other month. But we been talkin' strike out in the yard 'cause they gonna lay off a hundred and fifty men."

He stopped talking as if everything should have been clear.

"So this list was the men they were going to lay off?"

"That's what I thought. I grabbed it an' took it out wit' me. It's only later that I seen the seal."

"What seal?"

"Top Secret, man." Andre started tearing. "Top Secret."

"Why not just take it back?"

"I swear, man, I got outta there quick 'cause I didn't want no one t'see me. It wasn't till I got home and opened it up that I seen that government seal. Then I was too scared t'bring it back." Andre mixed his fingers together to show the complexity of his situation.

"But the envelope was the kind they used for the distribution list?" I asked.

"Yeah."

"Could be a setup," I said, noncommittally.

Andre looked at me hopefully. "I tole you."

"Or you could just be a poor fool," I said. "What you do with them papers?"

"I ain't sayin' nuthin' 'bout that."

It was Andre's turn to be quiet. We drove on toward the outskirts of L.A. proper. It was high noon. The desert sun was so bright that even the blue in the sky seemed to fade.

I pulled off the road at a restaurant called Skip's. I gave Andre a pullover sweater I kept in the trunk to hide the blood on his shirt. We couldn't do anything about his head, though. At first I thought the waitress wasn't going to serve us. We ordered chicken-fried steaks and beer. Andre was polite, but other than that he was silent.

I didn't want to push too hard, because Andre was highstrung and he had been through quite a lot already.

When the waitress left the check Andre just stared at it.

"What's it gonna be, Andre?"

"What do you mean?"

"I mean, you gonna tell me about Chaim Wenzler or what?"

It was a pleasure surprising Andre. His face registered emotion like mercury gauging a match.

"How'd you know that?"

"I got my ways. I need to know about you an' this dude."

"Why you gotta know?"

"I'm working' fo' a man, okay? Leave it at that an' you might stay outta jail."

Andre huffed and clenched his fists, but I could tell that he was broken.

"He's a guy I met, that's all."

"How?"

"When I was elected steward. This white guy, Martin Vost, district union president, introduced me at a monthly meetin'. Chaim was there as a adviser."

"Yeah? So he advise you t'go steal top secrets."

"Man, he was just like a friend. We go out drinkin' an' talkin' an' aftah while he took me t'this study group he got."

"An' what they be studyin'?"

"Union newspapers an' like that."

"So he didn't tell you t'steal them papers?"

"He said that strikin' was a war. He said that we gotta do ev'rything we could t'win fo' our side. So when I seen that distribution list I took it. It's kinda like he told me to; like he primed me fo' it."

"What he say when you bring it to 'im?"

"Who said I did?"

"Com'on, man, I ain't got time fo' this play shit."

"His eyes got all wide an' he asked me where I got it from. I told 'im. He said that stealin' that document was a fed'ral charge. He told me t'disappear."

"That's it?"

"All I gotta say, man."

"But there's one more thing," I said.

"What's that?"

"Where's what you stole?"

It was then that I noticed the sweat on Andre's upper lip. Maybe it was there the whole time.

"You gotta swear you ain't gonna tell where you got this from."

"Where is the shit, man?" I was losing patience with Andre's fears.

"You know the brick-walled car graveyard down at the far end of Vernon?"

"Yeah."

"We went down there. They got this emerald-green Dodge truck down along the back wall. We put the papers 'hind the seat."

"Wenzler go with you?"

"Yeah, man, we went there together. I said that we was lookin' fo' a muffler and then we snuck back there an' hid it."

"What if they sell it?"

"Shit, man, that ole thang is just a wreck. It's been back there fo' years."

When we got back in the car I told Andre that I'd try to help him.

"I work for a guy named Mofass. He manages a few 'partment buildin's," I said.

"Yeah?"

"I'ma call him an' ask him to put you up in one of his Mexican buildin's. I'll call Juanita too, send her over there." I took the three hundred dollars from my shirt pocket and handed it to Andre. "Use it slow, man. You might have to be gone for a while."

I let Andre off at a hotel on Buena Vista Boulevard. When I got home I called Mofass and told him to prepare a room somewhere for Andre.

"Who gonna pay me?" Mofass asked.

"I will."

"Ain't good business, Mr. Rawlins. Landlord should never pay nobody's rent."

Then I called Juanita.

"That you, Easy?" she said, softening when she heard my voice.

"Andre's in a hotel downtown, honey," I said, and then I gave her the address. "He got a little money an' he pretty scared too."

"You want me to go to him?" she asked, as if I had a say in how she spent the rest of her life.

"Yeah," I said. "And, Juanita?"

"Huh, Easy?"

"Maybe you could go easy on the boy an' not tell 'im 'bout us."

"Don't worry, honey, I'ma keep that secret right in here."

I couldn't see her but I could imagine where her hand was.

• 18 •

I came home to loud hammering. There were three men on my porch. Two of them were doing the carpentry. Boards had already been laced over the windows; there were bright yellow ribbons of paper across them. Right then the men were driving nails into fresh timbers across my front door.

"What the fuck you think it is you doin' here!" I shouted.

All of the men were white and wore dark suits. When they turned around I recognized only one of them, but that was enough.

Agent Lawrence said, "We're sealing the house against the threat of you liquidating property that may rightfully belong to the federal government."

"What?"

Instead of talking Lawrence tore off a sheet of paper that had been tacked to the wall. He handed me the federal marshal's warrant. It said that my property was temporarily confiscated by the federal marshal until such time that my tax responsibility had been determined; I made that much out. Two judges had signed the document; also the tax agent involved, Reginald Arnold Lawrence.

I ripped the warrant in half and pushed my way past the tax man. I went up to the closest marshal and said, "Brother, I don't know what you'd do if a man threatened to take your home, but I've been told by the FBI that I don't have to worry 'bout this until I done some work for them."

The marshal was short. He had blue eyes and thinning sandy hair that lay down and stuck to his scalp because of the sweat he'd built up driving nails into my walls.

"I don't know anything about that, Mr. Rawlins. All I know is that I got this warrant to execute."

"But this is my house, man! All my clothes are in there. My shoes, my address book, I don't have anything."

The two officers looked at each other. I could see that they sympathized with me. Nobody likes to kick a man out of his home. Nobody decent, that is.

"Come on, Aster," Agent Lawrence said. "I have to get home."

"He's got a right to hear something," Aster complained. "I mean, here we are locking up his house and he doesn't have anything but what's on his back."

"This is the law, mister," Lawrence said. "All we have is the law, that's why I'm here. I'm doing my job. And that's what I want from you."

Lawrence gave the men a hard stare and they turned back to their hammers.

I watched them for a minute. And while I did my breath came up short. Something started shaking in my chest.

"You cain't do this, man." I said it because I was afraid of what might happen if I didn't talk.

Lawrence ignored me, though. He took the two halves of the warrant and tacked them back up against the wall.

"I said, you cain't do this, man!"

The tone of my own voice in my ears reminded me of Poinsettia; her crying to Mofass that she needed another chance.

The marshals were almost done with their job, so I put my hand on Lawrence's shoulder.

He didn't bother with the hand. He drove his fist into my temple and followed with an uppercut that I managed to avoid. The adrenaline was already pumping, so I hit him somewhere in the chest and then in the side of his head. When he doubled over I pushed him down the stairs.

I was just ready to go after him when I remembered the two men behind me. I was about to turn but then they grabbed me by both arms.

As they dragged me down the stairway Lawrence cried, "He hit me! He assaulted me!" He said that over and over. He didn't sound outraged, though. It was more like he was glad that I had assaulted him.

The marshals wrestled me to the fence and forced me to my knees before handcuffing me to one of the metal posts. I was struggling and fighting, and maybe screaming a little. There may have been tears in my eyes and my voice as I warned those men to stay away from my house.

A small crowd of my neighbors gathered at the front gate. A few men even entered and approached the white peacekeepers.

The marshal who had talked to me approached the men. He had a calmness about him and was holding up his identification. As I watched him I felt a blow to the side of my head. When I looked around I saw the other marshal holding Agent Lawrence back.

"Stop it!" the black-haired, Mediterranean-looking man ordered.

". . . we're just doing our job," Marshal Aster was saying to the men. He was backing them up. No guns were drawn. "Everybody go on home. Mr. Rawlins will explain himself after we're gone . . ."

"I want him arrested for attacking a federal agent!" Lawrence shrieked. His lips stuck straight out and he shook as if he were freezing.

"Next time I'll kill your ass!" I shouted from my knees.

The black-haired marshal dragged Lawrence out to the gate and the other man came to my side.

"You cain't do this to me, man!" I said to him. "I ain't gonna lose my house, my clothes . . ."

"Shut up, man!" he ordered. He must have been an officer somewhere, because the tone of his voice demanded obedience.

He knelt there beside me and reached for the cuffs.

"We're going off duty after this, Mr. Rawlins. If you break the seal we'll have to come by tomorrow and arrest you, if you're still here, that is."

He took off the cuffs and I jumped to my feet. I advanced on the two men at the gate with Aster at my heel.

"What's goin' on, Easy?" Melford Thomas, my across-the-street neighbor, asked.

"I want you to arrest him," Lawrence said again.

"Why?" Aster asked. "All I saw was you fall on your ass."

"I won't take this!" Lawrence said, spitting over all of us.

Aster wiped his face. "We're going home now. You want to come with us you better get in the car, or else you can stay here and arrest him yourself."

Lawrence looked as if he might try it. But when he saw all of my angry-looking black neighbors he backed down.

"Don't break that seal, Rawlins," he said. "That's an official barrier."

And then they were off in their car.

I had the planks pulled off my door before they turned the corner.

Craxton was working late that night. Maybe he worked late every night, sitting up in some vast office plotting strategies against the enemies of America. I didn't need to worry about communists, though—the police were enough for me.

"What's that?" he laughed. "He had the federal marshal out there?"

"I don't find it too funny. He kicked me upside the head."

"Sorry, Easy. It's just that you've got to admire a man who wants to do the job right."

"What about me? I'm supposed to work for you and I don't even have a place to sleep or clothes to wear."

"I'll make some calls. You just climb into your bed, Easy, and get ready to work tomorrow. Agent Lawrence will not bother you again."

"Okay. Just as long you keep that man away from my house. I don't want him in here again."

"You got it. I thought Lawrence had more sense than that. My request for your help was informal. I didn't want to have to step on him. But I'll do that now."

I was satisfied with that much. There was a moment when we were both quiet.

Finally I asked, "So you still want me to look into this Wenzler thing?"

"Certainly do, Easy. You're my ace in the hole."

"Well then, I was thinkin' . . ."

"Yes?"

"About this, um, Andre Lavender guy."

"What about him?"

"Well, I asked a couple'a guys I still know down there about him. They said that he got in trouble with the law down there and disappeared."

"What kind of trouble was that?"

I was pretty sure that he already knew the answer, so I said, "I don't know."

"Well, Easy, I don't know about any trouble he had. I know that he's working with Wenzler and we'd like to talk to him. If you get a line we'd sure appreciate it. As a matter of fact, if you could lead us to Lavender we might not need you any more at all."

It was a tempting offer. Andre didn't mean anything to me. But he was innocent of anything but being a fool and Craxton wasn't promising me anything anyway. So I said, "Nobody seems to know where he's gone to, but I'll keep my eyes peeled."

I paced the rooms of my tiny house all night. I walked and cursed and loaded all my pistols. When the sun came up I sat out on the front porch, waiting for marshals.

They didn't come, though. That was better all the way round.

• 19 •

My life was pretty crazy in the days I worked for the FBI. I spent most of my late evenings in the arms of EttaMae. Those nights I spent exploring Etta's body and her love; either one was worth dying for. Being with EttaMae was the most exciting and dreadful time I ever had. I had to overcome my guilt and my fear of Mouse to be with her. I'd come to her apartment in the late evening looking all around to make sure that no one saw me. LaMarque would be sleeping in his little room and Etta would come to me slowly like a horse trainer trying to tame a skitterish buck. My heart was always racing from fear when I got there, but the fear soon turned to passion. Sometimes in the middle of our lovemaking Etta would hold me behind my neck and ask, "Do you really love me, Easy?" And I'd cry out, "Yeah, yeah, baby!" in a powerful surrender to the forces that built in me.

In the daytime I worked with Chaim Wenzler. He was a hard worker and a good man. We'd go from door to door in Hollywood and Beverly Hills and Santa Monica. I'd wait in the car and Chaim would go beg for clothes and other items. I offered to go up with him once but he said, "These people wouldn't put it in your hand, my friend. They wanna give maybe, but not direct. Give it to the kike and then he could give to the *schwartze*, that's what they're thinking." Then he spat.

We always went to coffee-shop restaurants for lunch. Chaim paid one day I and I would pay the next. The people running the restaurants were willing to take our money, but you could see that they were bothered by us. It was probably because we were so boisterous and intimate.

Chaim liked to tell stories and laugh, or cry. He told me about his childhood in Vilna. I had heard about Vilna because I had gone through Germany *liberating* the death camps. When I told Chaim about my experiences he talked to me about his times among the Germans, Poles, and Jews. In that way we grew close. We shared experience through memories that, although we were never in the same place, had the very real feelings of desperation and death that consumed us both during World War Two.

Chaim had been part of the communist underground during the German occupation of Vilna. He organized and fought against the Nazis. When the frightened Jewish population denounced the underground he and his comrades fled the city and formed a Jewish platoon that slew Nazis, blew up trains, and liberated every Jew that they could.

"We fought side by side with the Russian guerrillas," Chaim told me once. "They were soldiers of the people," he said, and he touched his chest with one hand and my arm with the other. "Like you and me."

I knew that the Russians abandoned the Warsaw Ghetto and I was sure that Chaim knew it too, but I couldn't say anything because I never knew a white man who thought that we were *really* the same. When he touched my arm he might as well have stuck his hand in my chest and grabbed my heart. Agent Craxton might have liked what I was doing for him, but he didn't think I was on his level.

Chaim carried a steel hip flask full of vodka. He liked to chip at it during the day. His high was pleasant and his friendliness was real. Sometimes he'd bring up his "organizing" at Champion. Once he even mentioned Andre Lavender. But whenever he did that I changed the subject. I acted like I was afraid to know about politics or unions. And I was afraid; afraid of what I might do to save myself from jail.

"What you do for money, Chaim?" I asked him one day. We were sitting at a tiny strip of park that overlooked the Pacific Ocean.

He looked out over the blue air and blue water for a long time before saying, "They won't let me work."

"Who?"

"America. They come and they tell the weak boss that I'm a bad man and he fires me. They wouldn't let me wash shit from the floor. So my friends help me, and my family."

"Who you talkin' 'bout?"

"The Cossack," he spat. "The Nazi, the FBI."

"You mean they come out to yo' job an' tell the boss that you did sumpin'?"

"They say I am not American. They say I am communist."

I found myself shaking my head. "Don't you know that's some shit."

"That is why I work for charity, for First African. The white people don't understand being treated like this. They think that they are free because nobody comes to their job. They see that I am bad because the police follow me. They have no idea." Chaim pointed at his head. "In here they are stupid with what they are told."

"You could say that again. You all the time hearin' 'bout how free America is, but it ain't."

"No. But they are free. They have a job and they keep it. When things get bad, my friend, it is you and I that are out of work."

I nodded. There had been many a time I'd seen the Negro staff of a company laid off when money was tight. It didn't always happen like that, but it did often enough.

Chaim grabbed my hand in a viselike grip. There were tears in his eyes. We sat there holding hands and looking at each other until I got a little uncomfortable. Then he said, "I saw them hang my brother when I was a child. He was accused of spitting in a soldier's path. They hung him and burned down my mother's house."

I won't say that those few words alone made us friends, but I understood Chaim Wenzler then.

*

I talked to Agent Craxton later that same night. He asked all sorts of questions about where we picked up clothes and who handled the money. He was looking for spies everywhere. If I hadn't talked to Andre Lavender I would have thought the FBI man was crazy.

But even though I had the proof I needed to set myself free I balked at bringing down Chaim Wenzler.

"What is it that you want on the man?" I asked Craxton.

"I'll know it when you tell me, Easy. Has he invited you to any meetings?"

"What kinda meetin's?"

"That's what I'm asking you."

"Uh-uh, no. All we do is collect clothes and then give 'em away."

"Don't you worry, Mr. Rawlins, he'll slip up. And then we'll have him."

There wasn't much consolation for me in that.

"I talked to your friend the other day, Easy," Agent Craxton said.

"Who's that?"

"Lawrence. He's singing a new tune now that Washington called his boss. He says that everything's okay and that he would be happy to process a schedule of payments when this thing is over."

"You not gonna let him do that, are you?"

"No, I don't think so. I told him that Washington should have your paperwork by the end of next week."

I sighed. "Thanks."

"You see, Easy, we're helping each other."

I could still feel that powerful grip on my hand.

• 20 •

I knew that I was bound to suffer a fall. In a perfect world I would have had Etta for my bride and Chaim for my best man. But after that last talk with Craxton my hopes for a happy life just sank. Everything I was doing seemed wrong. The police were suspicious. The IRS wanted me in jail. Even Craxton was lying to me, and I didn't know why. There was no room for escape, so I turned to alcohol. I had a drink or two and went through the motions of cleaning up. But the bath didn't cleanse and the whiskey didn't work.

I wasn't only worried about Mouse and what he might do to exact vengeance on me. I'm not a meek man and I will fight for what I believe is right, regardless of the odds. If I'd felt it was right for me to love Etta, then I wouldn't have cared about what Mouse might do; at least I would have been at peace with myself. But Mouse was my friend and he was in pain; I knew that when I looked into his eyes at Targets. But I hadn't worried about him at all. All I cared about was how I felt. The fact that I was so selfish sickened me.

It was the same with Chaim Wenzler. He might have been a communist but he was a friend to me. We'd drink out of the same glass sometimes, and we talked from our hearts. Craxton and Lawrence had me so worried about my money and my freedom that I had become their slave. At least Mouse and Chaim acted from their natures. They were the innocent ones while I was the villain.

Finally, when I succumbed to the whiskey, I began to think about Poinsettia Jackson.

All I could think about was that young woman and how my cold-heartedness had caused her to take her own life. I liked what the detective Quinten Naylor was doing, but I didn't agree with him. Why would someone want to kill a woman whose every moment was torture and pain? If it was someone who wanted to put her out of her misery they wouldn't have hung her. A bullet in the head would have been more humane. No. Poinsettia took her own life because she lost her beauty and her job, and when she begged me to let her at least have a roof over her head I took that too.

I was in a foul mood when I went down to First African that evening. I was more than a little drunk and willing to blame anybody else for the wrong that was in me.

I'd promised Odell that I'd come down to the elementary school that the church ran and do something about their ants. They had a problem with red ants.

Los Angeles had a special breed of red ant. They were about three times the size of the regular black ant and they were fire-engine red. But the real problem with them was their bite. The red ant's bite was painful, and on many people it made a great welt. That would have been bad enough, but children seemed to be especially bothered by the ants. And little kids loved to play in the dirt where red ants made their nests.

I had a poison that killed them in the hive. And I was so upset about everything, and so drunk, that I didn't have the sense to stay home.

I used the key Odell had given me and went down to the basement of the church, looking for a funnel. When I got to the cafeteria I saw that the lights were on. That didn't bother me, though. There were often people working in the church.

I got the funnel from a hopper room, then headed for the exit at the back of the basement. When I walked through the main room I saw them. Chaim Wenzler and a young woman who had black hair and pale skin.

"Easy," Chaim said with a smile. He rose and crossed the room to shake my hand.

"Hi, Chaim," I said.

He pulled me across the room by my hand, saying, "This is my daughter, Shirley."

"Pleased to meet you," I said. "But listen, Chaim, I got some work I gotta do an' there's a problem back home."

I must have sounded sincere, because Chaim and Shirley both frowned. They had identical dimples at the center of their chins.

I wanted to get away from there. The room seemed to be too dark and too hot. Just the idea that I was there to fool those people, the same way I fooled Poinsettia with my lies about being a helpless janitor, made my stomach turn. Before they could say their words of concern I threw myself toward the exit.

The schoolyard was a vast sandy lot that had three bungalows placed end to end at the northern side. The ants dug their nests against the salmon brick walls at the back. I set up my electric torch and took out the amber bottle of poison. I also had a flask of Teachers. I took a sip of my poison and then poured the ants a dram of theirs through the funnel.

What followed was a weird scene.

I'd never watched to see what happened after the poison hit a hive. Under electric light the sand looked like a real desert around the mound. At first there was just a wisp of smoke rising from the hole, but then about twenty of the ants came rushing out. They were frantic, running in widening arcs and stamping on the sand like parading horses held under a tight rein. These ants ran off into the night but were followed by weaker, more confused ants.

I saw no more than four of them actually die, but I knew that the hives were full of the dead. I knew that they had fallen where they stood, because the poison is very deadly in close quarters. Like in Dachau when we got there, the dead strewn like chips of wood at a lumberyard.

There were six holes in all. Six separate hives to slaughter. I went through the ritual, drinking whiskey and staring hard at the few corpses.

They were all the same except for the last one. For some reason, when I gave that one the dose of poison the ants flooded out of there in the hundreds. There were so many that I had to back away to avoid them swarming over me. I was so scared that I ran, stumbling twice.

I ran all the way back to the church. Before I went in, I drained the scotch and threw the bottle in the street.

I made it down into the basement, tripping on my own feet and the stairs. Chaim and his daughter were still there. The way they looked at me I wondered if I had been talking to myself.

Chaim gazed into my face with almost colorless eyes. I imagined he knew everything. About the FBI and Craxton, about the ants, about Poinsettia and daddyReese. He probably knew about the time I fell asleep and when I woke up my mother was dead.

"What's wrong, Mr. Rawlins?" he asked.

"Nuthin'," I said. I took a step forward. The impact of my foot on the floor sounded in my head like a giant kettle drum. "It's just that . . ."

"What?" Chaim grunted as he caught me by my arms. I realized that I was falling and tried to regain a foothold.

I kept talking too. "Ain't nuthin'," I said. I tried to back away but the wall stopped me.

Shirley, his daughter, moved in close behind Chaim. There was concern in her porcelain face.

"Stand still, Easy," Chaim was saying. Then he laughed. "I don't think you'll be sorting clothes tomorrow morning."

I laughed with him. "You be better off wit' somebody else helpin' you anyways, man."

He shook me the way people do when they're trying to awaken someone. "*You* are my friend, Easy." His somber look saddened me even more. I thought of the victims I had seen. Men wasted to the size of boys, mass graves full of innocence.

"I ain't no friend'a yours, man. Uh-uh. Th'ew her outta her own place. Th'ew her out an' now she's dead. You cain't trust no niggah like me, Chaim. You do better jus' t' shine me on."

With that I leaned against the wall and slid down to the floor.

"We can't just leave him here, Poppa," Shirley said. He said something back, but it sounded like music to me, a song that I forgot the words to. I thought for a moment that he understood my confession, that he intended to kill me in the church basement.

But instead they got me to my feet, and pushed me toward the door. I walked under my own steam for the most part but every now and then I tripped.

There was a loud drumming in my head and lamplights hanging against a completely black sky. I could hear the moths banging against the glass covers in between the thunder of my footsteps.

The light snapped on in the car and I fell into the backseat; Chaim pushed my legs in behind me.

I remember motion and soothing words. But I don't remember going into the house. Then I fell again, this time into a soft bed. I had been crying for a long time.

• 21 •

I heard a door slam somewhere below me. Sometime after that I opened my eyes.

The window had a lace curtain over its lower half. There were big white clouds moving fast across a perfectly blue sky in the upper panes. Watching that sky helped my breathing. I remember how deeply I inhaled, not even wanting to let it out.

"Good morning, Mr. Rawlins." It was a woman's voice. "How are you feeling?"

"What time is it?" I asked, sitting up. I wasn't wearing a shirt and the blankets came down to my stomach. Shirley Wenzler's eyes were fast to my chest.

"Ten, I guess."

She wore a no-sleeve one-piece cotton dress that had slanting stripes of blue, green, and gold, all very bright. Squinting at those bright colors let me know that I had a hangover.

"This your house?" I asked.

"Kind of. I rent. Poppa lives all the way in Santa Monica so we thought we'd take you here for the night."

"How'd I get in bed?"

"You walked."

"I don't remember." It was partially true.

"You were kind of drunk, Mr. Rawlins." She giggled and covered her mouth. She was a very pretty young woman with extremely pale skin against jet-black hair. Her face was heart-shaped, everything seemed to point at her smile.

"Poppa just shouted at you, and told you where to go, and he kept on shouting until you did it. You . . ." She hesitated.

"Yeah?"

"You were kind of like crying."

"Did I say anything?"

"About a dead woman. You said she killed herself because you made her leave. Is that true?"

"No, no it's not. She got evicted from a place I clean for. That's all."

"Oh," she whispered and then looked at my chest.

I liked the attention, so I left the blankets alone.

"Is Chaim here?" I asked.

"I took him to the church. I just got back. He said that you'd come later if you weren't too sick."

"Is this your room?" I asked, looking around.

"Uh-huh. But I stayed in the spare room in the attic. It has a bed and I like to go up there and read sometimes. Especially in the spring or fall when it isn't too hot or too cold.

"Poppa slept on the couch," she added. "He does that sometimes."

"Oh," I said, partly because I didn't know what to say, and partly because my head hurt.

I watched her watching me for a few moments until she finally said. "I've never seen a man's chest, I mean, like yours."

"All it is is brown, honey. Ain't that different."

"Not that, I mean the hair, I mean you don't have much and it's so curly and . . ."

"And what?"

Just then the doorbell rang. Three short chimes that sounded like they were in some other world. Shirley, who had turned bright red, made to leave. I guess that she was kind of flustered. I was too.

When she was gone I looked around the room. The furniture was all hand-crafted from a yellowish-brown wood that I couldn't identify. Not a surface was flat. Everything curved and arced, from the mirrored bureau to the chest of drawers.

There was a thick white carpet and a few upholstered chairs. It was a small, feminine room; just exactly the right size and gender for my hangover.

After a while I heard men's voices. I went to the window and saw Shirley Wenzler standing outside of a wire fence in front of a well-manicured little yard. She was talking to two men who were wearing dark suits and short-brimmed hats. I remember thinking that the men must have gone shopping together to get clothes that were so similar.

Shirley got angry and shouted something that I couldn't make out. Finally she walked away from them, turning every now and then to see if they'd gone. But they just stared at her attentively, like sentinels of a wolf pack.

While I watched I hustled on my pants. When I heard the door slam I wanted to go ask her what had happened, but the twins interested me. They walked slowly across the street and got into a dark blue or black Buick sedan. They didn't start the car and drive away; they just sat there, watching the house.

"So you're up?" Shirley Wenzler said from the doorway. She was smiling again.

I turned from the window and said, "Nice neighborhood you live in. Hollywood?"

"Almost." She smiled. "We're near La Brea and Melrose."

"That's a long drive from where you got me."

She laughed, a little too loudly, and came into the room. She sat in a plush-bottomed chair across from the bed. I sat down on the mattress to keep her company.

"Did some woman really die?" she asked.

"Woman over where I clean couldn't pay the rent and she killed herself."

"You saw it?"

"Yeah." But all I could remember was Poinsettia's dripping toe.

"My poppa saw things like that." There was a strange light in her eyes. Not haunted like Chaim's, but empty.

"Many Jews," she continued, as if reciting a prayer she'd gone to bed with her whole life. "Mothers and sons."

"Yeah," I said, also softly.

At Dachau I'd seen many men and women like Wenzler; small and slight from starvation. Most of them were dead, strewn across the paths between bungalows like those ants, I imagined, stretched out in their hives.

"You think you could have saved her?" she asked. I had the crazy feeling that I was talking to her father, not her.

"What?"

"The woman who died. You think you could have saved her?"

"I know it. I got the ear'a the man run the place. He'da let 'er stay."

"No," she said simply.

"What you mean, no?"

"We are all of us trapped, Mr. Rawlins. Trapped in amber, trapped in work. If you can't pay the rent you die."

"That ain't right," I said.

Her eyes brightened even more and she smiled at me. "No, Mr. Rawlins. It is wrong."

It sounded so true and so final that I couldn't think of anything to say. So I held my peace, staring at her pale delicate hands. I could see the trace of blue veins pulsing just under the white skin.

"Come on down when you're ready," she said, rising and moving toward the door. "I'm making breakfast now."

As if she'd conjured it, I suddenly smelled coffee and bacon.

She sat at a maple table in an alcove that looked out onto a very green back yard. There was a tangerine tree right out the window. It was covered with waxy white blossoms. The flowers were being picked over by dozens of hovering bees.

"Come have a seat," she said to me. She got up and took my arm just above the elbow. It was a friendly gesture, and it gave me a pang of guilt in the chest.

"Thanks," I said.

"Coffee?" Shirley asked. She wouldn't meet my eye.

"Love it," I said as sexy as I could with a hangover.

She poured the coffee. She had long, lovely arms and skin as white as the sandy beaches down in Mexico. White-skinned women amazed me back in those days. They were worth your life just to look at in the South. And anything that valuable held great allure.

"Before the war started my father sent me out of Poland in a box," she said as if continuing a conversation.

"He's a pretty smart guy, your father."

"He said that he could smell it—the Nazis coming." She looked like a young girl. I had the urge to kiss her but I held it in check.

"That's why my father works with you. Mr. Rawlins. He knows that the trouble he felt in Poland is just like what you feel here." There were tears in Shirley's eyes.

I thought of why I was there and the toast dried on my tongue.

"Your father is a good man," I said, meaning it. "He wants to make things better."

"But he has to think of himself too!" she blurted out. "He can't keep doing things that will take him away from his family. He has to be here. He's getting old, you know, and you can't keep taking things out of him."

"I guess he might spend a little too much time out on his charities, huh?"

"And what if no one worries about him? What happens when the Cossack comes to his door? Is anybody going to stand up for him?"

I could feel her tears in my own eyes. Nothing had changed since the night before. I was still traitorous and evil.

Shirley got up and went into the kitchen. Actually she ran there.

"Would you like some more toast, Mr. Rawlins?" Shirley asked when she'd come back in from the kitchen. Her eyes were red.

"No thanks," I said. "What time you got?"

"Almost twelve."

"Damn. I better get down there to help your father or he's gonna wonder what we been doin'."

Shirley smiled. "I can drive you."

It was a nice smile. I shuddered to see her trust me, because her father's ruin was my only salvation.

"You're pretty quiet," Shirley Wenzler said in the car.

"Just thinkin'."

"About what?"

"About how you got the advantage on me."

"What do you mean?"

I leaned over and whispered, "Well, you got to give your opinion on my chest but the jury still out on yours."

She focused her attention back on the road and blushed nicely.

"I'm sorry," I said. "I always like to flirt with pretty girls."

"I think that was a little bit more than flirting."

"'Pends on where you come from," I said. "Down here that was just a little compliment from an admirer." That was a lie, but she didn't know it.

"Well, I'm not used to men talking to me like that."

"I said I'm sorry."

She let me out at First African. I shook her hand, holding it a little longer than I should have. But she smiled and was still smiling as she left.

I watched the little Studebaker drive away. After that I noticed the dark Buick with the two dark-suited men. They were parked across from the church then. Just sitting there as if they were salesmen breaking for an afternoon lunch.

• 22 •

First African had an empty look to it on weekdays. Christ still hung over the entrance but he looked like more of an ornament when the churchgoers weren't gathered around the stairs. I always stopped to look up at him, though. I understood the idea of pain and death at the hands of another—most colored people did. As terrible as Poinsettia's death was, she wasn't the first person I'd seen hung.

I'd seen lynching and burnings, shootings and stonings. I'd seen a man, Jessup Howard, hung for looking at a white woman. And I'd seen two brothers who were lynched from two nooses on the same rope because they complained about the higher prices they were charged at the county store. The brothers had ripped off their shirts and gouged deep scratches in each other's skin in their struggles to keep from strangling. Both of their necks, broken at last, were horribly enlongated as they hung.

Part of that powerful feeling that black people have for Jesus comes from understanding his plight. He was innocent and they crucified him; he lifted his head to tell the truth and he died.

While I looked at him I heard something, but it was like something at the back of my mind. Like a crackle of a lit match and the sigh of an old timber in a windstorm.

Chaim was down in the basement, already working on boxes of clothes. He was holding up an old sequined dress, squinting at the glitter.

"Looks good," I said.

"Not bad, eh, Easy? Maybe Mrs. Cantella could find a new husband?" His smile was conspiratorial.

"Probably won't be no better than the last nine men she had."

We both laughed. Then I started helping him. We moved clothes from one box to another while putting prices on them with little eight-sided paper tags and safety pins. For plain dresses we charged a dollar and for a fancy one we charged one seventy-five. All pants were sixty-five cents, and hats and handkerchiefs ran about a quarter.

"Shirley's a good girl," Chaim said after a while.

I nodded. "I guess so. Takes a generous woman to take in some drunk that she don't even know."

"Sometimes you have to drink."

"Yeah, I guess that's true too."

"You're a good man, Easy. I'm glad to have you in my daughter's house."

We moved boxes around for another few minutes in silence.

I was just beginning to think seriously about how I could stay out of jail without getting Chaim in trouble when we heard the scream. It sounded far off but you could tell that it was full of terror.

Chaim and I looked at each other and then I headed for the stairs. I was halfway to the second floor when Winona Fitzpatrick came at me. She was running down with her arms out so I couldn't avoid her. She was crying and yelling and one of her shoes was off.

"Winona!" I cried. "Winona!"

"Blooddead," she moaned and then she fell into my arms.

Winona weighed at least two hundred pounds. I did my best to slow her fall till we came to the first floor. Then I let her down as gently as I could, but I still had to put her on the floor.

"Dead," she said.

"Who?"

"Dead. Blood," she said.

I decided that Chaim would come and take care of her and so I sprinted up the stairs. When I got to the minister's apartment on the second floor I slowed a bit. I began to wonder, at that very moment, what was happening to me. I gazed at the plywood door and thought about the Texas swamplands southeast of Houston. I thought about how a man could lose himself in those swampy lands for years and nobody could find him. I knew things had to be bad if I was missing that hard country.

Reverend Towne was sprawled back on the couch. His pants were down around his ankles and his boxer shorts were just below his knees. His penis was still half erect and I'm sure the pious men and women of the congregation would have been surprised that it was so small. You think of a Baptist minister as being a virile man, but I'd seen little boys that had more than him.

Another strange thing was the color of his skin. Most black men's skin gets darker in the genital area, but his was lighter, some strange quirk in his lineage.

The blood on his white shirt and his stunned expression told me that he was dead. I would have run to him to check it out but my way was blocked by the woman doubled over her own lap, sitting on her heels, at his feet. There was blood at the back of her head.

Nothing seemed to be out of place other than the two corpses. It was a modern apartment, there were no walls separating the rooms. The pink kitchen to the left had an electric range and a window that looked out the front of the church. On the right the bedroom, all made up and neat, sported African masks, shields, and tapestries on the far wall. A bright red blanket lay at the foot of the bed. The center of the apartment had a floor that was lower than the rooms that flanked it.

The center room was carpeted in white. The dead man reclined on a white leather couch. Towne's empty gaze lay on the modern fireplace that was shielded by a golden screen.

Everything was clean and made up except in a corner by the door; there was a pile of vomit. The murderer had eaten cole slaw and meatloaf for lunch. The strong smell of alcohol emanated from that corner.

When I looked out of the kitchen window I saw the stairs where

I'd stood not fifteen minutes before; I remembered the crackle and sigh. I wondered if it could have been a volley of small-caliber shots. Could have been.

I went back to the lovers, if that's what you could call them. It looked more like the convenience that we GIs enjoyed across Europe when there wasn't much time or money. She was still fully dressed, she even wore her shoes. It was the same woman I had seen him with in the basement.

Then I wondered who would be investigating the case. Magnolia Street wasn't that far away.

While I considered the telephone and the east Texas swamps, Chaim entered.

"What's this?" he stammered.

"Dead."

"Who?" he asked back. In real life you don't need very much language.

"I dunno, man. Winona was comin' down an' yellin' an' here they was."

"She kill them?"

"You wanna call the police, Chaim?"

"Where?" he asked. I was happy that he didn't ask why.

I pointed out the phone and looked around while he dialed. When he'd finished talking to the police dispatcher I asked him if he'd seen anything strange downstairs. He said no. Then I asked if he'd seen anyone other than me. He said that he saw one of the younger deacons, Robert Williams, earlier in the day.

The uniformed police came in around ten minutes. They called in the same report that Chaim had made, then they separated us and began asking questions.

Winona was led upstairs. She sat on the floor just outside the apartment crying and mumbling about blood.

My cop asked if Winona had known the minister. I said that I didn't know what their relationship was, and he got suspicious.

"You don't know her? Then how do you know her name?"

"I know her to say hello, I just don't know if she knew the minister. I mean, she's on the church council, so she knew him, but I don't know what they had to do with each other."

"How long was she up there with him?"

"Beats me."

He started pacing and clenching his fists. He was a fat man with a red face and bright blue eyes. He was taller than I was, and he had a habit of talking to himself.

"He knows her name," he said. "But after that he's stupid."

I said, "I was down in the basement," but he didn't even hear it.

He went, "Something wrong with that. Yes, something wrong."

Then he asked me, "You know where she lives?"

"No."

That started him pacing again.

"Boy's fooling around here, hiding something. Yeah, hiding something."

It was said that there were still crocodiles deep in the Texas swamps. I would have preferred a cuddly reptile right then.

"Fine," someone said from the door.

The crazy policeman turned as if someone had called him. It was Andrew Reedy.

"What's happening here?" Reedy asked.

"Two spooks blasted and salt-and-pepper here acting like it was God done it. Girl out in the hall found them."

Quinten Naylor came in behind Reedy. I don't know if he heard what the crazy cop had said but you could see that there was no love lost between the two. They didn't even acknowledge each other.

"Well, well, well," Reedy was saying. "Here you are again, Mr. Rawlins. Were they evicting these two?"

"That's the minister of the church on the couch. I don't know the girl."

I could see the mood shift in Reedy's face. A dead minister was a political problem, no matter what color he was.

"And why were you here?"

"Just workin' downstairs, that's all."

"Working?" Naylor said. "People always turn up dead when you're working?"

"No, sir."

"Did you know the minister?"

"To speak to, that's all."

"You a member of this church?"

"Yes, sir."

Naylor turned his head to the uniforms.

"Cover them up," he said. "Don't you guys know procedure?"

The fat cop made like he was going to go at Naylor but Reedy grabbed him by the arm and whispered to him. Then the uniforms left with the fat cop swaggering through the door.

On the way out the fat one said to Naylor, "Don't worry, son, lotsa killin's on nigger patrol. Wait till you see how the nigger bitches cut up on each other." Then he was gone.

"I'll kill that son of a bitch," Naylor said.

Reedy didn't say anything. He'd gone up to the bedroom and gotten sheets to cover the dead.

"What about you?" Naylor asked Chaim.

"I am Wenzler, officer. Easy and I are working in the basement and we hear the screams. He runs up, I come in, and poor Dr. Towne was here, and the girl. It's terrible."

"Mr. Rawlins work for you?"

"Together," Chaim said. "We do charity for the church."

"And you were down there when you heard the screams?"

"Yes."

"What about shots?"

"No shots, just screams. Weak little screams like she was far away, in a hole."

"Let's take 'em all down and get statements, Quint," Reedy said. "I'll call for more uniforms and we'll take 'em. I'll call the ambulance and the coroner, too."

• 23 •

I hadn't been to the Seventy-seventh Street station for *questioning* in many years. It looked older in the fifties but it smelled the same. A sour odor that wasn't anything exactly. It wasn't living and it wasn't dead, it wasn't food and it wasn't excrement. It wasn't anything I knew, but it was wrong, as wrong as the smells in Poinsettia's apartment.

The last time I was taken there I had been under arrest and the police put me in a raw-walled room that was made for questioning prisoners. The kind of questioning that was punctuated by fists and shoes. This time, though, they sat me at a desk with Quinten Naylor. He had a blue-and-white form in front of him and he asked me questions.

"Name?"

"Ezekiel Porterhouse Rawlins," I answered.

"Date of birth."

"Let's see now," I said. "That would be November third, nineteen hundred and twenty."

"Height."

"Close to six feet, almost six-one."

"Weight."

"One eighty-five, except at Christmas. Then I'm about one ninety."

He asked more questions like that and I answered freely. I trusted a Negro, I don't know why. I'd been beaten, robbed, shot at, and generally mistreated by more colored brothers than I'd ever been by whites, but I trusted a black man before I'd even think about a white one. That's just the way things were for me.

"Okay, Ezekiel, tell me about Poinsettia, Reverend Towne, and that woman."

"They all dead, man. Dead as mackerel."

"Who killed them?"

He had an educated way of talking. I could have talked like him if I'd wanted to, but I never did like it when a man stopped using the language of his upbringing. If you were to talk like a white man you might forget who you were.

"I'ont know, man. Poinsettia kilt herself, right?"

"Autopsy report on her will be in this evening. You got something to say about it now?"

"They ain't got to that yet?" I was really surprised.

"The coroner's working a little hard these days, Mr. Rawlins. There was that bus accident on San Remo Street and the fire in Santa Monica. Up until now we were only half sure that this was even a case," Quinten said. "He's been butt-high in corpses, but your turn is coming up."

"I don't know nuthin', man. I know the minister and the girl was murdered 'cause I seen the blood. I'ont know who killed 'em an' if I get my way I ain't gonna know. Murder ain't got nuthin' t'do wit' me."

"That's not how I hear it."

"How's that?"

"I hear that there were quite a few murders that you were intimate with a few years ago. Your testimony put away one of the killers."

"That's right! Not me." I pointed at my chest. "Somebody else did a killin' an' I told the law. If I knew today I'd tell you now. But I was dumb-assed in the basement, movin' some clothes, when I heard Winona yell. I went up to help but I could see that they was beyond what I could do."

"You think Winona did it?"

"Beats me."

"You see anybody else around?"

"No," I said. Chaim had mentioned Robert Williams, but I hadn't seen him.

"Nobody?"

"I seen Chaim, an' Chaim seen me. That's it."

"Where were you before you got to work?"

"I was at breakfast, with a friend'a mines."

"Who was that?"

"Her name was Shirley."

"Shirley what?"

"I don't know the girl's last name but I know where she lives."

"How long were you at the church before you went down to the basement?"

"I went right down."

So we started from the top again. And again.

One time he asked me if I heard the shots.

"Shots?"

"Yeah," he answered gruffly. "Shots."

"They were shot?"

"What did you think?"

"I'ont know, man, they coulda been stabbed fo' all I know."

That was it for officer Naylor. He got up and left in disgust. A few minutes later he returned and told me I could go. Chaim and Winona had been gone for hours. The police didn't suspect them. Winona was too hysterical to be faking it, and nobody knew that Chaim was part of the Red Terror.

I went out on the street and caught a bus down Central to the church, then I drove home. Nothing seemed quite right. Everything was off. It was strange enough that so much had happened. But now people were dying and still it didn't make sense.

As if to prove my fears, Mouse was on my swinging sofa on the front porch, drinking whiskey. I could smell him from ten feet away.

He was usually a natty dresser. He wore silk and cashmere as another man might wear cotton. Women dressed him and then took him out to show the world what they had.

He told me once that a woman had the pockets in his pants taken out and replaced them with satin so that she could stroke him under the table, or at a show, the way she did at home.

But it wasn't the smooth dresser I saw on my porch. He hadn't shaved in days, and Mouse had that kind of sparse beard that looked ratty on a man. His clothes were soiled, his disposition was taciturn. And he was drunk. Not the one-night kind of drunk but a drunk that you can only get from days of booze.

"Hiya, Easy."

"Mouse."

I sat down next to him and all of a sudden I had the feeling that we were young men again, as if we'd never left Texas. I guess that's what I was hoping for, simpler times.

"I ain't got my gun, man," Mouse said.

"No?"

"Naw."

"How come?"

"Might kill somebody, Easy. Somebody I don't wanna kill."

"Whas wrong wit' you, Ray? You sick?"

He laughed, hunching forward as if he were having a seizure.

"Yeah," he said. "Sick. Sick t' death of all this pain."

"What pain is that?"

He looked into my eyes with a steely gray gaze. "You seen my boy?"

"Yeah, when Etta come she brought him."

"He's a beautiful boy, ain't he?"

I nodded.

"He got big feet and a big mouf. Shit, that's all you need in this world. That's all you need."

Mouse stopped talking, so I said, "He's a great boy. Strong, and he's smart too."

"He's the devil hisself," Mouse whispered to his left arm.

"What's that you said?"

"Satan. Evil angel'a hell. You could tell the way his eyebrows goes up, makin' like horns."

"LaMarque kinda mischievous, but he ain't bad, Raymond."

"Satan in hell. Black cats and voodoo curse. You 'member Mama Jo?"

"Yeah."

I'd never forget her.

Mouse had conned me into driving him, in a stolen car, to a small bayou town in eastern Texas called Pariah. We were barely in our twenties but Mouse's true nature was already fully developed. He wanted a dowry his mother had promised him before she died. He was to marry EttaMae and he said, "I will get that money or daddyReese will be dead." Reese was Mouse's stepfather.

But before we ever got to Pariah, Mouse had me drive to a place out in the middle of the swamplands. There we came to a house hidden on all sides by pear trees that doubled as pillars. And in that house lived the country witch, Mama Jo. She was a six-foot-six witch who lived by her wits out beyond the laws of normal men. She was twenty years older than I, and I was barely twenty. But she put a spell on me when we stayed with her for a night. Mouse was out planning the murder and Mama Jo had me by the hair. I was screaming love for her and talking out of my head. I remembered the smell of her breath: sweet chili and garlic, bitter wine and stale tobacco.

"She always told me," Mouse said, "that sometimes evil come down on ya when you live bad. Evil come out in your chirren if you don't pay fo' what you done."

"LaMarque ain't like that, Ray."

"How you know?" he shouted, rearing up belligerently. "That boy done give me the eye, Easy. He tole me hisself that he hates me. He tole me hisself that he wisht I was dead. Now tell me it don't take a evil son to make that kinda wish on his own daddy."

I was thinking about Etta. I was trying to figure out how I thought I could get away with being her lover and Mouse's friend too.

"He don't hate you, Ray. He just a boy an' he mad that you an' Etta cain't be together."

"Devil outta hell," he whispered again. Then he said, "I did what a daddy's s'posed, Ease, I mean, I ain't ever seen my own daddy, an' you know I killed Reese."

Mouse had finally murdered his stepfather despite my attempts to stop him.

"Yeah," Mouse continued. "Kilt 'im dead. But you know him an' his son Navrochet beat me reg'lar an' laughed on it too."

Mouse had also killed his stepbrother, Navrochet.

"LaMarque don't think'a you like that, Ray," I said.

"Yes he do. Yes he do. An' you know I ain't given him no reason, man. You know I loved that boy an' I done right by him." There were tears streaming down his face. "You know sometimes I pick him up an' take 'im down t' Zelda's big-timin' house. The ho's there love it when you bring a boy. They jus' fuss over him an' give 'im chocolates. An' I shows 'im how t'gamble an' dance. But you know he start t'actin' shy an' scared an' shit. Embarrass me in front'a Zelda herself.

"But you know he always runnin' after me t'go t'the bafroom at the same time." Mouse smiled then. "He look at Dick like he ain't never seen nuthin' that big. Then, right after the las' time we went, he tole me that he don't wanna go nowhere wit' me no mo'. He won't even talk t' me an' if I try an' make 'im he scream like a demon, right out there in the middle'a the street just like I was a bad man, like Reese."

Before Mouse got the drop on Reese the old farmer had us on the run through the swamp. Raymond had killed one of his hunting dogs, but he had two more and they were chasing us down through the trees. We finally escaped, but by then it was nightfall and we had to stay outside for the night. I had the grippe and Mouse curled around me like a momma cat, keeping me warm through the night. I might have died if he hadn't cared for me.

I reached out my hands and held him by the forearms while he cried. It was loud and embarrassing but I didn't let go.

"I'm sorry, Raymond," I said after he stopped. He looked up at me, his eyes were red and his nose was running.

"I love that boy, Easy."

"He loves you too, man. That's your son, your blood. He loves you."

"Then why he act like that?"

"He just a li'l boy, that's all. You go down wit' all them wild folks you know an' he get so scared an' worked up that he wanna get outta there. He cain't stand it."

"Why don't he tell me that? I take 'im fishin'."

"He prob'ly don't know, man. You know kids don't really think, 'cept 'bout what feel good, and what don't."

Mouse sat back and stared at me as if I had just pulled a rabbit out of my ear. I could see the change come about in him. He sat up a little straighter, his eyes cleared.

I said, "Why don't you come on in? You get a shower and a good night's sleep. I'll talk wit' LaMarque the next time I'm over there."

I made the call while Mouse was in the shower.

"How's it going, Mr. Rawlins?" Special Agent Craxton asked.

"Minister and his girlfriend got killed."

"What?"

I told him about the murders. He asked all sorts of questions about the room.

Finally he said, "Sounds like a professional job."

"Could just be a good shot."

"Then why wasn't anything moved around, messed up?"

"She was down on his peter, man, maybe her husband found 'em. Maybe Winona found 'em and she thought Towne was hers."

"Maybe. Hear me," he said. "I'll look into things on my end. Meanwhile, you find out what you can about the minister. Who has he been seeing, what kind of political connections does he have?"

Craxton was the boss, so I said, "Okay."

Raymond came out of the shower with a towel around his hips and a smile on his face.

"You look better," I said.

"And you look like you just swallowed a pig. What's wrong, Easy?"

"You might as well ask what's right."

"You gonna talk to LaMarque fo' me?"

"Soon as I can, man."

He laughed like a small boy, younger even than his son.

"Then tell me what's wrong."

"I owe a man some money an' he holds the deed t'my houses. He want me to find some stuff on some men work down at First African."

I lied to Mouse because I was afraid that if I told him the truth he might decide to do me a Louisiana kind of favor, like burning down the IRS office, records and all.

"Yeah?"

"So then the minister, Reverend Towne, and some girl gets killed and I was there when it happened. And another man work for the first man's company still wants my houses and a girl live in one'a my places hung herself on account of I wanted t'throw her out. Or maybe she was murdered."

"You talk wit' the boy an' I kill the men, Easy."

"Naw, man. They work fo' big companies. You know, cut off one an' two take his place."

"White men?"

"Yeah."

"You think about it, man. If you want sumpin' just call me."

He dressed in the bathroom and left soon afterwards. He didn't stay, because his good clothes were at Dupree's and he was ready to look good again.

After he'd gone I went to my bed and drank three glasses of whiskey too fast. I passed out thinking that I should call EttaMae.

• 24 •

The fat ambulance attendant stood awkwardly on a high kitchen chair, a butcher's knife in his hand. He was sawing at the rope Poinsettia hung from. The sound was loud, like two men hacking at a tree. Finally she fell to the floor. The dead weight hit with a terrible impact. Her body had become soft and so punky that one of her arms and her head flew off. But it was the sound as she hit the floor that was the worst. The floorboards started rattling and the walls shook. The whole house vibrated with the power of an earthquake.

When I started awake it was barely dawn. The sky out my window had that weak blue of the early sun, but the racket hadn't stopped. For a moment I thought that I was really in an earthquake. But then I realized that it was someone knocking at the door.

When that someone shouted, "Police!" I thought that I would rather it be a natural disaster.

"Hold on!" I shouted back. I hauled on some slacks and a T-shirt and stepped into a beat-up pair of slippers.

When I opened the door Naylor and Reedy each took hold of an arm.

"You're under arrest," Naylor said, then he spun me around and put on the handcuffs.

I wasn't surprised, so I didn't say anything. If somebody had taken me out behind the house and put a bullet in my head I wouldn't have been surprised. There was nothing I could do, so I just hung my head and hoped I could ride out the storm.

I rode it out to the Seventy-seventh Street station. There they put me in a small room with the handcuffs still on. After a while the fat policeman with the red face, Officer Fine, came in to keep me company.

I asked him, "Am I under arrest?"

He showed me a mouth full of bad teeth.

"Well if I am I should be allowed a call, right?"

That didn't even get him to smile.

After a short while Reedy came in and asked the fat man to sit in the hall. He looked at me with sad green eyes and said, "Do you want to confess, Mr. Rawlins?"

"I wanna make a call is all."

Naylor came in then. They pulled up chairs on either side of me.

"I don't have much patience with murderers, Mr. Rawlins, especially when those murderers have killed a woman. A Negro woman at that," Naylor said. "So I want to know what happened or Reedy and I are going to go for coffee and we're going to leave Fine to ask the questions."

"That's mighty white'a you, brother," I grinned.

He slapped my face, not too hard though. I got the feeling that Quinten Naylor was trying to save me from real injury.

"Wanna get Fine?" Reedy asked while stifling a yawn.

"Who killed the minister and the girl?" Naylor asked me.

"I'ont know, man, I'ont know."

"Who killed Poinsettia Jackson?"

"She killed herself, right?"

They both were looking at me hard.

"I found 'er hangin' there, thas it, hangin'. I ain't killed nobody."

"But somebody hit her on the head, Easy. They knocked her unconscious and hung her from the light fixture," Naylor said. "Then they knocked the chair over to make it look like she'd used it to hang herself, but the chair was too far from the body, that's how we got onto them. They murdered her, Easy. Now do you know why anybody would want to do that?"

Philadelphia! It came to me just that fast. Quinten was an eastern Negro from Philadelphia, I'd've bet anything.

"Mr. Rawlins," Reedy said.

"How should I know?"

"Maybe you know someone who had a motive, a reason," Reedy continued. Naylor sat back and stared.

"Why anybody wanna kill a sick girl?"

"Maybe to get her ass outta that apartment."

"How should I know? Why don't you ask the owner?"

"I'm asking," Reedy said. He was looking me in the eye.

I pretended that I was alone on a raft in a rough sea. The policemen were sharks cruising my craft. I was safe for the moment, but I was taking on water.

"I wanna lawyer, I wanna make some calls."

"Why'd you lie to us, man?" Naylor asked. He sounded embarrassed, as if my little trick made him look bad at the station.

"Just gimme a phone, alright?"

"We'll give you Officer Fine," Reedy said.

"Send the mothahfuckah in then," the voice in my head said. "Let's see us some blood."

I didn't say a word but stared bullets at the cops instead. I knew how to take a beating. My old man used to take me out behind the house many a time before he finally left for good. Sometimes, when I was still a boy, I missed his whipping stick.

Reedy said, "Shit!" and walked out. Officer Fine replaced him by the door.

Naylor leaned close to me and said, "This could turn ugly, Ezekiel. I can't protect you if you don't give."

"Cut that shit out, man. You one'a them. You dress like them an' you talk like them too."

"Detective Reedy wants you in the hall, Naylor," Fine said. He was almost polite.

"Let me get a call or two, man," I hissed at Naylor. "You wanna save my ass, gimme some rights."

I held my breath while the black cop thought. Fine would have liked to kill me, I could tell that by the way he smelled.

"Come on," Naylor finally said.

"Hey wha . . ." Fine started to say, but Quinten stood up to him, and Quinten Naylor looked to be made from bricks.

"He's going to make a call. That's his right," Naylor said.

Naylor unlocked my handcuffs and led me down the hall toward a small area that was partitioned off by three frosted glass walls. Each one was about six feet high. There was a phone on a wooden stool in the cubicle.

"There you go," Naylor said to me, then he stood back to show me some privacy. Reedy came down with Fine and the three men started to haggle. I was a dead longhorn and those men were vultures, every one of them.

I dialed Mofass' office. No answer.

I dialed the boarding house he lived in. On the third ring Hilda Bark, the owner's daughter, answered. "Yeah?"

"Mofass there?"

"He's gone."

"Gone where?"

"Gone. Don't you understand English?" she scolded me the way her mother must have scolded her. "He left."

"You mean he moved out?"

"Uh-huh," she grunted and then she hung up.

The men were still haggling over my bones, so I quickly dialed Craxton's number.

"FBI," a bright male voice said.

"Yeah, yeah, right. Can I talk to Agent Craxton?"

"Agent Craxton is in the field today. He'll be back tomorrow. Would you like to leave a message?"

"Is he gonna call in?"

"Hard to say, sir. Agent Craxton is a field agent. He goes where he wants to and calls when he feels like it."

"Please tell him that this is Ezekiel Rawlins calling from the Seventy-seventh Street police station. Tell him that I need to see him down here right away."

"What's the nature of your business?"

"Just tell 'im, man."

He hung up on me too.

The next place I dialed was First African Day School. The phone was ringing when Fine came up and grabbed me by the shoulder.

"Nobody else was home," I told him.

"Okay," he smiled. He'd wait until I was finished with this call and then he'd see how loud I could scream.

"Hello?" a voice I didn't recognize said.

"May I speak to Odell Jones, please?"

There was a long wait but Odell finally came on the line.

"Yes?"

"Odell?"

"Easy?"

"Man, I'm in trouble."

"That's how you was born, man. Born to trouble an' bringin' everybody else down wit' you."

"They got me in jail, Odell."

"That's where criminals belong, Easy, in jail." He even raised his voice!

"Listen, man, I ain't had nuthin' t' do wit' Towne. It wasn't me, not at all."

"If it wasn't you then tell me this," he said. "If you didn't go out there to the church in the first place would he be dead now?"

It was a good question. I didn't have an answer.

"So what you want?" he asked curtly.

"Come get me outta here, man."

"How'm I gonna do that? I ain't got no money. All I got is God."

"Odell," I pleaded.

"Call on someone else, Easy Rawlins, this well is dry."

Three strikes and Fine took me by the arm.

"I'm off duty now, Mr. Rawlins," Quinten Naylor said. "Officer Fine will continue your interrogation."

• 25 •

Officer Fine was a patient man. Patient and delicate. He and his partner, a wan-faced rookie called Gabor, taught me little secrets like how far an arm can be twisted before it will break.

"All you gotta do is take your time," Fine said to no one in particular, as he twisted my right hand toward the base of my skull. "I could get these here fingers over the head and into the mouth and he'd probably bite 'em off t' stop the hurt."

"Don't give in, Easy!" the voice screamed in my head.

"Why'd you kill her?" Gabor asked me. I wanted to hit him but my feet and my left hand were manacled to the chair.

We'd been playing the game for over an hour. I'd been slapped, kicked, beaten with a rolled-up magazine, and twisted like a licorice stick.

When I grimaced from the arm twisting I felt dry blood crack across my cheek.

That nearly broke me. I was almost ready to confess, confess to anything they'd say. But the voice kept screaming for me.

The door opened and a tall silver-haired man walked in. I was grateful for the respite, but when Fine released me it felt as if he'd torn the arm from its socket.

I moaned, humiliated and in pain as I gazed at those shiny black shoes.

"Captain," Gabor said.

Then I saw a second pair of shoes that were as bright as polished onyx.

"This is what you call questioning, John?" Special Agent Craxton asked.

"It's a hard case, uh, Agent Craxton," the silver-haired man answered. Then he said to Fine, "Agent Craxton here is with the FBI. He needs Mr. Rawlins for a case he's working on."

"What about the murders?" Fine asked.

"Unchain him and apologize or I tear off your prick and shove it down your throat," Craxton said simply, almost sweetly.

Fine didn't like that, he brought his fists up to his chest and pushed his body forward a little, but when he peered into Craxton's eyes he backed down. He even unlocked my manacles, but he didn't apologize and he looked defiant, like a child angered at his father.

Craxton just smiled. The spaces between his teeth made him look like an alligator that had evolved to human form.

"Send me this officer's file, John."

"Apologize, Charlie," Captain John said.

The fat cop who had caused me so much pain said, "I'm sorry." And even though I was so hurt, that sounded good to me. His humiliation was like sweet, cold ice cream on hot apple pie.

I rubbed the dried blood from my face and said, "Fuck you, mothahfuckah. Fuck you twice."

It wasn't smart but I never imagined that I'd live to be an old man.

Agent Craxton was with two men who looked like real FBI. They wore dark suits and ties with white shirts and short-brimmed hats. They had black shoes and white socks and small bulges on the left side of their bulky jackets. They were cleanshaven and silent as stones.

They were also the same men that I saw Shirley talking to in front of her house.

The twins got in the front seat of a black Pontiac. Craxton and I got in behind. We headed out into the street, turning every three blocks or so. I don't think we had a destination; at least not a place we were going to.

"They think you killed all of them, Easy. Killed the girl at your place and killed the minister too."

"Yeah, I know."

"Did you?"

"Did I what?"

"Kill your tenant?"

"What for? Why I wanna kill her?"

"You tell me. She was your tenant. She wasn't paying your rent."

"Ain't nuthin' to tell. I found Poinsettia dead and I found the minister too. Bad luck, that's all."

"I can understand why they suspect you, though. If I hadn't sent you into that church myself I'd think it pretty strange."

"Yeah, that's how things happen—strange. I seen all kindsa things happen you wouldn't believe."

"Somebody's on to you, Mr. Rawlins. Somebody knows you're working with us."

"Why you say that?"

"Because this murder in the church was professional. Either they hired it out or one of the Russians did it themselves."

"Did? You mean shot them? Why would anybody wanna come kill Towne?"

"The reverend must've been involved. They thought they could cover their tracks by killing him."

"Why not just kill me?"

"Kill a weed at its root, that's what they do. He could have been their prize pupil but they cut him short if they think he'd jeopardize even one thing."

I decided to take a chance with Craxton.

"Man, they gotta be sumpin' you ain't tellin' me."

He paused, looking at me for a few moments before speaking.

"Why do you say that?"

"Well, I been on Wenzler for some days now an' I cain't see where he's any big thing. So I gotta wonder why you wanna get me out of a fed'ral charge just to spy on some small-time union guy. Then, on top'a that, this man gets himself killed an' you sure it's got somethin' t'do with what I'm doin'. Like I said—sumpin' don't add up."

Craxton leaned back against the window and began to outline his jaw with a hairy index finger. He started from the center of his chin and worked his way up the left side of his face. As his finger progressed a smile began to form. It was a full-fledged grin by the time he'd reached the earlobe.

"You're a smart one, eh, Rawlins?"

"Yeah," I said. "So smart that I'm here with you worryin' 'bout my liberty, my money, and my life. If I was any smarter I wouldn't even have to breathe."

"Wenzler's got something," Craxton said.

"Yeah? What's that?"

"You don't really need to now that, Easy. All you need to know is that we're playing for high stakes here. We're playing for keeps."

"You sayin' I could get killed?"

"That's right."

"So why the fuck didn't you say that before?" One of the robots in the front seat cocked his head a little. But I didn't let that bother me. "Here you lettin' me walk around like everything is goin' on accordin' t'plan an' really they's people drawin' a bead on me."

Craxton wasn't bothered by me, though.

"You want to go to prison, Easy?" he asked. "Just say the word and we can hand you back to Agent Lawrence."

"Listen," I said. "If you know what it is that Wenzler has got why don't you just take him?"

"We have, Easy. We arrested him and interrogated him. But he gave us nothing and we haven't got any proof. We don't have a fiber of evidence. I can't tell you what it is that we think he has but I can tell you that it's something important. I can tell you that it would hurt America to let it slip through our fingers."

"So you ain't gonna tell me what it is I'm lookin' for?"

"It's better if you don't know, Easy. Believe me, you don't want to know."

"Okay then, tell me this," I said. "Does whatever this is have to do with Andre Lavender?"

"I can tell you that if you know where Lavender is you should tell us. This isn't about race, Easy, it's about your country."

"So I should go out there with a bull's-eye on my back 'cause you say so?"

"You can pull out anytime."

He knew the chances of me doing that. "So you want me to stay on Wenzler?"

"That's right. And now you have the knowledge that Towne was somehow linked. We already have his involvement with the antiwar people. You can work from his relationship with Wenzler. For all we know Wenzler is the one who killed him."

Chaim had been a killer in Poland. The war wasn't so far back that a good soldier would forget his trade.

"What about Poinsettia? You think the Russians killed her?"

He gave me a hard look then.

"You could have killed her, or maybe somebody else did. I don't know and I don't care, because I don't have that job."

"You better believe those cops care."

Craxton shifted in his seat and gazed out the window.

"When this is over I'll explain why you were at the church," he said, leaning so close to the glass that steam clouded his already dim reflection. "I'll tell them that you're a hero. If they have no physical evidence you did the girl, then . . ." He hunched his shoulders and turned from the window to look at me. I felt a trickle of blood come down the side of my face.

"Ever been out in a cold foxhole, Ezekiel?"

"More times than I'd like t' remember."

"It's cold and alone out there, but that sure makes coming home sweet."

I didn't say anything, but I could have said, "Amen to that."

"Yeah," he continued. "Pain makes men out of scared little boys."

The sun was a big red ball just over the city. The underbellies of the clouds over our heads were long black hanging things, like stalactites in a great cave, but above those clouds was a bright orange that was almost religious it was so warm. I could almost hear the church organs.

"Yeah, Ezekiel, we have a real job to do. And it might get kind of painful."

I couldn't twitch my baby finger without a jolt going through my arm, but I asked, "How you figure?"

"We got to get Wenzler. He's a tough man and he's in with people worse than that. I know that you're taking a chance, but we need that to get this job done."

"What if I do all this you say an' I still don't find nuthin'?"

"If I don't get what I want, Mr. Rawlins, then my job isn't worth a cent. If I can't make this case you'll be shit out of luck along with me."

"And if you do find it?"

"Then I help you, Easy. Sink or swim."

"I have your word, Mr. Craxton?"

Instead of answering me he asked, "Home?"

"Yeah."

On the ride all he talked about was how he was going to buy some bonita, cut the fish in chunks, scald it, and then marinate it in a vinegar and soya sauce. It was a dish he'd learned to make while on duty in Japan.

"Nips know how to do fish," he said.

• 26 •

"What you thinkin' 'bout, Easy?" Etta asked.

We were laying back in her bed. I had my hands together behind my head and she was running her fingers along my erection, under the covers. I felt strange. It was one of those feelings that doesn't quite make sense. My body was excited but my mind was calm and wondering about the next move I should make. If Etta hadn't kept her fingers going like that I would have been nervous, unable to think about anything.

I came to her house in the evening, after LaMarque had gone to bed. She bathed me and then I loved her, again and again until it was close to sunrise. I don't think there was much pleasure in it for her, except maybe the pleasure of helping me dull the fear and pain I felt.

"'Bout them people. 'Bout how they dead but still I gotta worry 'bout 'em. That's what makes us different from the animals."

"How's that?" she whispered and, at the same time, she gave me a little squeeze.

"If a dog see sumpin' dead he just roll around on the corpse a few times an' move on, huntin'. But I find a dead man an' it's like he's alive, followin' me around an' pointin' his finger at me."

"What you gonna do, baby?"

"FBI man thinks Reverend Towne was mixed up in somethin'. He thinks that Towne was messed up wit' communists."

"What com'unists?"

"Uh, that feels good," I said. "The Jew I been workin' for, communist."

"What they gotta do wit' Towne?"

She sat up a little.

I said, "Put your hand back, Etta, put it back."

She grinned at me and settled back against my chest.

"That's why the government got me outta jail. They want the Jew," I said, clearheaded again.

"So? Let them do it. You ain't gotta go out an' do they job."

"Yeah," I said. Then I sat back and smiled because so much pleasure could come after pain.

"Mofass is gone," I said after a while.

"Gone where?"

"Nobody knows."

"Outta his house?"

"Uh-huh. He left some kinda half-assed note at the office. Said his mother was sick down in New Orleans and he was going to care for her. He let his room go too. That's some strange shit."

"Ain't nuthin' wrong wit' that."

"I guess. But I cain't see Mofass runnin' out without a word."

"People change when it comes t'family."

"But that's just it, Mofass never even liked his momma."

"You just cain't tell, Easy, blood is strong."

I knew she was right about that. I loved my father more than life even though he abandoned me when I was eight years old.

"But you know it is funny," Etta said.

"What?"

"You know that boy tried to beat up on you after church?"

"Willie Sacks?"

"Uh-huh. His momma, Paulette, come by here today."

"Why's that?"

"I asked her 'cause I wanted her to know how Willie had come after you. I told her but she already knew it. She said Willie had gone bad after he met Poinsettia."

"Bad how?"

"She had 'im runnin' after her an' spendin' all his money. Willie used t'take his money home. He ain't got no father an' Paulette relied on him t'pay the rent."

"Boys grow up, Etta. LaMarque do the same thing when some girl get him to feelin' like this." I touched her hand.

"But you know Willie never made enough an' Mofass was payin' fo' that girl too."

"What?"

"Mofass been payin' her rent the last year. Poinsettia told Willie 'bout it. She said how sometimes she had to go out with him but that they never did any more than kiss."

"No lie?" I never thought Mofass chased the ladies.

"But she also said how Mofass had her go out with other men sometimes."

"You mean like he was her pimp?"

"I don't know, Easy. I just know what Paulette said. Now you know she heard it from her son an' he got it from Poinsettia. Willie broke up with her when he found out. At least that's what Paulette thought. But after her accident she started callin' again. Maybe Mofass did somethin' to that girl."

"I don't know," I said. "But I can't see it. What could she have on him to make him wanna do that?"

"You'll find out."

"What makes you think so?"

"I just know it, that's all. You're a smart man, and you care too."

"Yeah?"

"Uh-huh."

She tossed back the blankets so that I could see her handiwork. She watched it too.

"I want some more, baby." She said it loudly and bold as if she were announcing to an audience.

I knew she didn't but I asked, "You do?"

"Yeah." It was almost a growl in my ear.

"Where?"

And she guided me. And I turned into a rutting pig again, trying to rut myself to safety.

I woke up with a start. There was a sound somewhere in the apartment. I worried that Mouse was in the other room with his revolver but at the same moment I looked at EttaMae. I looked at her feeling how spent I was and I realized that I wanted her more than just for sex. That was new to me. Usually sex was the first and last thing with me, but I wanted her with the same ardor when I was all used up.

I snaked out of bed and slithered into my pants. There was no light from outside or from the other room. I eased the door open and saw him sitting in the living room. He was swinging his head back and forth and kicking the heels of his feet against the couch.

"LaMarque!"

"Hi, Unca Easy," he said, looking around me to the room I came from.

"What you doin' up?"

"You sleep wit' my momma?"

"Yeah." I couldn't think of anything else to say. I could only hope that he would never repeat it to Mouse. I would have liked to ask him to keep it quiet, but it was a sin, I thought, to make a child lie.

"Oh."

"Why you up?" I asked again.

"Dreams."

"What kinda dreams?"

"'Bout a big ole monster wit' a hunert eyes."

"Yeah? He chase you?"

"Uh-uh. He ax me if I wanna ride an' then he take me flyin' so high an' then he start fallin' like we gonna crash."

LaMarque's eyes opened wide with fear as he spoke.

"Then," he went on, "he stop jus' fo' we crash an' he laugh. An' I ax 'im t'let me go but he jus' keep on flyin' high an' scarin' me."

I sat next to him and let him crawl into my lap. He was panting at first.

I waited until he'd calmed down and then I asked, "Do you like it when your daddy takes you to Zelda's?"

"Uh-uh, it's smelly there."

"Smell like what?"

"Dookey an' vomick." He stuck out his tongue.

"You tell your momma 'bout what it smells like there?"

"Uh-uh, I never telled. I's ascared ta."

"How come?"

"I'ont know."

"You think that they might fight if you told?"

"Uh-huh, yeah."

He'd grabbed a fistful of the fabric of my pants and wrung it.

"You know if you told your daddy that you didn't wanna go there no more he wouldn't take you."

"Yeah he would. He like to be gamblin' an' gettin' pussy."

When LaMarque said the last word he ducked down as if I might hit him.

"No, honey," I said and I patted his head. "Your daddy wanna see you more than them folks. He wants to play ball wit' you, an' watch TV too."

He didn't say anything to that, so we just sat for a while. He was wringing my pants hard enough to pinch me.

"Your daddy gonna come visit you an' Etta in a coupla days," I said after a long while.

"When?"

"Prob'ly day after tomorrow, I bet."

"He gonna bring me a present?"

"I bet he does."

"Are you gonna be in my momma's bed?"

I laughed and hugged him to my chest.

"No," I said. "I got work to do."

We sat there and watched the sun come up. Then we both fell

asleep. I dreamed about Poinsettia again. The flesh was coming off her. She was deteriorating in my dreams from one night to the next; soon she'd just be bones.

I awoke maybe half an hour after we'd gone to sleep. LaMarque was snoring. I carried him to his room and then I looked in on Etta. She was in the same position, one powerful hand thrown up next to her beautiful, satin-brown face. I still wanted her the way I had for so many years, but for the first time in my life I considered marriage.

I left a note in the kitchen telling Etta that Mouse would be by to visit his son in a couple of days. I told her that everything was fine. I signed it, "I love you."

• 27 •

From EttaMae's I went over to Mercedes Bark's house on Bell Street. Bell was a short block of large houses with brick fences and elaborate flower gardens. During Christmas everyone on Bell put out thousands of colored lights around their trees and bushes and along the frames of their houses. People lined up in their cars to see that street for three weeks either side of Christmas Day. It was just that kind of a neighborhood. Everybody worked together to make it nice.

It was all good and well but there was a down side to the Bell Street crowd; they were snobs. They thought that their people and their block were too good for most of the rest of the Watts community. They frowned on a certain class of people buying houses on their street and they had a tendency to exclude other people from their barbecues and whatnot. They even encouraged their children to shun other kids they might have met at school or at the playground, because it was the Bell Street opinion that most of the black kids around there were too coarse and unsophisticated.

Mercedes had a three-story house in the middle of the block. The walls were painted white and the trim was a deep forest green. There were chairs and sofas set out along the porch and a bright green lawn surrounded by white and purple dahlias, white sweetheart roses, and dwarf lemon trees.

Mercedes' husband, Chapman, had been a dentist and could afford the upkeep on so large a domicile. But when he died the widow was quick to realize that his life insurance wasn't enough to maintain the family in the way they had lived before. So she took the money and turned the upper floors into a boarding house. She could accommodate as many as twelve tenants at one time.

The neighborhood association took Mercedes to court. They complained that their beautiful street would be ruined by the kind of riffraff that had to live in a single room for weekly rent. But the county court didn't agree and Mrs. Bark started her rooming house.

Mofass was her first and most long-lasting tenant. He didn't need a kitchen because he took his meals at the Fetters Real Estate Office. And he certainly didn't want to be bothered with leaky roofs and shaggy lawns after doing that kind of work all day.

I got to the Bell Street Boardinghouse at about nine-thirty that morning. I knew that Mrs. Bark was sitting in a stuffed chair just inside the front door but I couldn't see her. She was hidden in the shadow of a stairwell and by the screen door, but she still had a good view of whoever came to visit.

I waited patiently ringing the bell even though I knew damn well that she could see me. I carried a tan rucksack in which I had two quart bottles of Rainier Ale.

"Who is that?" Mrs. Bark asked after the fourth ring.

"Easy Rawlins, ma'am. On some business for Mofass."

"You too late, Easy Rawlins. Mofass done moved out already."

"I know that, ma'am, that's why I'm here. Mofass called me from down south and said that I should get some papers that he left in his room by mistake."

I wasn't taking much of a chance. If Mofass had moved out all of a sudden he might have left something that would give me an idea about his relationship with Poinsettia. If he'd moved out clean I would have just been caught in a white lie by one of the snobs of Bell Street.

"What?" she cried. The audacity of Mofass forced Mercedes Bark to her feet, which was no easy task. She waddled her great body to the door and then rested by leaning her upper arm against the jamb. Mercedes wasn't tall, and if you only looked at her bespectacled face you would never have guessed how large she was. Even her shoulders were small, you might have called them slender. But from there on down Mercedes Bark was a titan. Her breasts and buttocks were tremendous. She took up the entire lower half of the doorway.

"He got some nerve," she said. "Sendin' you here when he left me a room fulla mess and now I cain't even rent the place until I hire somebody to clean it out."

"But that's just it, ma'am. Mofass told me that he was sorry but that his mother got sick so fast that he didn't have time to think things out. He don't wanna move outta this place. He told me to pay you the sixty dollars for his next month's rent."

I had the money in my hand. Mrs. Bark turned from a snapping wolf to a loon, crooning her sorrows for Mofass' poor mother and complimenting a son's deep love.

She got the key, after taking my money, and even came out of her apartment to point me on the way.

Mofass' room was far from being a mess. It was neat as a pin and as orderly as a pharaoh's tomb. In the center drawer of his desk were his pencils, pens, pads of paper, and ink pads. In the right-hand drawers were all of the receipts of his bills for his entire life. He still kept ticket stubs for movies he'd seen in New Orleans twenty years before. In the lower left drawer he kept folders detailing his daily business. One folder was for expenses, another for expenditures, and like that.

He also had a drawer full of cigars. I knew something was wrong when I saw them. For Mofass to leave fifty good cigars he must have been really shaken.

I searched the rest of the place without finding very much. Nothing under the bed or between the mattresses or even in his clothes. No loose boards or envelopes taped under the drawers.

Finally I sat down at his desk again and put my hand flat on top of it. Really it wasn't flat because there was a blotter there. I lifted it but there was nothing underneath so I let it fall back. And it made a little sound: flap flap. Not a single flap but two, as if there were two blotter sheets.

Mofass had slit his blotter in two and then taped it back together so he could keep things in there secret without calling any attention to them. But the tape had worn thin and the pages had separated.

I found a few items of interest there. First there was a receipt signed by William Wharton (Mofass' real name) from the Chandler Ambulance Service of Southern California. The bill was $83.30, issued for the transmission of a patient from Temple Hospital to 487 Magnolia Street on January 18, 1952. There was another hospital bill for $1,487.26 for two weeks of hospitalization of a P. Jackson. I couldn't imagine Mofass spending twenty dollars on a date and here he was spending six months' salary for a girl he urged me to evict.

The last two items were both envelopes. One had a hundred dollars in twenty-dollar bills and the other had a list of eight names, addresses, and phone numbers. The addresses were widely spread around the city.

While I was trying to make sense of what I'd found I sensed someone, or maybe I heard him there behind me.

Chester Fisk was standing in the doorway. A tall and slender elderly gentleman, Mr. Fisk was Mercedes' father and a permanent resident of the Bell Street Boardinghouse. His skin color was somewhere between light brown and a light gray highlighted in certain places, like his lips, with a brownish yellow.

"Mr. Rawlins."

"Hey, Chester. How's it goin'?"

"Oh." He contemplated a few seconds. "Alright. Sun's a li'l too strong and the night's a li'l too long. But it beats the hell outta bein' dead."

"Maybe I could take a little of that heat off," I said. Then I pulled out the two bottles of ale.

For a moment I thought Chester might cry. His eyes filled with gratitude so docile that it was almost bovine.

"Well, well, well," he said. He rested his hand around the neck of the closest bottle.

"You seen Mofass just before he moved out, Chester?"

"Sure did. Everybody else was asleep but old men hardly need t'sleep no more."

"Was he upset?"

"Powerful." Chester accented his answer with a nod.

"Did you talk with him?"

"Not too much I didn't. He just had this one li'l bag packed. Prob'ly just had a toothbrush and a second pair a drawers in it. I ast 'im was somethin' wrong an' he said that things were bad. Then he said that they was *real* bad."

"That's it? Did he say anything about his mother?"

"Nope. Didn't say nuthin' else 'bout nuthin'. Just rush in in a hurry an' run out the same way."

On the drive back to my house I tried to figure what it all meant. I knew that Mofass had paid for Poinsettia's hospital bill and probably for her rent, maybe for a year or more. I also had some names that I didn't know all around L.A.

Maybe his mother was sick.

Maybe he killed Poinsettia. Maybe Willie did. Everything was just cockeyed.

• 28 •

The phone rang eight times before Zaree Bouchard answered. "Hello?"

She sounded bored or fed up.

I said, "Hey, Zaree, how you doin'?"

"Oh, it's you, Easy." She didn't sound happy. "Which one of 'em you want?"

"Which one you wanna part wit'?"

"You could have 'em both fo'a dollar twenty-five."

I could see that we weren't going to play, so I said, "Let me have Dupree."

I heard her yell his name and then I winced at the hard knock of the receiver as she dropped it.

After a minute of quiet the phone started banging around again until finally Dupree said, "Yeah?"

"Mr. Bouchard," I exclaimed. "Easy here."

"Well, well, well." His voice reminded me of an alto sax going down the scale. "Mr. Rawlins. What can I do for you?"

"You heard about Towne?"

"Ain't done nuthin' but hear about it. That was a shame."

"Yeah. I was the one found the body, at least the one after Winona."

"I heard that, Easy. I heard that an' it made me think all over again how you was the last one saw Coretta 'fore Joppy Shag did her in."

Dupree always blamed me for his girlfriend's death. I never got mad at him, though, because I always felt a little responsible for it myself.

"Cops brought me in and I'm scared they might try an' pin it on me."

"Uh-huh," Dupree said. Maybe he wouldn't have minded the police finding me dirty.

"Yeah. Anybody know who the girl was they found with 'im?"

"Couple'a folks I heard said that her name was Tania, somethin' like that. But nobody said where she come from, or where she been."

Dupree was a good man. No matter how he felt about me we were still friends. He wouldn't lie.

"What's goin' on with Zaree?" I asked.

"She mad on Raymond."

"How come?"

"First he all wild over Etta. Then he start drinkin' an' get all slouchy an' filthy. Then, just yestiday, he gets all dressed up an' last night he come in wit' two white girls."

"Yeah?"

"I tell ya, Easy." The old friendliness returned to Dupree's voice. "I couldn't sleep wit' the kinda racket they was makin'. I mean he had 'em beggin' fo' it! An' if they asted fo' a little more in a soft voice he'd say, 'What you say?' and they had to scream."

"That got to Zaree?"

"Well, yeah," Dupree chuckled. "But what really got to 'er was that I got hard up ev'ry time he got one of 'em, and then I'd go after her. I told 'er that if she didn't want it then one'a them girls out there would."

Mouse was a bad influence on anything domestic.

"Lemme talk to 'im, okay, Dupree?"

"Yeah." Dupree was still laughing when he got off the phone.

"Whas happenin', Ease?" Mouse asked in his cool tone.

"You gotta call Etta, Ray."

"Yeah?" You could hear the satisfaction in his voice.

"Yeah. Call 'er an' take LaMarque out, to the park or somethin'."

"When?"

"Soon as you can, man, but you gotta remember somethin'."

"What's that?"

"LaMarque ain't hardly more than a baby, Ray. Don't go showin' him yo' business or takin' him out wit' one'a yo' girlfriends."

"What should I do?"

"Take him swimmin', or fishin'. Take 'im to the park an' play ball. What did you do when you was a boy?"

"Sometimes I'd sneak up on one'a them big river rats sunnin' hisself on the pier. You know I'd grab 'im by the tail and swing the mothahfuckah 'round till I smash his ass on the pilin'."

"LaMarque is sensitive, Ray. He wanna play little kid games. All you gotta do is remember that an' he ain't gonna want you dead."

Mouse was quiet for a few moments, and then he said, "Okay," softly.

"So you gonna call?"I asked.

"Yeah."

"An' you gonna play wit' him?"

"Uh-huh, yeah, play."

"Okay then," I said.

"Easy?"

"Yeah?"

"You alright, man. You might got a nut or sumpin' loose, but you alright."

I didn't know just what he meant but it sounded as if we had become friends again.

• 29 •

I was still laughing about Dupree and Zaree when I got off the phone. A good story or joke seems funnier when you're surrounded by death. I never laughed harder than when I rode along with Patton's army into the Battle of the Bulge.

I don't know how long he'd been knocking at the front door. Whoever it was he was a patient man. Knock knock knock, then a pause, then three more raps.

I can't say I was surprised to see Melvin Pride standing there. He wore black cotton pants, a white T-shirt, and a black sweater vest. It had been years since I had seen Melvin informally dressed.

"Melvin."

"Could I come in, Easy?"

There was an occasional twitch in his right cheek. A large nerve that connected his bloodshot eye with his ear.

I offered him coffee instead of liquor. After I'd served it we sat opposite each other in the living room, white porcelain cups cradled in our laps.

Then, instead of talking, we lit cigarettes.

After a long while Melvin asked, "How long you been living here?"

"Eight years."

Melvin and I were both serious men. We stared each other in the eye.

"Do you want something from me, Melvin?" I asked.

"I don't know, Brother Rawlins. I don't know."

"Must be somethin'. I'm surprised that you even knew my address."

Melvin took a deep draw on his cigarette and held it for a good five seconds. When he finally spoke, wisps of smoke escaped his nostrils, making his craggy face resemble a dragon.

"We do a lot of good work at First African," he said. "But there's lotsa pressure behind that good work. And you know all men don't act the same under pressure."

I nodded while gauging Melvin's size and strength.

"Who you been talkin' to, Melvin?" I asked. A spasm ran through the right side of his face.

"I don't need to be talkin' t'nobody, Easy Rawlins. I know *you*. Fo' years you been stickin' yo' nose in people's business. They say you got Junior Fornay sent up to prison. They say you'n Raymond Alexander done left a trail'a death from Pariah, Texas, right up here to Watts."

Even though what he said was true I acted like it wasn't. I said, "You don't know what you talkin' 'bout, man. All I do is take care'a some sweepin' here and there."

"You smart." Melvin smiled and winced at the same time. "I give ya that. I seen you cock your ear when me an' Jackie was talkin' on the church stair. Then I see you gettin' tight wit' Chaim Wenzler. You don't be givin' stuff away, Easy. Ev'rybody knows you a horse trader, man. So whatever you doin' up there I know it ain't gotta do wit' no Christian love. An' this time somebody talked. This time I *know* it's you."

"Who said?"

"Ain't no need fo' me t'tell you nothin', man. I know, and that's all gotta be said."

"There's a name fo' the shit you talkin', Melvin," I said. "I learned it at LACC. They call it paranoid. You see, a man wit' paranoia be scared'a things ain't even there."

Melvin's cheek jumped and he smiled again.

"Yeah," he said. "I be scared alright. An' you know it's the scared animal you gotta watch out for. Scared animals do things you don't expect. One minute he be runnin' scared an' the nex' he scratchin' at yo' windpipe."

"That's what you gonna do?"

Melvin stood up quickly, setting his cup on the arm of his chair. I matched him, move for move.

"Let it be, Easy. Let it be."

"What?"

"We both know what I'm talkin' 'bout. Maybe we made some mistakes but you know we did some good too."

"Well," I said, trying to sound reasonable. "Let's just lay it out so we both know what's happening."

"You heard all I got to say."

Melvin was finished talking. He didn't have a hat so he just turned around and walked away.

I went after him to the door and watched as he went between the potato and strawberry patches. His gait was grim and deliberate. After he'd gone I went to the closet, got my gun, and put it in my pocket.

An hour later I was pulling up to a house on Seventy-sixth Street. The house belonged to Gator Wade, a plumber from east Texas. Gator always parked his car in the driveway, next to his house, so he had no use for the little garage in the back yard. He floored the little shack, wired and plumbed it, and let it out for twenty-five dollars a month.

Jackie Orr, the head deacon at First African, had been living there for over three years.

Gator was at work. I parked out front and made my way back to Jackie's house. Nobody answered my knock, so I pried open the lock and let myself in. Jackie worked during the day time as a street sweeper for the city. I was fairly sure that he wouldn't interrupt me. And even if he did I doubted if he'd be armed.

The place was a mess but I couldn't be sure if someone had searched it or if Jackie was just a poor housekeeper, like most bachelors.

Next to his bed was a thick sheaf of purple-printed mimeographed papers. The title line read, "Reasons for the African Migration." It was a long rambling essay about Marcus Garvey and slavery and our ancestors back home in Africa. It wasn't the kind of literature I expected Jackie to read.

His clothes surprised me too. He had at least thirty suits hanging in the closet, and a different-color pair of shoes to match each one. I noticed a nice ring on his nightstand and a good watch too. I knew his salary wouldn't have covered the payments, and a woman would have to hear wedding bells to lay that kind of cash on a man's back.

Underneath the bottom drawer of his bureau was a thick envelope that contained more than a thousand dollars in denominations of twenty or less. There was also another list of names. This one included amounts of cash:

L. Towne,	-0-
M. Pride,	1,300
W. Fitzpatrick,	1,300
J. Orr,	1,300
S.A.,	3,600

There was money changing hands. And in Jackie's case the money turned into clothes. I didn't know who S.A. was but I had it in mind to find out.

I left the money but I took the list with me. Sometimes words are worth more than money; especially if your ass is on the line.

• 30 •

John's place was empty except for Odell sitting in his corner, eating a sandwich. He wouldn't even return my nod. It was hard to lose a friend like that, but things were so twisted that I couldn't really feel it, except as a pang in my lower gut.

As John served me whiskey I asked him, "You seen Jackson t'day?"

"No," John answered. "But he be here. Jackson need to be in a bar where they don't allow no fightin'."

"You gotta save his butt a lot?"

John shrugged. "Lotta people cain't stand the man. He smart but he stupid too."

I took the drink to the far end of his bar and waited.

John always had his share of drunks and a few businessmen plying their various trades. Every once in a while there'd be a woman doing business, but that was rare, as John didn't want trouble with the police.

Jackson Blue came through the door at about four-thirty.

"Hey, Easy," he squealed in his high, crackly voice.

"Jackson. Come on over here and have a seat."

He was wearing a loose and silvery sharkskin suit. His coal-black skin against the light but shadowy fabric made him look like the negative of a photograph of a white man.

"S'appenin', Ease?" Jackson greeted me like I was his best friend.

Once, five years earlier, I came close to being murdered by a hijacker named Frank Green. I was never sure if Jackson was the one who told Frank Green, now deceased, that I was on his trail. All I know is that one day I was talking to Jackson about it and that night Frank had a knife to my throat. It really didn't matter if it was Jackson, because he didn't have anything against me personally. He was just trading in the only real business he knew—information.

"It's bad, Jack, bad as it could be. You wanna drink?"

"Yeah."

"Bring Jackson his milk, John."

While John served the triple shot of scotch, Jackson smiled and said, "Whas the problem?"

"You know what happened at First African, right?"

"Yeah, yeah, sure. You know Rita dragged me there Sunday 'fore last. Said she'd keep me company on Saturday if I took her t'church."

This satisfied look came over Jackson's face and I knew that he was about to start bragging on the acts of love Rita had performed.

I interrupted his reverie, saying, "You hear anything 'bout them killin's?"

"How come?"

"Poinsettia got herself hung a while back and I found the body."

"Yeah, I heard," he said. Then a light went on in his yellowy eyes. "An' you fount the minister too. They think it was you?"

"Yeah, and the cops don't even know who the girl was. They'd like to say it was me."

"Shit," Jackson snorted. "Mothahfuckahs couldn't fines no clue if it was nailed to they ass."

"You know sumpin' 'bout it, Jackson?"

Jackson looked over his shoulder, at the door. That meant he knew something and he was wondering if he should tell it. He rubbed his chin and acted cagey for a half a minute or so.

Finally he said, "What you doin' at City College, man?"

"What?"

"You go there, right?"

"Yeah."

"So what you takin'?"

"Basic like, remedial courses. Gettin' some basic history an'

English I missed in night school. I got a couple'a advanced classes too."

"Yeah? What kinda history?"

"European. From the Magna Carta on."

"War," he stated simply.

"What's that you say?"

"Whatever it is I read about Europe is war. Them white men is always fightin'. War'a the Roses, the Crew-sades, the Revolution, the Kaiser, Hitler, the com'unists. Shit! All they care 'bout, war an' money, money an' land."

He was right, of course. Jackson Blue was always right.

"You wanna go to school there?"

"Maybe you wanna take me t'class one night. Maybe I see."

"What about the church, Jackson?"

"You say the cops don't even know who that girl is?"

"Nope."

"Maybe I go t'school an' be a cop."

"You gotta be five-eight at least to be a cop, Jack."

"Shit, man. If I ain't a niggah I'm a midget. Shit. You wanna get me another one, Ease?"

He pointed a long ebony finger at his empty glass.

I signaled for John to bring another. After he'd moved away Jackson said, "Tania's her name. Tania Lee."

"Where she live?"

"I'ont know. I just got it from one'a the young deacon boys—Robert Williams."

"He didn't know where she from?"

"Uh-uh. She just always tellin' him t'be proud'a his skin and to worship Africa."

"Yeah?"

"Yeah." Jackson grinned. "You know I'preciate a girl like a dark-skinned man but you ain't gonna find me in no Africa."

"Why not, Jackson? You 'fraid'a the jungle?"

"Hell no, man. Africa ain't got no mo' wild than America gots. But you know I cain't see how them Africans could take kindly t'no

American Negro. We been away too long, man." Jackson shook his head. He almost looked sorry. "Too long."

Jackson could have lectured me on the cultural rift between the continents all night, but an idea came to me.

"You ever hear of a group called the African Migration, Blue?"

"Sure, ain't you ever seen it? Down on Avalon, near White Horse Bar and Grill."

I had seen the place. It used to be a hardware store, but the owner died and the heirs sold it to a real estate broker who rented it out to storefront churches.

"I thought that was just another church."

"Naw, Easy. These is Marcus Garvey people. Back to Africa. You know, like W. E. B. Du Bois."

"Who?"

"Du Bois. He's a famous Negro, Easy. Almost a hundred years old. He always writin' 'bout gettin' back t'Africa. You prob'ly ain't never heard'a him 'cause he's a com'unist. They don't teach ya 'bout com'unists."

"So how do you know, if they don't teach it?"

"Lib'ary got its do' open, man. Ain't nobody tellin' you not to go."

There aren't too many moments in your life when you really learn something. Jackson taught me something that night in John's, something I'd never forget.

But I didn't have time to discuss the political nature of information right then. I had to find out what was happening, and it was the African Migration that was my next stop.

"Thanks, Jackson. You gonna be 'round fo'a while?" I put a five-dollar bill on the counter; Jackson covered it with his long skinny hand. Then he tipped his drink at me.

"Sure, Ease, sure I be here. You prob'ly find 'em too. They got a meetin' there just about ev'ry night."

There was a meeting going on in the gutted hardware store that evening. About forty people were gathered around a platform toward the back of the room to listen to the speakers.

A big man stopped me at the front door.

"You comin' to the meetin'?" he asked. He was tall, six-four or more, and fat. His big outstretched hand looked like the stuffed hand of a giant brown doll.

"Yeah."

"We like a little donation," the big man said, unconsciously rubbing the tips of his fingers together.

". . . they don't want us and we don't want them," I heard the female speaker in the back of the large room say.

"How little?" I asked.

"One dollar for one gentleman," he smiled.

I gave him two Liberty half-dollars.

The people in the room were a serious sort on the whole. Most of the men wore glasses, and every other person had a book or papers under their arm. Nobody noticed me. I was just another brother looking for a way to hold my head up high.

Among the crowd I made out Melvin Pride. He was intent on the speaker and so didn't notice me. I moved behind a pillar, where I could watch him without being seen.

The speaker was talking about home, Africa. A place where everybody looked like the people in that room. A place where the kings and presidents were black. I was moved to hear her.

But not so moved that I didn't keep an eye on the deacon. Melvin kept looking around nervously and rubbing his hands.

After a while the crowd broke out into a kind of exultant applause. The woman speaker, who wore wraparound African robes, bowed her head in recognition of the adulation before giving up the podium to the man behind her. She was chubby and light brown and had the face of a precocious schoolgirl, serious but innocent. Melvin went up to her, whispering while the next speaker prepared to address the crowd.

What looked to be a wad of folding money changed hands.

The man on the platform spoke in glowing terms about a powerful Negro woman who had shown leadership beyond her years. I knew it had to be Melvin's friend, because she took out a moment from her transaction to make eye contact with the speaker.

Melvin had finished his business anyway, he headed for the exit.

". . . Sonja Achebe," the speaker said. The crowd applauded again and the young woman headed for a doorway at the back of the room.

"Miss Achebe?"

"Yes?"

She smiled at me.

"Excuse me, ma'am, but my name is Easy, Easy Rawlins."

She frowned a bit as if the name meant something to her but she couldn't quite remember why.

"Yes, Brother Rawlins."

The mood of the Migration, like that of so many other black organizations, was basically religious.

"I need to talk to you 'bout Tania Lee."

She knew who I was then. She didn't say anything, just pointed at a doorway. We walked toward it as another speaker began to preach.

"What is it you wanted to know about Sister Lee?" she asked. We were in a large storeroom that was cut into tiny aisles by rows of slender, empty shelves. It was like a rat's maze, dimly lit by sparse forty-watt bulbs.

"I need to know who killed her, and why."

"She's dead?" Miss Achebe made a lame attempt at surprise.

"Com'on lady, you know what happened. She's one'a you people." I was reaching but I thought I might be right.

"You tell the police that?"

I stuck out my bottom lip and shook my head. "No reason. Least not yet."

Miss Achebe didn't look like a little girl anymore. The lines of an older woman etched her face.

"What do you want with me?" she asked.

"Who killed your friend and my minister?"

"I don't know what you're talking about. I don't have anything to do with killings."

"I saw you with Melvin and I seen him with Tania and Reverend Towne. Somethin's goin' on wit' you and the church. I know they gave you at least thirty-six hundred dollars, honey, but you see I don't care about that. The police lookin' at me for murder an' I cain't be worried 'bout you-all's li'l thing."

"We didn't kill Towne."

"Why'm I gonna believe that?"

"I don't care what you believe, Mr. Rawlins. I didn't kill anyone—nobody I know killed anyone."

"Maybe not." I nodded at her. "But all I gotta do is whisper a word to the man and he might just wanna prove that you did."

She snorted in place of a laugh. "We live with danger here, Mr. Rawlins. The police and the FBI make weekly visits. They don't scare me and you don't either."

"I don't wanna scare ya, Miss Achebe. What you got here looks good to me, but I was in the wrong place at the wrong time an' I gotta have some answers."

"I can't help you. I know nothing."

"Didn't Melvin say anything?"

"Nothing." She shrugged and glanced over my shoulder.

"Okay. But I gotta know . . ." I was interrupted by a heavy hand on my shoulder.

I turned to look up into the face of the man who took my money at the door.

"Anything wrong?" he asked.

"Yes, Bexel," Sonja said. "Mr. Rawlins here thinks that we're somehow involved with the murder of Reverend Towne."

"He do?" You could see how it hurt the big man that I could think such a thing.

Sonja smiled. "He wants to tell the police that."

"Naw?" When Bexel balled his hands into fists the knuckles of his fingers did an impression of popping corn.

I guess that my fights with Willie and Agent Lawrence had made me a little cocky. I made like I was going to step away from the sergeant-at-arms and then I dropped my right shoulder to deliver an uppercut to his lower gut.

It was a perfectly executed blow that I followed with an overhand left just below Bexel's heart. I danced backward until I felt a row of shelves behind me. It wasn't far but I didn't expect my quarry to be in any shape to trap me.

Then I looked up into his placid, smiling face.

Bexel leaned forward and pushed me with his great padded paw. My hurtling body shattered the shelves behind and the shelves behind them. My lungs collapsed in my chest and I felt pain in places that I'd never felt before.

Still smiling, the big man grabbed me roughly by both shoulders and lifted me until our faces almost touched.

I kicked him. Hard. And, to give myself a little credit, his left eye winced for a split second. But then he let go of my shoulders and grabbed me by the head.

"Bexel!" Sonja Achebe shouted. "Release him!"

I hit the floor certain, at least for that moment, that these were not the killers. I was fool enough to go into their den and blame them for the crime of murder. They could have killed me. Should have done.

I was on the floor thinking about cooked spaghetti and wondering if I was bleeding when Sonja asked, "Are you alright, Mr. Rawlins?"

"No, I sure ain't that."

Bexel was still standing before me. I was looking at his bloated black brogans. They were the largest shoes I had ever seen. He grabbed me by my jacket and lifted me to my feet. That was the first time that night that I had the sensation of flight.

"You should go now," Sonja Achebe said. "We didn't do anything wrong, but I don't expect you to believe that. It doesn't matter what you think, however, because we are not afraid."

I looked at Bexel. He wasn't even breathing hard. I remember hoping that I had finally learned to be cautious. But somewhere in my heart I knew that I'd never learn.

"Sorry," I said.

I shook Sonja Achebe's hand. "I know you might not believe this, but I was moved by your speech. There's a lotta people need what you have to offer."

"Not you?" She smiled for the first time and became a young girl again.

"I got me a home already. It might be in enemy lands, but it's mine still and all."

I liked Sonja Achebe and what the Migration stood for. I didn't want to see them come to harm. I found myself hoping that they hadn't been involved in Towne's death. I found myself wishing the same thing about Chaim Wenzler. It seemed to me that I was on everybody's side but my own.

• 31 •

Melvin Pride lived on Alaford Street. A quiet block of one-family homes behind a row of well-kept lawns and trimmed bushes. There was a smell of smoke in the air. I wondered at that, because it was unusual for anyone to be burning trash at that time of night.

I had to knock for a full minute before Melvin came to the door.

"What you want, Easy?" he asked through the screen, as hushed and stony as the grim reaper.

"I wanna talk to you about Reverend Towne and Tania Lee and the African Migration."

"Who?"

"I saw you there tonight, Melvin. I know you were siphoning off money to them 'cause you were all officers. Thing is, I cain't see why you would do it. I mean, Towne's got religion and a social conscience. But you just care about the church, and Winona an' Jackie be happy with a mirror. But even if I knew why they would do it I can't figure why you'd wanna kill anybody."

Melvin looked mean, but actually he was paralyzed. I pulled open the screen door and stepped past him into the house.

"You talkin' crazy, Easy Rawlins." Melvin moved to the side, and I took a step back from him. We were dancing like wary boxers in the first round of a title fight.

"That's right, I'm talking murder, Melvin."

"Murder who? I got someone t'say where I was fo' when they was killed. The po-lice already questioned me."

"I bet that was Jackie, or one'a his girls."

When I said "Jackie," Melvin's cheek jumped.

Then I said, "Come on, Melvin! You know all you people was stealin' from the church." It was just a guess but it was a good one. There weren't many places where a man like Jackie Orr could lay his hands on a thousand dollars. "You was all takin' money. Towne for the Migration, Winona and you for Towne, and Jackie . . . well, Jackie just caught on to a good thing."

"You cain't prove I killed nobody. And you cain't prove I stole nuthin'."

"You right 'bout the stealin'. I cain't prove that, not wit' you burnin' the books out back I cain't."

Melvin gave me a twitchy smile.

"But it's murder I can burn you on."

"Hell no! I ain't killed nobody! Never!"

"Maybe not, but all I gotta do is tell the cops an' they will beat you till you confess. That's how the game is played, Melvin."

Melvin turned his head as if he wanted to look into the door behind him. That door probably led to a bedroom.

He licked his lips. "You think I killed Towne? That's a laugh."

"I ain't laughin', Melvin. What I wanna know is why. You workin' with Wenzler or what?"

The look on Melvin's face was either a perfect job of acting or he knew nothing.

"You the one most prob'ly killed Towne, Easy." His tone was so certain that my sweat glands turned cold.

"Me?"

"Yeah, you. We got the lowdown on you, Easy."

"You said that before, Melvin. What does that mean?"

"It means that somebody blabbed on you, man. They told."

"Who?"

"I ain't sayin'. But it ain't just one, and I ain't the onliest one who knows, so you better not be thinkin' nuthin' like you gonna get at me. I know and Jackie does and the white man know too."

There was a righteous tone to Melvin's voice. He actually thought that I was the killer.

It took me a couple of days to decide on what happened next.

Melvin pushed me backwards, yelling, "You got him but you hain't gonna get me!" My foot turned on the carpet. Melvin stepped over me and connected with a solid right against my jaw. I was already falling and so I twisted over trying to roll out of the way. I hit a chair though and fell with my head toward the ground. Then there was a dull thud against my left thigh and I realized that Melvin had kicked me and probably meant to stomp me into the floor. I let myself roll sideways and stuck my legs between Melvin's so that when he tried to kick me again he fell forward, and I slammed my fist into the side of his head.

That's when we fell together, wrestling. Melvin was biting and growling like a dog. His attack was ferocious but it was unplanned. I kept giving him rabbit punches to the back of the neck. I did that until he removed his teeth from my left shoulder. Then I got to my feet holding Melvin by the shirt. I was terribly angry, because his attack scared me and because my mouth was in tremendous pain. I hit Melvin with everything I had. He went backwards across the room and I expected him to go down into a cold heap, but instead he kept on going and ran from the room.

At first I thought the fight was over. I had put all of my anger into that one blow and my violence was sated. But then, in the same moment, I remembered Melvin looking toward that door earlier.

By the time I burst through the doorway Melvin was turning from the night table next to his bed. There was a coal-colored pistol in his hand.

And for the second time that night I took flight; right into Melvin Pride.

The force of our bodies hitting the wall broke through the plaster. The sensation was the stutter effect of stepping on ice and then having that ice give way to free-fall. Melvin grunted, so did I. A timber sighed. Gravel slithered down my cheek and the pistol barked mutely, packed between the girth of our two bodies.

I felt the bite of the shot and automatically pushed away from Melvin to block up the hole in my chest.

I was covered with blood. I knew from my experiences in the war that I would soon lose consciousness. Melvin would murder me. Everything was over.

Then I heard Melvin slump down and I gave a wide grin in spite of the terrible pain in my jaw. It was Melvin who had taken the bullet; I had just felt the concussion of the shot.

Melvin's face was contorted in pain. A dark patch was forming on his shirt.

He was sucking down air and groaning, but Melvin was still trying to lift the pistol to shoot me. I took the gun from his blood-streaked hand and threw it on the bed. The craggy man groaned in fear as I stood over him. My jaw hurt me so bad that I had no desire to quell his fear. I tore a pillowcase in half and shoved it under Melvin's bloody shirt until it was directly over the wound.

"Hold this tight," I said. I had to lift his other arm and show him what to do.

"Don't kill me, man," he whispered.

"Melvin, you gotta get a hold of yourself. If you don't start thinkin' straight you gonna go into shock an' die."

I held his hand down hard over the wound to cause a little pain for him to focus on and to show him what he should be doing. The pistol he had was a .25-caliber so the wound wasn't too bad.

"Please don't kill me, please don't kill me," Melvin chanted.

"I don't want you dead, Melvin. I ain't gonna kill you, even though I should after this shit."

"Please," Melvin said again.

I pocketed the pistol and went to the bathroom, where I washed the blood off my shoes and from the cuffs of my black pants. Then I took an overcoat from Melvin's closet and used it to cover the rest of me.

In the back yard the incinerator was smoking away at various official papers from First African. Melvin had been trying to erase the accounting trail of the theft he and the others had perpetrated against the church. I hosed down what was left.

Back inside I found that Melvin had crawled into the kitchen. He was holding himself erect at the kitchen counter. I figured that he was trying to get a weapon, so I helped him to a chair. Then I went to the phone on the kitchen table and dialed Jackie Orr. He answered on the seventh ring.

"Hello."

"Hey, Jackie, this is Easy. Easy Rawlins."

"Yeah?" he said warily.

"Melvin's been shot." There was silence on the other end of the line. "I didn't shoot him, man. It was an accident. Anyway he's got a bullet in his shoulder and he needs a doctor."

"You ain't gettin' me over there with that lie, Easy. I ain't no fool."

"What I want with you, man?"

"You want my money."

"You got a thousand dollars in yo' bottom drawer, right? If I didn't take that then I don't need no money you got."

"I just call the cops, man."

"You do an' I hope you ready fo' jail, Jackie, 'cause I got all the proof I need that you been takin' money out the church. But here, talk to Melvin."

I cradled the phone next to Melvin's ear and left them to whisper their fears to each other.

On the drive back to my house I almost passed out from the pain in my mouth. At home I changed clothes, downed a few mouthfuls of brandy, and got back in my car.

Jackson was still spending my five dollars on whiskey at John's bar.

"Ease!" he shouted as I was coming across the room. Odell looked up from his drink. I nodded at him and he made to leave.

So I turned toward Jackson.

"I need you to come with me, Jackson," I said as fast as I could. The pain was unbearable. John stared at me, but when I didn't say anything he turned away.

"You know where I could get some painkillers?" I asked Jackson.

"Yeah."

I handed him my keys when we got out to the car. "You drive," I said. "I got a toothache."

"What's wrong, man?"

"Dude busted my tooth. He busted my fuckin' mouth!"

"Who?"

"Some guy wanted to rob me outside of the African Migration. I fixed him. Oh shit, it hurts."

"I got some pills at my place, man. Let's go get 'em."

"Oh," I answered. I guess he knew that meant yes.

Jackson had morphine tablets. He said all I needed was one, but I took four against the bright red hurt in my mouth. I was doubled over in pain.

"How long 'fore it kicks in, Jackson?"

"If you ain't et nuthin', 'bout a hour."

"An hour!"

"Yeah, man. But listen," he said. He had a fifth of Jim Beam by the neck. "We sit here and drink an' talk an' fo' long you will have fo'gotten you even had a tooth."

So we passed the bottle back and forth. Because he was drinking, Jackson loosened up to the point where he'd tell me anything. He told stories that many a man would have killed him for. He told me about armed robberies and knifings and adulteries. He named names and gave proofs. Jackson wasn't an evil man like Mouse, but he didn't care what happened as long as he could tell the tale.

"Jackson," I said after a while.

"Yeah, Ease?"

"What you think 'bout them Migration people?"

"They alright. You know it could get pretty lonely if you think 'bout how hard we got it 'round here. Some people just cain't get it outta they head."

"What?"

"All the stuff you cain't do, all the stuff you cain't have. An' all the things you see happen an' they ain't a damn thing you could do."

He passed the bottle to me.

"You ever feel like doin' sumpin'?" I asked the little cowardly genius.

"Pussy ain't too bad. Sometime I get drunk an' take a shit on a white man's doorstep. Big ole stinky crap!"

We laughed at that.

When everything was quiet again I asked, "What about these communists? What you think about them?"

"Well, Easy, that's easy," he said and laughed at how it sounded. "You know it's always the same ole shit. You got yo' people ain't got nuthin' but they want sumpin' in the worst way. So the banker and the corporation man gots it all, an' the workin' man ain't got shit. Now the workin' man have a union to say that it's the worker makes stuff so he should be gettin' the money. That's like com'unism. But the rich man don't like it so he gonna break the worker's back."

I was amazed at how simple Jackson made it sound.

"So," I said. "We're on the communist side."

"Naw, Easy."

"What you mean, no? I sure in hell ain't no banker."

"You ever hear 'bout the blacklist?" Jackson asked.

I had but I said, "Not really," in order to hear what Jackson had to say.

"It's a list that the rich people got. All kindsa names on it. White people names. They movie stars and writers and scientists on that list. An' if they name on it they cain't work."

"Because they're communist?"

Jackson nodded. "They even got the guy invented the atomic bomb on that paper, Easy. Big ole important man like that."

"So? What you sayin'?"

"Yo' name ain't on that list, Easy. My name ain't neither. You know why?"

I shook my head.

"They don't need yo' name to know you black, Easy. All they gotta do is look at you an' they know that."

"So what, Jackson?" I didn't understand and I was so drunk and high that it made me almost in a rage.

"One day they gonna th'ow that list out, man. They gonna need some movie star or some new bomb an' they gonna th'ow that list away. Mosta these guys gonna have work again," he said, then he winked at me. "But you still gonna be a black niggah, Easy. An' niggah ain't got no union he could count on, an' niggah ain't got no politician gonna work fo' him. All he got is a do'step t'shit in and a black hand t'wipe his black ass."

• 32 •

I woke up in my house, hungover and in profound pain. I got Jackson's bottle of morphine from my pants on the floor and took three pills. Then I went into the bathroom to wipe off the grime and smell of the night before.

Jackson's words stuck in my head like the pain of my tooth. I wasn't on either side. Not crazy Craxton and his lies and half-truths and not Wenzler's either, if indeed Wenzler even had a side.

I thought of going to a dentist. I was even looking in the phone book when the knocking came at my door.

It was Shirley Wenzler, and she was in worse shape that I was.

"Mr. Rawlins," she said, her lower lip trembling. "Mr. Rawlins, I came here because I didn't know. I mean, what else could I do?"

"What's wrong?" I asked.

"Come with me, Mr. Rawlins, please. It's Poppa, he's hurt."

I got my pants and my pullover sweater. She walked me to the car.

"Where to?"

"Santa Monica," she said.

I asked her if she had called a doctor and she answered, "No."

On the ride out she gave me more instructions, but that was it. I was nauseous and in pain, so I didn't push her. If Chaim needed a doctor I could figure that out when we got there.

It was a small house across the street from a park. The park was small too. Just one little grassy hill that rose up to the street on the other side. No trees or benches. Just a hill that was only fit for the two little children who rolled down it, pretending that they'd lost control.

I expected Shirley to have a key in her hand but she just pushed the door open and walked in. I limped behind her. The morphine dulled the hurt in my jaw, but then I could feel the tenderness of my left ankle and thigh.

The house was decorated in some cool, dull color, green or blue. The ceiling was so low that I remember ducking to go through the door from the living room to the bedroom.

The color there was red death.

Chaim was hunched over a chair. Most of the blood was right there under him. But there was also blood on the dresser and in the bathroom. Blood on the phone, in the dial. There were bloody handprints on the wall. He'd gone all the way around the room, propping himself up with his bloody hand.

Next to his body was a light green cushion, splattered and clotted with blood. He'd pressed the cushion to his chest, trying to staunch the bleeding, but he must have known that it wasn't going to work.

Shirley's eyes were wide and she wrung her hands. I pushed her back through the door. It was then I noticed the few drops of blood on the living-room carpet. I hadn't seen them before in the unlit room.

"He's dead," I told her. Even though she already knew it, she needed someone else to pronounce him gone.

There were two small-caliber bullet holes in the door. Maybe somebody had knocked and when Chaim asked who, they shot him through his own door.

"Let's get to the car," I said. I tried smudging any surface I'd touched, but there was no telling where a fingerprint might show up. I let my head hang down when we left the house and when we got in the car I sat so low that I could barely see over the dash. I didn't sit up straight until we were far from there.

We got to a small coffee shop in Venice Beach. A little place that had sandy floors and nets with seashells that hung from the ceiling. Our window looked out onto the shore. It was a cool morning, no one was out yet.

"When'd you find 'im?"

"This morning. Poppa," she said and then choked on a sob. "He wanted me to bring him something."

"What?"

"Money."

"How'd you know where to find me?"

"I called the church."

I had a coffee. I had to drink it carefully, because if I let the warm liquid on the wrong side I got a stabbing pain from my tooth.

"What did he need the money for?"

"He had to run, Easy. The government wanted him."

"Government?" I said as if I had never heard of the FBI.

"Poppa's a member of the Communist Party," she said, looking down into her knotted fists. "He got something, some papers, and the FBI has been hounding him. The last time they came by, last night, they said that they'd be back. Dad thought they'd take him, so he called me to bring him some money."

"Those FBI men at the house when I was there last week?" I asked just to see what she'd say.

"Yes."

"What is it he had?"

She looked reluctant to talk, so I said. "He's dead, Shirley. What we do now we gotta do for you."

"Some kind of plans. He got them from a guy at Champion Aircraft."

"What kind of plans?"

"Poppa didn't know but he thought that they were for weapons. He was sure that the government was making weapons to kill more people. Poppa hates the atomic bomb. He thinks that America will kill millions more due to imperialism. He says the plans are for a new bomber, maybe for atomic weapons."

The fact that she spoke of her father as if he were still alive bothered me, but I couldn't see setting her straight.

"What was he going to do with them?"

She shook her head, weeping.

"I don't know," she moaned. "I don't know."

"You gotta know."

"Why? Why is it important? He's dead."

"I didn't know him too long, but Chaim was my friend. I'd like to know that he wasn't a traitor."

"But he was, Mr. Rawlins. He believed that the kind of government we have only wants to make war. He wanted to take America's secret weapons plan and give them to a socialist newspaper, maybe in France, and to have everybody know about them. He wanted to make it so everybody was aware of the danger. He . . ." She began crying again.

Chaim was my friend and he was dead. Poinsettia was my tenant and she was dead too. One way or another both deaths were my fault. Even if it was only because of me not telling the truth or not having compassion when I could have.

She was shivering, so I put my hand out to cover hers.

The white cook came out from behind the counter and a few people turned all the way around in their chairs to watch.

Shirley didn't notice it.

She said. "He wanted to get out of the country, Easy."

"An' we gotta get outta here," I said.

When we got back to my house I asked her in. I don't know why. I was dirty and hurting and the last thing I wanted was to be entertaining some young woman, but I asked and she accepted, so we walked past the daylilies and the potatoes and strawberries up the dirt path to my house. And when I was fishing around in my pocket for the key she looked up at me and I stopped to look at her for a moment or two. Then I decided to kiss her. I leaned forward kind of quickly . . .

It wasn't the shot that bothered me.

It wasn't the hole torn in my front door or the car taking off down the street; nor was it the little yell or the look in Shirley Wenzler's eye, the look that could break a man's heart, that got to me. It wasn't bad luck or broken teeth or the remnants of a hangover or the whisper of a breeze that suggested death at the back of my neck. It wasn't political ideas that I didn't care about or understand that made me mad.

It was the idea that I suffered all of this because I wasn't, and hadn't been, my own man. I didn't even know who it was who was shooting at me in front of my own house! People hanging and shot dead for no real reason; that's what got me mad. Real mad. Something I could feel, like I felt the stirrings of an erection for Shirley when what I really wanted was a good night's sleep, a competent dentist, a peaceful death at the hands of a jealous husband or a racist cop.

Like most men, I wanted a war I could go down shooting in. Not this useless confusion of blood and innocence.

I stood there looking into Shirley's frightened face. She was shivering. I put my arms around her and said, "It's alright." Then I took her into my house without even looking after who it was that shot at us. I decided then that he was a dead man, whoever he was. I was going to start killing him at the soles of his feet. Whoever he was, he was going to remember me in hell.

"Do you think it was the government?" Shirley stammered as I helped her get the glass of whiskey to her lips.

"Prob'ly," I said, but I really didn't believe it. "They think you might get away wit' them papers."

"Oh, Easy!" She grabbed my arm. "What can we do?"

"You gots to run. Run hard."

"Where? Where can I go?"

"There's a hotel downtown called the Filbert. You go there and take a room. Call yourself Diane Bowers. I once had a girlfriend called that. Call me when you check in. I might not be here right when you call, but if I'm not I'll get to you under that same name, Diane Bowers."

She shuddered and pulled close to me.

"Let me stay for a while before I go. I'm too scared to drive."

And so we took off everything but our underclothes and my pistol.

We lay in my bed holding each other until she stopped shivering and we both fell asleep. I held her tightly, more for my own comfort than hers.

I dreamt that there was a trapdoor next to my mother's deathbed. I fell a long way down a passage that was similar to a well. At the bottom was a long river, but I knew it was a sewer, and there were men, desperate white men, searching for me. Sometimes the men would change into crocodiles and search for me in the water, sometimes the crocodiles would change into men. I was pressing back against a rocky wall, hiding. My hand, every now and then, unconsciously pushed into the recess of the wall, and every time that happened the wall hurt. It was a terrible pain and I came half awake massaging the side of my jaw where Melvin had broken my tooth.

I winced in pain, almost coming awake when I saw Mofass laughing behind his desk and then asking me about how could the IRS let me off. I saw him bad-mouthing Poinsettia and refusing to help sign my papers over to him.

Dreams are wonderful things, because they're a different way of thinking. I came to, for just a moment, with a clear idea of the path I should take. I knew who killed Poinsettia and I knew why. Even in my dream I knew it; even in my dreams I was plotting revenge.

• 33 •

We began kissing in our sleep. It was passionate and sloppy kissing while we were still unaware. When we came awake it was still dearly felt but neither of us wanted it to go anywhere. She got up and wandered around the room, maybe as her father had. I went up to her and kissed her again. I pressed her against the wall, she wrapped her legs around my hips and held on tight . . .

Rather than sex it was a kind of spasm, like vomiting or cramps. The sounds we made were the sounds boxers make when they take a blow to the body.

We didn't whisper about love. We didn't say anything until it was over.

Then all I said was that I'd call at the Filbert as soon as I could. I gave her EttaMae's number and told her to call if she couldn't get to me.

"Tell Etta what you need and tell her I said to call Mouse."

"Who?"

"A friend'a mines," I said.

"Oh, I remember." She smiled for the first time. "He's the man you said reminded you of Poppa."

"Yeah, that's right."

I didn't know what was going to happen with Shirley. All I could think about was vengeance, and, I thought, I knew how to go about getting it.

It was just getting dark outside and I saw Shirley to her car, pretending all the while that I was looking out for a bad guy. But I knew that shot was meant for me. And I knew who took that shot.

There was ice in my veins.

Primo's place was out in East Los Angeles, the Mexican neighborhood. He used to own a big house and rent out rooms to illegal aliens, but the board of health got down on him and condemned the place. So he put three hundred dollars down on a two-story house on Brooklyn Boulevard in Boyle Heights and tore out all the walls on the first floor. He and his wife, Flower, and all their eleven children lived on the upper level while Primo and Flower ran an informal luncheon café downstairs.

It was a dark room with bare, unfinished beams that were once hidden by walls. A few mismatched tables and chairs here and there. Flower was from Panama originally, but she knew her Mexican cooking well enough to make an egg-and-potato burrito and fried sausages to make you cry. Any Mexican day laborer within three miles came to Primo's for lunch. There was tequila and beer from the package store next door and smells so good that a Tijuana man might think he was back home with his family.

It was late when I got there, but I knew the family would be downstairs. Dinner with Primo started at about five and went on until the older children carried their sleeping brothers and sisters to bed.

"Easy! *Hola!*" Flower shouted when I stuck my head in the door. I never knocked at the family hour because there was too much noise for that type of pleasantry.

She crossed the large room and folded me in her soft embrace. Flower was bigger than EttaMae, and obviously a Negro, but we still considered her Mexican because she was from south of the border and cursed in Spanish when she got mad.

"Easy!" Primo said. He shook my hand and pounded my shoulder. "Get him a drink, somebody. Jesus! It's your godfather Ezekiel. Get him a bottle of beer."

Silent and shy, the little child jumped up, running the obstacle course of children, dogs, and furniture for the kitchen in back. Jesus Peña. Most of the Peña children were light-colored, honey, like their father, with big moonlike eyes. But Jesus was a duller hue with more Asiatic eyes. He wasn't their natural child. He was a boy I found eating raw flour from a five-pound bag. He'd been abused by an evil white man; a white man who had paid for his evil with a bullet in his heart. I brought Jesus to Primo and Flower. They kept him as long as I promised to take him back if anything ever happened to them. We'd drawn up the papers and Jesus was my godchild. I was proud of him, because he was smart and strong and loved animals. The only thing wrong about Jesus was that he wouldn't talk. I never knew if he remembered anything about his past, because I couldn't get him to talk, and whenever I asked him about it he hugged me and kissed me, then he ran away.

"What's wrong, Easy?" Primo asked.

"Somethin' gotta be wrong fo' me to wanna see my friends and my godchild?"

"Something wrong if you got a jaw that big."

It must've swollen while I napped.

"Got in a fight," I said. "I won, though."

Flower frowned at me. She jabbed the side of my mouth with her finger, and I nearly fainted.

"That's infected," she said. "You gotta see somebody or it'll get bad."

"Soon as I take care of some business."

"That tooth going to take care of you," she said, making her eyes big and round. The children all laughed and mimicked her.

"Okay!" Primo shouted, then he yelled something in Spanish and waved his hands as if he were making a breeze to blow the children upstairs.

At first the children resisted, but then Primo started slapping them and shouting.

Flower got them up the stairs and turned to see Primo waving at her. "You too, woman. Easy's here to talk to me."

Flower laughed and stuck out her tongue, then she turned and stuck her butt at us. She ran up the stairs before Primo could grab something to throw.

I pulled out the little glass bottle I'd gotten from Jackson Blue. There were five or six tablets left.

"What you taking for that, Easy?"

"Morphine," I said.

Primo made like he was going to gag. "That's bad stuff, man, I seen it in the war, in the Pacific. They give the boys that till they got the monkey on the back."

The morphine was wearing off. I felt like there was a gorilla in my mouth.

"I got a serious problem, Primo. After I take care of that maybe I could see a dentist."

"Oh." He nodded. "What's that?"

"Somebody been on my ass, man. I'ma have t'satisfy myself who it is, an' then I'ma kill 'im."

"Who?"

"I ain't gonna tell ya, Primo. If you don't know nuthin' then cain't nobody blame you fo' nuthin'."

I think that the lack of sleep, the pain, the morphine and liquor were all factors in my craziness then. I could tell that Primo thought I was less than rational, because he spoke softly and in short sentences. He didn't laugh or make jokes as he usually did.

"So what can I do for you?"

"Me and my girlfriend, EttaMae, might have to get away after it's done. I thought maybe you wanna take a vacation down in Mexico, back to that town in the badlands you always talk about."

Primo loved to talk about Anchou. It was a town in central Mexico that wasn't on any map; no one knew where it was but the people who came from there, or the rare few who were invited by one of the inhabitants. He once told me that the town was mobile; that if they knew trouble was coming they could pack up and move in just a couple of hours. But the Federales didn't want to mess with Anchou.

An Anchou woman, Primo said, would bite off a Federal's prick and serve it to her man for a love potion.

"Why don't you just go down to Texas? They won't find you."

"Cain't. Government in this. They ain't thought they gone to work 'less they cross a state border."

Mr. Peña frowned at me for a while. He took a drink from his beer and then frowned at me some more.

I was massaging the hinge of my jaw.

"Take the pills, Easy," he said at last.

I took three, washing them down with the beer Jesus had brought. There were three left in the bottle.

"Take the rest of them," Primo urged.

"This is all I got left."

"I got more. Take them so it really stops hurting."

I downed the rest of the bottle, hoping that the aching would stop and I could sleep well enough to do what had to be done the next day.

"I've got five hundred dollars right here, man," I said. I pulled a folded envelope from my back pocket and handed it to him.

Money always made Primo laugh. The more he had the more he laughed. He counted the twenties and tens I'd squirreled away in my walls. Every bill made his grin wider, his eyes glassier.

Maybe it was the dope kicking in, but I got a flash of fear that Primo was up to no good. Maybe he was in on all that bad luck I was having.

"You gonna help me, man?" I asked.

The fears must've shown in my voice, because Primo said, "Yes," very seriously. He handed me a clay jug from the side of his chair.

"Tequila?" I asked.

"Mescal."

I took a swig. I knew that it was potent liquor because I felt it even through the descending opiate haze.

Primo told me stories about Anchou.

"It's an old town," I remember him saying. "There was a chief there forty years ago who ran with Zapata before he was hung."

Every now and again he'd reach out to poke my jaw. If I told him it hurt he'd pass the jug over. But after a while there wasn't any pain.

Primo laughed too. After a while Flower came down and drank with us. She kept me company while Primo rummaged through some old boxes he kept in the corner of the large room.

"She's a mighty fine lady, Primo," I said when he came back. He had something like pruning shears in his hand.

"I found it," he said.

"Yeah," I continued. I heard him but I was too intent on my own purpose to heed. "I got a woman like 'er down in one'a my buildin's. She got a strong arm like yo' woman here and she smell like sweet flowers too."

I fell forward in my chair, trying to kiss Mrs. Peña on the lips if I remember right. I landed on her and got about as close as her shoulder. Then the room started spinning. I found myself on my back, on the floor with Flower above my head. She was pinning my shoulders down with her considerable weight.

". . . my cousin was a dentist in Guadalajara many years ago. I kept his tools," I heard Primo say. My stomach was flopping around, and I would have followed it but for Mrs. Peña's grip.

"Open wide, Easy," Primo was saying. He held my nostrils closed with one hand as he held the deadly-looking shears in the other. But they weren't shears really, they were more like streamlined pliers with an extended, toothy clamp at the nose.

"This is the one," Primo said as he frowned.

That's when I started fighting. I couldn't yell because of that damned tool and I couldn't turn away because of Flower's hold. But I bucked. I humped and bucked under Primo like he was my first love. I fought him and bit until all the fight went out of me and I felt something far off in my mouth like boulders rolling around in there.

Jesus Peña was squatting down next to my head. He was staring intently into my face. When he saw that my eyes were open he smiled.

I saw that he was missing a tooth, and I moved my own tongue toward the pain in my mouth; at least toward where the pain had been. What I found was a bitter-tasting gauze.

I sat up and spat the wad of cheesecloth to the floor. Jesus jumped back like a frightened kitten. The cloth was tooth-shaped and filled with tiny branches and leaves. It was also deeply stained with blood.

The blood reminded me of Poinsettia's feet and floor, of the hand marks on Chaim's walls. I lurched up off the cot. They had put me behind some boxes toward the back of the café. A few men were already there, eating buttered wheat tortillas and drinking beer for their breakfasts.

At least it's only morning, I remember thinking.

Flower was standing at the stove, off to my right. She was smiling in the steam that rose from a black kettle.

"Come over, Easy."

She handed me a bowl of broth topped with a skin of tiny crackers. There was a poached egg toward the bottom of the bowl.

"Garlic soup," she smiled.

I sat on a stool next to her. The first swallow made me gag, but I kept on eating the stuff. I hadn't been eating very much and I thought I needed the strength.

The sun was coming through a little window in the back of the kitchen. Tiny motes of dust, like a school of minute silvery fish, floated in the ray. I thought of the Magnolia Street apartments and of Mofass, that shit-brown carp, pulling himself up the long stairs.

After a while my stomach settled down. My tooth socket barely ached.

"Here you are," Flower said. She was holding out a handful of tea bags. "If it hurts, bite down on one of these until it goes away."

I pocketed the bags and asked, "Where's Primo?"

"He went to see his brother in San Diego. They gonna come up here while we're down south."

So the plan was in action.

"Thanks for the dentist work, Flower. I guess I was a little outta my head what with the pain and the dope."

"We love you, Easy," was her reply.

It was all I could do to keep from crying.

• 34 •

When I got home I took a long shower and calmed down. Murder was quieter in my heart. It was still there but softer, a little less insistent. I took a long time toweling off and dressing. I took time to appreciate the crisp lines of my walnut chairs and the spirally grain of the pine floor in the bedroom.

I put on a nice tan pair of slacks that an old girlfriend had bought me but I had only worn once, and a red Jamaican shirt that was hand-painted with designs of giant green palm leaves. I put on white nylon socks and basketlike woven black leather shoes. My .38 was the last item I chose. It hung unnoticed at the back of my pants, under the billowing red blouse.

Once I was dressed I went out into the yard to appreciate the garden. I sat, hidden from the street, in the cast-iron chair for half an hour watching a jay dance in the grass. He was proud and happy in moist grass that had gotten too tall in past weeks. He didn't have a natural enemy in sight, and that was all he needed to be happy.

I thought about the Mexican badlands. They sounded pretty good.

Roberta Jefferson, Mofass' sister, didn't live far from my house. She and her husband, George, had a small place. They both worked for the Los Angeles Board of Education. He was with the board's internal delivery service and she was a breakfast cook at Lincoln High School.

She was home when I got there, wearing a big yellow handkerchief around her round brown face. I took my time walking up to the door.

She was inside ironing shirts, there was the smell of collard greens in the air. Dozens of iridescent green flies hovered around the screen door. Flies love the smell of cooked greens.

There was no need to knock.

"Hi, Easy," Roberta said. "How you doin'?"

"Fine, Ro, just fine."

I stood there in the doorway, taking my time, waiting.

"Come on in, baby, what brings you here?"

"Lookin' fo' Mofass is all."

"I ain't seen 'im in two or three days. But you know sometimes a month go by an' he don't come round."

"Yeah," I said. I pulled up a high stool next to where she was ironing. "He left me a note to pull a refrigerator out of one'a his places, but he didn't say what apartment. You know I don't wanna be pullin' out no po' son's icebox. I might be takin' his last po'k chop."

We laughed nicely and then Roberta said, "Well, I ain't seen 'im, Easy. He show up though. You know Billy-boy don't trust nobody an' he will make sure you did it right."

"That's what you call 'im?"

Roberta laughed. "Yeah. Billy-boy Wharton. That's why he don't like seein' us, 'cause I ain't about t'let him fo'get his Christian name."

"Yeah," I said. "Yeah."

I asked her about her husband and children. They were fine. George Jr. had just gotten over a case of the chicken pox and little Mozelle had grown titties and said she wanted a baby to go with them. Normal things. Roberta said that the board was hiring and maybe it was time for me to get a regular job. I said I'd look into it.

"Your momma down Louisiana, ain't she, Ro?" I asked to finish off the questions about her family.

"She'll live there till she dies."

"How old is she now?"

"Close enough to seventy so she could kiss it, but she always say sixty-two. Not that she don't look young enough to lie 'bout it. My sister Regina tole me jus' yestiday that Momma got a new boyfriend down there."

"At seventy!" I was scandalized.

"I guess it ain't worn out yet."

"She must be in good health."

"Strong as a hog," Roberta answered.

We traded some more pleasantries and then I excused myself.

I rode down to the Magnolia Street apartments next. It was like walking into the past. Nothing had changed. I saw an aluminum gum wrapper that had been in the gutter across the street the last time I had been there. I was amazed to think that the apartments were still my property. Who had maintained my rights on them while I was gone these long days?

"Good morning, Mr. Rawlins," Mrs. Trajillo said.

"Mornin', ma'am. How are you today?"

She smiled in answer and I walked up to her window. There was a portrait of Christ on the wall behind her. His chest was cut open, revealing a Valentine's heart crowned in thorns. He was staring at me, holding up two fingers as if to say, "Go slow, child, find your nemesis."

"Have the police been back?" I asked.

"Sealed off the apartment and asked us all questions about who did it."

"Did they know? Did they find the killer?"

"I don't think so, Mr. Rawlins, but they asked a lot about you and Mr. Mofass."

"Mofass was here that day?"

"I didn't see him, and I told that nice colored man that Mr. Mofass wouldn't crawl through a window."

Only just on his belly, like a snake, I thought.

"I told them everything I saw, Mr. Rawlins. There was only the people that live here and the postman with a special delivery and a white insurance salesman."

"What salesman was that?" I asked.

"Just some white man in an old suit. He said that it was life insurance he was selling." Mrs. Trajillo snorted. "Just trying to steal poor people's money." She didn't like white people too well.

"Did he try to sell any to you?"

"I wasn't interested, but he went up and down in here looking for somebody to rob."

I wasn't interested in an insurance man, though. "So that was it, huh?"

"I think so, Mr. Rawlins. That white policeman was checking the door around back. He said that it looked like it had been forced open not too long ago."

I thanked her and bid her goodbye. But I must have looked grim, because she said after me, "You take care now, Mr. Rawlins. You know it is nobody's fault when someone dies."

"No?"

"It is only God who takes life."

I kept the laughter inside of me, like a caged wolf.

I still felt dirty when I got home, so I took a long bath. I wanted to be clean, perfect. I put a chair beside the tub and laid my .38 on it. I left the door open and all the lights on. Shadows would be my alarm.

I called Dupree but Mouse was out, playing with LaMarque.

There was one chance that I had of staying in Los Angeles. That chance depended on some creative handling of the top-secret papers.

So I dressed in dark worker clothes, loaded a squirt gun with ammonia, wrapped a canvas tarp I used for painting, and bought three steaks from the corner store. Then I went to the car graveyard on Vernon and went around the back, because it was nighttime and the place was closed. I made it over the barbed-wire fence by laying the canvas tarp over it. I didn't have time for the regular business hours.

The yard was made up of wide alleys formed by stacks of automobiles. I had worked my way down three lanes before the dogs got my scent. I saw two of them, a boxerlike monster and a shepherd, round the aisle of cars. The first one was growling and running at me fast, his brother hot on his tail. I squirted them both directly on their snouts with my ammonia gun. A dog would rather gnaw off his tail than have a snout full of that poison.

The papers were right where Andre had said they'd be. They were bound in a leather notebook, the kind that zips up the side, behind the seat of an ancient Dodge pickup truck. I tucked them under my arm, thinking about how Chaim put those papers there. I hadn't really said goodbye to my friend.

By the time I reached the tarp-covered fence the dogs were on me again. The boxer/greyhound showed his teeth and snarled, but he was tentative for all that and hung back behind the three or four other dogs. I took out the squirt gun and splashed the first snapping dog—no breed would describe him—on the snout.

He couldn't get away from me fast enough. The other dogs were on their way soon after, and I got out of the whole thing with no more than a small cut I suffered opening the truck's door. I left the steaks on the ground near the fence. Those dogs couldn't bark after me, causing unwanted attention, if they had their mouths full of T-bone.

Before I knocked on the door I heard screaming. High-pitched yelling mixed with words like "no" and "no mo'."

I knocked. When Etta opened the door the yelling was still going on behind her. Mouse and LaMarque were wrestling on the couch. They were both yelling, but LaMarque was on top, playfully pounding the sides of Mouse's head. Mouse was bowing low, pretending to be in pain and screeching like his namesake.

Etta put her hand to my chest, which I felt all the way down to my knees, and said, "Thank you, baby, Raymond done come back t'life fo' him."

"Etta, do you love me?" I whispered.

"Yes, Easy, I do," she whispered back.

I wanted to ask her to run with me, to go down to Mexico, but I'd wait until Mouse was somewhere else.

"Easy!" Mouse shouted from inside.

"Hi, Unca Easy," LaMarque said.

I wondered if LaMarque would come with Etta and me down to

Mexico or would she leave him with her sister. He was still young enough to pick up a language if he had to.

"Hi, boys," I said. Then, "Raymond."

"Yeah, Ease?"

"I need yo' help on sumpin'."

LaMarque had looked away from us to a round table that they used for meals. Across it lay Mouse's long .41-caliber pistol. It looked obscene there, but I supposed it was safer than if Mouse wore it while they tussled.

"I'll make tea," Etta said. Raymond's artillery didn't seem to bother her. She just pushed it to one side and another as she wiped off the table.

"No, honey," I said. "Raymond an' me got business. We gots to go."

And so we left.

In the hall I said, "I need some help, Mouse."

"Who you want me to kill?" he asked, pulling out his pistol to prove his readiness.

"I just need you to come with me, Raymond. I gotta look into a couple'a things and I could use somebody at my back."

Raymond was smiling as he holstered his long gun.

We drove out to Mofass' office. I had the key, so it wouldn't be a case of burglary.

"What we lookin' fo', Ease?" Mouse asked me. He was working at his golden teeth with an ivory toothpick that he carried.

"Just sit'own, Raymond. I gotta search Mofass' files."

"You don't need me fo' that."

"Somebody tried t'shoot me out in front'a my house yesterday," I told him. "I was standin' out there with a friend and I just happened t'bend over or the lights woulda been out on my show."

"Oh," Mouse said simply. He felt for his pistol under his coat and sat back in Mofass' swivel chair. He put his feet up on the desk and smiled at me as I went through the filing cabinet.

In his files Mofass kept a book of all the properties he managed.

There were twelve columns to the right of each address or unit, where he indicated, on a monthly basis, if the place was occupied or not. If the property was vacant for that month there was an *x* marked in pencil.

There were about twenty unoccupied apartments, the longest vacancy being on Clinton Street. I listed them, but I really didn't think Mofass would try to hide in an apartment. People didn't like Mofass, and they were likely to blab his whereabouts if given the opportunity.

Mofass also managed a group of business properties and seven warehouses. All of them were rented. One warehouse was rented to Alameda Fruits and Vegetables Incorporated. Mofass had told me when they had gone out of business. The president, Anton Vitali, also owned the building. He'd cleared out the building but kept paying the rent, to himself, because he needed people to believe he was solvent as a real estate owner. Mofass was happy with that, because he still got his percentage and didn't have to lift a finger.

I gave Mouse all the addresses, telling him to check the warehouse first.

"You want me to kill 'im, Ease?" Mouse asked as simply as if he were offering me a beer.

"Just hold him, Ray. I'll do what killin's gotta be done."

• 35 •

He answered the phone himself on the first ring. "Craxton!"

"Hello, Mr. Craxton."

"Well, well, Mr. Rawlins, I thought you might've run out on me."

"No, sir. Where'm I gonna go?"

"No further than I can reach, that's for sure."

"I been kinda busy, gettin' news."

"What kind of news?"

"Chaim Wenzler is dead."

"What?"

"They shot him through his front door. Shot him dead."

"How do you know about it?"

"Shirley Wenzler, Chaim's daughter, brought me there. Seems like I'm the only one she trusts."

"Does she know who did it?"

"She thinks it was you."

"Horseshit!"

"Don't get me wrong, I ain't sayin' no government man gonna do somethin' like that. All I'm sayin' is that she really thinks that the government did it."

"You got anything I can use?"

"I think he was in it with somebody down here. Like you said, he was working with somebody colored. But I don't know who it is. Whoever it is, though, they pegged me early on."

"How'd they do that, Easy?" Craxton asked.

"I don't know, but I think I know how to find out."

"Did you find anything in his house?"

"Like what?"

"Anything," he said evasively. "Anything I might be interested in."

"No sir. But then again I didn't spend any too long checkin' it out either. I don't like keepin' company with the dead."

"But you're working for me, Rawlins. If you can't get your hands dirty, then why should I help you?"

"Maybe if I knew what it was you were lookin' for I could nose around. But you ain't told me shit, man, Agent Craxton."

That cut our conversation for a moment. When he finally spoke again it was in forced calm and measured tones.

"What about the girl, Easy? Does she know why he was killed?"

"She don't know nuthin'. But I heard a thing or two down at First African."

"What things?"

"You got your secrets, Mr. Craxton, and I got mines. I'ma look this thing down until I find out who killed Wenzler. When I find out I'ma tell you, alright?"

"No." I could almost hear him shaking his head. "That's not alright at all. You're working for me—"

I cut him off, "Uh-uh. You ain't payin' me an' you ain't done a damn thing fo' me neither. I will find your killer and I figure he will be the key to whatever it is you lookin' for. At that time you an' me will come to a deal."

"I'm the law, Mr. Rawlins. You can't bargain with the law."

"The fuck I cain't! Somebody put a bullet two inches from my head yesterday afternoon. This is my life we speakin' on, so either you take my deal or we call it quits."

For the most part I was blowing smoke. But I knew things that Craxton didn't know. I had the papers and I knew who Chaim and Poinsettia's killer was. One thing had nothing to do with the other, but when I was finished everything would be as neat as a buck private's bunk bed.

I had Craxton over a barrel. He finally said, "When will you have something for me?"

"Six o'clock tomorrow. I got some irons in the fire right now. By six tomorrow I should know everything. If not then, then the day after."

"Six tomorrow?"

"That's the time."

"Alright. I'll expect a call then." He was trying to sound like he was still in charge.

"One more thing," I blurted out before he could hang up.

"What?"

"You gotta make sure the police don't mess wit' me before then."

"You got it."

"Thanks."

In the darkness of my house I spun plans. None of them seemed real. Mofass was all I had. He was the only one who connected everything. He had been up to something with Poinsettia, and I was the one who told him about the taxes and First African. He was the only one I could suspect. If I was guessing right he told Jackie and Melvin about me nosing around First African. So he was really to blame for Reverend Towne and Tania Lee, or maybe he killed them too. And Mofass was the only one with a reason. He wanted my money. He knew that the government would take my property and that he could buy it before it ever went to auction. He knew how to make payoffs. That's why he didn't want to sign, because he wanted it all.

I was going to kill Mofass, mainly because he had killed my tenant and I felt that I owed her something. But also because he had killed Chaim and I had come to like that man. He had destroyed my life, and I felt I owed him something for that.

All the things I'd told Craxton were half-truths and lies for him to follow down while I was on my way to Mexico.

Mexico. EttaMae and I and maybe even LaMarque. It was like a dream. It was better than what I had, at least that's what I told myself.

I sat waiting for a call. No radio and no television. I turned a single light on in the bedroom and then went to the living room to sit in shadows. I had been reading a book on the history of Rome, but I didn't have any heart for it that night. The history of Rome didn't move me the way it usually did. I didn't care about the Visigoths and the Ostrogoths sacking the Empire; I didn't even care about the Vandals, how they were so terrible that the Romans made a word out of their name.

I didn't even believe in history, really. Real was what was happening to me right then. Real was a toothache and a man you trusted who did you dirt. Real was an empty stomach or a woman saying yes, or a woman saying no. Real was what you could feel. History was like TV for me, it wasn't the great wave of mankind moving through an ocean of minutes and hours. It wasn't mankind getting better either; I had seen enough murder in Europe to know that the Nazis were even worse than the barbarians at Rome's gate. And even if I was in Rome they would have called me a barbarian; it was no different that day in Watts.

Chaim wanted to make it better for me and my people. Chaim was a good man; better than a lot of people in Washington, and a lot of black people I knew. But he was dead. He was history, as they say, and I was holding my gun in the dark; being real.

• 36 •

I was jolted awake by Mouse's call.

"Got 'im, man," he said. There was pride in his voice. The kind of pride a man has when he's paid off a bank note or brought a paycheck home to his wife.

"Where is he?"

"Right here in front'a me. You know, this boy sure is ugly."

I heard Mofass' gruff voice in the background, but I couldn't make out what he said.

"Shut up, fool!" Mouse shouted in my ear. "We don't need to hear from you."

"Where are you, Raymond?"

"On Alameda, at that warehouse you said. I come in a window an' fount his stuff. You know all I hadda do was wait an' he come grubbin' up the slide."

The entrance to the building was in the alley off the main street. Two tall doors held together through the handles with a chain and padlock. When I rattled the door a window opened above and Mouse stuck his head out.

"Hey, Easy. Go on down the alley a little ways and they's a chute for loadin'. It's open."

It was a two-foot-square aluminum slat, reinforced by a wooden frame, that lifted away from the wall. It opened on a metal slide, leading up into the building. That slide was slick from all the merchandise they dropped down into delivery trucks.

When I made it up to the second floor I dusted off and released the safety on my pistol. There were aisles formed by huge stacks of cardboard boxes and wooden crates. There was some light, but the long rows melted into darkness, giving the place the feeling of great depth. I could have been in Solomon's mines.

"Over here, Easy," Mouse called.

I followed the sound of his voice until I came to a little square kiosk. From inside that office the light came. Thick and yellow electric light, and cigarette smoke. There was a large gray metal desk with a thick green blotter. Mofass was behind the desk, sweating and looking generally undignified. Mouse was leaning against a wall, smiling at me.

"Here he is, Easy. I put a apple in his mouth if you want it."

"What's the idea, Mr. Rawlins?" Mofass started up. "Why you got this man to kidnap me? What I do to you?"

I simply lifted the pistol and pointed it at his head. Mouse flashed his friendliest smile at no one in particular. Mofass' jaw started to quiver because of the spasm going through his neck and shoulders.

"You got this wrong, Mr. Rawlins. You pointin' that peacemaker at the wrong man."

"Go on, Easy, kill 'im," Mouse whispered.

That's what saved Mofass' life. Mouse didn't even know why I had that man there, he didn't care either. All he knew was that killing satisfied some nerve he had somewhere. I was growing the same nerve, and I didn't like that idea at all.

"What you mean, wrong man?" I asked.

Instead of answering, Mofass broke wind.

Then he said, "It's that tax man, Easy, it's Lawrence."

"What?" I hadn't thought anything he could say would surprise me. "Com'on, man. You could do better than that."

"You don't lie to no loaded gun at your head, Mr. Rawlins. It was Lawrence sure as I'm sitting here."

The smell of Mofass' flatulence filled the room. Mouse was waving his hand under his nose.

"You better come up with somethin' better than that, Mofass. This is your life right here in my hand."

I moved the muzzle of the gun closer to Mofass' sweaty brow. He opened his eyes a little wider.

"It's the truth, Mr. Rawlins. He pulled me down on a tax charge ovah a year ago."

Mouse kicked a chair around so that he could sit on it. Mofass leaped up out of his seat.

"Sit down," I said. "An' go on."

"Yeah." A smile appeared on Mofass' lips and vanished just as fast. "I ain't paid no tax, not ever. I filed it but I always looked like I didn't make nuthin'. Lawrence caught on, though. He had me by the nuts."

"Uh-huh, yeah, I know what you mean."

"He told me that he was goin' t'court wit' what he had. So I ast 'im could we talk it over, over a drink." Mofass smiled again. "You see, Mr. Rawlins, if he let me buy him a drink then I knowed I could buy him. I got to a phone an' called Poinsettia. She hadn't paid no rent even way back then. She told me she'd be nice t'me if I let 'er slide, but you know I don't play it like that."

For no reason Mouse grabbed Mofass by his wrist, roughly, and then let him go. The surprise made the fat man yelp like a dog.

"It's the t-t-truth, man. I called 'er an' told 'er that if she was nice to my friend I'd let her slip by the summer."

"So you put 'em together?"

"Yeah. Lawrence couldn't hold his liquor worth a damn. An' you know when Poinsettia got there, an' started strokin' 'im, he was drinkin' it like water an' swaggerin' in his chair. I took 'em down to a hotel that night."

"So?"

"What could I do?" Mofass hunched his sloped shoulders. "He had me run her out to 'im much as three times a week. They always be drinkin'. Sometimes I didn't even take 'em nowhere but they just do it in the car."

"While you drivin', man?" Mouse asked.

"Yeah!"

"Shit! Thas some white boy you got there, Easy."

"I don't believe a word of this shit," I said. "I seen Agent Lawrence, he straight as a pin."

Mofass put his hands up to placate me. Mouse, as usual, smiled at the sign of surrender.

"You ain't seen 'im when he gets to drinkin', Mr. Rawlins. He get crazy-like. An' you know Poinsettia be gettin' him so high on love. Then sometimes he'd get mean an' beat her till she stayed inside fo' a week."

I remembered seeing Poinsettia in sunglasses on cloudy days.

"Alright, Mofass. You got a story here but I still don't see what it gotta do wit' me."

"'Bout six months ago they was shackin' up in a house I was brokerin' down on Clark. Lawrence got drunk an' th'ew Miss Jackson down the stairs. She was hurt pretty bad an' we hadda take her to a doctor I know."

"She didn't have no accident?"

Mofass shook his head, swallowed to wet his throat, and continued. "At first he was guilty an' wanted t'pay fo' her. Thas when he set up Rufus Johnson."

"I know him. He's one'a the men on that list in yo' desk."

"Yeah, a colored man. Live in Venice Beach. Lawrence set him up for tax fraud, and then I snuck in and tole Mr. Johnson that I could free him up fo' some cash."

"An' you split the money?" I asked.

"Lawrence took most of it, I swear."

"An' now he's after me."

"We worked that job on five other people. Never nobody I knew. An' he was okay for a while but then he got like he needed money fo' him. He started complainin' 'bout how Poinsettia an' his own wife an' child were anchors on his neck. He started on me about findin' one rich Negro an' then he could leave for good."

"An' you give 'im me?"

Mofass' eyes filled with tears but he didn't say a word.

"How did he think he could get my money?"

"We was gonna get you t'sign yo' property ovah t'me an' then we'd play like he got the tax law on me, but really we'd sell off the property and he'd get the money on the sly. He was gonna take it all. He knowed how black people don't hardly ever fight with the law."

"But if that's true, why didn't you let me sign my money over when I asked?"

"You ain't no fool, I should know that, right? I figured that if I jumped at yo' idea you'd know sumpin' was up. So I told Lawrence t' sweat ya. Make you scared and you'd beg me t'take what you got. Then when I had tax troubles later on an' the IRS took my money you'd know what it was like an' jus' be happy it wasn't you."

"But you lyin', man. Even if this tax shit is true, why would he kill anybody?"

"Why'd I kill 'em, man?" he yelled.

Mouse, holding up a solitary finger, said, "Keep cool, brother." Then he slapped Mofass across his face with the pistol.

Mofass' head whipped around hard and his big body followed it down to the floor. He got up holding his bloody cheek with both hands.

"What you hit me fo'?" he screamed like a child.

Mouse held his finger up again, and Mofass was silent.

"Answer me, Mofass," I warned.

"I don't know. All I know is that he called me to his house right after that FBI man cut you loose. He told me he wanted to know ev'rything you did. So I tole 'im 'bout you workin' fo' the church. You know how you said you was keepin' tabs on Towne?"

"An' how come you didn't come t'me wit' none'a this?"

"He had me by my balls, Mr. Rawlins. I was a tax evader an' I helped him rob them people. An' you know he was crazy too.

"He tole me that if the FBI got hold of his files on you they would know what we were up to. That's why he had me go to Jackie and Melvin. He went t'Towne hisself."

"An' killed him?"

"I don't know. All I know is that he went there and that Towne is dead."

I went on, "But you didn't say nuthin' when people started gettin' killed, did you, Mofass?" The muscles in my arm twitched, and I shifted the pistol so as not to shoot him before I knew it all.

"At first I didn't know. I mean, why would I think that he gonna kill Poinsettia? An' by the time Towne got it I was scared about me."

"Why'd Poinsettia get killed? What she have to do with this?"

"He offered her money, money so that she would call the po-lice an' blame you for beatin' her."

Mofass lifted his hands in a gesture of helplessness. The side of his face was swelling around the deep red welt on his cheek.

"You know how that girl was. She said sumpin' to 'im. Like how she gonna go to you if he don't pay her some more. She blamed him fo' her bein' sick an' she wanted to be taken care of."

"Man, that don't make no sense. Why he want her to blame me fo' hittin' her in the first place?"

"If you was in jail the FBI would have to find somebody else and then he could still get your money and save his ass."

Mofass began to weep.

"And you were going to let me give it to 'im, huh?"

"What was you gonna do fo' that FBI, man? Ain't that what he had you doin'? He said he'd save yo' money if you do somebody else dirt, ain't that right? How come you any different than me?"

Mofass hurt me with that.

"Let's get it over, Ease," Mouse said. He waved his pistol in the general direction of Mofass. I wouldn't have believed such a fat man could cower in his chair.

"No, man."

"I thought you wanted this boy's blood?" Mouse sounded indignant. "He fucked wit' you, right?"

"Yeah, he did do that."

"Then le's kill the mothahfuckah."

"That's alright. I got a better idea."

Mofass let another fart go.

"Like what?" Mouse asked.

"I want you to give me Lawrence's address, Mofass."

"You got it."

"And I want his home phone number too."

"Yes, sir, Mr. Rawlins, I got it right here," he said, tapping his temple.

"Don't mistake me, Mofass," I warned. "This ain't no merry-go-round here. You go fast right to the grave if you make a bad step. My man Raymond here is death, yo' death if you do sumpin' wrong."

"You don't have to warn me on that account," Mofass said in his business voice. "But can I ask you what it is you plan to do?"

"Same as you'd get if you play this wrong."

After he'd written the information I told him, "Go home, Mofass. Go somewhere. It will all be over by this time tomorrow."

After Mofass fled, Mouse said, "We shoulda killed 'im."

"No reason," I answered.

"He tried to cheat you man, Tried to steal yo' money."

"Yeah, he did. But you know we wasn't never friends. Uh-uh, Mofass an' me was in business. Businessmen steal just to keep in practice fo' they legal work."

I was glad the big man had left. He was so gaseous that he'd smelled up the whole office.

"Thank you, Raymond," I said. We shook hands.

"You my friend, Easy, you ain't gotta thank me. Shit! You the one set my head straight about LaMarque. You my best friend, man."

As I drove for home I thought about how I intended to take Mouse's wife and son and disappear in the Mexican hills. I couldn't kill Mofass, because I was no better than he was.

Once I got home I dialed the number Mofass had given me.

"Hello?" a timid woman's voice said.

"May I speak to Reggie Lawrence, please?" I asked.

"Who is this?" she asked. There was fear in her voice; fear so great that it shook me.

But still I told her who I was and she went to fetch my nemesis.

"Rawlins?"

"I want twenty-five hundred dollars," I said. "Don't gimme no shit, 'cause I know you got it. I want it in tens and twenties and I want it tomorrow evening."

"What the hell—" he started.

But I cut him off. "Listen man, I ain't got no time fo' yo' shit. I know what you been doin' an' I could prove it too. Mofass spilled his guts, an' I know you cain't afford no close look. So drop this shit an' bring me the money or they gonna turn yo' office into a jail cell."

"If this is some trick to get out of your taxes . . ." He said. He was trying to sound like he was still the boss, but I could hear the sweat on his tongue.

"Griffith Park, Reggie. Down below the observatory just inside the woods. Eight P.M. An army man will know how to be on time."

I told him how to get there, and before he could say another word, I hung up on him.

And you know that felt sweet.

• 37 •

At about seven A.M. I was parked down the street from 1135½ Stanley Street. It was a block or so north of Olympic Boulevard, and a solidly white neighborhood, but I took the chance that the police wouldn't see me. I had most of the plans wrapped up in an envelope, his name lightly taped in the center, next to me in the front seat. I wore black gloves, a porter's cap, and a uniform from a hotel Dupree once worked for in Houston.

At eight-fifteen Lawrence walked out his front door. I scooted down, squinted, and jammed my tongue into the socket Primo and Flower had created in my jaw. He went to his car and drove off, leaving his wife and child at home.

I waited another half an hour so she wouldn't be suspicious, and then I knocked at the door. There was crying in the background. It got louder when the door opened.

Mrs. Lawrence was small and redheaded, though there was lots of gray in the red. She seemed to be young, but her head hung forward as though it were weighed down. She had to lift her head and screw up her eyes to look at me. The stitched scar coming down the left side of her mouth was jagged, the flesh around her right eye puffy and discolored. There was bright red blood in the white of her eye.

"Can I help you?" she asked.

"Delivery, ma'am," I said in the crisp tone I used to address officers in WWII.

"Delivery for whom?"

"I got it here for a Reginald A. Lawrence," I said. "It's from a law firm in Washington."

She tried to smile, but the child started hollering. She turned away and then back to me, quickly. She put her hand out and said, "I'm his wife, I'll take it."

"I don't know . . ." I stalled.

"Hurry, please, my baby's sick."

"Well . . . okay, but I still need one ninety-five for the COD."

"Hold on," she sighed on an exasperated note. She went back into the house, running in the direction of the crying.

I slipped in the front door, taking out a sheet of government secrets that I'd folded into eighths. The door opened into a little entrance hall that was designed to make the house seem larger. There was a coat rack and lacquered ornamental desk in the hall. I opened the drawer to the desk and shoved the little slip of evidence under a pile of maps.

I moved into the living room, where the lady was fretting over a folding bed. The bed wasn't big, but the child in it was so slight that you could have gotten four or five children his width to lie there. He was almost as long as the bed, but his arms and legs were so skinny that they could have belonged to an infant. His wrists were torn and scabrous; his naked chest was covered with sharp, blue-green bruises. One of his eyes drifted around and the other fastened onto me as he moaned.

"Ma'am?" I said.

"Yes?" She didn't even turn to me, just cried as she wilted next to the child, who was weeping softly now that his mother was near.

I helped her to her feet.

"What happened to him?" I asked.

"Polio," she replied.

Who knows? Maybe she believed it.

She shot a quick glance at the child and stood up.

"He needs me," she said. "I have to be here. He needs me, he needs me."

I folded my arms around her, thinking of how her husband tried to shoot me the last time I'd held a woman. I helped her to a chair.

I removed Lawrence's name from the envelope and put the evidence in her lap.

"This ain't nuthin' important," I whispered. "Just give it to him when you got the chance."

I was at Griffith Park by seven P.M. I stopped my car on a fire trail below the observatory and hiked up through the trees behind the great domed building. It was a long hike, but I thought that it was worth the extra insurance to have a vantage point before the government man showed. There was a rustling of branches in the trees behind me as I made my way, but that didn't worry me.

It was almost eight-fifteen before Lawrence showed. He walked right down the grassy hill behind the lower wall and walked almost to the line of trees. He stretched out his left arm and snapped his wrist to his face to look at his watch. He was still gawky and awkward, but there was a new kind of aggressiveness in his gait. He strutted like a rooster, cocking his head from side to side as if he were spoiling for a fight.

"Evenin', Reggie," I called out from behind a scraggly pine. I walked out of the trees to meet him with both hands in my pockets.

He made a gesture toward his breast, but I brought my right hand out to show him the little pistol I held, then I shoved it back in my jacket pocket. He gave me a lopsided smile and hunched his shoulders. His big, bruising hands hung peacefully at his side.

"You got the money?" I asked.

He leaned forward slightly, indicating a brown paper parcel he held in his jacket.

"But if I give you this money, what guarantee do I have that you'll let me be?" he asked.

"I know you a killer, man. I'ma run wit' this here money. Run someplace you cain't find me."

He smiled at me, and we both froze in time. I could see that he didn't plan to move until I said something else, so I asked, "Why, man?"

He jumped slightly from a tremor running through his body.

"Hey! Fuck you!" he said, twisting his neck from side to side. I could smell the gin.

"Uh-uh, really. I gotta know, man. Why do you do all this shit?" I asked. I knew he was crazy, but I just wanted to have some reason.

There was a fever in Agent Lawrence's eyes.

"Niggers and Jews," he said. It was a toss-up whether or not he was talking to me.

"Like your wife an' child?"

He looked me in the eye then. But he was quiet.

"I mean, why Towne? Why Poinsettia?"

"I told the nigger minister about you. You know what he did?"

Lawrence brought his fists to his shoulders, so I said, "Cool it, man."

"Yeah." Lawrence sputtered a laugh. "He threw me out. But I went back there. Yes sir, I did."

He giggled again. I took the pistol from my pocket.

"And the bitch lived like a pig." Agent Lawrence was breathing hard. "Filthy. And she acted like I could, could ever be like that . . . All you had to do was pay. All you had to do was follow the program. I didn't want to kill them. But it was my ass out there on the line."

"Chaim Wenzler wasn't nuthin' to you, man."

"He was something to the FBI. If he was out of the way then they wouldn't need you."

"But then you tried t'kill me!"

Lawrence giggled again, and bit his thumb.

Twilight was falling. Actually it felt as if the darkness was rising out of the trees. It was time for me to collect my money and leave.

"Okay," I said. I had my hand on the pistol like another time. "Gimme the money."

I'd planned to act nervous when I took his money; but I didn't need to act.

"I thought you might be a nigger with nuts," he said, suddenly somber.

I felt my gorge rise, but I didn't give in. The night was coming on faster, soon we'd just be shadows.

"You don't really think that I'm going to let you get away with blackmailing me, do you?"

"Do somethin' stupid an' you'll see what kinda nuts I got."

Suddenly he made his decision. He took the package from the recess of his jacket and handed it to me.

I said, "Nice to do business with ya. You could go now."

The moment I touched the envelope he lunged forward and shouldered me in the chest, hard. Because we were on a hill I had the feeling of flight again, but this time I landed on my backside, my hands shooting out behind.

I tried to bring my gun around but couldn't. Lawrence ran down and kicked my shoulder. He grinned at me as he yanked awkwardly at the pistol in his pocket.

"Don't do it, man!" I shouted in warning. But he had the pistol out.

He said the word, nigger, and then he flew backwards about six feet. When he was in the air I heard the cannonlike pistol shot from down among the trees. I was running before the echoes were through shouting my name.

As fast as I ran, Mouse was already in the car by the time I got there.

He smiled at me and said, "You a damn fool, Easy Rawlins. We shoulda kilt that man the minute he showed his ugly face."

"I had to know, Raymond. I had to know for me."

We were driving down away from the observatory, through the forestlike park.

"You like some stupid cowboy, Easy. You wanna yell 'Draw!' 'fore you fire. That kinda shit gets ya killed."

He was right, of course, but that way I convinced myself that I wasn't a murderer. I gave him a chance to walk away from it—at least until I'd told the police about him.

"Was he the one?" Mouse asked. He really didn't care.

"He did the killin's."

"What you gonna do now?"

"Pray nobody saw us an' tell the FBI man that Lawrence forced me to tell about the work I was doin'. That he stole the papers from Wenzler. That he turned into a spy for profit. And I'll prove it by sayin' he was into tax cases fo' profit."

While I talked I counted out a five-hundred-dollar pile for Mouse.

I didn't intend to keep anything. I gave to the families of the dead people, including Shirley Wenzler. I figured that Lawrence should at least pay dollars for the havoc he'd caused. I even donated a thousand dollars to the African Migration. Sonja Achebe has sent me postcards from Nigeria for over thirty years.

Mouse stuck out his lower lip. "Not too bad. Not too bad."

I lit a couple of cigarettes while he drove. There were no sirens or any special activities on the road. I handed a cigarette to Mouse and breathed deep.

"Where you goin' now?" he asked after five or six miles of driving. We were on Adams Boulevard and all the police cars ignored our progress.

"I tole LaMarque I'd come by and take him for hot dogs."

And then I'd take him to Mexico, I thought.

• 38 •

But there was no reason to run anymore. There wasn't a killing they could pin on me. When they found Lawrence and uncovered his crimes they hushed up the whole thing. His pistol was matched for Reverend Towne, Tania Lee, and Chaim Wenzler. I gave them a list of hotels that Mofass had driven Lawrence and Poinsettia to. They found his fingerprints in her apartment. Mrs. Trajillo recognized the photograph of the annoying insurance man.

I was ashamed of what I'd done to Mouse and what I planned to do. Mofass shamed me because we were just alike. I made like I was friends with people and then I planned to do them dirt.

I was at the Filbert Hotel that night. I knocked at the door and was admitted by Shirley. She was dressed in a simple pink shift that came down to her knee. She smiled shyly at me. I was surprised to remember that we had been lovers.

"Hi," she said and then ducked her head.

The room was just large enough for two single beds and a chair and dresser.

"I was afraid that you might be the government men," she said. "I was sure that they'd kill you and then come to get me."

"No," I said. "They know who did it now. The man that killed your father, that is. It wasn't the government at all. Just a man who wanted to make some fast money. He thought he could take those plans and sell 'em."

"Who was it?"

"Nobody. Nobody you'd know."

I sat on one of the beds and Shirley settled beside me. I could feel her weight.

"It's okay now. You don't have to worry. I don't think the government wants to mess with you."

She didn't respond. I knew she wanted me to hold her, but I didn't. I'd already gotten her father killed, already destroyed her world.

After a long while I asked, "What are you going to do now?"

"I don't know. Go home, I guess. But are you sure it's true?"

"Yeah, this guy was involved with First African. He was kind of crazy. He hated communists and black people and things like that."

"He killed Reverend Towne?"

"Yeah."

"Have they caught him?"

"Not yet."

"What's his name?"

"I didn't get that. But whoever he was he thought I knew somethin'. That's why he shot at me in front of the house. He wasn't tryin' t'kill you at all."

I saw the relief in her face and then the guilt she felt for being glad that I was the target. I touched her hand.

"You can go home now, Shirley. It's alright."

She trusted me. I might as well have been the one to shoot her poor father through the door, but she didn't know that. And I wasn't going to tell her.

Primo trusted me too. I told him that the bad man was dead but that I didn't need to leave anymore.

"I already spent half the money, Easy," he said, acting a little cagey. "And I got my brother up here to take care of the place."

"That's okay, man. You an' Flower have a good time down there."

"Okay," Primo said. He was laughing, so I figured that he had my five hundred dollars in his pocket. "But you know Jesus will be too sad if he knows you ain't coming, Easy. That boy loves you. I think you should take him until we get back."

"What?"

"He's your boy, Easy. He loves you. Take him and if you want I'll take him back when we come."

"How long?"

"Three months, maybe four."

So I said goodbye to Primo and Flower and I got Jesus in the bargain.

They were gone for three years. By then Jesus was my son.

Craxton was just as happy as Primo. They had found Lawrence face-down beside the observatory. He called me to his office, one floor above Lawrence's room on Sixth Street.

"You say that Lawrence was in it with Wenzler? How can that be when he could only know Wenzler through you?"

"He tried to bribe me, Mr. Craxton. He put the squeeze on Mofass and then when you got involved he tried to get me in trouble."

"How did you find out about it?"

"Mofass finally broke down and told me."

Craxton nodded.

"I told him that I was going against a white guy doin' charities for the church. I didn't know that he was crazy."

"What about the girl, your tenant?"

"He knew about my buildin' and he wanted to squeeze me for a payoff, so he killed her I guess to put me in jail. If I was in jail I couldn't work for you."

"But if you were in jail for murder, how could he get your money?"

"I don't think he meant to kill her, really. I think he only wanted to hurt her. That's why her face was so bruised up. When she died he tried to make it look like suicide."

That last little bit of thinking was a little too sophisticated for what Craxton thought a Negro could come up with. He looked at me suspiciously but didn't say anything. Craxton didn't want to rock the boat. He had a dead communist and a man dealing in espionage. He had the evidence I planted at Lawrence's house and two bodies. I imagined that he'd get a promotion out of it.

"And where is Shirley Wenzler?" he asked.

"She's home, Mr. Craxton, and you know she don't have nuthin' t'do with this. She didn't have anything to do with what her father was doing."

"You like her, huh, Easy?"

"She's clean, man."

Craxton chuckled. He was on top of the world.

"But let me ask you somethin'," I said.

"Yes, Easy?"

"Why didn't you tell me about them papers Wenzler had?"

"Because you weren't supposed to know. Nobody was. It was a secret project that Champion had scrapped. Lindquist was supposed to have destroyed the copies he had. I was supposed to make sure that he had done that. We both slipped up."

"You mean they weren't even anything you were gonna use?"

"It would still have looked bad if they showed up in Russia."

"Look bad?"

I didn't tell anybody about Jackie Orr and Melvin Pride, or about Winona. I sent a letter to Odell, though; I didn't want to burn my brothers and sisters but I didn't want them to continue stealing from the church either. I left the African Migration out of it completely.

"I don't know, Mr. Rawlins, I don't know. It's all real neat, but who killed Lawrence?"

"I don't know," I said. "I wasn't there."

Craxton was true to his word and I took two years to pay off the money that the IRS said I owed. He also took the heat off of Shirley Wenzler and gave me his private number where I could get to him anytime.

Andre Lavender and Juanita got back into circulation. He never stood trial because Craxton never brought up his name. The FBI man wanted smooth sailing over a sea of death and silence.

Everything was fine.

The night after I spoke to Craxton I went to see Etta. I opened the door with my key. The apartment was dark, but I expected that. The door to LaMarque's room was open. I looked in to see him smiling in the arms of a giant teddy bear that I was sure came from Mouse.

"That's it, Etta," I heard him say. His voice came right through the wall, as if he were whispering in my ear. "Oh yeah, yeah. You know I missed that."

Then a loud smacking sound and then, "I love you, Daddy."

"You say what?" Raymond Alexander asked his wife, his woman.

"I love you, Daddy. I *need* you."

"You need this?"

And she made a sound that I cannot duplicate. It was deep and guttural and so charged with pleasure that I got dizzy and lowered myself to the floor.

The sounds Etta made got louder and even more passionate. She never made those sounds because of me; no woman ever had.

Mouse is crazy, I thought, just crazy!

But I wished for his insanity.

Etta did too.

• 39 •

The boy and I went to Mofass' office a few days later.

Jesus went through the door first and pulled out the chair for me to sit in front of my employee.

Mofass was staring at a plate of eggs and ham, with hash browns on the side. He'd probably been doing that for a quarter of an hour.

"Mo'nin, Mr. Rawlins." He had a leery look in his eye. Any man who survived a death threat from Raymond Alexander was leery.

"Mofass. What's goin' on?"

"They took me down to the federal detention center fo' a couple'a days there."

I opened my eyes as if I was surprised.

"Yeah, they did," he continued. "But I guess I gotta thank you fo' not pressin' no charge at the IRS."

"Part'a the deal the FBI guy made. I don't cause no trouble and they let me pay off my back taxes, on the quiet side."

"Well, I guess I should thank you anyway. That was a tight spot we was all in. You coulda taken it out on me."

"Should have too," I said.

Mofass glared.

"Jesus," I said. I fished a quarter out of my shirt pocket and flipped it to him. "Go get us some candy at that store we saw."

He gave me a mute grin and ran for the door.

I waited for the sound of his steps down the stairs to fade before talking again.

"That's right, Mofass, I shoulda let Raymond waste your ass. I should have but I couldn't, 'cause you my own personal hell. But it don't matter. You see, I lost sumpin' since that day we talked about that letter. I lost a lot. I got a good friend who hates me now 'cause he think I got his minister killed. An' I cain't go to him 'cause it was my fault, really. An' I lost my woman because I wasn't good enough. There's a lotta people dead 'cause'a me. And I turnt Poinsettia out. You told me to do it, but it's on my head, 'cause—"

He interrupted me. "I don't see what all this gotta do with me. If you want my keys to the places, I got 'em here."

"I made a good friend, Mofass, but yo' friend cut 'im down. Didn't even look in his face. Shot him through the door."

"What you want from me, Mr. Rawlins?"

"I ain't got no friends, man. All I got is Jackson Blue, who'd give me up fo' a bottle 'a wine, and Mouse; you know him. And a Mexican boy who cain't speak English hardly an' if he did he cain't talk no ways."

Sweat had appeared on Mofass' brow. I must've sounded pretty crazy.

"I want you to keep on workin' fo' me, William. I want you to be my friend."

Mofass put the cigar between his fat lips and puffed smoke. I don't think he knew how big his eyes were.

"Sure," he said. "You my best customer, Mr. Rawlins."

"Yeah, man. Yeah."

We sat there staring at each other until Jesus came back. He brought three tubes of chocolate disks, Flicks they were called. The three of us ate the chocolate in silence.

Jesus was the only one smiling.

• III •

WHITE BUTTERFLY

For the stories he keeps on telling

I dedicate this book to Leroy Mosley.

• 1 •

"Easy Rawlins!" someone called.

I turned to see Quinten Naylor twist the handle of my front gate.

"Eathy," my baby, Edna, cooed as she played peacefully with her feet in her crib next to me on the front porch.

Quinten was normal in height but he was broad and powerful-looking. His hands were the size of potholders, even under the suit jacket his shoulders were round melons. Quinten was a brown man but there was a lot of red under the skin. It was almost as if he were rage-colored.

As Quinten strode across the lawn he crushed a patch of chives that I'd been growing for seven years.

The violent-colored man smiled at me. He held out his beefy paw and said, "Glad I caught you in."

"Uh-huh." I stepped down to meet him. I shook his hand and looked into his eyes.

When I didn't say anything there was an uncomfortable moment for the Los Angeles police sergeant. He stared up into my face wanting me to ask him why he was there. But all I wanted was for him to leave me to go back into my home with my wife and children.

"Is this your baby?" he asked. Quinten was from back east, he spoke like an educated white northerner.

"Yeah."

"Beautiful child."

"Yeah. She sure is."

"She sure is," Quinten repeated. "Takes after her mother, I bet."

"What do you want wit' me, officer?" I asked.

"I want you to come with me."

"I'm under arrest?"

"No. No, not at all, Mr. Rawlins."

I knew when he called me mister that the LAPD needed my services again. Every once in a while the law sent over one of their few black representatives to ask me to go into the places where they could never go. I was worth a precinct full of detectives when the cops needed the word in the ghetto.

"Then why should I wanna go anywhere wit' you? Here I am spendin' the day wit' my fam'ly. I don't need no Sunday drive wit' the cops."

"We need your help, Mr. Rawlins." Quinten was becoming visibly more crimson under his brown shell.

I wanted to stay home, to be with my wife, to make love to her later on. But something about Naylor's request kept me from turning him down. There was a kind of defeat in the policeman's plea. Defeat goes down hard with black people; it's our most common foe.

"Where we gonna go?"

"It's not far. Twelve blocks. Hundred and Tenth Street." He turned as he spoke and headed for the street.

I yelled into the house, "I'm goin' fo' a ride with Officer Naylor. I'll be back in a while."

"What?" Regina called from her ironing board out back.

"I'm goin' out for a while," I yelled. Then I waved at my forty-foot avocado tree.

Little Jesus peeked out from his perch up there and smiled.

"Come on down here," I said.

The little Mexican boy climbed down the tree and ran up to me with a silent smile stitched across his face. He had the face of an ancient American, dark and wise.

"I don't want you off exploring today, Jesus," I said. "Stay around here and look after your mother and Edna."

Jesus looked at his feet and nodded.

"Look up here at me." I did all the talking when around Jesus because he hadn't said a word in the eight years I'd known him.

Jesus squinted up at me.

"I want you close to home. Understand me?"

Quinten was at his car, looking at his watch.

Jesus nodded, looking me in the eye this time.

"All right." I rubbed his crew-cut peach fuzz and went out to meet the cop.

Officer Naylor drove me to an empty lot in the middle of the 1200 block of 110th Street. There was an ambulance parked out front, flanked by patrol cars. I noticed a bright patent-leather white pump in the gutter as we crossed the street.

A crowd had gathered on the sidewalk. Seven white police officers stood shoulder to shoulder across the front of the property, keeping everybody out. The feeling was festive. The policemen were all at ease, smoking cigarettes and joking with the Negro gawkers.

The lot itself was decorated with two rusted-out Buicks that were hunkered down on broken axles in the weeds. A knotty oak had died toward the back end of the lot.

Quinten and I walked through the crowd. There were men, women, and children stretching their necks and bobbing back and forth. A boy said, "Lloyd saw 'er. She dead."

When we walked past the line of policemen one of them caught me by the arm and said, "Hey you, son."

Quinten gave him a hard stare and the officer said, "Oh, okay. You can go on."

Just one of the many white men I've shrugged off. His instinctive disrespect and arrogance hardly even mattered. I turned away and he was gone from my life.

"Right this way, Mr. Rawlins," Quinten Naylor said.

There were four plainclothes policemen looking down at the back of the tree. I couldn't make out what it was that they saw.

I recognized one of the cops. He was a burly white man, the kind of fat man who was fat everywhere, even in his face and hands.

"Mr. Rawlins," the burly man said. He held out a pillowy hand.

"You remember my partner," Quinten said. "Roland Hobbes."

We'd come around the tree by then. There was a woman in a pink party dress, a little open at the breast, sitting with her back against the trunk. Her legs were straight out in front of her, a little apart. Her head tilted to the side, away from me, and her hands were on either side of her thighs with the palms up. Her left foot sported a white pump, her right foot was bare.

I remember the softness and the underlying strength of Roland Hobbes' hand and the insect I saw perched on the woman's temple. I wondered why she didn't bat it away.

"Nice to see you," I was saying to Hobbes when I realized that the insect was a dried knot of blood.

When Roland let go of my hand he listed toward Quinten and said, "Same thing."

"Both?" Quinten asked.

Roland nodded.

The girl was young and pretty. It was hard for me to think that she was dead. It seemed as if she might get up from there any minute and smile and tell me her name.

Somebody whispered, "Third one."

• 2 •

They carried the body on a stretcher when the photographers were through—police photographers, not newsmen. A black woman getting killed wasn't photograph material for the newspapers in 1956.

After that Quinten Naylor, Roland Hobbes, and I got into Naylor's Chevrolet. He was still driving a 1948 model. I imagined him on his day off, in short sleeves, slaving and struggling under the hood to keep that jalopy running.

"Don't they give you a car when you with the police?" I asked.

"They called me from home. I came straight here."

"Then why'ont you buy yourself a new car?"

I was sitting in the front seat. Roland Hobbes had gotten in the back. He was deferential kind of a person, always polite and correct; I didn't trust him worth a damn.

"I don't need a new car. This car is just fine," Naylor said.

I looked down at the ruptured vinyl seat between my thighs. The gold-colored foam rubber gushed forth under my weight.

We drove quite a way down Central Avenue. That was before the general decline of the neighborhood. The streets were clean and the drunks were few. I counted fifteen churches between 110th Street and Florence Boulevard. At that corner was the Goodyear Rubber Plant. It was a vast field with two giant buildings far off to the northern end. There was also the hangar for the Goodyear Blimp there. Across the street sat a World gas station. World was a favorite hangout for Mexican hot-rodders and motorcycle enthusiasts who decorated their German machines with up to three hundred pounds of chrome piping and doodads.

Naylor drove to the gate of the Goodyear plant and flashed his badge at the guard. We drove to a large asphalt parking lot where hundreds of cars were parked neatly in rows like they were on sale. There were always cars parked there, because the Goodyear plant worked twenty-four hours a day, seven days a week.

"Let's take a walk," Naylor said.

I got out of the car with him. Hobbes stayed in the backseat. He picked up a *Jet* magazine that Naylor had back there and turned directly to the centerfold, the bathing-suit picture.

We walked out into the center of the grassy field. The sky was tending toward twilight. Every fourth or fifth car driving the boulevards had turned on their lights.

I didn't ask Quinten what we were doing. I knew it was something important for him to want to impress me with the fact that he could get onto that fancy lawn.

"You hear about Juliette LeRoi?" Quinten asked.

I had heard about her, her death, but I asked, "Who?"

"She was from French Guiana. Worked as a cocktail waitress for the Champagne Lounge."

"Yeah?" I prompted him.

"About a month ago she was killed. Throat cut. Raped too. They found her in a trash can on Slauson."

It was back-page news. TV and radio didn't cover it at all. But most colored people knew about it.

"Then there was Willa Scott. We found her tied to the pipes under a sink in an abandoned house on Hoover. She had her mouth taped shut and her skull caved in."

"Raped?"

"There was semen on her face. We don't know if that happened before or after she died. The last time she was seen was at the Black Irish."

I felt a knot in my gut.

"And now we have Bonita Edwards."

I was watching the field and the row of businesses beyond on Florence. The air darkened even as Naylor spoke. Lights twinkled on in the distance.

"That this girl's name?" I asked him. I was sorry I had come. I didn't want to care about these women. The rumors around the neighborhood were bad enough, but I could ignore rumors.

"Yes." Quinten nodded. "A *dancer*, another bar girl. Three party girls. So far."

The grass shifted from green to gray with the dusk.

I asked, "So why you talkin' t'me?"

"Juliette LeRoi had been in that can for two days before somebody called in the smell. Rigor mortis had set in. They didn't find the marks until after the news story was out."

My stomach let out a little groan.

"Willa Scott and Bonita Edwards had the same marks."

"What marks do you mean?"

Quinten darkened like the night. "Burns," he said. "Cigar burns on their, their breasts."

"So it's all the same man?" I asked. I thought of Regina and Edna. I wanted to get home, to make sure the doors were locked.

The policeman nodded. "We think so. He wants us to know he's doing it."

Quinten stared me in the eye. Behind him L.A. sizzled into a net of electric lights.

"What you lookin' at?" I dared him.

"We need you on this one, Easy. This one is bad."

"Just who do you mean when you say 'we'? Who is that? You and me? We gonna go'n hire somebody?"

"You know what I mean, Rawlins."

In my time I had done work for the numbers runners, churchgoers, businessmen, and even the police. Somewhere along the line I had slipped into the role of a confidential agent who represented people when the law broke down. And the law broke down often enough t keep me busy. It even broke down for the cops sometimes.

The last time I worked with Naylor he needed me to lure a killer named Lark Reeves out of Tijuana.

Lark had been in an illegal crap game in Compton and was down twenty-five dollars to a slumming white boy named Chi-Chi MacDonald. When Chi-Chi asked for his money he was a little too cocky and Lark shot him in the face. The shooting wasn't unusual but the color line had been crossed and Quinten knew that he could make a case for a promotion if he could pull Lark in.

As a rule I will not run down a black man for the law. But when Quinten came to me I had a special need. It was a week before Regina and I were to be married, and her cousin Robert Henry was in jail for robbery.

Robert had argued with a market owner. He said that a quart of milk he'd bought had soured in the store. When the grocer called him a liar Robert just picked up a gallon jug and made for the door. The grocer grabbed Bob by the arm and called to the checker for help.

Bob said, "You got a friend, huh? That's okay, 'cause I got a knife."

It was the knife that put Bob in jail. They called it armed robbery.

Regina loved her cousin, so when Quinten came to me about Lark I made him an offer. I told him that I'd set up a special poker game down in Watts and get the word out to Lark. I knew that Lark couldn't resist a good game.

High-stakes poker put Lark in San Quentin. He never connected me with the cops who busted the game and dragged him off to be identified at the station.

Quinten got his promotion because the cops thought that he had his thumb on the pulse of the black community. But all he really had was me. Me and a few other Negroes who didn't mind playing dice with their lives.

But I had stopped taking those kind of chances after I got married. I wasn't a stool for the cops anymore.

"I don't know nuthin' 'bout no dead girls, man. Don't you think I'd come tell ya if I did? Don't you think I'd wanna stop somebody killin' Negro women? Why, I got me a pretty young wife at home right now . . ."

"She's all right."

"How do you know?" I felt the pulse in my temples.

"This man is killing good-time girls. He's not after a nurse."

"Regina works. She comes home from the hospital, sometimes at night. He could be stalkin' her."

"That's why I need your help, Easy."

I shook my head. "Uh-huh, man. I cain't help you. What could I do?"

My question threw Naylor. "Help us," he said feebly.

He was lost. He wanted me to tell him what to do because the police didn't know how to catch some murderer who didn't make sense to them. They knew what to do when a man killed his wife or when a loan shark took out a bad debt. They knew how to question witnesses, white witnesses. Even though Quinten Naylor was black he didn't have sympathy among the rough crowd in the Watts community; a crowd commonly called *the element.*

"What you got so far?" I asked, mostly because I felt sorry for him.

"Nothing. You know everything I know."

"You got some special unit workin' it?"

"No. Just me."

Th cars passing on the distant streets buzzed in my ears like hungry mosquitoes.

"Three girls dead," I said. "An' you is all they could muster?" 

"Hobbes is on it with me."

I shook my head, wishing I could shake the ground under my feet.

"I cain't help you, man," I said.

"Somebody's got to help. If they don't, who knows how many girls will die?"

"Maybe you' man'll just get tired, Quinten."

"You've got to help us, Easy."

"No I don't. You livin' in a fool's nightmare, Mr. Policeman. I can't help you. If I knew this man's name or if I knew somethin', anything.

But it's the cops gotta gather up evidence. One man cain't do all that."

I could see the rage gathering in his arms and shoulders. But instead of hitting me Quinten Naylor turned away and stalked off toward the car. I ambled on behind, not wanting to walk with him. Quinten had the weight of the whole community on his shoulders. The black people didn't like him because he talked like a white man and he had a white man's job. The other policemen kept at a distance too. Some maniac was killing Negro women and Quinten was all alone. Nobody wanted to help him and the women continued to die.

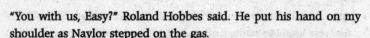

"You with us, Easy?" Roland Hobbes said. He put his hand on my shoulder as Naylor stepped on the gas.

I kept my silence and Hobbes took his friendly hand back. I was in a hurry to get to my house. I felt bad about turning down the policeman. I felt miserable that young women would die. But there was nothing I could do. I had my own life to attend to—didn't I?

• 3 •

I asked Naylor to let me off at the corner, intending to walk the last few steps home. But instead I stood there looking around. Night was coming on and I imagined that people were scurrying for shelter from a storm that was about to explode around them.

Not everybody was in a hurry.

Rafael Gordon was running a shell game in front of the Avalon, a tiny bar down toward the end of my block. Zeppo, the half-Italian, half-Negro spastic, was standing watch at the corner. Zeppo, who was always in a writhing fit, couldn't finish a sentence but he could whistle louder than most horn players could blow.

I waved at Zeppo and he shimmied at me, grimacing and winking. I tried to catch Rafael's eye but he was intent on the two rubes he'd snagged. Rafael was a short Negro, more gray in hue than he was brown. He was missing the greater portion of his front teeth and his left eye was dead in its socket. Rubes would look at Rafael and know that they could outsmart him. And maybe they thought they wouldn't have to pay even if they lost; Rafael didn't look like he could whip a poodle.

But Rafael Gordon carried a cork-hafted black iron fishing knife in his sleeve, and he always had a few feet of tempered steel chain in his pocket.

"Just show me where the red ball lands," he sang. "Just show me the red ball and two dollars. Double your money and howl tonight." He moved the fake walnut shells from side to side, lifting them at various times to show what was, and what wasn't.

A big man I'd never seen before pointed at a shell. I turned away and walked toward my home.

I was thinking about the dead party girl; about how she was killed with no reason except maybe how she looked or who she looked like. I shuddered at the memory of how natural she appeared. When a woman forgets that she's supposed to be pretty and on display she looks like that murdered girl did; just somebody who's tired and needs to rest.

That got me thinking about Regina and what she looked like. There was no comparison, of course. Regina was royal in her bearing. She never wore cheap shiny clothes or costume jewelry. When she danced it was not in that herky-jerky way that most young women moved. Regina's dancing was fluid and graceful like a fish in water or a bird on air.

The memory of that dead girl hung around me. I made it down to my front gate and looked to see that Regina and Edna were okay in the living room. I could see them through the window, then I got into my car and headed out to Hooper Street. Mofass had his real estate office on Hooper at that time. It was on the second floor of a two-story building. I owned the building, though nobody but Mofass knew that. The bottom floor was rented to a Negro bookstore that specialized in inspirational literature. Chester and Edwina Remy rented the place. Like all the tenants in my seven buildings, the Remys paid their rent to Mofass. He gave it to me sometime after that.

I knew Mofass would be in, because he worked late seven nights a week. All he ever did was work and smoke cigars.

The staircase that led to Mofass' door was exposed to the outside. It groaned and sagged as I made my way. Before I ever got to the door I could hear Mofass coughing.

I came in to find him crumpled over his maple desk, making a sound like an engine that won't turn over.

"I told ya to stop that smoking, Mofass. That cigar gonna kill you."

Mofass lifted his head. His jowly face made him resemble a bulldog. His pathetic gesture made him look even more canine. Tears from all that coughing fell from his rheumy eyes. He held the cigar out in front of his face and stared at it in terror. Then he smashed the black stogie in a clear glass ashtray and pushed himself upright in his swivel chair.

He stifled a cough and clenched his fists.

"How you doin'?" I asked.

"Fine," he whispered, and then he gagged on a cough.

I took the chair he had for clients and waited for any business he might have had to discuss. We'd known each other for many years. Maybe that's why I had two minds about Mofass' illness. On one hand I was always sorry to see a man in misery. But then again, Mofass was a coward who had betrayed me once. The only reason I hadn't killed him was that I hadn't proven to be a better man.

"What's goin' on?" I asked.

"Ain't nuthin' happenin' but the rent."

We both smiled at that.

"I guess that's okay," I said.

Mofass held up his hand for me to be quiet and took a porcelain jar from his desk. He unscrewed it, held it to his nose and mouth, and took a deep breath. The smell of camphor and menthol stung my nose.

"You hear 'bout the latest girl?" Mofass asked, his voice back from death's door.

"No, uh-uh."

"They found her on a Hundred and Tenth. Out near you. They said that there was nearly twenty cops out there."

"Yeah?"

"Good-time girls. Ain't havin' such a good time no more," he said. "Crazy man killin' young things. It's a shame."

Mofass pulled a cigar from his vest pocket. He was about to bite off the tip when he saw me staring. He put the death stick back and said, "Gonna be trouble fo' us."

"Trouble how?"

"Lotsa yo' young tenants these girls, man. Single girls or deserted ones. They got a baby and a job, and on Friday night they go out with they friends lookin' fo' a man."

"So what? You think whoever doin' this gonna kill all our renters?"

"Naw, naw. I ain't all that stupid. I might not got no college under my belt like you but I could see what's in front'a my nose just as good as the next man."

"An' what is that?"

"Georgette Wykers and Marie Purdue told me that they movin' in together—for p'otection. They said that they could take care of their kids better an' be safe too. Course they only be payin' half the rent."

"So? What could I do about that?"

Mofass smiled. Grinned. I could see all the way back to his last, gold-capped molar. When Mofass showed that kind of pleasure it meant that he had been successful where money was concerned.

"You don't need to do nuthin', Mr. Rawlins. I told 'em that the rules didn't 'low no doublin' up. Then I told Georgette that if she moved in with Marie, then Marie could th'ow her out 'cause Georgette's name wouldn't be on the contract."

If Mofass made money on the day he died he would die a happy man.

"Don't bother with it, man," I said. "Let them girls do what they want. You know they's a thousand people comin' out here ev'ry day. Somebody move out an' somebody else just move in."

Mofass shook his head sadly and slow. He couldn't take a deep breath but he felt sorry for me. How could I be so stupid and not bleed the whole world for a dollar and some change?

"You got anything else t'say, Mofass?"

"Them white men called again today."

A representative of a company called DeCampo Associates had been calling Mofass about some property I owned in Compton. They'd offered to buy it twice; the last time for more than twice what the land was worth.

"I don't wanna hear about it. If they want that property it must be worth more than they wanna pay."

I walked over to the window, because I didn't want to argue about it again. Mofass thought that I should sell the land because there was a quick profit. He was good in business from day to day, but Mofass didn't know how to plan for the future.

"They got another deal now," he said. "You wanna say no to a hundred thousand dollars?"

Out the window I saw a little boy pulling a blue wagon past a streetlamp. He had thick soda bottles in the wagon. Six or seven of them. At most that was fourteen cents, enough for three candy bars, just about. The boy was brown with bare feet and short pants and a striped T-shirt. He was deep in thought as he pulled that wagon. Maybe he was thinking about his spelling lesson from last week. Maybe he wondered at the right way to spell kangaroo. But I suspected that that boy was wondering how to get the one cent he needed to buy a third candy bar.

"A hundred thousand?"

"They wanna meet with you," Mofass rasped.

I heard him lighting a match and turned just in time to see him take his first drag.

"What is it they want from us, William?" Mofass' real name was William Wharton.

Mofass, taking on a conspiratorial tone, said, "The county gonna develop Willoughby Place into a main road, a four-lane avenue."

I owned nine acres on one side of Willoughby. It came as part of a deal I made to find an old Japanese gardener's lost property.

"So what?" I asked.

"These men will lend you the money for development. Hundred thousand dollars and they take you for a partner."

"Cain't wait t'give me money, huh?"

"All you gotta do is give me the okay, Mr. Rawlins, an' I'll tell 'em that the board done voted."

Whenever anybody wanted to do business with me they did it through Mofass. He represented the corporation I'd formed to do business. The *board* was a committee of one.

I had to laugh to myself. Here I was a woodchopper's son. A Negro and an orphan and from the South too. There was never a chance in hell that I'd ever see five thousand dollars but here I was being courted by white real estate men.

"Set up a meeting with them," I said. "I want to get a look at these men. But don't get yo' greedy hopes up, Willy, prob'ly won't nuthin' come from it."

Mofass grinned, breathing in smoke through his teeth.

• 4 •

It was a warm evening. I parked down toward the end of my block. Zeppo and Rafael were gone. The cardboard box that Rafael had used for his table was flattened on the sidewalk. A dollop of blood festooned by a cracked tooth adorned the curb. Somebody had learned a bitter lesson in Rafael Johnson's school of sleight-of-hand.

The drying blood made me think of the dead party girl again.

I still needed to be alone after all that had happened. So I decided to have a shot before I went back to my wife.

On the inside the Avalon was about the size of a walled-up display window. There was a bar and six stools—that's it. Rita Coe served bottled beer and drinks mixed with water or ice.

There was only one customer, a big man facing the wall and hunkered down over a pay phone at the end of the bar.

"What you doin' here, Easy Rawlins?" Rita was hard and small with beady eyes and thin lips.

"Whiskey was what I had in mind."

"I thought you didn't drink in no bar so close to your house?"

"Well, I will today."

"Why not?" the big man asked the phone. "I'm ready."

Rita poured my scotch into a bullet glass.

"How's Regina and the baby?" Rita asked.

"Fine, both fine."

She nodded and looked down at my hands. "You hear about them girls been gettin' killed?"

"Nuthin' but, seems like."

"You know, I'm scared to walk out to my car when I close up at night."

"You close up alone?" I asked her. But before she could answer the big man hung up the phone so hard that it gave out a brief ring of complaint.

Dupree Bouchard stood up and turned toward us—all six feet five inches of him. He saw me and then looked around as if he were searching for a back door. But the only door was the one I'd come through.

Dupree and I had been friends when we were younger men. One night he drank too much and passed out—leaving me and his girlfriend, Coretta, with nothing to hold but each other.

Maybe he heard our hushed cries through his alcoholic stupor. Or maybe he blamed me for her murder the next day.

"Hey, Dupree. How's Champion treatin' you?"

We'd both worked at Champion Aircraft ten years earlier. Dupree was a master machinist.

"They ain't no good up there, Easy. Every time you turn around they got another rule to hold you up. And if you a niggah, they got two rules."

"That's true," I said. "That's true. Everywhere you go it's the same."

"It's better back down home. At least down south a colored brother won't stab you in the back." He looked me in the eye when he said that. Dupree could never prove that I had done anything with or to Coretta. He just knew that I was with them one night and then she was gone from him forever.

"I don't know, Dupree," I said. "There hasn't been all that many lynchings up here in L.A. County."

"You wanna drink, Dupree?" Rita asked.

The big man sat down, two stools away from me, and nodded to her.

"How's your wife?" I asked to get him talking about something brighter.

"She's okay. I work at Temple Hospital now," he said.

"Really? My wife works there. Regina."

"What she look like?"

"Dark-complected. Pretty and kind of slim. She works in the maternity ward."

"What time she work?"

"Eight to five usually."

"Then I prob'ly ain't even seen 'er. I only been there two months and I'm on the graveyard shift. They got me doin' laundry in the basement."

"You like it?"

"Yeah," he said bitterly. "Love it."

Dupree took the drink that Rita brought and downed it in one swallow. He slapped two quarters on the bar and said, "I gotta go."

He went past me and out the door, silent and sullen. I remembered how loud he had laughed that last night with Coretta and me. His laugh was like thunder in those days.

I wished I could take back what had happened to my friend, my part in his lifelong despair. I wished it but wishes don't count for much in flesh and blood.

"Andre Lavender," I said to Rita.

"Say what?"

"Andre. You know him?"

"Uh-uh."

"Gimme some paper."

I wrote Andre's name and phone number and said, "Call him and say that I'd like him to come by and see you to your car at night."

"He work for you?"

"I did him a favor once. Now he could help you."

"Do I gotta pay him?"

"Shot of whiskey do him just fine."

I pushed my glass closer to her and she filled it again.

Jesus was doing cartwheels across the lawn in the porch light. Little Edna kept herself upright by holding the bars of her crib. She laughed and sputtered at her mute brother. I came in the gate and picked up a football that was nestled in among the dahlia bushes along the fence. I whistled, then threw the ball just when Jesus turned to see me. He caught the football, held it in one hand, and waved to Edna as if he were beckoning her with the other. She rattled her baby bars, bounced on the balls of her feet, and yelled as loud as she could, "Akach yeeee!"

Jesus kicked the ball so hard that it crashed against the far link fence. The jangling of steel was a kind of music for city children.

"What's goin' on out here?" Regina was framed for a moment by the gray haze of the screen door. She came out on the porch and stood in front of our little girl as if protecting her. Edna let out a howl. She couldn't see Jesus and the yard past her mother's skirts.

"Aw, com'on, honey. She's okay," I said as I mounted the three stairs to the porch.

"He could miss a kick out there an' tear her head off!"

Edna let herself fall hard on her diapered bottom. Jesus climbed up into the avocado tree.

"You got to be more careful, Easy," my wife of two years said.

"Eathy," echoed Edna.

I found it hard to answer, because it was always hard for me to think when looking at Regina. Her skin was the color of waxed ebony and her large almond-shaped eyes were a half an inch too far apart. She was tall and slender but, for all that she was beautiful, it was something else that got to me. Her face had no imperfection that I could see. No blemish or wrinkle. Never a pimple or mole or some stray hair that might have grown out of the side of her jaw. Her eyes would close now and then but never blink as normal people do. Regina was perfect in every way. She knew how to walk and how to sit down. But she was never flustered by a lewd comment or shocked by poverty.

I fell in love with Regina Riles each time I looked at her. I fell in love with her before we ever exchanged words.

"I thought it was okay, honey." I reached for her unconsciously and she moved away, a graceful dancer.

"Listen, Easy, Jesus don't know how to think about what's right for Edna. You got to do that for him."

"He knows more than you think, baby. He's been around little children more than most women have. And he understands even if he doesn't talk."

Regina shook her head. "He got problems, Easy. You sayin' that he's okay don't make it so."

Jesus climbed down out of the tree and went to the side of the house to get into his room.

"I don't know what you mean, honey," I said. "Everybody got problems. How you handle your problems means what kinda man you gonna be."

"He ain't no man. Jesus is just a little boy. I don't know what kind of trouble he's had but I do know that it's too much for him, that's why he can't talk."

I let it drop there. I could never bring myself to tell her the real story. About how I rescued the boy from a missing woman's house after he had been bought and abused by an evil man. How could I explain that the man who mistreated Jesus had been murdered and I knew who'd done it, but kept quiet?

Regina hoisted Edna into her arms. The baby screamed. I wanted to grab them both and hug them so hard that all this upset would squeeze out.

Talking to Regina was painful for me sometimes. She was so sure about what was right and what wasn't. She could get me stirred up inside. So much so that sometimes I didn't know if I was feeling rage or love.

I waited outside for a moment after they went in, looking at my house. There were so many secrets I carried and so many broken lives I'd shared. Regina and Edna had no part of that, and I swore to myself that they never would.

I went in finally, feeling like a shadow, stalking himself into light.

• 5 •

"You been drinkin'," Regina said when I walked through the door. I didn't think she could smell it and I hadn't had enough to stagger. Regina just knew me. I liked that, it made my heart kind of wild.

Edna and Regina were both on the couch. When the baby saw me she said, "Eathy," and pulled away to crawl in my direction. Regina grabbed her before she fell to the floor.

Edna hollered as if she had been slapped.

"You been down to the police station?"

"Quinten Naylor wanted to talk with me." I always felt bad when the baby cried. I felt that something had to be done before we could go on. But Regina just held her and talked to me as if there were no yelling.

"Then why you come home all liquored up?"

"Com'on, baby," I said. Everything seemed slow. I felt that there was more than enough time to explain to her, to calm everything down. If only Edna would stop crying, I thought, everything would be okay. "I just took a drink down at the Avalon."

"Musta been a long swallow."

"Yeah, yeah. I needed a drink after what Officer Naylor showed me."

That got her attention, but her stare was still hard and cold.

"He took me over to a vacant lot on a Hundred and Tenth. Dead girl over there. Shot-in-the-head dead. It's the same man killed them other two girls."

"They know who did it?"

I had to suppress my smile. Taking that angry glare off her face made me want to dance.

"Naw," I said, as soberly as I could.

"Then how do they know it's the same man?"

"He crazy, that's why. He marks 'em with a hot cigar."

"Rape?" she asked in a small voice. Edna stopped crying and looked at me with her mother's questioning eye.

"That," I said, suddenly sorry that I had said anything. "And other stuff."

I took Edna to my chest and sat there next to my wife.

"Naylor wanted me to help him. He thought I mighta heard somethin'."

When Regina put her hand on my knee I could have cheered.

"Why'd he think that?"

"I don't know. He knows that I used to get around pretty good. He just thought I might have heard somethin'. I told him that I couldn't help, but by then I needed a drink."

"Who was it?"

"Girl named Bonita Edwards."

Her hand moved to my shoulder.

"I still don't see why a policeman would come here to ask you about it. I mean, unless he thought you had something to do with it."

Regina always wanted to know why. Why did people call me for favors? Why did I feel I had to help certain people when they were in trouble? She never did know how I got her cousin out of jail.

"Well, you know," I said. "He probably thought that I was still in the street a lot. But I told him that I'm workin' for Mofass full-time now and that I don't get out too much."

I had lived a life of hiding before I met Regina. Nobody knew about me. They didn't know about my property. They didn't know about my relationship to the police. I felt safe in my secrets. I kept telling myself that Regina was my wife, my partner in life. I planned to tell her about what I'd done over the years. I planned to tell her that Mofass really worked for me and that I had plenty of money in bank accounts around town. But I had to get at it slowly, in my own time.

The money wasn't apparent in my way of living. So there was no need for her to be suspicious. I intended to tell her all about it someday. A day when I felt she could accept it, accept me for who I was.

"He knows that I get around the neighborhood is all, honey. They found that girl just twelve blocks from here."

"Could you help them?"

Edna stuck her hand down my shirt pocket and drooled on my chest.

"Uh-uh. I didn't know nuthin'. I told him that I'd ask around, though. You know it's an ugly thing."

Regina studied me like a pawnbroker looking for a flaw in a diamond ring. I bounced Edna in my arms until she started to laugh. Then I smiled at Regina. She just shook her head a little and studied me some more.

Edna felt like she weighed a hundred pounds and I laid her across my lap. I lay back myself.

Regina put her cool hand to my cheek. I could count each knuckle. I thought about that poor dead girl and the others.

Edna fell asleep. Regina took her to her crib. And I followed her to our bedroom. A room that was so small it was mostly bed.

She undressed and then moved to put on her nightclothes. But I embraced her before she got to her gown, my pants were down around my ankles. We fell back onto the bed with her on top. She tried, weakly, to pull away but I held her and stroked her in the ways she liked. She gave in to my caresses but she wouldn't kiss me. I rolled up on top of her and held her head between my hands. She let my leg slip between hers but when I put my lips to hers she wouldn't open her mouth or her eyes. My tongue pushed at her teeth but that was as far as I got.

Regina let me hold her. She buried her face against my neck while

I worked off my shorts and shirt. But when I moved to enter her she turned away from me. All of this was new. Regina wasn't as wild about sex as I was but she would usually come close to matching my ardor. Now it was like she wanted me but with nothing coming from her.

It excited me all the more, and even though I was dizzy with the alcohol in my blood, I cozied up behind her and entered her the way dogs do it.

"Stop, Easy!" she cried, but I knew she meant "Go on, do it!"

She writhed and I clamped my legs around hers. I bucked up against her and she grabbed the night table with such force that it was knocked over on to the floor. The lamp was pulled from the electric plug and the room went dark.

"Oh, God no!" she cried and she came, shouting and bucking and elbowing me hard.

When I relaxed my hold she pushed away and got up. I remember the light coming on and her standing there in the harsh electric glare. There was sweat on her face and glistening in her pubic hair. She looked at me with an emotion I could not read.

"I love you," I said.

I passed into sleep before her answer came.

It was afternoon in my dream. That golden sort of sunny day that they only get in southern California. Bonita Edwards was sitting under that tree with her legs out in front of her and her hands, palms up, at her side. There were birds, sparrows and jays, foraging through the grasses behind her. A little breeze put the tiniest chill in the air.

"Who did this?" I asked the dead girl.

She turned to me. The bullet hole showed sky-blue in her head.

"What?" she asked in a timid little voice.

"Who did this to you?"

Then she started to cry. It was strange because it wasn't the sound that a woman makes when she cries.

Regina was leaning up against the tree with both hands. Her skirt was hiked up above her buttocks and a large naked man was taking her from behind. Her head whipped from side to side and she had a powerful orgasm but making the same kind of strange crying noises that Bonita Edwards made.

I hated them all. I could feel the hatred down in my body like a deep breath. I grabbed Bonita by the lapels of her pink party dress and lifted her. She hung down, heavy like the corpse she was, still crying.

Crying in that strange way. Like a kitten maybe. Or an inner tube squealing from a leak. Like a baby.

I opened my eyes, feeling chilly because I had kicked off the blankets. Edna was crying in little bursts. I got up and stumbled to the door. At the door I looked back to see that Regina had her eyes open. She was looking at the ceiling.

I was frightened by her. But I dismissed the fear as part of my dream.

Soon it will all be over, I thought. They'll catch the killer and my nightmares will go away.

• 6 •

I went to the kitchen to put Edna's formula on the stove. Then I got a diaper from the package that Jesus brought home every other day from LuEllen Stone.

Edna was crying in the corner of the living room where we'd set up her crib. I turned on the small lamp and loomed over her. That silenced the cries for a moment. Then I leaned over and kissed her on the cheek. That got a smile and a coo. I carried her back to the kitchen, where I laid her on a sheet rolled out over the kitchen table. I filled a red rubber tub with tepid water and undid the safety pin of her diapers.

She was crying again but not angrily. She was just telling me that she felt bad. I could have joined her.

I washed her with a soft chamois towel, saying little nonsense things and kissing her now and again. By the time she was clean all the tears were gone. The bottle was ready and I changed her fast. I held her to my chest again and gave her the bottle. She suckled and cooed and clawed at my nose.

I turned toward the door to see Regina there staring at us.

"You really love her, don't you, baby?" she asked.

I would rather her call me that sweet name than make love to any other woman in the world. It was like she opened a door, and I was ready to run in.

I smiled at her and in that moment I saw something shift in her eyes. It was as if a light went out, like the door closed before I got the chance to make it home.

"Baby," I said.

Edna shifted in my arms so that she could see her mother. She held one arm out to her and Regina took her from me.

"I need some money," Regina said.

"How much?"

"Six hundred dollars."

"I could do that." I nodded and sat down.

"How?"

I looked up at her, not really understanding the question.

"I asked you how, Easy."

"You asked if I could get you six hundred dollars."

When she shook her head her straightened hair flung from one side to the other and then froze there at the left side of her head.

"Uh-uh, I said that I needed that money. I ain't ax you fo' nuthin'. You coulda wanted t'know why I needed it. You coulda wanted to know how much I already have."

Out of the small back window, over the sink, the sky was turning from night to a pale whitish color. It felt like the world was getting larger and I wanted to run outside.

"Okay. All right. What you need it for?"

"I need clothes for me an' the baby, I got bills t'pay for my car, and my auntie down in Colette is sick and needs money t'go to the hospital."

"What's wrong with 'er?"

"Stones. That's what the doctor said."

"An' how much you already got?" I almost felt like I was in charge.

"Uh-uh, Easy. I wanna know where you could get yo' hands on six hundred dollars," she snapped her fingers, "just like that."

"I don't ask you 'bout the money in yo' pocket, baby. That's your money," I said. "It ain't got nuthin' t'do with me."

"You don't need t'ask me nuthin', Easy Rawlins. You know I work right down at Temple. I get there at eight every mo'nin' an' I'm home at five-thirty every day. You know where my money came from."

"An' you know I work fo' Mofass," I argued. "I might not have reg'lar hours like you but I work just the same."

She snapped her fingers at me again. It made her furious that I could tell such a lie. "Ain't nobody clean an' sweep fo' a livin' could come up wit' that kinda money. You think I'm a fool?"

We had both come from hard times.

Regina was the eldest of fourteen Arkansas children. Her mother died giving birth to their last child. Her father disintegrated into a helpless drunk. Regina raised those children. She worked and farmed and smiled for the white store owners. I don't know the half of it but I do know that her life was hard.

She had once told me that she'd done things that she wasn't proud of to feed those hungry mouths.

"I ain't no criminal," I said. "That's all you gotta know. I could get your money if you need it. You want it?"

Edna, who was now cradled in her mother's arms, laughed loudly and threw her bottle to the floor. Her eyes and smile were bright and mischievous.

Regina bit her lip. That might have been a small concession for some women but for her it was capitulation to a bitter foe.

"You should tell me what I wanna know, Easy."

"I ain't hidin' nuthin' from you, baby. You need money an' I could get it. That's because I love you an' Edna and I would do anything for you."

"Then why won't you tell me what I wanna know?"

I stood up fast and Regina flinched.

"I don't ask you about Arkansas, do I? I don't ask you what you had to do? When you tell me your auntie needs money I don't ask you why, at least I don't care. If you love me you just take me like I am. I ain't never hurt you, have I?"

Regina just stared.

"Have I?"

"No. You ain't laid a hand on me. Not that way."

"What's that s'posed to mean?"

"You don't hit me. It wouldn't matter if you did, though, 'cause I be out the door right after I shoot you if you ever laid a hand on me or my daughter." The defiance was back. It was better than her pain. "You don't hit me but you do other things just as bad."

"Like what?"

Regina was looking at my hands. I looked down myself to see clenched fists.

"Last night," she said. "What you call that?"

"Call what?"

"What you did to me. I didn't want none'a you. But you made me. You raped me."

"Rape?" I laughed. "Man cain't rape his own wife."

My laugh died when I saw the angry tears in Regina's eyes.

Edna stared at her mother wide-eyed, wondering who this new mother was.

"An' that ain't all, Easy. I wanted to name our daughter Pontella after her great-grandmother. But you made us call her Edna. You said you just liked the name, but I know that you namin' her after that woman yo' crazy friend was married to."

She meant EttaMae.

She was right.

"All I wanna know," I said, "is if you want that six hundred dollars. I'm willin' t'get it but you gotta ask me."

Regina raised her beautiful black face and stared at me. She nodded after a while; it was a small, ungrateful gesture.

And an empty victory for me. I wanted to be happy that I could help when she needed. But what she needed was something I couldn't give.

• 7 •

I made myself scarce for the next few evenings. I'd go out to different bars and drink until almost eleven and then come home. Everybody was in bed by then. I could breathe a little easier with no one to ask me questions.

Never, in my whole life, had anyone ever been able to demand to know about my private life. There was many a time that I'd give up teeth rather than answer a police interrogator. And here I was with Regina's silence and her distrust.

At night I dreamed of sinking ships and falling elevators.

It got so bad that on the third night I couldn't sleep at all.

I could hear every sound in the house and the early traffic down Central Avenue. At six-thirty Regina got out of bed. A moment later Edna cried in the distance, then she laughed.

At seven the baby-sitter, Regina's cousin Gabby Lee, came over. She made loud noises that Edna liked and that always woke me up.

"Ooooo-ga wah!" the big woman cried. "Oooogy, oogy, oogy, wah, wah, wah!"

Edna went wild with pleasured squeals.

At seven-fifteen the front door slammed. That was Regina going to her little Studebaker. I heard the tinny engine turn over and the sputter her car made as she drove off.

Gabby Lee was in the bathroom with Edna. For some reason she thought that babies had to be changed in the bathroom. I guess it was her idea of early toilet training.

When she came out I said, "Good morning."

Gabby Lee was a big woman. Not very fat really but barrel-shaped and a lighter shade than about half of the white people you're ever likely to meet. She had wiry strawberry hair and definite Negro features. She reserved her smile for other women and babies.

"You here today?" she asked me—the man who paid her salary.

"It's my house, ain't it?"

"Honeybell"—that was one of the nicknames she had for Regina—"wanted me to do some cleanin' today. You bein' here just be in my way."

"It is my house, ain't it?"

Gabby Lee harrumphed and snarled.

I went around her to relieve myself in the bathroom. There was a dirty diaper steaming in the sink.

The newspaper on the front porch was folded into a tube shape held by a tiny blue rubber band. I got it and started a pot of coffee in the old percolator that I bought three days after my discharge in 1945.

Jesus kissed me good morning. He had his book bag and wore tennis shoes, jeans, and a tan short-sleeved shirt.

"You be good today and study hard," I said.

He nodded ferociously and grinned like a candidate for office. Then he ran out of the door and tore down out to the street.

He was never a great student. But since the fifth grade they put him in a special class. A class for kids with learning problems. His classmates ran a range from juvenile delinquent to mildly retarded. But his teacher, Keesha Jones, had taken a special interest in Jesus' reading. He sat up nearly every night with a book in his bed.

I poured myself a cup of coffee and settled down to the breakfast table intent on making some decision on what to do about Regina. Who knows, I might gotten somewhere if it wasn't for the headline of the *Los Angeles Examiner.*

WOMAN MURDERED
4TH VICTIM
KILLER
STALKS SOUTHLAND

Robin Garnett was last seen near a Thrifty's drugstore near Avalon. She was talking to a man who wore a trench coat with the collar turned up and a broad-rimmed Stetson hat. The article explained how she was later found in a small shack that sat on an abandoned lot four blocks away. She was beaten and possibly raped. She had been disfigured but the article didn't specify how. The article did explain why this murder was front-page news where the previous three were garbage liners—Robin Garnett was a white woman.

I found out that Robin was a coed at UCLA. She lived with her parents and had attended L.A. High. What the article didn't say was why she was down in that neighborhood in the first place.

I lit a Camel and drank my coffee. I opened the shades so that I could see them coming when they came.

At about nine, Gabby Lee emerged from my bedroom with Edna all dressed up for the park. I held out my arms and Edna screamed joyously. She reached for me but Gabby Lee held back.

"Bring my baby here to me," I said simply.

I held Edna and she held my nose. We made sounds at each other and laughed and laughed.

"We gotta go," Gabby Lee said after a while.

"I thought you was gonna clean?"

"I gotta be alone for that," she snapped. "Anyway it's a nice day out there and babies need some sun."

I handed my daughter back to the sour woman. Gabby lit up with Edna in her arms. That baby was so beautiful she could make a stone statue smile.

When they left the phone started ringing. It rang for a full minute before the caller disconnected. After that I took the phone off the hook.

I pulled a copy of Plato's writings from my shelf and read the *Phaedo* by the sunlight coming in my living-room window. My eyes hazed over when he died on that stone bench. I wondered at how it would be to be a white man; a man who felt that he belonged. I tried to imagine how it would feel to give up my life because I loved my homeland so much. Not the hero's death in the heat of battle but a criminal's death.

At eleven forty-seven a long black sedan parked in front of my house. Four men got out. Three of them were white men in business suits of various hues. The fourth was Quinten Naylor. They all got out of the car and looked around the neighborhood. They weren't timid about being deep in Watts. That's how I knew that they were all cops.

Quinten led the procession up to my door. They were all big men. The kind of white man who is successful because he towers over his peers. Almost every boss I had ever had was a white man and he was either a tall man or very fat, intimidation being the first requirement for obedience on the job.

I was at the door, behind a latched screen, when they mounted the porch.

"Good morning, Easy," Naylor said. He wasn't smiling. "We tried to call. I brought some men who want to discuss the news with you."

"I got to be somewhere in forty-five minutes," I said, not budging an inch.

"Open up, Rawlins." That came from a tight-lipped, Mediterranean-looking man in a two-piece silvery suit. I thought I recognized him but most cops blended into one brutal fist for me after a while.

"You got some paper for me to read?" I asked, not impolite.

"This is Captain Violette, Easy," Quinten said. "He's precinct captain."

"Oh," I mocked surprise. "An' these the other Pep Boys?"

Violette was my height, around six-one. The man next to him, behind Naylor, wore a threadbare baby-blue suit. He was an inch shorter and blunt in his appearance. His pasty white face was meaty and his ears were large. Black hairs sprouted everywhere on him. From his eyebrows, from his ears. He pushed his hand past Naylor to my door. It was blunt and hairy too.

"Hello, Mr. Rawlins. My name is Horace Voss. I'm a special liaison between the mayor's office and the police."

I could see that there was no turning this crowd away, so I unlatched the screen and shook Mr. Voss' hand.

"Well, come on in if you want, but I ain't even dressed yet, an' I gotta be somewhere soon."

Five big men made my living room seem like a small public toilet. But I got them all sitting somewhere. I leaned against the TV cabinet.

The man I hadn't met yet was the tallest one of all. He wore a tan wash-and-wear Sears suit. My uncle, Ogden Willy, owned one exactly like it in the Louisiana swamplands thirty years before.

He was thin and bony with long tapered fingers and deep green eyes. He was hatless and nearly bald with just a little black hair around his ears.

He crossed his long legs easily and smiled. He reminded me of a porcelain devil that was popular around that time in the Chinatown curio shops. "My name is Bergman, Mr. Rawlins. I work for the state—the governor. I'm not here in an official capacity. Just keeping an eye on these terrible events."

"Anybody want something to drink?" I asked.

"No," Violette said for everyone. But I think Mr. Voss would have liked to use his blunt fingers on a glass.

"We're here—" Quinten Naylor started to say but he was cut off by his superior, Violette.

"We're here to find out who's killing these girls," Violette said. He spoke with his upper lip tight against his teeth. "We don't want this crazy man running our streets."

"That's some shit," I said. "Excuse me, but I'ma have to go get me a beer if I gotta listen to this."

I went to the kitchen. Being independently employed I didn't have to worry about those officials getting me fired. I didn't have to worry about them beating me either. They were too important for that. Of course, they might have sent some goons later on. Maybe I should have been a little more deferential. But those men coming into my house turned my gut.

I filled the largest tumbler I had with ale and went back to the room. Voss looked at the foamy head, barely restraining himself from licking his lips.

"What the hell are you trying to do, Rawlins?" Violette yelled.

"Man, I'm in my own house, right? I ain't ask you over. Here you come crowdin' up my livin' room an' talkin' t'me like you got a blackjack in your pocket"—I was getting hot—"an' then you cryin' 'bout some dead girl an' I know they's been three before this one but you didn't give one good goddam! Because they was black girls an' this one is white!" If I had been on television every colored man and woman in America would have stood from their chairs and cheered.

Violette was up from his chair, but not to applaud. His face had turned bright red. That's when I remembered him. He was only a detective when he dragged Alvin Lewis out of his house on Sutter Place. Alvin had beaten a woman in an alley outside of a local bar and Violette had taken the call. The woman, Lola Jones, refused to press charges and Violette decided to take a little justice into his own hands. I remembered how red his face got while he beat Alvin with a police stick. I remembered how cowardly I felt while three other white policemen stood around with their hands on their pistols and grim satisfaction on their faces. It wasn't the satisfaction that a bad man had paid for his crime; those men were tickled to have power like that. A Nazi couldn't have done it better.

"Calm down, Anthony," the spectator Bergman ordered. "Mr. Rawlins, we're sorry to interrupt your day, but there is an emergency in the city. A man is killing women and we have to do something. I didn't know about this matter of the other women getting killed until today, but I promise you that we'll be looking into that. Still, no matter what way you look at it, we have a job to do."

"Police got a job to do. I'm just a citizen, a civilian. All I gotta do is cross on the green."

Mr. Bergman probably didn't even have a temper. He just smiled and nodded. "That's right, of course. It's Anthony's job to bring this man to justice. But you know that he could use some help, don't you, Mr. Rawlins?"

"I cain't help him. I'm not the police."

"But you can. You know all kinds of people in the community.

You can go where the police can't go. You can ask questions of people who aren't willing to talk to the law. We need every hand we can get in on this, Mr. Rawlins." He held his hand out toward me but I left it alone.

"I'm in the middle of my own business, man. I cain't do nuthin'."

"Yes you can," Violette said in a guttural voice. I realized that I was wrong about men in that position. If Captain Violette had me alone I'd have been eating teeth about then.

"They already got a list of suspects, Easy," Quinten said.

"What do I care?" I answered him. "Go get 'em, put 'em in jail."

He mentioned a couple of names that I knew. But I told him that if he knew who did it there was no need to worry.

"We're also looking into Raymond Alexander," he said.

I felt every man in the room staring at me.

"You gotta be kiddin'," I said. Raymond Alexander, known to his friends as Mouse, was crazy and a killer, no doubt. He was also the closest thing I had to a best friend.

"No, Easy." Naylor was gritting his teeth. He was as mad as I was at those men. "Alexander frequents all the bars that the Negro women went to and he is known to go after white women."

"Him an' about thirty thousand other black men under the age of eighty."

"Do you think there's a flaw in the police approach, Mr. Rawlins?" Horace Voss asked.

"You just makin' up names, man. Mouse didn't kill no girls."

"Then who did?" Voss' blunt smile didn't seem quite human, it was more like the cross of a hungry bear and a happy man.

"How you expect me to know?"

"I expect it," Violette said. "Because if you don't you're going to find it very hard living down here among the blues."

A policeman with a sense of poetry.

"Is that a threat?"

Violette glared at me.

"Of course it isn't, Mr. Rawlins," Bergman said. "No one wants to threaten you. We all want the same thing here. There's a man killing women and he has to be brought to justice. That's what we all want."

Quinten was at the window peering out at the street. He knew that I had to go along with the program set out there before me. Captain Violette would run me to ground if I didn't. And Quinten was fuming because I refused to help when there were only black victims. Now that a white woman was dead I would agree to help. The air we breathed was racist.

"Lay off Raymond Alexander until I have time to nose around. He ain't killed no woman an' arrestin' him won't do nobody no good."

"If he's guilty, Rawlins, he'll fry like anybody else," Violette growled.

"I ain't tryin' to protect nobody, man," I said. "Just lemme look if that's what you want, an' sit on these arrests for a couple'a days."

Bergman stood up straight and tall. "That's it for me then. I'm sure the police and the mayor can give you all the help you need, Mr. Rawlins."

The other men rose.

Violette wouldn't even look at me, he just went to the door. Naylor looked but he didn't say anything. Bergman smiled and shook my hand warmly.

"Why are you down here, Mr. Bergman?" I asked.

"Just routine." His bottom lip jutted out an eighth of an inch. "Just routine."

Horace Voss took my hand in both of his.

"Call me at the Seventy-seventh," he said. "I'm there until this thing is over."

Then they were all gone from my house.

I hadn't hit the streets since my wedding. I tried to bury that part of my life. In one way, looking for this killer was like coming back from the dead for me.

• 8 •

I fried blood sausages with onions and heated up a saucepan of red beans and rice for lunch. After I ate I mowed the lawn. It really didn't need it, but I wanted my new job to sink in and working in the garden calmed my nerves.

I couldn't seem to think of Bonita Edwards without seeing Regina crying. The dead woman's tragedy somehow resonated with Regina's anger.

I decided that I'd work out my problems with Regina after I'd seen to the job that L.A.'s representatives had given me.

But then I had to wonder at the strangeness of all those important white men thinking that they had to come all the way to my house in order to draft me.

I'd worked for city hall before but usually they called me downtown. They would have me wait on a cold marble bench while they preened and primped. Sometimes they'd call me to the police station and threaten me before asking my favors. But I'd never had a delegation at my house.

I expected Quinten Naylor, and maybe his white sidekick, but the people that had come were important. They were more important than one dead white girl. Women got killed all the time, and unless they were innocent mothers raped in their husbands' beds, the law didn't kick up such a big fuss.

Even though I'd eaten I had an empty feeling in the pit of my stomach. I filled the hole with three straight shots of bourbon. After that I felt calmer. Enough whiskey can take the edge off sunshine.

By one-thirty I was ready to go. I'd put on gray slacks and a gray square-cut shirt. My lapels were crimson, my shoes yellow suede. I had a light buzz on and my new Chrysler floated down the side streets like a yacht down some inland canals.

There was a small public library on Ninety-third and Hooper. Mrs. Stella Keaton was the librarian. We'd known each other for years. She was a white lady from Wisconsin. Her husband had a fatal heart attack in '34 and her two children died in a fire the year after that. Her only living relative had been an older brother who was stationed in San Diego with the navy for ten years. After his discharge he moved to L.A. When Mrs. Keaton had her tragedies he invited her to live with him. One year after that her brother, Horton, took ill, and after three months he died spitting up blood, in her arms.

All Mrs. Keaton had was the Ninety-third Street branch. She treated the people who came in there like her siblings and she treated the children like her own. If you were a regular at the library she'd bake you a cake on your birthday and save the books you loved under the front desk.

We were on a first-name basis, Stella and I, but I was unhappy that she held that job. I was unhappy because even though Stella was nice, she was still a white woman. A white woman from a place where there were only white Christians. To her Shakespeare was a god. I didn't mind that, but what did she know about the folk tales and riddles and stories colored folks had been telling for centuries? What did she know about the language we spoke?

I always heard her correcting children's speech. "Not 'I is,' " she'd say. "It's 'I am.' "

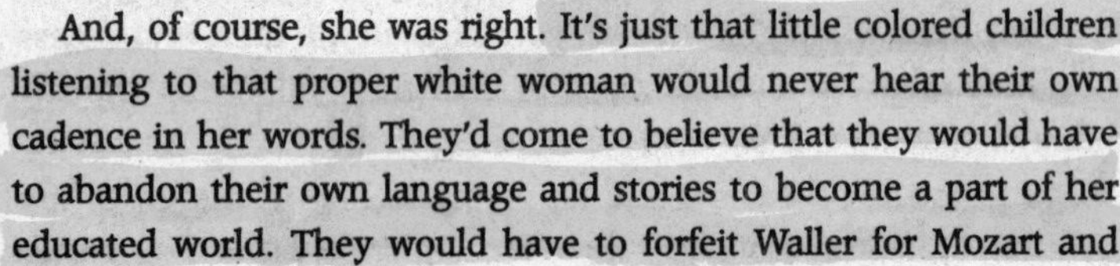

And, of course, she was right. It's just that little colored children listening to that proper white woman would never hear their own cadence in her words. They'd come to believe that they would have to abandon their own language and stories to become a part of her educated world. They would have to forfeit Waller for Mozart and

Remus for Puck. They would enter a world where only white people spoke. And no matter how articulate Dickens and Voltaire were, those children wouldn't have their own examples in the house of learning—the library.

I had argued with Stella about these things before. She was sensitive about them but when you told her that some man standing on a street corner telling bawdy tales was something like Chaucer she'd crinkle her nose and shake her head. She was always respectful, though. They often take the kindest white people to colonize the colored community. But as kind as Mrs. Keaton was, she reflected an alien view to our people.

"Good morning, Ezekiel," Mrs. Keaton said.

"Stella."

"How is that little Jesus?"

"He's fine, just fine."

"You know, he's in here every Saturday. He always wants to help more than he reads, but I think he's getting somewhere. Sometimes I come up on him and it seems as if he's mouthing the words and reading to himself."

There was nothing wrong with the boy's larynx, the doctors had told me that. He could have talked if he wanted to.

"Maybe he'll get around to it one day," I said, more finishing the thought in my head than talking to her.

She smiled with perfect little pearls along her pink gums. Mrs. Keaton was small and wiry. She had the same color hair as Gabby Lee. But Mrs. Keaton's color came out of a bottle, whereas Gabby's had come from the genetic war white men have waged on black women for centuries.

"You got the newspapers for the last two months, Stella?"

"Sure do. *Times* and *Examiner.*"

She took me into a back room that had a long oak reading table. The room smelled of old newspaper. Along all the shelves were stacks of the papers I wanted.

The papers pretty much said what Naylor told me. The articles were buried in the back pages and there was no connection made between the crimes.

Willa Scott's and Juliette LeRoi's whereabouts on the nights of their deaths were unknown. Their occupations were listed as waitress. Willa though, it seemed, was unemployed.

Bonita Edwards was in a bar the night she died. She'd had quite a few drinks and had been seen with quite a few men. But, witnesses said, she left alone. Of course, that didn't mean anything—she could have made a date with some man who was married and didn't want it to get around what he was doing. She could have made a date with a murderer who had the same reasons for not being seen.

I put that information together with what I'd already read, and heard, about Robin Garnett.

Robin Garnett didn't make any sense at all. She lived with her parents on Hauser, way over in the western part of L.A. Her father was a prosecuting attorney for the city and her mother stayed home. Robin was a coed at UCLA. She was twenty-one and still a sophomore. She'd just recently returned from a trip to Europe, the paper said, and was expecting to major in education.

She was a pretty girl. (Robin was the only victim to have a photograph printed.) She had sandy hair and a very nice, what old folks call a healthy, smile. Her hair was pulled back, very conservative. Her blouse was of the button-down-the-front variety, and every button was buttoned. The photo was for her parents, for a yearbook, it didn't give the slightest hint of what she might have really been like.

It certainly didn't say why she was the fourth of a series of murders that started out with three black women. Even if a white woman somehow fit into this scheme of murders, why would somebody kill three good-time girls and then go after a bobbysoxer?

I went out to the main room perplexed.

"Did you find what you were looking for, Ezekiel?"

"Naw." I shook my head. "I mean, yeah . . ." She frowned when I said that. I knew she wanted to correct me with "Yes."

John McKenzie's bar had grown over the years. He'd added a kitchen and eight plush booths for dinner. He even hired a short-order cook to burn steaks and boil vegetables. There was a stage for blues and jazz performances. And waitresses, three of them, serving the bar and the round tables that surrounded the stage.

John still owned Targets but Odell Jones' name was on the deeds. John had had too much trouble with the law to get a liquor license, so he needed a front man. Odell was ideal. He was a mild-mannered man, semiretired, two years shy of sixty, and twenty-two years older than I.

Odell was sitting in his regular booth toward the back. He was sipping at a beer and reading the *Sentinel*—L.A.'s largest Negro publication. We hadn't exchanged words in over three years and it still broke my heart that I had lost such a good friend. But when you're a poor man struggling in this world you rub up against people pretty hard sometimes. And the people you hurt the most are poor sons just like yourself.

Once I was deep in trouble and I asked Odell to lend me a hand. How was I to know that his minister would end up dead? How could I blame him for hating me either?

"Easy," John greeted me. His dark face was stony and expressionless.

"John. Gimme a fist of little Johnnie Walker." That meant four fingers.

While he poured I asked him, "You hear anything about them girls gettin' killed?"

"I knowed all them girls, Easy. Every one."

I thought again of Bonita Edwards. I slugged back half of my drink. "All of 'em?"

John looked me in the eye and nodded.

"Even Robin Garnett?"

"I don't know nuthin' 'bout no Robin what-have-ya but I know that white girl got her picture in the paper. That was Cyndi Starr an' they ain't no lyin' 'bout that." He looked at a stool next to me. Maybe a stool she'd once sat in. "Yeah, Cyndi—the White Butterfly."

"The what?"

"That was her stage name. She was a damned stripper, man."

"And you say her name was Cyndi Starr?"

"That was her name, least that's what they called her. You know, she was just like all these other girls. It's only these white people makin' all that fuss. They coulda been sayin' somethin' 'fore she got killed."

"You sure, John? Paper says she want to college in West L.A. They said she lived with her parents out there."

"I read it. But just 'cause you read it in the paper don't make it true. If she went t'college she studied takin' off her clothes fo'men to watch 'er, an' if she lived wit 'er parents they lived right down here on Hollywood Row."

"You mean she lived down here?"

"Uh-huh, right down on the Hollywood Row. An' that ain't all I know either."

"Yeah?"

"That other one, that Juliette LeRoi, she was down at Aretha's right around the night she got killed."

"How do you know?"

"I know 'cause she got into a fight wit' some boy or sumpin'. Coy Baxter told me that the boy was so messed up that he had to go to the emergency room at Temple."

"Aretha's, you say?"

John nodded again.

I asked him a few other questions and he answered them as well as he could.

My car started up with a roar. I hit the gas and felt the tug of gravity as she pulled toward the corner. I turned the steering wheel and felt the swing of the back end as I straightened out for the main drag.

That's when I saw the woman. She was jaywalking and pushing a baby carriage.

I hit the brakes and felt the back end fishtail. I got a panorama of the shops and stores on the east side of the street. The car turned completely around. By the time I was facing the young mother again, she was yelling, "Motherfucker! Motherfucker! Who in hell! Fuck you!" and things like that.

Another car behind me hit his brakes. The squeal seemed to go on forever, but it didn't hit anything. The woman stopped screaming and gathered her baby up in her arms. She ran for the sidewalk, leaving the carriage in the middle of the street.

My heart was beating fast. The woman was trying to calm down the hollering baby.

I started my engine back up and drove off thinking about how my life had gone out of control.

• 9 •

Bone Street was local history. A crooked spine down the center of Watts' jazz heyday, it was four long and jagged blocks. West of Central Avenue and north of 103rd Street, Bone Street was broken and desolate to look at by day, with its two-story tenementlike apartment buildings and its mangy hotels. But by night Bones, as it was called, was a center for late-night blues, and whiskey so strong that it could grow hairs on the glass it was served in. When a man said he was going to get down to the bare Bones he meant he was going to lose himself in the music and the booze and the women down there.

The women, in the late forties and even into the early fifties, were all beautiful; young and old, in satins, silks, and furs. They came in the back-room clubs fine and sassy, and daring any man to wipe the snarl from their lips. They'd come in and listen to Coltrane, Monk, Holiday, and all the rest, drinking shot for shot with their men.

It was a bold and flashy time. But by that evening all the shine had rubbed off to expose the base metal below. The sidwalks were broken, sporting hardy weeds in their cracks. Some clubs were still there but they were quieter now. The jazzmen had found new arenas. Many had gone to Paris and New York. The blues was still with us. The blues would always be with us. The blues will always be with us.

Sonny Terry, Brownie McGee, Lightnin' Hopkins, Soupspoon Wise, and a hundred others passed through the hotels and back-street dives that still cluttered Bone. In the old days the jazzmen came in fancy cars like Cadillacs. The bluesmen came by Greyhound, sometimes by thumb.

The women were still there. But their clothes didn't fit right anymore. Their eyes were more hungry than wild. All the promise after the war had drained away and a new generation was asking, "Where's ours?"

Rock and roll waged a war over the radio and in the large dance clubs. Bone Street was forgotten except by those lost souls who wanted a taste of the glitter of their day.

Aretha's was in an alley halfway down the 1600 block of Bone. It had other names over the years, and different addresses too. It was a legal bar, more or less. But the waitresses were all scantily clad girls and the police found it proper to shut Charlene Mars down every once in a while. Charlene ran Aretha's, or whatever it was called at the time. Over the years it had been named the Del-Mar, the Nines, Swing, And Juanita's. The name and the address changed but it was always the same club. The girls had different names too and even different faces, but they did the same work.

That year they wore a very short black skirt over a one-piece brown bathing suit and black fishnet stockings. The room was long and narrow with a very high ceiling and a stage at the far end. Down the left side of the room ran an oak bar tended by Westley.

Westley and Charlene had started as lovers. She was skinny and he wore fine clothes. They both loved jazz and, along with John from Targets, had the best hornmen and vocalists in the country. But a lot of whiskey and fine men, and fine women, moved through their lives. Charlene bought a small house in Compton, where she took care of her retarded brother. Westley, a tall large-handed man, took to sleeping in the bar.

The whites of his eyes were yellow and he stooped over. His arms were as strong as iron cables.

He looked at me and nodded at an empty table, but I walked up to the bar.

"Hey, West."

"Easy."

"Johnnie Walker," I said.

He turned away to grant my request.

The room was dark. The phonograph played a light and lively version of "Lady Blue." With no introduction a buxom woman, well into her fifties, jiggled out onstage. She wasn't wearing much and all of that was a shiny banana yellow against high-brown skin. She carried a long yellow plume, which she waved along with her breasts and thighs.

There were eight small tables opposite the bar and a cluster of them before the stage. Black men and women sat here and there. Fragile ribbons of smoke rose from gaudy aluminum ashtrays. A waitress moved petulantly from table to table. "You want sumpin' else t'drink?" was the question I heard her ask most often. The answer was almost always "No."

This was the early crowd, not huge tippers. They were kind of a warm-up act for the customers, mostly men, who came later.

Charlene sat right up next to the stage, sipping at a lime-colored drink. She had always claimed that the girls never did anything that they didn't want to do, but I'd known women who'd been fired from there because a customer had complained that they were "unfriendly."

I took the whiskey and moved toward the stage. Closer up you could see the makeup that the banana dancer wore. Her face looked like a carved wooden mask.

"Easy Rawlins!" Charlene squealed.

I took her hands and kissed her moist face.

"Charlene."

In a fit of improvisation the banana dancer moved downstage and brushed the back of my neck with her plume.

"Sit'own, baby." Charlene pulled an empty chair away from a table where an old man had his head resting on his hands.

"Kinda slow, huh?" I asked.

She pawed at me with a pudgy red-fingered hand. "It's early, Easy. Fern just do her li'l thing out there to get the stage ready for the young girls tonight."

I smiled and finished my drink. Before ordering another one I lit a Camel and inhaled deeply.

I didn't have a plan. I wasn't a policeman. I didn't have a notepad. Maybe we'd talk about the night that Juliette LeRoi was murdered. Maybe not.

"Could I get you somethin', mister?" the waitress asked. She was a high-yellow woman with straightened hair that came down and curled around her ears, like black modeling clay. She had light brown skin and freckles. Her large lips were in a permanent pout. She stood very close to me.

"Ask Westley what he had, Elaine, an' bring that," Charlene said for me. Then she said, "I thought you was married, Easy Rawlins."

I was watching Elaine move toward the bar.

"What would you do if you got married, Charlene?" I asked.

"Same things I do now, I guess."

"I mean, you got all this property an' stuff. What would you do if your husband didn't have all what you have?"

Charlene had big round cheeks that crowded her eyes when she smiled. "We'd have to sign us some papers before we got together. Yo know a po' niggah get next to that much money an' he's liable to go crazy. You know he'd be just like you."

"What you mean?" As I spoke Elaine returned and put the glass down in front of me.

Charlene took the waitress by the wrist and pulled her so close that the young woman was almost on her lap. She turned Elaine toward me so that I could get a good look at her. Elaine looked down at her breasts and smiled. Her long fake lashes enchanted me. I didn't know whether to take a drag off of my cigarette or a sip from my glass.

"Just like you, Easy. Here you are lookin' at Elaine. Now just think if you saw my deeds an' my cash register an' then this here girl's titties an' legs . . ."

I couldn't take my eyes off what Charlene was talking about. Elaine looked up at me. She was smiling but her eyes were cold.

I actually felt myself beginning to sweat.

Charlene slapped the girl on the butt and pushed her toward the bar. Elaine brushed me with one of those thighs as she went by. She even put a hand on my shoulder before walking away.

"Man got nuthin' cain't never get enough, Easy."

"What about a woman?" I asked. My throat was tight.

"What you worried 'bout?" Charlene smiled a warm, friendly smile. "You don't make enough to have no problem like that."

"I got a house," I said. "I got a car and a job that pays me a paycheck. That's enough fo'some women, ain't it?"

"I guess." She nodded. "Some women will take the dirty underwear right out of the hamper before they go. But unless you got sumpin' worth takin', Easy, I wouldn't be worried 'bout it. An' if you is worried, maybe you should cut it off now. That why you here?"

"Say what?"

"You wanna start playin' 'round?" Charlene's business wasn't a subtle one. "'Cause you know Elaine likes you."

"Naw." I shook my head and smiled. "I just wanted to ask you that question, that's all."

"Okay. But if you need anything, you know where t'come to. Gettin' people together is my business."

"Business good?" I asked.

Charlene nodded. She was watching two men come in. Westley was watching too. He could pour and look at the same time.

"'Cause I thought things mighta gotten kinda hard for you."

"Why?"

"After that thing with Julie LeRoi."

"What you mean?"

"Hey!" I put my hands in the air. "It's just that people been talkin' 'bout how she was here the night she was killed an' how the man that killed her was probably here, an' then he killed all them other girls."

"Caintnobodyprovethat," she said in machine-gun talk.

"Hey, like I said, it's just what I heard."

"Listen." She held a fat finger up to my face. "That Julie LeRoi was a tramp. She come here tryin' t'get her rent money. Now you know she be in five places in any night an' out on the corner if that don't work."

"But I heard she was here with a boyfriend." I snapped my fingers trying to remember something I didn't know.

"That boy Gregory?" she exploded. "He was her john. It's just that another one wanted her too an' he had more muscles, that's all."

I nodded, sipped.

"I see," I said, very seriously. "Anyway, it's cool now, right? Nobody's scared."

"Don't let 'em fool ya," Charlene said and pointed down the long room. "They all scared. Scared t'death. But what could they do? Poor woman all alone needs men fo'sumpin'. Maybe it's that night's rent an' maybe more, but she need sumpin'. An' these men is hungry too. Hungry fo'drink an' hungry fo'love."

I let her wisdom settle for a moment, then I said, "Well, I better be goin'."

When I stood up I felt the room bob a little as if I were on a ship.

"See ya," I said.

"Bye, Easy." Charlene smiled. "You take care now, baby."

I paid Westley on the way out. At the bar I tapped Elaine's shoulder and gave her a rolled-up dollar bill. When she smiled in the stronger light of the bar I noticed that she was missing one of her lower front teeth. That one simple, human fact excited me more than all of Charlene's bold talk.

When I staggered out of the door it wasn't only the whiskey that had me drunk.

• 10 •

The bars and clubs on and around Bone Street were many. I wouldn't have been able to hit all of them in one night, but I didn't have to, because I was looking for a special kind of joint. A place like Charlene's that catered to love-starved and sex-starved men, and sometimes women. A place that offered a little more than whiskey and blues. There were just a handful of clubs that fit those needs.

There was the Can-Can, run by Caleb Varley. At one time Caleb had a regular revue. But he had to cut back to a piano player and two sisters, Wanda and Sheila Rollet, who danced around artistically in golden glitter and glue. Then there was Pussy's Den, a pickup bar where B-girls had a couple of drinks before heading for an apartment, an alley, or an hourly motel.

DeCatur's still had Dixieland musicians.

The Yellow Dog and Mike's were one step down on the evolutionary scale. These were bars where the criminal element hung out. Gangsters and gamblers. Men who had done hard time for every crime you could think of. But there was a place for them, there were women for them too. Mostly your larger women. The kind who could take the punishment; either physical or grief. Both of these bars had back rooms where doctors sometimes came to patch a gunshot or knife wound. Where lawyers met clients that couldn't be seen going into an office in the daylight. And where women got on their knees for five minutes and five dollars, for a man who might not have seen a woman in five years.

I had been out of the bar scene since I got married, so most people were happy to see me. They were happy to talk. But nobody knew a thing.

I saw a fight in DeCatur's. A young boy named Jasper Filagret decided to take his woman, Dorthea, off the streets. He came in blustering and he went out bleeding. Dorthea left ten minutes later with another man. She had her fingers in his pocket while he rubbed the knuckles of his right hand.

I ran into an old acquaintance at the Yellow Dog. Roger Vaughn was his name. Roger was only five-six, but he had the shoulders of a heavyweight. He'd been drunk in a bar on Myrtle Street some years before. He'd wanted another drink but the bartender wanted to go home to his wife. He told Roger that he had to go and Roger said, "After one more drink." That's when the six-foot barman made his mistake. He grabbed Roger and Roger socked him, twice. The bartender was dead before he hit the floor. Roger did seven straight years for manslaughter. If the bartender had been a black man Roger wouldn't have done half that.

"Easy," Roger Vaughn said. He was hunched over his table with his big hands around a tumbler full of beer.

"Roger. You out at last, huh, man?"

"Not fo'long," he said, nodding in a way that made him seem wise.

"You paid your time, man. They cain't take you back unless you want 'em to." I pulled a chair up to his lonely table.

"Motherfucker took my money."

Roger was drunk and loose in the tongue. I knew that if I let him talk he would help me all he could. But I might have to hear things I didn't want to hear to get there. I was half drunk myself, otherwise I'd have bowed out right then.

"Motherfucker been doin' my wife. Right there in my own house. She come up to Soledad an' be smilin' at me. But all the time she comin' home to him. She comin' home t'him."

The glass broke in Roger's grip; more like it just crumbled. Beer, mixed with a little blood, ran over the table. I threw some paper napkins from the dispenser on the spill and handed Roger my handkerchief. He looked at me with a depth of gratitude.

"Thank you, Easy. You're a friend, man. A real friend."

You could buy a drunk's friendship with a handful of feathers and a sprinkle of salt.

"Thanks, Roger," I said. I patted his rocky shoulder across the table. "I was tryin' t'find somethin' out."

"What's that?"

"You knew Bonita Edwards?"

"Uh-huh, yeah, I knew 'er. You know that was a shame what happened that girl."

Blood soaked more and more into my rag.

"Hold that thing tight, Roger. You bleedin' pretty good there."

He gazed down at his hand and seemed surprised to see the bloody cloth. Then he clenched the hand into a fist and the whole thing disappeared.

"What you wanna know 'bout Bonnie?"

"She was a friend'a mines, Roger, so I'm askin' if anybody seen 'er 'round 'fore she got killed."

He shook his head slowly, his eyes moved loosely as he did. "Nope," he said. "An' you know if I did I'da kilt him jus' like I'ma kill . . ."

"Did you know what she was doin' that last week?" I asked, partly because I wanted to know and partly to distract him.

"I don't wanna cause you no pain, Easy, but I think she was down on Bethune."

I tried to look like I was bothered by this information. When somebody said Bethune they meant a whorehouse run by a white man named Max Howard and his wife, Estelle.

"Thank you, Roger," I said, as seriously as I could.

"Woman tear your heart out, man." Roger shook his head again. "An' that's what I'ma do to Charles Warren. He got my kids callin' him Daddy. He got my wife callin' him Daddy too. She be fuckin' me like it's all that love an' stuff. But she goin' t'see him Friday. I seen it on a note in her purse."

It was time for me to go. I should have gone. But instead I said, "Man, you don't know what it is."

Roger's head moved slowly as he turned his face upward to look at me. The rest of his body was rock-solid and tense.

He said, "What?"

"All I'm sayin' is give 'er a chance, man. Maybe it ain't what you think. I mean, she did come up to Soledad to see ya, right?"

Roger just stared.

"Woman wanna leave a man don't come up t'see him but the first few months," I continued. "But yo' wife come up the whole time, right?"

He wouldn't nod. We weren't friends anymore.

"Think about it, Roger. Talk to her."

I got up and backed away from the table. Roger followed me with his eyes. I decided to let him keep the handkerchief. Maybe when he looked at the bloody rag he'd remember what I said and refrain from killing Charles Warren.

The Howards' house was a big yellow thing. It had been a plain, single-story house at one time but they kept adding to it. First they made the garage into their living quarters so that the rest of the house could be used for business. Then they added a room on the other side. A second floor was put on in 1952 with a flat roof supporting a flower garden that Estelle tended. At some point they bought the house next door and annexed it by building a long hall-like structure across the yard. The original house was wood but the new addition was brick. The city started giving them zoning problems in '55 so they farmed out the girls for a while and had the whole thing painted yellow so that it would at least look of a piece.

I guess the city agent backed off or, more likely, was paid off. The girls came back, and along with them their regular customers. Nobody complained. Max, Estelle, and twelve women lived there—raising families, working hard, and going to church on Sundays.

I was drunk. The only reason I didn't have an accident driving the eight blocks to Bethune was that I didn't think about driving and somehow steered from instinct. I pushed the button in the center of the lion's mouth at the front door but I didn't feel my finger. I didn't hear the bell either, but, as I said, it was a big house.

A mule-faced woman answered the door. She was more than forty and less than sixty-five but that was all I could say about her age. Her platinum-blond hair cascaded to her shoulders like Marlene Dietrich's. Her skin was black. Her face had many folds in it. And her eyes were the color and sheen of wet mud. Her small hands, which she held before her pink bathrobe, looked as if they could crush stones.

"Estelle," I said. I had a stupid grin on my face. I could see it in the bronze-framed mirror that dominated the wall at Estelle's back. She peered at me as if I might have been a dream that would disappear.

I grinned on.

"What you want?" she asked, not in a friendly way at all.

"Thought I might have a drink an' some company." I shuddered. "It's cold out tonight."

"You already had enough t'drink, an' you got a wife t'keep you warm."

"Business so good you turnin' it away?"

Estelle pushed at a loose lock of her wig and the whole thing turned askew on her head. She didn't seem to notice, though.

"Ain't nuthin' that good. I just don't trust you, Easy. I hear all kindsa things 'bout you. What you want? I ain't axin' no mo'."

I tried to make the grin a little more sincere by looking into my own eyes in the mirror.

"Like I said. I want a drink an' some soft friendship. That's all."

"Why come here?"

"I been told that that girl . . ." I snapped my fingers again, looking for something I didn't know again. "You know, that li'l one, Bonita Edwards' friend."

The mud in Estelle's eyes hardened to stone. "Nita Edwards is dead."

"I ain't lookin' fo'her, it's just that I cain't remember her li'l friend's name."

"You mean Marla?" The look on Estelle Howard's mug would have deterred a rhinoceros.

"I don't know." I held up my hands. The smile muscles in my cheeks ached. "Jackson Blue told me 'bout her, but all he remembered was that she was Bonita's friend."

I smiled and she scowled for another thirty seconds or so, then she said, "You better com'on in fo' you let all the heat out."

• 11 •

We went down a long hall that was papered with yellow and orange velvet. There were small dark-stained tables every few feet with clean ashtrays and dishes of hard candy on them. This led to a largish room that had blue sofas along each cream wall. There were lamps here and there, all of them turned on. A woman and a boychild sat on a sofa before wall-length maroon drapes. She was Mexican with a lot of cleavage and makeup, backed by a mane of luxurious black hair. He was black and scrawny but had the largest brown eyes I'd ever seen—his mother's eyes.

"Wait here," Estelle said, batting at her wig.

She exited out a door on the opposite side of the room.

"Hey, mister?"

She was looking at me, smiling. The boy had something that came close to hatred in his beautiful eyes.

"Yeah?"

"Is it 'Peter and me went' or 'Peter and I went'?" She curled her lip and flared her nostril on the last sentence. I noticed that the boy had a straight-backed pad of paper on his lap.

" 'Peter and I,' like, 'Peter and I went to the store.' You see, you know because if you cut it down and said 'I went to the store' it would be better than 'Me went to the store.' "

The mother looked leery. The boy wanted to tear my heart out.

"You live here?" I asked.

"Yes." Her smile dazzled. She wasn't beautiful but she projected warmth.

"Hey, Pedro!"

The boy stopped scowling at me long enough to peer at the old white man coming through the door.

"Come here, boy!"

I was surprised that such an old and feeble-looking man could produce such volume.

He was tall and stooped over like Westley, but even more. He could almost look little Pedro in the eye. Max Howard fished a coin out of his pocket and flipped it at the boy. Pedro caught it and checked to see what it was—he didn't look disappointed.

Max had a full head of long white hair. During that time only old men could get away with that kind of hairstyle. He kept his head up, reminding me of a vulture scanning the horizon for the spectacle of death. He wore an old-fashioned three-button black suit with a starched white shirt and a silken blue-and-black tie. His shoes were older than I was but they were in perfect repair.

"Mr. Howard," I said.

"Rawlins, isn't it?"

"Yes, sir. Easy Rawlins." I didn't hold out my hand and he kept his claws in his pockets.

Max pressed his lips out and swiveled his head toward the mother and child. He might have nodded, maybe he silently mouthed something, but Pedro's mother gathered the boy up and hurried out of the room.

"Have a seat, Easy," Max Howard said.

I sat and he stood before me. His skin was like bleached onion parchment, crinkled and ghastly white.

He blinked. I crossed my legs. Somewhere far away a motor cruised down the street.

"What do you want here, Easy?" The question was straightforward.

"A woman," I said in kind.

His smiling lips quivered like a pair of light blue earthworms. "I don't think so," he said.

He blinked again. I uncrossed my legs.

After what seemed like a long time he said, "Twenty dollars."

I took out the bill and handed it over. He brought it right up to his face and squinted. Then he nodded and went back the way he'd come.

A few minutes later a short woman wearing a checkered muumuu that barely came down to her legs walked in. She had big red lips and round thighs. Her hair was permed into big floppy curls. Her eyes were big and round and ready to look into mine.

"Com'on," she said. Then she turned and walked away.

I followed her up the stairs. Her dress didn't hide a thing.

We went down a hallway that looked like it belonged in a hotel. There were doors on each side with numbers on them. She opened door seven and ushered me in.

"How you wan'it?" she asked my back.

When I turned around she'd taken off the dress.

"Just a little talk." I don't think I stuttered, but the girl smiled as if I had.

"What you wanna talk about?" One of her upper front teeth was solid gold. There was a nipple-sized mole just above her left nipple.

"You Marla?"

"Com'on." She pointed at the bed. "Sit'own."

We sat side by side with her thigh against my pant leg.

"You Marla?" I asked again.

"Uh-huh."

"I wanna know about Bonita Edwards."

"She dead."

Marla took my hand in hers and rubbed the knuckles against her nipple. It hardened and became very long.

Marla smiled. "She like you."

"I wanna know about Bonita Edwards."

"What you wanna know?"

"Did somebody want her dead? Anybody you know?"

Marla sat back with her hands propping her body from behind. "You workin' for the cops? 'Cause the cops already came here an' we told 'em that we didn't know nuthin'. Bonita had the day off an' she just never came back."

"I just wanna find out what happened to her. That's all."

"Max an' Estelle say I better watch out about you. They say you bad news an' I jus' better fuck you an' keep my mouf shut."

"S'pose I want you to use yo' mouf on me?"

Marla laughed and grabbed my arm. It was a very good laugh, lots of feeling behind it.

"That was a good one." She smiled at me and I realized that I was sitting on the bed with a naked young woman.

Then came three raps at the door. "Five minutes!" a man's voice said. It wasn't Max Howard.

"You got forty mo' dollars, mister?" Marla asked.

"How come?"

"They only give ya ten minutes for twenty an' they knock after five, you know, to hurry up. But if you pay again they let you go forty-five minutes fo' just sixty bucks."

I gave her the money.

She ran out in the hall without putting on a stitch.

In the room alone I considered going out of the window. Maybe she'd tell them what I asked her and they'd come back with a gun. I hadn't come armed. The whiskey was wearing off and I wasn't so brave anymore. I wasn't so sure.

The door opened and Marla came back with a bottle of scotch, two glasses, and her natural charm.

She was grinning. "We got almost a hour an' this bottle. You wan'it?"

She poured the two glasses full and settled on the bed beside me, her legs open wide enough to expose a thick mat of pubic hair. "So what you wanna know?"

"Same thing. A guy wants me t'find out about Bonita. He's upset about what happened and maybe he'd like t'say sumpin' to the guy that did it."

"What guy?"

"That ain't none'a yo' business, honey." I took a long drink and poured another glass full. Marla did the same and laughed.

"Bonita didn't have no boyfriend," she said speculatively. "She didn't even like men, not like me. An' I cain't think'a nobody wanna do that."

I sloshed back another drink. "Had to be somebody. Nobody kills you fo'nuthin'."

"Baby, you ain't never been in this business if you think that." Marla leaned forward to shake her head, and I realized that her curls were a wig.

"How old are you?" I demanded.

"Nineteen. An' I seen girls killed before. I seen men come at 'em with a baseball bat and a razor blade. I seen men come up these here steps with a dog they want the girl t'get friendly wit'. Uh-huh. I might just be a girl but I'm a woman too. I been a woman since I was eleven."

We both drank some more. Marla put her hand way up on my thigh.

"Who wanna know 'bout Bonita?" she asked.

"I can't say. They payin' me an' I ain't s'posed t'tell."

"You wanna fuck me?"

"Did Bonita know them other girls got killed?" I took another drink.

"Uh-uh."

"How do you know?"

"She told me. I know'd Julie LeRoi myself an' when I told Nita 'bout her she said, 'Who?' " Marla laughed. " 'Who?' Just like a owl."

I don't know how we started kissing, but there I was on my back and Marla was on top of me. I was so drunk I could barely feel our lips or tongues but something stronger than feeling was driving me.

When she was pulling down my pants I said, "How 'bout the other ones, Willa Scott or a stripper named Cyndi Starr?"

"You want me t'suck this thing or talk?"

I didn't say anything and she didn't either.

A long time later the knocks came on the door again.

"You gotta get dressed," Marla said.

I put on my pants and she slipped on her shift.

I got my money's worth. Bonita Edwards was from Dallas and had only been in L.A. three months. She came right to Max and Estelle's. She had an apartment but hardly ever went there. She didn't know Willa Scott, but Marla wasn't sure about Cyndi Starr.

"Marla?"

"What?"

"You ever do any work outside of here? I mean, does anybody ever hire you to meet 'em on you' day off or sumpin'?"

"Sometimes."

I knew from her smile that she'd hate me.

"Did Bonita?"

"That what you wanna know?" she snapped. "Why'ont you go on down to the mortuary an' jump on her?"

"Com'on, Marla. This is how I get paid."

"I don't know."

"You don't know what?"

"I don't know nuthin'!" she yelled, putting her fists up to her ears. Then she jumped up and ran out of the door.

I took a moment to grab my shirt before going after her.

When I made it to the hallway, a snakish white man was standing where Marla was supposed to be. He wore a tapered green suit that was large in the shoulders and thin at the hips. The suit matched his eyes. He smiled the way a snake would smile if serpents had lips.

"Hold on there, son," he hissed. "Playtime is over."

I was drunk, but not so drunk I didn't know that my reflexes were shot. I became as quiet as I could be, gathering all of my strength for one move.

"Why you after Marla?" Snake-lips was almost polite.

He raised his eyes a little, glancing over my right shoulder.

I heard the man behind me grunt. That was enough warning for me to avoid the blackjack aimed at my head. I moved to the right long enough to see a squat Negro stumble behind the force of his thrust. I let him fall and I threw a punch that landed on the side of Snake-lips' jaw. He fell back against the wall.

Little men are, on the whole, more agile than larger ones. The little Negro was already on his feet and swinging his sap. I moved enough not to take the full brunt of the blow but it did graze my head above the left ear.

The impact felt much like when a large vehicle, a bus for example, hits its brakes and sends you reeling. Then came the colors: red amoebae cut by yellow shards and peppered with black holes.

I aimed my fist for the place that I had last seen the little man's face. I felt a meaty impact.

Then I was stumbling down the stairs. I ran into a woman wearing a black negligee in the room where the Mexican woman and her child had been learning to read.

"Oh!" she exclaimed with a laugh in her voice. But when she looked at my face she backed away. I reached out to her after we'd collided; as she pulled away the material of her gown felt rough against my palms.

My bare feet were cold on the pavement outside. Marla's strong perfume and her female scent permeated my clothes. Maybe she liked me? I laughed and hurt and almost threw up. I shouldn't go home smelling like I did but I had to go home.

It took a long time for me to read the time off my copperfaced Gruen "very thin" watch. By then it was two forty-five. I took a deep breath and started the engine.

I drove very slowly down to my street, parking far enough away that Regina wouldn't be awakened by the familiar sound of my motor. I spent a whole minute opening the gate so it wouldn't squeak. Then I went in through Jesus' side door.

Jesus lay on his back with his mouth open. He would have slept through an earthquake. I took off my clothes and shoved them under his bed.

I sat in the bathtub letting the water trickle in slowly. Marla's smell was down my legs and under my fingernails. It was in my hair and on my breath.

After a long time I came out of the tub. I put on a robe and went to the baby's crib. Edna was hunched over one arm on her stomach and sucking her thumb. There was a dried web of mucus on the rim of her nostril. As I came close she sniffed at the air and frowned.

Regina was turned away from the door. The covers were up to her ears and she was taking in the deep breaths of sleep.

I got into the bed softly, so lightly that hardly a spring creaked. The pain in my head throbbed with each heartbeat.

The green fluorescent arms of the clock next to my bed said three-thirty.

It was the first time I had been with another woman since we'd been married. And it was a prostitute. I didn't even like it. But I had gotten dark pleasure from that girl.

Whoever had killed Bonita Edwards had probably met her at Bethune Street. I imagined all the ways I could question Max. I imagined sapping him and waiting until he awoke, and then hitting him again. Maybe I wouldn't let him talk for hours. Maybe I never would.

At three-forty she said, "Did you get the money, Easy?"

"No, baby. I been askin' questions fo' Officer Naylor t'day. I ain't hadda chance t'look into it yet."

I thought that I'd make it look hard to get the money. I planned to tell Regina everything about my money after I was finished with the police.

I just needed time to get all the words straight.

I stayed very still in hopes that she'd lull back into sleep. I purged all thoughts of sex, violence, and death from my mind.

After a while I couldn't even remember what Marla looked like.

"You smell like you been in a whorehouse," she said at four-oh-five.

Neither one of us had moved.

"You know I love you, Regina," I said.

"I know you think you do."

"You'n Edna mean more to me than anything."

"Uh-huh."

"Is that all you could say?"

I waited up until dawn but she never said another word.

• 12 •

My tongue felt like a cactus pad and the blood was pounding in my head. I got out of bed and walked along the walls into the living room.

They were all there.

Jesus was sitting in the light of the window reading a book and holding the fingers of his left hand against his head. I recognized his pose as the posture I took while reading.

Regina had on a turquoise housecoat. Edna, dressed only in diapers, sat in her lap. Mother and daughter sat staring at each other in awe. Just as I came into the room Edna reached for her mother's face and Regina leaned forward to be touched.

They were all so beautiful that I started to back away. But then somebody took the stairs in two steps and knocked at our door.

When Regina rose she saw me. A look of confusion crossed her face as if, maybe, I shouldn't have been there at all. Then she frowned and went to answer the door.

It was Gabby. She grinned at my daughter and wife, kissing them and making silly faces.

The smile died on her face when she saw me. I turned away and went back into the bedroom.

Regina came soon after saying, "You should be civil to Gabby Lee, Easy."

"Did she say somethin' to me?"

I noticed blood on the white pillowcase. The little Negro's

memento from the night before. My right arm ached as I made to cover the pillow with the sheet.

"Gabby Lee had plenty of trouble with men, Easy. She might not know how to be civil to a man but that don't excuse you."

"Could I drive you today?"

Regina had taken off her robe and was about to step into her yellow dress.

"Why?"

"Like we used to do. Then I'll pick you up tonight."

"Why today?" She sounded suspicious.

"Listen, honey," I said. I put out my hand to zip her back. She hesitated a moment before allowing my touch. "I know I been wrong with you. I know that. But I wanna make it right."

"Yeah?"

"It's just that I gotta get through this thing with Quinten Naylor first."

She touched my ear where the blackjack had struck. "What happened to you?"

"I love you, Regina."

I sat down on the bed. My head hurt so much that it was past pain. It felt more like a kind of motion; like a razor-backed viper slithering through my brain. Regina saw the agony in my face and sat down next to me.

"What's wrong, baby?"

"I wanna drive you to work and I want you to do something for me too."

"What?"

"On October fourteenth you got a patient at the Temple emergency room. It was a boy named Gregory. I don't know his last name. I need to find out where he lives."

"What for?"

"He knew one'a them girls got killed."

"Why don't you just tell Quinten Naylor about it? He could find out himself."

"Maybe, but if I could come up with a name and an address then I would know for sure that Quinten could find him. You know the police make so much noise when they doin' anything and this Gregory might have a friend at Temple."

"But I need my car," Regina said.

"I'll pick you up at five, I swear I will."

"Well . . . I guess," she said finally. "But we gotta hurry if you wanna go. You know I got a timetable to keep."

Temple Hospital is a big gray building at the top of a hill on Temple Street. Edna was born there on a rainy January night. Regina was in a lot of pain during labor and the nurses were so nice that she decided to become a nurse's aide herself. She never worried about a profession before then. But you couldn't pry her away from that job with gold or honey.

I took a left turn before we came to the main entrance.

"What you doin'?" Regina asked.

"Parking. I thought we could get some coffee like we used to."

"I gotta get to work."

"It's only eight-thirty. You don't have to be on shift until nine-fifteen."

Regina shook her head. "I don't have the time this mornin'," she said.

I made a turn in the middle of the street and pulled into a loading zone in front of the main entrance.

Regina said, "You been off in yo' own thing all this time, baby. You know I got girlfriends in there who expect me to sit wit' them."

"But I'm your husband."

She patted my cheek, then kissed it. "I'll find out what I can about your emergency boy, honey. I'll call you 'round ten, okay?"

"I guess."

She kissed me on the lips and opened the door. I felt so bad to be alone that I almost called out to her. I watched her walk away. The moment she was out of the car her mind was fully on the job she had to do. She didn't look back. I waited until the large door she went through had closed.

By the time I was back home that razor-backed viper was boring at my skull. Gabby Lee and Edna were playing in the living room.

Jesus was packing his lunch in the kitchen.

"How you doin'?" I asked him.

Jesus looked up at me and smiled.

"Let me see your hands."

He flashed his palms at me quickly and then reached for his lunch bag. But I reached out to touch his shoulder.

"Let's have a good look now," I said.

He'd been eating something sticky in the last twenty-four hours. Mottled dirt ran down the seams between his fingers.

"You gotta wash your hands every night, Jesus Rawlins. If you go to bed like that you could attract ants, maybe even a rat."

Jesus glanced fearfully down at the floor.

"Go on now, wash up and get on down to school."

He ran to the bathroom.

I went back to bed counting heartbeats and breathing as slowly as I could.

When Gabby Lee started making loud cooing noises with Edna in the other room I shouted, "Cut out that noise! Cut it out!"

Edna began to cry. I wanted to go out there and hold my hand over her little mouth, but I knew it was the hangover. I knew it was all the guilt I felt over the whore and me. Me, the whore-man, the fool.

"Now you made that baby cry," Gabby Lee said from the bedroom door.

She had a hard stare for me but when I looked up into her eye she backed down. She backed all the way out of the room. I pulled myself from bed and cursed Quinten Naylor. I hated that man. If it wasn't for him I'd be fine. I actually believed that. Way past thirty and I was still a fool.

I went into Jesus' room with a denim bag and gathered up my clothes. Then I went to the bedroom to get the sheets.

Gabby Lee watched me silently as I went from room to room.

I made coffee and toast. I drank the brew but the toast went uneaten. I washed and shaved and then washed again. I said good morning to my baby girl when I was halfway human. She laughed and played with my fingers. It's a shame the way children will forgive parents their sins.

I didn't say another word to Gabby Lee. She went around the house suddenly hating me like she hated all men. But I couldn't blame her that morning. It seemed like I was on the warpath against women and that all the men I knew, and those I didn't know, were too. I treated Marla like a piece of meat. I wasn't honest with my wife and I yelled at my baby. Somebody was going around killing women and the police hardly cared until a white girl got it. I wasn't even sure that they cared about her.

The phone ringing nearly tore my head off. Gabby Lee didn't answer it. She wasn't going to be my secretary. The bell reminded me of machine-gun bursts. When I finally staggered up to it I had to restrain myself from throwing the goddam thing out of the window.

"Yeah," I whispered.

"Easy?" said Regina. "Is that you?"

"Uh-huh."

"His last name is Jewel and he lives at one sixty-eight Harpo. They said somebody really worked him over. All kinds of broken bones. Um. He got a young wife came and got him the next day."

"Thanks, babe," I said. I'd written down the address and name on the tabletop in the dining room. Gabby Lee stared daggers at me but she didn't say a word.

"Easy?" Regina asked.

"Yeah?"

"Do you like doin' this?"

"Doin' what?"

"This. This workin' with the cops an' lookin' for people like this boy."

"Uh-uh, no, baby. I just wanna be home with you. That's what I like."

There was a neighborhood tomcat stalking across the front lawn. I was watching him through the front window when all of a sudden he froze and stared at me from a half-crouch. His eyes were Regina's, staring through my lies.

"But you do it 'cause you have to?"

"What?"

"I had to have me a baby. I had to. I like this job and I like a lotta things but I had to have Edna. I'd die without her."

"I'd die without you, honey," I said.

"I gotta go now, Easy. You be here at five?"

"Yeah. I'll be there."

When I went out the front door L.A. was waiting for me. You could see as far as the mountains would let you. I didn't deserve it, but it was mine just the same.

• 13 •

Gregory Jewel lived in a California-style tenement. The project was a deep lot with a row of white-and-green bungalows facing each other. At the end of the aisle of sixteen dwellings was a solitary bungalow. That was Gregory Jewel's house. A little bronze tab over the door buzzer said "assistant manager."

A young woman opened the door. She had light brown skin with dark brown freckles around her broad nose. She had spaces between her teeth which enhanced her smile and you could see that she always smiled. Even when she was sad she smiled. Her eyes were wet and there were creases in her young face, the creases of days of crying. Her solemn, creased face told of how she'd look when she became an older woman—Gregory would be a lucky man if he held on to her that long.

"Yes?" she said.

"Gregory Jewel," I said in a gruff tone. The hangover was talking for me.

"No, sir. No Gregory Jewel here."

"Com'on, honey. I know this is his house. An' I know Greg ain't goin' nowhere 'cause he's all beat up. So tell 'im that Easy Rawlins is here an' unless he wants the police on 'im he better talk wit' me now."

She listened to my speech patiently and when I finished she said, "Sorry, mistah, but they ain't no Gregory Jewel in this house."

"Ella!" came a shout from the house.

"What?"

"Who is that?"

"Just some man lookin' fo'a Gregory Jewel. I told 'im that they wasn't any here."

"Come on back here," the voice shouted.

Ella closed the door in my face. I took it. I felt like pushing past her and dragging Gregory from wherever he was hiding but I kept the anger caged. I was saving it for a stronger foe.

When the door opened again Ella's smile was gone.

"Com'on," she said.

The rooms in the bungalow were like a ship's cabin. There was hardly enough space to turn around. The furniture was mismatched and the linoleum on the floor was rotted around the corners. There was a professional photograph of Ella in the arms of a skinny, buck-toothed man tacked to the wall. There was a hot plate and a stack of dishes next to the front door.

Through that room was an even tinier bedroom. There was probably a toilet in a closet off from there. I never found out though, because the buck-toothed man was laid up in the small bed.

Gregory's left arm went straight out to the side and was wrapped, up past the shoulder, in a thick white cast. His right hand was bandaged and both of his feet were in casts. The casts were all scuffed and frayed. There was a bandage around Gregory's head and there was blood in both of his eyes.

"What you want?" he asked.

There was only enough room for a squat upholstered chair with their bed. I sat in it and Ella slumped against the door.

"You Gregory Jewel?"

My official tone made him nervous.

"How come?" he asked.

I looked at him for a few seconds. I didn't feel sorry for the man, because he called this misery on himself. But I felt kindred to his misery. It seemed to me that my whole life had been spent walking into shabby little houses with poor people bleeding or hacking or just dying quietly under the weight of our "liberation." I was born in a house no larger than that one. I lived there with two half-sisters and one step-brother. I watched my mother die of pneumonia on a bed like Gregory's.

All of a sudden my hangover was gone. I took a deep breath of sour air and said, "I gotta know 'bout how you was beaten, man."

"How come? You a cop?"

"The cops will be here 'less you tell me sumpin'."

"How I know that?"

"Listen, I ain't gonna mess around wit' you. If you want the cops here I'll send 'em. I need t'know 'bout how you got messed up. They do too."

The young couple looked at each other, then Gregory asked, "What's up?"

"This is deep, Greg. Real deep. You don't want yo' name nowhere around it. You could take that from me. I ain't gonna tell ya nuthin', but it's better fo'you that way. Now this is the last time I'm gonna ask it. After this I'm gone an' ev'rybody gonna know yo' name."

Gregory tried to laugh. "Wasn't nuthin'. Ain't nuthin' t'tell. I run inta him at a bar an' he said sumpin' I didn't like."

"What about Juliette LeRoi? I heard that the fight was over her."

Ella opened the door and went out.

"What you wanna go an' do that fo', man?" Gregory squealed. "That ain't right."

"What about Juliette LeRoi?" I asked again. I took a twenty-dollar bill from my pocket and put it on the cast.

Only great concentration kept Gregory from snatching that bill with the two available fingers of his bandaged hand. "What you wanna know?"

"What happened with you that night you got beat up?"

Gregory looked away from me at the small window near the top of the low ceiling. He brought to mind a chick that had fallen from the nest.

"I know 'er. That's all. I went with 'er down to Aretha's t'get some drinks. We did that sometimes and then maybe I'd get some, you know what I mean?

"So there was this dude with a beard there an' he said that he wanted her t'come wit' him. I stood up an' he pushed me across the room. Then he goes out the door pullin' on Julie. I got a bad temper so I runs on out an' goes after 'em. But he grabs me an' th'ows me in the alley." Tears came to Gregory's face. "First he broke my arm, man. Then he stomped my feet. Doctor said I might not even be able to walk right, an' you know we get our rent free if I look after things here an' they gonna throw us out if I don't get back to it soon."

"What about the man an' Juliette?" I didn't want to hear about his problems. There was nothing I could do.

"She saved me, man. She yelled at 'im an' pulled him back. I mean, he let her pull him. He was big an' real strong. He hit me in the head a couple of times with a trash can. The last I seen they was goin' off together."

"She call 'im anything?"

"She did but I don't remember." Gregory shook his head but that hurt him so he winced.

"Did he pull her away?"

"Uh-uh. She said she'd go with 'im if he let up."

"That's all?"

"He sounded funny."

"Like what?"

"He'd say 'mon' instead'a 'man.' He almost sounded like he was an English nigger."

That was enough for me. I stood up to go and Gregory said, "What's this all about?"

"You don't know?"

"Know what? What should I know?"

"Juliette is dead. She got killed sometime after she went off with this dude who busted you up."

"Naw, uh-uh, Julie ain't dead." Gregory gave a little laugh to prove it.

"Don't you talk to nobody, man?" I asked.

"Ella's all since this." He raised his broken arm about three inches.

I left him there to lie in his coffin-sized bedroom and consider how close he had come to death.

Ella was on the matchbook sofa crying when I left. I didn't say anything to her. There's no cure for living a life of poverty. There's nothing to say either.

Willa Scott lived with her parents on Eighty-third Street. They were two small people who owned a modest house. They'd had Willa late in life and were now of retirement age. All they could do was ask me why. "Why would somebody do that to our girl?"

"Did she ever have friends come to the house?" I asked. "Men friends."

Her mother, a hen-shaped woman, shook her head. The father, who never got out of his chair as long as I was there, said, "She was kinda private. She told us that most'a these men she meets out there wasn't good enough t'bring on home. But you know she was gonna get a job for the schools. She said she was."

"Did she know a man, a Negro man with a beard?"

"No sir," Mrs. Scott answered. "Did you want to see the pictures of her?"

Mrs. Scott brought out a handmade photograph album. She and her husband beamed at the photos while I stood behind them. She kneeled at his side and they both cooed and clucked.

I thanked them about halfway through.

When I went through the front door they were still admiring Willa's memory.

• 14 •

Between Eighty-sixth Street and Eighty-seventh Place on Central Avenue, not far from the Scotts' house, was a long stucco building that we called Hollywood Row. It was nowhere near Hollywood but we called it that because of its showy residents. It was only two stories high but it took up the whole length of the block. The bottom floor was made up of a mom-and-pop store called Market, two liquor stores, three bars, and a Chinese laundry called Lin Chow. The upper floor was a long hall of studio apartments populated by transient gangsters, whores, and musicians who'd seen their day come and go. The musicians were the only long-term residents. Lips McGee, a man I'd known since I was a youngster in Houston, had lived there for thirteen years.

First I went to Lin Chow, where a small woman wearing a blue quilted jacket and red cotton pants was ironing. She looked at me and gave me a toothless grin. I handed her the denim bag and she emptied it on the counter. She jotted something down on a white pad and tore the slip off for me.

I couldn't read it.

"How long?" I shouted.

She held up two fingers and shouted back, "Two day."

"Today?" I pointed at the floor indicating now.

She shook her head and held up two fingers again.

I used her sign language as a kind of omen and went to one of the liquor stores, where I purchased two pints of Johnnie Walker Red Label scotch.

The only entrance to the dwellings of Hollywood Row was a rickety door that opened into an alley behind the building. To the left of the door there was a corral of trash cans breeding ants, roaches, and flies. The cans were all overflowing with aluminum TV dinner plates and liquor bottles. The wooden stairs were spongy. The long hall was covered with a carpet that once was green. Now it was simply edged with color like a dry brown riverbed with dying grasses along its banks.

Hollywood Row wasn't a private place. People treated it like one big house. Most of the studio apartment doors were open. One door I passed revealed a man fully dressed in an antique zoot suit and a white ten-gallon hat. As I passed by we regarded each other as two wary lizards might stare as they slithered across some barren stone.

There were smells of cooking and incense and various human odors. And then there was a long and clear note made by a silver trumpet. The note broke into a ripple of sounds that somehow ended up at the same clear cry. And then came an earthy "wah-wah" that drowned out all the mortality in that hall.

I followed the sound to a door toward the end of the hall. On my way I passed shabby scenes of men and women in various states of undress. Some were lovers oblivious of my passage. Others were looking for someone to come down the hall and deliver them from their lives.

Lips McGee's door was ajar. I knocked gently and his trumpet answered, "Wah?"

"It's me, Lips, Easy Rawlins," I said.

"Com'on in, Easy."

The room wasn't big but it was larger than Gregory Jewel's whole house. There was a couch, a maple table with two oak chairs, and a sink over which a window peeked out onto Central Avenue. The walls were all covered with photographs of Lips' life. The larger ones were of him and the jazz greats. But there were older, brownish pictures of him playing in the one-room clubs and jazz parades down in Houston. He was old by then but in his heyday Lips was what every black man wanted to be. He was dapper and self-assured, articulate, and had money in his pocket. He was always surrounded by beautiful women, but what really made me jealous was the way he looked when he played his horn.

He'd stand straight and tall and play that horn as if every bit of his soul could be concentrated through a silver pipe. Sweat shone across his wide forehead and his eyes became shiny slits. When Lips hit the high notes he made that horn sound like a woman who was where she wanted to be when she was in love with you.

The smell of marijuana permeated the room. Lips was standing next to the sink; he'd probably been serenading the street. He wore blue jeans and a yellow T-shirt that hung loose on his bony frame. His hair was longish and combed backwards. His orangy-brown chin was whiskered with black and white stubs.

"Wah-wah," he blew. And then, "What you doin' here, Easy Rawlins?"

I sat down in one of the chairs.

"Makin' a social call," I said.

Lips laughed. He took a plate of something that looked like chili-out-of-a-can from the stove and placed it across from me on the table. Far away I heard sirens, lots of sirens. They were police sirens, not fire trucks.

"That's what the snake says t'the hare when he comin' down his hole," Lips said.

"What's that?"

"Makin' a social call." Lips chuckled. "An' the first thing he do is eat his host."

"That might be," I said. "But I ain't hungry t'night." I took a pint bottle from my jacket pocket. Lips grinned a little wider.

"I see," the old man said.

He brought out two jelly jars and filled them with my scotch. He blew a kiss to his glass before sipping. Then he smiled up at the ceiling.

Lips told me stories that I'd heard a hundred times before but I still laughed heartily. When we got quiet Lips would take a sip of whiskey, then a bite of chili. Then he'd blow a few notes, maybe even the beginning of a song—a nursery rhyme or jazz hit. He asked me about Mouse and Dupree Bouchard and Jackson Blue.

After we cracked the seal on the second bottle, Lips asked, "What you want here wit' me, man?"

"You hear 'bout these women gettin' killed?"

"Yeah?"

"I'm lookin' around with Quinten Naylor to find out who did it."

"Uh-huh?"

"One'a them girls, the last one, was called Robin Garnett in the newspaper, but the name she used down here was Cyndi Starr."

For a moment the old man looked even older. Then he licked his lips.

"Yeah," he said. "That white girl lived down here sometimes. I wondered where she went. Cyndi Starr, I wonder where you are, baby. I wonder wonder where." He smiled a different, softer smile for her memory.

"You knew her?" I asked.

When Lips looked me in the eye I knew he was going to go off on what we used to call his "wild talk." But that was the only way he knew how to say what he meant, so I took another drink and wished that I had been seated on the more comfortable couch.

"I been here thirteen years and there ain't never been no change. I mean, somebody moves out but then someone just like him, or her or what-have-you, moves in and it's the same. It's like you get so high like in a dream where you flyin', an' sometimes you think, 'What am I doin' up here?' And you go crashin' down on the ground, an' sometimes you don't even care. 'Cause nuthin' matters when a wave pulls out. The sand smooths over any footprint that was there.

"You ast me if I know Cyndi Starr but you ain't askin' 'bout Hilda Wildheart. You ain't askin' 'bout Curtis Mayhew. You know what happened t'them?"

I shook my head.

"Same fuckin' thing. Same fuckin' thing. They gone. Gone. That's all she wrote fo'them. Beautiful girl all sad inside want some man t'make her feel good. Put on some silky clothes an' some makeup. All the wolves up an' down the street make some noise an' she fo'get how bad she feel. Whas wrong with that? Huh? Whas wrong?"

There wasn't an answer.

"Hilda Wildheart, Sonia Juarez, Yakeesha Lewis . . ." He counted them off on his fingers as he went. "Tiffany Marlowe, even yo' Lois Chan been up here. Broken hearts, broken jaws, broken necks. All the pussy you could ever wanna be 'round. You know, mo' than one'a them girls kept me company when I was so low I couldn't even go outside. They brew some tea an' love me. Yeah," he shrugged, "they mighta lifted five bucks after I was asleep but they didn't take it all. Uh-uh. Them girls was all beautiful, an' here you go askin' 'bout Cyndi Starr like this is the first thing you know 'bout them po' girls. Young boys like you come up here t'get some pussy an' that's it. You gone."

Lips shrugged again. I poured him another glass of whiskey.

"She come up here laughin' an' singin' with her girlfriends an' her boyfriends," Lips said. I knew that he was talking about Cyndi because now he seemed to be talking to me rather than at me. "She used to come in here an' tell me things till even my old dick would get hard. She liked to say how she could handle two men till they was like jelly. She had a foul mouth but she was so sweet sometimes."

"When was the last time she was here?"

"Maybe I seen 'er about three weeks ago. She was gone for a while before that."

"Gone where?"

"She was just gone there fo'while. She had this other white girl stayin' there. Sylvia."

"How long was she gone?"

"I dunno. Three, four months. 'Bout that. Maybe more."

"What was this Sylvia girl like?"

"Raven. Long raven hair and black eyes and white skin so pale that it was always a shock t'look at her."

"Where's she now?"

Lips shook his head. "Don't know that either. She stayed a couple'a days when Cyndi got back but then she went. That was 'bout two months ago. Yeah, them girls was thick."

"Cyndi have a job?"

"She'd take off her clothes down at Melodyland."

"What room was hers?"

"The purple. Three doors down on the other side."

I thanked him for his help and toasted his virility.

Before I left he said, "You drinkin' pretty heavy there, boy. Better slow it down some."

"I got a lot on my mind, old man. Too much."

"You ain't gonna have much of a mind left if you keep on like that."

I laughed. "I'm still young, Lips. I can take it."

"I seen men turn old in six months under that bottle, man. I seen 'em die in a year."

I used my pocketknife, pried open the lock with no trouble.

Cyndi Starr's room had no history. Everything was right then. The single mattress on the floor in the corner. The signed photographs of Little Richard and Elvis Presley tacked to the wall. There were three partially eaten cans of pork and beans in the sink, each one with a spoon handle sticking out. A cardboard box made her night table. The Formica-top dining table was covered with movie magazines and one hard-cover book. That was a thick brown tome entitled *Industrial Psychology.*

"Can I help you?" The voice behind me was musical and delicate.

When I turned I was met by a small, fair man. His skin was almost white. He had a sparse goatee, long eyelashes, and brown suede pants and shirt. His shoes were made from blue fake alligator skin.

"No," I told him.

He cocked his head to the side and looked me up and down with a hint of a smile on his lips. He met my eye and blinked slowly. "Then what you doin' in here?"

"Lookin' fo' Cyndi."

He looked around the room. "She ain't here. An' even if she was, why you be openin' her do' if she don't answer?"

I was nervous in front of this brazen little man. His frank stares and insinuating smiles, coupled with the alcohol, made me uncomfortable.

"Ain't you heard, man?" I asked.

"Heard what?" His eyes hardened into the question.

"She's dead. Murdered by the man been killin' them girls."

"No." His lower lip trembled. His clasped his hands and took a step toward me.

"Raped her and brutalized her and then mutilated her body." I nodded. I felt better now that my inquisitor was disturbed.

He took another step and grabbed my sleeve.

"No," he said again. His eyes were begging me.

"An' I'm here fo' the police . . ."

He didn't give me enough time to finish. The little man stepped away from me, putting his hands on his thighs. His face was hard and unyielding. He backed straight into the door and then turned. He was gone in less than three heartbeats.

I looked around a little bit more. I found a yearbook from Los Angeles High School, the class of '55, and a folder full of *professional* photos of Cyndi. In one shot she posed naked, except for a G-string and her fingertips, feigning surprise on an empty stage. The spot light on her was in the shape of a butterfly against the black back drop. The White Butterfly. In a corner there was a box of clothes. She had everything in there, from a UCLA letter sweater to a pair of glitter-encrusted high heels.

I studied another of the photos for a while. It was her looking over her bare shoulder at the camera. The face was hard and beautiful. She wasn't healthy in that photograph. None of the force or sensuality in that snarl appeared in her college photo. I understood why no one but John had recognized her. Cyndi Starr was a different woman on Hollywood Row.

I felt like a child's pallbearer going down the stairs with her box of memories.

• 15 •

I called the police station from a phone booth in the street. Quinten agreed to wait for me at his office. He was all starch and good manners.

When I was going up the stairs to the station door I saw five men coming down. Four of them were policemen surrounding Roger Vaughn. He was manacled, hand and foot. He looked up at me and I remembered all the sirens I'd heard at Hollywood Row.

When Roger saw me he put both hands out to me. Instinctively I reached out too. But two of the cops clubbed him. He slumped down and they dragged him off to a van in the street.

The desk sergeant knew who I was and waved me by as I went up to him. But I stopped to ask, "What they got that man out there for?"

"Double killing. He found some guy on top of his wife."

By that time Quinten had his own office with a clouded glass door that had his name and rank stenciled on it in green paint. I lifted my hand but he must have recognized the shadow against the pane.

"Come on in, Ezekiel," he said.

It had been two days and he was five years older. His cannonball shoulders sagged down a little further and his head tilted to the side as if he found it too heavy to keep erect. When I came into the room he sighed like a dogface at the end of a thirty-mile forced march.

"You look half dead, Q-man," I said, coining the nickname that was to follow him the rest of his life.

"And you're drunk," was his reply.

"It's a hard world out there, brother. A little booze keeps ya from sinkin' to the bottom of the barrel."

"What do you want?"

"I'm feeling generous, officer. I've come to share what I know with you-all." I took a seat in a chair set by the door.

"What's that?"

"Them first three women was killed just about two weeks apart, right?"

Quinten nodded and his eyes drooped as if he might nod off on me.

"But then this Robin Garnett is dead just a couple days after you find Bonita Edwards."

"Yes, you're right about that," Naylor said in his prim Philadelphia accent. "Not only that. She was white, she was a college student, and she didn't live anywhere near this neighborhood; no one seems to know what she was doing down here. That's one of the reasons the brass is so upset. They think some crazy Negro is going to go on a rampage killing white women."

"Yeah," I smiled. "But I don't think you got it all. You see, this li'l darlin' got kilt wasn't all so pure as some might wanna think."

"What's that mean?"

I threw down one of Cyndi's stripper photographs.

Naylor studied it for a minute.

"Why didn't anybody show me this?"

"Nobody knew, man. That picture in the *Times* an' *Examiner* didn't look nuthin' like this stripper. An' mosta the people knew her prob'ly don't buy the mo'nin' news no way. An' even if they did, why they wanna come down here when you prob'ly th'ow them in jail fo'bad thoughts?"

"Where'd you get this?" Maybe he was going to throw *"me"* in the slam.

"At her pad, man. You know the Hollywood Row, right?"

"How'd you know where to go, Easy?"

"Listen." I held up my palm for him to admire. "I got my secrets. That's why you need me."

Quinten looked at me hard for a minute.

Finally he said, "All right. I'll go look into it. Makes it a little neater for us. I don't know what the man's going to think, though. You know they get real upset when these white women cross the line."

"Why don't we drive on down to where that girl's parents are at? You know, just for some questions. We could bring that picture down there an' see what they got say." I didn't mention the box of belongings I had out in the car.

"Why?"

"It just don't smell right, Quinten. Why she get killed two days after the other one when they gettin' murdered ev'ry two weeks or more 'fore that? How come this is a white one an' all the rest'a them is black? An' how come they kill this coed an' they killin' B-girls all before this?"

"You got the proof here that she was one of those kind of women." He held up the photograph to prove his point.

"Yeah," I said. "But maybe that's not the girl he killed."

"What?" Quinten slammed the picture down on his desk.

"I mean, it's the same body, the same life, but it was Robin Garnett got killed, not Cyndi Starr. I mean, they found her all dressed up like a coed, right? If it was the coed who was killed and not the stripper, then maybe there was some other reason fo'the murder, right?"

"Maybe the killer knew her. Maybe he knew about her double life." Quinten didn't want any complications.

"Yeah, I guess. He knew Juliette LeRoi, all right."

"What's that?"

I told him about the fight at Aretha's and Gregory Jewel. Also about how Bonita Edwards didn't know the other girls.

"You got all this and you're just coming in here now?"

"Hey, man, calm down. I'm here. Pass what I told you to your partner an' then let's you an' me go over to see the Garnetts."

"I don't think so. I appreciate you wanting to help, but police work should be kept in the house. They have enough trouble with a Negro cop. What are they going to think about you?"

I didn't like the way he said that. "What do you think about me, Quinten?"

A sneer flashed across Quinten's face. He sat forward placing his big fists on the desk. "I think you're rotten, Mr. Rawlins. You and your friend Raymond Alexander. Both of you belong in the penitentiary. But nobody wants to make that a priority. Everybody's always got something better. Maybe you'll help us catch this guy, probably you will. But whoever he is, he's just crazy. He can't help it. But you could. You're a criminal, Ezekiel Rawlins. I might have to work with you, I do have to. But just because you have to wipe your ass doesn't mean that you have to love shit."

Maybe if I hadn't been drinking it wouldn't have hurt. I don't know. But everybody was on me. Regina and Gabby Lee and Quinten Naylor. I felt like I needed a drink. I did need a drink.

The Los Angeles phone book was my best friend in those days. I went north to Pico Boulevard and then west until I hit Hauser. The Garnetts were five blocks further north from there.

They lived in a two-story Spanish-style house that shared a large lawn with a weeping willow and sloppy-looking St. Bernard on a long chain. The whole yard was surrounded by a low cement fence that had been treated to look like adobe. The roof was made from curved red tiles. Terra-cotta. Probably imported from Mexico or maybe even Italy. Two sharkish-looking Caddies were parked in the driveway. Five boy's bicycles were parked on the lawn.

I took the sweater, the yearbook, and the envelope of her working photos and put them in a large brown paper bag. Then I went up to the door and pressed the button. A buzzer went off in the house. That surprised me. I expected bells, Spanish bells to toll or chime, at least to ring. A buzzer was what you heard in a hardware store.

A boy in his early teens swung the door open wide. He was still young enough to have feminine features and so greatly resembled his dead sister's photographs. His face darkened for a moment when he saw me. Maybe he was expecting one of his little boyfriends rambling up on a J. C. Higgins.

"Hi." He had a beautiful all-American-boy grin.

"I'm lookin' fo'your mother or father." I smiled too.

"Dad's out but Mom's here. I'll get her."

"Mom!" he shouted as soon as he was out of sight.

He left the door open, either out of trust or ignorance, and I could see clear through the house. The living room was sunken and plush with white furry furniture. The back wall was mostly glass and looked out into the patio, backyard, and swimming pool.

The white woman, who was scolding the boy as she made her way from the patio, wasn't much older than I. But she seemed to have weathered many years. Mothers age more quickly than fathers do.

She was tall for a woman and erect. She wore a midcalf one-piece dress that was green with little horses printed in a spiral line from her neck to the hem. I could tell that the dress was expensive because the pattern wasn't askew. Somebody paid attention when they sewed it.

"Yes?" she asked. Her smile was tentative.

"Mrs. Garnett?"

"Yes?" Her hand moved toward the doorknob.

"My name is Easy, Easy Rawlins," I said.

"If you're from one of the papers, I'm sorry but we're not giving interviews. We . . ." She pulled the door close to her side and moved forward.

"No ma'am, I found some things that belong to you."

"I'm sorry, Mr. Rawlins, but I haven't lost anything."

As she made ready to shut the door I said, "Your daughter's things, ma'am."

"What are you talking about?" Her face and voice would have made a good final Friday scene on *As the World Turns.*

"She lived down in my neighborhood. Down on Central Avenue, and she left some clothes an' pictures down there."

"You're mistaken, sir. My daughter lived right here."

"No, ma'am. I mean, maybe she did, but she lived down on Central, too. I got her things right here in this bag."

When I pulled the blue sweater out of the bag she cried, "Oh my God!" and ran back into the house.

She yelled, "Milo! Milo!" and then she ran back to the door. "Who are you?"

It hurt to look in her eyes, so I stared at the mint weed that had pressed its way through the cracks at the base of the wall. I didn't want to be there but I'd be damned if I could question black people and not white ones.

The boy and a few of his friends ran to her side. Actually they came up behind her.

"Mom," Milo said.

"Go on back to your room, honey." She was in control again. She turned and led them away from the door and came back.

"Who are you?"

"I'm Easy Rawlins, ma'am, and I've been helping the police since your daughter's death."

"You're a policeman?" She didn't sound relieved.

"Not exactly, ma'am. But I've been working with them. Some Negro women have also been killed and I know the neighborhood. I just wanted to ask you a couple of questions about these things I found."

"Excuse me, Mr. Rawlins," she said with a perfect facsimile of a smile. "I've been upset, you can imagine. Come in and show me what you have."

I let her lead me into the sunken living room and took a seat on the furry couch.

"Can I get you something?" she asked.

"No. Just lemme show what I got here." I was less sure of my convictions now that I was in the house with her. She was no longer some white person put out of bounds by a racist world. She'd become a mother who had lost a child and I was on the verge of making that injury worse.

"We have pop and milk and beer," she recited. It was her regular list for a guest.

"I'd take a beer."

She squared her shoulders and turned for a door near the glass wall.

"All right," she said. "I'll just be a minute."

She went quickly through the door.

I looked at my watch. She was gone for six minutes.

She came back with a platter on which sat a soda-fountain glass full of amber brew. She smiled and put the platter in front of me.

"Did you know my daughter?" she asked. She probably wanted to wail.

"No, ma'am."

I emptied the bag on the table before us. She had taken a seat on the couch at an angle so that she faced me. She was a brave woman, I'll hand her that.

She picked up the high school yearbook and pressed it between her two hands. She looked for a moment at the letters. I was getting nervous. She got to the envelope of photographs. At first she looked quizzical. Like, "What could Robin have wanted with these?" But then the avalanche fell. She threw the photographs on the floor.

Her breaths stared to come in sharp little gasps. I could almost hear her bird's heart.

She swallowed and brought both hands to the back of her neck. Before her lay a patchwork, in photographs, of her daughter's life. A come-on smile, a bare breast. A sinuous pose that made her mother sit even straighter. The White Butterfly.

"Why?" Her voice was so full of feeling that it took me a moment to decipher the word.

"Ma'am?" I said after a while.

And, after another wait, "Ma'am?"

"Yes?"

"Is that Robin?"

She didn't deny it.

"Didn't the police ask you what she did on the weekends, ma'am? Did you know?"

"Would you like something to drink, Mr., Mr. . . ." She turned her body fully toward me. I was sure that if she'd turned her neck her head would have twisted off and shattered on the floor.

"Sure," I said.

She got up slowly and went back into the kitchen. My beer still sat on the table—untouched.

After about fifteen minutes I looked in on her. The kitchen was white linoleum and waxed maple. She was sitting at the table with her head cradled in her arms.

• 16 •

I had to ask about Cyndi. Maybe it made sense that she was killed by this man. Maybe it did.

But when I left that house I was finished with the case. Quinten and the police had my best shot. The bearded man was a good candidate for the killings. And I had a life to get back to.

I could hear Mofass hacking before I was halfway up the stairs. When I came into the room I found him holding his chest and breathing hard.

He looked up at me with hangdog, yellowy eyes. His lips formed a crooked grimace. There was a cigar between the fingers of his left hand.

"Sick," he whispered.

Mofass lolled back like a wounded sea lion. The skin around his lips was ashen. He wheezed instead of breathed. His eyes were focused somewhere outside the room.

I'd seen dead men that looked healthier.

"We better get you a doctor, man," I said. I even reached for the phone.

"What for?"

He took a shallow breath and opened his eyes wide as saucers. Then he stifled a cough. He revved his lungs for a few moments, then said, "Just gimme a minute. I be okay."

"You need a doctor."

"I need to pay the rent. That's what I need."

He got up by leaning against the desk and pushing himself up. He stood by holding the chair and then the wall. When he went through the small door that led to his toilet I wondered if he would die in there.

A tiny black ant was foraging among the crumbs and ashes of Mofass's desk. I put my finger next to him. He crawled all along the crevices between my fingers. I watched him and marveled that some god watched me like that. I got the urge to crush the insect but just then the toilet flushed and Mofass came banging into the room.

His face was cleaned up and his eyes were alive again. There was a waver in his walk but he didn't hold on to anything.

"We gonna go?" he asked me.

The building we went to was called the Dorado, deep in Culver City. The walls were yellow plaster edged by weathered timbers. Terracotta pots lined the walkway to the front door. Each one overflowed with serpentine vines. The door said "DeCampo Associates."

A round-faced Japanese woman sat at a round desk in the middle of a large entrance. She was placid and fat and golden. Her eyes went from Mofass to me.

"Afternoon, Mrs. Narotaki," Mofass said.

She smiled wider and looked him in the eye.

"Are they here?" Mofass nodded at the large oak door behind her.

Mrs. Narotaki said, "Have a seat. I'll tell them."

There were large red velvet chairs near the front door. Mofass and I went to them and sat side by side.

The small table next to me held a crystal vase that held seven white tulips. The ceiling was high and painted with a counterfeit Renaissance scene. There was a light blue sky complete with cotton-candy clouds and fat-boy angels with fig leaves to keep them modest.

"I want you to follow the program here, Mo," I whispered.

"Don't worry, Mr. Rawlins, I know what to do. But you got to remember that these here people in business t'make money. They ain't got no time t'be worried 'bout any li'l ole thang."

"Like what?"

"The Bontemps family."

The Bontempses were an elderly couple who lived in one of my apartment buildings. The Magnolia Street apartments. They were in their eighties and their only son was dead. I let them pay me what they could for the rent and accepted the rest in labor. Of course, there was only so much that they could do in advanced age. Henry watered the lawn and swept the front porch every day. Crystal kept tabs on neighbors who might have wanted to skip the rent by moving out in the middle of the night. She was insomniac, so every night noise drove her from her bed.

"I can't help what I do, Mofass. If I gots to give a man a break, that's what I do. I done it for you."

He swallowed deeply.

"Anyway, I just want you to tell 'em what we agreed on. Okay?"

"Yes sir."

Mofass lost all sense when it came to money. Money was his god and it wasn't a kindly deity.

Mrs. Narotaki looked up from her desk and smiled. "You can go in now."

The first thing you saw when going through the door was the garden. The ceiling-to-floor windows of the opposite wall looked out on a large garden with an Olympic-sized marble pond at its center. Two snowy swans preened at the center of the pond. The glass was tinted, which made the sky seem a deeper shade of blue. Mature willows trailed their sad leaves across the grounds, and a large white rabbit held one ear aloft as he nibbled in the grass and stared into the window.

The room was large and sunny. The walls were covered with paintings. The kind of paintings old European lords had made to glorify their possessions. There was a small scene of dead game hung upside down from a peg on a wall. Below the fowl and hares an attentive hunting dog sat. Behind him a rifle leaned against the wall.

A voluptuous maid carried a jug of milk and smiled from one frame. A white servant stood in a fancy den in another.

There were stuffed chairs against the wall like the chairs we had outside. But the room was dominated by a long ash table that was surrounded by six wooden chairs. Four of the chairs were already occupied.

"Mr. Wharton," one of the men said. He sat nearest the door and rose to shake Mofass' hand. He was short, simply dressed in a yellow cardigan sweater and dark brown slacks. His shirt was a cotton pullover with three buttons at the throat.

Mofass grinned and nodded. "Mr. Vie," he said. "I'd like you to meet Mr. Ezekiel Rawlins. Mr. Rawlins is one of the men who works for me. He also has a small share in that property you're interested in."

Mofass took my elbow and guided it until the little white man and I were shaking hands.

His eyes were a grayish blue. They told me that he was very happy to meet me and that we should be friends.

"Very happy to meet you, Mr. Rawlins," he said.

I was ushered into a seat between Mr. Vie and Mofass. Over the table Mofass and I were introduced to the other men, who all leaned over to shake our hands.

There was Fargo Baer, a big man in a proper brown suit. He had red hair everywhere. It was manageable and short on his head but it sprouted like weeds from his ears and throat and even from the backs of his hands.

Next to Fargo sat Bernard Seavers. Bernard was skinny, shifty-eyed, and bone-colored. His thick black hair made him look as if he were wearing a hat.

Finally, at the head of the table sat Jack DeCampo. Jack was the leader. His skin was olive-colored and smooth. His eyes were any light color you wanted them to be.

He formed his long fingers into a tent that met at its apex between his eyes and looked at Mofass for a long time.

Then he looked at me. "It's a pleasure to meet you, sir."

I nodded shyly and ducked my head in reverence. It was the way I used to grease white men in the south.

"We represent an investment syndicate interested in real estate."

The rest of the men, including Mofass, were like hungry jays eyeing a newly seeded lawn.

"Mr. Rawlins owns less than five percent of the property you're interested in, gentlemen. But since he and I work together I figure that he'd do well to hear what we had to say here." Mofass could talk like a white man when he had to.

DeCampo smiled at me.

"We're glad to have you here."

I grinned as foolishly as I could.

"We think we can help you, Mr. Wharton," Bernard Seavers said. The focus left me as soon as they knew how worthless I was. Five percent wouldn't stand in their way. If Mofass wanted to impress his hired hand they didn't mind.

"We want to make you money," Mr. Vie chirped.

"You'll have to pardon me if I don't believe you," Mofass said. He knew what I wanted. He knew how to squeeze.

"I know it sounds strange, Mr. Wharton," DeCampo said. "But our interests have crossed here."

"You mean about that property I got over on Willoughby?"

"You have the land. We have the capital." He put his hands together and pressed.

"What do you get out of this? Interest on a loan?"

His laugh was the sizzle of acid on skin. "Well, maybe a little more than that."

"How much more?"

"We get seventy-five percent of the corporation we make here. You sit back and let the money roll in."

"Seventy-five percent?"

"Yes, Mr. Wharton," Mr. Vie put in. "We're bringing in the capital and also the information that will make that investment most lucrative."

I could see the swans flirting. They stirred up the water so that it threw off powerful flashes of the afternoon sun.

"What is this information?"

Mr. DeCampo smiled. "The county is going to make Willoughby into a main street. Five lanes wide. And almost all of your nine acres will still be intact after the construction."

"So the value of the property will go up then?" Mofass asked. I could tell by the way he asked that he understood why I didn't want to sell before.

"In ten years it will be worth more than all of us here in this room could raise. We're talking supermarkets and department stores, Mr. Wharton. Maybe an office building in the future. Who knows?"

"But if we just wait, wouldn't the property be its own collateral?" Mofass asked innocently.

The jays started fidgeting. There was suddenly danger in the room.

"I mean," Mofass continued, "why should we take this kind of deal when we could own everything ourselves?"

"The truth is, " Fargo Baer said, "we're letting you in on the ground floor with this information. The land is unzoned now. As soon as the county planner lays out the new construction, the council is going to limit what you can do. I mean, you could push something through if you wanted, but it will cost you a prime penny then."

"And," Bernard Seavers put in. "Letting the banks know about the plans would cause other development projects. Right now we have the jump on everybody. Whatever we build will make us the business center of the neighborhood."

"So you wouldn't want us to tell anybody about this here meeting?" Mofass asked.

"Our partners wouldn't like that," DeCampo said as pleasantly as he could.

"And just who is that?"

The acid hiss issued from his mouth again. Then, "Men who know about land sales and new roads. Men who don't like to be cheated."

"But it's cheating to use this information to make a profit, ain't it? It's my taxes building that road?"

"In five years your twenty-five percent will be worth a million dollars," DeCampo said.

Mofass started to wheeze.

I imagined Edna and Regina playing in the grass with the swans stroking them. I even worried for a moment that a swan might hurt my baby girl.

"So you want me to give you three-quarters of what I own?"

"That's one way of looking at it." DeCampo shrugged. "But a better way is to say that we are going to increase your current wealth twentyfold."

The room was pretty quiet for a while. The only sound was Mofass' harsh breath.

I once thought that businessmen had some kind of honor or code. But I was straightened out about that long before I met Mr. DeCampo and his friends. I knew that there was something shady going on, and I had Mofass set up that meeting to find out exactly what it was. The next step I'd planned would give us a little time to look into their claims.

Mofass cleared his throat.

"Well, gentlemen," he said as we both rose. "I will have to discuss this with my board."

"What?" Mr. Vie asked.

"I represent a syndicate of my own, sir. Mr. Rawlins here owns a small part of that organization, and there are others. Businessmen down in our own community."

"But you led us to believe that you owned that property?" Fargo's question sounded more like a threat.

"I'm sorry if I misrepresented myself. You see, my partners like their privacy too."

"How soon will you have an answer, Mr. Wharton?" DeCampo asked, though his mouth didn't seem to move.

"Two days at the outside. I might know by this afternoon."

With that Mofass and I went to the door.

DeCampo followed us there. He shook my hand and beamed his cold smile into my eyes. Then he took Mofass' hand and held on to it.

"This information is to be held in confidence, Mr. Wharton. Nobody who doesn't need to know should be told."

I made it out of the door without having said a word.

• 17 •

We were driving down Venice Boulevard, heading back toward Watts. The trolley had already been shut down but the tracks still ran down the center of the street. Everybody had to have a car without the trolley running.

They were drinking champagne in Detroit.

"What do you want me to tell them, Mr. Rawlins?"

"When he calls ya tell 'im that we'll take a forty-sixty deal. We get the sixty."

"An' what if he don't buy that?"

"Then he's fucked. We go to Bank of America and lay it out to them the way DeCampo laid it out to us."

"I don't know," Mofass said tentatively.

"You don't know what?"

"A million dollars is a lotta money. My broker's fee of nine percent look pretty good. Why you wanna shake that up?"

"If they could give me one million, then they could make three. If they can do that then I could do it."

"I guess," Mofass said. But I'm not sure that he agreed with me.

For the rest of the ride we were quiet. Mofass hacked a little. I dreamed about being one of the few black millionaires in America. It was a strange kind of daydream, because whenever I thought of some Beverly Hills shopkeeper smiling at me I also thought that he was lying, that he really hated me. Even in my dreams I was persecuted by race.

When we were back in the office I asked, "How much money we got in the floor?"

"Nine hunnert eighty-seven."

"Gimme it."

Ordinarily Mofass would have questioned me on that hefty withdrawal but after talking six and seven figures he didn't bat an eye.

He lifted the carpet that lay before the desk. Under that was a plain pine floor. But if you slid a screwdriver between two of the boards you could pop out the small trapdoor. Down there is where we kept a certain percentage of cash receipts. That was our expense money.

Mofass pulled out the cash box and handed me what folding money there was.

When I was halfway down the stairs Mofass' phone rang. I figured it was Jack DeCampo checking to see if Mofass had an answer yet.

"Hey, baby!" I said out of the car window.

Regina looked trim and neat in her orange-and-white dress. She was standing in front of Temple. It was five o'clock exactly.

She didn't smile, just ran across the street and jumped in. We both leaned into an awkward kiss and said hello.

Her mood was nervous, jumpy.

"What's wrong?" I asked.

"It's just that I been workin' all day an' I wanna get away from here now."

So I pulled away from the curb and turned back toward home.

"Did you find that boy?" she asked me.

"Yeah."

"Did he know who the killer was?"

"Maybe he knew somethin', but we got to see yet. All he saw was a big man with a beard. Then all he saw was stars."

"You tell Quinten Naylor that?"

"Sure did," I said. Then, "Hey, honey, I'll tell you what. Why don't you tell Gabby Lee t'stay a couple'a days with Edna and Jesus?"

"Why?"

"Then we could go up to Frisco for two nights."

"Uh . . . not tomorrow, baby," she said, looking for other words. "I can't right now."

"Is it 'cause you want that money for your auntie?"

"No, it ain't that. I got a letter from my Uncle Andrew. He said that her husband came up with what they needed anyway."

"Then what is it?"

"Do you love me, Easy?"

I felt the afternoon sun burning on my face. It was like a red-hot slap that lingers long after you've been hit.

"Sure . . . I mean, yeah, of course I do."

"Maybe you don't. Maybe you just think you do."

"Don't do this, Regina. Don't play with me."

"I ain't playin' with you. It's just a feelin' I got, that's all."

"What feelin'?" I was sitting down but I might just as well have been on my knees.

"You don't talk to me. I mean, you don't say nuthin'."

"What am I doin' right now? Ain't this talk?"

"What's my auntie's name?"

"What?"

"You know that today is the first time you ever asked me to do anything for you, Easy? You never talk to me about what you be doin'. I mean, you say you work for Mofass but I don't have no idea where you are most of the time."

"So now I gotta sign in with you?"

"You was readin' a book the other day," she said, ignoring my question.

"Yeah . . ."

"I don't know what it was. I don't know what your mother's name was or who your friends are, not really."

"You don't wanna know them," I said. I laughed a little and shook my head.

"But I do wanna know. How can you know a man if you don't know his friends?"

"They ain't really friends, Gina. They more like business partners," I said. "I ain't got what you call any real friends left. My mother is dead and there ain't no more to say about that."

I turned on Ninety-sixth Street and parked. ". . . and I love you."

I don't know how I expected her to take that. She sat as far away from me as she could, with her back against the door. She shook her fine head and said, "I know you feel about me, but I don't know if it's love."

"What's that supposed to mean?"

"Sometimes you look at me the same way a dog be lookin' after raw meat. I get scared'a the way you look at me, scared'a what you might do."

"Like what?"

"Like the other night."

I didn't know what to say then. I thought about what she called rape. I didn't think that it was like some of these men do to women, how they grab them off the street and brutalize them. But I knew that if she was unwilling then I made her against that will. I was wrong but I didn't have the heart to admit it.

My silence infuriated her.

"Do you wanna fuck me right here?" she spat.

"Com'on, baby. Don't talk like that."

"Oh? I ain't s'posed t'say it? I'm just s'posed to shut my mouf while you fuck me raw?"

"I'm sorry."

"What?"

"I'm sorry."

"You sorry? Is that what you have to say? You want to apologize for raping me?"

I was facing her. I flung backward with my elbow and shattered the glass in the door. There was a sharp pain in my upper arm; I was glad for the distraction.

"What the hell you think you doin', Easy?" Regina screamed. There was fear in her voice.

"We gotta slow this down, Gina. We gotta stop before we go

someplace we cain't get down from." My voice was small and careful.

I started the car and drove off again. She gazed ahead. I looked out too, looked out for anything that would take my mind away from the anger in that car.

The thing I struck on was the palm trees. Their silhouettes rose above the landscape like impossibly tall and skinny girls. Their hair a mess, their posture stooped. I tried to imagine what they might be thinking but failed.

"You gotta talk to me," Regina said. "You gotta hear me too."

"What do you want me to say?"

She looked out the window but I don't think she was seeing anything. "I raised thirteen hungry brothers and served my father eggs to go with his whiskey in the morning."

"I know that."

"NO YOU DON'T!"

I'd never heard her shout like that.

"I said, no you don't," Regina said again. I could hear the breath ripping from her nostrils. "I mean, you know it happened but you don't know what it is to have fourteen men leanin' on you and cryin' to you. Beggin' you all the time for everything, everything you got. Your last nickel, your Saturday night. An' they never once asked about me. They come in hungry or beat up or drunk and needin' me t'make it right."

I pulled up in front of our house. When I moved my left arm to open the door there came the sound of broken glass settling.

"But they was better than you," Regina said. "At least they needed me for somethin'. I mean, maybe you want some pussy. Maybe you even wanna make me crazy and make me come. But if I do that and fall in love with you, all you gonna do is walk outta the house in the mornin' goin' who knows where."

"Everybody goes to work, baby."

"You don't understand. I want to be part of something. I ain't just some girl to suck your dick an' have your babies."

When Marla talked like that I got excited. But hearing it from my wife made me want to tear off her head. I held my temper, though. I knew I deserved her abuse.

She stared dead ahead and I kept silent, watching the clock on the dashboard. After four minutes had gone by I said, "I got that money if you need it."

"I don't want it."

"I'll bring you down to the places I work at and show you what I do."

"Yeah . . ." she said, waiting for more.

"We could throw a party and invite the people I know."

She turned fifteen degrees and softened just a little. It was then that I caught the scent of fried okra. They had served fried okra at the wake for my mother. I was barely seven years old and I hated the minister's eyes.

I hadn't eaten fried okra in twenty-nine years, but I smelled it sometimes. Usually when I was feeling strong emotions about a woman who was almost within my reach, just beyond touch.

"I do love you, Easy." It hurt her to say it.

The glass fell out onto the ground when I got out of the car. I had to brush the shards away in order to close the door again.

"You're bleeding," Regina said.

The blood had run down my arm, making a red seam all the way down to the tip of my baby finger.

Gabby was watching the evening news from the couch and Edna was examining the frills of a small pillow under the big woman's head.

"Give us a minute, Lee," Regina said. Then she led me to the bathroom, where she made me take off my shirt.

"There's glass in this." Her probing fingers made me jump. "Does it hurt?"

"Only when you mash on it," I whimpered.

When she cleaned out the cut the blood flowed more easily.

I watched Regina's face in the cabinet mirror as she wrapped the bandage around my upper arm. The pain was welcome. So was her touching me.

We made dinner together and played with the children. Jesus showed us his quizzes. A D in spelling but an A in math. Edna tore back and forth across the floor and screeched. Nobody talked much.

At about nine o'clock the phone rang.

"Hello?"

"Is this Mr. Rawlins?"

"Who's this?" I answered.

"My name is Vernor Garnett. You nearly gave my wife a heart attack today."

"How did you get this number, Mr. Garnett?"

"I work downtown, Rawlins. I can get just about anything I want."

"Okay, sir. Maybe I shouldn't have been so hard on your wife. But I've been working with the police on this thing and I felt I needed to find out some things."

"The police say that you were to be helping them with problems in the colored community. You had no business at my house."

"Your daughter was in my community, Mr. Garnett. She worked down here."

"You leave my family alone, Rawlins. You keep out of my life. Do you understand that?"

"Yessir. Right away, sir."

I cradled the phone and it started ringing in my hand. It was too fast to be Garnett calling back so I was civil.

"Yes?"

"What's wrong with you, Rawlins?"

"Who is this?" I asked for the second time in as many minutes.

"This is Horace Voss. Who gave you permission to go into that family's house and to leave evidence with them?"

"I guess you don't wanna work wit' me, right?"

"I want you out of this thing completely. All the way out!"

I hung up the phone again. Then I left if off the hook until about eleven, when we went to bed.

I got up at one to change the bandage. It was too tight, but I didn't want Regina to feel that I didn't appreciate her work.

I bathed the cut in witch hazel and wrapped it loosely with gauze and tape. I was just finishing up when the telephone rang.

It only rang once.

Regina was waiting for me in the hall.

"One'a your girlfriends," she informed me.

I followed her back into the bedroom and picked the receiver up off my pillow.

"Hello?"

"Thank God it's you, Easy. They got Raymond in jail."

"Who is this?" I asked for the third time.

"Minnie Fry."

That was Raymond "Mouse" Alexander's most-the-time girlfriend.

"Okay, Minnie. Now calm down. Who got Mouse?"

"The po-lice do!"

"Is he dead?"

"They holdin' him. He want me to call you first off."

"Down here at the Seventy-seventh?"

"Um-huh. You gotta go down there right now."

"It's almost two . . ."

"You gotta go right now, Easy! That's what Raymond said."

Mouse had faced loaded guns for me more than once. He had been my friend since we were young men, and even though Raymond was always close to mayhem, I knew he was the closest to family that I had outside of my wife and kids.

"All right," I sighed. "I'll go down there."

"You gonna go right now?" Minnie asked.

"I said all right, didn't I?"

"Okay. But you gotta go now."

We went back and forth like that three or four times before I could get her off the phone.

I got my clothes from the closet.

"My dressing wasn't good enough for you?" Regina asked as I put on my pants.

"A little tight is all. I just changed it."

"Where you goin' now?"

"Down to the police station."

"You gonna get drunk and fuck that girl down there?"

"That was Minnie Fry on the phone, babe. That's Mouse's girl. She said that Mouse was in jail."

"What's that got to do with you?"

"He's my friend, Regina. An' I could get him out."

"You cain't wait till mornin'?"

"He wouldn't wait for me."

Regina sucked her tooth and went back to bed. I leaned over her, to kiss her before I left, but she wasn't interested.

• 18 •

The night sergeant didn't believe that I worked for Quinten Naylor. But he didn't mind making an early-morning call to his superior officer either. So I waited while he tried to get through.

It was a quiet night at the station.

An old man nodded in and out of sleep on the long wooden bench where we both sat. He was a white wino, not uncommon in our neighborhood. His coat had once been brown but now it was worn to gray at places. He smelled of sweat and that made me like him. Across from us sat a middle-aged black woman. She was weeping into a blue handkerchief. Her cheeks and nose were bright black plums. I never knew why either one of them was there. I've spent my whole life passing by little tragedies like that and ignoring them.

"Mr. Rawlins," the desk sergeant called.

"Yeah?"

"Lieutenant Naylor said to let you see the man. Just fill this out and I'll get somebody to bring you back." He held out a clipboard with a mimeographed sheet of paper on it.

I put down my name and address and relationship with the incarcerated. I put down my social security number and my telephone number and the reason for my visit. I signed at the bottom and returned the clipboard to the sergeant.

He didn't even read it, just folded the page into quarters and pushed it down a slot behind him. Then he picked up the phone and pushed a button on the desk.

"Come on out here, Rivers," was all he said into the receiver.

A moment later a small white man in a short-sleeved khaki police shirt came out of a door behind the sergeant's desk. The man had a gaunt and pitted face. He was probably in his mid-thirties but he could have been sixty with a ravaged face like that.

"This the guy?"

The sergeant nodded.

"Come on," the ravaged man said. "I'm in a goddamned rush."

First he took me down a long gray-plaster hall. We came to a white wooden door that the policeman had a key for. Just beyond that door was another one, an iron door with evil-looking bolts all around it. He had a key for this door too. Then we were in another hall made of steel-grated floors, walls, and ceilings.

We came to a big room made all out of metal and glass. There was a table in the middle of the floor with a chair on either side. The table and chairs were all bolted to the floor.

I heard the gruff voice of one man talking and the pathetic sobs of another man.

"Sit down. Wait here," the little policeman said. Then he went through a door on the other side.

"I ain't tellin' you again!" It was the gruff voice.

In answer a man moaned. Then there was a loud crash and more crying. I heard the voice again but I couldn't make out what was being said.

The noise was coming from behind an iron door to my right.

The door behind me opened and Mouse, manacled hand and foot, shuffled in, followed by the warder.

It made me sick at heart to see Raymond like that. He was the only black man I'd ever known who had never been chained, in his mind, by the white man. Mouse was brash and wild and free. He might have been insane, but any Negro who dared to believe in his own freedom in America had to be mad. The sight of his incarceration made me shudder inside.

Rivers pushed Mouse toward the chair. Once Raymond was seated the policeman padlocked his chains through two metal loops in the floor. Then he went to sit on a stool in the corner, giving us as little privacy as he could.

I could still hear the arguing, moaning, and fighting from behind the iron door, but the guard and Mouse seemed unconcerned.

"You got a piece, Easy?" he whispered.

"What?"

"You got a gun?"

"No, no. I ain't comin' in no jail with a gun."

"I need to get out of here," Mouse said slowly. "They want to change my address to Folsom Prison an' that ain't gonna happen."

"Why they got you in here, Raymond?"

"They wanna frame me on them killin's. They need somebody t'hang."

"Why you?"

"I don't know, man. They say I knowed a couple'a them girls. Maybe I did, you know I always be after that stuff. But that don't mean I kilt no girls."

"So you didn't do it?"

"Do what?"

"What they said, man. Kill them girls."

"What? You think I'm crazy?"

Yes, I thought. Crazy and a killer in everything he did. He was a slight man, not over five-seven, with gold-edged teeth and a pencil-thin mustache. The police hadn't issued him jail clothes. He was decked out in green suede shoes, drab green pants, and a loose bright pink shirt that flopped around his wrists because they had taken his cufflinks.

He'd murdered his stepfather for a wedding dowry. He would have lied to God with his final breath.

"I just wanna know why they pulled you in here," I said. "That's all."

"Please, no," came a cry from behind the iron door.

I looked around at the guard but he was reading a paperback western.

"It don't matter why I'm here, Easy," Mouse said. "What matters is that you get me out."

Every now and then there was a dull thud against the iron door.

"Gimme a few hours," I said.

When the little guard led me back out of that hell I could have almost kissed the floor.

I was reading the morning paper at the sergeant's desk when Quinten Naylor arrived. It was seven-sixteen in the morning.

He motioned me to follow him and we both walked back to his office.

We sat with our coffee and cigarettes. Quinten nodded and asked, "What can I do for you?"

"Why you got Mouse down here, man?"

"Mr. Alexander is suspected of having information about a homicide." His face was wooden.

"You ain't got a damn thing on him."

"Do you know who did the killings?"

"What about that bearded guy I told you 'bout? He coulda done it."

"No corroboration. The owners of Aretha's denied the story."

"What about Gregory Jewel?"

"He says that he never saw the man that hit him."

"And you believe that?"

"Do you have something for me, Rawlins? Because if you don't I have business to take care of." He motioned his head toward the door, then he picked up a pencil and started writing on a white legal pad.

"What about Mouse?"

"He stays in jail until we have something better."

"On what charges?"

Naylor put down his pencil and looked at me. "No charge. He stays here two more days, then he gets transferred to the Hollywood station. After that we send him downtown. We could keep him tied up for months and even the commissioner wouldn't be able to find him."

"You proud'a that?"

"Are you going to find our killer?"

"I thought Voss wanted me out."

"He's not the only one involved. Violette wants you in. He's willing to kill your friend to make sure of it."

"Let Mouse out," I said.

"No can do."

"Let 'im out an' we'll find this killer together. I'ma need a helper if this thing gets full-time with me."

"He's a prime suspect, Easy. He's been everywhere those girls were. Even your Cyndi Starr."

"I don't think he did it."

"How would you know?"

"Raymond wouldn't kill those girls like that. But if you leave him in jail people gonna die for sure. Anyway, he told me he didn't have nuthin' t'do with it. He ain't got no reason t'lie t'me. Gimme a week with Raymond and we'll turn up what you need."

Quinten shook his head. "I don't know."

"Call Violette. Ask him," I said. "I'll be out at the bench when you get an answer."

I waited an hour and fifteen minutes for Naylor to come out. He had Mouse with him. Mouse was fastening his cufflinks and smiling at me. It was a killer's smile that reminded all the ladies of a sweet loving child.

• 19 •

Mouse was living with Minnie Fry at that time. They had a one-room cottage on Vernon.

She was sleeping in the Murphy bed when we got there.

"Hey, Minnie! Yo' boy is home," Mouse called as we came crashing into the room.

The only thing I could see of Minnie was her head. The rest of her was just a lump under a thick pink quilt. But when Mouse announced himself she yelled (I swear), "Oh boy!" and threw the bedding aside. All she wore was a tiny pair of pink panties but she didn't mind my eyes. She ran up to Mouse and hugged him to her large bosom as if he were the Lord called up from the dead.

"Baby!" she cried. She kissed him and hugged him some more. "Baby!"

Minnie was a head taller and fifty pounds heavier than Mouse. She swung him from side to side until he stopped holding on to her and started trying to push away.

"Stop it, Minnie. Stop it fo' you send me to the hospital."

She just kept crooning and swaying. I don't think anybody ever missed me as much as that woman missed him. I was away from home for years in World War Two and nobody waited at the shore to hold me like that.

"Put me down, girl," Mouse pleaded. I could see that he was smiling, though. "Go get decent fo' you shame ole Easy here."

Minnie didn't mind showing off her generous black figure as long as we didn't mention it, but when he said that she folded her arms around her chest and ducked a little as she scooped some clothes from a chair. She held these in front of her and tiptoed into the bathroom.

Mouse smiled after her. "She sumpin', huh, Easy?"

Minnie was out of the bathroom in two minutes. She wore a plain blue dress that she'd probably sewn from a pattern in home economics when she was still in high school. You could see the uneven seams along the blue straps that covered her shoulder. The dress was a little snug, because she'd gained a few pounds in the two years since she'd gotten her diploma.

"Place is a pigsty," Mouse said, curling his lip with distaste. "I only been in jail one day. How could you do all this?"

Minnie just wilted.

Mouse held out his hands in a helpless gesture. "What's that you say?"

"I didn't say nuthin', baby."

"Then what do you have to say? I mean, I come home to a hog barn an' you just gonna wave yo' titties in Easy's face?"

I felt for Minnie's shame but there was nothing I could do to help her. What Mouse wanted to say was that we were going to have to talk business so we were going out again. But he couldn't say something straightforward like that, so he criticized her cleaning in order that he could excuse himself while she got the house together.

"Now we gonna start over," Mouse said. "I'ma go with Easy now an' get some breakfast—"

"I'll cook for ya, baby," Minnie interrupted.

"Uh-uh, no. We gonna go down to the Pie Pan an' get us some food, and when we get back the house and you is gonna be just fine. Ain't that right?"

"Uh-huh. But I could get cleaned up real quick, Raymond . . ."

Mouse shook his head and frowned. "I don't wanna hear it, Minnie. We goin' now."

We did go to the Pie Pan. Mouse had toast, jelly, and hot chocolate. I ordered grits, sausages, and eggs scrambled with cubed potatoes and onions. We didn't talk at first because Mouse's hands were shaking. Over the years I had learned that as long as Mouse's hands were still shaking he could kill over the smallest slight. When he got nervous, violence was his easiest and first outlet. That's why I didn't take Minnie's part in the house. He might have struck her, or me, if he felt that his will was being questioned.

So we ate and smoked and waited for the jailhouse shakes to subside.

After the meal was over and we were both drinking tea with lemon I said, "We gotta find the man did them killin's, Raymond."

"All right wit' me. You know I wanna kill me some mothahfuckah. I don't take to no cell."

"We can't kill 'im, Raymond. I want the law off both of us an' the only way we could do that is t'give 'em somebody t'hang."

"I might not have t'kill 'im, but you know I might shoot 'im a li'l just the same. S'pose he a big boy don't respect my pistol?"

I didn't argue. If Mouse wanted to hurt somebody there was no way to stop him. I had to accept his insane violence if I wanted his help.

I told him everything that I'd learned. I told him about Aretha's and the whorehouse. I told him about Gregory Jewel and Cyndi Starr. In forty-five minutes he knew everything I did.

"What this white girl gotta do with it?"

"Bad luck, I guess."

"Bad luck my ass."

"What you mean?"

"I don't know, Easy. But we gonna find out. Who we gonna talk to first? You wanna try them boys who beat up on you?"

"Not right now. They were just hands. Probably come after me 'cause Max thought it would keep me off them. It's just bad for business have somebody 'round talkin' 'bout killin'."

"Gregory Jewel?"

"Uh-uh. He don't know nuthin'. No. It's Charlene Mars and Westley we talk to. Charlene told the cops that she never saw no man go up against Gregory Jewel. I don't know why, she could just be lyin' to fuck with 'em, but I think she knows somethin' too. Otherwise she'd tell 'em the little bit she knew."

"Sound good to me. You wanna go over there now?"

"Uh-uh. Tonight, after they close."

Mouse's eyes lit up. "I'll meet ya out front at two."

I nodded and shook his hand. Then I took him over to Minnie's house so he could spend the afternoon making up to her.

When I got home there was a note waiting from Jesus' gym teacher.

Jesus had gotten into a fight with two boys who were taunting him. When the gym teacher tried to stop them Jesus hit him in the nose.

"Don't be too hard on 'im, Easy," Regina said after I'd read the note. "You know children always be ridin' a child who's different."

"He gotta learn to keep his anger in check," I answered. I was always happy that Regina cared about Jesus. She just accepted him.

I might have sounded tough to her but I wasn't very upset by Jesus' crime.

Still, I put on a severe face and went into the boy's room. But when I saw him, curled up behind his knees on the bed, I knew that he'd already learned more than I could bully him into.

He shuddered when I sat next to him. I patted his shoulder and smiled as softly as I could.

"Don't worry, boy," I said. "We gonna go straighten this out in the morning."

Jesus looked at me with frightened eyes. He nodded as if to say, "Really?"

"Yeah. I know you a good boy, Jesus. You wouldn't fight unless you thought you had to. But I want you to promise me that you won't never fight unless somebody hits you or tries to hit you."

His gaze gained confidence. He smiled and nodded.

"'Cause you know a man can control you if he can drive you to fight over some shit he talks."

Jesus nodded again.

Jesus put his cold hands on my neck and kissed me just off to the left of my nose. When he hugged me I was amazed at how hot his cheek was.

"Let's go get some dinner now," I said.

At dinner Regina and I sat across the table avoiding eye contact like strangers who are uncertain about striking up a conversation.

When the baby and Jesus were asleep I brought a thick envelope with nine hundred dollars in it to her.

"Here's all the money you wanted and then some," I said.

She looked at me with clear serious eyes. I waited for her to say something but the words never came. Instead her face softened and she pulled me down in the bed, on top of her.

We didn't make love, just lay there like spoons with me holding her from behind. At one o'clock I moved away and dressed. I looked back at her from the door as I left. Her eyes were open wide, taking me in. I put my finger in front of my lips and waved. She just stared after me. God knows what she was thinking.

• 20 •

I parked down the block from Aretha's. Bone Street's denizens staggered alone and in pairs. There was shouting and kissing and vomiting on the sidewalk. The last ones to leave Aretha's were the strippers. Big women on the whole who trudged toward their homes like tired soldiers returning from the front lines.

It was two-twenty when I looked at my watch but that didn't bother me. I knew Mouse would be there when I needed him. He would always be there in my life, smiling and ready to commit mayhem.

The door to Aretha's hadn't opened in a while when he strolled out. He was wearing a bright yellow double-breasted jacket and dark brown pants. His silk shirt was blue and stamped all over with bright orange triangles. His close-cropped head was hatless. I guess Mouse figured that a man dressed like that just couldn't be killed.

He walked up to my window and said, "It's only them two now, Easy. I'da gotten what you wanted myself but I didn't wanna cheat you outta the fun."

"Door open?" I asked.

"Naw. They locked up when I left but I put a wedge on the back do'. We could go in when you want to."

We cut down the alley that ran parallel to Bone and through a little gate that led to the back door of the bar. Mouse straight-handed the door, pushing it open into a large dark room. Then we went through a doorway that came to another door. This door was edged in light. I could hear Charlene and Westley talking on the other side.

Mouse was the first one through. I heard Charlene gasp and Westley say, "What?" and then I came in.

They were seated at a small round table in front of the stage. Both of them staring at both of us. There was an electricity in the air. Westley looked like he wanted to make a break for the door.

If Charlene was going to break something it would be our heads. "What are you doin' in here?" It was more of a warning than a question.

"Easy got sumpin' t'ask," Mouse said in his friendliest tone.

"Get the hell outta here," Charlene said, but then she froze. I looked over and saw that Mouse had drawn his pistol.

"I ain't here t'play, Charlene. We need t'know what we need t'know an' you is gonna tell us," Mouse said.

"What you want from us?" Westley asked. His eyes were moving from side to side in a shifty manner. I knew that he was up to something and that scared me. I wasn't worried about him hurting us or getting away. What worried me was that Mouse might kill poor Westley and then I'd be struggling to get *myself* out of jail.

"Tell me 'bout the fight with that man and Gregory Jewel," I said quickly. Maybe we'd get what we wanted and get out before things got out of hand.

"I told you what I know already, Easy Rawlins." That was Charlene. "And then you go tryin' to get me in bad with the police."

"I wanna know who that man was, Charlene. Either you tell me or you convince me that you don't know."

"And what if I don't?" the big woman dared.

Mouse's grin was a boy's joy on a hot summer's day. Westley brought his foot up to his seat and put his hands together at the ankle. He had on red socks but I caught a glimpse of brown leather too. Westley pulled a small pistol from his pant leg. I yelled, "No!" and shoved my hand against Mouse's gun-bearing arm. Charlene called, "Oh no." The shots, big and small, deafened me. I saw Westley pitch sideways out of his chair.

Charlene cried, "West!" and ran to his side.

Mouse swung the barrel of his pistol at my head but I stepped out of the way. "What the fuck is wrong with you, Easy?" he cried.

I knew better than to answer. Mouse glared at me while Charlene was desperate over Westley. There was blood oozing down the bartender's arm.

Mouse went up to them and pushed Charlene aside. He checked the bartender's wound and moved away again taking the bartender's pistol with him.

"He ain't gonna die," Mouse said.

"Tell me," I said to Charlene.

Mouse clacked back the hammer of his pistol.

"His name is Saunders," she said in even, defeated tones. "He's bad news from here to St. Louis. Get inta fights and use his knife. I didn't want no trouble with him."

"Even if he was killin' girls?" I asked.

"I didn't know nuthin' 'bout no killin's. I see men and women do what he did to Gregory Jewel almost every night."

I remembered how Jasper Filagret was beaten over Dorthea.

"He got any friends?" I asked.

"One time he brought this cousin'a his down here. Red-headed man he called Abernathy. He works at Federal Butcher's with my nephew, Tiny. That's all I know."

Mouse turned friendly then. He got a rag from behind the bar and handed it to Charlene.

"He only got it in the shoulder," Mouse said. "He lucky Easy hit me."

Outside Mouse wasn't smiling. "Don't you never do that again, Easy Rawlins."

"You might have killed him."

"Westley coulda got us both if I didn't get him in the arm. Next time I shoot you too."

He wasn't lying.

With that over, Mouse's anger faded away. "We gotta take this butcher boy first thing, Easy. We could lay for him 'fore he even go into work."

"I can't till later."

"How come?"

"I gotta go to school with Jesus in the mornin'. He got trouble with some teacher and I have to go with him." All of a sudden I was very tired. I almost dozed off while we spoke.

"All right. Why don't you come on around Minnie's after that?"

I agreed. We said our goodbyes, then I drove home. I parked in front of my house but didn't have the strength to open the door.

I was thinking about a dead woman sitting peacefully under a tree. Mouse was talking to her. Talking and talking. Whatever he was saying he read from a little black book, like a telephone diary.

She just sat there, peacefully listening. Mouse went on talking. A thousand birds gathered in the trees. They were waiting silently for Mouse to finish talking so they could descend on the corpse and pluck the flesh from her bones.

• 21 •

I heard loud snoring and wondered that I had never heard Regina snore like that before. I lifted my hand to nudge her and touched something that was hard and smooth, the steering wheel. It was my own breathing that I heard. I stared up out of the windshield at the overcast skies. Even that dim light hurt my eyes.

It took many minutes for me to sit up.

Breathing slowly and taking small steps, I made it to the house. Regina was still asleep. It was five A.M. I stayed in the bathtub until I heard her moving around. Then I shaved and toweled off.

I was in the kitchen drinking coffee when she came in. She wore a flowered housecoat that had a bright orange-and-blue painting of a macaw down the left side.

"You didn't come home last night," she said.

I felt like a man who'd walked off the street and into a play. Nobody would let me off the stage until I said my lines, but I'd forgotten them.

Regina got a mugful of coffee and sat across from me. "Well?"

"The cops need me to find a toehold. They put Mouse in jail so I'd tell 'em I'd do it."

She just stared.

"I went to Aretha's with Mouse last night . . ."

"Who?"

"It's a bar."

"Where?"

"On Bone Street." I tried to keep my voice normal but it lowered when I named that name.

"Oh." She nodded and her beautiful eyes closed, shutting me out for the moment.

"It ain't like that, baby. We had to get somebody to talk to us. There was a fight, it got pretty bad. I made it home but I passed out in the car. You don't have to believe me, baby. I know you might wonder at how crazy I'm actin'. But I swear it's gonna get better. I swear it."

She put the coffee mug down and got up slowly. I sat there looking up at her.

"You don't have to swear at me, Easy," she said. "I ain't yo' keeper."

"But you know it's been kinda hard on me lately."

"Don't worry. Ain't nuthin' gonna happen if you miss one night at home. That ain't gonna bother me. All I wanna know is what happened. Maybe you in love with somebody else. I just asked."

"I love you."

She picked up the mug and went into the kitchen to fix Jesus' lunch. Later Jesus came out and sat by the front door.

Regina brought him his sack. She knelt down in front of him and straightened his shirt. She ran a finger along his cheek and he smiled; more from love than the tickle he felt. When she stood up and turned I saw that there were tears in Regina's eyes.

Regina went into our room and dressed quickly. She left the house without saying goodbye. Gabby Lee came and took Edna away.

I drove up to the Eighty-ninth Street school with Jesus. It was one big blue stucco building. Three floors of classrooms and a big asphalt field behind that. To the left of the field was a small bungalow where the children would go at various times during the week for an hour of calisthenics. They'd do jumping jacks and sit-ups and running in place. I knew because I had asked Jesus what he did in each of his subjects. He showed me in books for most things but when it came to PE he did the exercises to entertain both me and Edna.

Mr. Arnet, the coach, was standing in front of a group of little boys that were lying on their backs with their hands behind their heads. They were struggling to pull themselves up by their necks.

"One, two," Mr. Arnet said. "One, two."

I don't know what he was counting. The little heads and young bellies just strained and strained.

When Mr. Arnet saw Jesus and me he said in a loud voice, "All right, everybody, elimination ball in the big square."

The children all jumped up and started screaming. Arnet pulled a white volleyball out of a canvas bag behind him and threw it into a tall boy's waiting arms. All the children went into a large white square and started throwing the ball at each other. It looked like fun.

"Mr. Rawlins?" It was Arnet. He was a tall white man with strawlike blond hair, an extremely long neck, and a potbelly. When he walked up to me I saw that he wasn't nearly my height, but the long neck made him seem tall from the distance.

"Mr. Arnet," I said. "Looks like we had a little problem."

He ran his hand back through the straw, shook his head, and gave me a rueful grin.

"I had to bend over the sink for fifteen minutes with the bloody nose your boy gave me, Rawlins."

The way he used my name, the way he said it, rubbed me wrong. I took a deep breath and tried to overcome my anger.

"He's real sorry about that, Mr. Arnet. He feels bad and I told him that I won't have him fighting like that."

The gym teacher shook his head again and shoved his hands in his pockets. He clucked his tongue, giving the impression that I had failed the test.

"Is Jesus your natural son?" he asked.

I turned to Jesus, who had been looking up at us with a scowl of concentration. "Go on to your class now, honey," I said. "Me and Mr. Arnet gonna talk a little more."

He smiled quickly and ran off toward the big blue building.

"He's a beautiful boy," I said.

"Is he yours?" Mr. Arnet asked again.

That white man's eyes were mostly yellow but clotted with little gray dots which made them seem green. They were small, cagey eyes.

"Yes," I said. "He's my boy."

"Your wife a Mexican?"

I knew what was coming. Jesus had been with me for years but he wasn't my natural son. He was a poor soul that had been kidnapped to satisfy a rich man's evil appetites. I had saved Jesus from all that and, finally, I had taken him as my son. Mr. Arnet wanted to cause trouble about that. Maybe it was because he was humiliated by Jesus or maybe it was because he had a bleeding heart.

"Do you like your job, Mr. Arnet?" I asked.

The question caught him a little off guard. He said, "What?"

"I just ask because I know that a man who feels strongly about his work will stand up and be counted no matter what. I mean, take me and Jesus. He's my boy. I love him. It was a hard thing for me to get here this morning because I'm a working man and I had to stay late on the job last night. But you know I got my ass outta bed to come here and see what's what. I love Jesus. If a man or anybody wanted to hurt him I don't know what I might do."

I looked Mr. Arnet in the eye, then I shook my head. "No. No, that's not right. If somebody fucked with my boy I would kill the bastard. Because you see I'm committed to him. I love him. He's my son."

The coach had blanched a little while I spoke. When I finished he swallowed to lubricate his vocal chords, knowing that his next words were important ones.

"I understand you, Mr. Rawlins," he said. "It's a rare parent nowadays who takes such a deep concern with their children's welfare. I'm sure Jesus will be fine now."

"You call me if he isn't," I said. "I want Jesus to grow up right."

I looked him in the eye for a moment more. He got fidgety, clasping his hands together.

"Well, it was good to meet you, Mr. Rawlins." He held his hand out. I shook it. "I've got to get back to the kids now."

He pulled a police whistle out of his pocket and blew it at the kids. Then he yelled, "All right! Line up!" and was off running toward the large white square.

I stalked out of that schoolyard with my head throbbing and my heart going fast. It seemed like everything had to happen the hard way.

I called Quinten Naylor from a phone booth. I told him that the guy who beat Gregory Jewel and went off with Juliette LeRoi was called Saunders.

By the time I got home there was a message with Gabby Lee that fifteen thousand dollars had been offered for information leading to the capture of the killer and that a bearded man named Saunders was the prime suspect.

• 22 •

I went to meet Mouse at eleven-fifteen. Minnie was at the beauty shop where she worked but there was another woman there. Maxine Cone, Mouse's other girlfriend.

They were sitting on the bed drinking beers when I got there. Mouse offered me one and I took it.

I was halfway through the third beer when Mouse said, "Our boy be leavin' for lunch soon."

I put the bottle down on the floor and got up.

"Where you all going?" Maxine asked. She was very dark and slight with shoulder-length coarse hair that was combed straight back and down.

"We got work to do, Maxie. You go on home an' I call later on," Mouse told her.

I thought we were going to have another fight right there. I could see Maxine's jaw clenching and her eyes narrow like gun turrets. But she kept quiet. As a matter of fact she hardly said another word. She got a sweater from a nail on the wall and walked out before us.

Mouse and I went to my car and I called to Maxine, "Could I give you a ride somewhere?"

She just walked on down the sidewalk ignoring us both. I don't think she ever talked to Mouse again. In four months she was married to Billy Tyler.

Mouse ran through women like a boy going through toys on

Christmas morning. The whole year was Christmas for Mouse, his whole life was.

Federal Butcher's was in a building that I frequented in the late forties. It was a butchers' warehouse mainly, but there used to be a little bar on the third floor. Joppy's place.

Joppy had been a friend of mine for many years. He was an old friend from back in the Fifth Ward in Houston and he was a pal in L.A. when I first got there in the mid-forties. But when we did business at a bad angle Joppy ended up dead. My life had dire consequences; there were reminders of it all over Los Angeles.

Lunch hour came and went but we didn't see any redheaded black men. I went down to a package store and bought a half pint of Seagram's and two plastic cups.

By afternoon I couldn't keep my eyes open.

"Go on to sleep, Easy," Mouse said.

When the sounds of traffic got heavier and the quality of light shifted on my eyelids, I woke up. Men were coming out of the big double doors of Federal Butcher's. Some of them still wore their bloody white coats. I thought that Federal probably didn't have a laundry service and these men had to wash the blood away themselves.

"There he is," Mouse said.

A sharp-looking man in tan shirt and pants was walking quickly down Central. He had very light hair that was blond with fuzzy light-brown highlights. He was tall and well-built with an angular light brown face. He walked right past our car. Mouse started the engine and made a U-turn to follow.

When he stopped at a red light at 110th Street we parked and followed him on foot.

He went all the way to 125th Street before he turned. Then he went half the way down the block to an apartment building that was built exactly to the plans of my own Magnolia Street apartments. We waited for him to go in and then went to check the names on the mailboxes.

Randall Abernathy lived on the top floor in apartment 3C.

"Go on home, Raymond," I said.

"What?"

"I wanna talk to this one alone."

Mouse must have had something else to do, because he didn't argue with me. I was glad he didn't. I wanted to be quiet and subtle for a change.

When I knocked on the door to 3C there were footsteps across the room to the door and then a moment of silence.

"Who is it?" a careful voice asked.

"Roger Stockton," I answered in a loud, hollow voice that I used sometimes.

"I don't know any Roger."

"I'm from Star Meat Packing in Santa Clara, Mr. Abernathy. I want to discuss a job opportunity with you."

A poor man can always use a job. He might already have a job, a good one, but he can never count on that going on forever. The boss might go crazy and fire him tomorrow. Or maybe his mother will get sick and he'll need that extra cash.

I don't know for sure that Abernathy came from poverty, but he did open that door.

I put on a smile that could have gotten me elected, if I was a white man.

"Mr. Abernathy!" I grabbed his hand and pumped it. "It's good to finally meet you face to face."

A grin stumbled at his lips and Randall tried to return my warmth. But then he frowned for a second and pulled back a bit. In that same second I saw the pewter crucifix hanging around his neck, and I smelled the alcohol of my own breath.

"I wanna get right down to it, Brother Abernathy, because I don't wanna disturb your home. I got a job opportunity for a head butcher out at Star and you're the one I think I want."

"What?"

"Could I come in a minute and go over this with you?"

I limped past him into the middle of the room. I knew the layout of the apartment because of my own building. It was an efficiency unit. One moderate-sized room with a nook for a bed, an alcove for the kitchen, and a small bathroom on the side.

I could see by the decor that Abernathy was a solitary man. He had a table and one chair and a chest of drawers. The floor was swept, never mopped, and bare.

Favoring my left leg, I went to the straight-backed chair and lowered myself delicately.

"You hurt?" Abernathy asked.

There was an open Bible on the table in front of me. Half of the verses were underlined in blue ink.

"What? Oh, you mean my leg."

Abernathy stood over me and I got ready to give him my lies.

"In a way this here war wound is why I'm here. I got more shrapnel than bone in this leg. Chinese mortar from a North Korean regular did it . . ."

Abernathy perched himself on the edge of his neatly made bed.

". . . I heard the sucker comin' and jumped for the nearest hole . . . only there was this white boy named Tooms in the way so I knocks him over and takes it in the leg."

I grimaced a little and touched the imaginary wound.

Randall asked, "And that's why you're here?"

"This Tooms boy didn't know that he was in my way. He thought that I saved him on purpose." I winked. "He thinks that he owes me his life."

"If you saved him then I guess he does owe you something," Abernathy said. He was still confused about the direction of my story but he wanted to sound like he knew what was going on.

"That's how I see it too. So when his daddy told him that he wanted him to run the family business, Eugene, that's the white boy I saved, came right to me and said that he wanted me to be his manager."

"And this business is Star Meat Packing?"

I nodded with a knowing grin on my face.

"That doesn't tell me why you here, Mr. Stockton," the butcher said.

"Well." I looked around, a little uncomfortable. "I can see that you're a religious man, brother, but I can't lie to you. I was in a bar, I can't remember the name of it but it was down on Slauson. Anyway, I met this man down there. I told him this same story I told you and he's the one give me your name. He said that you was a damn good butcher but that a Negro never has no chance if the man he works for is white. I talked to a few people about you and they all said that you was a good worker and smart about meat."

"Who was this man?"

I managed to keep the excitement out of my voice as I said, "I forget his first name but the bartender kept callin' him Mr. Saunders."

Randall couldn't have stood up faster if he'd been sitting on hot coals.

"A big man?"

"With a beard," I replied, nodding.

"When did you say this was?"

I hunched my shoulders. "I don't know. Two weeks ago, maybe three."

"Then why you gettin' to me just now?" Abernathy was mad about something.

"I told you. Eugene made me the manager out at Star. He got me workin', tryin' t'learn the trade. You know they got me studyin' saws an' scales an' how t'read the black mold on beef. I tell ya, I never knew there was so much to cuttin' a steak. What's wrong with callin' on you three weeks later?"

"It's just that I can't see Saunders braggin' about me to nobody."

"He *was* actin' kinda strange, now that you mention it. But I thought it was just how much he was drinkin'. He kept on talkin' 'bout women too."

"Women," Abernathy said as if it were a curse. "Women is what destroyed that man." His tone approached that of a minister infused with the Holy Spirit.

"He looked okay to me."

"But on the inside he's rotten. Rotting away for all the evil he's done. There's no hiding from the Lord's retribution. Without faith them sulfa drugs won't do a thing. No no. Syphilis is the Lord's punishment for fornication."

His face flushed and his lips quivered. There was some insanity in Saunders' family, that much was clear.

"Well, at least he told me about you," I said. "Why don't we talk about you coming out to Star."

I told him all about Star and how much I needed a head butcher I could trust. We set a date two weeks away for him to come out and meet Eugene Tooms. I gave him a fake number and address.

Randall was happy by the end of our talk. He was going to double his salary and get a chance to be a partner in the business.

"Where can I get in touch with your cousin?" I asked at the door.

"J.T.? Why?"

"I don't know. He was good to me. Bought me a few drinks and gave me your name. That's worth a thank-you I suppose."

"He's gone."

"Gone? Gone where?"

"Up north."

"Frisco?"

"His family lives up in Oakland. They live up there but I've never been."

Regina, Jesus, and Edna were all on the front porch. Jesus was lying across Regina's lap and Edna sat next to them playing with a pink-and-blue ball. They all looked at me as I came up the four steps.

"Hi, honey," Regina said. Her voice was happy but she didn't look me in the eye.

Edna squealed and threw the ball at me.

"Hi, everybody."

Edna tried to run off her chair but Jesus caught her and tickled her so she wouldn't cry.

"Jesus," I said. "Take Edna in the house and play horse for a while."

Jesus and Edna loved the horse game. They'd both crawl around on all fours, crashing into things. Regina never let them play it, but I would when I needed to be alone for a while.

I kissed my wife and led her by the hand to the fence at the front of the yard. Some ignorant city gardener had planted an oak in the unpaved part of the sidewalk. The tree had grown and its roots were buckling the sidewalk on one side and the street on the other. Its trunk was gnarly and dark and it was shady there.

"What can you tell me about syphilis?" I asked.

"Why?" Regina's hand stiffened and she pulled away from me.

"Not because'a me, baby," I said. "But maybe this killer has it. I heard that he had been taking sulfa drugs."

"How long has he had it?"

"I don't know really. But they say that it's pretty bad."

"If it is bad then all kinda things could be wrong with him. VD can make you insane."

"Do they have special records of people been on these things?" I asked. "I know they had special hospitals down in Texas."

"I could find out."

"His name is Saunders, J. T. Saunders. And he was on the cure before they came up with penicillin."

We kissed lightly but then she moved away from me as we walked back to the house. Jesus and Edna had knocked over a table and there was water all over the floor.

• 23 •

The next morning I went around checking on my various proper-ties. I had a carpenter from Guatemala laying a floor in an apartment on Quigley Street and a gardener to talk to who hadn't mown a lawn in six weeks. I looked at the different places, picked up some trash, and noted certain infractions for Mofass to follow up.

Then I took a ride over to Mofass' office.

I found him hacking from deep in his lungs into a big yellow rag. He was coughing when I came into the room and he coughed while he told me that the DeCampo people had agreed to my demands.

"Mr. DeCampo called me himself," Mofass wheezed.

"That was mighty white of him."

I regretted saying that, because it sent Mofass into an even more virulent bout of coughing. Coughs racked his whole frame and tears nearly spurted from his eyes.

After long moments barking up sputum Mofass finally rasped out a question. "You gonna sign with them?"

I was afraid to tell him the truth. I thought he would drop dead if I refused him then.

I said, "Well, let's meet again and see what they got on paper."

I had no intention of letting those thieves steal what was mine. If a major road went near my property then I could deal with a bank and keep a hundred percent of my business.

"I'm gonna use your phone," I said.

"I need to go home anyways," he said. "This cold got me by the nuts."

I watched him put on his overcoat and hat. The weight of his garments seemed to drag him almost to the floor. I watched him go out the door and then I listened as his cough retreated down the stairs.

I sat down and dialed the number that I knew best.

"Temple Hospital," a nasally white woman informed me.

"Sixth-floor maternity, please."

There was a pause and then some clicks and buzzes. Finally another, richer voice said, "Nurse's station."

"Regina Rawlins, please."

"She's kinda busy right now. Who is it?"

"Louise," I said, "will you please go get my wife?"

"Easy?"

"How you doin', Louise? Regina said you were workin' again."

"Fine, baby." I could hear her gap-toothed grin. "I sure do miss you."

"You got Regina around there?"

"Mm. Too in love for a kind word?"

"With a woman as beautiful as you a man cain't take no chances, Louie."

"Okay. That's good enough."

After another wait my wife finally came on the line.

"Hi, honey," she said.

"Babe."

"He was tested in a hospital in Oxnard. It was a public hospital but affiliated with the navy. He was an able-bodied seaman in the merchant marines and they paid for his treatments."

"Does he still go there?"

"Not in a long time. His last visit was in 1938. He only went for three months. The clerk there said that he'd be really sick by now if he didn't get treatment somewhere."

"You get an address?"

"Just what he left back then. Twenty-four eighty-nine Stockard Street, Oakland, California. The phone was Axminister 3–854."

I wrote all that down on a pad that Mofass kept on his desk.

"I'll take you out for steaks if you get Gabby Lee to sit for the kids," I said.

"I can't tonight, baby." She sounded upset about it. "I spent so much time on this stuff for you that I had to promise Miss Butler that I'd stay late."

"Can't you do it tomorrow?"

"I gotta go now, honey. Good luck."

When I cradled the phone I felt very lonely. All of what I had and all I had done was had and done in secret. Nobody knew the real me. Maybe Mouse and Mofass knew something but they weren't friends that you could kick back and jaw with.

I thought that maybe Regina was right. But the thought of telling her all about me brought out a cold sweat; the kind of sweat you get when your life is in mortal danger.

Quinten Naylor was at his desk when I called. "What is it, Rawlins?"

"That reward go for me too?"

"If you catch him it does."

"What if he ain't in town?"

"Where is he?"

"Up north."

"Oakland?"

"What makes you ask that? I mean, why wouldn't you think San Francisco?"

"What have you found, Rawlins?" Quinten said in his cop voice.

"I told you 'bout Aretha's and Gregory Jewel an' you couldn't do nuthin' with it, officer. Now I'ma go find the man myself."

Maybe he had something to say about that, but I didn't hear it because I'd hung up the phone.

I called Mouse and told him about the reward. He said to meet him in front of Minnie's at four in the morning.

"Why do you have to go up there?" Regina asked. I was packing a small bag for the two-or-three-day trip.

"I told you. They offerin' fifteen thousand dollars for the ones turn him in. That's a lot of money."

"But you already told them he was up there. Now if they catch him you'll get the money anyway."

What could I say? She was right. But this was a job I'd taken on and I felt that I had to see it through. Anyway, being at home before we got things straight was torture for me. I needed some time away.

"You just wouldn't understand," I said lamely.

"Oh, I understand, all right. You're a crook just like that Mouse. You like criminals and bein' in the street."

"What are you talking about?"

"You think I don't know about you? Is that what you think? Your life ain't no secret, Easy. I heard about you and Junior Fornay and Joppy Shag and Reverend Towne. I can see with my own eyes how you're in business with Mofass and not workin' for him. Baby, you cain't hide in your own house."

"I gotta go an' that's all there is to it," I said. "Anything else we can talk about after I get back."

Regina put her hand on my chest and then brought her fingers together until they were all pointing at me.

We stood still for a moment, her nails poised above my heart.

I wanted to tell her that I loved her but I knew that wasn't what she wanted to hear.

"You got to let a woman see the weak parts, Easy. She gotta see that you need her strength. Woman cain't just be a thing that you th'ow money at. She just cain't be yo' baby's momma."

"I'll let . . ." was all I could say until the pressure of her nails stopped me.

"Shhh," she hissed. "Let me talk now. A woman don't care but that you need her love. You know I got a job an' you ain't ever even asked me fo'a penny. So why do I work? You change the baby and water the lawn and even sew up yo' own clothes. You know you ain't never asked me for a thing, Easy. Not one damn thing."

I always thought that if you did for people they'd like you; maybe even love you. Nobody cared for a man who cried. I cried after my mother died; I cried after my father left. Nobody loved me for that. I knew that a lot of tough-talking men would go home to their wives at night and cry about how hard their lives were. I never understood why a woman would stick it out with a man like that.

• 24 •

Mouse was sleeping in the passenger's seat next to me. The stone and sand cliffs of the California coast loomed on one side with the sun just coming over them. The ocean to our left rose out of its gray sleep into deep blue wonder.

I watched the terns and gulls wheel awkwardly between wisps of morning mist. Cactus pads grew at crazy angles as if they had rooted while tumbling down the mountainside. Bright and tiny purple flowers beamed from succulent vines at the side of the road.

My Chrysler was the only car in sight on the Pacific Coast Highway. I felt exhilarated and strong and ready to put everything in its proper place.

The hum of the engine was in my bones. I could have driven forever.

"Hey, Ease," Mouse croaked.

"You up?"

"Why you grinnin' like that, man?"

"Happy to be alive, Raymond. Just happy to be alive."

He uncurled in his seat and yawned. "You gotta be crazy t'be grinnin' like that this time'a mornin'. Damn. It's too early for that shit."

"I got some coffee in a thermos on the backseat. Some toast and jelly sandwiches too."

Mouse attacked the sandwiches and poured a cup of coffee for me. The sun rose over the crest and sparkled on the water's surface. For the first time in a week I was excited without the help of whiskey. But that thought made me want a drink.

We went through Oxnard, Ventura, and Santa Barbara. Highway 1 wended inland and by the coast in turns. It was a snaky pathway taken mostly by cars because Highway 101 was a more direct route between San Francisco and L.A.

We'd been going for some hours before starting to talk. I was happy looking at the scenery, and Mouse's nature was more suited to the nighttime.

When we were two hundred miles up the coast he asked, "What happens up north?"

"J. T. Saunders in Oakland. That's all I know."

"What you wanna do when we find 'im?" Mouse asked.

"We don't know nuthin' 'bout him, Raymond. He may be just a bad-luck dude in the wrong place at the wrong time. All we do is watch 'im an' give the police his address."

"S'pose he runs?"

"He ain't gonna run."

"What make you say that?"

"He ain't gonna see us so he ain't gonna run."

Mouse nodded and hunched his shoulders. "We'll see," he said.

By twelve we had gone past San Jose and were entering the Santa Cruz mountain range.

"You ever know anybody who went in for the sulfa-drug syphilis cure?" I asked.

"Me."

"What?"

"Me. I went down to that damned place for six months. They had me down for five years."

"And you stopped going?"

"Sure did. Damn! I hated that shit. You know, you go in there an' they give you that shot and the next thing you know you get this foul-assed nasty taste in your mouf. Shit! I hate even thinkin' about it."

"Raymond, you gotta go see a doctor."

"Why?"

"'Cause syphilis gets all in your body and comes out later on."

"I ain't got syphilis."

"But you just said . . ."

". . . I said that I went in for the treatment. I was a kid and I had this here pimple on my dick. I had this girl, Clovis, who said she wouldn't fuck me so I went to the doctor. He looked at my dick and said, 'Syphilis.' Then they made me go every week for that shot."

"Maybe he could tell just from looking." But I didn't believe that.

"Uh-uh. I know 'cause I got drunk one night and tried t'sign up for the army with Joe Dexter the next mornin'. When it came time to go I went down all smug and told 'em that they couldn't take me 'cause I had the syph. But this big ole cracker told me that my tests turned up clear. I ain't never had it."

White doctors at one time thought that almost all Negroes were rife with venereal disease. I could believe that they wouldn't bother with a test.

"So," I asked. "Why didn't you go into the army?"

"They got my jail record the same day. They said t'come back when the fightin' was worse. It never did get bad enough for them to wanna take me."

The past few years I had been staying at the Galaxy Motel on Lombard. It was only ten dollars a night and the old couple there knew me. Mr. and Mrs. Riley. They were an old Irish couple whose parents had immigrated. They had soft brogues and gentle smiles.

"Well hello, Easy," Mr. Riley greeted me as I came into his glass-walled office. "Haven't seen you in quite a while."

Wine racks on the wall held maps, ferry schedules, and tourist guides to parts of the city.

"Workin' too hard down there. Too hard."

"How's the wife?"

"Fine. How's Mrs. Riley?"

"At home with the grandchildren. Cecily had twins last June."

I checked us into a room with two double beds and a television.

I had Mr. Riley dial Axminister 3–854 from the switchboard. Karl Bender answered. He didn't know a J. T. Saunders and he didn't know me. I tried to find out how long he'd had that phone number and his address but that didn't get me anywhere.

"What now?" Mouse asked.

"I don't know. I got a twenty-year-old address for him."

"Twenty years! Man, I lived in over a hundred places in twenty years."

"And every one of them remembers you."

Mouse's boyish grin was disarming. Not that he needed it; I'd seen him cut down more than one armed man in his day.

It had gotten dark outside. The headlights lined up on the Lombard. Two prostitutes took the room next to ours and started doing business. Mouse and I had to laugh, because they could get a john in and out of that room in five minutes flat. The walls were like paper so we could hear it all.

"Uh-uh, money first," one of the girls would say. You could hear the man breathing and then the rustle of clothes.

"Oh!" she'd cry before he had time to get in her, and then, "Do it!" And the guy would all of a sudden scream or grunt or groan. His tone would always be a little sorry like a rube at a carnival who'd hit the pyramid of milk bottles dead center but couldn't knock them over.

"What you wanna do, Easy?" Mouse said at about eight o'clock. "'Cause you know I gotta do sumpin' or I'ma go give my money to them girls next door."

"Let's go over to Oakland and see where this J. T. Saunders used to live," I said.

"Do it!" one of the girls next door replied.

• 25 •

We went across on the lower level of the Bay Bridge. It was Friday night and ten thousand cars followed our example. In the rearview mirror I saw the shimmering lights of San Francisco above the herd of shifting, speeding cars.

Oakland was a full fifteen degrees warmer than San Francisco. We went from comfortable weather to where I had to open the collar of my shirt.

2489 Stockard Street was a three-decker apartment building. The paint had peeled off so long ago that the wood siding had weathered to gray.

A fat woman sat on the porch fanning herself with a church fan. Two small boys ran around her with slats of wood in their hands.

"Bangbangbangbangbangbangbangbang," said one of the boys.

"Kachoom, kachoom," the other one volleyed in deep tones, reminiscent of cannon fire.

The woman was oblivious to the war going on around her. She was very dark with gray hair and a young face.

"Ma'am?" I said. I took two steps up. The boys stopped dead, the slat-guns forgotten in their hands.

The woman kept fanning. She was concentrating on something across the street.

I took another step and said again, "Ma'am?"

The boys' mouths were what my mother used to call flytraps.

"Yes?" She still had her eyes glued out across the street.

I looked in that direction. The only thing I could make out was the shifting light of a TV through a window. I couldn't make out the picture. I doubted that she could either.

"What you want?" the woman asked.

"Does a family named Saunders live around here?"

"No." She leaned forward to show me that she was busy watching. "Bangbangbang."

"Did a family by that name ever live here?"

"Maybe they did, mister. How you expect me to know?"

The artillery boy was using me for cover. He lobbed charges from his cannon-slat as his nemesis sought cover behind the young-old woman.

I could see Mouse down by the car smoking a cigarette and sitting on the hood.

And I stood there, watching her watch television.

After a minute the woman craned her neck back and cried, "Nate!"

A window opened on a floor above and a raspy voice called out, "Yeah?"

"Man down here wanna know if somebody called . . ." She turned to me and asked, "Whashisname?"

I told her.

"Saunders!" she shouted. "Ever lived here?"

"Come on up," the sandpaper voice said. "Number twenty-seven."

"Sir?" I called from the latched screen of his front door.

Nate, whoever he was, lived in his living room. He had a bed in there and a table with a hot plate and toaster on it. There was a two-tiered bookshelf that was stacked high with pamphlets.

The old man, with the help of two canes, got up slowly from his chair at the window and slowly made it to the door. It was a whole minute watching him move the cane in his right hand to his left. I wondered if he had the strength to pop the latch on the door.

"Evenin', young man," he greeted.

We took the long journey back to his chair at the window.

"Hot out, ain't it?" he asked.

I nodded. "How come you got a screen on the front door? You got flies in the building?"

"I like the door open but sometimes them damn kids come in here and steal my cake if I take a nap."

"Oh."

"You interested in the Saunderses, is you?"

"Did you know them?"

"Nathaniel Bly," he said.

I was confused for a moment and then I realized that he was telling me his name.

"Vincent Charles," I replied.

"Why you want them after all these years, Mr. Charles?"

"I knew their son, J.T."

He nodded and my heart jumped a little. "We did some time in the merchant marines. This is the only address I got for him."

Nate sat there nodding at me. He had a wistful smile on his face almost as if he were remembering something I'd mentioned.

"I don't even know if any'a them is still alive," he said. "His daddy died even before they moved. You know Viola couldn't pay the rent here on such a big apartment. I don't know why somebody want a place so big anyways. I like to have everything right with me. But my chirren pays the rent so I stay here. They live right down here, you know. Willie's on Morton and Betty live on Seventeenth. Willie's a car mechanic in San Francisco an' Betty caterin'. Lotta folks say that caterin' is domestic work and they turn up their nose but Betty could buy and sell mosta them. Last year she made more than ten thousand dollars . . ."

"Did she play with J.T. when they were small?"

The question caught Nate up short. He'd forgotten that I'd come there looking for somebody.

"No," he said. "Willie an' Betty was a couple years younger than J.T. and Squire."

"Squire?"

"I thought you said you was J.T.'s buddy? How come you don't know about his brother?"

I laughed agreeably. "We was on a boat, man. J.T. didn't talk about his family, except this address, and I didn't ask."

"He was somethin' else." Nate shook his head. "Always torturin' li'l animals and beatin' up my kids."

"J.T?"

"Squire. J.T. was a timid little boy. He had some kinda fright when he was a baby and he was scared'a all kindsa things—especially bugs. I mean, he couldn't take seein' a ant on the sidewalk. An' Squire'd go out and catch a ole dead dragonfly and run after J.T. with it. And when Viola would come out Squire'd jes' say, 'I try'n give him a pretty.' Sweet and evil, just like a angel from hell.

"One time I come up on them in the basement. Squire was beatin' on J.T. with a piece'a rubber hose. He kept tellin' J.T., 'Do it! Do it!' And finally J.T. whimpers and cries and picks up this big half-dead waterbug and puts it down the front of his own pants. You know that poor boy falled down on the ground, cried for all he had. Squire danced around him like a witch. Like a witch."

"Why didn't you stop him, Nate?"

Nate gave me an inquiring look. "Where you from, son?"

"Texas. Texas an' Louisiana."

"Was that hard back then while you was comin' up?" he asked.

I had to grin when I nodded.

"I used to think that Negroes was niggers. And them niggers had to be hard to make it in this here hard world. I always worried that if a child seen me doin' for him he might grow up thinkin' that the world would do for him. I raised my kids hard. And now they pay my rent and drop off the groceries but they ain't never got no time to talk with me. I know they think I was mean."

"But they're doin' all right," I said.

"When I seen Squire torturin' J.T. I told myself that the boy had to learn how to fight. But you know my heart was dancin' along with Squire while that poor boy suffered. It was dancin' up a storm."

He looked out the window after that speech.

After a while I asked, "Do you know where Viola Saunders lives today?"

"Cain't say that I do."

When I got downstairs the boys were eating out of a quart container of ice milk and the woman was still gazing across the street.

None of them looked up to watch me go.

• 26 •

Viola Saunders was in the phone book: 386$\frac{3}{4}$ Queen Anne's Lane.

Queen Anne's Lane was a short street, only one block in length, that was crowded with apartment buildings. There was a big vacant lot on one side and eight large apartment buildings, built into a hill, on the other.

We went up and down the block but 386$\frac{3}{4}$ wasn't to be found. Finally we went into 386 and knocked on a screen door on the first floor. A television was playing somewhere in the apartment and we could see its shadowy light play down the long dark hallway.

A small boy, almost a baby, came running down the hall. He stopped at the screen and looked up at us.

"Wah!" he exclaimed.

All he wore was a striped T-shirt that barely came down to his distended belly button.

"Arnold!" a woman screamed from inside the house. She came down the hall with a baby in each arm and two more trailing at her skirts.

She was of medium height and attractively built. She wore a muumuu with a neckline cut lower than most that clung to her figure because of the perspiration. She had slack lips, that accented the carelessness of her eyes, and light skin. Her children were all different colors. The baby we first met was light like his mother but the infants she held were both black, twins. One little girl, who was about five and stood peering at us from behind her mother's right leg, was a solid brown color. Her little sister, on the other side, was almost white with dirty-blond hair and greenish eyes. You could see that they were all siblings by their eyes. They all had their mother's vacant, slightly wondering stare.

The young mother gave me a brief once-over and then she looked at Mouse. He wore a deep blue square-cut shirt that hung out over loose gray trousers. His shoes were gray suede. His smile sparkled from behind the diamond in his front tooth.

"Yeah?" she asked Mouse in a slow, meaningful way.

He smiled, bowed almost imperceptibly, and said, "We lookin' fo'a man named J.T. Saunders. You know 'im?"

"Uh-uh," she said. She didn't care either.

One of the babies started crying and the mother said, "Vanessa, Tiffany, here," and she leaned over to hand the crying baby and his docile brother to the two little girls. "Take Henry an' them back in the big room."

The little girls, both of them almost toppling under the weight of their brothers, staggered back toward the shadowy TV light.

Little Arnold stayed until they were almost around the corner and then he turned to run after.

"You wanna come in?" she asked Mouse. She took the latch off the screen and we followed her into the hall. We walked down to where the TV was and turned in the opposite direction.

It was a small kitchen lit by a bare sixty-watt bulb. The walls were a greasy yellow. The floor was covered by pitted yellow linoleum. The yellow tile sink was piled high with dishes. There was a big pan of dirty rice, open and crusty, sitting on the two-burner stove. The ceiling, which was once white, was blackened by smoke and grease.

I was the only one who noticed the dirt, though. Our hostess had taken a bottle of beer from her little refrigerator and handed it to Mouse. They weren't talking but their eyes were exchanging promises.

"You know where three eighty-six and three-quarters is?" I asked before they could fall into an embrace.

"Huh?" she asked.

"What's your name?" Mouse asked her.

"Marlene."

"We lookin' fo' three eighty-six and three-quarters, Marlene," Mouse said. He might have been talking about her eyes, or maybe her breasts.

Marlene pointed through a small window above the sink.

"Up there," she said. "It's one'a them."

Through the window I saw a small concrete path that led past 386 to a small bank of houses nestled behind the larger apartment buildings.

Arnold was at the door looking at us. Greenish mucus welled at his left nostril.

Mouse was looking hard at Marlene.

I moved toward the door. I was halfway down the hall when Mouse came after me.

"Wait up, Easy, you cain't go up against him by yo'self," he said.

"I thought you was busy."

Marlene followed us until we were out of the door. Mouse stopped at the door and looked at her meaningfully. "What you doin' later on, Marlene?"

"Nuthin'."

"You mind if I come back?"

"Uh-uh, I be here."

The concrete pathway was dark but there was a half-moon. On the left side of the path an unpainted picket fence protected any strollers from a sixty-foot drop down into the backyard of Marlene's apartment building.

It was a steep climb and Mouse and I were both puffing by the time we made the summit.

There were seven little houses with all kinds of numbers on them.

There was a light on inside 386¾

Mouse and I looked at each other before going up the short dirt path to the front door. He unbuttoned the two lower buttons of his shirt and shrugged so that he could reach his pistol if he needed it. I went on ahead of him to the door.

A woman answered this door too. She was tall and imposing. She seemed all the more noble because her salt-and-pepper hair was wrapped high on her head with a bright red-and-purple scarf. Her nightdress was a long coral gown. It set off her dark skin in a way that spoke of the islands.

"Yes?" Her voice was musical and deep.

"J.T. here?" I could feel Mouse tense up behind me.

"Who are you?" she asked.

"Martin," I said. "Martin Greer. This is my cousin Sammy." I moved aside to point at Mouse. He smiled.

"Hm! What you want here?"

"We came up from L.A. Abernathy told us we should look up J. T. when we got here."

"Randall Abernathy?"

"Yeah, Randy."

"He don't even like us."

"He didn't say nuthin' like that to me. Matter'a fact he said that J.T. got him a job. Yeah, Randy said that J.T. was good at havin' some fun."

"And what about you?" she asked Mouse. "What do you want?"

"Uh . . . well . . ." Mouse gaped at her. There was a certain kind of woman that just had him cowed. She could have slapped his face and he would have apologized for hurting her hand.

"What do you want?" Viola Saunders asked again. She was older than us, sixty or more, and commanding.

"Could we come inside?" I asked.

For a moment she stared at me. I tried to open my face, to let her know that I was going to be honest with her. Later, when we sat down in her house, I could lie.

Viola opened the door and I felt a touch at my shoulder.

"I'ma wait out here, Ease," Mouse whispered at my ear.

The room she led me to was large but there was very little floor space because of the crowd of furniture. Bookshelves covered with knickknacks and books lined every wall. Two couches, three stuffed chairs, a walnut coffee table, a cherry dining table, and a piano were stabled there. The deep green carpet was thick. It swallowed up the sounds walking might have made. The walls were green too.

"Have a seat, Mr. Greer."

"Thank you, ma'am. You sure have a nice house."

"What do you want with my son?" She stood next to the piano.

"Nuthin' special. I just heard that he knew how to have a good time in Oakland and . . ."

"Don't lie to me, son. What James do to you?"

My muscles went lax and my ability to lie just flowed away from me.

"Nothing to me personally, Mrs. Saunders. But maybe he knows something about a girl he was with a few weeks ago."

"She pregnant?"

"She's dead."

Viola Saunders pulled back on her neck like a viper does before she strikes. Her eyes glassed over and her shoulders rose.

"What her die from?"

"Somebody killed her. She wasn't the only one."

"And you t'ink it were James?"

"All I know is that somebody saw her with him and there was a fight."

The elegant woman from the islands closed her eyes. Her lips went in and out a little and her neck quivered ever so slightly.

"Is James staying here, ma'am?"

"He's a good son, Mr. Greer. He always bring me somet'ing when he goes away. He always bring me somet'ing."

The house was empty, silent and sad.

"He's a good son," she said again. "But he's different now. It's like he's not himself no more. He get so angry sometimes that I worry. I lock my door against him, sometimes. My own son."

I knew that she'd tell me anything I wanted as long as I let her talk.

"You going to hurt my son, Mr. Greer?" She used my fake name to have power over me. Even that one lie was almost too much to bear.

"No, ma'am."

"What about your friend?"

"We just want to talk to him, that's all."

"He was always a gentle boy."

"Do you know where I could find him?"

"I don't want to hear that you hurt my boy 'cause I help you, Mr. Greer."

"I just want to ask him what happened."

"Was it a young girl?"

"Yeah, she was seen with your son but nobody says that he killed her. I just want to ask him a few questions."

Mrs. Saunders trusted me. But she was worried.

"If I tell him about this he will be warned, Mrs. Saunders. He'll know that he was the last one to see her."

"You find him at Tiny Bland's. It's down there on Chino Street near Lake Merritt. He go down there for the whores on Friday."

Viola walked with me out into the front yard.

"You let my son be, hoodlum," she said to Mouse.

He scuffed his toe on the sidewalk and watched the ground. "Yes, ma'am."

"Look at me," Viola demanded.

Mouse looked her in the eye; the fact of him feeling fear frightened me.

"Don't you hurt my son."

"You got it." Mouse nodded and turned away.

When she had gone back into the house Mouse relaxed again. He was fully calm as we descended toward the street.

"You think Marlene wanna go with us?" he asked when we'd gotten to the car.

"I think she got five kids need a momma stay with 'em, Raymond."

He scratched his chin and said, "Yeah. You right." Then he smiled. "I come back after they in bed."

• 27 •

The broad red neon sign said Tiny Bland's in bold script. It shone behind a black glass wall that made up the facade of the nightclub.

Cars drove up letting out fancy Negro men and Negro women dressed in furs and silk. The women also wore gaudy costume jewelry and carried bags made of soft leather.

Across the street winos shambled and skinny teenagers played. Two young men in T-shirts and jeans leaned against an old Chevrolet and eyed the patrons of Tiny Bland's with sullen stares. The kind of stares that say, "I wanna fuck you or kill you or eat you." Or maybe all three.

But the club-goers weren't bothered. They were telling jokes and laughing. Two weeks' pay went into one evening at Tiny Bland's.

A tall black man wearing a metallic gold suit stood at the front door. He greeted the patrons and warded off any undesirable element that might seek entry.

A young man who worked parking the cars was at the bouncer's beck and call. He wore a dark blue uniform with gold satin stripes along the sides of his pants. He was full of "yessir" and "yes'm." He had more teeth than all of those smiling women. He had a pocketful of tip change and his body danced with expectations.

"How we gonna get in here?" I asked Mouse. "I didn't think our boy'd go someplace like this."

Mouse shrugged. "Just walk in the front door, man, like everybody else."

"We ain't dressed fo'it, Raymond."

But Mouse ignored me. He got on the short line that had formed at the door. I stood there with him, glad that we were going to be refused entry. I had sobered a little and thought that we'd do better following Saunders at a distance. We could wait across the street with the winos and muggers and follow our quarry to wherever he lived.

The doorman was letting a couple up at the front of the line go in. It was an orangish Negro, who sported a crew cut, and his blonde date. Everybody on the line was let in.

Until the guard laid eyes on me, that is.

I was wearing ocher slacks and a gray shirt that had two tiny cigarette holes in the pocket.

He looked at those holes like they might have been plague warts and asked, "Yeah? What you want?"

"I wanna come in. You got air conditioning in there?"

"Don't matter if I do, 'cause you ain't comin' in." He looked over my shoulder, indicating that our audience was through and that he was ready for the next applicant.

"Open that do', man, fo' I put you' head th'ough it." That was Mouse.

He hadn't noticed Mouse before. Maybe he thought that the short one was my ugly date.

Anyway, he looked down then and said, "What?"

"You heard me, Leonard, I said open up that door."

Mouse had a big grin on his face. The man in the gold suit was grinning too.

"Mouse," he said.

"Thatta be Mr. Mouse to you." They shook hands and laughed some.

Then Mouse asked, "Man, what they got you wearin'?"

Leonard spread a big hand across his golden chest and looked down shyly.

"That's what they pay me for, brother," he said.

"I hear ya," Mouse intoned.

We were waved in.

The hostess at the podium was black. As were the waiters, the musicians on the platform up front, and most of the patrons.

Mouse asked for a table but I interrupted and said that we'd stand at the bar for a while.

I ordered a triple shot of scotch. Mouse ordered beer.

"Nice place, huh, Easy?"

He was grinning and looking around the room. It was a large room with low ceilings, painted black from the floor up. The waitresses wore white satin gowns and the waiters wore tuxedos.

There were people and more people. The band was playing upbeat jazz, not like the religious refrains of Lips McGee. A crystal globe hung in the center of the room throwing off bright fragments of light that made everything seem a little unreal. Maybe Tiny Bland's was worth two weeks' pay.

"How'd you know that dude?" I asked Mouse.

"I hung out here for a while."

"When?"

"When Terry Peters got kilt."

It was in the street that Mouse had killed Terry in a dispute over two thousand dollars.

"How long you up here?"

"Until somebody else got killed and the cops started worryin' 'bout that."

The bar was long and shiny black. A few feet down from us, Crew Cut was drinking and telling a story to his white date.

She was making eyes at the man next to them.

I don't know if the woman wanted to start trouble but she was well on her way with that flirtation. The man she was making eyes at was of normal height but you could tell by looking at him that he was brawny and full of violence. He had shaggy hair and a thin mustache. His eyes were murky and unfocused even though he stared directly in the white woman's face. But none of these features matched the gash in his neck. There was a wide and jagged scar at his throat, made all the more unsightly because it was lighter, yellowish actually, than his medium-brown skin.

I wondered what kind of accident or war could have caused such a catastrophe. I was more than a little awed that this burly fellow, or anyone, could have survived that pain and bloodletting.

But he just smiled and flirted with the white woman while Crew Cut talked about how he had installed a shortwave radio in his Pontiac.

"Easy," Mouse said. I turned back to him. He was looking around the room.

"Yeah?"

"He ain't here, man."

"We ain't even looked good yet, Raymond."

"I looked."

"You mean you wanna get back to that sloppy girl's house. That's what you mean."

Mouse beamed and smoothed his mustache. "I know what's waitin' back at home, man."

"An' what if she got a boyfriend come in at twelve? What you gonna do then?"

"I do what I do, Easy. An' you know I do it good."

"Hey, man, back off," someone behind me declared. It was said with such anger that I turned quickly and took a step back.

The orange man was pulling his date's hand from the scarred man's caress. The scarred man held his hands out, palms up, and smiled just like Mouse had smiled. I felt the force of the triple shot hit my hands; they felt weak and impotent.

The woman in front of me got out of the way but I was too slow. The scarred man flipped his right hand over and made it into a fist that went crashing into Crew Cut's face. The next thing I knew I was being struck in the chest by the orange man's back. His fuzzy head was at my chin. He pushed against me and went back up against his foe.

It was a mistake he paid for.

By the time he was on the floor he was bleeding from the mouth and nose. There was a circle around the two men. Nobody moved for a brief moment. The orange man was panting on his back, propped up by both elbows. The scarred man was in a crouch with a vacant look in his face. The last time I had seen a look like that was in the Battle of the Bulge. It was on a German foot soldier who intended to send me to hell.

The scarred man reached into his gray jacket.

The orange man smiled.

The scarred man came out with a short thick-bladed knife and took a step.

Somebody screamed.

The orange man took out a pistol and pointed it.

I could see the knife-wielder's eyes change. He was defeated and the murder was gone from him; maybe he even started to lower the blade.

I'll never know, because the smiling orange man began pulling off shots. At the first shot the scarred man started to genuflect. Pow! . . . and a cursory bow. Pow! . . . and chin comes down to hide the scar. By the sixth shot he was prostrate over his knees on the floor.

The orange man never stopped smiling.

People were either running or kissing the floor. One very fat woman in a vast sky-blue gown tried to squeeze herself down into a corner. I saw the orange man's date run out the front door, but her boyfriend hardly moved.

After a few moments he got to his feet. He dusted himself off in a ritual fashion, slightly patting his forearms and knees. He put the gun in his pocket and sat down at the bar. The room had almost emptied out by then.

"Com'on, man, let's get outta here," Mouse said at my side. "Cops be here any minute. An' you know I ain't gonna answer no questions when I could be with Marlene."

Being at the scene of a murder meant no more to Mouse than a dead cow meant to Randall Abernathy. All us poor southern Negroes had lived and breathed death since we were children, but Mouse was different—he accepted it. To him death was as natural as rain.

I agreed that we should leave but I was bothered by the murder. Everything seemed logical. I mean, one man has been killing the other over women for a hundred thousand years. But why didn't he even look for his date? Why didn't he run?

Outside we joined the crowd across the street. I thought that we might catch a glimpse of Saunders.

The ambulance was there in under ten minutes. The police were there before that. They hustled the killer off. I couldn't be sure but the orange man's hands seemed to be free. Unshackled.

While Mouse talked to the doorman I moved around looking for the bearded man. I didn't catch sight of him.

I did see the two toughs who were eyeing the club earlier. They were talking to some of the men from the club. Thinking that they might know why the killing was so unusual I moved near to them and listened.

At first a big man in a tan cotton suit was talking.

He said, "Yeah. The short-haired dude seen that man you said holding on to his girl's hand. You know he was lookin' right down her dress an' lickin' his lips . . ."

"Yeah, yeah," a smaller, mutt-faced man said. "I'da kilt him too. You see that? Guy says leggo my-my girl and here-here he go kickin' his ass. Th-that ain't right."

"Yow main," said one of the T-shirts. "Sand'r'n them allus like'n take it. Shit, he fock my cousin an' a'most kilt Bobby Lee."

"Who you said that was?" I asked the boy.

He glared at me because of my tone. Maybe I reminded him of his truant officer.

"Sander," he said, almost swallowing the word.

"Did he useta wear a beard?" I held my hand under my chin to show him what I meant.

"Yeah."

"Where he from?"

"Who the fuck're you, man?" the other boy shouted.

The mutt-faced man and his friend walked away. I remember thinking that they were smart men. I thought that I'd never do this kind of work again.

Then I thought about fighting those youngsters. They were in their late teens, maybe one was older. The one on the left had well-defined arms in the lamplight. I was still young enough that I could take them. I might have gotten a bloody nose but those boys' lives were in my hands.

They moved apart, watching my hands and eyes. Maybe they did this for a living. More probably for fun.

I reached into my pocket and pulled out two five-dollar bills, handing one to each of them.

"Where'd you say that man Saunders was from? I mean where was he born?" I asked.

"He talk funny," the first boy said. He snatched the bill at the same as his partner did.

"Yeah," the other boy said. "He always say 'mon' insteada 'main.' "

"He been gone for a while?" I asked them. But now that they had my five dollars they had somewhere to go. I could see it in their eyes again.

"Hell, main, I ain't been' paid t'watch that crazy mothahfuckah. Shit!"

With that they both took off.

• 28 •

I was thinking about what I had to say while the phone rang. The girls next door were having a party with two men and the neon light from the motel sign was flashing through the gauzelike curtains.

Mouse was at Marlene's house. I'd let him off there.

"Hello?" Quinten's voice was thick.

"Sorry t'be botherin' you, man, but I got somethin'."

"Where you calling from?"

"San Francisco."

"You find Saunders?"

"Yeah, I found 'im."

"It's late, Easy. I don't have time to play with you."

His father probably said the same words when Quinten was just a baby cop.

"He's dead."

"Where?"

"Probably in the morgue over in Oakland."

"You sure?"

"Pretty much so. I saw 'im get shot. I saw them carry him off with a sheet over his eyes."

"Who killed him?"

"Nobody I know. The police got him too."

There was a silence on the other end of the line. Maybe I was needlessly worrying about how the man I sought out in another city was murdered before my eyes.

"You go to police headquarters office downtown, in Oakland, at about noon. Where are you now?"

I gave him the number of the motel.

"You be at police headquarters at noon unless I call you to say something else."

"Okay, Quinten. All right, man. I'll be there. But if this is the dude I want the reward and I want you people to get off my ass and to stay off it too."

"Noon," he said and then he hung up.

"Hello." Her voice was soft and sweet and inviting.

"Hey, honey, I wake you?"

"Easy?"

"Yeah, baby."

"When you comin' home?"

"Prob'ly not till day after tomorrow. Around dinner. Did I get you outta bed?"

"No."

"You up at midnight?"

"I couldn't sleep so I was cleanin' the kitchen."

"I love you, honey. You know I got a lot t'tell when I get home."

"Okay," she said so softly that I almost didn't hear.

"You know I got money, baby, but it's yours too. I never . . ."

"Tell me when you get here, Easy."

"Cain't we talk now?"

"I don't wanna talk like this, on the phone. You come on home, Easy."

"I love you," I said.

"We'll talk when you get home," she whispered back.

The next morning found me at Marlene's apartment door.

"Momma an' them in the bedroom," the dirty-blonde girl told me. She had the disdain of a woman in her voice. She was learning early to hate men for their indifference, and to lament the treachery of her mother.

"Will you tell the man, Mouse, something for me?"

She just stared at the floor.

I took a silver fifty-cent piece from my pocket and handed it to her.

Her frown never left her face but her eyes widened and she took the coin. She started to run but I touched her arm.

"You tell him that I will be back at four. Okay?"

"'Kay," she told my wrist. Then she ran hard into the house calling her sister's name.

"Ezekiel Rawlins," I told Miss Cranshaw for the third time.

"How do you spell that?" the gray-haired, stick-figured old secretary asked.

"I don't know."

"What?"

"I ain't never been to school an' my momma us'ly signs all my papers. Ain't nobody evah axed me t'spell it at all really. You the first one."

I had been standing there in my best brown suit with a cream-colored shirt, real gold cufflinks, brown blucher shoes, and argyle socks. I had on a hand-painted silk tie, double-knotted to perfection. And this woman had called everybody but me. I had been there, and in the chair in front of her, for over an hour.

I had told her, in my best white man's English, "I would like to be announced to the chief's office. I know that this is an unusual request, but a police officer from Los Angeles, a Sergeant Quinten Naylor, told me to meet him, with the chief, concerning a case in Los Angeles that seems to overlap with a case in your lovely city."

"You should go to your own precinct to give information you have there, sir," she said and then opened a drawer to look in, giving me a chance to withdraw.

I insisted.

She asked me my name.

I gave it, and spelled it, and she called the aide to the captain of the precinct we were in.

She told me that he had never heard of me.

I restated my speech.

She asked me my name.

We might have gotten to hate each other if one of the aides to the assistant mayor hadn't been informed that there actually was an L.A. cop in with the chief. They were waiting on an informant from L.A.

Miss Cranshaw almost spit bile as she made the call for me. Her jaws clenched so that I thought her teeth might crack.

It might have been the first time she'd had to serve a Negro. I was working for progress.

"Is this the man you were looking for from Los Angeles?" Chief Wayland T. Hargrove asked me.

We were in the Oakland City morgue standing over a lab table that bore the remains of J.T. Saunders. He was naked and mottled. He smelled sour like old vegetables smell just before they sprout fungus.

His eyes were open and his head turned slightly toward the left. The gash in his neck was less pronounced in death.

"I think he is, sir," I said. "He certainly is the one I saw getting shot. I saw the man that shot him too. I don't know whether I'd call it self-defense or what."

"No need to bother about that," spectator Bergman from the governor's office said. He appeared at the Oakland morgue a few minutes after we did. "What we want to know is if this is the man who killed those women in the South Bay."

"You mean in L.A."

"No, Easy," Quinten Naylor said. "There were three murders up here last year. This man is a suspect."

"Black women?"

"All of them." Quinten was looking me straight in the eye. He wanted me to keep quiet, and I knew why. He had to answer for the murders in L.A. before hysteria eroded his ability to work there. Trouble with Wayland T. Hargrove or, more especially, Mr. Bergman was the last thing he needed.

But I was mad. "What?"

Chief Hargrove lifted his eyebrows at my indignation. He was wearing gray pinstripes and had a headful of blue-gray hair.

"This man has been a problem in the Bay for fifteen years," Hargrove said to no one in particular. "He spent five years away for manslaughter. He was suspected in the killing of his first wife but there was no evidence. We'd even brought him in on these mutilation killings, but . . ."

"You mean women been gettin' killed up here the same way and nobody knows?"

"That's why the governor had me go to Los Angeles, Mr. Rawlins," Mr. Bergman said. "We were aware of the killings in Oakland, but when it started down in Los Angeles too we became nervous."

"'Specially when he started in on white girls," I sneered.

"It was prudent, Mr. Rawlins, to keep the investigation secret. We had no hard evidence that it was a single perpetrator."

I was quiet because it took every ounce of willpower I had to keep from tearing that head from those shoulders.

"We understand," Roland Hobbes said. "All we want is to lift this guy's prints and check them against the ones we got at the site of the Scott killing."

"Of course," the chief said. "Of course."

"What about the guy killed this man?" I asked.

"That's Oakland police business," said Bergman.

"I saw it, man. I saw it, and it looked like a setup to me."

"Watch it, Easy," Naylor said under his breath. "You're just a guest here."

"Ain't you guys here to find crime and stop it? What if that other guy was part of it?"

"He wasn't," the spectator said.

"How do you know?"

"He's a cop."

He might as well have hit me with a sledgehammer. My brain turned to jelly. My heart almost stopped in my chest.

Bergman's any-color eyes complemented the smile he aimed at me. "A cop?"

The chief cleared his throat. "I hope you men get what you need here," he said. "If there's anything else I can do for you, please ask. Give my regards to Mr. Voss and Captain Violette."

He turned, as did his entourage of two plainclothes bodyguards, two uniformed policemen, and the assistant. Bergman, the porcelain devil, accompanied them. Quinten Naylor, Roland Hobbes, and I were left with a white-coated morgue assistant and a diminutive doctor who'd come in from a game of golf to oversee this postmortem.

"Do you have the materials you need?" the little doctor asked Quinten.

"Um," Quinten answered, looking rather squeamishly at the corpse.

"I'll do it," Roland Hobbes said.

He began bringing out fingerprinting paraphernalia from a small tan suitcase that he carried. Quinten touched my arm and said, "Let's talk outside for a minute."

In the morgue corridor Quinten looked a little healthier. He wasn't so afraid of dead people as long as he didn't have to touch them.

"It's over, Easy," he said in the wide green hall.

"It is?"

"For you. There might be questions. There might be an investigation as to the killing of Saunders. But you've done your job. You can stay here if you want, but I don't think you'll be welcome. I don't think you'll be welcome at all."

I thought of Marlene opening the door for Mouse. She welcomed him.

"What about the reward?"

"It's got to be verified, but if the investigation points at this guy then the money is yours."

"Me and Mouse. He's been lookin' with me."

Quinten frowned. "Where is he?"

"Where he belongs. More than I can say for us."

"Well." Quinten wouldn't meet my gaze. "We're gone after this. You want tickets to fly home?"

"I got a car, and some unwelcome questions to ask."

"They'll kill you up here, Easy. It's just that simple."

"Who sent that man, Quinten?"

"I don't know. I called Violette and he called Voss and Bergman. After that there was a meeting down at city hall and a call was made to Oakland. Nobody asked me a thing."

29

Queen Anne's Lane was ugly in the light of day. People sat out in front of their apartments staring at me. They would have stared at each other if I wasn't there. Children screamed and ran in the empty lots across the street. Boys played war while the little girls watched, half in envy and half bewildered.

I went up to Marlene's apartment building. I was about to go in when I remembered why we had come there in the first place. So instead of going back to the apartment of dirty children, I went up the slender cement passageway to the address we'd looked up the day before.

The door was open and an old woman sat in front of it in a lawn chair. Behind her I could see people, mainly women moving quietly about the house.

"Yah?" the old woman said.

"Hi." I smiled and folded my hands in front of me. "I came to see Mrs. Saunders."

"An' why is that?"

I remembered the stick-figured Miss Cranshaw. She was white and this woman black, but they both had the same regard for me.

"I was here last night and she sent me down to deliver a message to James. I didn't get to talk with him but I saw him get killed."

Gray hairs battled with nappy white ones across the woman's head. There was a bald patch toward the top of her pate.

"What's your name?"

For a moment I froze, forgetting completely the name I had used. But then it came to me and I smiled. "Greer. Martin Greer."

"Don't you know your own name?" the elder lady asked. And I wondered if her mother had entertained a man like Mouse while she cared for her little brother.

I wondered but I didn't answer. Finally the woman got up and went back into the house. She took her chair with her and closed the front door.

When the door opened again I was ashamed. The woman from the night before wore an expansive black dress that came down to her bare feet. She was widest at the thighs and her eyes were swollen and vulnerable.

I was a dog.

"Yes?" she said, holding her chin up.

"I was here last night."

"I remember, Mr. Greer. But he's dead now. I can't send you to him now." If she'd cried I would have had to run. I couldn't comfort this woman.

"I know," I said. "I saw it. I saw it all."

"Why didn't you do something?" The tears stayed in her eyes.

"It was too fast . . ."

She nodded.

"It was like, like . . . I don't know . . ."

She put her hand out and I moved out of range.

"Tell me what happened," she said softly.

I did tell her. And as I talked I wondered again if I really was the cause of this fine woman's anguish.

"But you say that he had the gun and he was holding it on James Thomas?"

"Yeah."

"But why would he shoot him?"

"I don't know."

"No. No," she echoed.

"I went down to the police department to make a statement today. They said that they had been looking for J.T. havin' to do with some dead women in the South Bay."

She just looked at me.

"They said that he's the one who killed those girls down in L.A." I said.

I told her the dates of the last killings.

"It couldn't have been."

"He was here?"

"Not all those times, but the last one you said. He was here with me that day. All day."

"You sure?"

"He was right here with me."

Marlene kissed Mouse goodbye with such passion that I felt it across the room. Mouse had a way of bringing out the love in people. It was because there was no shame in him. For the desperate souls in us all, Mouse was the savior. He brought out the dreams you had as a baby. He made you believe in magic again. He was the kind of devil you'd sell your soul to and never regret the deal.

We went back to the hotel and had fried chicken and broiled ribs from a stand called Fat Charlie's. It was Sunday night, so Ed Sullivan was on television.

The food tasted like cardboard and the stories and acts didn't make any sense.

"What's wrong with you, Easy?" Mouse asked after we ate.

The women were working next door, but slower, as it was the Sabbath. There was a mild groan from the wall and an unconvincing "Ooo, baby."

"Ain't nuthin' wrong."

"No? Then why you droopin' like a puppy just got weaned?"

"They kilt 'im, man."

"Kilt who?"

"Saunders. They used me t'set 'im up."

"Who did?"

"I really don't know. Maybe it was Quinten or one'a them men he took t'my house. Maybe it was all of 'em. Probably was. Somebody killed 'im, though. They got his name from me an' killed him."

"So?" Mouse was already bored with talking about my problems.

"So that makes it my fault. That's so."

"He killed them girls, right?" Mouse sighed. "I mighta killed 'im my own self if I'da thought about it."

"But he shoulda gone to court. People up here shoulda found out that some man was killin' women and nobody even knew about it. That's probably why they killed him. They didn't want a trial to let people know that a killer had run free and nobody even knew."

"He's dead, Easy. It's over, man."

"But it ain't right."

"Naw, it ain't that. It ain't never right, Ease. Niggah ain't gonna get nuthin' right till they put 'im under six feet of loose dirt. That's as right as it gets round these parts."

"So you sayin' I should just drop it?"

"What else can you do?"

"I didn't drop it when you was in jail, Raymond. I got you outta there."

"Uh-huh. An' I thank you fo'that too. But you know we partners, brother. Shit! You better not fuck wit' my partner or I put you down."

There was nothing to argue about. Mouse didn't understand guilt or abstract responsibility. He'd go up against a platoon of men to protect me or EttaMae, his ex-wife, or their boy LaMarque. He'd shoot it out with the law for his own people, but Mouse couldn't hold a moral concept in his brain. Explaining right to him was like trying to explain the color red to a man who was born blind.

And he was right anyway. I tried my best. I did what I thought was right. I found the man killing black women. I did it all.

I couldn't take on the cops. I'd never work for them again, but that's all I could do. I had a wife and children of my own to look after. And Saunders was a killer; I knew that from the moment I laid eyes on him.

We went to sleep early, but Mouse got up in the middle of the night. He sat at the foot of his double bed and smoked a cigarette. I listened to him breathe and to the women talking to each other through the wall.

After a while Mouse went out the door. A moment later I heard a woman's voice say, "Who's there?"

"It's your neighbor," Mouse said. "I brought a bottle'a Jim Beam."

The door opened and the ladies laughed. They partied until six in the morning. Toward the end the women wanted to go to sleep. Finally they sent Mouse back home to me.

• 30 •

The ride down the Coast Highway was beautiful. Mouse slept almost the whole time.

Between the motor humming and the sea air coming in my window I started feeling better about J.T. Saunders. He was a killer, after all, and I had my life to go back to. It was wrong for the police to cover up the killings but I couldn't change the world.

It was a windy afternoon. White rags tore from the navy-blue sea. There was a sonic boom somewhere around Ventura. That roused Mouse for a moment.

"What was that?" he asked.

"Nuthin'. You must' been havin' a dream."

He gave a big grin and said, "Know what I'ma do, Easy?"

"What?"

"First thing I get that money I'ma buy me a '57 T-Bird."

I didn't argue with him. Mouse knew how to enjoy his life.

I got home at about five. Regina's car wasn't parked out front yet. Gabby Lee and Edna weren't to be seen. Jesus' scooter lay on its side near the garden. Everything looked very good.

I had owned that house for more than ten years, but since Regina had moved in, it was more like a home than ever.

I still remember the day I met her. It was at a club in Compton. I was following a man named Addison Prine for his fiancée's father. The old man, Tony Spigs, was sure that Addison had a girlfriend and he wanted me to find her name. Spigs was a jealous old man and he wanted to keep his only daughter at home as long as he could. Spigs was also Mofass' preferred carpenter and I thought I could get a good carpentry job out of him for a hefty favor.

Addison was at a small table with another man and a woman. Near to them a woman sat alone. She was wearing a simple brown dress. She had the dregs of a bright red drink with a straw in it before her.

"Can I sit here?" I asked her in a businesslike manner.

She looked up at me and her eyes laughed. That's when I fell in love. Her eyes laughed without a smile crossing her lips. Then she looked around the room. There were quite a few empty tables around, because it was late afternoon and the Toucan was still waiting for its crowd.

"I like this one," was my answer to her gaze.

She looked the other way and I sat down.

Addison put his hand over the hand of the woman at his table. A waiter came up and took my whiskey order.

Regina didn't avoid my face but she just looked straight ahead, past me rather than at me.

"No, Nancy," Addison said. "I ain't gonna forget you. I got the tickets right here in my pocket."

The woman, a chesty specimen in a checkered dress suit, laughed. I thought about Addison's fiancée. Iona Spigs was a pretty but tight-mouthed girl. She liked a neat house and churchfilled Sundays.

Nancy liked to get her hands dirty. When she leaned over to kiss Addison it was with her smile showing.

I shook my head and sighed.

My fake date glanced at me, but no more.

I sipped my drink.

Nancy swabbed Addison's mouth with her tongue.

I motioned for the waiter to come over. When he stood there before me I asked my wife-to-be, "Would you like something else?"

She nodded at her empty glass and the waiter went away.

I sighed again.

"What would you do?" I asked my glass.

"What?"

"What would you do if you had a friend and his daughter was gonna marry that man over there?" I swung my head in Addison's direction.

The eyes did their laugh.

"Is that your friend's daughter he kissin'?"

"Not hardly."

She laughed for real then. It was a good laugh in a woman. She let her head fall backward and her mouth open wide. Then she bent forward and thrummed the table with her short, unpainted nails.

I laughed too. Not quite as hard. The waiter brought our drinks.

"I don't think you should do nuthin'," Regina said.

"Why not?" I asked.

"She picked that man. She got a reason that maybe even she don't know."

"But what if he break her heart?"

"She live with her daddy?"

"Yeah."

"At least she be on her own then. Maybe that's what she wants."

Jesus was sitting at the kitchen table. His hands were out in front of him and there was no food or anything else there. He looked up at me when I tousled his hair.

"Run on outside now. Go on an' play, boy. You shouldn't be inside," I said.

I was glad that Regina and Edna were still gone. I had them with me anyway. I enjoyed the feeling of them in the house. On the couch that Edna always jumped from. At the sink where Regina cleaned every night.

"I'm a poor woman and from a long line of proud poor people," she told me that night. I'd told Tony Spigs that I couldn't find anything on Addison.

Regina wasn't an inventive lover. She didn't do tricks or bellow or jibber. But when we came together it was like everything she had was mine. She came on me like waves on the shore. She was constant and strong.

There was a folded piece of paper on the TV. Under the note lay the nine hundred dollars I'd given her. When I saw the money I knew I was lost.

> *Dear Easy:*
>
> It is hard for me to say honey but I found a man that I love. And I am going away with him. You know I have tried but I cannot stay.
>
> You are wonderful Easy but I need something that we don't have. I love you. I do love you but I have to go.
>
> Don't hate me for taking Edna. She needs her mother.
>
> *Goodbye.*

The dictionary was on the coffee table. She'd looked up the words she couldn't spell. The tears came and my knees buckled. After a long while I looked up and saw Jesus sitting on his haunches. He was sitting watch over me.

• 31 •

I went to the Safeway market the next morning and bought a gallon of vodka and an equal amount of grapefruit soda. Jesus slipped off to school and I drank. I drank deliberately as if I were working.

Lift hand to lip and sip, swallow and sip again, put glass on table but don't let it go. After twenty-one double-sips, refill and start over.

I slept in the afternoon.

Jesus came back at about three-thirty. He came banging in the front door and ran across to his room dropping books and clothes as he went. When he came back I grabbed him by the arm and hefted him into the air.

"What the hell do you think this is, boy, a pigsty?"

He shied away from me after that. I felt wrong about handling him that way but whenever it bothered me I just drank some more.

The phone rang at four. Jesus ran in from the front. He stared worriedly after the bell. I kept up the sipping regimen. Double-sip, ring, double-sip, ring. Finally the phone stopped ringing but the liquor still flowed.

Jesus had warmed two cans of spaghetti for our dinner. I sat at the table but the smell made my stomach lurch. I leaned away from the smell in my chair.

There was a song playing in my head, "I Cover the Waterfront." I was humming the lyrics when I looked up and saw Mouse. He appeared as if by magic right there in my dinette.

"Hey, Easy," Mouse said.

Jesus jumped out of his chair and hugged the crazy killer-man.

"Mouse," I replied. I wasn't actually seeing double but Mouse's visage shimmied a little. My voice, and his, carried the slight quality of an echo chamber.

"Better sit up, man. That's how Blackfoot Whitey died."

"What?"

"Sittin' back, drunk in his chair, till he went too far one day an' busted his neck."

"She's gone, man."

"Yeah. I know."

"You do? How'd you find out?"

There were very few times that Mouse actually looked serious. The only times I had ever seen him somber was when he was getting ready to go out on a criminal job. So his grave stare made me wonder, almost forget my sorrow.

"It was Dupree," he said.

I watched my eyelids flutter. My heart did the same. I tried to think of her in that big man's arms. I tried to think of her not with me.

"He been after her at the hospital. You know how he always be bad-mouthin' California . . ."

"How you know?"

"Sophie said it. She was mad that a brother of hers could do that to a friend. She told me so I could tell you."

Up until that moment Regina was still with me. I still loved her and wanted her back. I planned to follow her first letter and beg for her to come back to me. But the thought of her in Dupree Bouchard's arms tainted my brain. There was a smell and an ugly color that became a part of everything we had been. I was sick.

Jesus was at my side with his slender boy's arm around my neck. He put his face against my cheek.

"Mind if I mix me one, Easy?" Mouse asked. He was already pouring a drink.

I nodded and bowed. My wife had left me, had taken my child, had gone off with my friend. There was no song on the radio too stupid for my heart.

That night is still mixed up in my mind. I remember Mouse getting me outside to see his canary-yellow '57 T-Bird. It was a classic from the day it came off the line.

He told me that a loan shark fronted him the money; that he couldn't wait for the reward to buy his new car.

I remember women's breasts held barely in check by loose blouses, and how seeing that sight made me sick inside.

I remember loud music and dancing so hard that my clothes were soaked through with sweat.

I remember a man with tears in his eyes and a kitchen knife in his hand. He was coming toward me. I moved to put my arm out but then I saw that I had my arm around a woman. She yelled in my ear, "Derek! Stop!"

There were other images but most of them were even less coherent. I saw Mouse smiling next to me in the car. He was driving fast and the night wind tore across my face. I was laughing too.

"Ohhhhh, Daddy," came a woman's voice. "Uh, uh, uh."

Every utterance pounded pain right in the center of my brain. I opened my eyes and saw that a woman was lying against my chest. Her dark face was barely visible under the straightened metallic-gold hair. But I could see that she was sleeping.

"Oh yeah yeah," the voice came again. The bed shook and bobbed.

I looked to my left and saw a woman I had never seen before. Her face could have been ugly or beautiful but I couldn't tell because it was contorted in the throes of a powerful orgasm. She was on her side with her eyes looking directly into mine but I don't think I registered for her. Above her left shoulder Mouse was grinning like a hound. His gaze was locked to her profile and his whole body hunched rhythmically while she moaned.

I sat up, pushing the woman on my chest aside. I climbed to the foot of the bed and walked across the sloppy room toward the door.

"Oh, yeah," Mouse called.

The woman yelled out something too but it didn't make any sense, like maybe it was a foreign language.

Outside the door I saw, in the very early morning light, a bathroom.

Even urinating made me feel sick. I could feel the puckered walls of my stomach with every motion. Even breathing made me salivate.

There was a box next to the bathroom door. I kicked it slightly upon leaving the toilet. Any contact sent pains rolling through my head. I put my hand to my eyes and the baby started crying. The baby that had been sleeping in the cardboard box on the floor.

I lifted the child, who was even younger than my own. I kicked open the door to the bedroom and shouted. "Who left this here baby on the flo'?"

Mouse and his girl were still cupped together, but peacefully. When the other woman heard the baby crying she sprang up to her hands and knees and stared at me.

She said, "Who?"

"This baby yours?" I asked, none too kindly.

She ran at me and took the baby away. "Mothahfuckah!" There was a slight slur to her voice but the hatred was pure.

"Why you gonna leave a baby on the floor, in the toilet?" I yelled.

She swung from side to side looking for a place to deposit her child.

"Bastid!" she yelled. "I kill you!"

We were both naked and not very far from being drunk.

"They should take that baby away from you," I screamed.

The look on the young mother's face was indecipherable. Her lips and eyes squirmed and shook, her whole body vibrated, and the baby hollered.

Mouse came right at me. He had our clothes in his arms. He rammed his body into mine and I fell out of the room. He slammed the door on the two women and threw me my clothes.

"Put 'em on, Easy."

I could still hear the baby crying through the door. I would have never put my child in harm's way.

In the car Mouse drove a few blocks without saying anything. I couldn't have spoken if I wanted to.

But at Crenshaw he stopped the car at the curb. It was no later than five-thirty and the traffic was still light.

"Easy, I gotta talk to you, man."

I sighed.

"You cain't keep up like this, man. All this drinkin' an' feelin' sorry fo' yo'self. I mean, it's done, man. The man is dead and the woman is gone."

I thought about Bonita Edwards sitting so peacefully by the tree. Mouse pulled out into the street and drove me home.

I never said a word and he didn't say anything else.

I stood out in front of the house for a while before going in.

Jesus was sleeping on the couch. He had some of Edna's toys around him on the floor. He used one of her baby pillows for his own head.

• 32 •

I laid in bed with my eyes open wide. At least that's how it felt. I must have been dreaming, though, because people were coming in and out of my room, bad-mouthing me. Regina came, and Saunders and Quinten Naylor. Everybody had something to say and I was in no condition to contradict them.

I watched the windowpane go from day to night.

There was a large, jagged stone in my lower intestines and my fingers were all numb.

I slept fitfully through the night. Waking up once to check on Jesus.

I felt an evil magic in the room. When I looked at the clock it said five-oh-five and the phone rang. It rang and rang.

By the time I went to the living room to answer it Jesus was already there. He was sitting next to the phone with his hands clasped before his chest as if he might have been in prayer.

I let it ring two more times before I picked it up.

I was thinking of all the things I would say to her. At one moment I imagined myself screaming, "Whore!" And in the next moment I was breaking down and taking her back. I felt great power and relief lifting the receiver.

I picked up the phone and held it to my ear. I wanted her to say the first words. From her words I could decide what to say.

"Mr. Rawlins?" a man's voice said. "Hello? Anybody there?"

"Who is this?"

"It's Vernor Garnett. Robin's father."

"What you callin' me at this time'a mornin' for?"

"I'm sorry. I'm really sorry. We're just worried, that's all."

Saunders' death and implication in the murders had already been in the paper and the news. They had said that Saunders was killed in a case of self-defense in a barroom brawl in Oakland. Due to the particularly violent nature of the man and due to excellent police work by Quinten Naylor, the man's fingerprints were taken and compared to partial prints left at the scene of the murder of Willa Scott. Saunders was the killer. The killings in Oakland went unknown.

They knew who killed their daughter and they knew that he was dead. Anyway, this man was a prosecuting attorney. What could I know that he couldn't find out?

"What's wrong?" I asked.

"I went down to that hotel where Robin lived. I went to find out about what was happening to her. To find out why."

I felt sorry for the man. To think of a man seeing his daughter lower herself to the squalor of Hollywood Row was an awful thought. I felt it even more because I knew then what it was like to lose a child.

"Mr. Rawlins?"

"I'm listenin', Mr. Garnett. I feel for ya, but that still don't answer why you wanna talk t'me."

"Robin had a baby. At least we think she did."

"What?"

"One of the, uh, people who lived there said that she was pregnant."

"Did he ask you for money?"

"I'm not a fool, Rawlins."

"That don't answer my question."

"He said that he'd tell us about her for twenty dollars and I told him that I'd hear what he had to say before I gave him a dime."

"An' he said she was with child?"

"He gave me the name of the hospital she went to. He took her there."

"Uh-huh." I stifled a yawn.

"We went to the hospital. They hadn't heard of her, but . . ." He hesitated. ". . . but they had done a test on a Cyndi Starr."

"No jive?"

"It was three months ago. She delivered there. I saw the birth certificate. My granddaughter's name is Feather Starr."

I felt the alcohol evaporating out of my pores. A chill climbed my shoulders, and for the first time that I could remember I was completely sober.

"You got this certificate?"

"Right here. Right here in my hand."

"Why you call me?"

"I don't know what to do, Mr. Rawlins. The police say that they'll look into it. We went to see that man Voss. But he told us that the chances are slim. He said that we should keep up hope but that the chances are slim. Hope for this baby is all that my wife has, Mr. Rawlins."

"An' you think I could help where the police cain't?"

"You found us. They say you found the man who killed our daughter."

"Cops tell you that?"

"Yes."

"They tell you to call me?"

"No. We talked it over. We want to hire you if that's okay."

"Hire me for what?"

"Find our granddaughter, Mr. Rawlins. She's all that's left of Robin."

I tried to think about it. But I couldn't. I just opened my mouth and said something. I decided that whatever came out would be what I should do. "I'll be by at around ten, Mr. Garnett. I cain't promise you nuthin'. I cain't promise you a thing, but I'll come on by."

I was at Mofass' office at eight. He was eating jelly doughnuts and sweating even though it wasn't that warm.

He skipped any pleasantries and asked, "You ready fo' me to go to that meetin', Mr. Rawlins?"

"Oh yeah, I'm ready."

"It's set for three-thirty."

"I'll tell ya what, Mofass."

"Yeah?"

"You go tell them boys that we don't need 'em."

"What?"

"You heard me. Tell 'em I don't give a shit what they want. If we make somethin' outta my places then it's gonna be us to do it."

"Mr. Rawlins, I cain't tell ya what to do with yo' own property, but . . ."

"That's right, man. You ain't got nuthin' t'say about it. It's my money and my life."

"But I promised 'em, Mr. Rawlins. I told 'em that I could get the partners t'say yeah. You told me you would."

"I never said nuthin' of the kind."

Mofass bit his lower lip, something he hadn't even done when I'd once held a pistol to his head.

"They give me five thousand dollars," he said.

"So?"

"I ain't got it, Mr. Rawlins. I spent it. I thought you was gonna go 'long with 'em."

His breathing was getting worse.

"That ain't my problem, William."

"But I took it on your behalf. I took it for our company."

"Shit," was all I had to say.

I left him gagging and coughing in his swivel chair.

The house looked almost the same. The Caddies were still in the driveway but the bicycles were gone. I didn't get a chance to use the buzzer—they had the door open before I was halfway up the walk.

They both came out to meet me. Mr. Garnett shook my hand. He even smiled.

"I'm sorry about the other day, Rawlins. But when I came home

Sarah couldn't even talk. Milo was sitting holding her hand and crying."

"Then I guess it's me who should be sorry." I looked at her when I said that.

"Coffee, Mr. Rawlins?" Mrs. Garnett asked.

"Sure, sure," I said.

We sat in the living room again. The couple sat side by side holding hands on the couch. I tried to remember the last time I had been with Regina like that.

"Would you prefer cream?" Mrs. Garnett asked.

"Naw." I looked at them for a few moments more. The man was big and powerful but he was uncertain. He stared at the floor while he patted his wife's hand. She was strength on the verge of collapse. Her brown hair was fading into gray. Her steely blue eyes were on mine, but somewhere else at the same time.

"Can you help us?" she asked.

"Let's see what you got."

The husband had the certificate in an official-looking envelope. It had a cellophane window that revealed a blank page that had been scrawled over by a harried hand.

Feather Starr was born on August 12. There was no father mentioned. Back in those days they included race on birth certificates. It was a little box labeled "Race." In Feather's little box there was written a small "w."

"Looks right," I said. "But I thought the paper said that Robin, or Cyndi or whatever you call her, was in Europe until about then?"

"She'd left home about six months ago," Vernor said. "We didn't want to admit it. We were ashamed."

"Did you go to the police?" I asked.

"She was twenty-one, Mr. Rawlins. She told us that she was dropping out of school. The police couldn't have done a thing. What's important now is that we have a granddaughter somewhere." Mr. Garnett had tears in his voice. "It means our baby isn't completely gone."

"Yeah, could be."

"What do you mean?" Mrs. Garnett asked. Her tone of voice was telling me that she might not be able to take one more thing. But I still had things to say.

"Who knows what a girl like this is gonna do with a baby?"

"Girl like what?" the father said.

"You're a prosecutor, man." I looked him right in the eye. "You know what it's like. Fo'them girls money is in their titties and in their legs." I felt myself sneering. Each word hit the man like a haymaker. He winced and cowered in his chair. "A woman up in Hollywood Row be brushin' out her hair for a man to wanna see. He's gonna pay fo'that. One way or the other he gonna pay. Either he gonna buy whiskey while she dancin' on a bar or he gonna hand it over before he walk through the door."

As I spoke I moved toward the edge of my seat. Mr. Garnett folded backwards—he even let go of his wife's hand.

"Why are you doing this?" Mrs. Garnett said. "Why are you torturing him?"

She caught me up short. I sat back to clear my head.

"Just tryin' t'make my point, that's all."

"What point?"

"Girls like the ones live down on the Row live by their bodies. Each piece got its purpose and each piece got its price."

She didn't know what I was talking about, but I was pretty sure that her husband did.

"Baby is just another piece," I said.

"What?"

"Baby got a price tag too. Baby got a big price tag if you know the right market."

"Are you saying that Robin might have sold her baby?" Mr. Garnett's tone was threatening to break out into fists.

"I seen a man pay a woman five dollars so he could put his head on her shoulder."

Garnett leaped to his feet. I didn't flinch though. I didn't flinch because I had a loaded .25 in my pocket.

"Get out my house!" he yelled. "Get out!"

I stood as tall as I could but Vernor still had an inch or two on me.

"All right," I said. "But this is just why I talked like that."

Mrs. Garnett stood and asked, "What do you mean?"

"This thing with yo' girl is ugly and you might not really wanna get into it. You might find out all kindsa things. You might find a dead baby someplace. You might find a pimp done sold your baby girl to some sex fiend in Las Vegas. You open up this can'a worms and you could find out anything. And if you cain't take it then better find out right now."

I felt for them. At least I knew that Regina would take care of my baby. They had one dead child and another one who could be dead or worse.

"You don't have to worry about me, Rawlins," Mr. Garnett said. "I can take whatever I have to."

I believed him. Garnett was large and kind of rugged-looking. His eyes weren't strong but they didn't seem to have much fear either. Like a doctor's eyes when he sees a man dying; just another day.

We were all standing and I didn't want to sit down again. I was afraid to death of sitting down again. I felt that the sadness of that woman would drown me if I stayed any longer.

"Okay, okay," I said. "I'll find the baby if she's there to be found."

"How much?" Mr. Garnett asked.

"I'll take five hundred dollars plus my expense on the day I deliver the baby to you."

Mrs. Garnett saw me to the door. She put her hand on my forearm and looked into my eyes. Her eyes were blue-gray. They shifted back and forth between colors even while I stared into them.

"When should we get in touch with you?" she asked.

"Wait for me. When I know somethin' you'll know it too."

"You're my hope, Mr. Rawlins. I didn't think I could go on until Vernor found out about the baby. If I could just have her."

There was gratitude in her eyes. Gratitude and maybe the desire to go with me.

"I'll call," I said and walked on down the path.

• 33 •

The toothless laundress at Lin Chow remembered me right away. She smiled and pulled out a bundle wrapped in brown paper and tied by white string. I paid her a dollar seventy-five and she showed me her gums.

The dirge was plaintive and high, then guttural, an almost human groan. I listened while I went up the stairs and down the hall.

Lips was seated at his table, his chest was bare and his feet were too. He played his horn in a way that would teach any man to love jazz.

The music washed over me like the air at the end of the first battle after D-Day. There were no more bullets or shards of metal flying through the air. The dead lay around in pieces and whole but I couldn't really mourn for them because I was alive. It was pure luck that I wasn't stretched out. I lived a little longer so that I could hurt a little more.

It was a sweet pain.

I sat at the window and listened to him play for a long time. I watched the cars and pedestrians wander while Lips made sense of their lives.

A nice-looking young woman was walking across the street being followed by a pear-shaped man. He was talking loudly and gesturing with his hands. After half a block she stopped and then she smiled. He smiled too. They walked side by side after that. I wondered if they had ever met. Then I wondered if they'd get married.

"What you need now?" Lips asked. I hadn't even realized that he had stopped playing.

"Did you know about her baby?"

"Who baby?"

"Cyndi's." I turned to meet his glassy stare.

"That's why she gone," he said finally.

"You didn't know?"

"Naw. Not me, man. People go in an' outta here all the time. You know they mo' likely be dead then pregnant."

"Anybody else know her good enough that she might tell them?"

"Sylvia."

"Who's that?"

"I already told you 'bout her. 'Nother white girl. Actress too. Sylvia Bride's what they calls her. I don't know where she is now, though."

"That all?"

"Boy live across the hall from her. Prancer."

"Little guy with a mustache?"

"Uh-huh, they was good friends."

I left twenty dollars on the table and made a note about it in this tiny spiral notepad I'd bought.

The door was unadorned. I knocked for a long time before I heard any sound whatever from inside.

He opened the door wearing crosshatched boxer shorts and brown slippers. His slick hair was tousled and his eyes were bloodshot. He looked at me for a long time trying to think who I might be.

"Yeah?" he said, giving up at last.

"You Prancer?"

"Who're you?"

"Can I come in?"

He stood there a few seconds and then backed up, letting me in the room.

I don't know what I was expecting but the room surprised me. It was very neat, with conservative furnishings, except for the bed. The bed had a wooden headboard painted blue with the figures of little cherubs at the top corners. There was also a sofa and chair set before a coffee table. The coffee table had magazines of various kinds, mainly movie magazines, spread across it.

The only adornment on the wall was a movie poster of James Dean looking tortured and vulnerable.

I sat in the chair and Prancer stood there before me rubbing his eyes. He had the body of a teenaged boy but he must have been in his late twenties, maybe even thirty.

"Do I know you?" he asked.

"I was in Cyndi's room the other day. You wanted me to leave."

"You the cop," he said, suddenly awake and none too pleased.

"Just a man," I said as cool as I could manage. "Lookin' fo' somethin'."

"Lookin' fo' what?"

"They say Cyndi had a baby."

"Who says?"

"You told her father that."

Prancer didn't say anything. He just stared at me with his right hand cupped under where his left breast would have been if he were a woman.

"They went to the hospital where you sent them. They found out that Cyndi Starr delivered."

He grinned defiantly and rocked back and forth. "I ain't lied t'them."

"You know where the child is?"

He shook his head like he was shaking water from his hair.

"You know anything could help me find her?"

"How come?"

"Grandparents want the child. It's all they got left."

For a moment Prancer's oblivious child's face showed feeling. "She had a girl?" he asked.

I nodded.

"Listen, man," he said. His face was empty again. "I feel for them, mother and child, but you know I got the rent t'pay. If I got sumpin' t'get you in here wit' me then you know they gotta have some money somewheres."

"I got thirty dollars in my pocket, boy. That's it. Can we deal?"

Prancer actually licked his lips when I laid out the six five-dollar bills in his hand.

"Where?"

"You know Bull Horker?"

It was a question, not an address, but that was all I needed. Much more, actually. Maybe too much.

• 34 •

Bull Horker owned a ribs-and-chicken joint on the southern outskirts of downtown. It was just an old bungalow that he and his brother owned. They set it on a vacant lot that they leased from a friend who was in jail for manslaughter.

Bull was a massive man. He resembled the sculptures of Balzac done by Rodin. His corpulence was indicative of strength of limb and of spirit. His large gut was a clenched fist. His beefy jowls looked as if they could gnash through pipe.

His skin was mottled like some fine Asian woodwork. It was pulled back tight across his wide, hippopotamus-like face.

"Sylvia who?" he said, cocking his head at such a severe angle that his left ear was almost parallel to the floor.

We were sitting at the back of the dive. The cook, an old ex-convict called Bailey, was frying short ribs and flour behind the counter.

Bull had migrated to Chicago from Mississippi but wound up in L.A. because of his intense dislike of the cold. He did favors for people; so did I. But Mr. Horker's favors always had a price attached up front. Sometimes it was cash; sometimes it was something more dear.

He had plenty of business because he'd do *anything,* from finding a cut-rate engagement ring to killing your worst enemy.

"Sylvia Bride," I said. "That's probably her working name. She does exotic dancing."

"Nope," he smiled. He looked around the room cautiously and

then pulled a fifth of some kind of pink liquor from under his chair. "Drink?"

I shook my head no.

"Mind if I try?"

"You sure you don't know her?" I asked again.

"Sure as this here booze." He slugged back a healthy shot. Suddenly there was a powerful odor of apricots.

"The police been lookin' for her in the worst way."

The lizard-skinned clown transformed into a bronze warrior before my eyes. His fists clenched and his jaw set. His eyes became so dull that it was hard to distinguish them from the rest of his face.

"Says which?" he breathed.

"Cops lookin' for this girl, this Sylvia."

"So?"

"They gonna go out t'look in my trail if I cain't locate 'er. We kinda workin' together on this one."

Bull was a big man. I didn't think I would stand a chance against him without a high-caliber gun. As he looked at me I considered my demise. One eye, his left one, nearly shut while the other one opened wide.

I girded myself for the stampede.

Then the right half of his upper lip curled back, revealing an especially feral-looking canine. The rest of his teeth slowly came into view until I saw, with little relief, that Bull was smiling.

"You comin' inta my place an' threatenin' me, Easy Rawlins?"

"I ain't threatenin' nobody. I ain't scared'a you neither. I'm lookin' for this girl and I heard your name. That's all. The police want her. That ain't no threat—it's the truth."

Bull poured another shot of schnapps and drank it.

We had never been at odds before. I wasn't afraid of him any more than I was afraid of any man. The problem wasn't men, it was death.

Death seemed to hound me. He was in Bull Horker's placid visage; he was on a slab in Oakland. She leaned up against a tree a few blocks from my house.

"If I tell you I don't know the girl, then that's all I gotta say," Bull said.

"And if I tell you that somebody got a thousand dollars for something they lost and Sylvia found, then you wouldn't be able to help me, huh?"

Bull just stared.

I wrote my number on the corner of his racing form. Then I walked out of there into the smog and sun of Los Angeles.

Jesus was still at school when I got home. He had emptied out all of my liquor bottles. Poured every one down the drain and set them neatly across the window sill. Even my hundred-dollar bottle of Armagnac.

I took off my clothes and got into the bed.

There was a child crying in my dreams.

• 35 •

In the morning I woke to find Jesus asleep at the foot of my bed. He was curled up into a little ball, fully dressed, with his mouth wide open. He was just a little boy and the world around him was whirling like a storm.

I never knew where Jesus was from. For a long time he lived with my friend Primo down in the barrio. But then Primo left for a while and Jesus came to live with me.

I was the closest thing to a father he had, and now that Regina was gone I didn't even come home regularly.

I got up and threw out the bottles that my son had emptied and made breakfast. We had pancakes and bacon. Jesus ate with silent glee.

"Don't worry, boy," I told him. "We're gonna get through this one just like we made it all them other times."

Jesus nodded solemnly. I tickled his ribs and he fell off the chair to the floor.

After he was gone to school I called Quinten Naylor.

"Yes?" he said in my ear.

"Yeah, man. Are you a cop or what?"

"Rawlins?"

"Robin Garnett, Cyndi Starr, or whatever you wanna call 'er, had a baby just three months ago. She never went to Europe and she dropped out of UCLA."

He was silent for a moment and then he said, "Go on."

"Viola Saunders said that J.T. was up there when Robin was killed."

"She's just trying to protect him, that's all."

I told him about Prancer and Sylvia.

"We got the killer, Easy."

"You ain't got shit. You just wanna shove yo' head in the dirt and make like it's gonna go away."

Quinten hung up on me and I sat back in my chair.

I wanted a drink. I thought of Regina and slapped myself hard against the head.

Then I called up the memory of the day we buried my mother. It was in St. Ives' graveyard four miles outside of New Iberia, Louisiana. My father wore a black suit and a black tie. He held a spray of honeysuckle in one hand and my hand in the other. My mother's sister and her children were there. The sky was clear and the air was heavy and hot. The minister said a lot of words and my father held my hand. He never let go.

Then, just a week later, he left for logging up in Mississippi. He never came back down. Nobody knew what had happened. Nobody knew a thing. Maybe he died. Maybe he found a new wife and moved away. Maybe he got in a fight one night and killed somebody and he was arrested and sent to jail for the rest of my boyhood.

I sat at the kitchen table and watched the sun edge across it. I watched the floor until I could see the trails of dried mop markings from the last time that Regina had cleaned.

Then I cried. I cried the same misery I had when I was a child. My eyes and nose ran. And I felt my father's hand and an old woman hovering behind me and cried for my loss.

I howled and banged the table. Whenever I let myself feel the pain of that loss I have no fear of Death. I hate him a little. I'd like for him to come meet me outside where I could poke out his eyes.

When it was over my feelings for Regina were gone. At least they weren't yelling in my ears. I still missed Edna like I missed my own childhood, such as it was.

The phone rang just as my breathing returned to normal. It was like a signal.

"Yeah?" I said. I knew that it wasn't Regina. I knew that I'd never hear from her again.

"Mr. Rawlins?"

"Yeah."

"This is Sylvia Bride."

"Uh-huh."

"Can you come up wit' somethin' if I give you the girl?"

"Whose girl is it?"

"Fuck you!"

"That don't tell me nuthin'. I ain't gonna scam nobody. If you could prove it then I might do somethin'. They might too."

She was quiet for a moment. I heard a baby stammer in the silence.

"You know the Beldin Arms?"

"Sure." It was an apartment building on Sixty-third Street.

"Meet me there in an hour."

"What apartment?"

"Just go there," she said and then she hung up.

I dressed casually for the meeting. Tan cotton slacks with a green-and-blue square-cut shirt. I wore sandals without socks. There was a .38 pistol hooked to the back of my belt and a .25 in my pocket.

The phone was ringing when I left but I let it ring. There was nothing so important that it couldn't wait.

I got to the front of the Beldin Arms in exactly one hour. I looked at the mailboxes in the entrance hall, but there was no Sylvia Bride.

While I stood there a small boy ran up the steps. He was short and stocky. He swaggered from side to side as boys are likely to do when they feel important. He seemed to be looking around for accolades on the beautiful job he was doing at playing the child.

He stopped in front of me. "You lookin' fo'a lady?"

"What?' I asked.

"She said you gimme a dollar if I show you."

I handed him a dollar and he started to run out the door, saying over his shoulder, "She in the park."

"What park?"

He waved his right hand indicating the direction and said, "Down there," as if he were talking to a very stupid little brother.

At the end of the block was Beldin Park. Mostly concrete. Four scraggly pines amid a small, balding patch of grass. Sylvia Bride sat on the bench.

She wore red silk pants tapered at the ankle and a red Chinese blouse. Her shoes were powder-blue and her hair could have used some work. It was unwashed and brushed back in bold strokes. She smoked Luckies. There was a half-empty pack in her lap.

"Where's the baby?" I asked, standing above her.

"Sit down." She was quiet and almost demure.

I sat down and asked her, "Where's the baby?"

She took a photograph from inside the cellophane wrapper of the Lucky pack and handed it to me. It was a picture of Cyndi Starr and a small, brown baby.

"I've got a whole album of pictures with them. Any blind fool could see that they're mother and child. I have her diary too. She wrote pages and pages about Feather."

"Is it a daily thing?"

"Huh?"

"Is it a daily journal or is it just about the baby?"

"Oh, no. Cyndi was real smart. She went to college, you know. Every day she'd write down poems and how she felt . . ."

"Is it up to the day she was killed?"

"I don't know. I didn't read it. I mean it was hers."

"But . . ." I began to say and then I held back. No reason to let her realize the book was worth anything.

"I want two thousand dollars. I want it in my hands, and then you can have the baby, the diary, and the album."

I reached for my pocket. "Now lemme see, you want that in tens or twenties?"

She smiled at me. I might have liked Sylvia Bride in another world.

"We could switch. But it has to be someplace safe. And I need two thousand."

"I'll get you the money if I can. We could do it in the zoo or at the beach. I don't care where. But before you see the money my people will have to look at what you got. If that convinces them, then we make the trade."

Sylvia bit her red lips with small, sharp teeth. "Okay," she said. "My number's on the back of that picture. Call me when you find out something."

"Tell me something before you go."

"What?"

"Who killed Cyndi?"

She fumbled for a cigarette. I lit it for her.

"I don't know. It was some crazy man, right?"

"I don't think so. It just doesn't make sense."

"Everybody loved her. She was great."

"Was Bull Horker a friend of hers too?"

"He let her stay at his place down near Redondo while she was pregnant. But that's all."

"He the father?"

"God knows who the father is, Mr. Rawlins."

"How was she living when she couldn't work?"

"She borrowed from Bull. But he didn't do it. She was going to pay him three thousand dollars."

"From where?"

"I don't know, honey. She said that she was going to get it from some man."

"A white man?"

"She never said. I mean . . ." Sylvia stopped talking and turned her head at an angle.

"She said," Sylvia continued, "that she didn't like somebody but that they had to pay up."

We both let that one sit until she got up to go.

"Why you come to me, Sylvia?" I said.

"You came to me. You're the one."

"But you could have called that girl's parents yourself. You could do it now."

"I'm not talking to white people about this," she said.

I'd heard that all the time. Half the black people I knew would walk an extra mile to avoid straightforward contact with white people. It didn't surprise me that white people might not trust each other. I couldn't trust them, so why should they trust each other?

Sylvia crossed the street and walked down the block. At the end of the street she got into the passenger's seat of a new Ford. I thought I knew who the driver was.

• 36 •

Jesus and I went to Pecos Bob's Barbecue Heaven for dinner. He had two servings of ribs. Then we went to the penny arcade at the Santa Monica pier. He played the little coin games and rode the merry-go-round. It was great fun.

I bought a beer but didn't drink it. Jesus had cotton candy and caramel corn, but that was okay, he needed to feel good. We went home feeling dizzy from the red flashing lights and bells.

He was kind of slow in the morning but at least he slept in his own bed. I watched him trail off toward school. He met up with two little girls from across the street. I never even knew that Jesus had friends he walked to school with.

Mrs. Garnett was home.

"Two thousand dollars?" she gasped.

"That's what she said. But first you get to see the diary, the photo album with all the pictures of Cyn—of Robin and her baby."

I didn't mention that the baby was black. Many times little black babies look white when they are born. The color sets in later on. I figured I'd let the shock of race set in on them without my trying to soften it. After all, a black baby didn't bother me.

"I don't know. I'll have to talk to my husband."

"Okay. I'll call you tonight. But if he says yeah, then how long before you get the money?"

"I don't know if he will agree."

"But if he does?"

She hesitated but then said, "Day after tomorrow, maybe."

I spent the day cleaning up. I threw Regina's things away. She'd left clothing and costume jewelry and knickknacks all over the house. I threw all of that out. Edna's toys and blankets, those that were left, I piled in her crib. I covered all of that with a big blanket and left it in the living room.

I spent the afternoon reading *The Souls of Black Folk* by W.E.B. Du Bois. It was a book Jackson Blue told me about years before.

Jesus came home at about three-thirty and we played catch until six. We had pork chops, mashed potatoes with sautéed onions, and canned asparagus for dinner. After that Jesus split a candy bar with me and I asked him to wash the dishes.

The phone rang at eight o'clock.

"Hello."

"Mr. Rawlins. My wife wells me that you've found our baby."

"Maybe, sir. I don't know. Woman had a picture of your daughter and a little baby. She says that she's got an album full of enough pictures to prove to anybody that it's your granddaughter."

"What's this woman's name and what does she have to do with Robin?"

"She was Robin's friend. Her name is Sylvia."

"Sylvia what?"

"You not gonna find her in any phone book, Mr. Garnett."

"But maybe I know her. If she was my daughter's friend I might know her."

"Bride," I said. "Sylvia Bride."

"No. I never heard that name before. You say she wants two thousand dollars?"

"She said that."

"It's a lot of money for something we don't even know for sure."

"Listen," I said. "I'll call her and make a meeting where she will show you the book. If you think the baby in the pictures is the daughter, then you can make a deal. You don't have to bring the money with you. Leave it with your lawyer. I'll call her after this an' say that we all gonna meet tomorrow at four on the front stairs of the main library downtown. Okay?"

"My wife said something about a diary."

"Yeah. It seems like she did a lot of writing about Feather. Sylvia seems to think that it will help to identify the baby." I paused for a moment.

"Listen, Mr. Garnett. I don't think that that crazy man killed your girl."

"What?"

"I can't go into all of it right now but I think that somebody killed her and made it seem like she was the crazy man's victim."

"But nobody knew about the crazy man until after she was dead."

"People all over my neighborhood did. Some of them might even have found out about those burns."

"It doesn't sound likely, Mr. Rawlins. That's all pretty elaborate."

"She was seen with some man the day she was killed. And Sylvia told me that somebody was going to give Cyndi some money. Maybe this diary will tell us who that is."

"My God," Garnett said. He sounded so broken up that I felt sorry I had confided in him. There was enough pain in his life.

After a long minute he said, "I hope you're wrong. I hope . . . Well, nothing to do but meet this woman and see what she's got."

"You sure now?"

"Yes. Yes, I'm certain."

"All right. Then I'll call her an' make the date. If sumpin' happens I'll call you back, all right?"

He took a deep breath and then said, "Okay."

Sylvia was unhappy at first. But I told her that she didn't have to have the baby there. All she had to have was the photographs and the diary. The library was as public and safe as she was about to get.

Jesus went to sleep early and was off to school before I was out of bed.

I was working in the garden around noon when Quinten Naylor

and Roland Hobbes drove up in front of my house. They walked abreast and each of them gave me a noncommittal stare.

"Ezekiel Rawlins . . ." Roland Hobbes started the speech.

"Hold it, man," I said. "Lemme get a call on the phone before you take me down. My wife is gone and my little boy is mute. Lemme call somebody down here 'fore you take me in."

Hobbes and Naylor exchanged glances. Neither one of them said a thing. Finally Naylor nodded and Hobbes accompanied me to the telephone.

"*Hola*," said Flower. Her voice was deep and dark as a South American rain forest. Even listening to her brought images of large white lilies on a black bough. I could hear children in the background. The children Jesus called brother and sister before he came to live with me.

I told her to send Primo, her husband, up for the boy. I told her that I was going to jail. She gave me a friendly sigh of sorrow and said okay. The thought that I still had a friend in the world lightened my heart a little.

I hung up the phone and Roland Hobbes said, "Ezekiel Rawlins, you are under arrest."

They didn't tell me a thing. Just cuffed me and drove me down to the station house.

They put me in a holding cell, where I sat until seven-thirty the next morning. It wasn't much of a cell. It was more like a high-ceilinged hopper room with a chair and a light fixture. There were no windows, nor even bars. Just a gray room with a chair. They took my cigarettes, so I was edgy.

There was an eye hole in the gray metal door. Every once in a while it seemed to darken a little, as if someone were looking in at me.

Two uniformed cops came to escort me to court. I met my court-appointed lawyer before the bench. I didn't catch his name. He didn't shake my hand.

Then my lawyer and the prosecution went to the bench and talked with the judge. They discussed my fate for thirty seconds and my lawyer came back to where I stood.

He was a sandy-haired, short man with ears that stood straight away from his head. He was middle-aged and skinny but he still had bad posture and shirttails that brimmed out of his pants.

"What's all this about?" I asked him.

He shuffled his papers together and walked away from the desk. The judge said, "Next case," just like on television, and the court officers started to hustle me off.

I grabbed at my lawyer's jacket.

"Lemme talk to my man a minute," I begged.

"What do you want, Mr. Rawlins?" the little lawyer, whose name I never knew, asked.

"What am I in here for an' what happens now?"

"You're in here for extortion, Mr. Rawlins, and you go to jail until somebody posts twenty-five thousand dollars or your trial comes up."

The lawyer turned away and I was dragged to a room where four other men slept. A half an hour later the sleeping men were roused by three court officers.

We were hustled into a bus that had wire mesh over all the windows and a cell door separating us from the driver. He didn't need that protection, though, because each of the prisoners was manacled by his handcuffs to a bolt under his seat.

We were driven to a flat building near the southern outskirts of town.

The building we were taken to wasn't originally a jail. Maybe they made ball bearings there, or apricot jam. The walls were made of concrete, probably reinforced with steel.

The prisoners were led to a large room, half a football field in size. In the middle of the big room the state had erected steel cages. Like the cages in the older zoos. There looked to be forty-five or fifty of the cells. About half of them were occupied.

One cage to a man. Each one was eight by eight by eight and furnished with a small cot. There were two pails on the floor. One had a cup to drink from, the other was there when you needed to relieve yourself.

One of the other prisoners sold me a pack of cigarettes for a five-dollar bill that I had palmed before leaving the house. When the guards were gone and I was safely locked away, I lit up.

I still remember how good that cigarette tasted. As bad as my life had turned in those few days I still remembered that moment as being one of the most satisfying in my life.

For a while the new inmates talked to the old ones. I asked the guy in the cell next to mine, "What kinda jail is this?"

"Temporary," the gray old white man said. "They're buildin' a new one and this is just the overflow."

I handed him a cigarette and lit it.

"Obliged," he said.

Then the guards told us to be quiet.

Somebody might not believe what happened to me. They might say that a prisoner in America always knows the specific crime of which he is accused. They might say that a man has a right to good counsel and at least a phone call.

At one time I would have said that white people had those rights but colored ones didn't. But as time went by I came to understand that we're all just one step away from an anonymous grave. You don't have to live in a communist country to be assassinated; just ask J.T. Saunders about that.

The police could come to your house today and drag you from your bed. They could beat you until you swallow teeth and they can lock you in a hole for months.

I knew all that but I put it far out of my mind. I just lay back on my cot and savored the cigarette.

• 37 •

I was in the cell but I wasn't alone. Naylor, Voss, Violette, and Hobbes were in there with me.

Naylor said, "You didn't want to help a black woman but you go out for some white whore."

"I saw you with her," Hobbes said.

Voss just shook his head and spit.

Then Violette unholstered his pistol. When he cocked back the hammer it made a squeaking sound instead of a crack.

Then I hear, outside of the dream, "Look out, boy!" And then I felt a cold spray against my face. Another voice curses but by that time I'm doubling up from the cot.

He went past me, driving the knife he held into the mattress rather than into me. His body was over mine and I gave him an uppercut to the groin that would have halted a gorilla.

My attacker fell to the floor, huffing and coughing. It was a white man in a gray jail suit. I kicked him once in the ribs and then I stamped my foot down on his right hand. I was barefoot and so could feel his fingers snapping along with the pain in my heel.

I broke his hand so I wouldn't have to kill him. I had to do something. I would have been within my rights, as I see them, to kill a killer. But instead I disabled him.

I picked him up and dragged him down the aisle of cages and threw him on the floor in front of the door that led to the guards' kiosk. As I went back toward my cell a commotion began among the waking prisoners. By the time I'd locked myself away there were seven guards stumbling over the would-be killer.

He was holding his hand over his groin and coughing. The guards looked around suspiciously.

I noticed a very sour odor. I wondered if it was my own fear that I smelled.

"He's got keys!" one of the guards shouted.

"Pssst!"

The man yelled in pain as they pulled him from the floor. I felt my toe and realized I had probably broken his rib too.

"Pssst!" It was the old white man next to me.

I looked at him and he smiled. He was missing teeth both upper and lower.

"Hope I didn't get your cigarettes with that piss." His smile broadened and I realized that he was the one who'd warned me, who'd thrown water—urine—in my face.

He giggled and said, "Lucky there warn't no turds in there."

It struck me as so funny that I had to laugh, but I couldn't laugh because that would have called attention from the guards, who were looking around for somebody to brutalize.

I sat there with tears coming from my eyes and my diaphragm beating against my chest. When the guards went past my cell I covered myself with the blanket to keep them from smelling the guilt. The foul odor made me gag harder.

After a while the guards took that groaning assassin away.

"You got a good friend somewhere," the old white man said. He wore jail gray also.

"What do you mean?"

"Somebody went to a lotta trouble to kill you." He gave me a wink. "Unless you know that bozo."

I handed my savior five cigarettes.

"What's your name?" I asked him.

"Alamo. Alamo Weir." He winked at me and I lit his cigarette.

I lay back in the squalor and began to think. I started with Quinten

Naylor coming up to my house and driving me to the scene of a crime.

They fitted me with jailhouse grays the next morning. We all went into a big room with a long table and ate thick oatmeal watered down with reconstituted milk. At midday they let us walk around outside of our cells. During that time Alamo stuck with the white prisoners and I moved with the colored brothers.

After we were back in our cells I was taken to a room where Anthony Violette was waiting for me.

"Glad to see that you're still alive, Rawlins." He smiled at me.

I couldn't say a word. A police captain wanted me dead. I was dead.

"No smart-assed joke? Maybe you could go get me a beer."

"I ain't done nuthin' this bad to you, man," I said.

"That's right. You haven't done a damn thing to me. I'm just a police officer, doing my duty."

"What am I in here for?"

"Extortion." Violette's smile was plastered to his face. The humiliation he felt from me was immense. One black man talking back to him in front of a superior; maybe that was enough to have me killed.

"I didn't extort anybody."

"That's not what Vernor Garnett says."

"He killed her." It jumped right out of my mouth. It was so fast and so natural that the smile was blasted from Violette's face.

"What?"

"He killed his own daughter and now he's using you and me to cover his track."

"Listen here, Rawlins . . ."

"No. You listen to me. Vernor was supposed to meet me yesterday afternoon in front of the main library. A woman who knew about Cyndi's daughter was going to bring proof that the baby was Cyndi's."

"What kind of proof? What baby?" the cop asked in spite of himself.

"A bunch'a pictures and a diary that might have identified the killer, the man who was going to bring her three thousand dollars."

"Who're you? Charlie Chan?"

"What'd he say I did?"

"What you did do. You threatened to go to the papers about his daughter. You were going to expose her life down in Watts."

"I bet that's what *she* did. I bet she was going to tell the family about her life and her daughter too. Yeah. He already knew about the baby."

"You're crazy, Rawlins. She didn't have a kid. And Vernor didn't know about her before you told him."

"She did have a baby. She'd left home and had it at one of Bull Horker's places."

He hadn't believed a word up until I mentioned Horker.

"Where were you going to meet this girl?" The cop was fully in charge now.

I told him my story again. He didn't tell me a thing. When I was finished he just stood up, in a hurry to leave.

"What about me?" I asked him.

"Come up with the bail."

"But I didn't extort nuthin'."

"That's what you say. Maybe you just read the papers. We'll see."

"Listen, captain," I said in a voice loud enough to stop him a moment. "There's somebody trying to kill me in here."

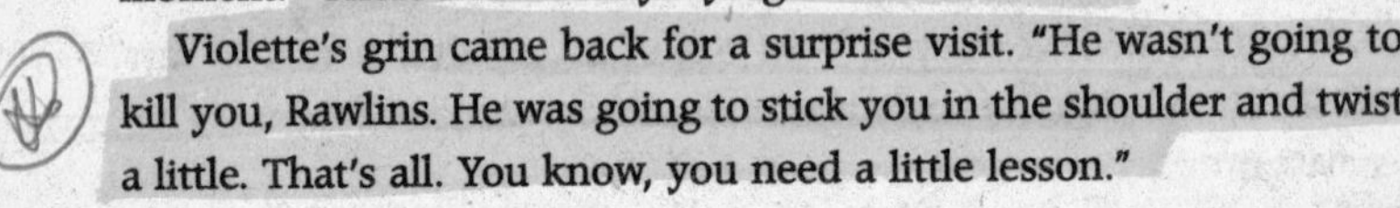

Violette's grin came back for a surprise visit. "He wasn't going to kill you, Rawlins. He was going to stick you in the shoulder and twist a little. That's all. You know, you need a little lesson."

Alamo and I shared a few cigarettes that he got and sat up all that night. He was a career criminal. He'd done everything, if you were to believe him, from petty larceny to first-degree murder.

He'd been born in a small town in Iowa and hit the road after he was let loose from the army after World War One.

"It just warn't never right after that. All them dead boys," Alamo told me. He shook his head in real remorse. "And all them people, never felt it, act like they know life. Damn. I could take their money or their life. They wouldn't even know it was gone."

He was kind of crazy but I was comforted by him. After all, it was sane men who had put me in jail.

The next morning the guard came and took me from the cell. Alamo had passed me a sharpened spoon in the night, and I had it up the long sleeve of my gray jail suit. We walked along the big tables and out through large double doors that led to a garage.

The guard told me to pick up a box that sat in a corner. I looked down in it to see my civilian clothes.

"Put 'em on," the porky, crew-cut white man said.

I stripped right there in front of him, carefully leaving the spoon in the sleeve of the shirt. After I was dressed in my normal clothes I threw the prison garb into a corner and retrieved my weapon.

Another guard came up and they escorted me to the driveway in front of the factory. There sat a squad car with two cops in it. The cops got out and put manacles on me, hand and foot.

"Where'm I goin'?" I asked once.

The police just laughed.

I sat in the backseat on the way downtown. Every moment was very important. I looked at windows with manikins in them and got weepy. I saw a man make a left turn and I imagined myself turning the steering wheel. I thought of my baby girl and felt my inner organs shift.

It must have taken an hour to drive all the way downtown but it seemed like fleet moments to me. They hustled me out of the car and then put me in another holding cell. I was sure that someone was going to kill me. I had the spoon hidden in my pocket. I didn't think that I could fight past guns with that spoon, but I could take somebody with me; at least I could do that.

In the afternoon they took me from the holding cell and brought me to a wire-cage kiosk. A young cop pushed a big manila envelope at me. Inside it I found my wallet and keys. Those simple items scared me so much that I began to tremble. I knew that I was being set up for the kill.

I walked out of the front door of the municipal building next to city hall with my shoulders hunched and my head down.

"Easy!" he yelled.

I looked up, ready to go down fighting, only to see Raymond Alexander in all his splendor. He wore a close-fitting bright checkered jacket and flared black slacks. He shoes were ivory and his hat close-brimmed. Mouse smiled for miles.

"You look terrible," he said.

"What you doin' here, Raymond?"

"I done made yo' bail, Easy. I got you out."

"What?"

"Com'on man, let's get outta here. Them cops prob'ly take us in fo'loiterin' fo'long."

In the car we went past the squat buildings of fifties L.A. down into Watts.

"Where you wanna go, Easy?" Mouse asked after a while.

"You came up with my bail?"

"Uh-huh."

"Twenty-five hundred dollars?"

"Uh-uh. Twenty-five thousand. Bail bondsman wouldn't touch it."

"Where you come up wit' money like that? You go to Mofass?"

"Tried to but he's in the hospital."

"Hospital?"

"Yeah. Some white boys tore him up. He told me to tell you that them men you been doin' business wit' is mad in the worst way."

"Shit. So where'd you get the money?"

"You sure you wanna know?" He was smiling.

"Where?"

"There's this private poker game out in Gardena. I robbed it."

"An' they had that much money?"

"An' some to boot."

"You kill anybody?"

"Shot this one guy but I don't think he gonna die. Maybe just walk funny fo'awhile."

• 38 •

Bull Horker was found in an alley in San Pedro. He'd been shot seven times in the chest. The police believed that he was killed somewhere else and dumped in that alley. He was found at eight P.M. on the day I was supposed to meet Sylvia and Vernor on the library steps.

The article said that there were signs of a struggle but there was no explanation of what the signs were.

Primo and Flower were glad to see us. Jesus was so happy I thought he might even talk. He ran up and put his arms around me and he just wouldn't let go. I had to walk with his embrace and sit with him on my lap.

Mofass looked pretty good in his hospital bed. The rest gave him a little strength and they wouldn't let him smoke in the ward. His only problems were a busted hand and three fractures in his left leg.

"They th'owed me down the steps, Mr. Rawlins. They didn't care if I was dead. They told me that if I lived I should tell my partners that they ain't playin'."

Mouse grinned.

"I'll take care of it, William. You just rest here and try to give up them cigars. You know they gonna kill you faster than DeCampo."

"It's killin' me *not* to smoke."

*

I gave Mouse the names of DeCampo and his associates. I told him their Culver City office address and asked him to visit each and every one of them, on the most private terms.

"I want them to understand that killing Mofass won't save their lives," I said. "And, Raymond," I pointed in his face, "I don't want nobody dead or even wounded."

I've read many a novel that extolled the virtues of capitalism. Not one of them ever came within a mile of the truth.

I was sitting at my desk in the early evening going over the accounts of the killing of Bull Horker. I was looking for something that might lead me to Vernor. But there was nothing I could see.

I was already used to the silence. The silence we'd lived with before Regina, and then Edna. Jesus was reading a red storybook. And I was still alive.

Then the screech of the gate brought me to the window. There was Quinten Naylor again. He was wearing the same suit he wore the day he brought me to see Bonita Edwards' body.

I blamed him for Regina leaving me. I blamed him but I knew I was wrong.

He wasn't surprised to see me open the door before he could knock. I nodded at a chair that stood where the crib had been and he sat down.

I lit a cigarette. He brushed his hand over the top of his head.

"The charges against you have been dropped," Naylor said.

"Oh? How come?"

"They got the wife in custody."

"What about Milo?" That little boy was the first one I thought of.

"Juvenile Hall."

"Yeah. Take it out on the kid. Put him in jail 'cause'a what his old man did."

"His mother was in on it. She confessed."

"What? Naw, I don't believe it. I saw how she acted when I showed her the pictures."

"She didn't know then. But after that she began to put th together. Garnett had told her something about the killings before their daughter was killed. She didn't think anything until after he told her about their granddaughter. He'd been in touch with Robin even after she'd left school. He had to know that she was pregnant."

"So she found out when he was planning to go after Sylvia?"

"He was scared over the diary. Robin had threatened to come to his office dressed like a whore and with a baby in her arms if he didn't give her enough money to care for her child."

"Killed his own child." I was saddened by even the possibility.

"She drove him to it," Quinten said. "She was a whore and she just wouldn't straighten out. Then she threatened him."

"She drove him to it," I said. "Well then, what drove her?"

Quinten didn't understand the question. There was right and wrong for him. He dealt with morality the way Mofass went after money. There is no such thing as a long-term investment, there's money right now, there's sin right now. Mofass didn't see past the money those crooks blinded him with and Quinten Naylor couldn't see that maybe Vernor Garnett had sown the seeds of his own destruction.

"Where is the father?" I asked.

"He ran after going to meet Sylvia. He killed Bull Horker, we're pretty sure of that. Then he disappeared with the girl. We found his car in West Hollywood yesterday. Bull's blood was all over the front seat."

"What happened to the girl?"

"Nothing yet. All we know is what I said. His name and picture are out there. We'll get him."

"I'm sure of that."

"What's that supposed to mean?"

"You're good at gettin' people, Quinten. You got J.T. Saunders good. When Violette thought I mighta done somethin' he had me set up faster than you could spit."

"What are you talking about, Rawlins? When a prosecutor says that someone is extorting him we believe it. Especially when . . ."

"When it's a nigger. Especially then. Yeah. What are you doing here anyway, man? You gonna me send down to jail again?"

Naylor studied a few fingernails before he answered. "I wanted to say I'm sorry." The words seemed to stick in his mouth. "I always thought that . . . I don't know. I just always thought that I could work inside the police and keep my hands clean. I put myself above you. Don't get me wrong, I'm not saying that I think you live right. But maybe I'm not so much better."

Maybe Naylor wasn't so bad either. I didn't tell him that, though. I didn't tell him a thing.

• 39 •

Over the next few days things came back into order, after a fashion. Anybody who asked me was told that Regina had gone to visit her sick aunt in Arkansas.

Jack DeCampo came to Mofass' hospital room—to apologize. He blamed the attack on *silent partners* and said that he didn't know about the mayhem until it was already too late.

Mofass didn't want to let him off at first but he remembered the kind of fear that Mouse could throw into a man.

"You know, Mr. Rawlins," Mofass told me on the phone, "that man was so pale that he could'a been two white men."

It was rare that Mofass and I laughed at the same joke.

"When I told 'im that our friend was on the payroll and that he didn't have to be scared I thought he mighta kissed me."

"Okay, William," I said. "Maybe next time you'll fly right."

"Uh-huh. But you know there is this one thing."

"What?"

"They still wanna be partners. They say they'll give a hunnert an' twenty-five thousand just to be twenty-five percent." He was making deals from what might have been his deathbed.

"Man . . ."

"They got good connections, Mr. Rawlins. They could get us deals that no bank ever gonna give a Negro."

The thought of DeCampo working for me sounded good. And I could use the cash for development.

"You tell 'im eighteen percent and he's got a deal."

"Okay, man." I could hear his grin over the phone.

The telephone rang four days after Quinten Naylor's visit. I still got butterflies whenever I had to answer a phone. I still thought, What can I say to her?

"Hello?"

"Is this a Mr. Rawlins?" a young man's voice said.

"Yeah."

"Well . . . I don't know, sir. This is kinda weird."

"What's that?"

"Well, you see this couple . . . have been eating here at the Chicken Pit for about a week now."

The butterflies were beating up a storm.

"And a couple of days ago the woman, just a girl really, comes up from the table to ask me for a glass of water. But when she reaches for the glass she grabs my finger and passes this note. I think she was worried . . ."

"What did this note say?"

"It was a corner of a newspaper, a racing form with your name and phone number in one margin and a note saying, 'Call the police, we're at the Seacrest,' and it's signed 'Sylvia.' "

"Why'd you wait two days, man?"

"I don't know. It was just so weird. I don't want any trouble. You see . . . I can't talk to the police."

"Where's this Seacrest place?"

"It's a motel at the corner of Adams and La Brea. Do you think . . ."

"Have they been in your place since then?"

"The next day I had off. I went to San Diego and really forgot about . . ."

"Was she in there today?"

"No. Just the man, I mean. That's why I called."

I hung up the phone and rushed to the closet to get my gun.

Jesus followed me around the house and kept grabbing me. Finally I stopped and asked him, "What?"

He just stared at the pistol in my hand.

"It's not Regina," I told him. "She's gone. It's not her."

At first Jesus didn't believe me. But I sat down and convinced him after a while. I told him that I'd be back soon. Then I drove off in the direction of the Seacrest.

At every red light I tried to persuade myself to call the cops. On every straightaway I imagined killing Vernor Garnett. He was everything I hated. He'd killed his own child and his wife still stayed behind him. He'd got me in jail by just telling a lie. A white man.

The Seacrest was a single-story motel facing a large parking lot with the entrances to all of the rooms facing out. I parked across the street at three in the afternoon and waited.

I sat there for three hours. And the whole time all I thought about was Regina. I'd tried to think about her before but all I encountered was pain. But somehow, waiting for that evil man, I didn't feel the pain. I only felt cold rage.

By the time Garnett walked out of the last room on the end I hadn't figured out a thing. I couldn't say for a fact why she left me. I couldn't say that I would have been different.

Garnett had grown some facial hair and wore a trench coat with the lapels turned up. He walked down the street to the Chicken Pit with his head down.

I jimmied his door and went in.

Sylvia was dead. He'd laid her out on the floor of the closet and closed the door. But she was already starting to smell. Her temple was caved in. The room was a shambles. Clothes and bags of food were thrown around. A newspaper spread on the bed was open to the travel section. Three special fares to Mexico were circled.

I turned out the light and stood behind the door. I just waited there forever. The gray forms of the bed and dresser got fainter. The pistol was cold on my fingers.

When Garnett came back he opened the door and closed it before flicking on the light. I hadn't expected to be blinded by the sudden light.

"What," Vernor called out loudly as if maybe he was with somebody. But he was alone.

Maybe if he had jumped me in that second I would have been keeping Sylvia company. But instead he clawed at the doorknob for two seconds, three.

I flat-handed him with the pistol. He shook his head as if assailed by a sudden and unpleasant memory. I hit him again and he went down to his knees like J.T. Saunders had done for the police assassin.

"Please," he said in a small voice.

A voice was screaming in my head, "Kill him!" Over and over. My neck quivered. I honestly felt that if I didn't pull the trigger I would die. The tears came from my eyes, a guttural cry escaped my lips. My diaphragm undulated so that it was hard to keep the pistol steady.

Garnett cowered against the door. He held his hands up before his face. We were both madmen at the end of our lives. We were madmen but only he was a lawyer.

He started talking. At first I was too upset to hear him but then after a while his gibbering began to make sense. He told me that he didn't mean it. He hadn't planned to kill his daughter. But after he had, he faked Saunders' MO, because he'd heard about it down at the courthouse.

He had killed her in his car also.

"What about Sylvia?"

"I just wanted the diary," he pleaded. "They didn't bring it with them."

"Why'd you kill her?"

"It was too late," he said. "She wouldn't give me. She wanted . . . wanted . . ."

I hog-tied Garnett and gagged him; put him in the closet with Sylvia Bride.

"Hello?" Quinten Naylor said.

I gave him the address and told him that somebody had called. I didn't know who.

Maybe to some people revenge is sweet. All I know is that I had to stop my car five blocks away and vomit for a full minute before I could breathe again.

Bull Horker's cook, Bailey, was more than happy to tell me where Cyndi stayed in Redondo Beach. For another fifty dollars he would have shed blood for me.

The house on Exeter was inhabited by an old woman named Charla Fine. She was holding the baby for Bull Horker and she was none too happy that the Bull had died. But Feather seemed hale and more or less happy. When I first saw her she was sucking her toe. I looked down and she smiled at me and said something in baby talk that I thought meant "Tickle my stomach and push my nose."

Five hundred dollars and the baby was mine.

The papers the next day detailed the crime. The dead stripper Sylvia Bride (her real name was Phyllis Weinstein) had her picture on the front page all over California.

The trial was front-page news for weeks. Everything the prosecutor wanted to avoid came out in public. His daughter's wild life, and death. The father's crime, the mother's cover-up.

Nobody cared much about the baby. Most of the speculation was that the child had probably been killed by the mother. This was substantiated by the fact that no one had seen the baby after she was born.

Anyway, the birth certificate had the baby listed as white. Feather was safe with me.

Vernor Garnett died in prison two years after he was sentenced. His wife moved back east somewhere after she was found innocent of conspiracy.

There wasn't much written about Milo.

• 40 •

We moved three months later. I bought a small house in an area near West Los Angeles called View Park. Middle-class black families had started colonizing that neighborhood, and I wanted to get away from people who knew me and Regina.

Jesus liked his new school, and all the work of moving got my mind off the trouble in my life. Regina still lived in my dreams. Sometimes I'd wake up in the middle of the night in despair.

But when I'd wake up, little Feather needed her bottle and a change of diapers. She wasn't my little Edna but she was beautiful and happy almost all of the time. I'd lost Regina and Gabby Lee, but Jackson Blue would baby-sit at least once a week and I didn't mind caring for her.

Jesus never got tired of playing with Feather. He'd take her everywhere once she started to walk.

And I decided to let Dupree and Regina leave for good. Mouse found out where they had gone. He offered to go down to kill Dupree, and Regina, and bring Edna back. But I told him to give me the address and let it lie.

Enough people had died. I would have been happy if not one more person in the world ever had to face that fate.